A Little Life

A Little Life

[A NOVEL]

Hanya Yanagihara

Doubleday

NEW YORK   LONDON   TORONTO   SYDNEY   AUCKLAND

This book is a work of fiction. Names, characters, businesses, organizations, places, events, and incidents either are the product of the author's imagination or are used fictitiously. Any resemblance to actual persons, living or dead, events, or locales is entirely coincidental.

Book design by Maria Carella
Jacket design by Cardon Webb
Jacket photograph: *Orgasmic Man* by Peter Hujar © 1987
The Peter Hujar Archive LLC. Courtesy Pace/MacGill Gallery,
New York and Fraenkel Gallery, San Francisco

Library of Congress Cataloging-in-Publication Data
Yanagihara, Hanya.
A little life : a novel / Hanya Yanagihara. — First edition.
pages ; cm
ISBN 978-0-385-53925-8 (hardcover)—ISBN 978-0-385-53926-5 (eBook)
1. Families—Fiction. 2. Domestic fiction. I. Title.
PS3625.A674L58 2015
813'.6—dc23   2014027379

MANUFACTURED IN THE UNITED STATES OF AMERICA

1 3 5 7 9 10 8 6 4 2

First Edition

To Jared Hohlt
in friendship; with love

Contents

A Little Life

[I]

Lispenard Street

1

THE ELEVENTH APARTMENT had only one closet, but it did have a sliding glass door that opened onto a small balcony, from which he could see a man sitting across the way, outdoors in only a T-shirt and shorts even though it was October, smoking. Willem held up a hand in greeting to him, but the man didn't wave back.

In the bedroom, Jude was accordioning the closet door, opening and shutting it, when Willem came in. "There's only one closet," he said.

"That's okay," Willem said. "I have nothing to put in it anyway."

"Neither do I." They smiled at each other. The agent from the building wandered in after them. "We'll take it," Jude told her.

But back at the agent's office, they were told they couldn't rent the apartment after all. "Why not?" Jude asked her.

"You don't make enough to cover six months' rent, and you don't have anything in savings," said the agent, suddenly terse. She had checked their credit and their bank accounts and had at last realized that there was something amiss about two men in their twenties who were not a couple and yet were trying to rent a one-bedroom apartment on a dull (but still expensive) stretch of Twenty-fifth Street. "Do you have anyone who can sign on as your guarantor? A boss? Parents?"

"Our parents are dead," said Willem, swiftly.

The agent sighed. "Then I suggest you lower your expectations. No one who manages a well-run building is going to rent to candidates with your financial profile." And then she stood, with an air of finality, and looked pointedly at the door.

When they told JB and Malcolm this, however, they made it into a comedy: the apartment floor became tattooed with mouse droppings, the man across the way had almost exposed himself, the agent was upset because she had been flirting with Willem and he hadn't reciprocated.

"Who wants to live on Twenty-fifth and Second anyway," asked JB. They were at Pho Viet Huong in Chinatown, where they met twice a month for dinner. Pho Viet Huong wasn't very good—the pho was curiously sugary, the lime juice was soapy, and at least one of them got sick after every meal—but they kept coming, both out of habit and necessity. You could get a bowl of soup or a sandwich at Pho Viet Huong for five dollars, or you could get an entrée, which were eight to ten dollars but much larger, so you could save half of it for the next day or for a snack later that night. Only Malcolm never ate the whole of his entrée and never saved the other half either, and when he was finished eating, he put his plate in the center of the table so Willem and JB—who were always hungry—could eat the rest.

"Of course we don't *want* to live at Twenty-fifth and Second, JB," said Willem, patiently, "but we don't really have a choice. We don't have any money, remember?"

"I don't understand why you don't stay where you are," said Malcolm, who was now pushing his mushrooms and tofu—he always ordered the same dish: oyster mushrooms and braised tofu in a treacly brown sauce—around his plate, as Willem and JB eyed it.

"Well, I can't," Willem said. "Remember?" He had to have explained this to Malcolm a dozen times in the last three months. "Merritt's boyfriend's moving in, so I have to move out."

"But why do *you* have to move out?"

"Because it's Merritt's name on the lease, Malcolm!" said JB.

"Oh," Malcolm said. He was quiet. He often forgot what he considered inconsequential details, but he also never seemed to mind when people grew impatient with him for forgetting. "Right." He moved the mushrooms to the center of the table. "But you, Jude—"

"I can't stay at your place forever, Malcolm. Your parents are going to kill me at some point."

"My parents love you."

"That's nice of you to say. But they won't if I don't move out, and soon."

Malcolm was the only one of the four of them who lived at home, and as JB liked to say, if he had Malcolm's home, he would live at home too. It wasn't as if Malcolm's house was particularly grand—it was, in fact, creaky and ill-kept, and Willem had once gotten a splinter simply by running his hand up its banister—but it was large: a real Upper East Side town house. Malcolm's sister, Flora, who was three years older than him, had moved out of the basement apartment recently, and Jude had taken her place as a short-term solution: Eventually, Malcolm's parents would want to reclaim the unit to convert it into offices for his mother's literary agency, which meant Jude (who was finding the flight of stairs that led down to it too difficult to navigate anyway) had to look for his own apartment.

And it was natural that he would live with Willem; they had been roommates throughout college. In their first year, the four of them had shared a space that consisted of a cinder-blocked common room, where sat their desks and chairs and a couch that JB's aunts had driven up in a U-Haul, and a second, far tinier room, in which two sets of bunk beds had been placed. This room had been so narrow that Malcolm and Jude, lying in the bottom bunks, could reach out and grab each other's hands. Malcolm and JB had shared one of the units; Jude and Willem had shared the other.

"It's blacks versus whites," JB would say.

"Jude's not white," Willem would respond.

"And I'm not black," Malcolm would add, more to annoy JB than because he believed it.

"Well," JB said now, pulling the plate of mushrooms toward him with the tines of his fork, "I'd say you could both stay with me, but I think you'd fucking hate it." JB lived in a massive, filthy loft in Little Italy, full of strange hallways that led to unused, oddly shaped cul-de-sacs and unfinished half rooms, the Sheetrock abandoned mid-construction, which belonged to another person they knew from college. Ezra was an artist, a bad one, but he didn't need to be good because, as JB liked to remind them, he would never have to work in his entire life. And not only would *he* never have to work, but his children's children's children would never have to work: They could make bad, unsalable, worthless art for generations and they would still be able to buy at whim the best oils they wanted, and impractically large lofts in downtown Manhattan that they could trash with their bad architectural decisions, and when they got sick of the artist's life—as JB was convinced Ezra someday would—all they would need to do is call their trust officers and be awarded an enormous lump sum of cash of an amount that the four of them (well, maybe not Malcolm) could never dream of seeing in their lifetimes. In the meantime, though, Ezra was a useful person to know, not only because he let JB and a few of his other friends from school stay in his apartment—at any time, there were four or five people burrowing in various corners of the loft—but because he was a good-natured and basically generous person, and liked to throw excessive parties in which copious amounts of food and drugs and alcohol were available for free.

"Hold up," JB said, putting his chopsticks down. "I just realized— there's someone at the magazine renting some place for her aunt. Like, just on the verge of Chinatown."

"How much is it?" asked Willem.

"Probably nothing—she didn't even know what to ask for it. And she wants someone in there that she knows."

"Do you think you could put in a good word?"

"Better—I'll introduce you. Can you come by the office tomorrow?"

Jude sighed. "I won't be able to get away." He looked at Willem.

"Don't worry—I can. What time?"

"Lunchtime, I guess. One?"

"I'll be there."

Willem was still hungry, but he let JB eat the rest of the mushrooms. Then they all waited around for a bit; sometimes Malcolm ordered jackfruit ice cream, the one consistently good thing on the menu, ate two bites, and then stopped, and he and JB would finish the rest. But this time he didn't order the ice cream, and so they asked for the bill so they could study it and divide it to the dollar.

—

The next day, Willem met JB at his office. JB worked as a reception-ist at a small but influential magazine based in SoHo that covered the downtown art scene. This was a strategic job for him; his plan, as he'd explained to Willem one night, was that he'd try to befriend one of the editors there and then convince him to feature him in the magazine. He estimated this taking about six months, which meant he had three more to go.

JB wore a perpetual expression of mild disbelief while at his job, both that he should be working at all and that no one had yet thought to recognize his special genius. He was not a good receptionist. Although the phones rang more or less constantly, he rarely picked them up; when any of them wanted to get through to him (the cell phone reception in the building was inconsistent), they had to follow a special code of ringing twice, hanging up, and then ringing again. And even then he sometimes failed to answer—his hands were busy beneath his desk, combing and plaiting snarls of hair from a black plastic trash bag he kept at his feet.

JB was going through, as he put it, his hair phase. Recently he had decided to take a break from painting in favor of making sculptures from black hair. Each of them had spent an exhausting weekend following JB from barbershop to beauty shop in Queens, Brooklyn, the Bronx, and Manhattan, waiting outside as JB went in to ask the owners for any sweepings or cuttings they might have, and then lugging an increasingly awkward bag of hair down the street after him. His early pieces had included *The Mace,* a tennis ball that he had de-fuzzed, sliced in half, and filled with sand before coating it in glue and rolling it around and around in a carpet of hair so that the bristles moved like seaweed underwater, and "The Kwotidien," in which he covered various household items—a stapler; a spatula; a teacup—in pelts of hair. Now he was working on a large-scale project that he refused to discuss with them except in snatches, but it involved the combing out and braiding together of many pieces in order to make one apparently endless rope of frizzing black hair. The previous Friday he had lured them over with the promise of pizza and beer to help him braid, but after many hours of tedious work, it became clear that there was no pizza and beer forthcoming, and they had left, a little irritated but not terribly surprised.

They were all bored with the hair project, although Jude—alone among them—thought that the pieces were lovely and would someday be considered significant. In thanks, JB had given Jude a hair-covered hairbrush, but then had reclaimed the gift when it looked like Ezra's father's friend might be interested in buying it (he didn't, but JB never returned the hairbrush to Jude). The hair project had proved difficult in

other ways as well; another evening, when the three of them had somehow been once again conned into going to Little Italy and combing
out more hair, Malcolm had commented that the hair stank. Which it
did: not of anything distasteful but simply the tangy metallic scent of
unwashed scalp. But JB had thrown one of his mounting tantrums,
and had called Malcolm a self-hating Negro and an Uncle Tom and
a traitor to the race, and Malcolm, who very rarely angered but who
angered over accusations like this, had dumped his wine into the nearest bag of hair and gotten up and stamped out. Jude had hurried, the
best he could, after Malcolm, and Willem had stayed to handle JB. And
although the two of them reconciled the next day, in the end Willem
and Jude felt (unfairly, they knew) slightly angrier at Malcolm, since the
next weekend they were back in Queens, walking from barbershop to
barbershop, trying to replace the bag of hair that he had ruined.

"How's life on the black planet?" Willem asked JB now.

"Black," said JB, stuffing the plait he was untangling back into the
bag. "Let's go; I told Annika we'd be there at one thirty." The phone on
his desk began to ring.

"Don't you want to get that?"

"They'll call back."

As they walked downtown, JB complained. So far, he had concentrated most of his seductive energies on a senior editor named Dean,
whom they all called DeeAnn. They had been at a party, the three
of them, held at one of the junior editor's parents' apartment in the
Dakota, in which art-hung room bled into art-hung room. As JB talked
with his coworkers in the kitchen, Malcolm and Willem had walked
through the apartment together (Where had Jude been that night?
Working, probably), looking at a series of Edward Burtynskys hanging
in the guest bedroom, a suite of water towers by the Bechers mounted
in four rows of five over the desk in the den, an enormous Gursky floating above the half bookcases in the library, and, in the master bedroom,
an entire wall of Diane Arbuses, covering the space so thoroughly that
only a few centimeters of blank wall remained at the top and bottom.
They had been admiring a picture of two sweet-faced girls with Down
syndrome playing for the camera in their too-tight, too-childish bathing suits, when Dean had approached them. He was a tall man, but he
had a small, gophery, pockmarked face that made him appear feral and
untrustworthy.

They introduced themselves, explained that they were here because they were JB's friends. Dean told them that he was one of the senior editors at the magazine, and that he handled all the arts coverage.

"Ah," Willem said, careful not to look at Malcolm, whom he did not trust not to react. JB had told them that he had targeted the arts editor as his potential mark; this must be him.

"Have you ever seen anything like this?" Dean asked them, waving a hand at the Arbuses.

"Never," Willem said. "I love Diane Arbus."

Dean stiffened, and his little features seemed to gather themselves into a knot in the center of his little face. "It's DeeAnn."

"What?"

"DeeAnn. You pronounce her name 'DeeAnn.'"

They had barely been able to get out of the room without laughing. "DeeAnn!" JB had said later, when they told him the story. "Christ! What a pretentious little shit."

"But he's *your* pretentious little shit," Jude had said. And ever since, they had referred to Dean as "DeeAnn."

Unfortunately, however, it appeared that despite JB's tireless cultivation of DeeAnn, he was no closer to being included in the magazine than he had been three months ago. JB had even let DeeAnn suck him off in the steam room at the gym, and still nothing. Every day, JB found a reason to wander back into the editorial offices and over to the bulletin board on which the next three months' story ideas were written on white note cards, and every day he looked at the section dedicated to up-and-coming artists for his name, and every day he was disappointed. Instead he saw the names of various no-talents and overhypes, people owed favors or people who knew people to whom favors were owed.

"If I ever see Ezra up there, I'm going to kill myself," JB always said, to which the others said: You won't, JB, and Don't worry, JB— you'll be up there someday, and What do you need them for, JB? You'll find somewhere else, to which JB would reply, respectively, "Are you sure?," and "I fucking doubt it," and "I've fucking invested this time— three whole months of my fucking life—I better be fucking up there, or this whole thing has been a fucking waste, just like everything else," everything else meaning, variously, grad school, moving back to New York, the hair series, or life in general, depending on how nihilistic he felt that day.

He was still complaining when they reached Lispenard Street. Willem was new enough to the city—he had only lived there a year—to have never heard of the street, which was barely more than an alley, two blocks long and one block south of Canal, and yet JB, who had grown up in Brooklyn, hadn't heard of it either.

They found the building and punched buzzer 5C. A girl answered, her voice made scratchy and hollow by the intercom, and rang them in. Inside, the lobby was narrow and high-ceilinged and painted a curdled, gleaming shit-brown, which made them feel like they were at the bottom of a well.

The girl was waiting for them at the door of the apartment. "Hey, JB," she said, and then looked at Willem and blushed.

"Annika, this is my friend Willem," JB said. "Willem, Annika works in the art department. She's cool."

Annika looked down and stuck out her hand in one movement. "It's nice to meet you," she said to the floor. JB kicked Willem in the foot and grinned at him. Willem ignored him.

"It's nice to meet you, too," he said.

"Well, this is the apartment? It's my aunt's? She lived here for fifty years but she just moved into a retirement home?" Annika was speaking very fast and had apparently decided that the best strategy was to treat Willem like an eclipse and simply not look at him at all. She was talking faster and faster, about her aunt, and how she always said the neighborhood had changed, and how she'd never heard of Lispenard Street until she'd moved downtown, and how she was sorry it hadn't been painted yet, but her aunt had just, literally just moved out and they'd only had a chance to have it cleaned the previous weekend. She looked everywhere but at Willem—at the ceiling (stamped tin), at the floors (cracked, but parquet), at the walls (on which long-ago-hung picture frames had left ghostly shadows)—until finally Willem had to interrupt, gently, and ask if he could take a look through the rest of the apartment.

"Oh, be my guest," said Annika, "I'll leave you alone," although she then began to follow them, talking rapidly to JB about someone named Jasper and how he'd been using Archer for *everything*, and didn't JB think it looked a little too round and weird for body text? Now that Willem had his back turned to her, she stared at him openly, her rambling becoming more inane the longer she spoke.

JB watched Annika watch Willem. He had never seen her like this, so nervous and girlish (normally she was surly and silent and was actually a bit feared in the office for creating on the wall above her desk an elaborate sculpture of a heart made entirely of x-acto blades), but he had seen lots of women behave this way around Willem. They all had. Their friend Lionel used to say that Willem must have been a fisherman in a past life, because he couldn't help but attract pussy. And yet most of the time (though not always), Willem seemed unaware of the attention. JB had once asked Malcolm why he thought that was, and Malcolm said he thought it was because Willem hadn't noticed. JB had only grunted in reply, but his thinking was: Malcolm was the most obtuse person he knew, and if even *Malcolm* had noticed how women reacted around Willem, it was impossible that Willem himself hadn't. Later, however, Jude had offered a different interpretation: he had suggested that Willem was deliberately *not* reacting to all the women so the other men around him wouldn't feel threatened by him. This made more sense; Willem was liked by everyone and never wanted to make people feel intentionally uncomfortable, and so it was possible that, subconsciously at least, he was feigning a sort of ignorance. But still—it was fascinating to watch, and the three of them never tired of it, nor of making fun of Willem for it afterward, though he would normally just smile and say nothing.

"Does the elevator work well here?" Willem asked abruptly, turning around.

"What?" Annika replied, startled. "Yes, it's pretty reliable." She pulled her faint lips into a narrow smile that JB realized, with a stomach-twist of embarrassment for her, was meant to be flirtatious. Oh, Annika, he thought. "What exactly are you planning on bringing into my aunt's apartment?"

"Our friend," he answered, before Willem could. "He has trouble climbing stairs and needs the elevator to work."

"Oh," she said, flushing again. She was back to staring at the floor. "Sorry. Yes, it works."

The apartment was not impressive. There was a small foyer, little larger than the size of a doormat, from which pronged the kitchen (a hot, greasy little cube) to the right and a dining area to the left that would accommodate perhaps a card table. A half wall separated this space from the living room, with its four windows, each striped with

bars, looking south onto the litter-scattered street, and down a short
hall to the right was the bathroom with its milk-glass sconces and worn-
enamel tub, and across from it the bedroom, which had another window and was deep but narrow; here, two wooden twin-bed frames had
been placed parallel to each other, each pressed against a wall. One of
the frames was already topped with a futon, a bulky, graceless thing, as
heavy as a dead horse.

"The futon's never been used," Annika said. She told a long story
about how she was going to move in, and had even bought the futon
in preparation, but had never gotten to use it because she moved in
instead with her friend Clement, who wasn't her boyfriend, just her
friend, and god, what a retard she was for saying that. Anyway, if Willem wanted the apartment, she'd throw in the futon for free.

Willem thanked her. "What do you think, JB?" he asked.

What did he think? He thought it was a shithole. Of course, he too
lived in a shithole, but he was in his shithole by choice, and because it
was free, and the money he would have had to spend on rent he was
instead able to spend on paints, and supplies, and drugs, and the occasional taxi. But if Ezra were to ever decide to start charging him rent,
no way would he be there. His family may not have Ezra's money, or
Malcolm's, but under no circumstances would they allow him to throw
away money living in a shithole. They would find him something better, or give him a little monthly gift to help him along. But Willem and
Jude didn't have that choice: They had to pay their own way, and they
had no money, and thus they were condemned to live in a shithole. And
if they were, then this was probably the shithole to live in—it was cheap,
it was downtown, and their prospective landlord already had a crush on
fifty percent of them.

So "I think it's perfect," he told Willem, who agreed. Annika let
out a yelp. And a hurried conversation later, it was over: Annika had
a tenant, and Willem and Jude had a place to live—all before JB had
to remind Willem that he wouldn't mind Willem paying for a bowl of
noodles for lunch, before he had to get back to the office.

—

JB wasn't given to introspection, but as he rode the train to his
mother's house that Sunday, he was unable to keep himself from expe-

riencing a vague sort of self-congratulation, combined with something approaching gratitude, that he had the life and family he did.

His father, who had emigrated to New York from Haiti, had died when JB was three, and although JB always liked to think that he remembered his face—kind and gentle, with a narrow strip of mustache and cheeks that rounded into plums when he smiled—he was never to know whether he only thought he remembered it, having grown up studying the photograph of his father that sat on his mother's bedside table, or whether he actually did. Still, that had been his only sadness as a child, and even that was more of an obligatory sadness: He was fatherless, and he knew that fatherless children mourned the absence in their lives. He, however, had never experienced that yearning himself. After his father had died, his mother, who was a second-generation Haitian American, had earned her doctorate in education, teaching all the while at the public school near their house that she had deemed JB better than. By the time he was in high school, an expensive private day school nearly an hour's commute from their place in Brooklyn, which he attended on scholarship, she was the principal of a different school, a magnet program in Manhattan, and an adjunct professor at Brooklyn College. She had been the subject of an article in *The New York Times* for her innovative teaching methods, and although he had pretended otherwise to his friends, he had been proud of her.

She had always been busy when he was growing up, but he had never felt neglected, had never felt that his mother loved her students more than she loved him. At home, there was his grandmother, who cooked whatever he wanted, and sang to him in French, and told him literally daily what a treasure he was, what a genius, and how he was the man in her life. And there were his aunts, his mother's sister, a detective in Manhattan, and her girlfriend, a pharmacist and second-generation American herself (although she was from Puerto Rico, not Haiti), who had no children and so treated him as their own. His mother's sister was sporty and taught him how to catch and throw a ball (something that, even then, he had only the slightest of interest in, but which proved to be a useful social skill later on), and her girlfriend was interested in art; one of his earliest memories had been a trip with her to the Museum of Modern Art, where he clearly remembered staring at *One: Number 31, 1950*, dumb with awe, barely listening to his aunt as she explained how Pollock had made the painting.

In high school, where a bit of revisionism seemed necessary in order to distinguish himself and, especially, make his rich white classmates uncomfortable, he blurred the truth of his circumstances somewhat: He became another fatherless black boy, with a mother who had completed school only after he was born (he neglected to mention that it was graduate school she had been completing, and so people assumed that he meant high school), and an aunt who walked the streets (again, they assumed as a prostitute, not realizing he meant as a detective). His favorite family photograph had been taken by his best friend in high school, a boy named Daniel, to whom he had revealed the truth just before he let him in to shoot their family portrait. Daniel had been working on a series of, as he called it, families "up from the edge," and JB had had to hurriedly correct the perception that his aunt was a borderline streetwalker and his mother barely literate before he allowed his friend inside. Daniel's mouth had opened and no sound had emerged, but then JB's mother had come to the door and told them both to get in out of the cold, and Daniel had to obey.

Daniel, still stunned, positioned them in the living room: JB's grandmother, Yvette, sat in her favorite high-backed chair, and around her stood his aunt Christine and her girlfriend, Silvia, to one side, and JB and his mother to the other. But then, just before Daniel could take the picture, Yvette demanded that JB take her place. "He is the king of the house," she told Daniel, as her daughters protested. "Jean-Baptiste! Sit down!" He did. In the picture, he is gripping both of the armrests with his plump hands (even then he had been plump), while on either side, women beamed down at him. He himself is looking directly at the camera, smiling widely, sitting in the chair that should have been occupied by his grandmother.

Their faith in him, in his ultimate triumph, remained unwavering, almost disconcertingly so. They were convinced—even as his own conviction was tested so many times that it was becoming difficult to self-generate it—that he would someday be an important artist, that his work would hang in major museums, that the people who hadn't yet given him his chances didn't properly appreciate his gift. Sometimes he believed them and allowed himself to be buoyed by their confidence. At other times he was suspicious—their opinions seemed so the complete opposite of the rest of the world's that he wondered whether they might be condescending to him, or just crazy. Or maybe they had bad taste. How could four women's judgment differ so profoundly from everyone else's? Surely the odds of theirs being the correct opinion were not good.

And yet he was relieved to return every Sunday on these secret visits back home, where the food was plentiful and free, and where his grandmother would do his laundry, and where every word he spoke and every sketch he showed would be savored and murmured about approvingly. His mother's house was a familiar land, a place where he would always be revered, where every custom and tradition felt tailored to him and his particular needs. At some point in the evening—after dinner but before dessert, while they all rested in the living room, watching television, his mother's cat lying hotly in his lap—he would look at his women and feel something swell within him. He would think then of Malcolm, with his unsparingly intelligent father and affectionate but absentminded mother, and then of Willem, with his dead parents (JB had met them only once, over their freshman year move-out weekend, and had been surprised by how taciturn, how formal, how *un-Willem* they had been), and finally, of course, Jude, with his completely nonexistent parents (a mystery, there—they had known Jude for almost a decade now and still weren't certain when or if there had ever been parents at all, only that the situation was miserable and not to be spoken of), and feel a warm, watery rush of happiness and thankfulness, as if an ocean were rising up in his chest. I'm lucky, he'd think, and then, because he was competitive and kept track of where he stood against his peers in every aspect of life, I'm the luckiest one of all. But he never thought that he didn't deserve it, or that he should work harder to express his appreciation; his family was happy when he was happy, and so his only obligation to them was to be happy, to live exactly the life he wanted, on the terms he wanted.

"We don't get the families we deserve," Willem had said once when they had been very stoned. He was, of course, speaking of Jude.

"I agree," JB had replied. And he did. None of them—not Willem, not Jude, not even Malcolm—had the families they deserved. But secretly, he made an exception for himself: He *did* have the family he deserved. They were wonderful, truly wonderful, and he knew it. And what's more, he *did* deserve them.

"There's my brilliant boy," Yvette would call out whenever he walked into the house.

It had never had to occur to him that she was anything but completely correct.

———

The day of the move, the elevator broke.

"Goddammit," Willem said. "I *asked* Annika about this. JB, do you
have her number?"

But JB didn't. "Oh well," said Willem. What good would texting
Annika do, anyway? "I'm sorry, guys," he said to everyone, "we're going
to have to take the stairs."

No one seemed to mind. It was a beautiful late-fall day, just-cold
and dry and blustery, and there were eight of them to move not very
many boxes and only a few pieces of furniture—Willem and JB and
Jude and Malcolm and JB's friend Richard and Willem's friend Carolina and two friends of the four of theirs in common who were both
named Henry Young, but whom everyone called Asian Henry Young
and Black Henry Young in order to distinguish them.

Malcolm, who when you least expected it would prove himself
an efficient manager, made the assignments. Jude would go up to the
apartment and direct traffic and the placement of boxes. In between
directing traffic, he would start unpacking the large items and breaking down the boxes. Carolina and Black Henry Young, who were both
strong but short, would carry the boxes of books, since those were of a
manageable size. Willem and JB and Richard would carry the furniture. And he and Asian Henry Young would take everything else. On
every trip back downstairs, everyone should take down any boxes that
Jude had flattened and stack them on the curb near the trash cans.

"Do you need help?" Willem asked Jude quietly as everyone began
dividing up for their assignments.

"No," he said, shortly, and Willem watched him make his halting,
slow-stepping way up the stairs, which were very steep and high, until
he could no longer see him.

It was an easy move-in, brisk and undramatic, and after they'd all
hung around for a bit, unpacking books and eating pizza, the others
took off, to parties and bars, and Willem and Jude were finally left
alone in their new apartment. The space was a mess, but the thought
of putting things in their place was simply too tiring. And so they lin-

gered, surprised by how dark the afternoon had grown so quickly, and that they had someplace to live, someplace in Manhattan, someplace they could afford. They had both noticed the looks of politely maintained blankness on their friends' faces as they saw their apartment for the first time (the room with its two narrow twin beds—"Like something out of a Victorian asylum" was how Willem had described it to Jude—had gotten the most comments), but neither of them minded: it was theirs, and they had a two-year lease, and no one could take it away from them. Here, they would even be able to save a little money, and what did they need more space for, anyway? Of course, they both craved beauty, but that would have to wait. Or rather, they would have to wait for it.

They were talking, but Jude's eyes were closed, and Willem knew— from the constant, hummingbird-flutter of his eyelids and the way his hand was curled into a fist so tight that Willem could see the ocean-green threads of his veins jumping under the back of his hand—that he was in pain. He knew from how rigid Jude was holding his legs, which were resting atop a box of books, that the pain was severe, and knew too that there was nothing he could do for him. If he said, "Jude, let me get you some aspirin," Jude would say, "I'm fine, Willem, I don't need anything," and if he said, "Jude, why don't you lie down," Jude would say, "Willem. I'm *fine*. Stop worrying." So finally, he did what they had all learned over the years to do when Jude's legs were hurting him, which was to make some excuse, get up, and leave the room, so Jude could lie perfectly still and wait for the pain to pass without having to make conversation or expend energy pretending that everything was fine and that he was just tired, or had a cramp, or whatever feeble explanation he was able to invent.

In the bedroom, Willem found the garbage bag with their sheets and made up first his futon and then Jude's (which they had bought for very little from Carolina's soon-to-be ex-girlfriend the week before). He sorted his clothes into shirts, pants, and underwear and socks, assigning each its own cardboard box (newly emptied of books), which he shoved beneath the bed. He left Jude's clothes alone, but then moved into the bathroom, which he cleaned and disinfected before sorting and putting away their toothpaste and soaps and razors and shampoos. Once or twice he paused in his work to creep out to the living room, where Jude remained in the same position, his eyes still closed, his hand still balled, his head turned to the side so that Willem was unable to see his expression.

His feelings for Jude were complicated. He loved him—that part was simple—and feared for him, and sometimes felt as much his older brother and protector as his friend. He knew that Jude would be and had been fine without him, but he sometimes saw things in Jude that disturbed him and made him feel both helpless and, paradoxically, more determined to help him (although Jude rarely asked for help of any kind). They all loved Jude, and admired him, but he often felt that Jude had let him see a little more of him—just a little—than he had shown the others, and was unsure what he was supposed to do with that knowledge.

The pain in his legs, for example: as long as they had known him, they had known he had problems with his legs. It was hard not to know this, of course; he had used a cane through college, and when he had been younger—he was so young when they met him, a full two years younger than they, that he had still been growing—he had walked only with the aid of an orthopedic crutch, and had worn heavily strapped splint-like braces on his legs whose external pins, which were drilled into his bones, impaired his ability to bend his knees. But he had never complained, not once, although he had never begrudged anyone else's complaining, either; their sophomore year, JB had slipped on some ice and fallen and broken his wrist, and they all remembered the hub-bub that had followed, and JB's theatrical moans and cries of misery, and how for a whole week after his cast was set he refused to leave the university infirmary, and had received so many visitors that the school newspaper had written a story about him. There was another guy in their dorm, a soccer player who had torn his meniscus and who kept saying that JB didn't know what pain was, but Jude had gone to visit JB every day, just as Willem and Malcolm had, and had given him all the sympathy he had craved.

One night shortly after JB had deigned to be discharged from the clinic and had returned to the dorm to enjoy another round of attention, Willem had woken to find the room empty. This wasn't so unusual, really: JB was at his boyfriend's, and Malcolm, who was tak-ing an astronomy class at Harvard that semester, was in the lab where he now slept every Tuesday and Thursday nights. Willem himself was often elsewhere, usually in his girlfriend's room, but she had the flu and he had stayed home that night. But Jude was always there. He had never had a girlfriend or a boyfriend, and he had always spent the night in their room, his presence beneath Willem's bunk as familiar and constant as the sea.

He wasn't sure what compelled him to climb down from his bed and stand for a minute, dopily, in the center of the quiet room, looking about him as if Jude might be hanging from the ceiling like a spider. But then he noticed his crutch was gone, and he began to look for him, calling his name softly in the common room, and then, when he got no answer, leaving their suite and walking down the hall toward the communal bathroom. After the dark of their room, the bathroom was nauseously bright, its fluorescent lights emitting their faint continual sizzle, and he was so disoriented that it came as less of a surprise than it should have when he saw, in the last stall, Jude's foot sticking out from beneath the door, the tip of his crutch beside it.

"Jude?" he whispered, knocking on the stall door, and when there was no answer, "I'm coming in." He pulled open the door and found Jude on the floor, one leg tucked up against his chest. He had vomited, and some of it had pooled on the ground before him, and some of it was scabbed on his lips and chin, a stippled apricot smear. His eyes were shut and he was sweaty, and with one hand he was holding the curved end of his crutch with an intensity that, as Willem would later come to recognize, comes only with extreme discomfort.

At the time, though, he was scared, and confused, and began asking Jude question after question, none of which he was in any state to answer, and it wasn't until he tried to hoist Jude to his feet that Jude gave a shout and Willem understood how bad his pain was.

He somehow managed to half drag, half carry Jude to their room, and fold him into his bed and inexpertly clean him up. By this time the worst of the pain seemed to have passed, and when Willem asked him if he should call a doctor, Jude shook his head.

"But Jude," he said, quietly, "you're in pain. We have to get you help."

"Nothing will help," he said, and was silent for a few moments. "I just have to wait." His voice was whispery and faint, unfamiliar.

"What can I do?" Willem asked.

"Nothing," Jude said. They were quiet. "But Willem—will you stay with me for a little while?"

"Of course," he said. Beside him, Jude trembled and shook as if chilled, and Willem took the comforter off his own bed and wrapped it around him. At one point he reached under the blanket and found Jude's hand and prised open his fist so he could hold his damp, callused palm. It had been a long time since he had held another guy's hand—not since his own brother's surgery many years ago—and he was surprised by how strong Jude's grip was, how muscular his fingers. Jude shuddered and chattered his teeth for hours, and eventually Willem lay down beside him and fell asleep.

The next morning, he woke in Jude's bed with his hand throbbing, and when he examined the back of it he saw bruised smudges where Jude's fingers had clenched him. He got up, a bit unsteadily, and walked into the common area, where he saw Jude reading at his desk, his features indistinguishable in the bright late-morning light.

He looked up when Willem came in and then stood, and for a while they merely looked at each other in silence.

"Willem, I'm so sorry," Jude said at last.

"Jude," he said, "there's nothing to be sorry for." And he meant it; there wasn't.

But "I'm sorry, Willem, I'm so sorry," Jude repeated, and no matter how many times Willem tried to reassure him, he wouldn't be comforted.

"Just don't tell Malcolm and JB, okay?" he asked him.

"I won't," he promised. And he never did, although in the end, it didn't make a difference, for eventually, Malcolm and JB too would see him in pain, although only a few times in episodes as sustained as the one Willem witnessed that night.

He had never discussed it with Jude, but in the years to come, he would see him in all sorts of pain, big pains and little ones, would see him wince at small hurts and occasionally, when the discomfort was too profound, would see him vomit, or pleat to the ground, or simply blank out and become insensate, the way he was doing in their living room now. But although he was a man who kept his promises, there was a part of him that always wondered why he had never raised the issue with Jude, why he had never made him discuss what it felt like, why he had never dared to do what instinct told him to do a hundred times: to sit down beside him and rub his legs, to try to knead back into submission those misfiring nerve endings. Instead here he was hiding in the bathroom, making busywork for himself as, a few yards away, one of his dearest friends sat alone on a disgusting sofa, making the slow, sad, lonely journey back to consciousness, back to the land of the living, without anyone at all by his side.

"You're a coward," he said to his reflection in the bathroom mirror. His face looked back at him, tired with disgust. From the living room, there was only silence, but Willem moved to stand unseen at its border, waiting for Jude to return to him.

—

"The place is a shithole," JB had told Malcolm, and although he wasn't wrong—the lobby alone made Malcolm's skin prickle—he nevertheless returned home feeling melancholy, and wondering yet again whether continuing to live in his parents' house was really preferable to living in a shithole of his own.

Logically, of course, he should absolutely stay where he was. He made very little money, and worked very long hours, and his parents' house was large enough so that he could, in theory, never see them if he chose. Aside from occupying the entire fourth floor (which, to be honest, wasn't much better than a shithole itself, it was so messy—his mother had stopped sending the housekeeper up to clean after Malcolm had yelled at her that Inez had broken one of his model houses), he had access to the kitchen, and the washing machine, and the full spectrum of papers and magazines that his parents subscribed to, and once a week he added his clothes to the drooping cloth bag that his mother dropped off at the dry cleaners on the way to her office and Inez picked up the following day. He was not proud of this arrangement, of course, nor of the fact that he was twenty-seven and his mother still called him at the office when she was ordering the week's groceries to ask him if he would eat extra strawberries if she bought them, or to wonder whether he wanted char or bream for dinner that night.

Things would be easier, however, if his parents actually respected the same divisions of space and time that Malcolm did. Aside from expecting him to eat breakfast with them in the morning and brunch every Sunday, they also frequently dropped by his floor for a visit, preceding their social calls with a simultaneous knock and doorknob-turn that Malcolm had told them time and again defeated the purpose of knocking at all. He knew this was a terribly bratty and ungrateful thing to think, but at times he dreaded even coming home for the inevitable small talk that he would have to endure before he was allowed to scruff upstairs like a teenager. He especially dreaded life in the house without Jude there; although the basement apartment had been more private than his floor, his parents had also taken to blithely dropping by when Jude was in residence, so that sometimes when Malcolm went downstairs to see Jude, there would be his father sitting in the basement apartment already, lecturing Jude about something dull. His father in particular liked Jude—he often told Malcolm that Jude had real intellectual heft and depth, unlike his other friends, who were essentially flibbertigibbets—and in his absence, it would be Malcolm whom his father would regale with his complicated stories about the market, and the shifting global financial realities, and various other topics about which Malcolm didn't much care. He in fact sometimes suspected that his father would have preferred Jude for a son: He and Jude had gone to the same law school. The judge for whom Jude had clerked had been his father's mentor at his first firm. And Jude was an assistant prosecutor in the criminal division of the U.S. Attorney's Office, the exact same place his father had worked at when he was young.

"Mark my words: that kid is going places," or "It's so rare to meet someone who's going to be a truly self-made star at the start of their career," his father would often announce to Malcolm and his mother after talking to Jude, looking pleased with himself, as if he was somehow responsible for Jude's genius, and in those moments Malcolm would have to avoid looking at his mother's face and the consoling expression he knew it wore.

Things would also be easier if Flora were still around. When she was preparing to leave, Malcolm had tried to suggest that he should be her roommate in her new two-bedroom apartment on Bethune Street, but she either genuinely didn't understand his numerous hints or simply chose not to understand them. Flora had not seemed to mind the excessive amount of time their parents demanded from them, which had meant that he could spend more time in his room working on his model houses and less time downstairs in the den, fidgeting through one of his father's interminable Ozu film festivals. When he was younger, Malcolm had been hurt by and resentful of his father's preference for Flora, which was so obvious that family friends had commented on it.

"Fabulous Flora," his father called her (or, at various points of her adolescence, "Feisty Flora," "Ferocious Flora," or "Fierce Flora," though
always with approval), and even today—even though Flora was practically thirty—he still took a special pleasure in her. "Fabulous said the
wittiest thing today," he'd say at dinner, as if Malcolm and his mother
did not themselves talk to Flora on a regular basis, or, after a brunch
downtown near Flora's apartment, "Why did Fabulous have to move
so far from us?" even though she was only a fifteen-minute car ride
away. (Malcolm found this particularly galling, as his father was always
telling him brocaded stories about how he had moved from the Grena-
dines to Queens as a child and how he had forever after felt like a man
trapped between two countries, and someday Malcolm too should go
be an expat somewhere because it would really enrich him as a person
and give him some much-needed perspective, etc., etc. And yet if Flora
ever dared move off the island, much less to another country, Malcolm
had no doubt that his father would fall apart.)

    Malcolm himself had no nickname. Occasionally his father called
him by other famous Malcolms' last names—"X," or "McLaren," or
"McDowell," or "Muggeridge," the last for whom Malcolm was supposedly named—but it always felt less like an affectionate gesture and
more like a rebuke, a reminder of what Malcolm should be but clearly
was not.

    Sometimes—often—it seemed to Malcolm that it was silly for him
to still worry, much less mope, about the fact that his father didn't seem
to like him very much. Even his mother said so. "You know Daddy
doesn't mean anything by it," she'd say once in a while, after his father
had delivered one of his soliloquies on Flora's general superiority, and
Malcolm—wanting to believe her, though also noting with irritation
that his mother still referred to his father as "Daddy"—would grunt or
mumble something to show her that he didn't care one way or another.
And sometimes—again, increasingly often—he would grow irritated
that he spent so much time thinking about his parents at all. Was this
normal? Wasn't there something just a bit pathetic about it? He was
twenty-seven, after all! Was this what happened when you lived at
home? Or was it just him? Surely this was the best possible argument
for moving out: so he'd somehow cease to be such a child. At night, as
beneath him his parents completed their routines, the banging of the
old pipes as they washed their faces and the sudden thunk into silence

as they turned down the living-room radiators better than any clock at indicating that it was eleven, eleven thirty, midnight, he made lists of what he needed to resolve, and fast, in the following year: his work (at a standstill), his love life (nonexistent), his sexuality (unresolved), his future (uncertain). The four items were always the same, although sometimes their order of priority changed. Also consistent was his ability to precisely diagnose their status, coupled with his utter inability to provide any solutions.

The next morning he'd wake determined: today he was going to move out and tell his parents to leave him alone. But when he'd get downstairs, there would be his mother, making him breakfast (his father long gone for work) and telling him that she was buying the tickets for their annual trip to St. Barts today, and could he let her know how many days he wanted to join them for? (His parents still paid for his vacations. He knew better than to ever mention this to his friends.)

"Yes, Ma," he'd say. And then he'd eat his breakfast and leave for the day, stepping out into the world in which no one knew him, and in which he could be anyone.

2

AT FIVE P.M. every weekday and at eleven a.m. every weekend, JB got on the subway and headed for his studio in Long Island City. The weekday journey was his favorite: He'd board at Canal and watch the train fill and empty at each stop with an ever-shifting mix of different peoples and ethnicities, the car's population reconstituting itself every ten blocks or so into provocative and improbable constellations of Poles, Chinese, Koreans, Senegalese; Senegalese, Dominicans, Indians, Pakistanis; Pakistanis, Irish, Salvadorans, Mexicans; Mexicans, Sri Lankans, Nigerians, and Tibetans—the only thing uniting them being their newness to America and their identical expressions of exhaustion, that blend of determination and resignation that only the immigrant possesses.

In these moments, he was both grateful for his own luck and sentimental about his city, neither of which he felt very often. He was not someone who celebrated his hometown as a glorious mosaic, and he made fun of people who did. But he admired—how could you not?— the collective amount of labor, *real* labor, that his trainmates had no doubt accomplished that day. And yet instead of feeling ashamed of his relative indolence, he was relieved.

The only other person he had ever discussed this sensation with, however elliptically, was Asian Henry Young. They had been riding out to Long Island City—it had been Henry who'd found him space in the studio, actually—when a Chinese man, slight and tendony and carrying a persimmon-red plastic bag that sagged heavily from the crook of the last joint of his right index finger, as if he had no strength or will left to carry it any more declaratively, stepped on and slumped into the seat across from them, crossing his legs and folding his arms around himself and falling asleep at once. Henry, whom he'd known since high school and was, like him, a scholarship kid, and was the son of a seamstress in Chinatown, had looked at JB and mouthed, "There but for the grace of god," and JB had understood exactly the particular mix of guilt and pleasure he felt.

The other aspect of those weekday-evening trips he loved was the light itself, how it filled the train like something living as the cars rattled across the bridge, how it washed the weariness from his seat-mates' faces and revealed them as they were when they first came to the country, when they were young and America seemed conquerable. He'd watch that kind light suffuse the car like syrup, watch it smudge furrows from foreheads, slick gray hairs into gold, gentle the aggressive shine from cheap fabrics into something lustrous and fine. And then the sun would drift, the car rattling uncaringly away from it, and the world would return to its normal sad shapes and colors, the people to their normal sad state, a shift as cruel and abrupt as if it had been made by a sorcerer's wand.

He liked to pretend he was one of them, but he knew he was not. Sometimes there would be Haitians on the train, and he—his hearing, suddenly wolflike, distinguishing from the murmur around him the slurpy, singy sound of their Creole—would find himself looking toward them, to the two men with round faces like his father's, or to the two women with soft snubbed noses like his mother's. He always hoped that he might be presented with a completely organic reason to speak to them—maybe they'd be arguing about directions somewhere, and he might be able to insert himself and provide the answer—but there never was. Sometimes they would let their eyes scan across the seats, still talking to each other, and he would tense, ready his face to smile, but they never seemed to recognize him as one of their own.

Which he wasn't, of course. Even he knew he had more in common with Asian Henry Young, with Malcolm, with Willem, or even with Jude, than he had with them. Just look at him: at Court Square he disembarked and walked the three blocks to the former bottle factory where he now shared studio space with three other people. Did *real* Haitians have studio space? Would it even occur to *real* Haitians to leave their large rent-free apartment, where they could have theoreti-cally carved out their own corner to paint and doodle, only to get on a subway and travel half an hour (think how much work could be accom-plished in those thirty minutes!) to a sunny dirty space? No, of course not. To conceive of such a luxury, you needed an American mind.

The loft, which was on the third floor and accessed by a metal staircase that made bell-like rings whenever you stepped on it, was white-walled and white-floored, though the floors were so extravagantly splintered that in areas it looked like a shag rug had been laid down. There were tall old-fashioned casement windows punctuating every side, and these at least the four of them kept clean—each tenant was assigned one wall as his personal responsibility—because the light was too good to squander to dirt and was in fact the whole point of the space. There was a bathroom (unspeakable) and a kitchen (slightly less horrifying) and, standing in the exact center of the loft, a large slab of a table made from a piece of inferior marble placed atop three sawhorses. This was a common area, which anyone could use to work on a project that needed a little extra space, and over the months the marble had been streaked lilac and marigold and dropped with dots of precious cadmium red. Today the table was covered with long strips of various-colored hand-dyed organza, weighted down at either end with paper-backs, their tips fluttering in the ceiling fan's whisk. A tented card stood at its center: DRYING. DO NOT MOVE. WILL CLEAN UP FIRST THING TOM'W P.M. TX 4 PATIENCE, H.Y.

There were no walls subdividing the space, but it had been split into four equal sections of five hundred square feet each by electrical tape, the blue lines demarcating not just the floor but also the walls and ceiling above each artist's space. Everyone was hypervigilant about respecting one another's territory; you pretended not to hear what was going on in someone else's quarter, even if he was hissing to his girl-friend on his phone and you could of course hear every last word, and when you wanted to cross into someone's space, you stood at the edge of the blue tape and called his name once, softly, and then only if you saw that he wasn't deep in the zone, before asking permission to come over.

At five thirty, the light was perfect: buttery and dense and fat some-how, swelling the room as it had the train into something expansive and hopeful. He was the only one there. Richard, whose space was next to his, tended bar at nights and so spent his time at the studio in the morning, as did Ali, whose area he faced. That left Henry, whose space was diagonal from his and who usually arrived at seven, after he left his day job at the gallery. He took off his jacket, which he threw into his corner, uncovered his canvas, and sat on the stool before it, sighing.

This was JB's fifth month in the studio, and he loved it, loved it more than he thought he would. He liked the fact that his studiomates were all real, serious artists; he could never have worked in Ezra's place, not only because he believed what his favorite professor had once told him—that you should never paint where you fucked—but because to work in Ezra's was to be constantly surrounded and interrupted by dilettantes. There, art was something that was just an accessory to a lifestyle. You painted or sculpted or made crappy installation pieces because it justified a wardrobe of washed-soft T-shirts and dirty jeans and a diet of ironic cheap American beers and ironic expensive hand-rolled American cigarettes. Here, however, you made art because it was the only thing you'd ever been good at, the only thing, really, you thought about between shorter bursts of thinking about the things everyone thought about: sex and food and sleep and friends and money and fame. But somewhere inside you, whether you were making out with someone in a bar or having dinner with your friends, was always your canvas, its shapes and possibilities floating embryonically behind your pupils. There was a period—or at least you hoped there was—with every painting or project when the life of that painting became more real to you than your everyday life, when you sat wherever you were and thought only of returning to the studio, when you were barely conscious that you had tapped out a hill of salt onto the dinner table and in it were drawing your plots and patterns and plans, the white grains moving under your fingertip like silt.

He liked too the specific and unexpected companionability of the place. There were times on the weekends when everyone was there at the same time, and at moments, he would emerge from the fog of his painting and sense that all of them were breathing in rhythm, panting almost, from the effort of concentrating. He could feel, then, the collective energy they were expending filling the air like gas, flammable and sweet, and would wish he could bottle it so that he might be able to draw from it when he was feeling uninspired, for the days in which he would sit in front of the canvas for literally hours, as though if he stared long enough, it might explode into something brilliant and charged.

He liked the ceremony of waiting at the edge of the blue tape and clearing his throat in Richard's direction, and then crossing over the boundary to look at his work, the two of them standing before it in silence, needing to exchange only the fewest of words yet understanding exactly what the other meant. You spent so much time *explaining* yourself, your work, to others—what it meant, what you were trying to accomplish, why you were trying to accomplish it, why you had chosen the colors and subject matter and materials and application and technique that you had—that it was a relief to simply be with another person to whom you didn't have to explain anything: you could just look and look, and when you asked questions, they were usually blunt and technical and literal. You could be discussing engines, or plumbing: a matter both mechanical and straightforward, for which there were only one or two possible answers.

They all worked in different mediums, so there was no competition, no fear of one video artist finding representation before his studiomate, and less fear that a curator would come in to look at your work and fall in love with your neighbor's instead. And yet—and this was important—he respected everyone else's work as well. Henry made what he called deconstructed sculptures, strange and elaborate ikebana arrangements of flowers and branches fashioned from various kinds of silk. After he'd finish a piece, though, he'd remove its chicken-wire buttressing, so that the sculpture fell to the ground as a flat object and appeared as an abstract puddle of colors—only Henry knew what it looked like as a three-dimensional object.

Ali was a photographer who was working on a series called "The History of Asians in America," for which he created a photograph to represent every decade of Asians in America since 1890. For each image, he made a different diorama representing an epochal event or theme in one of the three-foot-square pine boxes that Richard had built for him, which he populated with little plastic figures he bought at the craft store and painted, and trees and roads that he glazed from potter's clay, and backdrops he rendered with a brush whose bristles were so fine they resembled eyelashes. He then shot the dioramas and made C-prints. Of the four of them, only Ali was represented, and he had a show in seven months about which the other three knew never to ask because any mention of it made him start bleating with anxiety. Ali wasn't progressing in historical order—he had the two thousands done (a stretch of lower Broadway thick with couples, all of whom were white men and, walking just a few steps behind them, Asian women), and the nineteen-eighties (a tiny Chinese man being beaten by two tiny white thugs with wrenches, the bottom of the box greased with varnish to resemble a parking lot's rain-glossed tarmac), and was currently working on the nineteen-forties, for which he was painting a cast of fifty men, women, and children who were meant to be prisoners in the Tule Lake internment camp. Ali's work was the most laborious of all of theirs, and sometimes, when they were procrastinating on their own projects, they would wander into Ali's cube and sit next to him, and Ali, barely lifting his head from the magnifying mirror under which he held a three-inch figure on whom he was painting a herringbone skirt and saddle shoes, would hand them a snarl of steel wool that he needed shredded to resemble tumbleweeds, or some fine-gauge wire that he wanted punctuated with little ties so that it would look barbed.

But it was Richard's work that JB admired the most. He was a sculptor too, but worked with only ephemeral materials. He'd draw on drafting paper impossible shapes, and then render them in ice, in butter, in chocolate, in lard, and film them as they vanished. He was gleeful about witnessing the disintegration of his works, but JB, watching just last month as a massive, eight-foot-tall piece Richard had made—a swooping sail-like batwing of frozen grape juice that resembled coagulated blood—dripped and then crumbled to its demise, had found himself unexpectedly about to cry, though whether from the destruction of something so beautiful or the mere everyday profundity of its disappearance, he was unable to say. Now Richard was less interested in substances that melted and more interested in substances that would attract decimators; he was particularly interested in moths, which apparently loved honey. He had a vision, he told JB, of a sculpture whose surface so writhed with moths that you couldn't even see the shape of the thing they were devouring. The sills of his windows were lined with jars of honey, in which the porous combs floated like fetuses suspended in formaldehyde.

JB was the lone classicist among them. He painted. Worse, he was a figurative painter. When he had been in graduate school, no one really cared about figurative work: anything—video art, performance art, photography—was more exciting than painting, and truly *anything* was better than figurative work. "That's the way it's been since the nineteen-fifties," one of his professors had sighed when JB complained to him. "You know that slogan for the marines? 'The few, the brave . . .'? That's us, we lonely losers."

It was not as if, over the years, he hadn't attempted other things, other mediums (that stupid, fake, derivative Meret Oppenheim hair project! Could he have done anything cheaper? He and Malcolm had gotten into a huge fight, one of their biggest, when Malcolm had called the series "ersatz Lorna Simpson," and of course the worst thing was that Malcolm had been completely right), but although he would never have admitted to anyone else that he felt there was something effete, girlish almost and at any rate certainly not gangster, about being a figurative painter, he had recently had to accept that it was what he was: he loved paint, and he loved portraiture, and that was what he was going to do.

So: Then what? He had known people—he *knew* people—who were, technically, much better artists than he was. They were better draftsmen, they had better senses of composition and color, they were more disciplined. But they didn't have any ideas. An artist, as much as a writer or composer, needed themes, needed ideas. And for a long time, he simply didn't have any. He tried to draw only black people, but a lot of people drew black people, and he didn't feel he had anything new to add. He drew hustlers for a while, but that too grew dull. He drew his female relatives, but found himself coming back to the black problem. He began a series of scenes from Tintin books, with the characters portrayed realistically, as humans, but it soon felt too ironic and hollow, and he stopped. So he lazed from canvas to canvas, doing paintings of people on the street, of people on the subway, of scenes from Ezra's many parties (these were the least successful; everyone at those gatherings were the sort who dressed and moved as if they were constantly being observed, and he ended up with pages of studies of posing girls and preening guys, all of their eyes carefully averted from his gaze), until one night, he was sitting in Jude and Willem's depressing apartment on their depressing sofa, watching the two of them assemble dinner, negotiating their way through their miniature kitchen like a bustling lesbian couple. This had been one of the rare Sunday nights he wasn't at his mother's, because she and his grandmother and aunts were all on a tacky cruise in the Mediterranean that he had refused to go on. But he had grown accustomed to seeing people and having dinner—a real dinner—made for him on Sundays, and so had invited himself over to Jude and Willem's, both of whom he knew would be home because neither of them had any money to go out.

He had his sketch pad with him, as he always did, and when Jude sat down at the card table to chop onions (they had to do all their prep work on the table because there was no counter space in the kitchen), he began drawing him almost unthinkingly. From the kitchen came a great banging, and the smell of smoking olive oil, and when he went in to discover Willem whacking at a piece of butterflied chicken with the bottom of an omelet pan, his arm raised over the meat as if to spank it, his expression oddly peaceful, he drew him as well.

He wasn't sure, then, that he was really working toward anything, but the next weekend, when they all went out to Pho Viet Huong, he brought along one of Ali's old cameras and shot the three of them eating and then, later, walking up the street in the snow. They were moving particularly slowly in deference to Jude, because the sidewalks were slippery. He saw them lined up in the camera's viewfinder: Malcolm, Jude, and Willem, Malcolm and Willem on either side of Jude, close enough (he knew, having been in the position himself) to catch him if he skidded but not so close that Jude would suspect that they were anticipating his fall. They had never had a conversation that they would do this, he realized; they had simply begun it.

He took the picture. "What're you doing, JB?" asked Jude, at the same time as Malcolm complained, "Cut it out, JB."

The party that night was on Centre Street, in the loft of an acquaintance of theirs, a woman named Mirasol whose twin, Phaedra, they knew from college. Once inside, everyone dispersed into their different subgroups, and JB, after waving at Richard across the room and noting with irritation that Mirasol had provided a whole tableful of food, meaning that he'd just wasted fourteen dollars at Pho Viet Huong when he could've eaten here for free, found himself wandering toward where Jude was talking with Phaedra and some fat dude who might have been Phaedra's boyfriend and a skinny bearded guy he recognized as a friend of Jude's from work. Jude was perched on the back of one of the sofas, Phaedra next to him, and the two of them were looking up at the fat and skinny guys and all of them were laughing at something: He took the picture.

Normally at parties he grabbed or was grabbed by a group of people, and spent the night as the nuclei for a variety of three- or foursomes, bounding from one to the next, gathering the gossip, starting harm-less rumors, pretending to share confidences, getting others to tell him who they hated by divulging hatreds of his own. But this night, he trav-eled the room alert and purposeful and largely sober, taking pictures of his three friends as they moved in their own patterns, unaware that he was trailing them. At one point, a couple of hours in, he found them by the window with just one another, Jude saying something and the other two leaning in close to hear him, and then in the next moment, the three of them leaning back and all laughing, and although for a moment he felt both wistful and slightly jealous, he was also trium-phant, as he had gotten both shots. *Tonight, I am a camera,* he told himself, *and tomorrow I will be JB again.*

In a way, he had never enjoyed a party more, and no one seemed to notice his deliberate rovings except for Richard, who, as the four of them were leaving an hour later to go uptown (Malcolm's parents were in the country, and Malcolm thought he knew where his mother hid her weed), gave him an unexpectedly sweet old-man clap on the shoul-der. "Working on something?"

"I think so."

"Good for you."

The next day he sat at his computer looking at the night's images on the screen. The camera wasn't a great one, and it had hazed every picture with a smoky yellow light, which, along with his poor focusing skills, had made everyone warm and rich and slightly soft-edged, as if they had been shot through a tumblerful of whiskey. He stopped at a close-up of Willem's face, of him smiling at someone (a girl, no doubt) off camera, and at the one of Jude and Phaedra on the sofa: Jude was wearing a bright navy sweater that JB could never figure out belonged to him or to Willem, as both of them wore it so much, and Phaedra was wearing a wool dress the shade of port, and she was leaning her head toward his, and the dark of her hair made his look lighter, and the nubbly teal of the sofa beneath them made them both appear shining and jewel-like, their colors just-licked and glorious, their skin delicious. They were colors anyone would want to paint, and so he did, sketching out the scene first in his book in pencil, and then again on stiffer board in watercolors, and then finally on canvas in acrylics.

That had been four months ago, and he now had almost eleven

paintings completed—an astonishing output for him—all of scenes from his friends' lives. There was Willem waiting to audition, studying the script a final time, the sole of one boot pressed against the sticky red wall behind him; and Jude at a play, his face half shadowed, at the very second he smiled (getting that shot had almost gotten JB thrown out of the theater); Malcolm sitting stiffly on a sofa a few feet away from his father, his back straight and his hands clenching his knees, the two of them watching a Buñuel film on a television just out of frame. After some experimentation, he had settled on canvases the size of a standard C-print, twenty by twenty-four inches, all horizontally oriented, and which he imagined might someday be displayed in a long snaking single layer, one that would wrap itself around a gallery's walls, each image following the next as fluidly as cells in a film strip. The renderings were realistic, but photo-realistic; he had never replaced Ali's camera with a better one, and he tried to make each painting capture that gently fuzzed quality the camera gave everything, as if someone had patted away the top layer of clarity and left behind something kinder than the eye alone would see.

In his insecure moments, he sometimes worried the project was too fey, too inward—this was where having representation really helped, if only to remind you that *someone* liked your work, thought it important or at the very least beautiful—but he couldn't deny the pleasure he got from it, the sense of ownership and contentment. At times he missed being part of the pictures himself; here was a whole narrative of his friends' lives, his absence an enormous missing part, but he also enjoyed the godlike role he played. He got to see his friends differently, not as just appendages to his life but as distinct characters inhabiting their own stories; he felt sometimes that he was seeing them for the first time, even after so many years of knowing them.

About a month into the project, once he knew that this was what he was going to concentrate on, he'd of course had to explain to them why he kept following them around with a camera, shooting the mundane moments of their lives, and why it was crucial that they let him keep doing so and provide him with as much access as possible. They had been at dinner at a Vietnamese noodle shop on Orchard Street that they hoped might be a Pho Viet Huong successor, and after he'd made his speech—uncharacteristically nervous as he did so—they all found themselves looking toward Jude, who he'd known in advance would be the problem. The other two would agree, but that didn't help him. They all needed to say yes or it wouldn't work, and Jude was by far the most self-conscious among them; in college, he turned his head or blocked his face whenever anyone tried to take his picture, and whenever he had smiled or laughed, he had reflexively covered his mouth with his hand, a tic that the rest of them had found upsetting, and which he had only learned to stop doing in the past few years.

As he'd feared, Jude was suspicious. "What would this involve?" he kept asking, and JB, summoning all his patience, had to reassure him numerous times that of course his goal wasn't to humiliate or exploit him but only to chronicle in pictures the drip of all of their lives. The others said nothing, letting him do the work, and Jude finally consented, although he didn't sound too happy about it.

"How long is this going to go on for?" Jude asked.

"Forever, I hope." And he did. His one regret was that he hadn't begun earlier, back when they were all young.

On the way out, he walked with Jude. "Jude," he said quietly, so that the others couldn't hear him. "Anything that involves you—I'll let you see in advance. You veto it, and I'll never show it."

Jude looked at him. "Promise?"

"Swear to god."

He regretted his offer the instant he made it, for the truth was that Jude was his favorite of the three of them to paint: He was the most beautiful of them, with the most interesting face and the most unusual coloring, and he was the shyest, and so pictures of him always felt more precious than ones of the others.

The following Sunday when he was back at his mother's, he went through some of his boxes from college that he'd stored in his old bedroom, looking for a photograph he knew he had. Finally he found it: a picture of Jude from their first year that someone had taken and printed and which had somehow ended up in his possession. In it, Jude was standing in the living room of their suite, turned partway to the camera. His left arm was wrapped around his chest, so you could see the satiny starburst-shaped scar on the back of his hand, and in his right he was unconvincingly holding an unlit cigarette. He was wearing a blue-and-white-striped long-sleeved T-shirt that must not have been his, it was so big (although maybe it really was his; in those days, all of Jude's clothes were too big because, as it later emerged, he intentionally bought them oversized so he could wear them for the next few years, as he grew), and his hair, which he wore longish back then so he could hide behind it, fizzled off at his jawline. But the thing that JB had always remembered most about this photograph was the expression on Jude's face: a wariness that in those days he was never without. He hadn't looked at this picture in years, but doing so made him feel empty, for reasons he wasn't quite able to articulate.

This was the painting he was working on now, and for it he had broken form and changed to a forty-inch-square canvas. He had experimented for days to get right that precise shade of tricky, serpenty green for Jude's irises, and had redone the colors of his hair again and again before he was satisfied. It was a great painting, and he knew it, knew it absolutely the way you sometimes did, and he had no intention of ever showing it to Jude until it was hanging on a gallery wall somewhere and Jude would be powerless to do anything about it. He knew Jude would hate how fragile, how feminine, how vulnerable, how *young* it made him look, and knew too he would find lots of other imaginary things to hate about it as well, things JB couldn't even begin to anticipate because he wasn't a self-loathing nut job like Jude. But to him, it expressed everything about what he hoped this series would be: it was a love letter, it was a documentation, it was a saga, it was *his*. When he worked on this painting, he felt sometimes as if he were flying, as if the world of galleries and parties and other artists and ambitions had shrunk to a pinpoint beneath him, something so small he could kick it away from himself like a soccer ball, watch it spin off into some distant orbit that had nothing to do with him.

It was almost six. The light would change soon. For now, the space was still quiet around him, although distantly, he could hear the train rumbling by on its tracks. Before him, his canvas waited. And so he picked up his brush and began.

—

There was poetry on the subway. Above the rows of scooped-plastic seats, filling the empty display space between ads for dermatologists and companies that promised college degrees by mail, were long laminated sheets printed with poems: second-rate Stevens and third-rate Roethke and fourth-rate Lowell, verse meant to agitate no one, anger and beauty reduced to empty aphorisms.

Or so JB always said. He was against the poems. They had appeared when he was in junior high, and for the past fifteen years he had been complaining about them. "Instead of funding *real* art and *real* artists, they're giving money to a bunch of spinster librarians and cardigan fags to pick out this shit," he shouted at Willem over the screech of the F train's brakes. "And it's all this Edna St. Vincent Millay–type shit. Or it's actually good people they've neutered. And they're all white, have you noticed that? What the fuck is up with that?"

The following week, Willem saw a Langston Hughes poster and called JB to tell him. "Langston *Hughes*?!" JB groaned. "Let me guess— 'A Dream Deferred,' right? I knew it! That shit doesn't count. And anyway, if something really *did* explode, that shit'd be down in two seconds flat."

Opposite Willem that afternoon is a Thom Gunn poem: "Their relationship consisted / In discussing if it existed." Underneath, some-one has written in black marker, "Dont worry man I cant get no pussy either." He closes his eyes.

It's not promising that he's this tired and it's only four, his shift not even begun. He shouldn't have gone with JB to Brooklyn the previous night, but no one else would go with him, and JB claimed he owed him, because hadn't he accompanied Willem to his friend's horrible one-man show just last month?

So he'd gone, of course. "Whose band is this?" he'd asked as they waited on the platform. Willem's coat was too thin, and he'd lost one of his gloves, and as a result he had begun assuming a heat-conserving posture—arms wrapped around his chest, hands folded into his arm-pits, rocking back on his heels—whenever he was forced to stand still in the cold.

"Joseph's," said JB.

"Oh," he said. He had no idea who Joseph was. He admired JB's Felliniesque command of his vast social circle, in which everyone was a colorfully costumed extra, and he and Malcolm and Jude were crucial but still lowly accessories to his vision—key grips or second art directors—whom he regarded as tacitly responsible for keeping the entire endeavor grinding along.

"It's hard core," said JB pleasantly, as if that would help him place Joseph.

"What's this band called?"

"Okay, here's the thing," JB said, grinning. "It's called Smegma Cake 2."

"What?" he asked, laughing. "Smegma Cake 2? Why? What happened to Smegma Cake 1?"

"It got a staph infection," JB shouted over the noise of the train clattering into the station. An older woman standing near them scowled in their direction.

Unsurprisingly, Smegma Cake 2 wasn't very good. It wasn't even hard core, really; more ska-like, bouncy and meandering ("Something happened to their sound!" JB yelled into his ear during one of the more prolonged numbers, "Phantom Snatch 3000." "Yeah," he yelled back, "it sucks!"). Midway through the concert (each song seeming to last twenty minutes) he grew giddy, at both the absurdity of the band and the crammedness of the space, and began inexpertly moshing with JB, the two of them sproinging off their neighbors and bystanders until everyone was crashing into one another, but cheerfully, like a bunch of tipsy toddlers, JB catching him by the shoulders and the two of them laughing into each other's faces. It was in these moments that he loved JB completely, his ability and willingness to be wholly silly and frivolous, which he could never be with Malcolm or Jude—Malcolm because he was, for all his talk otherwise, interested in propriety, and Jude because he was serious.

Of course, this morning he had suffered. He woke in JB's corner of Ezra's loft, on JB's unmade mattress (nearby, on the floor, JB himself snored juicily into a pile of peaty-smelling laundry), unsure how, exactly, they'd gotten back over the bridge. Willem wasn't normally a drinker or a stoner, but around JB he occasionally found himself behaving otherwise. It had been a relief to return to Lispenard Street, its quiet and clean, the sunlight that baked his side of the bedroom hot and loafy between eleven a.m. and one p.m. already slanting through the window, Jude long gone for the day. He set his alarm and fell instantly asleep, waking with enough time only to shower and swallow an aspirin before hurrying to the train.

The restaurant where he worked had made its reputation on both its food—which was complicated without being challenging—and the consistency and approachability of its staff. At Ortolan they were taught to be warm but not familiar, accessible but not informal. "It's not Friendly's," his boss, Findlay, the restaurant's general manager, liked to say. "Smile, but don't tell people your name." There were lots of rules such as these at Ortolan: Women employees could wear their wedding rings, but no other jewelry. Men shouldn't wear their hair longer than the bottom of their earlobes. No nail polish. No more than two days' worth of beard. Mustaches were to be tolerated on a case-by-case basis, as were tattoos.

Willem had been a waiter at Ortolan for almost two years. Before Ortolan, he had worked the weekend brunch and weekday lunch shift at a loud and popular restaurant in Chelsea called Digits, where the customers (almost always men, almost always older: forty, at least) would ask him if he was on the menu, and then laugh, naughty and pleased with themselves, as if they were the first people to ever ask him that, instead of the eleventh or twelfth that shift alone. Even so, he always smiled and said, "Only as an appetizer," and they'd retort, "But I want an entrée," and he would smile again and they would tip him well at the end.

It had been a friend of his from graduate school, another actor named Roman, who'd recommended him to Findlay after he'd booked a recurring guest role on a soap opera and had quit. (He was conflicted about accepting the gig, he told Willem, but what could he do? It was too much money to refuse.) Willem had been glad for the referral, because besides its food and service, the other thing that Ortolan was known for—albeit among a much smaller group of people—was its flexible hours, especially if Findlay liked you. Findlay liked small flat-chested brunette women and all sorts of men as long as they were tall and thin and, it was rumored, not Asian. Sometimes Willem would stand on the edge of the kitchen and watch as mismatched pairs of tiny dark-haired waitresses and long skinny men circled through the main dining room, skating past one another in a weirdly cast series of minuets.

Not everyone who waited at Ortolan was an actor. Or to be more precise, not everyone at Ortolan was *still* an actor. There were certain restaurants in New York where one went from being an actor who waited tables to, somehow, being a waiter who was once an actor. And if the restaurant was good enough, respected enough, that was not only a perfectly acceptable career transition, it was a preferable one. A waiter at a well-regarded restaurant could get his friends a coveted reservation, could charm the kitchen staff into sending out free dishes to those same friends (though as Willem learned, charming the kitchen staff was less easy than he'd thought it would be). But what could an actor who waited tables get his friends? Tickets to yet another off-off-Broadway production for which you had to supply your own suit because you were playing a stockbroker who may or may not be a zombie, and yet there was no money for costumes? (He'd had to do exactly that last year, and because he didn't have a suit of his own, he'd had to borrow one of Jude's. Jude's legs were about an inch longer than his, and so for the duration of the run he'd had to fold the pants legs under and stick them in place with masking tape.)

It was easy to tell who at Ortolan was once an actor and was now a career waiter. The careerists were older, for one, and precise and fussy about enforcing Findlay's rules, and at staff dinners they would osten-tatiously swirl the wine that the sommelier's assistant poured them to sample and say things like, "It's a little like that Linne Calodo Petite Sirah you served last week, José, isn't it?" or "Tastes a little minerally, doesn't it? This a New Zealand?" It was understood that you didn't ask them to come to your productions—you only asked your fellow actor-waiters, and if you were asked, it was considered polite to at least try to go—and you certainly didn't discuss auditions, or agents, or anything of the sort with them. Acting was like war, and they were veterans: they didn't want to think about the war, and they certainly didn't want to talk about it with naïfs who were still eagerly dashing toward the trenches, who were still excited to be in-country.

Findlay himself was a former actor, but unlike the other former actors, he liked to—or perhaps "liked" was not the word; perhaps the more accurate word would be simply "did"—talk about his past life, or at least a certain version of it. According to Findlay, he had once almost, almost booked the second lead in the Public Theater produc-tion of *A Bright Room Called Day* (later, one of the waitresses had told them that all of the significant roles in the play were for women). He had understudied a part on Broadway (for what production was never made clear). Findlay was a walking career memento mori, a caution-ary tale in a gray wool suit, and the still-actors either avoided him, as if his particular curse were something contagious, or studied him closely, as if by remaining in contact with him, they could inoculate themselves.

But at what point had Findlay decided he would give up acting, and how had it happened? Was it simply age? He was, after all, old: forty-five, fifty, somewhere around there. How did you know that it was time to give up? Was it when you were thirty-eight and still hadn't found an agent (as they suspected had happened to Joel)? Was it when you were forty and still had a roommate and were making more as a part-time waiter than you had made the year you decided to be a full-time actor (as they knew had happened to Kevin)? Was it when you got fat, or bald, or got bad plastic surgery that couldn't disguise the fact that you were fat and bald? When did pursuing your ambitions cross the line from brave into foolhardy? How did you know when to stop? In earlier, more rigid, less encouraging (and ultimately, more helpful) decades, things would be much clearer: you would stop when you turned forty, or when you got married, or when you had kids, or after five years, or ten years, or fifteen. And then you would go get a real job, and acting and your dreams for a career in it would recede into the evening, a melting into history as quiet as a briquette of ice sliding into a warm bath.

But these were days of self-fulfillment, where settling for something that was not quite your first choice of a life seemed weak-willed and ignoble. Somewhere, surrendering to what seemed to be your fate had changed from being dignified to being a sign of your own cowardice. There were times when the pressure to achieve happiness felt almost oppressive, as if happiness were something that everyone should and could attain, and that any sort of compromise in its pursuit was some-how your fault. Would Willem work for year upon year at Ortolan, catching the same trains to auditions, reading again and again and again, one year maybe caterpillaring an inch or two forward, his prog-ress so minute that it hardly counted as progress at all? Would he some-day have the courage to give up, and would he be able to recognize that moment, or would he wake one day and look in the mirror and find himself an old man, still trying to call himself an actor because he was too scared to admit that he might not be, might never be?

According to JB, the reason Willem wasn't yet successful was because of Willem. One of JB's favorite lectures to him began with

"If I had your looks, Willem," and ended with, "And now you've been so fucking spoiled by things coming to you so easily that you think everything's just going to *happen* for you. And you know what, Willem? You're good-looking, but *everyone* here is good-looking, and you're just going to have to try harder."

Even though he thought this was sort of ironic coming from JB (Spoiled? Look at JB's family, all of them clucking after him, pushing on him his favorite foods and just-ironed shirts, surrounding him in a cloud of compliments and affection; he once overheard JB on the phone telling his mother he needed her to get him more underwear, and that he'd pick it up when he went to see her for Sunday dinner, for which, by the way, he wanted short ribs), he understood what he meant as well. He knew he wasn't lazy, but the truth was that he lacked the sort of ambition that JB and Jude had, that grim, trudging determination that kept them at the studio or office longer than anyone else, that gave them that slightly faraway look in their eyes that always made him think a fraction of them was already living in some imagined future, the contours of which were crystallized only to them. JB's ambition was fueled by a lust for that future, for his speedy arrival to it; Jude's, he thought, was motivated more by a fear that if he didn't move forward, he would somehow slip back to his past, the life he had left and about which he would tell none of them. And it wasn't only Jude and JB who possessed this quality: New York was populated by the ambitious. It was often the only thing that everyone here had in common.

Ambition and atheism: "Ambition is my only religion," JB had told him late one beery night, and although to Willem this line sounded a little too practiced, like he was rehearsing it, trying to perfect its careless, throwaway tone before he someday got to say it for real to an interviewer somewhere, he also knew that JB was sincere. Only here did you feel compelled to somehow justify anything short of rabidity for your career; only here did you have to apologize for having faith in something other than yourself.

The city often made him feel he was missing something essential, and that that ignorance would forever doom him to a life at Ortolan. (He had felt this in college as well, where he knew absolutely that he was the dumbest person in their class, admitted as a sort of unofficial poor-white-rural-dweller-oddity affirmative-action representative.) The others, he thought, sensed this as well, although it seemed to truly bother only JB.

"I don't know about you sometimes, Willem," JB once said to him, in a tone that suggested that what he didn't know about Willem wasn't good. This was late last year, shortly after Merritt, Willem's former roommate, had gotten one of the two lead roles in an off-Broadway revival of *True West*. The other lead was being played by an actor who had recently starred in an acclaimed independent film and was enjoying that brief moment of possessing both downtown credibility and the promise of more mainstream success. The director (someone Willem had been longing to work with) had promised he'd cast an unknown as the second lead. And he had: it was just that the unknown was Merritt and not Willem. The two of them had been the final contenders for the part.

His friends had been outraged on his behalf. "But Merritt doesn't even know how to act!" JB had groaned. "He just stands onstage and sparkles and thinks that's enough!" The three of them had started talking about the last thing they had seen Merritt in—an all-male off-off-Broadway production of *La Traviata* set in nineteen-eighties Fire Island (Violetta—played by Merritt—had been renamed Victor, and he had died of AIDS, not tuberculosis)—and they all agreed it had been barely watchable.

"Well, he *does* have a good look," he'd said, in a weak attempt to defend his absent former roommate.

"He's not *that* good-looking," Malcolm said, with a vehemence that surprised all of them.

"Willem, it'll happen," Jude consoled him on the way back home after dinner. "If there's any justice in the world, it'll happen. That director's an imbecile." But Jude never blamed Willem for his failings; JB always did. He wasn't sure which was less helpful.

He had been grateful for their anger, naturally, but the truth was, he didn't think Merritt was as bad as they did. He was certainly no worse than Willem himself; in fact, he was probably better. Later, he'd told this to JB, who responded with a long silence, stuffed with disapproval, before he started lecturing Willem. "I don't know about you sometimes, Willem," he began. "Sometimes I get the sense you don't even really want to be an actor."

"That's not true," he'd protested. "It's just that I don't think that every rejection is meaningless, and I don't think everyone who gets a job over me does so out of dumb luck."

There had been another silence. "You're too kind, Willem," JB said, darkly. "You're never going to get anywhere like this."

"Thanks, JB," he'd said. He was rarely offended by JB's opinions—often, he was right—but at that particular moment, he didn't much feel like hearing JB's thoughts on his shortcomings and his gloomy predictions about his future unless he completely changed his personality. He'd gotten off the phone and had lain in bed awake, feeling stuck and sorry for himself.

Anyway, changing his personality seemed basically out of the question—wasn't it too late? Before he was a kind man, after all, Willem had been a kind boy. Everyone had noticed: his teachers, his classmates, the parents of his classmates. "Willem is such a compassionate child," his teachers would write on his report cards, report cards his mother or father would look at once, briefly and wordlessly, before adding them to the stacks of newspapers and empty envelopes that they'd take to the recycling center. As he grew older, he had begun to realize that people were surprised, even upset, by his parents; a high-school teacher had once blurted to him that given Willem's temperament, he had thought his parents would be different.

"Different how?" he'd asked.

"Friendlier," his teacher had said.

He didn't think of himself as particularly generous or unusually good-spirited. Most things came easily to him: sports, school, friends, girls. He wasn't *nice*, necessarily; he didn't seek to be everyone's friend, and he couldn't tolerate boors, or pettiness, or meanness. He was humble and hardworking, diligent, he knew, rather than brilliant. "Know your place," his father often said to him.

His father did. Willem remembered once, after a late-spring freeze had killed off a number of new lambs in their area, his father being interviewed by a newspaper reporter who was writing a story about how it had affected the local farms.

"As a rancher," the reporter began, when Willem's father had stopped her.

"Not a rancher," he'd said, his accent making these words, as all words, sound brusquer than they should, "a ranch hand." He was correct, of course; a rancher meant something specific—a landowner—and by that definition, he wasn't a rancher. But there were plenty of other people in the county who then also had no right to call themselves ranchers and yet did so anyway. Willem had never heard his father say that they shouldn't—his father didn't care what anyone else did or didn't do—but such inflation was not for him, or for his wife, Willem's mother.

Perhaps because of this, he felt he always knew who and what he was, which is why, as he moved farther and then further away from the ranch and his childhood, he felt very little pressure to change or reinvent himself. He was a guest at his college, a guest in graduate school, and now he was a guest in New York, a guest in the lives of the beautiful and the rich. He would never try to pretend he was born to such things, because he knew he wasn't; he was a ranch hand's son from western Wyoming, and his leaving didn't mean that everything he had once been was erased, written over by time and experiences and the proximity to money.

He was his parents' fourth child, and the only one still alive. First there had been a girl, Britte, who had died of leukemia when she was two, long before Willem had been born. This had been in Sweden, when his father, who was Icelandic, had been working at a fish farm, where he had met his mother, who was Danish. Then there had been a move to America, and a boy, Hemming, who had been born with cerebral palsy. Three years later, there had been another boy, Aksel, who had died in his sleep as an infant for no apparent reason.

Hemming was eight when Willem was born. He couldn't walk or speak, but Willem had loved him and had never thought of him as anything but his older brother. Hemming could smile, however, and as he did, he'd bring his hand up toward his face, his fingers shaping themselves into a duck's bill claw, his lips pulling back from his azalea-pink gums. Willem learned to crawl, and then walk and run—Hemming remaining in his chair year after year—and when he was old and strong enough, he would push Hemming's heavy chair with its fat, stubborn tires (this was a chair meant to be sedentary, not to be nosed through grasses or down dirt roads) around the ranch where they lived with their parents in a small wooden house. Up the hill from them was the main house, long and low with a deep wraparound porch, and down the hill from them were the stables where their parents spent their days. He had been Hemming's primary caretaker, and companion, all through high school; in the mornings, he was the first one awake, making his parents' coffee and boiling water for Hemming's oatmeal, and in the evenings, he waited by the side of the road for the van that would drop his brother off after his day at the assisted-living center an hour's drive away. Willem always thought they clearly looked like brothers—they had their parents' light, bright hair, and their father's gray eyes, and both of them had a groove, like an elongated parentheses, bracketing the left side of their mouths that made them appear easily amused and ready to smile—but no one else seemed to notice this. They saw only that Hemming was in a wheelchair, and that his mouth remained open, a damp red ellipse, and that his eyes, more often than not, drifted skyward, fixed on some cloud only he could see.

"What do you see, Hemming?" he sometimes asked him, when they were out on their night walks, but of course Hemming never answered him.

Their parents were efficient and competent with Hemming, but not, he recognized, particularly affectionate. When Willem was kept late at school because of a football game, or a track meet, or when he was needed to work an extra shift at the grocery store, it was his mother who waited for Hemming at the end of the drive, who hefted Hemming into and then out of his bath, who fed him his dinner of chicken-and-rice porridge and changed his diaper before putting him to bed. But she didn't read to him, or talk to him, or go on walks with him the way Willem did. Watching his parents around Hemming bothered him, in part because although they never behaved objectionably, he could tell that they viewed Hemming as their responsibility but no more. Later he would argue with himself that that was all that could reasonably be expected of them; anything else would be luck. But still. He wished they loved Hemming more, just a little more.

(Although maybe love was too much to ask from his parents. They had lost so many children that perhaps they simply either wouldn't or couldn't surrender themselves wholly to the ones they now had. Eventually, both he and Hemming would leave them too, by choice or not, and then their losses would be complete. But it would be decades before he was able to see things this way.)

His second year of college, Hemming had had to have an emergency appendectomy. "They said they caught it just in time," his mother told him over the phone. Her voice was flat, very matter-of-fact; there was no relief in it, no anguish, but neither was there any—and he'd had to make himself consider this, even though he hadn't wanted to, was scared to—disappointment either. Hemming's caregiver (a local woman, paid to watch him during the night now that Willem was gone) had noticed him pawing at his stomach and moaning, and had been able to diagnose the hard truffley lump under his abdomen for what it was. While Hemming was being operated on, the doctors had found a growth, a few centimeters long, on his large intestine and had biopsied it. X-rays had revealed further growths, and they were going to excise those as well.

"I'll come home," he said.

"No," his mother had said. "You can't do anything here. We'll tell you if it's anything serious." She and his father had been more bemused than anything when he had been admitted to college—neither of them had known he was applying—but now that he was there, they were determined that he should graduate and forget the ranch as quickly as possible.

But at night he thought of Hemming, alone in a hospital bed, how he'd be frightened and would cry and listen for the sound of his voice. When Hemming was twenty-one, he'd had to have a hernia removed, and he had wept until Willem held his hand. He knew he'd have to go back.

The flights were expensive, much more than he'd anticipated. He researched bus routes, but it would take three days to get there, three days to get back, and he had midterm exams he had to take and do well in if he was to keep his scholarship, and his jobs to attend to. Finally, drunk that Friday night, he confided in Malcolm, who got out his checkbook and wrote him a check.

"I can't," he said, immediately.

"Why not?" asked Malcolm. They argued back and forth until Willem finally accepted the check.

"I'll pay you back, you know that, right?"

Malcolm shrugged. "There's no way for me to say this without sounding like a complete asshole," he said, "but it doesn't make a difference to me, Willem."

Still, it became important to him to repay Malcolm somehow, even though he knew Malcolm wouldn't accept his money. It was Jude who had the idea of putting the money directly into Malcolm's wallet, and so every two weeks after he'd cashed his check from the restaurant where he worked on the weekends, he'd stuff two or three twenties into it while Malcolm was asleep. He never quite knew if Malcolm noticed—he spent it so quickly, and often on the three of them—but Willem took some satisfaction and pride in doing it.

In the meantime, though, there was Hemming. He was glad he went home (his mother had only sighed when he told her he was coming), and glad to see Hemming, although alarmed by how thin he had become, how he groaned and cried as the nurses prodded the area around his sutures; he'd had to grab the sides of his chair to keep himself from shouting at them. At nights, he and his parents would have silent meals; he could almost feel them pulling away, as if they were unpeeling themselves from their lives as parents of two children and readying themselves to drift toward a new identity elsewhere.

On his third night, he took the keys to the truck to drive to the hospital. Back east, it was early spring, but here the dark air seemed to glitter with frost, and in the morning the grass was capped with a thin skin of crystals.

His father came onto the porch as he was walking down the steps. "He'll be asleep," he said.

"I just thought I'd go," Willem told him.

His father looked at him. "Willem," he said, "he won't know whether you're there or not."

He felt his face go hot. "I know you don't fucking care about him," he snapped at him, "but I do." It was the first time he'd ever sworn at his father, and he was unable to move for a moment, fearful and half excited that his father might react, that they might have an argument. But his father just took a sip from his coffee and then turned and went inside, the screen door smacking softly shut behind him.

For the rest of his visit they were all the same as they always were; they went in shifts to sit with Hemming, and when he wasn't at the hospital, Willem helped his mother with the ledgers, or his father as he oversaw the reshodding of the horses. At nights he returned to the hospital and did schoolwork. He read aloud from *The Decameron* to Hemming, who stared at the ceiling and blinked, and struggled through his calculus, which he finally finished with the unhappy certainty that he had gotten all of it wrong. The three of them had gotten used to Jude doing their calculus for them, working through the problems as quickly as if he were running arpeggios. Their first year, Willem had genuinely wanted to understand it, and Jude had sat with him for a string of nights, explaining again and again, but he had never been able to comprehend it.

"I'm just too stupid to get this," he'd said after what felt like an hours-long session, at the end of which he had wanted to go outside and run for miles, he was so prickly with impatience and frustration.

Jude had looked down. "You're not stupid," he said, quietly. "I'm just not explaining it well enough." Jude took seminars in pure math that you had to be invited to enroll in; the rest of them couldn't even begin to fathom what, exactly, he did in it.

In retrospect, he was surprised only by his own surprise when his mother called three months later to tell him that Hemming was on life support. This was in late May, and he was halfway through his final exams. "Don't come back," she'd told him, commanded him, almost. "Don't, Willem." He spoke with his parents in Swedish, and it wasn't until many years later, when a Swedish director he was working with pointed out how affectless his voice became when he switched into the language, that he recognized that he had unconsciously learned to adopt a certain tone when he talked to his parents, one emotionless and blunt, that was meant to echo their own.

Over the next few days he fretted, did poorly in his exams: French, comparative literature, Jacobean drama, the Icelandic sagas, the hated calculus all slurring into one. He picked a fight with his girlfriend, who was a senior and graduating. She cried; he felt guilty but also unable to repair the situation. He thought of Wyoming, of a machine coughing life into Hemming's lungs. Shouldn't he go back? He *had* to go back. He wouldn't be able to stay for long: on June fifteenth, he and Jude were moving into a sublet off-campus for the summer—they'd both found jobs in the city, Jude working on weekdays as a classics professor's amanuensis and on weekends at the bakery he worked at during the school year, Willem as a teacher's assistant at a program for disabled children—but before then, the four of them were going to stay at Malcolm's parents' house in Aquinnah, on Martha's Vineyard, after which Malcolm and JB would drive back to New York. At nights, he called

Hemming at the hospital, made his parents or one of the nurses hold the phone up to his ear, and spoke to his brother, even though he knew he probably couldn't hear him. But how could he not have tried?

And then, one morning a week later, his mother called: Hemming had died. There was nothing he could say. He couldn't ask why she hadn't told him how serious the situation had been, because some part of him had known she wouldn't. He couldn't say he wished he had been there, because she would have nothing to say in response. He couldn't ask her how she felt, because nothing she said would be enough. He wanted to scream at his parents, to hit them, to elicit from them *something*—some melting into grief, some loss of composure, some recognition that something large had happened, that in Hemming's death they had lost something vital and necessary to their lives. He didn't care if they really felt that way or not: he just needed them to say it, he needed to feel that something lay beneath their imperturbable calm, that somewhere within them ran a thin stream of quick, cool water, teeming with delicate lives, minnows and grasses and tiny white flowers, all tender and easily wounded and so vulnerable you couldn't see them without aching for them.

He didn't tell his friends, then, about Hemming. They went to Malcolm's house—a beautiful place, the most beautiful place Willem had ever seen, much less stayed in—and late at night, when the others were asleep, each in his own bed, in his own room with his own bathroom (the house was that big), he crept outside and walked the web of roads surrounding the house for hours, the moon so large and bright it seemed made of something liquid and frozen. On those walks, he tried very hard not to think of anything in particular. He concentrated instead on what he saw before him, noticing at night what had eluded him by day: how the dirt was so fine it was almost sand, and puffed up into little plumes as he stepped in it, how skinny threads of bark-brown snakes whipsawed silently beneath the brush as he passed. He walked to the ocean and above him the moon disappeared, concealed by tattered rags of clouds, and for a few moments he could only hear the water, not see it, and the sky was thick and warm with moisture, as if the very air here were denser, more significant.

Maybe this is what it is to be dead, he thought, and realized it wasn't so bad after all, and felt better.

He expected it would be awful to spend his summer around people

who might remind him of Hemming, but it was actually pleasant, helpful even. His class had seven students, all around eight years old, all
severely impaired, none very mobile, and although part of the day was
ostensibly devoted to trying to teach them colors and shapes, most of
the time was spent playing with them: reading to them, pushing them
around the grounds, tickling them with feathers. During recess all the
classrooms opened their doors to the school's central courtyard, and the
space filled with children on such a variety of wheeled contraptions and
vessels and vehicles that it sometimes sounded as if it was populated by
mechanical insects, all of them squeaking and whirring and clucking
at once. There were children in wheelchairs, and children on small,
scaled-down mopeds that putted and clicked along the flagstones at a
tortoise's speed, and children strapped prone atop smooth lengths of
wood that resembled abbreviated surfboards on wheels, and who pulled
themselves along the ground with their elbowed stumps, and a few children with no means of conveyance at all, who sat in their minders' laps,
the backs of their necks cupped in their minders' palms. Those were
the ones who reminded him most keenly of Hemming.

Some of the children on the motorcycles and the wheeled boards
could speak, and he would toss, very gently, large foam balls to them
and organize races around the courtyard. He would always begin these
races at the head of the pack, loping with an exaggerated slowness
(though not so exaggerated that he appeared too broadly comic; he
wanted them to think he was actually trying), but at some point, usually
a third of the way around the square, he would pretend to trip on something and fall, spectacularly, to the ground, and all the kids would pass
him and laugh. "Get up, Willem, get up!" they'd cry, and he would,
but by that point they would have finished the lap and he would come
in last place. He wondered, sometimes, if they envied him the dexterity
of being able to fall and get up again, and if so, if he should stop doing
it, but when he asked his supervisor, he had only looked at Willem and
said that the kids thought he was funny and that he should keep falling.
And so every day he fell, and every afternoon, when he was waiting with
the students for their parents to come pick them up, the ones who could
speak would ask him if he was going to fall the next day. "No way," he'd
say, confidently, as they giggled. "Are you kidding? How clumsy do you
think I am?"

It was, in many ways, a good summer. The apartment was near

MIT and belonged to Jude's math professor, who was in Leipzig for the season, and who was charging them such a negligible rent that the two of them found themselves making small repairs to the place in order to express their gratitude: Jude organized the books that were stacked into quavering, precarious skyscrapers on every surface and spackled a section of wall that had gone puddingy with water damage; Willem tightened doorknobs, replaced a leaky washer, changed the ballcock in the toilet. He started hanging out with another of the teacher's aides, a girl who went to Harvard, and some nights she would come over to the house and the three of them would make large pots of spaghetti alle vongole and Jude would tell them about his days with the professor, who had decided to communicate with Jude in only Latin or ancient Greek, even when his instructions were things like, "I need more binder clips," or "Make sure you get an extra shot of soy milk in my cappuccino tomorrow morning." In August, their friends and acquaintances from college (and from Harvard, and MIT, and Wellesley, and Tufts) started drifting back to the city, and stayed with them for a night or two until they could move into their own apartments and dorm rooms. One evening toward the end of their stay, they invited fifty people up to the roof and helped Malcolm make a sort of clambake on the grill, blanketing ears of corn and mussels and clams under heaps of dampened banana leaves; the next morning the four of them scooped up the shells from the floor, enjoying the castanety clatter they made as they were tossed into trash bags.

But it was also that summer that he realized he wouldn't go home again, that somehow, without Hemming, there was no point in him and his parents pretending they needed to stay together. He suspected they felt the same way; there was never any conversation about this, but he never felt any particular need to see them again, and they never asked him. They spoke every now and again, and their conversations were, as always, polite and factual and dutiful. He asked them about the ranch, they asked him about school. His senior year, he got a role in the school's production of *The Glass Menagerie* (he was cast as the gentleman caller, of course), but he never mentioned it to them, and when he told them that they shouldn't bother to come east for graduation, they didn't argue with him: it was nearing the end of foal season anyway, and he wasn't sure they would have been able to come even if he hadn't excused them. He and Jude had been adopted by Malcolm's and JB's families for the weekend, and when they weren't around, there were plenty of other people to invite them to their celebratory lunches and dinners and outings.

"But they're your *parents*," Malcolm said to him once a year or so. "You can't just stop talking to them." But you could, you did: he was proof of that. It was like any relationship, he felt—it took constant pruning, and dedication, and vigilance, and if neither party wanted to make the effort, why wouldn't it wither? The only thing he missed—besides Hemming—was Wyoming itself, its extravagant flatness, its trees so deeply green they looked blue, the sugar-and-turd apple-and-peat smell of a horse after it had been rubbed down for the night.

When he was in graduate school, they died, in the same year: his father of a heart attack in January, his mother of a stroke the following October. Then he *had* gone home—his parents were older, but he had forgotten how vivid, how tireless, they had always been, until he saw how diminished they had become. They had left everything to him, but after he had paid off their debts—and then he was unsettled anew, for all along he had assumed most of Hemming's care and medical treatments had been covered by insurance, only to learn that four years after his death, they were still writing enormous checks to the hospital every month—there was very little left: some cash, some bonds; a heavy-bottomed silver mug that had been his long-dead paternal grandfather's; his father's bent wedding ring, worn smooth and shiny and pale; a black-and-white portrait of Hemming and Aksel that he'd never seen before. He kept these, and a few other things, too. The rancher who had employed his parents had long ago died, but his son, who now owned the ranch, had always treated them well, and it had been he who employed them long after he might reasonably be expected to, and he who paid for their funerals as well.

In their deaths, Willem was able to remember that he had loved them after all, and that they had taught him things he treasured knowing, and that they had never asked from him anything he wasn't able to do or provide. In less-charitable moments (moments from just a few years prior), he had attributed their lassitude, their unchallenging acceptance of whatever he might or might not do, to a lack of interest: what parent, Malcolm had asked him, half jealously, half pityingly, says nothing when their only child (he had apologized later) tells them he wants to be an actor? But now, older, he was able to appreciate that they had never even suggested he might owe them a debt—not success, or fealty, or affection, or even loyalty. His father, he knew, had gotten into some sort of trouble in Stockholm—he was never to know what—that had in part encouraged his parents' move to the States. They would never have demanded he be like them; they hardly wanted to be themselves.

And so he had begun his adulthood, the last three years spent bobbing from bank to bank in a muck-bottomed pond, the trees above and around him blotting out the light, making it too dark for him to see whether the lake he was in opened up into a river or whether it was contained, its own small universe in which he might spend years, decades—his life—searching bumblingly for a way out that didn't exist, had never existed.

If he had an agent, someone to guide him, she might be able to show him how to escape, how to find his way downstream. But he didn't, not yet (he had to be optimistic enough to think it was still a matter of "yet"), and so he was left in the company of other seekers, all of them looking for that same elusive tributary, through which few left the lake and by which no one ever wanted to return.

He was willing to wait. He *had* waited. But recently, he could feel his patience sharpening itself into something splintery and ragged, chipping into dry little bits.

Still—he was not an anxious person, he was not inclined toward self-pity. Indeed, there were moments when, returning from Ortolan or from a rehearsal for a play in which he would be paid almost nothing for a week's work, so little that he wouldn't have been able to afford the prix fixe at the restaurant, he would enter the apartment with a feeling of accomplishment. Only to him and Jude would Lispenard Street be considered an achievement—for as much work as he had done to it, and as much as Jude had cleaned it, it was still sad, somehow, and furtive, as if the place was embarrassed to call itself a real apartment—but in those moments he would at times find himself thinking, *This is enough. This is more than I hoped.* To be in New York, to be an adult, to stand on a raised platform of wood and say other people's words!—it was an absurd life, a not-life, a life his parents and his brother would never have dreamed for themselves, and yet he got to dream it for himself every day.

But then the feeling would dissipate, and he would be left alone to scan the arts section of the paper, and read about other people who were doing the kinds of things he didn't even have the expansiveness, the arrogance of imagination to dream of, and in those hours the world would feel very large, and the lake very empty, and the night very black, and he would wish he were back in Wyoming, waiting at the end of the road for Hemming, where the only path he had to navigate was the one back to his parents' house, where the porch light washed the night with honey.

—

First there was the life of the office you saw: forty of them in the main room, each with their own desk, Rausch's glass-walled room at one end, closest to Malcolm's desk, Thomasson's glass-walled room at the other. Between them: two walls of windows, one that looked over Fifth Avenue, toward Madison Square Park, the other of which peered over Broadway, at the glum, gray, gum-stamped sidewalk. That life existed officially from ten a.m. until seven p.m., Monday through Friday. In this life, they did what they were told: they tweaked models, they drafted and redrew, they interpreted Rausch's esoteric scribbles and Thomasson's explicit, block-printed commands. They did not speak. They did not congregate. When clients came in to meet with Rausch and Thomasson at the long glass table that stood in the center of the main room, they did not look up. When the client was famous, as was more and more the case, they bent so low over their desks and stayed so quiet that even Rausch began whispering, his voice—for once—accommodating itself to the office's volume.

Then there was the second life of the office, its real life. Thomasson was less and less present anyway, so it was Rausch whose exit they awaited, and sometimes they had to wait for a long time; Rausch, for all his partygoing and press-courting and opining and traveling, was in reality a hard worker, and although he might go out to an event (an opening, a lecture), he might also return, and then things would have to be hastily reassembled, so that the office he walked back into would resemble the office he had left. It was better to wait for the nights he would disappear completely, even if it meant waiting until nine or ten o'clock. They had cultivated Rausch's assistant, brought her coffees and croissants, and knew they could trust her intelligence on Rausch's arrivals and departures.

But once Rausch was definitively gone for the day, the office transformed itself as instantaneously as a pumpkin into a carriage. Music was turned on (they rotated among the fifteen of them who got to choose), and takeout menus materialized, and on everyone's computers, work for Ratstar Architects was sucked back into digital folders, put to sleep, unloved and forgotten, for the night. They allowed themselves an hour of waste, of impersonating Rausch's weird Teutonic boom (some of them thought he was secretly from Paramus and had adopted the name—Joop Rausch, how could it not be fake?—and the extravagant accent to obscure the fact that he was boring and from Jersey and his name was probably Jesse Rosenberg), of imitating Thomasson's scowl and way of marching up and down the length of the office when he wanted to perform for company, barking at no one in particular (them, they supposed), "It's ze vurk, gentlemen! It's ze vurk!" They made fun of the firm's most senior principal, Dominick Cheung, who was talented but who was becoming bitter (it was clear to everyone but him that he would never be made a partner, no matter how often Rausch and Thomasson promised him), and even of the projects they worked on: the unrealized neo-Coptic church wrought from travertine in Cappadocia; the house with no visible framework in Karuizawa that now wept rust down its faceless glass surfaces; the museum of food in Seville that was meant to win an award but didn't; the museum of dolls in Santa Catarina that never should've won an award but did. They made fun of the schools they'd gone to—MIT, Yale, Rhode Island School of Design, Columbia, Harvard—and how although they'd of course been warned that their lives would be misery for years, how they had all of them, to a one, assumed they'd be the exception (and now all, to a one, secretly thought they still would be). They made fun of how little money they made, how they were twenty-seven, thirty, thirty-two, and still lived with their parents, a roommate, a girlfriend in banking, a boyfriend in publishing (a sad thing, when you had to sponge off of your boyfriend in publishing because he made more than you). They bragged of what they would be doing if they hadn't gone into this wretched industry: they'd be a curator (possibly the one job where you'd make even less than you did now), a sommelier (well, make that two jobs), a gallery owner (make it three), a writer (all right, four—clearly, none of them were equipped to make money, ever, in any imagining). They fought about buildings they loved and buildings they hated. They debated a photography show at this gallery, a video art show at another. They shouted back and forth at one another about critics, and restaurants, and philosophies, and materials. They commiserated with one another about peers who had become successes, and gloated over peers who had quit the business entirely, who had become llama farmers in Mendoza, social workers in Ann Arbor, math teachers in Chengdu.

During the day, they played at being architects. Every now and then a client, his gaze helicoptering slowly around the room, would stop on one of them, usually either Margaret or Eduard, who were the best-looking among them, and Rausch, who was unusually attuned to shifts in attention away from himself, would call the singled-out over, as if beckoning a child to the adults' dinner party. "Ah, yes, this is Margaret," he'd say, as the client looked at her appraisingly, much as he had minutes before been looking at Rausch's blueprints (blueprints finished in fact by Margaret). "She'll be running me out of town someday soon, I'm sure." And then he'd laugh his sad, contrived, walrus-bark laugh: "Ah! Ha! Ha! Ha!"

Margaret would smile and say hello, and roll her eyes at them the moment she turned around. But they knew she was thinking what they were all thinking: Fuck you, Rausch. And: When? When will I replace you? When will it be my turn?

In the meantime, all they had was play: after the debating and the shouting and the eating, there was silence, and the office filled with the hollow tappings of mice being clicked and personal work being dragged from folders and opened, and the grainy sound of pencils being dragged across paper. Although they all worked at the same time, using the same company resources, no one ever asked to see anyone else's work; it was as if they had collectively decided to pretend it didn't exist. So you worked, drawing dream structures and bending parabolas into dream shapes, until midnight, and then you left, always with the same stupid joke: "See you in ten hours." Or nine, or eight, if you were really lucky, if you were really getting a lot done that night.

Tonight was one of the nights Malcolm left alone, and early. Even if he walked out with someone else, he was never able to take the train with them; they all lived downtown or in Brooklyn, and he lived uptown. The benefit to walking out alone was that no one would witness him catching a cab. He wasn't the only person in the office with rich parents—Katharine's parents were rich as well, as, he was pretty sure, were Margaret's and Frederick's—but he lived with his rich parents, and the others didn't.

He hailed a taxi. "Seventy-first and Lex," he instructed the driver. When the driver was black, he always said Lexington. When the driver wasn't, he was more honest: "Between Lex and Park, closer to Park." JB thought this was ridiculous at best, offensive at worst. "You think they're gonna think you're any more gangster because they think you live at Lex and not Park?" he'd ask. "Malcolm, you're a dumbass."

This fight about taxis was one of many he'd had with JB over the years about blackness, and more specifically, his insufficient blackness. A different fight about taxis had begun when Malcolm (stupidly; he'd recognized his mistake even as he heard himself saying the words) had observed that he'd never had trouble getting a cab in New York and maybe people who complained about it were exaggerating. This was his junior year, during his and JB's first and last visit to the weekly Black Students' Union meeting. JB's eyes had practically engorged, so appalled and gleeful was he, but when it was another guy, a self-righteous prick from Atlanta, who informed Malcolm that he was, number one, barely black, number two, an oreo, and number three, because of his white mother, unable to wholly understand the challenges of being *truly* black, it had been JB who had defended him—JB was always harassing him about his relative blackness, but he didn't like it when other people did it, and he certainly didn't like it when it was done in mixed company, which JB considered everyone except Jude and Willem, or, more specifically, other black people.

Back in his parents' house on Seventy-first Street (closer to Park), he endured the nightly parental interrogation, shouted down from the second floor ("Malcolm, is that you?" "Yes!" "Did you eat?" "Yes!" "Are you still hungry?" "No!"), and trudged upstairs to his lair to review once again the central quandaries of his life.

Although JB hadn't been around to overhear that night's exchange with the taxicab driver, Malcolm's guilt and self-hatred over it moved race to the top of tonight's list. Race had always been a challenge for Malcolm, but their sophomore year, he had hit upon what he considered a brilliant cop-out: he wasn't black; he was post-black. (Postmodernism had entered Malcolm's frame of consciousness much later than everyone else's, as he tried to avoid taking literature classes in a sort of passive rebellion against his mother.) Unfortunately, no one was convinced by this explanation, least of all JB, whom Malcolm had begun to think of as not so much black but *pre*-black, as if blackness, like nirvana, was an idealized state that he was constantly striving to erupt into.

And anyway, JB had found yet another way to trump Malcolm, for just as Malcolm was discovering postmodern identity, JB was discovering performance art (the class he was in, Identity as Art: Performative Transformations and the Contemporary Body, was favored by a certain kind of mustachioed lesbian who terrified Malcolm but for some reason flocked to JB). So moved was he by the work of Lee Lozano that for his midterm project, he decided to perform an homage to her entitled *Decide to Boycott White People (After Lee Lozano)*, in which he stopped talking to all white people. He semi-apologetically, but mostly proudly, explained his plan to them one Saturday—as of midnight that night, he would stop talking to Willem altogether, and would reduce his conversational output with Malcolm by a half. Because Jude's race was undetermined, he would continue speaking to him, but would only do so in riddles or Zen koans, in recognition of the unknowability of his ethnic origins.

Malcolm could see by the look that Jude and Willem exchanged with each other, brief and unsmiling though, he observed irritatedly, full of meaning (he always suspected the two of them of conducting an extracurricular friendship from which he was excluded), that they were amused by this and were prepared to humor JB. For his part, he supposed he should be grateful for what might amount to a period of respite from JB, but he wasn't grateful and he wasn't amused: he was annoyed, both by JB's easy playfulness with race and by his using this stupid, gimmicky project (for which he would probably get an A) to make a commentary on Malcolm's identity, which was really none of JB's business.

Living with JB under the terms of his project (and really, when were they *not* negotiating their lives around JB's whims and whimsies?) was actually very much like living with JB under normal circumstances. Minimizing his conversations with Malcolm did not reduce the number of times JB asked Malcolm if he could pick up something for him at the store, or refill his laundry card since Malcolm was going anyway, or if he could borrow Malcolm's copy of *Don Quixote* for Spanish class because he'd left his in the basement men's room in the library. His not speaking to Willem didn't also mean that there wasn't plenty of non-verbal communication, including lots of texts and notes that he'd scribble down ("Scrning of *Godfather* at Rex's—coming?") and hand him, which Malcolm was positive was not what Lozano had intended. And his poor-man's Ionesconian exchanges with Jude suddenly dissolved when he needed Jude to do his calculus homework, at which point Ionesco abruptly transformed into Mussolini, especially after Ionesco realized that there was a whole other problem set he hadn't even begun because he had been busy in the men's room in the library, and class began in forty-three minutes ("But that's enough time for you, right, Judy?").

Naturally, JB being JB and their peers easy prey for anything that was glib and glittery, JB's little experiment was written up in the school paper, and then in a new black literary magazine, *There Is Contrition*, and became, for a short tedious period, the talk of the campus. The attention had revived JB's already flagging enthusiasm for the project—he was only eight days into it, and Malcolm could see him at times almost wanting to explode into talk with Willem—and he was able to last another two days before grandly concluding the experiment a success and announcing that his point had been made.

"What point?" Malcolm had asked. "That you can be as annoying to white people without talking to them as when you *are* talking to them?"

"Oh, fuck you, Mal," said JB, but lazily, too triumphant to even engage with him. "You wouldn't understand." And then he headed off to see his boyfriend, a white guy with a face like a praying mantis's who was always regarding JB with a fervent and worshipful expression that made Malcolm feel slightly sick.

At the time, Malcolm had been convinced that this racial discomfort he felt was a temporary thing, a purely contextual sensation that was awakened in everyone in college but then evaporated the further from it you moved. He had never felt any particular agita about or pride in being black, except in the most remote ways: he knew he was supposed to have certain feelings about certain things in life (taxicab drivers, for one), but somehow that knowledge was only theoretical, not anything he had experienced himself. And yet blackness was an essential part of

his family's narrative, which had been told and retold until it was worn
to a shine: how his father had been the third black managing director at
his investment firm, the third black trustee at the very white boys' pre-
paratory school that Malcolm had attended, the second black CFO of a
major commercial bank. (Malcolm's father had been born too late to be
the *first* black anything, but in the corridor in which he moved—south
of Ninety-sixth Street and north of Fifty-seventh; east of Fifth and west
of Lexington—he was still as rare as the red-tailed hawk that sometimes
nested in the crenellations of one of the buildings opposite theirs on
Park Avenue.) Growing up, the fact of his father's blackness (and, he
supposed, his own), had been trumped by other, more significant matters, factors that counted for more in their slice of New York City than
his father's race: his wife's prominence in the Manhattan literary scene,
for example, and, most important, his wealth. The New York that Malcolm and his family occupied was one divided not along racial lines but
rather tax brackets, and Malcolm had grown up insulated from everything that money could protect him from, including bigotry itself—or
so it in retrospect seemed. In fact, it wasn't until college that he was
made to truly confront the different ways in which blackness had been
experienced by other people, and, perhaps more stunningly, how apart
his family's money had set him from the rest of the country (although
this assumed you could consider his classmates representative of the
rest of the country, which you of course couldn't). Even today, almost
a decade after meeting him, he still had trouble comprehending the
sort of poverty that Jude had been raised in—his disbelief when he
finally realized that the backpack Jude had arrived to college with had
contained, literally, everything on earth in his possession had been so
intense that it had been almost physical, so profound that he had mentioned it to his father, and he was not in the habit of revealing to his
father evidence of his naïveté, for fear of provoking a lecture about his
naïveté. But even his father, who had grown up poor in Queens—albeit
with two working parents and a new set of clothes every year—had been
shocked, Malcolm sensed, although he had endeavored to conceal it
by sharing a story of his own childhood deprivation (something about
a Christmas tree that had to be bought the day after Christmas), as if
lack of privilege were a competition that he was still determined to win,
even in the face of another's clear and inarguable triumph.

However, race seemed less and less a defining characteristic when one was six years out of college, and those people who still nursed it as the core of their identity came across as somehow childish and faintly pathetic, as if clinging to a youthful fascination with Amnesty International or the tuba: an outdated and embarrassing preoccupation with something that reached its potent apotheosis in college applications. At his age, the only truly important aspects of one's identity were sexual prowess; professional accomplishments; and money. And in all three of these aspects, Malcolm was also failing.

Money he set aside. He would someday inherit a huge amount. He didn't know how huge, and he had never felt the need to ask, and no one had ever felt the need to tell him, which is how he knew it was huge indeed. Not Ezra huge, of course, but—well, maybe it *was* Ezra huge. Malcolm's parents lived much more modestly than they might, thanks to his mother's aversions to garish displays of wealth, so he never knew if they lived between Lexington and Park because they couldn't afford to live between Madison and Fifth, or whether they lived between Lexington and Park because his mother would find it too ostentatious to live between Madison and Fifth. He would like to make his own money, he would. But he wasn't one of those rich kids who tortured himself about it. He would try to earn his way, but it wasn't wholly up to him.

Sex, and sexual fulfillment, however, was something he *did* have to take responsibility for. He couldn't blame his lack of a sex life on the fact that he'd chosen a low-paying field, or on his parents for not properly motivating him. (Or could he? As a child, Malcolm had had to endure his parents' long groping sessions—often conducted in front of him and Flora—and he now wondered whether their show-offy competence had dulled some competitive spirit within him.) His last real relationship had been more than three years ago, with a woman named Imogene who dumped him to become a lesbian. It was unclear to him, even now, whether he had actually been physically attracted to Imogene or had simply been relieved to have someone else make decisions that he had been happy to follow. Recently, he had seen Imogene (also an architect, although at a public interest group that built experimental low-income housing—exactly the sort of job Malcolm felt he should *want* to have, even if he secretly didn't) and had teasingly told her—he had been joking!—that he couldn't help but feel that he had driven her to lesbianism. But Imogene had bristled and told him that she had *always* been a lesbian and had stayed with him because he had seemed so sexually confused that she thought she might be able to help educate him.

But since Imogene, there had been no one. Oh, what was wrong with him? Sex; sexuality: these too were things he should have sorted out in college, the last place where such insecurity was not just tolerated but encouraged. In his early twenties, he had tried falling in and out of love with various people—friends of Flora's, classmates, one of his mother's clients, a debut novelist who had written a literary roman à clef about being a sexually confused firefighter—and yet still didn't know to whom he might be attracted. He often thought that being gay (as much as he also couldn't stand the thought of it; somehow it, like race, seemed the province of college, an identity to inhabit for a period before maturing to more proper and practical realms) was attractive mostly for its accompanying accessories, its collection of political opinions and causes and its embrace of aesthetics. He was missing, it seemed, the sense of victimization and woundedness and perpetual anger it took to be black, but he was certain he possessed the interests that would be required if he were gay.

He fancied himself already half in love with Willem, and at various points in love with Jude too, and at work he would sometimes find himself staring at Eduard. Sometimes he noticed Dominick Cheung staring at Eduard as well, and then he would stop himself, because the last person he wanted to be was sad, forty-five-year-old Dominick, leering at an associate in a firm that he would never inherit. A few weekends ago, he had been at Willem and Jude's, ostensibly to take some measurements so he could design them a bookcase, and Willem had leaned in front of him to grab the measuring tape from the sofa, and the very nearness of him had been suddenly unbearable, and he had made an excuse about needing to get into the office and had abruptly left, Willem calling after him.

He had in fact gone to the office, ignoring Willem's texts, and had sat there at his computer, staring without seeing the file before him and wondering yet again why he had joined Ratstar. The worst thing was that the answer was so obvious that he didn't even need to ask it: he had joined Ratstar to impress his parents. His last year of architecture school, Malcolm had had a choice—he could have chosen to work with two classmates, Jason Kim and Sonal Mars, who were starting their own firm with money from Sonal's grandparents, or he could have joined Ratstar.

"You've got to be kidding me," Jason had said when Malcolm had told him of his decision. "You realize what your life is going to be like as an associate at a place like that, don't you?"

"It's a great firm," he'd said, staunchly, sounding like his mother, and Jason had rolled his eyes. "I mean, it's a great name to have on my résumé." But even as he said it, he knew (and, worse, feared Jason knew as well) what he really meant: it was a great name for his parents to say at cocktail parties. And, indeed, his parents liked to say it. "Two kids," Malcolm had overheard his father say to someone at a dinner party celebrating one of Malcolm's mother's clients. "My daughter's an editor at FSG, and my son works for Ratstar Architects." The woman had made an approving sound, and Malcolm, who had actually been trying to find a way to tell his father he wanted to quit, had felt something in him wilt. At such times, he envied his friends for the exact things he had once pitied them for: the fact that no one had any expectations for them, the ordinariness of their families (or their very lack of them), the way they navigated their lives by only their own ambitions.

And now? Now Jason and Sonal had had two projects appear in *New York* and one in *The New York Times*, while he was still doing the sort of work he had done in his first year of architecture school, working for two pretentious men at a firm they had pretentiously named after a pretentious Anne Sexton poem, and getting paid almost nothing to do it.

He had gone to architecture school for the worst reason of all, it seemed: because he loved buildings. It had been a respectable passion, and when he was a child, his parents had indulged him with tours of houses, of monuments wherever they had traveled. Even as a very young boy, he had always drawn imaginary buildings, built imaginary structures: they were a comfort and they were a repository—everything he was unable to articulate, everything he was unable to decide, he could, it seemed, resolve in a building.

And in an essential way, this was what he was most ashamed of: not his poor understanding of sex, not his traitorous racial tendencies, not his inability to separate himself from his parents or make his own money or behave like an autonomous creature. It was that, when he and his colleagues sat there at night, the group of them burrowed deep into their own ambitious dream-structures, all of them drawing and planning their improbable buildings, he was doing nothing. He had lost the ability to imagine anything. And so every evening, while the others created, he copied: he drew buildings he had seen on his travels, buildings other people had dreamed and constructed, buildings he had lived in or passed through. Again and again, he made what had already been made, not even bothering to improve them, just mimicking them. He was twenty-eight; his imagination had deserted him; he was a copyist.

It frightened him. JB had his series. Jude had his work, Willem had his. But what if Malcolm never again created anything? He longed for the years when it was enough to simply be in his room with his hand moving over a piece of graph paper, before the years of decisions and identities, when his parents made his choices for him, and the only thing he had to concentrate on was the clean blade stroke of a line, the ruler's perfect knife edge.

3

IT WAS JB who decided that Willem and Jude should host a New Year's Eve party at their apartment. This was resolved at Christmas, which was a three-part affair: Christmas Eve was held at JB's mother's place in Fort Greene, and Christmas dinner itself (a formal, organized event, at which suits and ties were required) was at Malcolm's house, and succeeded a casual lunch at JB's aunts' house. They had always followed this ritual—four years ago, they had added Thanksgiving at Jude's friends Harold and Julia's house in Cambridge to the lineup—but New Year's Eve had never been assigned. The previous year, the first post-school-life New Year's that they had all been in the same city at the same time, they had all ended up separate and miserable—JB lodged at some lame party at Ezra's, Malcolm stuck at his parents' friends' dinner uptown, Willem trapped by Findlay into a holiday shift at Ortolan, Jude mired in bed with the flu at Lispenard Street—and had resolved to actually make plans for the next year. But they hadn't, and hadn't, and then it was December and they still hadn't done anything.

So they didn't mind JB deciding for them, not in this case. They figured they could accommodate twenty-five people comfortably, or forty uncomfortably. "So make it forty," said JB, promptly, as they'd known he would, but later, back at their apartment, they wrote up a list of just twenty, and only their and Malcolm's friends, knowing that JB would invite more people than were allotted him, extending invitations to friends and friends of friends and not-even friends and colleagues and bartenders and shop clerks, until the place grew so dense with bodies that they could open all the windows to the night air and still not dispel the fog of heat and smoke that would inevitably accumulate.

"Don't make this complicated," was the other thing JB had said, but Willem and Malcolm knew that was a caution meant solely for Jude, who had a tendency to make things more elaborate than was necessary, to spend nights making batches of gougères when everyone would have been content with pizza, to actually clean the place beforehand, as if anyone would care if the floors were crunchy with grit and the sink was scummed with dried soap stains and flecks of previous days' breakfasts.

The night before the party was unseasonably warm, warm enough that Willem walked the two miles from Ortolan to the apartment, which was so thick with its rich butter scents of cheese and dough and fennel that it made him feel he had never left work at all. He stood in the kitchen for a while, pinching the little tumoric blobs of pastry off their cooling racks to keep them from sticking, looking at the stack of plastic containers with their herbed shortbreads and cornmeal gingersnaps and feeling slightly sad—the same sadness he felt when he noticed that Jude had cleaned after all—because he knew they would be devoured mindlessly, swallowed whole with beer, and that they would begin the New Year finding crumbs of those beautiful cookies everywhere, trampled and stamped into the tiles. In the bedroom, Jude was already asleep, and the window was cracked open, and the heavy air made Willem dream of spring, and trees afuzz with yellow flowers, and a flock of blackbirds, their wings lacquered as if with oil, gliding soundlessly across a sea-colored sky.

When he woke, though, the weather had turned again, and it took him a moment to realize that he had been shivering, and that the sounds in his dream had been of wind, and that he was being shaken awake, and that his name was being repeated, not by birds but by a human voice: "Willem, Willem."

He turned over and propped himself up on his elbows, but was able to register Jude only in segments: his face first, and then the fact that he was holding his left arm before him with his right hand, and that he had cocooned it with something—his towel, he realized—which was so white in the gloom that it seemed a source of light itself, and he stared at it, transfixed.

"Willem, I'm sorry," said Jude, and his voice was so calm that for a few seconds, he thought it was a dream, and stopped listening, and Jude had to repeat himself. "There's been an accident, Willem; I'm sorry. I need you to take me to Andy's."

Finally he woke. "What kind of accident?"

"I cut myself. It was an accident." He paused. "Will you take me?"

"Yeah, of course," he said, but he was still confused, still asleep, and it was without understanding that he fumblingly dressed, and joined Jude in the hallway, where he was waiting, and then walked with him up to Canal, where he turned for the subway before Jude pulled him back: "I think we need a cab."

In the taxi—Jude giving the driver the address in that same crushed, muted voice—he at last gave in to consciousness, and saw that Jude was still holding the towel. "Why did you bring your towel?" he asked.

"I told you—I cut myself."

"But—is it bad?"

Jude shrugged, and Willem noticed for the first time that his lips had gone a strange color, a not-color, although maybe that was the streetlights, which slapped and slid across his face, bruising it yellow and ocher and a sickly larval white as the cab pushed north. Jude leaned his head against the window and closed his eyes, and it was then that Willem felt the beginnings of nausea, of fear, although he was unable to articulate why, only that he was in a cab heading uptown and something had happened, and he didn't know what but that it was something bad, that he wasn't comprehending something important and vital, and that the damp warmth of a few hours ago had vanished and the world had reverted to its icy harshness, its raw end-of-year cruelty.

Andy's office was on Seventy-eighth and Park, near Malcolm's parents' house, and it was only once they were inside, in the true light, that Willem saw that the dark pattern on Jude's shirt was blood, and that the towel had become sticky with it, almost varnished, its tiny loops of cotton matted down like wet fur. "I'm sorry," Jude said to Andy, who had opened the door to let them in, and when Andy unwrapped the towel, all Willem saw was what looked like a choking of blood, as if Jude's arm had grown a mouth and was vomiting blood from it, and with such avidity that it was forming little frothy bubbles that popped and spat as if in excitement.

"Jesus fucking Christ, Jude," said Andy, and steered him back to the examining room, and Willem sat down to wait. Oh god, he thought, oh god. But it was as if his mind was a bit of machinery caught uselessly in a groove, and he couldn't think beyond those two words. It was too bright in the waiting room, and he tried to relax, but he couldn't for the phrase beating its rhythm like a heartbeat, thudding through his body like a second pulse: *Oh god. Oh god. Oh god.*

He waited a long hour before Andy called his name. Andy was eight years older than he, and they had known him since their sophomore year, when Jude had had an episode so sustained that the three of them had finally decided to take him to the hospital connected with the university, where Andy had been the resident on call. He had been the only doctor Jude agreed to see again, and now, even though Andy was an orthopedic surgeon, he still treated Jude for anything that went wrong, from his back to his legs to flu and colds. They all liked Andy, and trusted him, too.

"You can take him home," Andy said. He was angry. With a snap, he peeled off his gloves, which were crusty with blood, and pushed back his stool. On the floor was a long, messy paint-swipe streak of red, as if someone had tried to clean up something sloshed and had given up in exasperation. The walls had red on them as well, and Andy's sweater was stiff with it. Jude sat on the table, looking slumped and miserable and holding a glass bottle of orange juice. His hair was glued together in clumps, and his shirt appeared hard and shellacked, as if it was made not from cloth but from metal. "Jude, go to the waiting room," Andy instructed, and Jude did, meekly.

Once he was gone, Andy shut the door and looked at Willem. "Has he seemed suicidal to you?"

"What? No." He felt himself grow very still. "Is that what he was trying to do?"

Andy sighed. "He says he wasn't. But—I don't know. No. I don't know; I can't tell." He went over to the sink and began to scrub violently at his hands. "On the other hand, if he had gone to the ER—which you guys really should've fucking done, you know—they most likely would've hospitalized him. Which is why he probably didn't." Now he was speaking aloud to himself. He pumped a small lake of soap onto his hands and washed them again. "You know he cuts himself, don't you?"

For a while, he couldn't answer. "No," he said.

Andy turned back around and stared at Willem, wiping each finger dry slowly. "He hasn't seemed depressed?" he asked. "Is he eating regularly, sleeping? Does he seem listless, out of sorts?"

"He's seemed fine," Willem said, although the truth was that he didn't know. *Had* Jude been eating? *Had* he been sleeping? Should he have noticed? Should he have been paying more attention? "I mean, he's seemed the same as he always is."

"Well," said Andy. He looked deflated for a moment, and the two of them stood quietly, facing but not looking at each other. "I'm going to take his word for it this time," he said. "I just saw him a week ago, and I agree, nothing seemed unusual. But if he starts behaving strangely at all—I mean it, Willem—you call me right away."

"I promise," he said. He had seen Andy a few times over the years, and had always sensed his frustration, which often seemed directed toward many people at once: at himself, at Jude, and especially at Jude's friends, none of whom, Andy always managed to suggest (without ever saying it aloud), were doing a good enough job taking care of him. He liked this about Andy, his sense of outrage over Jude, even as he feared his disapproval and also thought it somewhat unfair.

And then, as it often did once he had finished rebuking them, Andy's voice changed and became almost tender. "I know you will," he said. "It's late. Go home. Make sure you give him something to eat when he wakes up. Happy New Year."

—

They rode home in silence. The driver had taken a single, long look at Jude and said, "I need an extra twenty dollars on the fare."

"Fine," Willem had said.

The sky was almost light, but he knew he wouldn't be able to sleep. In the taxi, Jude had turned away from Willem and looked out of the window, and back at the apartment, he stumbled at the doorway and walked slowly toward the bathroom, where Willem knew he would start trying to clean up.

"Don't," he told him. "Go to bed," and Jude, obedient for once, changed direction and shuffled into the bedroom, where he fell asleep almost immediately.

Willem sat on his own bed and watched him. He was aware, suddenly, of his every joint and muscle and bone, and this made him feel very, very old, and for several minutes he simply sat staring.

"Jude," he called, and then again more insistently, and when Jude didn't answer, he went over to his bed and nudged him onto his back and, after a moment's hesitation, pushed up the right sleeve of his shirt. Under his hands, the fabric didn't so much yield as it did bend and crease, like cardboard, and although he was only able to fold it to the inside of Jude's elbow, it was enough to see the three columns of neat white scars, each about an inch wide and slightly raised, laddering up his arm. He tucked his finger under the sleeve, and felt the tracks continuing onto the upper arm, but stopped when he reached the bicep, unwilling to explore more, and withdrew his hand. He wasn't able to examine the left arm—Andy had cut back the sleeve on that one, and Jude's entire forearm and hand were wrapped with white gauze—but he knew he would find the same thing there.

He had been lying when he told Andy he hadn't known Jude cut himself. Or rather, he hadn't known for certain, but that was only a technicality: he knew, and he had known for a long time. When they were at Malcolm's house the summer after Hemming died, he and Malcolm had gotten drunk one afternoon, and as they sat and watched JB and Jude, back from their walk to the dunes, fling sand at each other, Malcolm had asked, "Have you ever noticed how Jude always wears long sleeves?"

He'd grunted in response. He had, of course—it was difficult not to, especially on hot days—but he had never let himself wonder why. Much of his friendship with Jude, it often seemed, was not letting himself ask the questions he knew he ought to, because he was afraid of the answers.

There had been a silence then, and the two of them had watched as JB, drunk himself, fell backward into the sand and Jude limped over and begun burying him.

"Flora had a friend who always wore long sleeves," Malcolm continued. "Her name was Maryam. She used to cut herself."

He let the silence pull between them until he imagined he could hear it come alive. There had been a girl in their dorm who had cut herself as well. She had been with them freshman year, but, he realized, he hadn't seen her at all this past year.

"Why?" he asked Malcolm. On the sand, Jude had worked up to JB's waist. JB was singing something meandering and tuneless.

"I don't know," Malcolm said. "She had a lot of problems."

He waited, but it seemed Malcolm had nothing more to say. "What happened to her?"

"I don't know. They lost touch when Flora went to college; she never spoke about her again."

They were quiet again. Somewhere along the way, he knew, it had been silently decided among the three of them that he would be primarily responsible for Jude, and this, he recognized, was Malcolm's way of presenting him with a difficulty that needed a solution, although what, exactly, the problem was—or what the answer might be—he wasn't certain, and he was willing to bet that Malcolm didn't know, either.

For the next few days he avoided Jude, because he knew if he were alone with him, he wouldn't be able to stop himself from having a conversation with him, and he wasn't sure that he wanted to, or what that conversation would be. It wasn't hard to do: in the daytime, they were together as a group, and at night, they were each in their own rooms. But one evening, Malcolm and JB left together to pick up the lobsters, and he and Jude were left on their own in the kitchen, slicing tomatoes and washing lettuce. It had been a long, sunny, sleepy day, and Jude was in one of his light moods, when he was almost carefree, and even as he asked, Willem experienced a predictive melancholy at ruining such a perfect moment, one in which everything—the pink-bled sky above them and the way the knife sliced so cleanly through the vegetables beneath them—had conspired to work so well, only to have him upset it.

"Don't you want to borrow one of my T-shirts?" he asked Jude.

He didn't answer until he had finished coring the tomato before him, and then gave Willem a steady, blank gaze. "No."

"Aren't you hot?"

Jude smiled at him, faintly, warningly. "It's going to be cold any minute now." And it was true. When the last daub of sun vanished, it would be chilly, and Willem himself would have to go back to his room for a sweater.

"But"—and he heard in advance how absurd he would sound, how the confrontation had wriggled out of his control, catlike, as soon as he had initiated it—"you're going to get lobster all over your sleeves."

At this, Jude made a noise, a funny kind of squawk, too loud and too barky to be a real laugh, and turned back to the cutting board. "I think I can handle it, Willem," he said, and although his voice was mild, Willem saw how tightly he was holding the knife's handle, almost squeezing it, so that the bunch of his knuckles tinged a suety yellow.

They were lucky then, both of them, that Malcolm and JB returned before they had to continue talking, but not before Willem heard Jude begin to ask "Why are—" And although he never finished his sentence (and indeed, didn't speak to Willem once throughout dinner, through which he kept his sleeves perfectly neat), Willem knew that his question would not have been "Why are you asking me this?" but "Why are *you* asking me this?" because Willem had always been careful not to express too much interest in exploring the many cupboarded cabinet in which Jude had secreted himself.

If it had been anyone else, he told himself, he wouldn't have hesitated. He would have demanded answers, he would have called mutual friends, he would have sat him down and yelled and pleaded and threatened until a confession was extracted. But this was part of the deal when you were friends with Jude: he knew it, Andy knew it, they all knew it. You let things slide that your instincts told you not to, you scooted around the edges of your suspicions. You understood that proof of your friendship lay in keeping your distance, in accepting what was told you, in turning and walking away when the door was shut in your face instead of trying to force it open again. The war-room discussions the four of them had had about other people—about Black Henry Young, when they thought the girl he was dating was cheating on him and were trying to decide how to tell him; about Ezra, when they *knew* the girl he was dating was cheating on him and were trying to decide how to tell him—they would never have about Jude. He would consider it a betrayal, and it wouldn't help, anyway.

For the rest of the night, they avoided each other, but on his way to bed, he found himself standing outside Jude's room, his hand hovering above the door, ready to knock, before he returned to himself: What would he say? What did he want to hear? And so he left, continued on, and the next day, when Jude made no mention of the previous evening's almost-conversation, he didn't either, and soon that day turned to night, and then another, and another, and they moved further and further from his ever trying, however ineffectively, to make Jude answer a question he couldn't bring himself to ask.

But it was always there, that question, and in unexpected moments it would muscle its way into his consciousness, positioning itself stubbornly at the forefront of his mind, as immovable as a troll. Four years ago, he and JB were sharing an apartment and attending graduate school, and Jude, who had remained in Boston for law school, had come down to visit them. It had been night then, too, and there had been a locked bathroom door, and him banging on it, abruptly, inexplicably terrified, and Jude answering it, looking irritated but also (or was he imagining this?) strangely guilty, and asking him "What, Willem?" and he once again being unable to answer, but knowing that something was amiss. Inside the room had smelled sharply tannic, the rusted-metal scent of blood, and he had even picked through the trash can and found a curl of a bandage wrapper, but was that from dinner, when JB had cut himself with a knife while trying to chop a carrot in his hand (Willem suspected he exaggerated his incompetency in the kitchen in order to avoid having to do any prep work), or was it from Jude's nighttime punishments? But again (again!), he did nothing, and when he passed Jude (feigning sleep or actually asleep?) on the sofa in the living room, he said nothing, and the next day, he again said nothing, and the days unfurled before him as clean as paper, and with each day he said nothing, and nothing, and nothing.

And now there was this. If he had done something (what?) three years ago, eight years ago, would this have happened? And what exactly was *this*?

But this time he would say something, because this time he had proof. This time, to let Jude slip away and evade him would mean that he himself would be culpable if anything happened.

After he had resolved this, he felt the fatigue overwhelm him, felt it erase the worry and anxiety and frustration of the night. It was the last day of the year, and as he lay down on his bed and closed his eyes, the last thing he remembered feeling was surprise that he should be falling asleep so fast.

—

It was almost two in the afternoon when Willem finally woke, and the first thing he remembered was his resolve from earlier that morning. Certainly things had been realigned to discourage his sense of initiative: Jude's bed was clean. Jude was not in it. The bathroom, when he visited it, smelled eggily of bleach. And at the card table, there was Jude himself, stamping circles into dough with a stoicism that made Willem both annoyed and relieved. If he was to confront Jude, it seemed, it would be without the benefit of disarray, of evidence of disaster.

He slouched into the chair across from him. "What're you doing?"

Jude didn't look up. "Making more gougères," he said, calmly. "One of the batches I made yesterday isn't quite right."

"No one's going to fucking care, Jude," he said meanly, and then, barreling helplessly forward, "We could just give them cheese sticks and it'd be the same thing."

Jude shrugged, and Willem felt his annoyance quicken into anger. Here Jude sat after what was, he could now admit, a terrifying night, acting as if nothing had happened, even as his bandage-wrapped hand lay uselessly on the table. He was about to speak when Jude put down the water glass he'd been using as a pastry cutter and looked at him. "I'm really sorry, Willem," he said, so softly that Willem almost couldn't hear him. He saw Willem looking at his hand and pulled it into his lap. "I should never—" He paused. "I'm sorry. Don't be mad at me."

His anger dissolved. "Jude," he asked, "what were you doing?"

"Not what you think. I promise you, Willem."

Years later, Willem would recount this conversation—its contours, if not its actual, literal content—for Malcolm as proof of his own incompetence, his own failure. How might things have been different if he spoke only one sentence? And that sentence could have been "Jude, are you trying to kill yourself?" or "Jude, you need to tell me what's going on," or "Jude, why do you do this to yourself?" Any of those would have been acceptable; any of those would have led to a larger conversation that would have been reparative, or at the very least preventative.

Wouldn't it?

But there, in the moment, he instead only mumbled, "Okay."

They sat in silence for what felt like a long time, listening to the murmur of one of their neighbors' televisions, and it was only much later that Willem would wonder whether Jude had been saddened or relieved that he had been so readily believed.

"*Are* you mad at me?"

"No." He cleared his throat. And he wasn't. Or, at least, *mad* was not the word he would have chosen, but he couldn't then articulate what word would be correct. "But we obviously have to cancel the party."

At this, Jude looked alarmed. "Why?"

"*Why?* Are you kidding me?"

"Willem," Jude said, adopting what Willem thought of as his litigatory tone, "we can't cancel. People are going to be showing up in seven hours—less. And we really have no clue who JB's invited. They're going to show up anyway, even if we let everyone else know. And besides"—he inhaled sharply, as if he'd had a lung infection and was trying to prove it had resolved itself—"I'm perfectly fine. It'll be more difficult if we cancel than if we just go forward."

Oh, how and why did he always listen to Jude? But he did, once again, and soon it was eight, and the windows were once again open, and the kitchen was once again hot with pastry—as if the previous night had never happened, as if those hours had been an illusion—and Malcolm and JB were arriving. Willem stood in the door of their bedroom, buttoning up his shirt and listening to Jude tell them that he had burned his arm baking the gougères, and that Andy had had to apply a salve.

"I told you not to make those fucking gougères," he could hear JB say, happily. He loved Jude's baking.

He was overcome, then, with a powerful sensation: he could close the door, and go to sleep, and when he woke, it would be a new year, and everything would be wiped fresh, and he wouldn't feel that deep, writhing discomfort inside of him. The thought of seeing Malcolm and JB, of interacting with them and smiling and joking, seemed suddenly excruciating.

But, of course, see them he did, and when JB demanded they all go up to the roof so he could get some fresh air and have a smoke, he let Malcolm complain uselessly and halfheartedly about how cold it was without joining in, before resignedly following the three of them up the narrow staircase that led to the tar-papered roof.

He knew that he was sulking, and he removed himself to the back of the building, letting the others talk without him. Above him, the sky was already completely dark, midnight dark. If he faced north, he could see directly beneath him the art-supply store where JB had been working part-time since quitting the magazine a month ago, and in the distance, the Empire State Building's gaudy, graceless bulk, its tower aglow with a garish blue light that made him think of gas stations, and the long drive back to his parents' house from Hemming's hospital bed so many years ago.

"Guys," he called over to the others, "it's cold." He wasn't wearing his coat; none of them were. "Let's go." But when he went to the door that opened into the building's stairwell, the handle wouldn't turn. He tried it again—it wouldn't budge. They were locked out. "Fuck!" he shouted. "Fuck, fuck, *fuck!*"

"Jesus, Willem," said Malcolm, startled, because Willem rarely got angry. "Jude? Do you have the key?"

But Jude didn't. "Fuck!" He couldn't help himself. Everything felt so wrong. He couldn't look at Jude. He blamed him, which was unfair. He blamed himself, which was more fair but which made him feel worse. "Who's got their phone?" But idiotically, no one had his phone: they were down in the apartment, where they themselves should have been, were it not for fucking JB, and for fucking Malcolm, who so unquestioningly followed everything JB said, every stupid, half-formed idea, and for fucking Jude as well, for last night, for the past nine years, for hurting himself, for not letting himself be helped, for frightening and unnerving him, for making him feel so useless: for everything.

For a while they screamed; they pounded their feet on the rooftop in the hopes that someone beneath them, one of their three neighbors whom they'd still never met, might hear them. Malcolm suggested throwing something at the windows of one of the neighboring buildings, but they had nothing to throw (even their wallets were downstairs, tucked cozily into their coat pockets), and all the windows were dark besides.

"Listen," Jude said at last, even though the last thing Willem wanted to do was listen to Jude, "I have an idea. Lower me down to the fire escape and I'll break in through the bedroom window."

The idea was so stupid that he initially couldn't respond: it sounded like something that JB would imagine, not Jude. "No," he said, flatly. "That's crazy."

"Why?" asked JB. "I think it's a great plan." The fire escape was an unreliable, ill-conceived, and mostly useless object, a rusted metal skeleton affixed to the front of the building between the fifth and third floors like a particularly ugly bit of decoration—from the roof, it was a drop of about nine feet to the landing, which ran half the width of their living room; even if they could safely get Jude down to it without triggering one of his episodes or having him break his leg, he'd have to crane over its edge in order to reach the bedroom window.

"Absolutely not," he told JB, and the two of them argued for a bit until Willem realized, with a growing sense of dismay, that it was the only possible solution. "But not Jude," he said. "I will."

"You can't."

"Why? We won't need to break in through the bedroom, anyway; I'll just go in through one of the living-room windows." The living-room windows were barred, but one of them was missing, and Willem thought he might be able to squeeze between the remaining two bars, just. Anyway, he'd have to.

"I closed the windows before we came up here," Jude admitted in a small voice, and Willem knew that meant he'd also locked them, because he locked anything that could be: doors, windows, closets. It was reflexive for him. The bedroom window's lock was broken, however, so Jude had fashioned a mechanism—a complex, blocky thing made from bolts and wire—that he claimed secured it completely.

He had always been mystified by Jude's hyper-preparedness, his dedication to finding disaster everywhere—he had long ago noticed Jude's habit of, upon entering any new room or space, searching for the nearest exit and then standing close to it, which had initially been funny and then, somehow, became less so—and his equal dedication to implementing preventative measures whenever he could. One night, the two of them had been awake late in their bedroom, talking, and Jude had told him (quietly, as if he was confessing something precious) that the bedroom window's mechanism could in fact be opened from the outside, but that he was the only one who knew how to unjam it.

"Why are you telling me this?" he'd asked.

"Because," Jude had said, "I think we should get it fixed, properly."

"But if you're the only one who knows how to open it, why does it matter?" They didn't have extra money for a locksmith, not to come fix a problem that wasn't a problem. They couldn't ask the superintendent: After they had moved in, Annika had admitted that she technically wasn't allowed to sublet the apartment, but as long as they didn't cause any problems, she thought the landlord wouldn't bother them. And so they tried not to cause problems: they made their own repairs, they patched their own walls, they fixed the plumbing themselves.

"Just in case," Jude had said. "I just want to know we're safe."

"Jude," he'd said. "We're going to be safe. Nothing's going to happen. No one's going to break in." And then, when Jude was silent, he sighed, gave up. "I'll call the locksmith tomorrow," he'd said.

"Thank you, Willem," Jude had said.

But in the end, he'd never called.

That had been two months ago, and now they were standing in the cold on their roof, and that window was their only hope. "Fuck, fuck," he groaned. His head hurt. "Just tell me how to do it, and I'll open it."

"It's too difficult," Jude said. By now they had forgotten Malcolm and JB were standing there, watching them, JB quiet for once. "I won't be able to explain it."

"Yeah, I know you think I'm a fucking moron, but I can figure it out if you only use small words," he snapped.

"Willem," said Jude, surprised, and there was a silence. "That's not what I meant."

"I know," he said. "Sorry. I know." He took a deep breath. "Even if we were to do this, though—and I don't think we should—how would we even lower you down?"

Jude walked to the edge of the roof, which was bordered on each side by a flat-topped shin-high wall, and peered over it. "I'll sit on the wall looking out, directly above the fire escape," he said. "Then you and JB should both sit by it. Each of you hold one of my hands with both of your own, and then you'll lower me down. Once you can't reach anymore, you'll let go and I'll drop the rest of the way."

He laughed, it was so risky and dumb. "And if we did this, how would you reach the bedroom window?"

Jude looked at him. "You're going to have to trust I can do it."

"This is stupid."

JB stopped him. "This is the only plan, Willem. It's fucking freezing out here."

And it was; only his rage was keeping him warm. "Have you not noticed his whole fucking arm is completely bandaged up, JB?"

"But I'm fine, Willem," said Jude, before JB could respond.

It was ten more minutes of the two of them bickering until Jude finally marched back over to the edge. "If you won't help me, Willem, Malcolm will," he said, although Malcolm looked terrified as well.

"No," he said, "I will." And so he and JB knelt and pressed themselves against the wall, each holding one of Jude's hands with both of their own. By now it was so cold that he could barely feel his fingers close around Jude's palm. He had Jude's left hand, and all he could sense anyway was its cushion of gauze. As he squeezed it, an image of Andy's face floated before him, and he was sick with guilt.

Jude pushed off the side of the ledge, and Malcolm gave a little moan that ended in a squeak. Willem and JB leaned over as far as they could, until they were in danger of tipping over the edge themselves, and when Jude called to them to let go, they did, and watched him land in a clatter on the slat-floored fire escape beneath them.

JB cheered, and Willem wanted to smack him. "I'm fine!" Jude shouted up to them, and waved his bandaged hand in the air like a flag, before moving over to the edge of the fire escape, where he pulled himself up onto its railing so he could start untangling the implement. He had his legs twined around one of the railing's iron spindles, but his position was precarious, and Willem watched him sway a little, trying to keep his balance, his fingers moving slowly from numbness and cold.

"Get me down there," he said to Malcolm and JB, ignoring Malcolm's fluttery protests, and then he went over the edge himself, calling down to Jude before he did so his arrival wouldn't upset his equilibrium.

The drop was scarier, and the landing harder, than he had thought it would be, but he made himself recover quickly and went over to where Jude was and wrapped his arms around his waist, tucking his leg around a spindle to brace himself. "I've got you," he said, and Jude leaned out over the edge of the railing, farther than he could have done on his own, and Willem held on to him so tightly that he could feel the knuckles of Jude's spine through his sweater, could feel his stomach sink and rise as he breathed, could feel the echo of his fingers' movements through his muscles as he twisted and unkinked the twigs of wire that were fastening the window into its stile. And when it was done, Willem climbed onto the railing and into the bedroom first, and then reached out again to pull Jude in by his arms, careful to avoid his bandages.

They stood back on the inside, panting from the effort, and looked at each other. It was so deliciously warm inside this room, even with the cold air gusting in, that he at last let himself feel weak with relief. They were safe, they had been spared. Jude grinned at him then, and he grinned back—if it had been JB before him, he would've hugged him out of sheer stupid giddiness, but Jude wasn't a hugger and so he didn't. But then Jude raised his hand to brush some of the rust flakes out of his hair, and Willem saw that on the inside of his wrist his bandage was stained with a deep-burgundy splotch, and recognized, belatedly, that the rapidity of Jude's breathing was not just from exertion but from pain. He watched as Jude sat heavily on his bed, his white-wrapped hand reaching behind him to make sure he would land on something solid.

Willem crouched beside him. His elation was gone, replaced by something else. He felt himself weirdly close to tears, although he couldn't have said why.

"Jude," he began, but he didn't know how to continue.

"You'd better get them," Jude said, and although each word came out as a gasp, he smiled at Willem again.

"Fuck 'em," he said, "I'll stay here with you," and Jude laughed a little, although he winced as he did so, and carefully tipped himself backward until he was lying on his side, and Willem helped lift his legs up onto the bed. His sweater was freckled with more flecks of rust, and Willem picked some of them off of him. He sat on the bed next to him, unsure where to begin. "Jude," he tried again.

"Go," Jude said, and closed his eyes, although he was still smiling, and Willem reluctantly stood, shutting the window and turning off the bedroom light as he left, closing the door behind him, heading for the stairwell to save Malcolm and JB, while far beneath him, he could hear the buzzer reverberating through the staircase, announcing the arrival of the evening's first guests.

[II]

The Postman

1

SATURDAYS WERE FOR work, but Sundays were for walking. The walks had begun out of necessity five years ago, when he had moved to the city and knew little about it: each week, he would choose a different neighborhood and walk from Lispenard Street to it, and then around it, covering its perimeter precisely, and then home again. He never skipped a Sunday, unless the weather made it near impossible, and even now, even though he had walked every neighborhood in Manhattan, and many in Brooklyn and Queens as well, he still left every Sunday morning at ten, and returned only when his route was complete. The walks had long ceased to be something he enjoyed, although he didn't *not* enjoy them, either—it was simply something he did. For a period, he had also hopefully considered them something more than exercise, something perhaps restorative, like an amateur physical therapy session, despite the fact that Andy didn't agree with him, and indeed disapproved of his walks. "I'm fine with your wanting to exercise your legs," he'd said. "But in that case, you should really be swimming, not dragging yourself up and down pavement." He wouldn't have minded swimming, actually, but there was nowhere private enough for him to swim, and so he didn't.

Willem had occasionally joined him on these walks, and now, if his route took him past the theater, he would time it so they could meet at the juice stand down the block after the matinee performance. They would have their drinks, and Willem would tell him how the show had gone and would buy a salad to eat before the evening performance, and he would continue south, toward home.

They still lived at Lispenard Street, although both of them could have moved into their own apartments: he, certainly; Willem, probably. But neither of them had ever mentioned leaving to the other, and so neither of them had. They had, however, annexed the left half of the living room to make a second bedroom, the group of them building a lumpy Sheetrocked wall one weekend, so now when you walked in, there was only the gray light from two windows, not four, to greet you. Willem had taken the new bedroom, and he had stayed in their old one.

Aside from their stage-door visits, it felt like he never saw Willem these days, and for all Willem talked about how lazy he was, it seemed he was constantly at work, or trying to work: three years ago, on his twenty-ninth birthday, he had sworn that he was going to quit Ortolan before he turned thirty, and two weeks before his thirtieth birthday, the two of them had been in the apartment, squashed into their newly partitioned living room, Willem worrying about whether he could actually afford to leave his job, when he got a call, the call he had been waiting for for years. The play that had resulted from that call had been enough of a success, and had gotten Willem enough attention, to allow him to quit Ortolan for good thirteen months later: just one year past his self-imposed deadline. He had gone to see Willem's play—a family drama called *The Malamud Theorem*, about a literature professor in the early throes of dementia, and his estranged son, a physicist—five times, twice with Malcolm and JB, and once with Harold and Julia, who were in town for the weekend, and each time he managed to forget that it was his old friend, his roommate, onstage, and at curtain call, he had felt both proud and wistful, as if the stage's very elevation announced Willem's ascendancy to some other realm of life, one not easily accessible to him.

His own approach to thirty had triggered no latent panic, no fluster of activity, no need to rearrange the outlines of his life to more closely resemble what a thirty-year-old's life ought to be. The same was not true for his friends, however, and he had spent the last three years of his twenties listening to their eulogies for the decade, and their detailing of what they had and hadn't done, and the cataloging of their self-loathings and promises. Things had changed, then. The second bedroom, for example, was erected partly out of Willem's fear of being twenty-eight and still sharing a room with his college roommate, and that same anxiety—the fear that, fairy-tale-like, the turn into their fourth decade would transform them into something else, something out of their control, unless they preempted it with their own radical announcements—inspired Malcolm's hasty coming out to his parents, only to see him retreat back in the following year when he started dating a woman.

But despite his friends' anxieties, he knew he would love being thirty, for the very reason that they hated it: because it was an age of undeniable adulthood. (He looked forward to being thirty-five, when he would be able to say he had been an adult for more than twice as long as he had been a child.) When he was growing up, thirty had been a far-off, unimaginable age. He clearly remembered being a very young boy—this was when he lived in the monastery—and asking Brother Michael, who liked to tell him of the travels he had taken in his other life, when he too might be able to travel.

"When you're older," Brother Michael had said.

"When?" he'd asked. "Next year?" Then, even a month had seemed as long as forever.

"Many years," Brother Michael had said. "When you're older. When you're thirty." And now, in just a few weeks, he would be.

On those Sundays, when he was readying to leave for his walk, he would sometimes stand, barefoot, in the kitchen, everything quiet around him, and the small, ugly apartment would feel like a sort of marvel. Here, time was his, and space was his, and every door could be shut, every window locked. He would stand before the tiny hallway closet—an alcove, really, over which they had strung a length of burlap—and admire the stores within it. At Lispenard Street, there were no late-night scrambles to the bodega on West Broadway for a roll of toilet paper, no squinching your nose above a container of long-spoiled milk found in the back corner of the refrigerator: here, there was always extra. Here, everything was replaced when it needed to be. He made sure of it. In their first year at Lispenard Street he had been self-conscious about his habits, which he knew belonged to someone much older and probably female, and had hidden his supplies of paper towels under his bed, had stuffed the fliers for coupons into his briefcase to look through later, when Willem wasn't home, as if they were a particularly exotic form of pornography. But one day, Willem had discovered his stash while looking for a stray sock he'd kicked under the bed.

He had been embarrassed. "Why?" Willem had asked him. "I think it's great. Thank god you're looking out for this kind of stuff." But it had still made him feel vulnerable, yet another piece of evidence added to the overstuffed file testifying to his pinched prissiness, his fundamental and irreparable inability to be the sort of person he tried to make people believe he was.

And yet—as with so much else—he couldn't help himself. To whom could he explain that he found as much contentment and safety in unloved Lispenard Street, in his bomb-shelter stockpilings, as he did in the facts of his degrees and his job? Or that those moments alone in the kitchen were something akin to meditative, the only times he found himself truly relaxing, his mind ceasing to scrabble forward, planning in advance the thousands of little deflections and smudgings of truth, of fact, that necessitated his every interaction with the world and its inhabitants? To no one, he knew, not even to Willem. But he'd had years to learn how to keep his thoughts to himself; unlike his friends, he had learned not to share evidence of his oddities as a way to distinguish himself from others, although he was happy and proud that they shared theirs with him.

Today he would walk to the Upper East Side: up West Broadway to Washington Square Park, to University and through Union Square, and up Broadway to Fifth, which he'd stay on until Eighty-sixth Street, and then back down Madison to Twenty-fourth Street, where he'd cross east to Lexington before continuing south and east once more to Irving, where he'd meet Willem outside the theater. It had been months, almost a year, since he had done this circuit, both because it was very far and because he already spent every Saturday on the Upper East Side, in a town house not far from Malcolm's parents', where he tutored a twelve-year-old boy named Felix. But it was mid-March, spring break, and Felix and his family were on vacation in Utah, which meant he ran no risk of seeing them.

Felix's father was a friend of friends of Malcolm's parents, and it had been Malcolm's father who had gotten him the job. "They're really not paying you enough at the U.S. Attorney's Office, are they?" Mr. Irvine had asked him. "I don't know why you won't just let me introduce you to Gavin." Gavin was one of Mr. Irvine's law school friends, who now presided over one of the city's more powerful firms.

"Dad, he doesn't *want* to work for some corporate firm," Malcolm had begun, but his father continued talking as if Malcolm hadn't even spoken, and Malcolm had hunched back into his chair. He had felt bad for Malcolm then, but also annoyed, as he had told Malcolm to *discreetly* inquire whether his parents knew anyone who might have a kid who needed tutoring, not to *actually* ask them.

"Really, though," Malcolm's father had said to him, "I think it's ter-rific that you're interested in making your way on your own." (Malcolm slouched even lower in his seat.) "But do you really need the money that badly? I didn't think the federal government paid *that* miserably, but it's been a long time since I was in public service." He grinned.

He smiled back. "No," he said, "the salary's fine." (It was. It wouldn't have been to Mr. Irvine, of course, nor to Malcolm, but it was more money than he had ever dreamed he would have, and every two weeks it arrived, a relentless accumulation of numbers.) "I'm just saving up for a down payment." He saw Malcolm's face swivel toward him, and he reminded himself to tell Willem the particular lie he had told Mal-colm's father before Malcolm told Willem himself.

"Oh, well, good for you," said Mr. Irvine. This was a goal he could understand. "And as it happens, I know just the person."

That person was Howard Baker, who had hired him after interview-ing him for fifteen distracted minutes to tutor his son in Latin, math, German, and piano. (He wondered why Mr. Baker wasn't hiring pro-fessionals for each subject—he could have afforded it—but didn't ask.) He felt sorry for Felix, who was small and unappealing, and who had a habit of scratching the inside of one narrow nostril, his index finger tunneling upward until he remembered himself and quickly retracted it, rubbing it on the side of his jeans. Eight months later, it was still unclear to him just how capable Felix was. He wasn't stupid, but he suffered from a lack of passion, as if, at twelve, he had already become resigned to the fact that life would be a disappointment, and he a disap-pointment to the people in it. He was always waiting, on time and with his assignments completed, every Saturday at one p.m., and he obedi-ently answered every question—his answers always ending in an anx-ious, querying upper register, as if every one, even the simplest ("*Salve, Felix, quid agis?*" "Um . . . *bene?*"), were a desperate guess—but he never had any questions of his own, and when he asked Felix if there was any subject in particular he might want to try discussing in either language, Felix would shrug and mumble, his finger drifting toward his nose. He always had the impression, when waving goodbye to Felix at the end of the afternoon—Felix listlessly raising his own hand before slouching back into the recesses of the entryway—that he never left the house, never went out, never had friends over. Poor Felix: his very name was a taunt.

The previous month, Mr. Baker had asked to speak to him after their lessons were over, and he had said goodbye to Felix and followed the maid into the study. His limp had been very pronounced that day, and he had been self-conscious, feeling—as he often did—as if he were playing the role of an impoverished governess in a Dickensian drama.

He had expected impatience from Mr. Baker, perhaps anger, even though Felix was doing quantifiably better in school, and he was ready to defend himself if he needed—Mr. Baker paid far more than he had anticipated, and he had plans for the money he was earning there—but he was instead nodded toward the chair in front of the desk.

"What do you think's wrong with Felix?" Mr. Baker had demanded.

He hadn't been expecting the question, so he had to think before he answered. "I don't think anything's wrong with him, sir," he'd said, carefully. "I just think he's not—" *Happy*, he nearly said. But what was happiness but an extravagance, an impossible state to maintain, partly because it was so difficult to articulate? He couldn't remember being a child and being able to define happiness: there was only misery, or fear, and the absence of misery or fear, and the latter state was all he had needed or wanted. "I think he's shy," he finished.

Mr. Baker grunted (this was obviously not the answer he was looking for). "But you like him, right?" he'd asked him, with such an odd, vulnerable desperation that he experienced a sudden deep sadness, both for Felix and for Mr. Baker. Was this what being a parent was like? Was this what being a *child* with a parent was like? Such unhappinesses, such disappointments, such expectations that would go unexpressed and unmet!

"Of course," he had said, and Mr. Baker had sighed and given him his check, which the maid usually handed to him on his way out.

The next week, Felix hadn't wanted to play his assignment. He was more listless than usual. "Shall we play something else?" he'd asked.

Felix had shrugged. He thought. "Do you want me to play something for you?" Felix had shrugged again. But he did anyway, because it was a beautiful piano and sometimes, as he watched Felix inch his fingers across its lovely smooth keys, he longed to be alone with the instrument and let his hands move over its surface as fast as he could.

He played Haydn, Sonata No. 50 in D Major, one of his favorite pieces and so bright and likable that he thought it might cheer them both up. But when he was finished, and there was only the quiet boy sitting next to him, he was ashamed, both of the braggy, emphatic optimism of the Haydn and of his own burst of self-indulgence.

"Felix," he'd begun, and then stopped. Beside him, Felix waited. "What's wrong?"

And then, to his astonishment, Felix had begun to cry, and he had tried to comfort him. "Felix," he'd said, awkwardly putting his arm around him. He pretended he was Willem, who would have known exactly what to do and what to say without even thinking about it. "It's going to be all right. I promise you, it will be." But Felix had only cried harder.

"I don't have any friends," Felix had sobbed.

"Oh, Felix," he'd said, and his sympathy, which until then had been of the remote, objective kind, clarified itself. "I'm sorry." He felt then, keenly, the loneliness of Felix's life, of a Saturday spent sitting with a crippled nearly thirty-year-old lawyer who was there only to earn money, and who would go out that night with people he loved and who, even, loved him, while Felix remained alone, his mother—Mr. Baker's third wife—perpetually elsewhere, his father convinced there was something wrong with him, something that needed fixing. Later, on his walk home (if the weather was nice, he refused Mr. Baker's car and walked), he would wonder at the unlikely unfairness of it all: Felix, who was by any definition a better kid than he had been, and who yet had no friends, and he, who was a nothing, who did.

"Felix, it'll happen eventually," he'd said, and Felix had wailed, "But *when?*" with such yearning that he had winced.

"Soon, soon," he had told him, petting his skinny back, "I promise," and Felix had nodded, although later, walking him to the door, his little geckoey face made even more reptilian from tears, he'd had the distinct sensation that Felix had known he was lying. Who could know if Felix would ever have friends? Friendship, companionship: it so often defied logic, so often eluded the deserving, so often settled itself on the odd, the bad, the peculiar, the damaged. He waved goodbye at Felix's small back, retreating already into the house, and although he would never have said so to Felix, he somehow fancied that this was why Felix was so wan all the time: it was because Felix had already figured this out, long ago; it was because he already knew.

—

He knew French and German. He knew the periodic table. He knew—as much as he didn't care to—large parts of the Bible almost by memory. He knew how to help birth a calf and rewire a lamp and unclog a drain and the most efficient way to harvest a walnut tree and which mushrooms were poisonous and which were not and how to bale hay and how to test a watermelon, an apple, a squash, a muskmelon for freshness by thunking it in the right spot. (And then he knew things he wished he didn't, things he hoped never to have to use again, things that, when he thought of them or dreamed of them at night, made him curl into himself with hatred and shame.)

And yet it often seemed he knew nothing of any real value or use, not really. The languages and the math, fine. But daily he was reminded of how much he didn't know. He had never heard of the sitcoms whose episodes were constantly referenced. He had never been to a movie. He had never gone on vacation. He had never been to summer camp. He had never had pizza or popsicles or macaroni and cheese (and he had certainly never had—as both Malcolm and JB had—foie gras or sushi or marrow). He had never owned a computer or a phone, he had rarely been allowed to go online. He had never owned anything, he realized, not really: the books he had that he was so proud of, the shirts that he repaired again and again, they were nothing, they were trash, the pride he took in them was more shameful than not owning anything at all. The classroom was the safest place, and the only place he felt fully confident: everywhere else was an unceasing avalanche of marvels, each more baffling than the next, each another reminder of his bottomless ignorance. He found himself keeping mental lists of new things he had heard and encountered. But he could never ask anyone for the answers. To do so would be an admission of extreme otherness, which would invite further questions and would leave him exposed, and which would inevitably lead to conversations he definitely was not prepared to have. He felt, often, not so much foreign—for even the foreign students (even Odval, from a village outside Ulaanbaatar) seemed to understand these references—as from another time altogether: his childhood might well have been spent in the nineteenth century, not the twenty-first, for all he had apparently missed, and for how obscure and merely decorative what he *did* know seemed to be. How was it that apparently all of his peers, whether they were born in Lagos or Los Angeles, had had more or less the same experience, with the same cultural landmarks? Surely there was someone who knew as little as he did? And if not, how was he ever to catch up?

In the evenings, when a group of them lay splayed in someone's room (a candle burning, a joint burning as well), the conversation often turned to his classmates' childhoods, which they had barely left but about which they were curiously nostalgic and certainly obsessed. They recounted what seemed like every detail of them, though he was never sure if the goal was to compare with one another their similarities or to boast of their differences, because they seemed to take equal pleasure in both. They spoke of curfews, and rebellions, and punishments (a few people's parents had hit them, and they related these stories with something close to pride, which he also found curious) and pets and siblings, and what they had worn that had driven their parents crazy, and what groups they had hung out with in high school and to whom they had lost their virginity, and where, and how, and cars they had crashed and bones they had broken, and sports they had played and bands they had started. They spoke of disastrous family vacations and strange, colorful relatives and odd next-door neighbors and teachers, both beloved and loathed. He enjoyed these divulgences more than he expected—these were *real* teenagers who'd had the sorts of real, plain lives he had always wondered about—and he found it both relaxing and educational to sit there late at night and listen to them. His silence was both a necessity and a protection, and had the added benefit of making him appear more mysterious and more interesting than he knew he was. "What about you, Jude?" a few people had asked him, early in the term, and he knew enough by then—he was a fast learner—to simply shrug and say, with a smile, "It's too boring to get into." He was astonished but relieved by how easily they accepted that, and grateful too for their self-absorption. None of them really wanted to listen to someone else's story anyway; they only wanted to tell their own.

And yet his silence did not go unnoticed by everyone, and it was his silence that had inspired his nickname. This was the year Malcolm discovered postmodernism, and JB had made such a fuss about how late Malcolm was to that particular ideology that he hadn't admitted that he hadn't heard of it either.

"You can't just *decide* you're post-black, Malcolm," JB had said. "And also: you have to have actually *been black* to begin with in order to move *beyond* blackness."

"You're such a dick, JB," Malcolm had said.

"Or," JB had continued, "you have to be so genuinely uncategorizable that the normal terms of identity don't even apply to you." JB had turned toward him, then, and he had felt himself freeze with a momentary terror. "Like Judy here: we never see him with anyone, we don't know what race he is, we don't know anything about him. Post-sexual, post-racial, post-identity, post-past." He smiled at him, presumably to show he was at least partly joking. "The post-man. Jude the Postman."

"The Postman," Malcolm had repeated: he was never above grabbing on to someone else's discomfort as a way of deflecting attention from his own. And although the name didn't stick—when Willem had returned to the room and heard it, he had only rolled his eyes in response, which seemed to remove some of its thrill for JB—he was reminded that as much as he had convinced himself he was fitting in, as much as he worked to conceal the spiky odd parts of himself, he was fooling no one. They knew he was strange, and now his foolishness extended to his having convinced himself that he had convinced *them* that he wasn't. Still, he kept attending the late-night groups, kept joining his classmates in their rooms: he was pulled to them, even though he now knew he was putting himself in jeopardy by attending them.

Sometimes during these sessions (he had begun to think of them this way, as intensive tutorials in which he could correct his own cultural paucities) he would catch Willem watching him with an indecipherable expression on his face, and would wonder how much Willem might have guessed about him. Sometimes he had to stop himself from saying something to him. Maybe he was wrong, he sometimes thought. Maybe it would be nice to confess to someone that most of the time he could barely relate to what was being discussed, that he couldn't participate in everyone else's shared language of childhood pratfalls and frustrations. But then he would stop himself, for admitting ignorance of that language would mean having to explain the one he *did* speak.

Although if he were to tell anyone, he knew it would be Willem. He admired all three of his roommates, but Willem was the one he trusted. At the home, he had quickly learned there were three types of boys: The first type might cause the fight (this was JB). The second type wouldn't join in, but wouldn't run to get help, either (this was Malcolm). And the third type would actually try to help you out (this was the rarest type, and this was obviously Willem). Maybe it was the same with girls as well, but he hadn't spent enough time around girls to know this for sure.

And increasingly he was certain Willem knew something. (*Knows what?* he'd argue with himself, in saner moments. *You're just looking for a reason to tell him, and then what will he think of you? Be smart. Say nothing. Have some self-control.*) But this was of course illogical. He knew even before he got to college that his childhood had been atypical—you had only to read a few books to come to that conclusion—but it wasn't until recently that he had realized how atypical it truly was. Its very strangeness both insulated and isolated him: it was near inconceivable that anyone would guess at its shape and specificities, which meant that if they did, it was because he had dropped clues like cow turds, great ugly unmissable pleas for attention.

Still. The suspicion persisted, sometimes with an uncomfortable intensity, as if it was inevitable that he should say something and was being sent messages that took more energy to ignore than they would have to obey.

One night it was just the four of them. This was early in their third year, and was unusual enough for them all to feel cozy and a little sentimental about the clique they had made. And they *were* a clique, and to his surprise, he was part of it: the building they lived in was called Hood Hall, and they were known around campus as the Boys in the Hood. All of them had other friends (JB and Willem had the most), but it was known (or at least assumed, which was just as good) that their first loyalties were to one another. None of them had ever discussed this explicitly, but they all knew they liked this assumption, that they liked this code of friendship that had been imposed upon them.

The food that night had been pizza, ordered by JB and paid for by Malcolm. There had been weed, procured by JB, and outside there had been rain and then hail, the sound of it cracking against the glass and the wind rattling the windows in their splintered wooden casements the final elements in their happiness. The joint went round and round, and although he didn't take a puff—he never did; he was too worried about what he might do or say if he lost control over himself—he could feel the smoke filling his eyes, pressing upon his eyelids like a shaggy warm beast. He had been careful, as he always was when one of the others paid for food, to eat as little as possible, and although he was still hungry (there were two slices left over, and he stared at them, fixedly, before catching himself and turning away resolutely), he was also deeply content. I could fall asleep, he thought, and stretched out on the couch, pulling Malcolm's blanket over him as he did. He was pleasantly exhausted, but then he was always exhausted those days: it was as if the daily effort it took to appear normal was so great that it left energy for little else. (He was aware, sometimes, of seeming wooden, icy, of being boring, which he recognized that here might have been considered the greater misfortune than being whatever it was he was.) In the background, as if far away, he could hear Malcolm and JB having a fight about evil.

"I'm just saying, we wouldn't be having this argument if you'd read Plato."

"Yeah, but *what* Plato?"

"Have you read Plato?"

"I don't see—"

"*Have* you?"

"No, but—"

"See! See, see?!" That would be Malcolm, jumping up and down and pointing at JB, while Willem laughed. On weed, Malcolm grew both sillier and more pedantic, and the three of them liked getting into silly and pedantic philosophical arguments with him, the contents of which Malcolm could never recall in the morning.

Then there was an interlude of Willem and JB talking about something—he was too sleepy to really listen, just awake enough to distinguish their voices—and then JB's voice, ringing through his fug: "Jude!"

"What?" he answered, his eyes still closed.

"I want to ask you a question."

He could instantly feel something inside him come alert. When high, JB had the uncanny ability to ask questions or make observations that both devastated and discomfited. He didn't *think* there was any malice behind it, but it made you wonder what went on in JB's subconscious. Was *this* the real JB, the one who had asked their hallmate, Tricia Park, what it was like growing up as the ugly twin (poor Tricia had gotten up and run out of the room), or was it the one who, after JB had witnessed him in the grip of a terrible episode, one in which he could feel himself falling in and out of consciousness, the sensation as sickening as tumbling off a roller coaster in mid-incline, had snuck out that night with his stoner boyfriend and returned just before daybreak with a bundle of bud-furred magnolia branches, sawn off illegally from the quadrangle's trees?

"What?" he asked again, warily.

"Well," said JB, pausing and taking another inhalation, "we've all known each other a while now—"

"We have?" Willem asked in fake surprise.

"Shut up, Willem," JB continued. "And all of us want to know why you've never told us what happened to your legs."

"Oh, JB, we do not—" Willem began, but Malcolm, who had the habit of vociferously taking JB's side when stoned, interrupted him: "It really hurts our feelings, Jude. Do you not trust us?"

"Jesus, Malcolm," Willem said, and then, mimicking Malcolm in a shrieky falsetto, " 'It really hurts our feelings.' You sound like a girl. It's Jude's business."

And this was worse, somehow, having to have Willem, always Willem, defend him. Against Malcolm and JB! At that moment, he hated all of them, but of course he was in no position to hate them. They were his friends, his first friends, and he understood that friendship was a series of exchanges: of affections, of time, sometimes of money, always of information. And he had no money. He had nothing to give them, he had nothing to offer. He couldn't loan Willem a sweater, the way Willem let him borrow his, or repay Malcolm the hundred dollars he'd pressed upon him once, or even help JB on move-out day, as JB helped him.

"Well," he began, and was aware of all of their perked silences, even Willem's. "It's not very interesting." He kept his eyes closed, both because it made it easier to tell the story when he didn't have to look at them, and also because he simply didn't think he could stand it at the moment. "It was a car injury. I was fifteen. It was the year before I came here."

"Oh," said JB. There was a pause; he could feel something in the room deflate, could feel how his revelation had shifted the others back into a sort of somber sobriety. "I'm sorry, bro. That sucks."

"You could walk before?" asked Malcolm, as if he could not walk now. And this made him sad and embarrassed: what he considered walking, they apparently did not.

"Yes," he said, and then, because it was true, even if not the way they'd interpret it, he added, "I used to run cross-country."

"Oh, wow," said Malcolm. JB made a sympathetic grunting noise.

Only Willem, he noticed, said nothing. But he didn't dare open his eyes to look at his expression.

Eventually the word got out, as he knew it would. (Perhaps people really *did* wonder about his legs. Tricia Park later came up to him and told him she'd always assumed he had cerebral palsy. What was he supposed to say to *that*?) Somehow, though, over the tellings and retellings, the explanation was changed to a car accident, and then to a drunken driving accident.

"The easiest explanations are often the right ones," his math professor, Dr. Li, always said, and maybe the same principle applied here. Except he knew it didn't. Math was one thing. Nothing else was that reductive.

But the odd thing was this: by his story morphing into one about a car accident, he was being given an opportunity for reinvention; all he had to do was claim it. But he never could. He could never call it an accident, because it wasn't. And so was it pride or stupidity to not take the escape route he'd been offered? He didn't know.

And then he noticed something else. He was in the middle of another episode—a highly humiliating one, it had taken place just as he was coming off of his shift at the library, and Willem had just happened to be there a few minutes early, about to start his own shift—when he heard the librarian, a kind, well-read woman whom he liked, ask why he had these. They had moved him, Mrs. Eakeley and Willem, to the break room in the back, and he could smell the burned-sugar tang of old coffee, a scent he despised anyway, so sharp and assaultive that he almost vomited.

"A car injury," he heard Willem's reply, as from across a great black lake.

But it wasn't until that night that he registered what Willem had said, and the word he had used: injury, not accident. Was it deliberate, he wondered? What did Willem know? He was so addled that he might have actually asked him, had Willem been around, but he wasn't—he was at his girlfriend's.

No one was there, he realized. The room was his. He felt the creature inside him—which he pictured as slight and raggedy and lemur-like, quick-reflexed and ready to sprint, its dark wet eyes forever scanning the landscape for future dangers—relax and sag to the ground. It was at these moments that he found college most enjoyable: he was in a warm room, and the next day he would have three meals and eat as much as he wanted, and in between he would go to classes, and no one would try to hurt him or make him do anything he didn't want to do. Somewhere nearby were his roommates—his friends—and he had survived another day without divulging any of his secrets, and placed another day between the person he once was and the person he was now. It seemed, always, an accomplishment worthy of sleep, and so he did, closing his eyes and readying himself for another day in the world.

—

It had been Ana, his first and only social worker, and the first person who had never betrayed him, who had talked to him seriously about college—the college he ended up attending—and who was convinced that he would get in. She hadn't been the first person to suggest this, but she had been the most insistent.

"I don't see why not," she said. It was a favorite phrase of hers. The two of them were sitting on Ana's porch, in Ana's backyard, eating banana bread that Ana's girlfriend had made. Ana didn't care for nature (too buggy, too *squirmy*, she always said), but when he made the suggestion that they go outdoors—tentatively, because at the time he was still unsure where the boundaries of her tolerance for him lay—she'd slapped the edges of her armchair and heaved herself up. "I don't see why not. Leslie!" she called into the kitchen, where Leslie was making lemonade. "You can bring it outside!"

Hers was the first face he saw when he had at last opened his eyes in the hospital. For a long moment, he couldn't remember where he was, or who he was, or what had happened, and then, suddenly, her face was above his, looking at him. "Well, well," she said. "He awakes."

She was always there, it seemed, no matter what time he woke. Sometimes it was day, and he heard the sounds of the hospital—the mouse squeak of the nurses' shoes, and the clatter of a cart, and the drone of the intercom announcements—in the hazy, half-formed moments he had before shifting into full consciousness. But sometimes it was night, when everything was silent around him, and it took him longer to figure out where he was, and why he was there, although it came back to him, it always did, and unlike some realizations, it never grew easier or fuzzier with each remembrance. And sometimes it was neither day nor night but somewhere in between, and there would be something strange and dusty about the light that made him imagine for a moment that there might after all be such a thing as heaven, and that he might after all have made it there. And then he would hear Ana's voice, and remember again why he was there, and want to close his eyes all over again.

They talked of nothing in those moments. She would ask him if he was hungry, and no matter his answer, she would have a sandwich for him to eat. She would ask him if he was in pain, and if he was, how intense it was. It was in her presence that he'd had the first of his episodes, and the pain had been so awful—unbearable, almost, as if someone had reached in and grabbed his spine like a snake and was trying to loose it from its bundles of nerves by shaking it—that later, when the surgeon told him that an injury like his was an "insult" to the body, and one the body would never recover from completely, he had understood what the word meant and realized how correct and well-chosen it was.

"You mean he's going to have these all his life?" Ana had asked, and he had been grateful for her outrage, especially because he was too tired and frightened to summon forth any of his own.

"I wish I could say no," said the surgeon. And then, to him, "But they may not be this severe in the future. You're young now. The spine has wonderful reparative qualities."

"Jude," she'd said to him when the next one came, two days after the first. He could hear her voice, but as if from far away, and then, suddenly, awfully close, filling his mind like explosions. "Hold on to my hand," she'd said, and again, her voice swelled and receded, but she

seized his hand and he held it so tightly he could feel her index finger
slide oddly over her ring finger, could almost feel every small bone in
her palm reposition themselves in his grip, which had the effect of making her seem like something delicate and intricate, although there was
nothing delicate about her in either appearance or manner. "Count,"
she commanded him the third time it happened, and he did, counting up to a hundred again and again, parsing the pain into negotiable
increments. In those days, before he learned it was better to be still, he
would flop on his bed like a fish on a boat deck, his free hand scrabbling
for a halyard line to cling to for safety, the hospital mattress unyielding
and uncaring, searching for a position in which the discomfort might
lessen. He tried to be quiet, but he could hear himself making strange
animal noises, so that at times a forest appeared beneath his eyelids,
populated with screech owls and deer and bears, and he would imagine
he was one of them, and that the sounds he was making were normal,
part of the woods' unceasing soundtrack.

When it had ended, she would give him some water, a straw in the
glass so he wouldn't have to raise his head. Beneath him, the floor tilted
and bucked, and he was often sick. He had never been in the ocean,
but he imagined this was what it might feel like, imagined the swells of
water forcing the linoleum floor into quavering hillocks. "Good boy,"
she'd say as he drank. "Have a little more."

"It'll get better," she'd say, and he'd nod, because he couldn't
begin to imagine his life if it *didn't* get better. His days now were hours:
hours without pain and hours with it, and the unpredictability of this
schedule—and his body, although it was his in name only, for he could
control nothing of it—exhausted him, and he slept and slept, the days
slipping away from him uninhabited.

Later, it would be easier to simply tell people that it was his legs
that hurt him, but that wasn't really true: it was his back. Sometimes
he could predict what would trigger the spasming, that pain that would
extend down his spine into one leg or the other, like a wooden stake set
aflame and thrust into him: a certain movement, lifting something too
heavy or too high, simple tiredness. But sometimes he couldn't. And
sometimes the pain would be preceded by an interlude of numbness,
or a twinging that was almost pleasurable, it was so light and zingy, just
a sensation of electric prickles moving up and down his spine, and he
would know to lie down and wait for it to finish its cycle, a penance

he could never escape or avoid. But sometimes it barged in, and those were the worst: he grew fearful that it would arrive at some terribly inopportune time, and before each big meeting, each big interview, each court appearance, he would beg his own back to still itself, to carry him through the next few hours without incident. But all of this was in the future, and each lesson he learned he did so over hours and hours of these episodes, stretched out over days and months and years.

As the weeks passed, she brought him books, and told him to write down titles he was interested in and she would go to the library and get them—but he was too shy to do so. He knew she was his social worker, and that she had been assigned to him, but it wasn't until more than a month had passed, and the doctors had begun to talk about his casts being removed in a matter of weeks, that she first asked him about what had happened.

"I don't remember," he said. It was his default answer for everything back then. It was a lie as well; in uninvited moments, he'd see the car's headlights, twinned glares of white, rushing toward him, and recall how he'd shut his eyes and jerked his head to the side, as if that might have prevented the inevitable.

She waited. "It's okay, Jude," she said. "We basically know what happened. But I need you to tell me at some point, so we can talk about it." She had interviewed him earlier, did he remember? There had apparently been a moment soon after he'd come out of the first surgery that he had woken, lucid, and answered all her questions, not only about what had happened that night but in the years before it as well—but he honestly didn't remember this at all, and he fretted about what, exactly, he had said, and what Ana's expression had been when he'd told her.

How much had he told her? he asked at one point.

"Enough," she said, "to convince me that there's a hell and those men need to be in it." She didn't sound angry, but her words were, and he closed his eyes, impressed and a little scared that the things that had happened to him—to him!—could inspire such passion, such vitriol.

She oversaw his transfer into his new home, his final home: the Douglasses'. They had two other fosters, both girls, both young—Rosie was eight and had Down syndrome, Agnes was nine and had spina bifida. The house was a maze of ramps, unlovely but sturdy and

smooth, and unlike Agnes, he could wheel himself around without asking for assistance.

The Douglasses were evangelical Lutherans, but they didn't make
him attend church with them. "They're good people," Ana said. "They
won't bother you, and you'll be safe here. You think you can manage
grace at the table for a little privacy and guaranteed security?" She
looked at him and smiled. He nodded. "Besides," she continued, "you
can always call me if you want to talk sin."

And indeed, he was in Ana's care more than in the Douglasses'.
He slept in their house, and ate there, and when he was first learning
how to move on his crutches, it was Mr. Douglass who sat on a chair
outside the bathroom, ready to enter if he slipped and fell getting into
or out of the bathtub (he still wasn't able to balance well enough to take
a shower, even with a walker). But it was Ana who took him to most of
his doctor's appointments, and Ana who waited at one end of her backyard, a cigarette in her mouth, as he took his first slow steps toward her,
and Ana who finally got him to write down what had happened with
Dr. Traylor, and kept him from having to testify in court. He had said
he could do it, but she had told him he wasn't ready yet, and that they
had plenty of evidence to put Dr. Traylor away for years even without
his testimony, and hearing that, he was able to admit his own relief:
relief at not having to say aloud words he didn't know how to say, and
mostly, relief that he wouldn't have to see Dr. Traylor again. When he
at last gave her the statement—which he'd written as plainly as possible, and had imagined while writing it that he was in fact writing
about someone else, someone he had known once but had never had
to talk to again—she read it through once, impassive, before nodding at
him. "Good," she said briskly, and refolded it and placed it back in its
envelope. "Good job," she added, and then, suddenly, she began to cry,
almost ferociously, unable to stop herself. She was saying something to
him, but she was weeping so hard he couldn't understand her, and she
had finally left, though she had called him later that night to apologize.

"I'm sorry, Jude," she said. "That was really unprofessional of me. I
just read what you wrote and I just—" She was silent for a period, and
then took a breath. "It won't happen again."

It was also Ana who, after the doctors determined he wouldn't be
strong enough to go to school, found him a tutor so he could finish high

school, and it was she who made him discuss college. "You're really smart, did you know that?" she asked him. "You could go anywhere, really. I talked to some of your teachers in Montana, and they think so as well. Have you thought about it? You have? Where would you want to go?" And when he told her, preparing himself for her to laugh, she instead only nodded: "I don't see why not."

"But," he began, "do you think they'd take someone like me?"

Once again, she didn't laugh. "It's true, you haven't had the most—traditional—of educations"—she smiled at him—"but your tests are terrific, and although you probably don't think so, I promise you know more than most, if not all, kids your age." She sighed. "You may have something to thank Brother Luke for after all." She studied his face. "So I don't see why not."

She helped him with everything: she wrote one of his recommendations, she let him use her computer to type up his essay (he didn't write about the past year; he wrote about Montana, and how he'd learned there to forage for mustard shoots and mushrooms), she even paid for his application fee.

When he was accepted—with a full scholarship, as Ana had predicted—he told her it was all because of her.

"Bullshit," she said. She was so sick by that point that she could only whisper it. "You did it yourself." Later he would scan through the previous months and see, as if spotlit, the signs of her illness, and how, in his stupidity and self-absorption, he had missed one after the next: her weight loss, her yellowing eyes, her fatigue, all of which he had attributed to—what? "You shouldn't smoke," he'd said to her just two months earlier, confident enough around her now to start issuing orders; the first adult he'd done so to. "You're right," she'd said, and squinted her eyes at him while inhaling deeply, grinning at him when he sighed at her.

Even then, she didn't give up. "Jude, we should talk about it," she'd say every few days, and when he shook his head, she'd be silent. "Tomorrow, then," she'd say. "Do you promise me? Tomorrow we'll talk about it."

"I don't see why I have to talk about it at all," he muttered at her once. He knew she had read his records from Montana; he knew she knew what he was.

She was quiet. "One thing I've learned," she said, "you have to talk about these things while they're fresh. Or you'll never talk about them. I'm going to teach you how to talk about them, because it's going to get harder and harder the longer you wait, and it's going to fester inside you, and you're always going to think you're to blame. You'll be wrong, of course, but you'll always think it." He didn't know how to respond to that, but the next day, when she brought it up again, he shook his head and turned away from her, even though she called after him. "Jude," she said, once, "I've let you go on for too long without addressing this. This is my fault."

"Do it for me, Jude," she said at another point. But he couldn't; he couldn't find the language to talk about it, not even to her. Besides, he didn't want to relive those years. He wanted to forget them, to pretend they belonged to someone else.

By June she was so weak she couldn't sit. Fourteen months after they'd met, she was the one in bed, and he was the one next to her. Leslie worked the day shift at the hospital, and so often, it was just the two of them in the house. "Listen," she said. Her throat was dry from one of her medications, and she winced as she spoke. He reached for the jug of water, but she waved her hand, impatiently. "Leslie's going to take you shopping before you leave; I made a list for her of things you'll need." He started to protest, but she stopped him. "Don't argue, Jude. I don't have the energy."

She swallowed. He waited. "You're going to be great at college," she said. She shut her eyes. "The other kids are going to ask you about how you grew up, have you thought about that?"

"Sort of," he said. It was all he thought about.

"Mmph," she grunted. She didn't believe him either. "What are you going to tell them?" And then she opened her eyes and looked at him.

"I don't know," he admitted.

"Ah, yes," she said. They were quiet. "Jude," she began, and then stopped. "You'll find your own way to discuss what happened to you. You'll have to, if you ever want to be close to anyone. But your life—no matter what you think, you have nothing to be ashamed of, and none of it has been your fault. Will you remember that?"

It was the closest they had ever gotten to discussing not only the previous year but the years that preceded it, too. "Yes," he told her.

She glared at him. "Promise me."

"I promise."

But even then, he couldn't believe her.

She sighed. "I should've made you talk more," she said. It was the last thing she ever said to him. Two weeks later—July third—she was dead. Her service was the week after that. By this point he had a summer job at a local bakery, where he sat in the back room spackling cakes with fondant, and in the days following the funeral he sat until night at his workstation, plastering cake after cake with carnation-pink icing, trying not to think of her.

At the end of July, the Douglasses moved: Mr. Douglass had gotten a new job in San Jose, and they were taking Agnes with them; Rosie was being reassigned to a different family. He had liked the Douglasses, but when they told him to stay in touch, he knew he wouldn't—he was so desperate to move away from the life he was in, the life he'd had; he wanted to be someone whom no one knew and who knew no one.

He was put into emergency shelter. That was what the state called it: emergency shelter. He'd argued that he was old enough to be left on his own (he imagined, also illogically, that he would sleep in the back room of the bakery), and that in less than two months he'd be gone anyway, out of the system entirely, but no one agreed with him. The shelter was a dormitory, a sagging gray honeycomb populated by other kids who—because of what they had done or what had been done to them or simply how old they were—the state couldn't easily place.

When it was time for him to leave, they gave him some money to buy supplies for school. They were, he recognized, vaguely proud of him; he might not have been in the system for long, but he was going to college, and to a superior college at that—he would forever after be claimed as one of their successes. Leslie drove him to the Army Navy Store. He wondered, as he chose things he thought he might need—two sweaters, three long-sleeve shirts, pants, a gray blanket that resembled the clotty stuffing that vomited forth from the sofa in the shelter's lobby—if he was getting the correct things, the things that might have been on Ana's list. He couldn't stop himself from thinking that there was something else on that list, something essential that Ana thought he needed that he would now never know. At nights, he craved that list, sometimes more than he craved her; he could picture it in his mind, the funny up-and-down capitalizations she inserted into a single word, the mechanical pencil she always used, the yellow legal pads, left over from her years as a lawyer, on which she made her notes. Sometimes the letters solidified into words, and in the dream life he'd feel triumphant; ah, he'd think, of course! Of course that's what I need! Of course Ana would know! But in the mornings, he could never remember what those things were. In those moments he wished, perversely, that he had never met her, that it was surely worse to have had her for so brief a period than to never have had her at all.

They gave him a bus ticket north; Leslie came to the station to see him off. He had packed his things in a double-layered black garbage bag, and then inside the backpack he'd bought at the Army Navy Store: everything he owned in one neat package. On the bus he stared out the window and thought of nothing. He hoped his back wouldn't betray him on the ride, and it didn't.

He had been the first to arrive in their room, and when the second boy came in—it had been Malcolm—with his parents and suitcases and books and speakers and television and phones and computers and refrigerator and flotillas of digital gadgetry, he had felt the first sensations of sickening fear, and then anger, directed irrationally at Ana: How could she let him believe he might be equipped to do this? Who could he say he was? Why had she never told him exactly how poor, how ugly, what a scrap of bloodied, muddied cloth, his life really was? Why had she let him believe he might belong here?

As the months passed, this feeling dampened, but it never disappeared; it lived on him like a thin scum of mold. But as that knowledge became more acceptable, another piece became less so: he began to realize that she was the first and last person to whom he would never have to explain anything. She knew that he wore his life on his skin, that his biography was written in his flesh and on his bones. She would never ask him why he wouldn't wear short sleeves, even in the steamiest of weather, or why he didn't like to be touched, or, most important, what had happened to his legs or back: she knew already. Around her he had felt none of the constant anxiety, nor watchfulness, that he seemed condemned to feel around everyone else; the vigilance was exhausting, but it eventually became simply a part of life, a habit like good posture. Once, she had reached out to (he later realized) embrace him, but he had reflexively brought his hands up over his head to protect himself, and although he had been embarrassed, she hadn't made him feel silly or overreactive. "I'm an idiot, Jude," she'd said instead. "I'm sorry. No more sudden movements, I promise."

But now she was gone, and no one knew him. His records were sealed. His first Christmas, Leslie had sent him a card, addressed to him through the student affairs office, and he had kept it for days, his last link to Ana, before finally throwing it away. He never wrote back, and he never heard from Leslie again. It was a new life. He was determined not to ruin it for himself.

Still, sometimes, he thought back to their final conversations, mouthing them aloud. This was at night, when his roommates—in various configurations, depending on who was in the room at the time—slept above and next to him. "Don't let this silence become a habit," she'd warned him shortly before she died. And: "It's all right to be angry, Jude; you don't have to hide it." She had been wrong about him, he always thought; he wasn't what she thought he was. "You're destined for greatness, kid," she'd said once, and he wanted to believe her, even though he couldn't. But she was right about one thing: it *did* get harder and harder. He *did* blame himself. And although he tried every day to remember the promise he'd made to her, every day it became more and more remote, until it was just a memory, and so was she, a beloved character from a book he'd read long ago.

—

"The world has two kinds of people," Judge Sullivan used to say. "Those who are inclined to believe, and those who aren't. In my courtroom, we value belief. Belief in *all* things."

He made this proclamation often, and after doing so, he would groan himself to his feet—he was very fat—and toddle out of the room. This was usually at the end of the day—Sullivan's day, at least—when he left his chambers and came over to speak to his law clerks, sitting on the edge of one of their desks and delivering often opaque lectures that were interspersed with frequent pauses, as if his clerks were not lawyers but scriveners, and should be writing down his words. But no one did, not even Kerrigan, who was a true believer and the most conservative of the three of them.

After the judge left, he would grin across the room at Thomas, who would raise his eyes upward in a gesture of helplessness and apology. Thomas was a conservative, too, but "a *thinking* conservative," he'd remind him, "and the fact that I even have to make that distinction is fucking depressing."

He and Thomas had started clerking for the judge the same year, and when he had been approached by the judge's informal search committee—really, his Business Associations professor, with whom the judge was old friends—the spring of his second year of law school, it had been Harold who had encouraged him to apply. Sullivan was known among his fellow circuit court judges for always hiring one clerk whose political views diverged from his own, the more wildly, the better. (His last liberal law clerk had gone on to work for a Hawaiian rights sovereignty group that advocated for the islands' secession from the United States, a career move that had sent the judge into a fit of apoplectic self-satisfaction.)

"Sullivan hates me," Harold had told him then, sounding pleased. "He'll hire you just to spite me." He smiled, savoring the thought. "And because you're the most brilliant student I've ever had," he added.

The compliment made him look at the ground: Harold's praise tended to be conveyed to him by others, and was rarely handed to him directly. "I'm not sure I'm liberal enough for him," he'd replied. Certainly he wasn't liberal enough for Harold; it was one of the things—his opinions; the way he read the law; how he applied it to life—that they argued about.

Harold snorted. "Trust me," he said. "You are."

But when he went to Washington for his interview the following year, Sullivan had talked about the law—and political philosophy—with much less vigor and specificity than he had anticipated. "I hear that you sing," Sullivan said instead after an hour of conversation about what he had studied (the judge had attended the same law school), and his position as the articles editor on the law review (the same position the judge himself had held), and his thoughts on recent cases.

"I do," he replied, wondering how the judge had learned that. Singing was his comfort, but he rarely did it in front of others. Had he been singing in Harold's office and been overheard? Or sometimes he sang in the law library, when he was re-shelving books late at night and the space was as quiet and still as a church—had someone overheard him there?

"Sing me something," said the judge.

"What would you like to hear, sir?" he asked. Normally, he would have been much more nervous, but he had heard that the judge would make him do a performance of some sort (legend had it that he'd made a previous applicant juggle), and Sullivan was a known opera lover.

The judge put his fat fingers to his fat lips and thought. "Hmm," he said. "Sing me something that tells me something about you."

He thought, and then sang. He was surprised to hear what he chose—Mahler's "Ich bin der Welt abhanden gekommen"—both because he didn't even really like Mahler that much and because the lied was a difficult one to perform, slow and mournful and subtle and not meant for a tenor. And yet he liked the poem itself, which his voice teacher in college had dismissed as "second-rate romanticism," but which he had always thought suffered unfairly from a poor translation. The standard interpretation of the first line was "I am lost to the world," but he read it as "I have *become* lost to the world," which, he believed, was less self-pitying, less melodramatic, and more resigned, more confused. *I have become lost to the world / In which I otherwise wasted so much time.* The lied was about the life of an artist, which he was definitely not. But he understood, primally almost, the concept of losing, of loosing oneself from the world, of disappearing into a different place, one of retreat and safety, of the twinned yearnings of escape and discovery. *It means nothing to me / Whether the world believes me dead / I can hardly say anything to refute it / For truly, I am no longer a part of the world.*

When he finished, he opened his eyes to the judge clapping and laughing. "Bravo," he said. "Bravo! But I think you might be in the wrong profession altogether, you know." He laughed again. "Where'd you learn to sing like that?"

"The brothers, sir," he'd replied.

"Ah, a Catholic boy?" asked the judge, sitting up fatly in his chair and looking ready to be pleased.

"I was raised Catholic," he began.

"But you're not now?" the judge asked, frowning.

"No," he said. He had worked for years to keep the apology out of his voice when he said this.

Sullivan made a noncommittal grunting noise. "Well, whatever they gave you should have offered at least some sort of protection against whatever Harold Stein's been filling your head with for the past few years," he said. He looked at his résumé. "You're his research assistant?"

"Yes," he said. "For more than two years."

"A good mind, wasted," Sullivan declared (it was unclear whether he meant his or Harold's). "Thanks for coming down, we'll be in touch. And thanks for the lied; you have one of the most beautiful tenors I've heard in a long time. Are you *sure* you're in the right field?" At this, he smiled, the last time he would ever see Sullivan smile with such pleasure and sincerity.

Back in Cambridge, he told Harold about his meeting ("You *sing?*" Harold asked him, as if he'd just told him he flew), but that he was certain he wouldn't get the clerkship. A week later, Sullivan called: the job was his. He was surprised, but Harold wasn't. "I told you so," he said.

The next day, he went to Harold's office as usual, but Harold had his coat on. "Normal work is suspended today," he announced. "I need you to run some errands with me." This was unusual, but Harold was unusual. At the curb, he held out the keys: "Do you want to drive?"

"Sure," he said, and went to the driver's side. This was the car he'd learned to drive in, just a year ago, while Harold sat next to him, far more patient outside the classroom than he was in it. "Good," he'd said. "Let go of the clutch a little more—good. Good, Jude, good."

Harold had to pick up some shirts he'd had altered, and they drove to the small, expensive men's store on the edge of the square where Willem had worked his senior year. "Come in with me," Harold instructed him, "I'm going to need some help carrying these out."

"My god, Harold, how many shirts did you buy?" he asked. Harold had an unvarying wardrobe of blue shirts, white shirts, brown corduroys (for winter), linen pants (for spring and summer), and sweaters in various shades of greens and blues.

"Quiet, you," said Harold.

Inside, Harold went off to find a salesperson, and he waited, running his fingers over the ties in their display cases, rolled and shiny as pastries. Malcolm had given him two of his old cotton suits, which he'd had tailored and had worn throughout both of his summer internships, but he'd had to borrow his roommate's suit for the Sullivan interview, and he had tried to move carefully in it the entire time it was his, aware of its largeness and the fineness of its wool.

Then "That's him," he heard Harold say, and when he turned, Harold was standing with a small man who had a measuring tape draped around his neck like a snake. "He'll need two suits—a dark gray and a navy—and let's get him a dozen shirts, a few sweaters, some ties, socks, shoes: he doesn't have anything." To him he nodded and said, "This is Marco. I'll be back in a couple of hours or so."

"Wait," he said. "Harold. What are you doing?"

"Jude," said Harold, "you need something to wear. I'm hardly an expert on this front, but you can't show up to Sullivan's chambers wearing what you're wearing."

He was embarrassed: by his clothes, by his inadequacy, by Harold's generosity. "I know," he said. "But I can't accept this, Harold."

He would've continued, but Harold stepped between him and Marco and turned him away. "Jude," he said, "accept this. You've earned it. What's more, you need it. I'm not going to have you humiliating me in front of Sullivan. Besides, I've already paid for it, and I'm not getting my money back. Right, Marco?" he called behind him.

"Right," said Marco, immediately.

"Oh, leave it, Jude," Harold said, when he saw him about to speak. "I've got to go." And he marched out without looking back.

And so he found himself standing before the triple-leafed mirror, watching the reflection of Marco busying about his ankles, but when Marco reached up his leg to measure the inseam, he flinched, reflexively. "Easy, easy," Marco said, as if he were a nervous horse, and patted his thigh, also as if he were a horse, and when he gave another involuntary half kick as Marco did the other leg, "Hey! I have pins in my mouth, you know."

"I'm sorry," he said, and held himself still.

When Marco was finished, he looked at himself in his new suit: here was such anonymity, such protection. Even if someone were to accidentally graze his back, he was wearing enough layers so that they'd never be able to feel the ridges of scars beneath. Everything was covered, everything was hidden. If he was standing still, he could be anyone, someone blank and invisible.

"I think maybe half an inch more," Marco said, pinching the back of the jacket in around the waist. He swatted some threads off his sleeve. "Now all you need's a good haircut."

He found Harold waiting for him in the tie area, reading a magazine. "Are you done?" he asked, as if the entire trip had been his idea and Harold had been the one indulging his whimsy.

Over their early dinner, he tried to thank Harold again, but every time he tried, Harold stopped him with increasing impatience. "Has anyone ever told you that sometimes you just need to accept things, Jude?" he finally asked.

"You said to never just accept anything," he reminded Harold.

"That's in the classroom and in the courtroom," Harold said. "Not in life. You see, Jude, in life, sometimes nice things happen to good people. You don't need to worry—they don't happen as often as they should. But when they do, it's up to the good people to just say 'thank you,' and move on, and maybe consider that the person who's doing the nice thing gets a bang out of it as well, and really isn't in the mood to hear all the reasons that the person for whom he's done the nice thing doesn't think he deserves it or isn't worthy of it."

He shut up then, and after dinner he let Harold drive him back to his apartment on Hereford Street. "Besides," Harold said as he was getting out of the car, "you looked really, really nice. You're a great-looking kid; I hope someone's told you that before." And then, before he could protest, "Acceptance, Jude."

So he swallowed what he was going to say. "Thank you, Harold. For everything."

"You're very welcome, Jude," said Harold. "I'll see you Monday."

He stood on the sidewalk and watched Harold's car drive away, and then went up to his apartment, which was on the second floor of a brownstone adjacent to an MIT fraternity house. The brownstone's owner, a retired sociology professor, lived on the ground floor and leased out the remaining three floors to graduate students: on the top floor were Santosh and Federico, who were getting their doctorates in electrical engineering at MIT, and on the third floor were Janusz and Isidore, who were both Ph.D. candidates at Harvard—Janusz in biochemistry and Isidore in Near Eastern religions—and directly below them were he and his roommate, Charlie Ma, whose real name was Chien-Ming Ma and whom everyone called CM. CM was an intern at Tufts Medical Center, and they kept almost entirely opposite schedules: he would wake and CM's door would be closed and he would hear his wet, snuffly snores, and when he returned home in the evenings at eight, after working with Harold, CM would be gone. What he saw of CM he liked—he was from Taipei and had gone to boarding school in Connecticut and had a sleepy, roguish grin that made you want to smile back at him—and he was a friend of Andy's friend, which was how they had met. Despite his perpetual air of stoned languor, CM was tidy as well, and liked to cook: he'd come home sometimes and find a plate of fried dumplings in the center of the table, with a note beneath that read EAT ME, or, occasionally, receive a text instructing him to rotate the chicken in its marinade before he went to bed, or asking him to pick up a bunch of cilantro on his way home. He always would, and would return to find the chicken simmered into a stew, or the cilantro minced and folded into scallop pancakes. Every few months or so, when their schedules intersected, all six of them would meet in Santosh and Federico's apartment—theirs was the largest—and eat and play poker. Janusz and Isidore would worry aloud that girls thought they were gay because they were always hanging out with each other (CM cut his eyes toward him; he had bet him twenty dollars that they were sleeping together but were trying to pretend they were straight—at any rate, an impossible thing to prove), and Santosh and Federico would complain about how stupid their students were, and about how the quality of MIT undergraduates had really gone downhill since their time there five years ago.

His and CM's was the smallest of the apartments, because the landlord had annexed half of the floor to make a storage room. CM paid significantly more of the rent, so he had the bedroom. He occupied a corner of the living room, the part with the bay window. His bed was a floppy foam egg-carton pallet, and his books were lined up under the windowsill, and he had a lamp, and a folding paper screen to give him some privacy. He and CM had bought a large wooden table, which they placed in the dining-room alcove, and which had two metal folding chairs, one discarded from Janusz, the other from Federico. One half of the table was his, the other half CM's, and both halves were stacked with books and papers and their laptops, both emitting their chirps and burbles throughout the day and night.

People were always stunned by the apartment's bleakness, but he had mostly ceased to notice it—although not entirely. Now, for example, he sat on the floor before the three cardboard boxes in which he stored his clothes, and lifted his new sweaters and shirts and socks and shoes from their envelopes of white tissue paper, placing them in his lap one at a time. They were the nicest things he had ever owned, and it seemed somehow shameful to put them in boxes meant to hold file folders. And so finally, he rewrapped them and returned them carefully to their shopping bags.

The generosity of Harold's gift unsettled him. First, there was the matter of the gift itself: he had never, never received anything so grand. Second, there was the impossibility of ever adequately repaying him. And third, there was the meaning behind the gesture: he had known for some time that Harold respected him, and even enjoyed his company. But was it possible that he was someone important to Harold, that Harold liked him more than as just a student, but as a real, actual friend? And if that was the case, why should it make him so self-conscious?

It had taken him many months to feel truly comfortable around Harold: not in the classroom or in his office, but outside of the classroom, outside of the office. In life, as Harold would say. He would return home after dinner at Harold's house and feel a flush of relief. He knew why, too, as much as he didn't want to admit it to himself: traditionally, men—adult men, which he didn't yet consider himself among—had been interested in him for one reason, and so he had learned to be frightened of them. But Harold didn't seem to be one of those men. (Although Brother Luke hadn't seemed to be one of those men either.) He was frightened of everything, it sometimes seemed, and he hated that about himself. Fear and hatred, fear and hatred: often, it seemed that those were the only two qualities he possessed. Fear of everyone else; hatred of himself.

He had known of Harold before he met him, for Harold was known. He was a relentless questioner: every remark you made in his class would be seized upon and pecked at in an unending volley of Whys. He was trim and tall, and had a way of pacing in a tight circle, his torso pitched forward, when he was engaged or excited.

To his disappointment, there was much he simply couldn't remember from that first-year contracts class with Harold. He couldn't remember, for example, the specifics of the paper he wrote that interested Harold and which led to conversations with him outside the classroom and, eventually, to an offer to become one of his research assistants. He couldn't remember anything particularly interesting he said in class.

But he *could* remember Harold on that first day of the semester, pacing and pacing, and lecturing them in his low, quick voice.

"You're One Ls," Harold had said. "And congratulations, all of you. As One Ls, you'll be taking a pretty typical course load: contracts; torts; property; civil procedure; and, next year, constitutional and criminal law. But you know all this.

"What you may not know is that this course load reflects—beautifully, simply—the very structure of our society, the very mechanics of what a society, our particular society, needs to make it work. To have a society, you first need an institutional framework: that's constitutional law. You need a system of punishment: that's criminal. You need to know that you have a system in place that will make those other systems work: that's civil procedure. You need a way to govern matters of domain and ownership: that's property. You need to know that someone will be financially accountable for injuries caused you by others: that's torts. And finally, you need to know that people will keep their agreements, that they will honor their promises: and *that* is contracts."

He paused. "Now, I don't want to be reductive, but I'll bet half of you are here so you can someday wheedle money out of people—torts people, there's nothing to be ashamed of!—and the other half of you are here because you think you're going to change the world. You're here because you dream of arguing before the Supreme Court, because you think the real challenge of the law lies in the blank spaces between the lines of the Constitution. But I'm here to tell you—it doesn't. The truest, the most intellectually engaging, the *richest* field of the law is contracts. Contracts are not just sheets of paper promising you a job, or a house, or an inheritance: in its purest, truest, broadest sense, contracts govern every realm of law. When we choose to live in a society, we choose to live under a contract, and to abide by the rules that a contract dictates for us—the Constitution itself is a contract, albeit a malleable contract, and the question of just how malleable it is, exactly, is where law intersects with politics—and it is under the rules, explicit or otherwise, of this contract that we promise not to kill, and to pay our taxes, and not to steal. But in this case, we are both the creators of and bound by this contract: as citizens of this country, we have assumed, from birth, an obligation to respect and follow its terms, and we do so daily.

"In this class, you will of course learn the mechanics of contracts—how one is created, how one is broken, how binding one is and how to unbind yourself from one—but you will also be asked to consider law itself as a series of contracts. Some are more fair—and this one time, I'll allow you to say such a thing—than others. But fairness is not the only, or even the most important, consideration in law: the law is not always fair. Contracts are not fair, not always. But sometimes they are necessary, these unfairnesses, because they are necessary for the proper functioning of society. In this class you will learn the difference between what is fair and what is just, and, as important, between what is fair and what is necessary. You will learn about the obligations we have to one another as members of society, and how far society should go in enforcing those obligations. You will learn to see your life—all of our lives—as a series of agreements, and it will make you rethink not only the law but this country itself, and your place in it."

He had been thrilled by Harold's speech, and in the coming weeks, by how differently Harold thought, by how he would stand at the front of the room like a conductor, stretching out a student's argument into strange and unimaginable formations. Once, a fairly benign discussion about the right to privacy—both the most cherished and the foggiest of constitutional rights, according to Harold, whose definition of contracts often ignored conventional boundaries and bounded happily into other fields of law—had led to an argument between the two of them about abortion, which he felt was indefensible on moral grounds but necessary on social ones. "Aha!" Harold had said; he was one of the few professors who would entertain not just legal arguments but moral ones. "And, Mr. St. Francis, what happens when we forsake morals in law for social governance? What is the point at which a country, and its people, should start valuing social control over its sense of morality? *Is* there such a point? I'm not convinced there is." But he had hung in, and the class had stilled around them, watching the two of them debate back and forth.

Harold was the author of three books, but it was his last, *The American Handshake: The Promises and Failures of the Declaration of Independence*, that had made him famous. The book, which he had read even before he met Harold, was a legal interpretation of the Declaration of Independence: Which of its promises had been kept and which had not, and were it written today, would it be able to withstand trends in contemporary jurisprudence? ("Short answer: No," read the *Times* review.) Now he was researching his fourth book, a sequel of sorts to

The American Handshake, about the Constitution, from a similar perspective.

"But only the Bill of Rights, and the sexier amendments," Harold told him when he was interviewing him for the research assistant position.

"I didn't know some were sexier than others," he said.

"*Of course* some are sexier than others," said Harold. "Only the eleventh, twelfth, fourteenth, and sixteenth are sexy. The rest are basically the dross of politics past."

"The thirteenth is garbage?" he asked, enjoying himself.

"I didn't say it was *garbage,*" Harold said, "just not sexy."

"But I think that's what dross means."

Harold sighed dramatically, grabbed the dictionary off his desk, flipped it open, and studied it for a moment. "Okay, fine," he said, tossing it back onto a heap of papers, which slid toward the edge of the surface. "The third definition. But I meant the first definition: the leftovers, the detritus—the *remains* of politics past. Happy?"

"Yes," he said, trying not to smile.

He began working for Harold on Monday, Wednesday, and Friday afternoons and evenings, when his course load was lightest—on Tuesdays and Thursdays he had afternoon seminars at MIT, where he was getting his master's, and worked in the law library at night, and on Saturdays he worked in the library in the morning and in the afternoons at a bakery called Batter, which was near the medical college, where he had worked since he was an undergraduate and where he fulfilled specialty orders: decorating cookies and making hundreds of sugar-paste flower petals for cakes and experimenting with different recipes, one of which, a ten-nut cake, had become the bakery's best seller. He worked at Batter on Sundays as well, and one day Allison, the bakery's owner, who entrusted him with many of the more complicated projects, handed him an order form for three dozen sugar cookies decorated to look like various kinds of bacteria. "I thought you of all people might be able to figure this out," she said. "The customer's wife's a microbiologist and he wants to surprise her and her lab."

"I'll do some research," he said, taking the page from her, and noting the customer's name: Harold Stein. So he had, asking CM and Janusz for their advice, and had made cookies shaped like paisleys, like mace balls, like cucumbers, using different-colored frosting to draw their cytoplasms and plasma membranes and ribosomes and fashioning flagella from strands of licorice. He typed up a list identifying each and folded it into the box before closing it and tying it with twine; he didn't know Harold very well then, but he liked the idea of making something for him, of impressing him, even if anonymously. And he liked wondering what the cookies were meant to celebrate: A publication? An anniversary? Or was it simple uxoriousness? Was Harold Stein the sort of person who showed up at his wife's lab with cookies for no reason? He suspected he perhaps was.

The following week, Harold told him about the amazing cookies he'd gotten at Batter. His enthusiasm, which just a few hours ago in class had been directed at the Uniform Commercial Code, had found a new subject in the cookies. He sat, biting the inside of his cheek so he wouldn't smile, listening to Harold talk about how genius they'd been and how Julia's lab had been struck speechless by their detail and verisimilitude, and how he had been, briefly, the hero of the lab: "Not an easy thing to be with those people, by the way, who secretly think everyone involved in the humanities is something of a moron."

"Sounds like those cookies were made by a real obsessive," he said. He hadn't told Harold he worked at Batter, and didn't plan on doing so, either.

"Then that's an obsessive I'd like to meet," said Harold. "They were delicious, too."

"Mmm," he said, and thought of a question to ask Harold so he wouldn't keep talking about the cookies.

Harold had other research assistants, of course—two second-years and a third-year he knew only by sight—but their schedules were such that they never overlapped. Sometimes they communicated with one another by notes or e-mail, explaining where they'd left off in their research so the next person could pick it up and carry it forward. But by the second semester of his first year, Harold had assigned him to work exclusively on the fifth amendment. "That's a good one," he said. "Incredibly sexy." The two second-year assistants were assigned the ninth amendment, and the third-year, the tenth, and as much as he knew it was ridiculous, he couldn't help but feel triumphant, as if he had been favored with something the others hadn't.

The first invitation to dinner at Harold's house had been spontaneous, at the end of one cold and dark March afternoon. "Are you sure?"
he asked, tentative.

Harold had looked at him, curiously. "Of course," he said. "It's just
dinner. You have to eat, right?"

Harold lived in a three-story house in Cambridge, at the edge of the
undergraduate campus. "I didn't know you lived here," he said, as Harold pulled into the driveway. "This is one of my favorite streets. I used
to walk down it every day as a shortcut to the other side of campus."

"You and everybody else," Harold replied. "When I bought it just
before I got divorced, all these houses were occupied by grad students;
all the shutters were falling off. The smell of pot was so thick you could
get stoned just driving by."

It was snowing, just lightly, but he was grateful that there were only
two steps leading up to the door, and that he wouldn't have to worry
about slipping or needing Harold's help. Inside, the house smelled of
butter and pepper and starch: pasta, he thought. Harold dropped his
briefcase on the floor and gave him a vague tour—"Living room; study
behind it; kitchen and dining room to your left"—and he met Julia,
who was tall like Harold, with short brown hair, and whom he liked
instantly.

"Jude!" she said. "Finally! I've heard so much about you; I'm so happy
to be meeting you at last." It sounded, he thought, like she really was.

Over dinner, they talked. Julia was from an academic family from
Oxford and had lived in America since graduate school at Stanford; she
and Harold had met five years ago through a friend. Her lab studied a
new virus that appeared to be a variant of H5N1 and they were trying
to map its genetic code.

"Isn't one of the concerns in microbiology the potential weaponiza-
tion of these genomes?" he asked, and felt, rather than saw, Harold turn
toward him.

"Yes, that's right," Julia said, and as she explained to him the con-
troversies surrounding her and her colleagues' work, he glanced over at
Harold, who was watching him, and who raised an eyebrow at him in a
gesture that he couldn't interpret.

But then the conversation shifted, and he could almost watch as the
discussion moved steadily away from Julia's lab and inexorably toward
him, could see how good a litigator Harold would be if he wanted to,

could see his skill in redirecting and repositioning, almost as if their conversation were something liquid, and he was guiding it through a series of troughs and chutes, eliminating any options for its escape, until it reached its inevitable end.

"So, Jude," Julia asked, "where did you grow up?"

"South Dakota and Montana, mostly," he said, and he could feel the creature inside of him sit up, aware of danger but unable to escape it.

"So are your parents ranchers?" asked Harold.

He had learned over the years to anticipate this sequence of questioning, and how to deflect it as well. "No," he said, "but a lot of people were, obviously. It's beautiful countryside out there; have you spent any time in the West?"

Usually, this was enough, but it wasn't for Harold. "Ha!" he said. "That's the silkiest pivot I've heard in a long time." Harold looked at him, closely enough so that he eventually looked down at his plate. "I suppose that's your way of saying you're not going to tell us what they do?"

"Oh, Harold, leave him alone," said Julia, but he could feel Harold staring at him, and was relieved when dinner ended.

After that first night at Harold's, their relationship became both deeper and more difficult. He felt he had awakened Harold's curiosity, which he imagined as a perked, bright-eyed dog—a terrier, something relentless and keen—and wasn't sure that was such a good thing. He wanted to know Harold better, but over dinner he had been reminded that that process—getting to know someone—was always so much more challenging than he remembered. He always forgot; he was always made to remember. He wished, as he often did, that the entire sequence—the divulging of intimacies, the exploring of pasts—could be sped past, and that he could simply be teleported to the next stage, where the relationship was something soft and pliable and comfortable, where both parties' limits were understood and respected.

Other people might have made a few more attempts at questioning him and then left him alone—other people *had* left him alone: his friends, his classmates, his other professors—but Harold was not as easily dissuaded. Even his usual strategies—among them, telling his interlocutors that he wanted to hear about *their* lives, not talk about his: a tactic that had the benefit of being true as well as effective—didn't work with Harold. He never knew when Harold would pounce next, but whenever he did, he was unprepared, and he felt himself becoming more self-conscious, not less, the more time they spent with each other.

They would be in Harold's office, talking about something—the University of Virginia affirmative action case going before the Supreme Court, say—and Harold would ask, "What's *your* ethnic background, Jude?"

"A lot of things," he would answer, and then would try to change the subject, even if it meant dropping a stack of books to cause a distraction.

But sometimes the questions were contextless and random, and these were impossible to anticipate, as they came without preamble. One night he and Harold were in his office, working late, and Harold ordered them dinner. For dessert, he'd gotten cookies and brownies, and he pushed the paper bags toward him.

"No, thanks," he said.

"Really?" Harold asked, raising his eyebrows. "My son used to love these. We tried to bake them for him at home, but we never got the recipe quite right." He broke a brownie in half. "Did your parents bake for you a lot when you were a kid?" He would ask these questions with a deliberate casualness that he found almost unbearable.

"No," he said, pretending to review the notes he'd been taking.

He listened to Harold chewing and, he knew, considering whether to retreat or to continue his line of questioning.

"Do you see your parents often?" Harold asked him, abruptly, on a different night.

"They're dead," he said, keeping his eyes on the page.

"I'm sorry, Jude," Harold said after a silence, and the sincerity in his voice made him look up. "Mine are, too. Relatively recently. Of course, I'm much older than you."

"I'm sorry, Harold," he said. And then, guessing, "You were close to them."

"I was," said Harold. "Very. Were you close to yours?"

He shook his head. "No, not really."

Harold was quiet. "But I'll bet they were proud of you," he said, finally.

Whenever Harold asked him questions about himself, he always felt something cold move across him, as if he were being iced from the inside, his organs and nerves being protected by a sheath of frost. In that moment, though, he thought he might break, that if he said anything the ice would shatter and he would splinter and crack. So he waited until he knew he would sound normal before he asked Harold if he needed him to find the rest of the articles now or if he should do it in the morning. He didn't look at Harold, though, and spoke only to his notebook.

Harold took a long time to reply. "Tomorrow," Harold said, quietly, and he nodded, and gathered his things to go home for the night, aware of Harold's eyes following his lurching progress to the door.

Harold wanted to know how he had been raised, and if he had any siblings, and who his friends were, and what he did with them: he was greedy for information. At least he could answer the last questions, and he told him about his friends, and how they had met, and where they were: Malcolm in graduate school at Columbia, JB and Willem at Yale. He liked answering Harold's questions about them, liked talking about them, liked hearing Harold laugh when he told him stories about them. He told him about CM, and how Santosh and Federico were in some sort of fight with the engineering undergrads who lived in the frat house next door, and how he had awoken one morning to a fleet of motorized dirigibles handmade from condoms floating noisily up past his window, up toward the fourth floor, each dangling signs that read SANTOSH JAIN AND FEDERICO DE LUCA HAVE MICRO-PENISES.

But when Harold was asking the other questions, he felt smothered by their weight and frequency and inevitability. And sometimes the air grew so hot with the questions Harold *wasn't* asking him that it was as oppressive as if he actually had. People wanted to know so much, they wanted so many answers. And he understood it, he did—he wanted answers, too; he too wanted to know everything. He was grateful, then, for his friends, and for how relatively little they had mined from him, how they had left him to himself, a blank, faceless prairie under whose yellow surface earthworms and beetles wriggled through the black soil, and chips of bone calcified slowly into stone.

"You're really interested in this," he snapped at Harold once, frustrated, when Harold had asked him whether he was dating anyone, and then, hearing his tone, stopped and apologized. They had known each other for almost a year by then.

"*This?*" said Harold, ignoring the apology. "I'm interested in *you*. I don't see what's strange about that. This is the kind of stuff friends talk about with each other."

And yet despite his discomfort, he kept coming back to Harold, kept accepting his dinner invitations, even though at some point in every encounter there would be a moment in which he wished he could disappear, or in which he worried he might have disappointed.

One night he went to dinner at Harold's and was introduced to Harold's best friend, Laurence, whom he had met in law school and who was now an appellate court judge in Boston, and his wife, Gillian, who taught English at Simmons. "Jude," said Laurence, whose voice was even lower than Harold's, "Harold tells me you're also getting your master's at MIT. What in?"

"Pure math," he replied.

"How is that different from"—she laughed—"regular math?" Gillian asked.

"Well, regular math, or applied math, is what I suppose you could call practical math," he said. "It's used to solve problems, to provide solutions, whether it's in the realm of economics, or engineering, or accounting, or what have you. But pure math doesn't exist to provide immediate, or necessarily obvious, practical applications. It's purely an expression of form, if you will—the only thing it proves is the almost infinite elasticity of mathematics itself, within the accepted set of assumptions by which we define it, of course."

"Do you mean imaginary geometries, stuff like that?" Laurence asked.

"It can be, sure. But it's not just that. Often, it's merely proof of—of the impossible yet consistent internal logic of math itself. There's all kinds of specialties within pure math: geometric pure math, like you said, but also algebraic math, algorithmic math, cryptography, information theory, and pure logic, which is what I study."

"Which is what?" Laurence asked.

He thought. "Mathematical logic, or pure logic, is essentially a conversation between truths and falsehoods. So for example, I might say to you 'All positive numbers are real. Two is a positive number. Therefore, two must be real.' But this isn't *actually* true, right? It's a derivation, a supposition of truth. I haven't actually *proven* that two is a real number, but it must logically be true. So you'd write a proof to, in essence, prove that the logic of those two statements is in fact real, and infinitely applicable." He stopped. "Does that make sense?"

"*Video, ergo est,*" said Laurence, suddenly. *I see it, therefore it is.*

He smiled. "And that's exactly what applied math is. But pure math is more"—he thought again—"*Imaginor, ergo est.*"

Laurence smiled back at him and nodded. "Very good," he said.

"Well, I have a question," said Harold, who'd been quiet, listening to them. "How and why on earth did you end up in law school?"

Everyone laughed, and he did, too. He had been asked that question often (by Dr. Li, despairingly; by his master's adviser, Dr. Kashen, perplexedly), and he always changed the answer to suit the audience, for the real answer—that he wanted to have the means to protect himself; that he wanted to make sure no one could ever reach him again—seemed too selfish and shallow and tiny a reason to say aloud (and would invite a slew of subsequent questions anyway). Besides, he knew enough now to know that the law was a flimsy form of protection: if he *really* wanted to be safe, he should have become a marksman squinting through an eyepiece, or a chemist in a lab with his pipettes and poisons.

That night, though, he said, "But law isn't so unlike pure math, really—I mean, it too in theory can offer an answer to every question, can't it? Laws of anything are meant to be pressed against, and stretched, and if they can't provide solutions to every matter they claim to cover, then they aren't really laws at all, are they?" He stopped to consider what he'd just said. "I suppose the difference is that in law, there are many paths to many answers, and in math, there are many paths to a single answer. And also, I guess, that law isn't actually about the truth: it's about governance. But math doesn't have to be convenient, or practical, or managerial—it only has to be true.

"But I suppose the other way in which they're *alike* is that in mathematics, as well as in law, what matters more—or, more accurately, what's more memorable—is not that the case, or proof, is won or solved, but the beauty, the economy, with which it's done."

"What do you mean?" asked Harold.

"Well," he said, "in law, we talk about a beautiful summation, or a beautiful judgment: and what we mean by that, of course, is the loveliness of not only its logic but its expression. And similarly, in math, when we talk about a beautiful proof, what we're recognizing is the simplicity of the proof, its . . . elementalness, I suppose: its inevitability."

"What about something like Fermat's last theorem?" asked Julia.

"That's a perfect example of a non-beautiful proof. Because while it was important that it was solved, it was, for a lot of people—like my adviser—a disappointment. The proof went on for hundreds of pages, and drew from so many disparate fields of mathematics, and was so—tortured, *jigsawed*, really, in its execution, that there are still many people at work trying to prove it in more elegant terms, even though it's already been proven. A beautiful proof is succinct, like a beautiful ruling. It combines just a handful of different concepts, albeit from across the mathematical universe, and in a relatively brief series of steps, leads to a grand and new generalized truth in mathematics: that is, a wholly provable, unshakable absolute in a constructed world with very few unshakable absolutes." He stopped to take a breath, aware, suddenly, that he had been talking and talking, and that the others were silent, watching him. He could feel himself flushing, could feel the old hatred fill him like dirtied water once more. "I'm sorry," he apologized. "I'm sorry. I didn't mean to ramble on."

"Are you joking?" said Laurence. "Jude, I think that was the first truly revelatory conversation I've had in Harold's house in probably the last decade or more: thank you."

Everyone laughed again, and Harold leaned back in his chair, looking pleased. "See?" he caught Harold mouthing across the table to Laurence, and Laurence nodding, and he understood that this was meant about him, and was flattered despite himself, and shy as well. Had Harold talked about him to his friend? Had this been a test for him, a test he hadn't known he was to take? He was relieved he had passed it, and that he hadn't embarrassed Harold, and relieved too that, as uncomfortable as it sometimes made him, he might have fully earned his place in Harold's house, and might be invited back again.

With each day he trusted Harold a little more, and at times he wondered if he was making the same mistake again. Was it better to trust or better to be wary? Could you have a real friendship if some part of you was always expecting betrayal? He felt sometimes as if he was taking advantage of Harold's generosity, his jolly faith in him, and sometimes as if his circumspection was the wise choice after all, for if it should end badly, he'd have only himself to blame. But it was difficult to not trust Harold: Harold made it difficult, and, just as important, he was making it difficult for himself—he *wanted* to trust Harold, he *wanted* to give in, he *wanted* the creature inside him to tuck itself into a sleep from which it would never wake.

Late one night in his second year of law school he was at Harold's, and when they opened the door, the steps, the street, the trees were hushed with snow, and the flakes cycloned toward the door, so fast that they both took a step backward.

"I'll call a cab," he said, so Harold wouldn't have to drive him.

"No, you won't," Harold said. "You'll stay here."

And so he stayed in Harold and Julia's spare bedroom on the second floor, separated from their room by a large windowed space they used as a library, and a brief hallway. "Here's a T-shirt," Harold said, lobbing something gray and soft at him, "and here's a toothbrush." He placed it on the bookcase. "There's extra towels in the bathroom. Do you want anything else? Water?"

"No," he said. "Harold, thank you."

"Of course, Jude. Good night."

"Good night."

He stayed awake for a while, the feather comforter wadded around him, the mattress plush beneath him, watching the window turn white, and listening to water glugging from the faucets, and Harold and Julia's low, indistinguishable murmurs at each other, and one or the other of them padding from one place to another, and then, finally, nothing. In those minutes, he pretended that they were his parents, and he was home for the weekend from law school to visit them, and this was his room, and the next day he would get up and do whatever it was that grown children did with their parents.

The summer after that second year, Harold invited him to their house in Truro, on Cape Cod. "You'll love it," he said. "Invite your friends. They'll love it, too." And so on the Thursday before Labor Day, once his and Malcolm's internships had ended, they all drove up to the house from New York, and for that long weekend, Harold's attention shifted to JB and Malcolm and Willem. He watched them too, admiring how they could answer every one of Harold's parries, how generous they were with their own lives, how they could tell stories about themselves that they laughed at and that made Harold and Julia laugh as well, how comfortable they were around Harold and how comfortable Harold was around them. He experienced the singular pleasure of watching people he loved fall in love with other people he loved. The house had a private walk down to a private spit of beach, and in the mornings the four of them would troop downhill and swim—even he did, in his pants and undershirt and an old oxford shirt, which no one bothered him about—and then lie on the sand baking, the wet clothes ungluing themselves from his body as they dried. Sometimes Harold would come and watch them, or swim as well. In the afternoons, Malcolm and JB would pedal off through the dunes on bicycles, and he and Willem would follow on foot, picking up bits of shaley shells and the sad carapaces of long-nibbled-away hermit crabs as they went, Willem slowing his pace to match his own. In the evenings, when the air was soft, JB and Malcolm sketched and he and Willem read. He felt doped, on sun and food and salt and contentment, and at night he fell asleep quickly and early, and in the mornings he woke before the others so he could stand on the back porch alone looking over the sea.

What is going to happen to me? he asked the sea. *What is happening to me?*

The holiday ended and the fall semester began, and it didn't take him long to realize that over that weekend, one of his friends must have said something to Harold, although he was certain it wasn't Willem, who was the only one to whom he'd finally told something of his past—and even then, not very much at all: three facts, each more slender than the last, all meaningless, all of which combined to make not even a beginning of a story. Even the first sentences of a fairy tale had more detail than what he had told Willem: *Once upon a time, a boy and a girl lived with their father, a woodcutter, and their stepmother, deep in a cold forest. The woodcutter loved his children, but he was very poor, and so one day* . . . So whatever Harold had learned had been speculation, buttressed by their observations of him, their theories and guesses and fictions. But whatever it was, it had been enough to make Harold's questions to him—about who he had been and where he had come from—stop.

As the months and then the years passed, they developed a friendship in which the first fifteen years of his life remained unsaid and unspoken, as if they had never happened at all, as if he had been removed from the manufacturer's box when he reached college, and a switch at the base of his neck had been flipped, and he had shuddered to life. He knew that those blank years were filled in by Harold's own imaginings, and that some of those imaginings were worse than what had actually happened, and some were better. But Harold never told him what he supposed for him, and he didn't really want to know.

He had never considered their friendship contextual, but he was prepared for the likelihood that Harold and Julia did. And so when he moved to Washington for his clerkship, he assumed that they would forget him, and he tried to prepare himself for the loss. But that didn't happen. Instead, they sent e-mails, and called, and when one or the other was in town, they would have dinner. In the summers, he and his friends visited Truro, and over Thanksgiving, they went to Cambridge. And when he moved to New York two years later to begin his job at the U.S. Attorney's Office, Harold had been almost alarmingly excited for him. They had even offered to let him live in their apartment on the Upper West Side, but he knew they used it often, and he wasn't sure how real their offer was, and so he declined.

Every Saturday, Harold would call and ask him about work, and he'd tell him about his boss, Marshall, the deputy U.S. Attorney, who had the unnerving ability to recite entire Supreme Court decisions from memory, closing his eyes to summon a vision of the page in his mind, his voice becoming robotic and dull as he chanted, but never dropping or adding a word. He had always thought he had a good memory, but Marshall's amazed him.

In some ways, the U.S. Attorney's Office reminded him of the home: it was largely male, and the place fizzed with a particular and constant hostility, the kind of hissing acrimony that naturally arises whenever a group of highly competitive people who are all evenly matched are housed in the same small space with the understanding that only some of them would have the opportunity to distinguish themselves. (Here, though, they were matched in accomplishments; at the home, they were matched in hunger, in want.) All two hundred of the assistant prosecutors, it seemed, had attended one of five or six law schools, and virtually all of them had been on the law review and moot court at their respective schools. He was part of a four-person team that worked mostly on securities fraud cases, and he and his teammates each had something—a credential, an idiosyncrasy—that they hoped lifted them above the others: he had his master's from MIT (which no one cared about but was at least an oddity) and his circuit court clerkship with Sullivan, with whom Marshall was friendly. Citizen, his closest friend at the office, had a law degree from Cambridge and had practiced as a barrister in London for two years before moving to New York. And Rhodes, the third in their trio, had been a Fulbright Scholar in Argentina after college. (The fourth on their team was a profoundly lazy guy named Scott who, it was rumored, had only gotten the job because his father played tennis with the president.)

He was usually at the office, and sometimes, when he and Citizen and Rhodes were there late, eating takeout, he was reminded of being with his roommates in their suite at Hood. And although he enjoyed Citizen's and Rhodes's company, and the specificity and depth of their intelligence, he was in those moments nostalgic for his friends, who thought so differently than he did and who made him think differently as well. In the middle of one conversation with Citizen and Rhodes about logic, he recalled, suddenly, a question Dr. Li had asked him his freshman year, when he was auditioning to be accepted into his pure math seminar: *Why are manhole covers round?* It was an easy question, and easy to answer, but when he'd returned to Hood and had repeated Dr. Li's question to his roommates, they were silent. And then finally JB had begun, in the dreamy tones of a wandering storyteller, "Once, very long ago, mammoths roamed the earth, and their footprints left permanent circular indentations in the ground," and they had all laughed. He smiled, remembering it; he sometimes wished he had a mind like JB's, one that could create stories that would delight others, instead of the mind he did have, which was always searching for an explanation, an explanation that, while perhaps correct, was empty of romance, of fancy, of wit.

"Time to whip out the credentials," Citizen would whisper to him on the occasions that the U.S. Attorney himself would emerge onto the floor and all the assistant prosecutors would buzz toward him, mothlike, as a multitude of gray suits. They and Rhodes would join the hover, but even in those gatherings he never mentioned the one credential he knew could have made not only Marshall but the U.S. Attorney as well stop and look at him more closely. After he'd gotten the job, Harold had asked him if he could mention him to Adam, the U.S. Attorney, with whom Harold was, it happened, longtime acquaintances. But he'd told Harold he wanted to know he could make it on his own. This was true, but the greater reason was that he was tentative about naming Harold as one of his assets, because he didn't want Harold to regret his association with him. And so he'd said nothing.

Often, however, it felt as if Harold was there anyway. Reminiscing about law school (and its attendant activity, bragging about one's accomplishments in law school) was a favorite pastime in the office, and because so many of his colleagues had gone to his school, quite a few of them knew Harold (and the others knew of him), and he'd sometimes listen to them talk about classes they'd taken with him, or how prepared they'd had to be for them, and would feel proud of Harold, and—though he knew it was silly—proud of himself for knowing him. The following year, Harold's book about the Constitution would be published, and everyone in the office would read the acknowledgments and see his name and his affiliation with Harold would be revealed, and many of them would be suspicious, and he'd see worry in their faces as they tried to remember what they might have said about Harold in his presence. By that time, however, he would feel he had established himself in the office on his own, had found his own place alongside Citizen and Rhodes, had made his own relationship with Marshall.

But as much as he would have liked to, as much as he craved it, he was still cautious about claiming Harold as his friend: sometimes he worried that he was only imagining their closeness, inflating it hopefully in his mind, and then (to his embarrassment) he would have to retrieve *The Beautiful Promise* from his shelf and turn to the acknowledgments, reading Harold's words again, as if it were itself a contract, a declaration that what he felt for Harold was at least in some degree reciprocated. And yet he was always prepared: *It will end this month*, he would tell himself. And then, at the end of the month: *Next month. He won't want to talk to me next month.* He tried to keep himself in a constant state of readiness; he tried to prepare himself for disappointment, even as he yearned to be proven wrong.

And still, the friendship spooled on and on, a long, swift river that had caught him in its slipstream and was carrying him along, taking him somewhere he couldn't see. At every point when he thought that he had reached the limits of what their relationship would be, Harold or Julia flung open the doors to another room and invited him in. He met Julia's father, a retired pulmonologist, and brother, an art history professor, when they visited from England one Thanksgiving, and when Harold and Julia came to New York, they took him and Willem out to dinner, to places they had heard about but couldn't afford to visit on their own. They saw the apartment at Lispenard Street—Julia polite,

Harold horrified—and the week that the radiators mysteriously stopped working, they left him a set of keys to their apartment uptown, which was so warm that for the first hour after he and Willem arrived, they simply sat on the sofa like mannequins, too stunned by the sudden reintroduction of heat into their lives to move. And after Harold witnessed him in the middle of an episode—this was the Thanksgiving after he moved to New York, and in his desperation (he knew he wouldn't be able to make it upstairs), he had turned off the stove, where he had been sauteeing some spinach, and pulled himself into the pantry, where he had shut the door and laid down on the floor to wait—they had rearranged the house, so that the next time he visited, he found the spare bedroom had been moved to the ground-floor suite behind the living room where Harold's study had been, and Harold's desk and chair and books moved to the second floor.

But even after all of this, a part of him was always waiting for the day he'd come to a door and try the knob and it wouldn't move. He didn't mind that, necessarily; there was something scary and anxiety-inducing about being in a space where nothing seemed to be forbidden to him, where everything was offered to him and nothing was asked in return. He tried to give them what he could; he was aware it wasn't much. And the things Harold gave him so easily—answers, affection—he couldn't reciprocate.

One day after he'd known them for almost seven years, he was at the house in springtime. It was Julia's birthday; she was turning fifty-one, and because she had been at a conference in Oslo for her fiftieth birthday, she'd decided that this would be her big celebration. He and Harold were cleaning the living room—or rather, he was cleaning, and Harold was plucking books at random from the shelves and telling him stories about how he'd gotten each one, or flipping back the covers so he could see other people's names written inside, including a copy of *The Leopard* on whose flyleaf was scrawled: "Property of Laurence V. Raleigh. Do not take. Harold Stein, this means you!!"

He had threatened to tell Laurence, and Harold had threatened him back. "You'd better not, Jude, if you know what's good for you."

"Or what?" he'd asked, teasing him.

"Or—this!" Harold had said, and had leaped at him, and before he could recognize that Harold was just being playful, he had recoiled so violently, torquing his body to avoid contact, that he had bumped into the bookcase and had knocked against a lumpy ceramic mug that Harold's son, Jacob, had made, which fell to the ground and broke into three neat pieces. Harold had stepped back from him then, and there was a sudden, horrible silence, into which he had nearly wept.

"Harold," he said, crouching to the ground, picking up the pieces, "I'm so sorry, I'm so sorry. Please forgive me." He wanted to beat himself against the floor; he knew this was the last thing Jacob had made Harold before he got sick. Above him, he could hear only Harold's breathing.

"Harold, please forgive me," he repeated, cupping the pieces in his palms. "I think I can fix this, though—I can make it better." He couldn't look up from the mug, its shiny buttered glaze.

He felt Harold crouch beside him. "Jude," Harold said, "it's all right. It was an accident." His voice was very quiet. "Give me the pieces," he said, but he was gentle, and he didn't sound angry.

He did. "I can leave," he offered.

"Of course you're not going to leave," Harold said. "It's okay, Jude."

"But it was Jacob's," he heard himself say.

"Yes," said Harold. "And it still is." He stood. "Look at me, Jude," he said, and he finally did. "It's okay. Come on," and Harold held out his hand, and he took it, and let Harold pull him to his feet. He wanted to howl, then, that after everything Harold had given him, he had repaid him by destroying something precious created by someone who had been most precious.

Harold went upstairs to his study with the mug in his hands, and he finished his cleaning in silence, the lovely day graying around him. When Julia came home, he waited for Harold to tell her how stupid and clumsy he'd been, but he didn't. That night at dinner, Harold was the same as he always was, but when he returned to Lispenard Street, he wrote Harold a real, proper letter, apologizing properly, and sent it to him.

And a few days later, he got a reply, also in the form of a real letter, which he would keep for the rest of his life.

"Dear Jude," Harold wrote, "thank you for your beautiful (if unnecessary) note. I appreciate everything in it. You're right; that mug means a lot to me. But you mean more. So please stop torturing yourself.

"If I were a different kind of person, I might say that this whole incident is a metaphor for life in general: things get broken, and sometimes they get repaired, and in most cases, you realize that no matter what gets damaged, life rearranges itself to compensate for your loss, sometimes wonderfully.

"Actually—maybe I am that kind of person after all.

"Love, Harold."

—

It was not so many years ago—despite the fact that he knew otherwise, despite what Andy had been telling him since he was seventeen—that he was still maintaining a sort of small, steady hope that he might get better. On especially bad days, he would repeat the Philadelphia surgeon's words to himself—"the spine has wonderful reparative qualities"—almost like a chant. A few years after meeting Andy, when he was in law school, he had finally summoned the courage to suggest this to him, had said aloud the prediction he had treasured and clung to, hoping that Andy might nod and say, "That's exactly right. It'll just take time."

But Andy had snorted. "He told you *that?*" he asked. "It's not going to get better, Jude; as you get older, it'll get worse." Andy had been looking down at his ankle as he spoke, using tweezers to pick out shreds of dead flesh from a wound he'd developed, when he suddenly froze, and even without seeing Andy's face, he could tell he was chagrined. "I'm sorry, Jude," he said, looking up, still cupping his foot in his hand. "I'm sorry I can't tell you differently." And when he couldn't answer, he sighed. "You're upset."

He was, of course. "I'm fine," he managed to say, but he couldn't bring himself to look at Andy.

"I'm sorry, Jude," Andy repeated, quietly. He had two settings, even then: brusque and gentle, and he had experienced both of them often, sometimes in a single appointment.

"But one thing I promise," he said, returning to the ankle, "I'll always be here to take care of you."

And he had. Of all the people in his life, it was in some ways Andy who knew the most about him: Andy was the only person he'd been naked in front of as an adult, the only person who was familiar with every physical dimension of his body. Andy had been a resident when they met, and he had stayed in Boston for his fellowship, and his postfellowship, and then the two of them had moved to New York within months of each other. He was an orthopedic surgeon, but he treated him for everything, from chest colds to his back and leg problems.

"Wow," Andy said dryly, as he sat in his examining room one day hacking up phlegm (this had been the previous spring, shortly before he had turned twenty-nine, when a bout of bronchitis had been snaking its way through the office), "I'm so glad I specialized in orthopedics. This is such good practice for me. This is exactly what I thought I'd do with my training."

He had started to laugh, but then his coughing had begun again and Andy had thumped him on the back. "Maybe if someone recommended a real internist to me, I wouldn't have to keep going to a chiropractor for all my medical needs," he said.

"Mmm," Andy said. "You know, maybe you *should* start seeing an internist. God knows it'd save me a lot of time, and a shitload of headaches as well." But he would never go to see anyone but Andy, and he thought—although they had never discussed it—that Andy wouldn't want him to, either.

For all Andy knew about him, he knew relatively little about Andy. He knew that he and Andy had gone to the same college, and that Andy was a decade older than he, and that Andy's father was Gujarati and his mother was Welsh, and that he had grown up in Ohio. Three years ago, Andy had gotten married, and he had been surprised to be invited to the wedding, which was small and held at Andy's in-laws' house on the Upper West Side. He had made Willem come with him, and was even more surprised when Andy's new wife, Jane, had thrown her arms around him when they were introduced and said, "The famous Jude St. Francis! I've heard so much about you!"

"Oh, really," he'd said, his mind filling with fear, like a flock of flapping bats.

"Nothing like that," Jane had said, smiling (she was a doctor as well: a gynecologist). "But he adores you, Jude; I'm so glad you came." He had met Andy's parents as well, and at the end of the evening, Andy had slung an arm around his neck and given him a hard, awkward kiss on the cheek, which he now did every time they saw each other. Andy always looked uncomfortable doing it, but also seemed compelled to keep doing it, which he found both funny and touching.

He appreciated Andy in many ways, but he appreciated most his unflappability. After they had met, after Andy had made it difficult not to continue seeing him by showing up at Hood, banging on their door after he had missed two follow-up appointments (he hadn't forgotten; he had just decided not to go) and ignored three phone calls and four e-mails, he had resigned himself to the fact that it might not be bad to have a doctor—it seemed, after all, inevitable—and that Andy might be someone he could trust. The third time they met, Andy took his history, or what he would provide of it, and wrote down the facts he would tell him without comment or reaction.

And indeed, it was only years later—a little less than four years ago—that Andy had directly mentioned his childhood. This had been during his and Andy's first big fight. They'd had skirmishes, of course, and disagreements, and once or twice a year Andy would deliver a long lecture to him (he saw Andy every six weeks—though more frequently these days—and could always anticipate which appointment would be the Lecture Appointment by the terseness with which Andy would greet him and conduct his examination) that covered what Andy considered his perplexing and infuriating unwillingness to take proper care of himself, his maddening refusal to see a therapist, and his bizarre reluctance to take pain medication that would probably improve his quality of life.

The fight had concerned what Andy had retroactively come to consider a botched suicide attempt. This had been right before New Year's, and he had been cutting himself, and he had cut too close to a vein, and it had resulted in a great, sloppy, bloody mess into which he had been forced to involve Willem. In the examining room that night, Andy had refused to speak to him, he was so angry, and had actually muttered to himself as he made his stitches, each as neat and tiny as if he were embroidering them.

Even before Andy had opened his mouth at his next appointment, he had known that he was furious. He had actually considered not coming in for his checkup at all, except he knew if he didn't, Andy would simply keep calling him—or worse, calling Willem, or worse yet, Harold—until he showed up.

"I should fucking have had you hospitalized," were Andy's first words to him, followed by, "I'm such a fucking idiot."

"I think you're overreacting," he'd begun, but Andy ignored him.

"I happen to believe you weren't trying to kill yourself, or I'd've had you committed so fast your head would've spun," he said. "It's only because statistically, anyone who cuts themselves as much as you do, and for as many years as you have, is in less immediate danger of suicide than someone who's less consistently self-injurious." (Andy was fond of statistics. He sometimes suspected he made them up.) "But Jude, this is crazy, and that was way too close. Either you start seeing a shrink immediately or I'm going to commit you."

"You can't do that," he'd said, furious himself now, although he knew Andy could: he had looked up the laws of involuntary commitment in New York State, and they were not in his favor.

"You know I can," Andy had said. He was almost shouting at this point. Their appointments were always after office hours, because they sometimes chatted afterward if Andy had time and was in a good mood.

"I'll sue you," he'd said, absurdly, and Andy had yelled back at him, "Go right ahead! Do you know how fucked up this is, Jude? Do you have any idea what kind of position you're putting me in?"

"Don't worry," he'd said, sarcastically, "I don't have any family. No one's going to sue you for wrongful death."

Andy had stepped back, then, as if he had tried to hit him. "How dare you," he'd said, slowly. "You know that's not what I mean."

And of course he did. But "Whatever," he said. "I'm leaving." And he slid off the table (fortunately, he hadn't changed out of his clothes; Andy had started lecturing him before he'd had a chance) and tried to leave the room, although leaving the room at his pace was hardly dramatic, and Andy scooted over to stand in the doorway.

"Jude," he said, in one of his sudden mood changes, "I know you don't want to go. But this is getting scary." He took a breath. "Have you ever even talked to anyone about what happened when you were a kid?"

"That doesn't have anything to do with anything," he'd said, feeling cold. Andy had never alluded to what he'd told him, and he found himself feeling betrayed that he should do so now.

"Like hell it doesn't," Andy had said, and the self-conscious theatricality of the phrase—did anyone really say that outside of the movies?—made him smile despite himself, and Andy, mistaking his smile for mockery, changed directions again. "There's something incredibly arrogant about your stubbornness, Jude," he continued. "Your utter refusal to listen to anyone about anything that concerns your health or well-being is either a pathological case of self-destructiveness or it's a huge fuck-you to the rest of us."

He was hurt by this. "And there's something incredibly manipulative about you threatening to *commit* me whenever I disagree with you, and especially in this case, when I've *told* you it was a stupid accident," he hurled back at Andy. "Andy, I appreciate you, I really do. I don't know what I'd do without you. But I'm an adult and you can't dictate what I do or don't do."

"You know what, Jude?" Andy had asked (now he was yelling again). "You're right. I can't dictate your decisions. But I don't have to accept them, either. Go find some other asshole to be your doctor. I'm not going to do it any longer."

"Fine," he'd snapped, and left.

He couldn't remember when he had been angrier on his own behalf. Lots of things made him angry—general injustice, incompetence, directors who didn't give Willem a part he wanted—but he rarely got angry about things that happened or had happened to him: his pains, past and present, were things he tried not to brood about, were not questions to which he spent his days searching for meaning. He already knew why they had happened: they had happened because he had deserved them.

But he knew too that his anger was unjustified. And as much as he resented his dependence upon Andy, he was grateful for him as well, and he knew Andy found his behavior illogical. But Andy's job was to make people better: Andy saw him the way he saw a mangled tax law, as something to be untangled and repaired—whether *he* thought he could be repaired was almost incidental. The thing he *was* trying to fix—the scars that raised his back into an awful, unnatural topography, the skin stretched as glossy and taut as a roasted duck's: the reason he was trying to save money—was not, he knew, something Andy would approve of. "Jude," Andy would say if he ever heard what he was planning, "I promise you it's not going to work, and you're going to have wasted all that money. Don't do it."

"But they're hideous," he would mumble.

"They're not, Jude," Andy would say. "I swear to god they're not."

(But he wasn't going to tell Andy anyway, so he would never have to have that particular conversation.)

The days passed and he didn't call Andy and Andy didn't call him. As if in punishment, his wrist throbbed at night when he was trying to sleep, and at work he forgot and banged it rhythmically against the side of his desk as he read, a longtime bad tic he'd not managed to erase.

The stitches had seeped blood then, and he'd had to clean them, clumsily, in the bathroom sink.

"What's wrong?" Willem asked him one night.

"Nothing," he said. He could tell Willem, of course, who would listen and say "Hmm" in his Willem-ish way, but he knew he would agree with Andy.

A week after their fight, he came home to Lispenard Street—it was a Sunday, and he had been walking through west Chelsea—and Andy was waiting on the steps before their front door.

He was surprised to see him. "Hi," he said.

"Hi," Andy had replied. They stood there. "I wasn't sure if you'd take my call."

"Of course I would've."

"Listen," Andy said. "I'm sorry."

"Me too. I'm sorry, Andy."

"But I really do think you should see someone."

"I know you do."

And somehow they managed to leave it at that: a fragile and mutually unsatisfying cease-fire, with the question of the therapist the vast gray demilitarized zone between them. The compromise (though how this had been agreed upon as such was unclear to him now) was that at the end of every visit, he had to show Andy his arms, and Andy would examine them for new cuts. Whenever he found one, he would log it in his chart. He was never sure what might provoke another outburst from Andy: sometimes there were many new cuts, and Andy would merely groan and write them down, and sometimes there were only a few new cuts and Andy would get agitated anyway. "You've fucking ruined your arms, you know that, right?" he would ask him. But he would say nothing, and let Andy's lecture wash over him. Part of him understood that by not letting Andy do his job—which was, after all, to heal him—he was being disrespectful, and was to some degree making Andy into a joke in his own office. Andy's tallies—sometimes he wanted to ask Andy if he would get a prize once he reached a certain number, but he knew it would make him angry—were a way for him to at least pretend he could manage the situation, even if he couldn't: it was the accrual of data as a small compensation for actual treatment.

And then, two years later, another wound had opened on his left leg, which had always been the more troublesome one, and his cuttings were set aside for the more urgent matter of his leg. He had first developed one of these wounds less than a year after the injury, and it had healed quickly. "But it won't be the last," the Philadelphia surgeon had said. "With an injury like yours, everything—the vascular system, the dermal system—has been so compromised that you should expect you might get these now and again."

This was the eleventh he'd had, so although he was prepared for the sensation of it, he was never to know its cause (An insect bite? A brush against the edge of a metal filing cabinet? It was always something so gallingly small, but still capable of tearing his skin as easily as if it had been made of paper), and he was never to cease being disgusted by it: the suppuration, the sick, fishy scent, the little gash, like a fetus's mouth, that would appear, burbling viscous, unidentifiable fluids. It was unnatural, the stuff of monster movies and myths, to walk about with an opening that wouldn't, couldn't be closed. He began seeing Andy every Friday night so he could debride the wound, cleaning it and removing the dead tissue and examining the area around it, looking for new skin growth, as he held his breath and gripped the side of the table and tried not to scream.

"You have to tell me when it's painful, Jude," Andy had said, as he breathed and sweated and counted in his head. "It's a good thing if you can feel this, not a bad thing. It means the nerves are still alive and still doing what they're supposed to."

"It's painful," he managed to choke out.

"Scale of one to ten?"

"Seven. Eight."

"I'm sorry," Andy replied. "I'm almost done, I promise. Five more minutes."

He shut his eyes and counted to three hundred, making himself go slowly.

When it was over, he would sit, and Andy would sit with him and give him something to drink: a soda, something sugary, and he'd feel the room begin to clarify itself around him, bit by blurry bit. "Slowly," Andy would say, "or you'll be sick." He would watch as Andy dressed the wound—he was always at his calmest when he was stitching or sewing or wrapping—and in those moments, he would feel so vulnerable and weak that he would have agreed to anything Andy might have suggested.

"You're not going to cut yourself on your legs," Andy would say, more a statement than a question.

"No, I won't."

"Because that would be too insane, even for you."

"I know."

"Your anatomy is so degraded that it'd get really infected."

"Andy. I *know*."

He had, at various points, suspected that Andy was talking to his friends behind his back, and there were times when they would use Andy-like language and turns of phrase, and even four years after "The Incident," as Andy had begun calling it, he suspected that Willem was going through the bathroom trash in the morning, and he'd had to take extra cautions disposing of his razors, bundling them in tissue and duct tape and throwing them into garbage cans on the way to work. "Your crew," Andy called them: "What've you and your crew been up to these days?" (when he was in a good mood) and "I'm going to tell your fucking crew they've got to keep their eyes on you" (when he wasn't).

"Don't you dare, Andy," he'd say. "And anyway, it's not their responsibility."

"Of course it is," Andy would retort. As with other issues, they couldn't agree on this one.

But now it was twenty months after the appearance of this most recent wound and it still hadn't healed. Or rather, it had healed and then broken again and then healed again, and then he had woken on Friday and felt something damp and gummy on his leg—the lower calf, right above the ankle—and had known it had split. He hadn't called Andy yet—he would do so on Monday—but it had been important to him to take this walk, which he feared would be his last for some time, maybe months.

He was on Madison and Seventy-fifth now, very near Andy's office, and his leg was hurting him so much that he crossed to Fifth and sat on one of the benches near the wall that bordered the park. As soon as he sat, he experienced that familiar dizziness, that stomach-lifting nausea, and he bent over and waited until the cement became cement again and he would be able to stand. He felt in those minutes his body's treason, how sometimes the central, tedious struggle in his life was his unwillingness to accept that he would be betrayed by it again and again, that he could expect nothing from it and yet had to keep maintaining it. So much time, his and Andy's, was spent trying to repair something unfixable, something that should have wound up in charred bits on a slag heap years ago. And for what? His mind, he supposed. But there was—as Andy might have said—something incredibly arrogant about that, as if he was saving a jalopy because he had a sentimental attachment to its sound system.

If I walk just a few more blocks, I can be at his office, he thought, but he never would have. It was Sunday. Andy deserved some sort of respite from him, and besides, what he was feeling now was not something he hadn't felt before.

He waited a few more minutes and then heaved himself to his feet, where he stood for half a minute before dropping to the bench again. Finally he was able to stand for good. He wasn't ready yet, but he could imagine himself walking to the curb, raising his arm to hail a cab, resting his head against the back of its black vinyl banquette. He would count the steps to get there, just as he would count the steps it would take him to get from the cab and to his building, from the elevator to the apartment, and from the front door to his room. When he had learned to walk the third time—after his braces had come off—it had been Andy who had helped instruct the physical therapist (she had not been pleased, but had taken his suggestions), and Andy who had, as Ana had just four years before, watched him make his way unaccompanied across a space of ten feet, and then twenty, and then fifty, and then a hundred. His very gait—the left leg coming up to make a near-ninety-degree angle with the ground, forming a rectangle of negative space, the right listing behind—was engineered by Andy, who had made him work at it for hours until he could do it himself. It was Andy who told him he thought he was capable of walking without a cane, and when he finally did it, he'd had Andy to thank.

Monday was not very many hours away, he told himself as he struggled to stay standing, and Andy would see him as he always did, no matter how busy he was. "When did you notice the break?" Andy would say, nudging gently at it with a bit of gauze. "Friday," he'd say. "Why didn't you call me then, Jude?" Andy would say, irritated. "At any rate, I hope you didn't go on your stupid fucking walk." "No, of course not," he'd say, but Andy wouldn't believe him. He sometimes wondered whether Andy thought of him as only a collection of viruses and malfunctions: If you removed them, who was he? If Andy didn't have to take care of him, would he still be interested in him? If he appeared one day magically whole, with a stride as easy as Willem's and JB's complete lack of self-consciousness, the way he could lean back in his chair and let his shirt hoist itself from his hips without any fear, or with Malcolm's long arms, the skin on their insides as smooth as frosting, what would he be to Andy? What would he be to any of them? Would they like him less? More? Or would he discover—as he often feared—that what he understood as friendship was really motivated by their pity of him? How much of who he was was inextricable from what he was unable to do? Who would he have been, who would he be, without the scars, the cuts, the hurts, the sores, the fractures, the infections, the splints, and the discharges?

But of course he would never know. Six months ago, they had managed to get the wound under control, and Andy had examined it, checking and rechecking, before issuing a fleet of warnings about what he should do if it reopened.

He had been only half listening. He was feeling light that day for some reason, but Andy was querulous, and along with a lecture about his leg, he had also endured another about his cutting (too much, Andy thought), and his general appearance (too thin, Andy thought).

He had admired his leg, pivoting it and examining the place where the wound had at last closed over, as Andy talked and talked. "Are you listening to me, Jude?" he had finally demanded.

"It looks good," he told Andy, not answering him, but wanting his reassurance. "Doesn't it?"

Andy sighed. "It looks—" And then he stopped, and was quiet, and he had looked up, had watched Andy shut his eyes, as if refocusing himself, and then open them again. "It looks good, Jude," he'd said, quietly. "It does."

He had felt, then, a great surge of gratitude, because he knew Andy didn't think it looked good, would never think it looked good. To Andy, his body was an onslaught of terrors, one against which the two of them had to be constantly attentive. He knew Andy thought he was self-destructive, or delusional, or in denial.

But what Andy never understood about him was this: he was an optimist. Every month, every week, he chose to open his eyes, to live another day in the world. He did it when he was feeling so awful that sometimes the pain seemed to transport him to another state, one in which everything, even the past that he worked so hard to forget, seemed to fade into a gray watercolor wash. He did it when his memories crowded out all other thoughts, when it took real effort, real concentration, to tether himself to his current life, to keep himself from raging with despair and shame. He did it when he was so exhausted of trying, when being awake and alive demanded such energy that he had to lie in bed thinking of reasons to get up and try again, when it would be much easier to go to the bathroom and untape the plastic zipped bag containing his cotton pads and loose razors and alcohol wipes and bandages from its hiding place beneath the sink and simply surrender. Those were the very bad days.

It really had been a mistake, that night before New Year's Eve when he sat in the bathroom drawing the razor across his arm: he had been half asleep still; he was normally never so careless. But when he realized what he had done, there had been a minute, two minutes—he had counted—when he genuinely hadn't known what to do, when sitting there, and letting this accident become its own conclusion, seemed easier than making the decision himself, a decision that would ripple past him to include Willem, and Andy, and days and months of consequences.

He hadn't known, finally, what had compelled him to grab his towel from its bar and wrap it around his arm, and then pull himself to his feet and wake Willem up. But with each minute that passed, he moved further and further from the other option, the events unfolding themselves with a speed he couldn't control, and he longed for that year right after the injury, before he met Andy, when it seemed that everything might be improved upon, and that his future self might be something bright and clean, when he knew so little but had such hope, and faith that his hope might one day be rewarded.

—

Before New York there had been law school, and before that, college, and before that, there was Philadelphia, and the long, slow trip across country, and before that, there was Montana, and the boys' home, and before Montana was the Southwest, and the motel rooms, and the lonely stretches of road and the hours spent in the car. And before that was South Dakota and the monastery. And before that? A father and a mother, presumably. Or, more realistically, simply a man and a woman. And then, probably, just a woman. And then him.

It was Brother Peter, who taught him math, and was always reminding him of his good fortune, who told him he'd been found in a garbage can. "Inside a trash bag, stuffed with eggshells and old lettuce and spoiled spaghetti—and you," Brother Peter said. "In the alley behind the drugstore, you know the one," even though he didn't, as he rarely left the monastery.

Later, Brother Michael claimed this wasn't even true. "You weren't *in* the trash bin," he told him. "You were *next to* the trash bin." Yes, he conceded, there had been a trash bag, but he had been atop it, not in it, and at any rate, who knew what was in the trash bag itself, and who cared? More likely it was things thrown away from the pharmacy: cardboard and tissues and twist ties and packing chips. "You mustn't believe everything Brother Peter says," he reminded him, as he often did, along with: "You mustn't indulge this tendency to self-mythologize," as he said whenever he asked for details of how he'd come to live at the monastery. "You came, and you're here now, and you should concentrate on your future, and not on the past."

They had created the past for him. He was found naked, said Brother Peter (or in just a diaper, said Brother Michael), but either way, it was assumed he'd been left to, as they said, let nature have its way with him, because it was mid-April and still freezing, and a newborn couldn't have survived for long in that weather. He must have been there for only a few minutes, however, because he was still almost warm when they found him, and the snow hadn't yet filled the car's tire tracks, nor the footprints (sneakers, probably a woman's size eight) that led to the trash bin and then away from it. He was lucky they had found him (it was fate they had found him). Everything he had—his name, his birthday (itself an estimate), his shelter, his very life—was because of them. He should be grateful (they didn't expect him to be grateful to them; they expected him to be grateful to God).

He never knew what they might answer and what they might not. A simple question (Had he been crying when they found him? Had there been a note? Had they looked for whoever had left him?) would be dismissed or unknown or unexplained, but there were declarative answers for the more complicated ones.

"The state couldn't find anyone to take you." (Brother Peter, again.)

"And so we said we'd keep you here as a temporary measure, and then months turned into years and here you are. The end. Now finish these equations; you're taking all day."

But *why* couldn't the state find anyone? Theory one (beloved of Brother Peter): There were simply too many unknowns—his ethnicity, his parentage, possible congenital health problems, and on and on. Where had he come from? Nobody knew. None of the local hospitals had recorded a recent live birth that matched his description. And that was worrisome to potential guardians. Theory two (Brother Michael's): This was a poor town in a poor region in a poor state. No matter the public sympathy—and there had been sympathy, he wasn't to forget that—it was quite another thing to add an extra child to one's household, especially when one's household was already so stretched. Theory three (Father Gabriel's): He was meant to stay here. It had been God's will. This was his home. And now he needed to stop asking questions.

Then there was a fourth theory, invoked by almost all of them when he misbehaved: He was bad, and had been bad from the beginning. "You must have done something very bad to be left behind like that," Brother Peter used to tell him after he hit him with the board, rebuking him as he stood there, sobbing his apologies. "Maybe you cried so much they just couldn't stand it any longer." And he'd cry harder, fearing that Brother Peter was correct.

For all their interest in history, they were collectively irritated when he took interest in his own, as if he was persisting in a particularly tiresome hobby that he wasn't outgrowing at a fast enough rate. Soon he learned not to ask, or at least not to ask directly, although he was always alert to stray pieces of information that he might learn in unlikely moments, from unlikely sources. With Brother Michael, he read *Great Expectations*, and managed to misdirect the brother into a long segue about what life for an orphan would be like in nineteenth-century London, a place as foreign to him as Pierre, just a hundred-some miles away. The lesson eventually became a lecture, as he knew it would, but from it he did learn that he, like Pip, would have been given to a relative if there were any to be identified or had. So there were none, clearly. He was alone.

His possessiveness was also a bad habit that needed to be corrected. He couldn't remember when he first began coveting something that he could own, something that would be his and no one else's. "Nobody here owns anything," they told him, but was that really true? He knew that Brother Peter had a tortoiseshell comb, for example, the color of freshly tapped tree sap and just as light-filled, of which he was very proud and with which he brushed his mustache every morning. One day the comb disappeared, and Brother Peter had interrupted his history lesson with Brother Matthew to grab him by the shoulders and shake him, yelling that he had stolen the comb and had better return it if he knew what was good for him. (Father Gabriel later found the comb, which had slipped into the shallow wedge of space between the brother's desk and the radiator.) And Brother Matthew had an original clothbound edition of *The Bostonians*, which had a soft-rubbed green spine and which he once held before him so he could look at its cover ("Don't touch! I said *don't* touch!"). Even Brother Luke, his favorite of the brothers, who rarely spoke and never scolded him, had a bird that all the others considered his. Technically, said Brother David, the bird was no one's, but it had been Brother Luke who had found it and nursed it and fed it and to whom it flew, and so if Luke wanted it, Luke could have it.

Brother Luke was responsible for the monastery's garden and greenhouse, and in the warm months, he would help him with small tasks. He knew from eavesdropping on the other brothers that Brother Luke had been a rich man before he came to the monastery. But then something happened, or he had done something (it was never clear which), and he either lost most of his money or gave it away, and now he was here, and just as poor as the others, although it was Brother Luke's money that had paid for the greenhouse, and which helped defray some of the monastery's operating expenses. Something about the way the other brothers mostly avoided Luke made him think he might be bad, although Brother Luke was never bad, not to him.

It was shortly after Brother Peter accused him of stealing his comb that he actually stole his first item: a package of crackers from the kitchen. He was passing by one morning on the way to the room they had set aside for his schooling, and no one was there, and the package was on the countertop, just within his reach, and he had, on impulse, grabbed it and run, stuffing it under the scratchy wool tunic he wore, a miniature version of the brothers' own. He had detoured so he could hide it under his pillow, which had made him late for class with Brother Matthew, who had hit him with a forsythia switch as punishment, but the secret of its existence filled him with something warm and joyous. That night, alone in bed, he ate one of the crackers (which he didn't even really like) carefully, breaking it into eight sections with his teeth and letting each piece sit on his tongue until it became soft and gluey and he could swallow it whole.

After that, he stole more and more. There was nothing in the monastery he really wanted, nothing that was really worth having, and so he simply took what he came across, with no real plan or craving: food when he could find it; a clacky black button he found on the floor of Brother Michael's room in one of his post-breakfast prowlings; a pen from Father Gabriel's desk, snatched when, mid-lecture, the father had turned from him to find a book; Brother Peter's comb (this last was the only one he planned, but it gave him no greater thrill than the others). He stole matches and pencils and pieces of paper—useless junk, but someone else's junk—shoving them down his underwear and running back to his bedroom to hide them under his mattress, which was so thin that he could feel its every spring beneath his back at night.

"Stop that running around or I'll have to beat you!" Brother Matthew would yell at him as he hurried to his room.

"Yes, Brother," he would reply, and make himself slow to a walk.

It was the day he took his biggest prize that he was caught: Father Gabriel's silver lighter, stolen directly off his desk when he'd had to interrupt his lecturing of him to answer a phone call. Father Gabriel had bent over his keyboard, and he had reached out and grabbed the lighter, palming its cool heavy weight in his hand until he was finally dismissed. Once outside the father's office, he had hurriedly pushed it into his underwear and was walking as quickly as he could back to his room when he turned the corner without looking and ran directly into Brother Pavel. Before the brother could shout at him, he had fallen back, and the lighter had fallen out, bouncing against the flagstones.

He had been beaten, of course, and shouted at, and in what he thought was a final punishment, Father Gabriel had called him into his office and told him that he would teach him a lesson about stealing other people's things. He had watched, uncomprehending but so frightened that he couldn't even cry, as Father Gabriel folded his handkerchief to the mouth of a bottle of olive oil, and then rubbed the oil into the back of his left hand. And then he had taken his lighter—the same one he had stolen—and held his hand under the flame until the greased spot had caught fire, and his whole hand was swallowed by a white, ghostly glow. Then he had screamed and screamed, and the father had hit him in the face for screaming. "Stop that shouting," he'd shouted. "This is what you get. You'll never forget not to steal again."

When he regained consciousness, he was back in his bed, and his hand was bandaged. All of his things were gone: the stolen things, of course, but the things he had found on his own as well—the stones and feathers and arrowheads, and the fossil that Brother Luke had given him for his fifth birthday, the first gift he had ever received.

After that, after he was caught, he was made to go to Father Gabriel's office every night and take off his clothes, and the father would examine inside him for any contraband. And later, when things got worse, he would think back to that package of crackers: if only he hadn't stolen them. If only he hadn't made things so bad for himself.

His rages began after his evening examinations with Father Gabriel, which soon expanded to include midday ones with Brother Peter. He would have tantrums, throwing himself against the stone walls of the monastery and screaming as loudly as he could, knocking the back of his damaged ugly hand (which, six months later, still hurt sometimes, a deep, insistent pulsing) against the hard, mean corners of the wooden dinner tables, banging the back of his neck, his elbows, his cheeks— all the most painful, tender parts—against the side of his desk. He had them in the day and at night, he couldn't control them, he would feel them move over him like a fog and let himself relax into them, his body and voice moving in ways that excited and repelled him, for as much as he hurt afterward, he knew it scared the brothers, that they feared his anger and noise and power. They hit him with whatever they could find, they started keeping a belt looped on a nail on the schoolroom wall, they took off their sandals and beat him for so long that the next day he couldn't even sit, they called him a monster, they wished for his death, they told him they should have left him on the garbage bag. And he was grateful for this, too, for their help exhausting him, because he couldn't lasso the beast himself and he needed their assistance to make it retreat, to make it walk backward into the cage until it freed itself again.

He started wetting his bed and was made to go visit the father more often, for more examinations, and the more examinations the father gave him, the more he wet the bed. The father began visiting him in his room at night, and so did Brother Peter, and later, Brother Matthew, and he got worse and worse: they made him sleep in his wet night-shirt, they made him wear it during the day. He knew how badly he stank, like urine and blood, and he would scream and rage and howl, interrupting lessons, pushing books off tables so that the brothers would have to start hitting him right away, the lesson abandoned. Sometimes he was hit hard enough so that he lost consciousness, which is what he began to crave: that blackness, where time passed and he wasn't in it, where things were done to him but he didn't know it.

Sometimes there were reasons behind his rages, although they were reasons known only to him. He felt so ceaselessly dirty, so soiled, as if inside he was a rotten building, like the condemned church he had been taken to see in one of his rare trips outside the monastery: the beams speckled with mold, the rafters splintered and holey with nests of termites, the triangles of white sky showing immodestly through the ruined rooftop. He had learned in a history lesson about leeches, and how many years ago they had been thought to siphon the unhealthy blood out of a person, sucking the disease foolishly and greedily into their fat wormy bodies, and he had spent his free hour—after classes but before chores—wading in the stream on the edge of the monastery's property, searching for leeches of his own. And when he couldn't find any, when he was told there weren't any in that creek, he screamed and screamed until his voice deserted him, and even then he couldn't stop, even when his throat felt like it was filling itself with hot blood.

Once he was in his room, and both Father Gabriel and Brother Peter were there, and he was trying not to shout, because he had learned that the quieter he was, the sooner it would end, and he thought he saw, passing outside the doorframe quick as a moth, Brother Luke, and had felt humiliated, although he didn't know the word for humiliation then. And so the next day he had gone in his free time to Brother Luke's garden and had snapped off every one of the daffodils' heads, piling them at the door of Luke's gardener's shed, their fluted crowns pointing toward the sky like open beaks.

Later, alone again and moving through his chores, he had been regretful, and sorrow had made his arms heavy, and he had dropped the bucket of water he was lugging from one end of the room to the other, which made him toss himself to the ground and scream with frustra-tion and remorse.

At dinner, he was unable to eat. He looked for Luke, wondering when and how he would be punished, and when he would have to apologize to the brother. But he wasn't there. In his anxiety, he dropped the metal pitcher of milk, the cold white liquid splattering across the floor, and Brother Pavel, who was next to him, yanked him from the bench and pushed him onto the ground. "Clean it up," Brother Pavel barked at him, throwing a dishrag at him. "But that'll be all you'll eat until Friday." It was Wednesday. "Now go to your room." He ran, before the brother changed his mind.

The door to his room—a converted closet, windowless and wide enough for only a cot, at one end of the second story above the dining hall—was always left open, unless one of the brothers or the father were with him, in which case it was usually closed. But even as he rounded the corner from the staircase, he could see the door was shut, and for a while he lingered in the quiet, empty hallway, unsure what might be waiting for him: one of the brothers, probably. Or a monster, perhaps. After the stream incident, he occasionally daydreamed that the shadows thickening the corners were giant leeches, swaying upright, their glossy segmented skins dark and greasy, waiting to smother him with their wet, soundless weight. Finally he was brave enough and ran straight at the door, opening it with a slam, only to find his bed, with its mud-brown wool blanket, and the box of tissues, and his schoolbooks on their shelf. And then he saw it in the corner, near the head of the bed: a glass jar with a bouquet of daffodils, their bright funnels frilled at their tops.

He sat on the floor near the jar and rubbed one of the flowers' velvet heads between his fingers, and in that moment his sadness was so great, so overpowering, that he wanted to tear at himself, to rip the scar from the back of his hand, to shred himself into bits as he had done to Luke's flowers.

But why had he done such a thing to Brother Luke? It wasn't as if Luke was the only one who was kind to him—when he wasn't being made to punish him, Brother David always praised him and told him how quick he was, and even Brother Peter regularly brought him books from the library in town to read and discussed them with him afterward, listening to his opinions as if he were a real person—but not only had Luke never beaten him, he had made efforts to reassure him, to express his allegiance with him. The previous Sunday, he was to recite aloud the pre-supper prayer, and as he stood at the foot of Father Gabri-el's table, he was suddenly seized by an impulse to misbehave, to grab a handful of the cubed potatoes from the dish before him and fling them around the room. He could already feel the scrape in his throat from the screaming he would do, the singe of the belt as it slapped across his back, the darkness he would sink into, the giddy bright of day he would wake to. He watched his arm lift itself from his side, watched his fingers open, petal-like, and float toward the bowl. And just then he had raised his head and had seen Brother Luke, who gave him a wink, so solemn and brief, like a camera's shutter-click, that he was at first unaware he had seen anything at all. And then Luke winked at him again, and for some reason this calmed him, and he came back to himself, and said his lines and sat down, and dinner passed without incident.

And now there were these flowers. But before he could think about what they might mean, the door opened, and there was Brother Peter, and he stood, waiting in that terrible moment that he could never pre-pare for, in which anything might happen, and anything might come.

The next day, he had left directly after his classes for the green-house, determined that he should say something to Luke. But as he drew closer, his resolve deserted him, and he dawdled, kicking at small stones and kneeling to pick up and then discard twigs, throwing them toward the forest that bordered the property. What, really, did he mean to say? He was about to turn back, to retreat toward a particular tree on the north edge of the grounds in whose cleft of roots he had dug a hole and begun a new collection of things—though these things were only objects he had discovered in the woods and were safely nobody's: little rocks; a branch that was shaped a bit like a lean dog in mid-leap—and where he spent most of his free time, unearthing his possessions and holding them in his hands, when he heard someone say his name and turned and saw it was Luke, holding his hand up in greeting and walking toward him.

"I thought it was you," Brother Luke said as he neared him (dis-ingenuously, it would occur to him much later, for who else would it have been? He was the only child at the monastery), and although he tried, he was unable to find the words to apologize to Luke, unable in truth to find the words for anything, and instead he found himself cry-ing. He was never embarrassed when he cried, but in this moment he was, and he turned away from Brother Luke and held the back of his scarred hand before his eyes. He was suddenly aware of how hungry he was, and how it was only Thursday afternoon, and he wouldn't have anything to eat until the next day.

"Well," said Luke, and he could feel the brother kneeling, very close to him. "Don't cry; don't cry." But his voice was so gentle, and he cried harder.

Then Brother Luke stood, and when he spoke next, his voice was jollier. "Jude, listen," he said. "I have something to show you. Come with me," and he started walking toward the greenhouse, turning around to make sure he was following. "Jude," he called again, "come with me," and he, curious despite himself, began to follow him, walking toward the greenhouse he knew so well with the beginnings of an unfamiliar eagerness, as if he had never seen it before.

As an adult, he became obsessed in spells with trying to identify the exact moment in which things had started going so wrong, as if he could freeze it, preserve it in agar, hold it up and teach it before a class: *This is when it happened. This is where it started.* He'd think: Was it when I stole the crackers? Was it when I ruined Luke's daffodils? Was it when I had my first tantrum? And, more impossibly, was it when I did whatever I did that made her leave me behind that drugstore? And what had that been?

But really, he would know: it was when he walked into the greenhouse that afternoon. It was when he allowed himself to be escorted in, when he gave up everything to follow Brother Luke. That had been the moment. And after that, it had never been right again.

—

There are five more steps and then he is at their front door, where he can't fit the key into the lock because his hands are shaking, and he curses, nearly dropping it. And then he is in the apartment, and there are only fifteen steps from the front door to his bed, but he still has to stop halfway and bring himself down slowly to the ground, and pull himself the final feet to his room on his elbows. For a while he lies there, everything shifting around him, until he is strong enough to pull the blanket down over him. He will lie there until the sun leaves the sky and the apartment grows dark, and then, finally, he will hoist himself onto his bed with his arms, where he will fall asleep without eating or washing his face or changing, his teeth clacking against themselves from the pain. He will be alone, because Willem will go out with his girlfriend after the show, and by the time he gets home, it will be very late.

When he wakes, it will be very early, and he will feel better, but his wound will have wept during the night, and pus will have soaked through the gauze he had applied on Sunday morning before he left for his walk, his disastrous walk, and his pants will be stuck to his skin with its ooze. He will send a message to Andy, and then leave another with his exchange, and then he will shower, carefully removing the bandage, which will bring scraps of rotten flesh and clots of blackened mucus-thick blood with it. He will pant and gasp to keep from shouting. He will remember the conversation he had with Andy the last time this happened, when Andy suggested he get a wheelchair to keep on reserve, and although he hates the thought of using a wheelchair again, he will wish he had one now. He will think that Andy is right, that his walks are a sign of his inexcusable hubris, that his pretending that everything is fine, that he is not in fact disabled, is selfish, for the consequences it means for other people, people who have been inexplicably, unreasonably generous and good to him for years, for almost decades now.

He will turn off the shower and lower himself into the tub and lean his cheek against the tile and wait to feel better. He will be reminded of how trapped he is, trapped in a body he hates, with a past he hates, and how he will never be able to change either. He will want to cry, from frustration and hatred and pain, but he hasn't cried since what happened with Brother Luke, after which he told himself he would never cry again. He will be reminded that he is a nothing, a scooped-out husk in which the fruit has long since mummified and shrunk, and now rattles uselessly. He will experience that prickle, that shiver of disgust that afflicts him in both his happiest and his most wretched moments, the one that asks him who he thinks he is to inconvenience so many people, to think he has the right to keep going when even his own body tells him he should stop.

He will sit and wait and breathe and he will be grateful that it is so early, that there is no chance of Willem discovering him and having to save him once again. He will (though he won't be able to remember how later) somehow work himself into a standing position, get himself out of the tub, take some aspirin, go to work. At work, the words will blur and dance on the page, and by the time Andy calls, it will only be seven a.m., and he will tell Marshall he's sick, refuse Marshall's offer of a car, but let him—this is how bad he feels—help him into a cab. He will make the ride uptown that he had stupidly walked just the previous day. And when Andy opens the door, he will try to remain composed.

"Judy," Andy will say, and he will be in his gentle mode, there will be no lectures from him today, and he will allow Andy to lead him past his empty waiting room, his office not yet open for the day, and help him onto the table where he has spent hours, days of hours, will let Andy help undress him even, as he closes his eyes and waits for the small bright hurt of Andy easing the tape off his leg, and pulling away from the raw skin the sodden gauze beneath.

My life, he will think, my life. But he won't be able to think beyond this, and he will keep repeating the words to himself—part chant, part curse, part reassurance—as he slips into that other world that he visits when he is in such pain, that world he knows is never far from his own but that he can never remember after: My life.

2

YOU ASKED ME once when I knew that he was for me, and I told you that I had always known. But that wasn't true, and I knew it even as I said it—I said it because it sounded pretty, like something someone might say in a book or a movie, and because we were both feeling so wretched, and helpless, and because I thought if I said it, we both might feel better about the situation before us, the situation that we perhaps had been capable of preventing—perhaps not—but at any rate hadn't. This was in the hospital: the first time, I should say. I know you remember: you had flown in from Colombo that morning, hopscotching across cities and countries and hours, so that you landed a full day before you left.

But I want to be accurate now. I want to be accurate both because there is no reason not to be, and because I should be—I have always tried to be, I always try to be.

I'm not sure where to begin.

Maybe with some nice words, although they are also true words: I liked you right away. You were twenty-four when we met, which would have made me forty-seven. (Jesus.) I thought you were unusual: later, he'd speak of your goodness, but he never needed to explain it to me, for I already knew you were. It was the first summer the group of you came up to the house, and it was such a strange weekend for me, and for him as well—for me because in you four I saw who and what Jacob might have been, and for him because he had only known me as his teacher, and he was suddenly seeing me in my shorts and wearing my apron as I scooped clams off the grill, and arguing with you three about everything. Once I stopped seeing Jacob's face in all of yours, though, I was able to enjoy the weekend, in large part because you three seemed to enjoy it so much. You saw nothing strange in the situation: you were boys who assumed that people would like you, not from arrogance but because people always had, and you had no reason to think that, if you were polite and friendly, then that politeness and friendliness might not be reciprocated.

He, of course, had every reason to not think that, although I wouldn't discover that until later. Then, I watched him at mealtimes, noticing how, during particularly raucous debates, he would sit back in his seat, as if physically leaning out of the ring, and observe all of you, how easily you challenged me without fear of provoking me, how thoughtlessly you reached across the table to serve yourselves more potatoes, more zucchini, more steak, how you asked for what you wanted and received it.

The thing I remember most vividly from that weekend is a small thing. We were walking, you and he and Julia and I, down that little path lined with birches that led to the lookout. (Back then it was a narrow throughway, do you remember that? It was only later that it became dense with trees.) I was with him, and you and Julia were behind us. You were talking about, oh, I don't know—insects? Wildflowers? You two always found something to discuss, you both loved being outdoors, both loved animals: I loved this about both of you, even though I couldn't understand it. And then you touched his shoulder and moved in front of him and knelt and retied one of his shoelaces that had come undone, and then fell back in step with Julia. It was so fluid, a little gesture: a step forward, a fold onto bended knee, a retreat back toward her side. It was nothing to you, you didn't even think about it; you never even paused in your conversation. You were always watching him (but you all were), you took care of him in a dozen small ways, I saw all of this over those few days—but I doubt you would remember this particular incident.

But while you were doing it, he looked at me, and the look on his face—I still cannot describe it, other than in that moment, I felt something crumble inside me, like a tower of damp sand built too high: for him, and for you, and for me as well. And in his face, I knew my own would be echoed. The impossibility of finding someone to do such a thing for another person, so unthinkingly, so gracefully! When I looked at him, I understood, for the first time since Jacob died, what people meant when they said someone was heartbreaking, that something could break your heart. I had always thought it mawkish, but in that moment I realized that it might have been mawkish, but it was also true.

And that, I suppose, was when I knew.

—

I had never thought I would become a parent, and not because I'd had bad parents myself. Actually, I had wonderful parents: my mother died when I was very young, of breast cancer, and for the next five years it was just me and my father. He was a doctor, a general practitioner who liked to hope he might grow old with his patients.

We lived on West End, at Eighty-second Street, and his practice was in our building, on the ground floor, and I used to come by to visit after school. All his patients knew me, and I was proud to be the doctor's son, to say hello to everyone, to watch the babies he had delivered grow into kids who looked up to me because their parents told them I was Dr. Stein's son, that I went to a good high school, one of the best in the city, and that if they studied hard enough, they might be able to as well. "Darling," my father called me, and when he saw me after school on those visits, he would place his palm on the back of my neck, even when I grew taller than he, and kiss me on the side of my head. "My darling," he'd say, "how was school?"

When I was eight, he married his office manager, Adele. There was never a moment in my childhood in which I was not aware of Adele's presence: it was she who took me shopping for new clothes when I needed them, she who joined us for Thanksgiving, she who wrapped my birthday presents. It was not so much that Adele was a mother to me; it's that to me, a mother was Adele.

She was older, older than my father, and one of those women whom men like and feel comfortable around but never think of marrying, which is a kind way of saying she wasn't pretty. But who needs prettiness in a mother? I asked her once if she wanted children of her own, and she said I was her child, and she couldn't imagine having a better one, and it says everything you need to know about my father and Adele and how I felt about them and how they treated me that I never even questioned that claim of hers until I was in my thirties and my then-wife and I were fighting about whether we should have another child, a child to replace Jacob.

She was an only child, as I was an only child, and my father was an only child, too: a family of onlys. But Adele's parents were living—my father's were not—and we used to travel out to Brooklyn, to what has now been swallowed by Park Slope, to see them on weekends. They had lived in America for almost five decades and still spoke very little English: the father, timidly, the mother, expressively. They were blocky, like she was, and kind, like she was—Adele would speak to them in Russian, and her father, whom I called Grandpa by default, would unclench one of his fat fists and show me what was secreted within: a wooden birdcall, or a wodge of bright-pink gum. Even when I was an adult, in law school, he would always give me something, although he no longer had his store then, which meant he must have bought them somewhere. But where? I always imagined there might be a secret shop full of toys that went out of fashion generations ago, and yet was patronized, faithfully, by old immigrant men and women, who kept them in business by buying their stocks of whorl-painted wooden tops and little metal soldiers and sets of jacks, their rubber balls sticky with grime even before their plastic wrap had been torn.

I had always had a theory—born of nothing—that men who had been old enough to witness their father's second marriage (and, therefore, old enough to make a judgment) married their stepmother, not their mother. But I didn't marry someone like Adele. My wife, my first wife, was cool and self-contained. Unlike the other girls I knew, who were always minimizing themselves—their intelligence, of course, but also their desires and anger and fears and composure—Liesl never did. On our third date, we were walking out of a café on MacDougal Street, and a man stumbled from a shadowed doorway and vomited on her. Her sweater was chunky with it, that pumpkin-bright splatter, and I remember in particular the way a large globule clung to the little diamond ring she wore on her right hand, as if the stone itself had grown a tumor. The people around us gasped, or shrieked, but Liesl only closed her eyes. Another woman would have screeched, or squealed (*I* would have screeched or squealed), but I remember she only gave a great shudder, as if her body were acknowledging the disgust but also removing itself from it, and when she opened her eyes, she was recovered. She peeled off her cardigan, chucked it into the nearest garbage can. "Let's go," she told me. I had been mute, shocked, throughout the entire episode, but in that moment, I wanted her, and I followed her where she led me, which turned out to be her apartment, a hellhole on Sullivan Street. The entire time, she kept her right hand slightly aloft from her body, the blob of vomit still clinging to her ring.

Neither my father nor Adele particularly liked her, although they never told me so; they were polite, and respectful of my wishes. In exchange, I never asked them, never made them lie. I don't think it was because she wasn't Jewish—neither of my parents were religious—but, I think, because they thought I was too much in awe of her. Or maybe this is what I've decided, late in life. Maybe it was because what I admired as competence, they saw as frigidity, or coldness. Goodness knows they wouldn't have been the first to think that. They were always polite to her, and she reasonably so to them, but I think they would have preferred a potential daughter-in-law who would flirt with them a little, to whom they could tell embarrassing stories about my childhood, who would have lunch with Adele and play chess with my father. Someone like you, in fact. But that wasn't Liesl and wouldn't ever be, and once they realized that, they too remained a bit aloof, not to express their displeasure but as a sort of self-discipline, a reminder to themselves that there were limits, her limits, that they should try to respect. When I was with her, I felt oddly relaxed, as if, in the face of such sturdy competence, even misfortune wouldn't dare try to challenge us.

We had met in New York, where I was in law school and she was in medical school, and after graduating, I got a clerkship in Boston, and she (one year older than I) started her internship. She was training to be an oncologist. I had been admiring of that, of course, because of what it suggested: there is nothing more soothing than a woman who wants to heal, whom you imagine bent maternally over a patient, her lab coat white as clouds. But Liesl didn't want to be admired: she was interested in oncology because it was one of the harder disciplines, because it was thought to be more cerebral. She and her fellow oncological interns had scorn for the radiologists (too mercenary), the cardiologists (too puffed-up and pleased with themselves), the pediatricians (too sentimental), and especially the surgeons (unspeakably arrogant) and the dermatologists (beneath comment, although they of course worked with them frequently). They liked the anesthesiologists (weird and geeky and fastidious, and prone to addiction), the pathologists (even more cerebral than they), and—well, that was about it. Sometimes a group of them would come over to our house, and would linger after dinner discussing cases and studies, while their partners—lawyers and historians and writers and lesser scientists—were ignored until we slunk off to the living room to discuss the various trivial, less-interesting things with which we occupied our days.

We were two adults, and it was a happy enough life. There was no whining that we didn't spend enough time with each other, from me or from her. We remained in Boston for her residency, and then she moved back to New York to do her fellowship. I stayed. By that time I was working at a firm and was an adjunct at the law school. We saw each other on the weekends, one in Boston, one in New York. And then she completed her program and returned to Boston; we married; we bought a house, a little one, not the one I have now, just at the edge of Cambridge.

My father and Adele (and Liesl's parents, for that matter; mysteriously, they were considerably more emotive than she was, and on our infrequent trips to Santa Barbara, while her father made jokes and her mother placed before me plates of sliced cucumbers and peppered tomatoes from her garden, she would watch with a closed-off expression, as if embarrassed, or at least perplexed by, their relative expansiveness) never asked us if we were going to have children; I think they thought that as long as they didn't ask, there was a chance we might. The truth was that I didn't really feel the need for it; I had never envisioned having a child, I didn't feel about them one way or another. And that seemed enough of a reason not to: having a child, I thought, was something you should actively want, crave, even. It was not a venture for the ambivalent or passionless. Liesl felt the same way, or so we thought.

But then, one evening—I was thirty-one, she was thirty-two: young—I came home and she was already in the kitchen, waiting for me. This was unusual; she worked longer hours than I did, and I usually didn't see her until eight or nine at night.

"I need to talk to you," she said, solemnly, and I was suddenly scared. She saw that and smiled—she wasn't a cruel person, Liesl, and I don't mean to give the impression that she was without kindness, without gentleness, because she had both in her, was capable of both. "It's nothing bad, Harold." Then she laughed a little. "I don't think."

I sat. She inhaled. "I'm pregnant. I don't know how it happened. I must've skipped a pill or two and forgotten. It's almost eight weeks. I had it confirmed at Sally's today." (Sally was her roommate from their med-school days, her best friend, and her gynecologist.) She said all this very quickly, in staccato, digestible sentences. Then she was silent. "I'm on a pill where I don't get my periods, you know, so I didn't know." And then, when I said nothing, "Say something."

I couldn't, at first. "How do you feel?" I asked.

She shrugged. "I feel fine."

"Good," I said, stupidly.

"Harold," she said, and sat across from me, "what do you want to do?"

"What do *you* want to do?"

She shrugged again. "I know what I want to do. I want to know what you want to do."

"You don't want to keep it."

She didn't disagree. "I want to hear what you want."

"What if I say I want to keep it?"

She was ready. "Then I'd seriously consider it."

I hadn't been expecting this, either. "Leez," I said, "we should do what you want to do." This wasn't completely magnanimous; it was mostly cowardly. In this case, as with many things, I was happy to cede the decision to her.

She sighed. "We don't have to decide tonight. We have some time." Four weeks, she didn't need to say.

In bed, I thought. I thought those thoughts all men think when a woman tells them she's pregnant: What would the baby look like? Would I like it? Would I love it? And then, more crushingly: fatherhood. With all its responsibilities and fulfillments and tedium and possibilities for failure.

The next morning, we didn't speak of it, and the day after that, we didn't speak of it again. On Friday, as we were going to bed, she said, sleepily, "Tomorrow we've got to discuss this," and I said, "Absolutely." But we didn't, and we didn't, and then the ninth week passed, and then the tenth, and then the eleventh and twelfth, and then it was too late to easily or ethically do anything, and I think we were both relieved. The decision had been made for us—or rather, our indecisiveness had made the decision for us—and we were going to have a child. It was the first time in our marriage that we'd been so mutually indecisive.

We had imagined that it would be a girl, and if it was, we'd name it Adele, for my mother, and Sarah, for Sally. But it wasn't a girl, and we instead let Adele (who was so happy she started crying, one of the very few times I'd seen her cry) pick the first name and Sally the second: Jacob More. (Why More, we asked Sally, who said it was for Thomas More.)

I have never been one of those people—I know you aren't, either—who feels that the love one has for a child is somehow a superior love, one more meaningful, more significant, and grander than any other. I didn't feel that before Jacob, and I didn't feel that after. But it *is* a singular love, because it is a love whose foundation is not physical attraction, or pleasure, or intellect, but fear. You have never known fear until you have a child, and maybe that is what tricks us into thinking that it is more magnificent, because the fear itself is more magnificent. Every day, your first thought is not "I love him" but "How is he?" The world, overnight, rearranges itself into an obstacle course of terrors. I would hold him in my arms and wait to cross the street and would think how absurd it was that my child, that any child, could expect to survive this life. It seemed as improbable as the survival of one of those late-spring butterflies—you know, those little white ones—I sometimes saw wobbling through the air, always just millimeters away from smacking itself against a windshield.

And let me tell you two other things I learned. The first is that it doesn't matter how old that child is, or when or how he became yours. Once you decide to think of someone as your child, something changes, and everything you have previously enjoyed about them, everything you have previously felt for them, is preceded first by that fear. It's not biological; it's something extra-biological, less a determination to ensure the survival of one's genetic code, and more a desire to prove oneself inviolable to the universe's feints and challenges, to triumph over the things that want to destroy what's yours.

The second thing is this: when your child dies, you feel everything you'd expect to feel, feelings so well-documented by so many others that I won't even bother to list them here, except to say that everything that's written about mourning is all the same, and it's all the same for a reason—because there is no real deviation from the text. Sometimes you feel more of one thing and less of another, and sometimes you feel them out of order, and sometimes you feel them for a longer time or a shorter time. But the sensations are always the same.

But here's what no one says—when it's your child, a part of you, a very tiny but nonetheless unignorable part of you, also feels relief. Because finally, the moment you have been expecting, been dreading, been preparing yourself for since the day you became a parent, has come.

Ah, you tell yourself, *it's arrived. Here it is.*

And after that, you have nothing to fear again.

———

Years ago, after the publication of my third book, a journalist once asked me if you could tell right away whether a student had a mind for law or not, and the answer is: Sometimes. But often, you're wrong—the student who seemed so bright in the first half of the semester becomes steadily less so as the year goes on, and the student about whom you never thought one thing or another is the one who emerges as a dazzler, someone you love hearing think.

It's often the most naturally intelligent students who have the most difficult time in their first year—law school, particularly the first year of law school, is really not a place where creativity, abstract thought, and imagination are rewarded. In this way, I often think—based upon what I've heard, not what I know firsthand—that it's a bit like art school.

Julia had a friend, a man named Dennys, who was as a boy a tremendously gifted artist. They had been friends since they were small, and she once showed me some of the drawings he made when he was ten or twelve: little sketches of birds pecking at the ground, of his face, round and blank, of his father, the local veterinarian, his hand smoothing the fur of a grimacing terrier. Dennys's father didn't see the point of drawing lessons, however, and so he was never formally schooled. But when they were older, and Julia went to university, Dennys went to art school to learn how to draw. For the first week, he said, they were allowed to draw whatever they wanted, and it was always Dennys's sketches that the professor selected to pin up on the wall for praise and critique.

But then they were made to learn *how* to draw: to re-draw, in essence. Week two, they only drew ellipses. Wide ellipses, fat ellipses, skinny ellipses. Week three, they drew circles: three-dimensional circles, two-dimensional circles. Then it was a flower. Then a vase. Then a hand. Then a head. Then a body. And with each week of proper training, Dennys got worse and worse. By the time the term had ended, his pictures were never displayed on the wall. He had grown too self-conscious to draw. When he saw a dog now, its long fur whisking the ground beneath it, he saw not a dog but a circle on a box, and when he tried to draw it, he worried about proportion, not about recording its doggy-ness.

He decided to speak to his professor. We are meant to break you down, Dennys, his professor said. Only the truly talented will be able to come back from it.

"I guess I wasn't one of the truly talented," Dennys would say. He became a barrister instead, lived in London with his partner.

"Poor Dennys," Julia would say.

"Oh, it's all right," Dennys would sigh, but none of us were convinced.

And in that same way, law school breaks a mind down. Novelists, poets, and artists don't often do well in law school (unless they are *bad* novelists, poets, and artists), but neither, necessarily, do mathematicians, logicians, and scientists. The first group fails because their logic is their own; the second fails because logic is *all* they own.

He, however, was a good student—a great student—from the beginning, but this greatness was often camouflaged in an aggressive non-greatness. I knew, from listening to his answers in class, that he had everything he needed to be a superb lawyer: it's not accidental that law is called a trade, and like all trades, what it demands most is a capacious memory, which he had. What it demands next—again, like many trades—is the ability to see the problem before you . . . and then, just as immediately, the rat's tail of problems that might follow. Much the way that, for a contractor, a house is not just a structure—it's a snarl of pipes engorging with ice in the winter, of shingles swelling with humidity in the summer, of rain gutters belching up fountains of water in the spring, of cement splitting in the first autumn cold—so too is a house something else for a lawyer. A house is a locked safe full of contracts, of liens, of future lawsuits, of possible violations: it represents potential attacks on your property, on your goods, on your person, on your privacy.

Of course, you can't literally think like this all the time, or you'd drive yourself crazy. And so for most lawyers, a house is, finally, just a house, something to fill and fix and repaint and empty. But there's a period in which every law student—every good law student—finds that their vision shifts, somehow, and realizes that the law is inescapable, that no interaction, no aspect of daily life, escapes its long, graspy fingers. A street becomes a shocking disaster, a riot of violations and potential civil lawsuits. A marriage looks like a divorce. The world becomes temporarily unbearable.

He could do this. He could take a case and see its end; it is very difficult to do, because you have to be able to hold in your head all the possibilities, all the probable consequences, and then choose which ones to worry over and which to ignore. But what he also did—what he couldn't stop himself from doing—was wonder as well about the moral implications of the case. And that is not helpful in law school. There were colleagues of mine who wouldn't let their students even *say* the words "right" and "wrong." "*Right* has nothing to do with it," one of my professors used to bellow at us. "What is the *law*? What does the *law* say?" (Law professors enjoy being theatrical; all of us do.) Another, whenever the words were mentioned, would say nothing, but walk over to the offender and hand him a little slip of paper, a stack of which he kept in his jacket's inside pocket, that read: *Drayman 241.* Drayman 241 was the philosophy department's office.

Here, for example, is a hypothetical: A football team is going to an away game when one of their vans breaks down. So they ask the mother of one of the players if they can borrow her van to transport them. Sure, she says, but I'm not going to drive. And so she asks the assistant coach to drive the team for her. But then, as they're driving along, something horrible happens: the van skids off the road and flips over; everyone inside dies.

There is no criminal case here. The road was slippery, the driver wasn't intoxicated. It was an accident. But then the parents of the team, the mothers and fathers of the dead players, sue the owner of the van. It was her van, they argue, but more important, it was she who appointed the driver of her van. He was only her agent, and therefore, it is she who bears the responsibility. So: What happens? Should the plaintiffs win their suit?

Students don't like this case. I don't teach it that often—its extremity makes it more flashy than it is instructive, I believe—but whenever I did, I would always hear a voice in the auditorium say, "But it's not fair!" And as annoying as that word is—*fair*—it is important that students never forget the concept. "Fair" is never an answer, I would tell them. But it is always a consideration.

He never mentioned whether something was fair, however. Fairness itself seemed to hold little interest for him, which I found fascinating, as people, especially young people, are very interested in what's fair. Fairness is a concept taught to nice children: it is the governing principle of kindergartens and summer camps and playgrounds and soccer fields. Jacob, back when he was able to go to school and learn things and think and speak, knew what fairness was and that it was important, something to be valued. Fairness is for happy people, for people who have been lucky enough to have lived a life defined more by certainties than by ambiguities.

Right and wrong, however, are for—well, not unhappy people, maybe, but scarred people; scared people.

Or am I just thinking this now?

"So were the plaintiffs successful?" I asked. That year, his first year, I had in fact taught that case.

"Yes," he said, and he explained why: he knew instinctively why they would have been. And then, right on cue, I heard the tiny "But it's not fair!" from the back of the room, and before I could begin my first lecture of the season—"fair" is never an answer, etc., etc.—he said, quietly, "But it's right."

I was never able to ask him what he meant by that. Class ended, and everyone got up at once and almost ran for the door, as if the room was on fire. I remember telling myself to ask him about it in the next class, later that week, but I forgot. And then I forgot again, and again. Over the years, I would remember this conversation every now and again, and each time I would think: I must ask him what he meant by that. But then I never would. I don't know why.

And so this became his pattern: he knew the law. He had a feeling for it. But then, just when I wanted him to stop talking, he would introduce a moral argument, he would mention ethics. Please, I would think, please don't do this. The law is simple. It allows for less nuance than you'd imagine. Ethics and morals do, in reality, have a place in law—although not in jurisprudence. It is morals that help us make the laws, but morals do not help us apply them.

I was worried he'd make it harder for himself, that he'd complicate the real gift he had with—as much as I hate to have to say this about my profession—thinking. *Stop!* I wanted to tell him. But I never did, because eventually, I realized I enjoyed hearing him think.

In the end, of course, I needn't have worried; he learned how to control it, he learned to stop mentioning right and wrong. And as we know, this tendency of his didn't stop him from becoming a great lawyer. But later, often, I was sad for him, and for me. I wished I had urged him to leave law school, I wished I had told him to go to the equivalent of Drayman 241. The skills I gave him were not skills he needed after all. I wish I had nudged him in a direction where his mind could have been as supple as it was, where he wouldn't have had to harness himself to a dull way of thinking. I felt I had taken someone who once knew how to draw a dog and turned him into someone who instead knew only how to draw shapes.

I am guilty of many things when it comes to him. But sometimes, illogically, I feel guiltiest for this. I opened the van door, I invited him inside. And while I didn't drive off the road, I instead drove him somewhere bleak and cold and colorless, and left him standing there, where, back where I had collected him, the landscape shimmered with color, the sky fizzed with fireworks, and he stood openmouthed in wonder.

3

THREE WEEKS BEFORE he left for Thanksgiving in Boston, a package—a large, flat, unwieldy wooden crate with his name and address written on every side in black marker—arrived for him at work, where it sat by his desk all day until he was able to open it late that night.

From the return address, he knew what it was, but he still felt that reflexive curiosity one does when unwrapping anything, even something unwanted. Inside the box were layers of brown paper, and then layers of bubble wrap, and then, wrapped in sheets of white paper, the painting itself.

He turned it over. "To Jude with love and apologies, JB," JB had scribbled on the canvas, directly above his signature: "Jean-Baptiste Marion." There was an envelope from JB's gallery taped to the back of the frame, inside of which was a letter certifying the painting's authenticity and date, addressed to him and signed by the gallery's registrar.

He called Willem, who he knew would have already left the theater and was probably on his way home. "Guess what I got today?"

There was only the slightest of pauses before Willem answered. "The painting."

"Right," he said, and sighed. "So I suppose you're behind this?"

Willem coughed. "I just told him he didn't have a choice in the matter any longer—not if he wanted you to talk to him again at some point." Willem paused, and he could hear the wind whooshing past him. "Do you need help getting it home?"

"Thanks," he said. "But I'm just going to leave it here for now and pick it up later." He re-clad the painting in its layers and replaced it in its box, which he shoved beneath his console. Before he shut off his computer, he began a note to JB, but then stopped, and deleted what he'd written, and instead left for the night.

He was both surprised and not that JB had sent him the painting after all (and not at all surprised to learn that it had been Willem who had convinced him to do so). Eighteen months ago, just as Willem was beginning his first performances in *The Malamud Theorem*, JB had been offered representation by a gallery on the Lower East Side, and the previous spring, he'd had his first solo show, "The Boys," a series of twenty-four paintings based on photographs he'd taken of the three of them. As he'd promised years ago, JB had let him see the pictures of him that he wanted to paint, and although he had approved many of them (reluctantly: he had felt queasy even as he did so, but he knew how important the series was to JB), JB had ultimately been less interested in the ones he'd approved than in the ones he wouldn't, a few of which—including an image in which he was curled into himself in bed, his eyes open but scarily unseeing, his left hand stretched open unnaturally wide, like a ghoul's claw—he alarmingly had no memory of JB even taking. That had been the first fight: JB wheedling, then sulking, then threatening, then shouting, and then, when he couldn't change his mind, trying to convince Willem to advocate for him.

"You realize I don't actually owe you anything," JB had told him once he realized his negotiations with Willem weren't progressing. "I mean, I don't *technically* have to ask your permission here. I could *technically* just paint whatever the fuck I want. This is a courtesy I'm extending you, you know."

He could've swamped JB with arguments, but he was too angry to do so. "You promised me, JB," he said. "That should be enough." He could have added, "And you owe me as my friend," but he had a few years ago come to realize that JB's definition of friendship and its responsibilities was different than his own, and there was no arguing with him about it: you either accepted it or you didn't, and he had decided to accept it, although recently, the work it took to accept JB and his limitations had begun to feel more enraging and wearisome and arduous than seemed necessary.

In the end, JB had had to admit defeat, although in the months before his show opened, he had made occasional allusions to what he called his "lost paintings," great works he could've made had he, Jude, been less rigid, less timid, less self-conscious, and (this was his favorite of JB's arguments) less of a philistine. Later, though, he would be embarrassed by his own gullibility, by how he had trusted that his wishes would be respected.

The opening had been on a Thursday in late April shortly after his thirtieth birthday, a night so unseasonably cold that the plane trees' first leaves had frozen and cracked, and rounding the corner onto Norfolk Street, he had stopped to admire the scene the gallery made, a bright golden box of light and shimmered warmth against the chilled flat black of the night. Inside, he immediately encountered Black Henry Young and a friend of theirs from law school, and then so many other people he knew—from college, and their various parties at Lispenard Street, and JB's aunts, and Malcolm's parents, and long-ago friends of JB's that he hadn't seen in years—that it had taken some time before he could push through the crowd to look at the paintings themselves.

He had always known that JB was talented. They all did, everyone did: no matter how ungenerously you might occasionally think of JB as a person, there was something about his work that could convince you that you were wrong, that whatever deficiencies of character you had ascribed to him were in reality evidence of your own pettiness and ill-temper, that hidden within JB was someone of huge sympathies and depth and understanding. And that night, he had no trouble at all recognizing the paintings' intensity and beauty, and had felt only an uncomplicated pride in and gratitude for JB: for the accomplishment of the work, of course, but also for his ability to produce colors and images that made all other colors and images seem wan and flaccid in comparison, for his ability to make you see the world anew. The paintings had been arranged in a single row that unspooled across the walls like a stave, and the tones JB had created—dense bruised blues and bourbon-ish yellows—were so distinctly their own, it was as if JB had invented a different language of color altogether.

He stopped to admire *Willem and the Girl*, one of the pictures he had already seen and had indeed already bought, in which JB had painted Willem turned away from the camera but for his eyes, which seemed to look directly back at the viewer, but were actually looking at, presumably, a girl who had been standing in Willem's exact sightline. He loved the expression on Willem's face, which was one he knew very well, when he was just about to smile and his mouth was still soft and undecided, somehow, but the muscles around his eyes were already pulling themselves upward. The paintings weren't arranged chronologically, and so after this was one of himself from just a few months ago (he hurried past the ones of himself), and following that an image of Malcolm and his sister, in what he recognized from the furniture was Flora's long-departed first West Village apartment (*Malcolm and Flora, Bethune Street*).

He looked around for JB and saw him talking to the gallery director, and at that moment, JB straightened his neck and caught his eye, and gave him a wave. "Genius," he mouthed to JB over people's heads, and JB grinned at him and mouthed back, "Thank you."

But then he had moved to the third and final wall and had seen them: two paintings, both of him, neither of which JB had ever shown him. In the first, he was very young and holding a cigarette, and in the second, which he thought was from around two years ago, he was sitting bent over on the edge of his bed, leaning his forehead against the wall, his legs and arms crossed and his eyes closed—it was the position he always assumed when he was coming out of an episode and was gathering his physical resources before attempting to stand up again. He hadn't remembered JB taking this picture, and indeed, given its perspective—the camera peeking around the edge of the doorframe—he knew that he wasn't meant to remember, because he wasn't meant to be aware of the picture's existence at all. For a moment, the noise of the space blotted out around him, and he could only look and look at the paintings: even in his distress, he had the presence of mind to understand that he was responding less to the images themselves than to the memories and sensations they provoked, and that his sense of violation that other people should be seeing these documentations of two miserable moments of his life was a personal reaction, specific only to himself. To anyone else, they would be two contextless paintings, meaningless unless he chose to announce their meaning. But oh, they were difficult for him to see, and he wished, suddenly and sharply, that he was alone.

He made it through the post-opening dinner, which was endless and at which he missed Willem intensely—but Willem had a show that night and hadn't been able to come. At least he hadn't had to speak to JB at all, who was busy holding court, and to the people who approached him—including JB's gallerist—to tell him that the final two pictures, the ones of him, were the best in the show (as if he were somehow responsible for this), he was able to smile and agree with them that JB was an extraordinary talent.

But later, at home, after regaining control of himself, he was at last free to articulate to Willem his sense of betrayal. And Willem had taken his side so unhesitatingly, had been so angry on his behalf, that he had been momentarily soothed—and had realized that JB's duplicity had come as a surprise to Willem as well.

This had begun the second fight, which had started with a confrontation with JB at a café near JB's apartment, during which JB had proven maddeningly incapable of apologizing: instead, he talked and talked, about how wonderful the pictures were, and how someday, once he had gotten over whatever issues he had with himself, he'd come to appreciate them, and how it wasn't even that big a deal, and how he really needed to confront his insecurities, which were groundless anyway, and maybe this would prove helpful in that process, and how everyone except him knew how incredibly great-looking he was, and so shouldn't that tell him something, that maybe—no, *definitely*—he was the one who was wrong about himself, and finally, how the pictures were already done, they were finished, and what did he expect should happen? Would he be happier if they were destroyed? Should he rip them off the wall and set them on fire? They had been seen and couldn't be un-seen, so why couldn't he just accept it and get over it?

"I'm not asking you to destroy them, JB," he'd said, so furious and dizzied by JB's bizarre logic and almost offensive intractability that he wanted to scream. "I'm asking you to apologize."

But JB couldn't, or wouldn't, and finally he had gotten up and left, and JB hadn't tried to stop him.

After that, he simply stopped speaking to JB. Willem had made his own approach, and the two of them (as Willem told him) had actually begun shouting at each other in the street, and then Willem, too, had stopped speaking to JB, and so from then on, they had to rely primarily on Malcolm for news of JB. Malcolm, typically noncommittal, had admitted to them that he thought JB was totally in the wrong, while at the same time suggesting that they were both being unrealistic: "You *know* he's not going to apologize, Judy," he said. "This is JB we're talking about. You're wasting your time."

"*Am* I being unreasonable?" he asked Willem after this conversation.

"No," Willem said, immediately. "It's fucked up, Jude. He fucked up, and he needs to apologize."

The show sold out. *Willem and the Girl* was delivered to him at work, as was *Willem and Jude, Lispenard Street, II,* which Willem had bought. *Jude, After Sickness* (the title, when he learned it, had made him so newly angry and humiliated that for a moment he experienced what the saying "blind with rage" meant) was sold to a collector whose purchases were considered benedictions and predictive of future success: he only bought from artists' debut shows, and almost every artist whose work he had bought had gone on to have a major career. Only the show's centerpiece, *Jude with Cigarette,* remained unplaced, and this was due to a shockingly amateurish error, in which the director of the gallery had sold it to an important British collector and the owner of the gallery had sold it to the Museum of Modern Art.

"So, perfect," Willem said to Malcolm, knowing Malcolm would ferry his words back to JB. "JB should tell the gallery that he's keeping the painting, and he should just give it to Jude."

"He can't do that," Malcolm said, as appalled as if Willem had suggested simply tossing the canvas into a trash can. "It's MoMA."

"Who cares?" Willem asked. "If he's that fucking good, he'll have another shot at MoMA. But I'm telling you, Malcolm, this is really the only solution he has left if he wants to keep Jude as a friend." He paused. "And me, too."

So Malcolm conveyed that message, and the prospect of losing Willem as a friend had been enough to make JB call Willem and demand a meeting, at which JB had cried and accused Willem of betraying him, and always taking Jude's side, and obviously not giving a shit about his, JB's, career, when he, JB, had always supported Willem's.

All of this had taken place over months, as spring turned into summer, and he and Willem had gone to Truro without JB (and without Malcolm, who told them he was afraid of leaving JB on his own), and JB had gone to the Irvines' in Aquinnah over Memorial Day and they had gone over the Fourth of July, and he and Willem had taken the long-planned trip to Croatia and Turkey by themselves.

And then it was fall, and by the time Willem and JB had their second meeting, Willem had suddenly and unexpectedly booked his first film role, playing the king in an adaptation of *The Girl with the*

Silver Hands and was leaving to shoot in Sofia in January, and he had gotten a promotion at work and had been approached by a partner at Cromwell Thurman Grayson and Ross, one of the best corporate firms in the city, and was having to use the wheelchair Andy had gotten him that May more often than not, and Willem had broken up with his girlfriend of a year and was dating a costume designer named Philippa, and his former fellow law clerk, Kerrigan, had written a mass e-mail to everyone he had ever worked with in which he simultaneously came out and denounced conservatism, and Harold had been asking him who was coming over for Thanksgiving this year, and if he could stay a night after whoever he invited had left, because he and Julia needed to talk about something with him, and he had seen plays with Malcolm and gallery shows with Willem and had read novels that he would have argued about with JB, as the two of them were the novel-readers of the group: a whole list of things the four of them would have once picked over together that they now instead discussed in twos or threes. At first, it had been disorienting, after so many years of operating as a foursome, but he had gotten used to it, and although he missed JB—his witty self-involvement, the way he could see everything the world had to offer only as it might affect him—he also found himself unable to forgive him and, simultaneously, able to see his life without him.

And now, he supposed, their fight was over, and the painting was his. Willem came down with him to the office that Saturday and he unwrapped it and leaned it against the wall and the two of them regarded it in silence, as if it were a rare and inert zoo animal. This was the painting that had been reproduced in the *Times* review and, later, the *Artforum* story, but it wasn't until now, in the safety of his office, that he was able to truly appreciate it—if he could forget it was him, he could almost see how lovely an image it was, and why JB would have been attracted to it: for the strange person in it who looked so frightened and watchful, who was discernibly neither female nor male, whose clothes looked borrowed, who was mimicking the gestures and postures of adulthood while clearly understanding nothing of them. He no longer felt anything for that person, but not feeling anything for that person had been a conscious act of will, like turning away from someone in the street even though you saw them constantly, and pretending you couldn't see them day after day until one day, you actually couldn't—or so you could make yourself believe.

"I don't know what I'm going to do with it," he admitted to Willem, regretfully, because he didn't want the painting, and yet felt guilty that Willem had axed JB out of his life on his behalf, and for something he knew he would never look at again.

"Well," said Willem, and there was a silence. "You could always give it to Harold; I'm sure he'd love it." And he knew then that Willem had perhaps always known that he didn't want the painting, and that it hadn't mattered to him, that he hadn't regretted choosing him over JB, that he didn't blame him for having to make that decision.

"I could," he said slowly, although he knew he wouldn't: Harold would indeed love it (he had when he had seen the show) and would hang it somewhere prominent, and whenever he went to visit him, he would have to look at it. "I'm sorry, Willem," he said at last, "I'm sorry to drag you down here. I think I'll leave it here until I figure out what to do."

"It's okay," Willem said, and the two of them wrapped it up again and replaced it under his desk.

After Willem left, he turned on his phone and this time, he did write JB a message. "JB," he began, "Thanks very much for the painting, and for your apology, both of which mean a lot." He paused, thinking about what to say next. "I've missed you, and want to hear what's been going on in your life," he continued. "Call me when you have some time to hang out." It was all true.

And suddenly, he knew what he should do with the painting. He looked up the address for JB's registrar and wrote her a note, thanking her for sending him *Jude with Cigarette* and telling her that he wanted to donate it to MoMA, and could she help facilitate the transaction?

Later, he would look back on this episode as a sort of fulcrum, the hinge between a relationship that was one thing and then became something else: his friendship with JB, of course, but also his friendship with Willem. There had been periods in his twenties when he would look at his friends and feel such a pure, deep contentment that he would wish the world around them would simply cease, that none of them would have to move from that moment, when everything was in equilibrium and his affection for them was perfect. But, of course, that was never to be: a beat later, and everything shifted, and the moment quietly vanished.

It would have been too melodramatic, too final, to say that after this JB was forever diminished for him. But it *was* true that for the first time, he was able to comprehend that the people he had grown to trust might someday betray him anyway, and that as disappointing as it might be, it was inevitable as well, and that life would keep propelling him steadily forward, because for everyone who might fail him in some way, there was at least one person who never would.

—

It was his opinion (shared by Julia) that Harold had a tendency to make Thanksgiving more complicated than it needed to be. Every year since he'd first been invited to Harold and Julia's for the holiday, Harold promised him—usually in early November, when he was still full of enthusiasm for the project—that this year he was going to blow his mind by upending the lamest of American culinary traditions. Harold always began with big ambitions: their first Thanksgiving together, nine years ago, when he was in his second year of law school, Harold had announced he was going to make duck à l'orange, with kumquats standing in for the oranges.

But when he arrived at Harold's house with the walnut cake he'd baked the night before, Julia was standing alone in the doorway to greet him. "Don't mention the duck," she whispered as she kissed him hello. In the kitchen, a harassed-looking Harold was lifting a large turkey out of the oven.

"Don't say a word," Harold warned him.

"What would I say?" he asked.

This year, Harold asked how he felt about trout. "Trout stuffed with other stuff," he added.

"I like trout," he'd answered, cautiously. "But you know, Harold, I actually *like* turkey." They had a variation on this conversation every year, with Harold proposing various animals and proteins—steamed black-footed Chinese chicken, filet mignon, tofu with wood ear fungus, smoked whitefish salad on homemade rye—as turkey improvements.

"No one *likes* turkey, Jude," Harold said, impatiently. "I know what you're doing. Don't insult me by pretending you do because you don't think I'm actually capable of making anything else. We're having trout, and that's it. Also, can you make that cake you made last year? I think it'd go well with this wine I got. Just send me a list of what you need me to get."

The perplexing thing, he always thought, was that in general, Harold wasn't that interested in food (or wine). In fact, he had terrible taste, and was often taking him to restaurants that were overpriced yet mediocre, where Harold would happily devour dull plates of blackened meat and unimaginative sides of gloppy pasta. He and Julia (who also had little interest in food) discussed Harold's strange fixation every year: Harold had numerous obsessions, some of them inexplicable, but this one seemed particularly so, and more so for its endurance.

Willem thought that Harold's Thanksgiving quest had begun partly as shtick, but over the years, it had morphed into something more serious, and now he was truly unable to stop himself, even as he knew he'd never succeed.

"But you know," Willem said, "it's really all about you."

"What do you mean?" he'd asked.

"It's a performance for you," Willem had said. "It's his way of telling you he cares about you enough to try to impress you, without actually saying he cares about you."

He'd dismissed this right away: "I don't think so, Willem." But sometimes, he pretended to himself that Willem might be right, feeling silly and a little pathetic because of how happy the thought made him.

Willem was the only one coming to Thanksgiving this year: by the time he and JB had reconciled, JB had already made plans to go to his aunts' with Malcolm; when he'd tried to cancel, they had apparently been so irked that he'd decided not to antagonize them further.

"What's it going to be this year?" asked Willem. They were taking the train up on Wednesday, the night before Thanksgiving. "Elk? Venison? Turtle?"

"Trout," he said.

"Trout!" Willem replied. "Well, trout's easy. We may actually end up with trout this year."

"He said he was going to stuff it with something, though."

"Oh. I take it back."

There were eight of them at dinner: Harold and Julia, Laurence and Gillian, Julia's friend James and his boyfriend Carey, and he and Willem.

"This is dynamite trout, Harold," Willem said, cutting into his second piece of turkey, and everyone laughed.

What was the point, he wondered, at which he had stopped feeling so nervous and out of place at Harold's dinners? Certainly, his friends had helped. Harold liked sparring with them, liked trying to provoke JB into making outrageous and borderline racist statements, liked teasing Willem about when he was going to settle down, liked debating structural and aesthetic trends with Malcolm. He knew Harold enjoyed engaging with them, and that they enjoyed it too, and it gave him the chance to simply listen to them being who they were without feeling the need to participate; they were a fleet of parrots shaking their bright-colored feathers at one another, presenting themselves to their peers without fear or guile.

The dinner was dominated by talk of James's daughter, who was getting married in the summer. "I'm an old man," James moaned, and Laurence and Gillian, whose daughters were still in college and spending the holiday at their friend's house in Carmel, made sympathetic noises.

"This reminds me," said Harold, looking at him and Willem, "when are you two ever going to settle down?"

"I think he means you," he smiled at Willem.

"Harold, I'm thirty-two!" Willem protested, and everyone laughed again as Harold spluttered: "What is that, Willem? Is that an explanation? Is that a defense? It's not like you're sixteen!"

But as much as he enjoyed the evening, a part of his mind remained abuzz and anxious, worrying about the conversation Harold and Julia wanted to have with him the next day. He had finally mentioned it to Willem on the ride up, and in moments, when the two of them were working together (stuffing the turkey, blanching the potatoes, setting the table), they would try to figure out what Harold might have to say to him. After dinner, they put on their coats and sat in the back garden, puzzling over it again.

At least he knew that nothing was wrong with them—it was the first thing he had asked, and Harold had assured him that he and Julia were both fine. But what, then, could it be?

"Maybe he thinks I'm hanging around them too much," he suggested to Willem. Maybe Harold was, simply, sick of him.

"Not possible," Willem said, so quickly and declaratively that he was relieved. They were quiet. "Maybe one of them got a job offer somewhere and they're moving?"

"I thought of that, too. But I don't think Harold would ever leave Boston. Julia, either."

There weren't, in the end, many options, at least many that would make a conversation with him necessary: maybe they were selling the house in Truro (but why would they need to talk to him about that, as much as he loved the house). Maybe Harold and Julia were splitting up (but they seemed the same as they always did around each other). Maybe they were selling the New York apartment and wanted to know if he wanted to buy it from them (unlikely: he was certain they would never sell the apartment). Maybe they were *renovating* the apartment and needed him to oversee the renovation.

And then their speculations grew more specific and improbable: maybe Julia was coming out (maybe Harold was). Maybe Harold was being born again (maybe Julia was). Maybe they were quitting their jobs, moving to an ashram in upstate New York. Maybe they were becoming ascetics who would live in a remote Kashmiri valley. Maybe they were having his-and-hers plastic surgery. Maybe Harold was becoming a Republican. Maybe Julia had found God. Maybe Harold had been nominated to be the attorney general. Maybe Julia had been identified by the Tibetan government in exile as the next reincarnation of the Panchen Lama and was moving to Dharamsala. Maybe Harold was running for president as a Socialist candidate. Maybe they were opening a restaurant on the square that served only turkey stuffed with other kinds of meat. By this time they were both laughing so hard, as much from the nervous, self-soothing helplessness of not knowing as from the absurdity of their guesses, that they were bent over in their chairs, pressing their coat collars to their mouths to muffle the noise, their tears freezing pinchingly on their cheeks.

In bed, though, he returned to the thought that had crept, tendril-like, from some dark space of his mind and had insinuated itself into his consciousness like a thin green vine: maybe one of them had discovered something about the person he once was. Maybe he would be presented with evidence—a doctor's report, a photograph, a (this was the nightmare scenario) film still. He had already decided he wouldn't deny it, he wouldn't argue against it, he wouldn't defend himself. He would acknowledge its veracity, he would apologize, he would explain that he never meant to deceive them, he would offer not to contact them again, and then he would leave. He would ask them only to keep his secret, to not tell anyone else. He practiced saying the words: *I'm so sorry, Harold. I'm so sorry, Julia. I never meant to embarrass you.* But of course it was such a useless apology. He might not have meant to, but it wouldn't make a difference: he would have; he had.

Willem left the next morning; he had a show that night. "Call me as soon as you know, okay?" he asked, and he nodded. "It's going to be fine, Jude," he promised. "Whatever it is, we'll figure it out. Don't worry, all right?"

"You know I will anyway," he said, and tried to smile back at Willem.

"Yeah, I know," said Willem. "But try. And call me."

The rest of the day he kept himself busy cleaning—there was always plenty to clean at the house, as both Harold and Julia were unenthusiastic tidiers—and by the time they sat down to an early dinner he'd made of turkey stew and a beet salad, he felt almost aloft from nervousness and could only pretend to eat, moving the food around his plate like a compass point, hoping Harold and Julia wouldn't notice. After, he began stacking the plates to take them to the kitchen, but Harold stopped him. "Leave them, Jude," he said. "Maybe we should have our talk now?"

He felt himself go fluttery with panic. "I should really rinse them off, or everything's going to congeal," he protested, lamely, hearing how stupid he sounded.

"Fuck the plates," said Harold, and although he knew that Harold genuinely didn't care what did or didn't congeal on his plates, for a moment he wondered if his casualness was *too* casual, a simulacrum of ease rather than the real thing. But finally, he could do nothing but put the dishes down and trudge after Harold into the living room, where Julia was pouring coffee for herself and Harold, and had poured tea for him.

He lowered himself to the sofa, and Harold to the chair to his left, and Julia to the squashed suzani-covered ottoman facing him: the places they always sat, the low table between them, and he wished the moment would hold itself, for what if this was the last one he would have here, the last time he would sit in this warm dark room, with its books and tart, sweet scent of cloudy apple juice and the navy-and-scarlet Turkish carpet that had buckled itself into pleats under the coffee table, and the patch on the sofa cushion where the fabric had worn thin and he could see the white muslin skin beneath—all the things that he'd allowed to grow so dear to him, because they were Harold and Julia's, and because he had allowed himself to think of their house as his.

For a while they all sipped at their drinks, and none of them looked at the other, and he tried to pretend that this was just a normal evening, although if it had been a normal evening, none of them would be so silent.

"Well," Harold began at last, and he set his cup down on the table, readying himself. *Whatever he says,* he reminded himself, *don't start making excuses for yourself. Whatever he says, accept it, and thank him for everything.*

There was another long silence. "This is hard to say," Harold continued, and shifted his mug in his hand, and he made himself wait through Harold's next pause. "I really did have a script prepared, didn't I?" he asked Julia, and she nodded. "But I'm more nervous than I thought I would be."

"I know," she said. "But you're doing great."

"Ha!" Harold replied. "It's sweet of you to lie to me, though," and smiled at her, and he had the sense that it was only the two of them in the room, and that for a moment, they had forgotten he was there at all. But then Harold was quiet again, trying to say what he'd say next.

"Jude, I've—we've—known you for almost a decade now," Harold said at last, and he watched as Harold's eyes moved to him and then moved away, to somewhere above Julia's head. "And over those years, you've grown very dear to us; both of us. You're our friend, of course, but we think of you as more than a friend to us; as someone more special than that." He looked at Julia, and she nodded at him once more. "So I hope you won't think this is too—presumptuous, I suppose—but we've been wondering if you might consider letting us, well, adopt you." Now he turned to him again, and smiled. "You'd be our legal son, and our legal heir, and someday all this"—he tossed his free arm into the air in a parodic gesture of expansiveness—"will be yours, if you want it."

He was silent. He couldn't speak, he couldn't react; he couldn't even feel his face, couldn't sense what his expression might be, and Julia hurried in. "Jude," she said, "if you don't want to, for whatever reason, we understand completely. It's a lot to ask. If you say no, it won't change how we feel about you, right, Harold? You'll always, always be welcome here, and we hope you'll always be part of our lives. Honestly, Jude—we won't be angry, and you shouldn't feel bad." She looked at him. "Do you want some time to think about it?"

And then he could feel the numbness receding, although as if in compensation, his hands began shaking, and he grabbed one of the throw pillows and wrapped his arms around it to hide them. It took him a few tries before he was able to speak, but when he did, he couldn't look at either of them. "I don't need to think about it," he said, and his voice sounded strange and thin to him. "Harold, Julia—are you kidding? There's nothing—nothing—I've ever wanted more. My whole life. I just never thought—" He stopped; he was speaking in fragments. For a minute they were all quiet, and he was finally able to look at both of them. "I thought you were going to tell me you didn't want to be friends anymore."

"Oh, Jude," said Julia, and Harold looked perplexed. "Why would you ever think that?" he asked.

But he shook his head, unable to explain it to them.

They were silent again, and then all of them were smiling—Julia at Harold, Harold at him, he into the pillow—unsure how to end the moment, unsure where to go next. Finally, Julia clapped her hands together and stood. "Champagne!" she said, and left the room.

He and Harold stood as well and looked at each other. "Are you sure?" Harold asked him, quietly.

"I'm as sure as you are," he answered, just as quietly. There was an uncreative and obvious joke to be made, about how much like a marriage proposal the event seemed, but he didn't have the heart to make it.

"You realize you're going to be bound to us for life," Harold smiled, and put his hand on his shoulder, and he nodded. He hoped Harold wouldn't say one more word, because if he did, he would cry, or vomit, or pass out, or scream, or combust. He was aware, suddenly, of how exhausted, how utterly depleted he was, as much by the past few weeks of anxiety as well as the past thirty years of craving, of wanting, of wishing so intensely even as he told himself he didn't care, that by the time they had toasted one another and first Julia and then Harold had hugged him—the sensation of being held by Harold so unfamiliar and intimate that he had nearly squirmed—he was relieved when Harold told him to leave the damn dishes and go to bed.

When he reached his room, he had to lie on the bed for half an hour before he could even think of retrieving his phone. He needed to feel the solidity of the bed beneath him, the silk of the cotton blanket against his cheek, the familiar yield of the mattress as he moved against it. He needed to assure himself that this was his world, and he was still in it, and that what had happened had really happened. He thought, suddenly, of a conversation he'd once had with Brother Peter, in which he'd asked the brother if he thought he'd ever be adopted, and the brother had laughed. "No," he'd said, so decisively that he had never asked again. And although he must have been very young, he remembered, very clearly, that the brother's dismissal had only hardened his resolve, although of course it wasn't an outcome that was his to control in the slightest.

He was so discombobulated that he forgot that Willem was already onstage when he called, but when Willem called him back at intermission, he was still in the same place on the bed, in the same comma-like shape, the phone still cupped beneath his palm.

"Jude," Willem breathed when he told him, and he could hear how purely happy Willem was for him. Only Willem—and Andy, and to some extent Harold—knew the outlines of how he had grown up: the monastery, the home, his time with the Douglasses. With everyone else, he tried to be evasive for as long as he could, until finally he would say that his parents had died when he was little, and that he had grown up in foster care, which usually stopped their questions. But Willem knew more of the truth, and he knew Willem knew that this was his most impossible, his most fervent desire. "Jude, that's amazing. How do you feel?"

He tried to laugh. "Like I'm going to mess it up."

"You won't." They were both quiet. "I didn't even know you could adopt someone who's a legal adult."

"I mean, it's not common, but you can. As long as both parties consent. It's mostly done for purposes of inheritance." He made another attempt at a laugh. (*Stop trying to laugh*, he scolded himself.) "I don't remember much from when I studied this in family law, but I do know that I get a new birth certificate with their names on it."

"Wow," said Willem.

"I know," he said.

He heard someone calling Willem's name, commandingly, in the background. "You have to go," he told Willem.

"Shit," said Willem. "But Jude? Congratulations. No one deserves it more." He called back at whoever was yelling for him. "I've got to go," he said. "Do you mind if I write Harold and Julia?"

"Sure," he said. "But Willem, don't tell the others, okay? I just want to sit with it for a while."

"I won't say a word. I'll see you tomorrow. And Jude—" But he didn't, or couldn't, say anything else.

"I know," he said. "I know, Willem. I feel the same way."

"I love you," said Willem, and then he was gone before he had to respond. He never knew what to say when Willem said that to him, and yet he always longed for him to say it. It was a night of impossible things, and he fought to stay awake, to be conscious and alert for as long as possible, to enjoy and repeat to himself everything that had happened to him, a lifetime's worth of wishes coming true in a few brief hours.

Back in the apartment the next day, there was a note from Willem telling him to wait up, and when Willem came home, he had ice cream and a carrot cake, which the two of them ate even though neither of them particularly liked sweets, and champagne, which they drank even though he had to wake up early the following morning. The next few weeks slid by: Harold was handling the paperwork, and sent him forms to sign—the petition for adoption, an affidavit to change his birth certificate, a request for information about his potential criminal record—which he took to the bank at lunch to have notarized; he didn't want anyone at work to know beyond the few people he told: Marshall, and Citizen, and Rhodes. He told JB and Malcolm, who on the one hand reacted exactly as he'd anticipated—JB making a lot of unfunny jokes at an almost tic-like pace, as if he might eventually land on one that worked; Malcolm asking increasingly granular questions about various hypotheticals that he couldn't answer—and on the other had been genuinely thrilled for him. He told Black Henry Young, who had taken two classes with Harold when he was in law school and had admired him, and JB's friend Richard, to whom he'd grown close after one particularly long and tedious party at Ezra's a year ago when the two of them had had a conversation that had begun with the French welfare state and then had moved on to various other topics, the only two semi-sober people in the room. He told Phaedra, who had started screaming, and another old college friend, Elijah, who had screamed as well.

And, of course, he told Andy, who at first had just stared at him and then nodded, as if he had asked if Andy had an extra bandage he could give him before he left for the night. But then he began making a series of bizarre seal-like sounds, half bark, half sneeze, and he realized that Andy was crying. The sight of it made him both horrified and slightly hysterical, unsure of what to do. "Get out of here," Andy commanded him between sounds. "I mean it, Jude, get the fuck out," and so he did. The next day at work, he received an arrangement of roses the size of a gardenia bush, with a note in Andy's angry blocky handwriting that read:

JUDE—I'M SO FUCKING EMBARRASSED I CAN BARELY
WRITE THIS NOTE. PLEASE FORGIVE ME FOR YESTERDAY. I
COULDN'T BE HAPPIER FOR YOU AND THE ONLY QUESTION
IS WHAT TOOK HAROLD SO FUCKING LONG. I HOPE
YOU'LL TAKE THIS AS A SIGN THAT YOU NEED TO TAKE
BETTER CARE OF YOURSELF SO SOMEDAY YOU'LL HAVE
THE STRENGTH TO CHANGE HAROLD'S ADULT DIAPERS
WHEN HE'S A THOUSAND YEARS OLD AND INCONTINENT,
BECAUSE YOU KNOW HE'S NOT GOING TO MAKE IT EASY
FOR YOU BY DYING AT A RESPECTABLE AGE LIKE A NORMAL
PERSON. BELIEVE ME, PARENTS ARE PAINS IN THE ASS LIKE
THAT. (BUT GREAT TOO, OF COURSE.) LOVE, ANDY

It was, he and Willem agreed, one of the best letters they'd ever read.

But then the ecstatic month passed, and it was January, and Willem left for Bulgaria to film, and the old fears returned, accompanied now by new fears. They had a court date for February fifteenth, Harold told him, and with a little rescheduling, Laurence would be presiding. Now that the date was so close, he was sharply, inescapably aware that he might ruin it for himself, and he began, at first unconsciously and then assiduously, avoiding Harold and Julia, convinced that if they were reminded too much, too actively of what they were in fact getting that they would change their minds. And so when they came into town for a play the second week in January, he pretended he was in Washington on business, and on their weekly phone calls, he tried to say very little, and to keep the conversations brief. Every day the improbability of the situation seemed to grow larger and more vivid in his mind; every time he glimpsed the reflection of his ugly zombie's hobble in the side of a building, he would feel sickened: Who, really, would ever want *this*? The idea that he could become someone else's seemed increasingly ludicrous, and if Harold saw him just once more, how could he too not come to the same conclusion? He knew it shouldn't matter so much to him—he was, after all, an adult; he knew the adoption was more ceremonial than truly sociologically significant—but he wanted it with a steady fervor that defied logic, and he couldn't bear it being taken away from him now, not when everyone he cared about was so happy for him, not when he was so close.

He had been close before. The year after he arrived in Montana, when he was thirteen, the home had participated in a tristate adoption fair. November was National Adoption Month, and one cold morning, they had been told to dress neatly and had been hurried onto two school buses and driven two hours to Missoula, where they were herded off the buses and into the conference room of a hotel. Theirs had been the last buses to arrive, and the room was already filled with children, boys on one side, girls on the other. In the center of the room was a long stripe of tables, and as he walked over to his side, he saw that they were stacked with labeled binders: Boys, Babies; Boys, Toddlers; Boys, 4–6; Boys, 7–9; Boys, 10–12; Boys, 13–15; Boys, 15+. Inside, they had been told, were pieces of paper with their pictures, and names, and information about themselves: where they were from, what ethnicity they were, information about how they did in school and what sports they liked to play and what talents and interests they had. What, he wondered, did his sheet of paper say about him? What talents might have been invented for him, what race, what origins?

The older boys, the ones whose names and faces were in the 15+ binder, knew they would never be adopted, and when the counselors turned away, they snuck out through the back exit to, they all knew, get high. The babies and toddlers had only to be babies and toddlers; they would be the first to be chosen, and they didn't even know it. But as he watched from the corner he had drifted toward, he saw that some of the boys—the ones old enough to have experienced one of the fairs before, but still young enough to be hopeful—had strategies. He watched as the sullen became smiling, as the rough and bullying became jocular and playful, as boys who hated one another in the context of the home played and bantered in a way that appeared convincingly friendly. He saw the boys who were rude to the counselors, who cursed at one another in the hallways, smile and chat with the adults, the prospective parents, who were filing into the room. He watched as the toughest, the meanest of the boys, a fourteen-year-old named Shawn who had once held him down in the bathroom, his knees digging into his shoulder blades, pointed at his name tag as the man and woman he had been talking with walked toward the binders. "Shawn!" he called after them, "Shawn Grady!" and something about his hoarse hopeful voice, in which he could hear the effort, the strain, to not sound hopeful at all, made him feel sorry for Shawn for the first time, and then angry at the man and woman, who, he could tell, were actually paging through the "Boys, 7–9" binder. But those feelings passed quickly, because he tried not to feel anything those days: not hunger, not pain, not anger, not sadness.

He had no tricks, he had no skills, he couldn't charm. When he had arrived at the home, he had been so frozen that they had left him behind the previous November, and a year later, he wasn't sure that he was any better. He thought less and less frequently of Brother Luke, it was true, but his days outside the classroom smeared into one; most of the time he felt he was floating, trying to pretend that he didn't occupy his own life, wishing he was invisible, wanting only to go unnoticed. Things happened to him and he didn't fight back the way he once would have; sometimes when he was being hurt, the part of him that was still conscious wondered what the brothers would think of him now: gone were his rages, his tantrums, his struggling. Now he was the boy they had always wished him to be. Now he hoped to be someone adrift, a presence so thin and light and insubstantial that he seemed to displace no air at all.

So he was surprised—as surprised as the counselors—when he learned that night that he was one of the children chosen by a couple: the Learys. Had he noticed a woman and man looking at him, maybe even smiling at him? Maybe. But the afternoon had passed, as most did, in a haze, and even on the bus ride home, he had begun the work of forgetting it.

He would spend a probationary weekend—the weekend before Thanksgiving—with the Learys, so they could see how they liked

each other. That Thursday he was driven to their house by a counselor named Boyd, who taught shop and plumbing and whom he didn't
know very well. He knew Boyd knew what some of the other counselors
did to him, and although he never stopped them, he never participated,
either.

But as he was getting out of the car in the Learys' driveway—a one-
story brick house, surrounded on all sides by fallow, dark fields—Boyd
snatched his forearm and pulled him close, startling him into alertness.

"Don't fuck this up, St. Francis," he said. "This is your chance, do
you hear me?"

"Yes, sir," he'd said.

"Go on, then," said Boyd, and released him, and he walked toward
Mrs. Leary, who was standing in the doorway.

Mrs. Leary was fat, but her husband was simply big, with large red
hands that looked like weaponry. They had two daughters, both in their
twenties and both married, and they thought it might be nice to have
a boy in the house, someone who could help Mr. Leary—who repaired
large-scale farm machinery and also farmed himself—with the field
work. They chose him, they said, because he seemed quiet, and polite,
and they didn't want someone rowdy; they wanted someone hardworking, someone who would appreciate what having a home and a house
meant. They had read in the binder that he knew how to work, and how
to clean, and that he did well on the home's farm.

"Now, your name, that's an unusual name," Mrs. Leary said.

He had never thought it unusual, but "Yes, ma'am," he said.

"What would you think of maybe going by a different name?" Mrs.
Leary asked. "Like, Cody, maybe? I've always liked the name Cody. It's
a little less—well, it's a little more us, really."

"I like Cody," he said, although he didn't really have an opinion
about it: Jude, Cody, it didn't matter to him what he was called.

"Well, good," said Mrs. Leary.

That night, alone, he said the name aloud to himself: Cody Leary.
Cody Leary. Could it be possible that he was entering this house as
one person and then, as if the place were enchanted, transformed into
another? Was it that simple, that fast? Gone would be Jude St. Francis,
and with him, Brother Luke, and Brother Peter, and Father Gabriel,
and the monastery and the counselors at the home and his shame and
fears and filth, and in his place would be Cody Leary, who would have

parents, and a room of his own, and would be able to make himself into whomever he chose.

The rest of the weekend passed uneventfully, so uneventfully that with each day, with each hour, he could feel pieces of himself awaken, could feel the clouds that he gathered around himself separate and vanish, could feel himself seeing into the future, and imagining the place in it he might have. He tried his hardest to be polite, and hardworking, and it wasn't difficult: he got up early in the morning and made breakfast for the Learys (Mrs. Leary praising him so loudly and extravagantly that he had smiled, embarrassed, at the floor), and cleaned dishes, and helped Mr. Leary degrease his tools and rewire a lamp, and although there were events he didn't care for—the boring church service they attended on Sunday; the prayers they supervised before he was allowed to go to bed—they were hardly worse than the things he didn't like about the home, they were things he knew he could do without appearing resentful or ungrateful. The Learys, he could sense, would not be the sort of people who would behave the way that parents in books would, the way the parents he yearned for might, but he knew how to be industrious, he knew how to keep them satisfied. He was still frightened of Mr. Leary's large red hands, and when he was left alone with him in the barn, he was shivery and watchful, but at least there was only Mr. Leary to fear, not a whole group of Mr. Learys, as there had been before, or there were at the home.

When Boyd picked him up Sunday evening, he was pleased with how he'd done, confident, even. "How'd it go?" Boyd asked him, and he was able to answer, honestly, "Good."

He was certain, from Mrs. Leary's last words to him—"I have a feeling we'll be seeing much more of you very soon, Cody"—that they would call on Monday, and that soon, maybe even by Friday, he would be Cody Leary, and the home would be one more place he'd put behind him. But then Monday passed, and then Tuesday, and Wednesday, and then it was the following week, and he wasn't called to the headmaster's office, and his letter to the Learys had gone unanswered, and every day the driveway to the dormitory remained a long, blank stretch, and no one came to get him.

Finally, two weeks after the visit, he went to see Boyd at his workshop, where he knew he stayed late on Thursday nights. He waited through dinner out in the cold, the snow crunching under his feet, until he finally saw Boyd walking out the door.

"Christ," Boyd said when he saw him, nearly stepping on him as he turned. "Shouldn't you be back in the dorms, St. Francis?"

"Please," he begged. "Please tell me—are the Learys coming to get me?" But he knew what the answer was even before he saw Boyd's face.

"They changed their minds," said Boyd, and although he wasn't known, by the counselors or the boys, for his gentleness, he was almost gentle then. "It's over, St. Francis. It's not going to happen." He reached out a hand toward him, but he ducked, and Boyd shook his head and began walking off.

"Wait," he called, recovering himself and running as well as he could through the snow after Boyd. "Let me try again," he said. "Tell me what I did wrong, and I'll try again." He could feel the old hysteria descending upon him, could feel inside him the vestiges of the boy who would throw fits and shout, who could still a room with his screams.

But Boyd shook his head again. "It doesn't work like that, St. Francis," he said, and then he stopped and looked directly at him. "Look," he said, "in a few years you'll be out of here. I know it seems like a long time, but it's not. And then you'll be an adult and you'll be able to do whatever you want. You just have to get through these years." And then he turned again, definitively, and stalked away from him.

"How?" he yelled after Boyd. "Boyd, tell me how! How, Boyd, how?" forgetting that he was to call him "sir," and not "Boyd."

That night he had his first tantrum in years, and although the punishment here was the same, more or less, as it had been at the monastery, the release, the sense of flight it had once given him, was not: now he was someone who knew better, whose screams would change nothing, and all his shouting did was bring him back to himself, so that everything, every hurt, every insult, felt sharper and brighter and stickier and more resonant than ever before.

He would never, never know what he had done wrong that weekend at the Learys'. He would never know if it had been something he could control, or something he couldn't. And of all the things from the monastery, from the home, that he worked to scrub over, he worked hardest at forgetting that weekend, at forgetting the special shame of allowing himself to believe that he might be someone he knew he wasn't.

But now, of course, with the court date six weeks, five weeks, four weeks away, he thought of it constantly. With Willem gone, and no one to monitor his hours and activities, he stayed up until the sun began lightening the sky, cleaning, scrubbing with a toothbrush the space beneath the refrigerator, bleaching each skinny grout-canal between the bathtub wall tiles. He cleaned so he wouldn't cut himself, because he was cutting himself so much that even he knew how crazy, how destructive he was being; even he was scared of himself, as much by what he was doing as by his inability to control it. He had begun a new method of balancing the edge of the blade on his skin and then pressing down, as deep as he could, so that when he withdrew the razor— stuck like an ax head into a tree stump—there was half a second in which he could pull apart the two sides of flesh and see only a clean white gouge, like a side of fatted bacon, before the blood began rushing in to pool within the cut. He felt dizzy, as if his body was pumped with helium; food tasted like rot to him, and he stopped eating unless he had to. He stayed at the office until the night shift of cleaners began moving through the hallways, noisy as mice, and then stayed awake at home; he woke with his heart thudding so fast that he had to gulp air to calm himself. It was only work, and Willem's calls, that forced him into normalcy, or he'd have never left the house, would have cut himself until he could have loosed whole pyramids of flesh from his arms and flushed them down the drain. He had a vision in which he carved away at himself—first arms, then legs, then chest and neck and face—until he was only bones, a skeleton who moved and sighed and breathed and tottered through life on its porous, brittle stalks.

He was back to seeing Andy every six weeks, and had delayed his most recent visit twice, because he dreaded what Andy might say. But finally, a little less than four weeks before the court date, he went uptown and sat in one of the examining rooms until Andy peered in to say he was running late.

"Take your time," he said.

Andy studied him, squinting a bit. "I won't be long," he said, finally, and then was gone.

A few minutes later, his nurse Callie came in. "Hi, Jude," she said. "Doctor wants me to get your weight; do you mind stepping on the scale?"

He didn't want to, but he knew it wasn't Callie's fault or decision, and so he dragged himself off the table, and onto the scale, and didn't look at the number as Callie wrote it down in his chart, and thanked him, and left the room.

"So," Andy said after he'd come in, studying his chart. "What should we talk about first, your extreme weight loss or your excessive cutting?"

He didn't know what to say to that. "Why do you think I've been cutting myself excessively?"

"I can always tell," Andy said. "You get sort of—sort of bluish under the eyes. You're probably not even conscious of it. And you're wearing your sweater over the gown. Whenever it's bad, you do that."

"Oh," he said. He hadn't been aware.

They were quiet, and Andy pulled his stool close to the table and asked, "When's the date?"

"February fifteenth."

"Ah," said Andy. "Soon."

"Yes."

"What're you worried about?"

"I'm worried—" he began, and then stopped, and tried again. "I'm worried that if Harold finds out what I really am, he won't want to—" He stopped. "And I don't know which is worse: him finding out before, which means this definitely won't happen, or him finding out after, and realizing I've deceived him." He sighed; he hadn't been able to articulate this until now, but having done so, he knew that this was his fear.

"Jude," Andy said, carefully, "what do you think is so bad about yourself that he wouldn't want to adopt you?"

"Andy," he pled, "don't make me say it."

"But I honestly don't know!"

"The things I've done," he said, "the diseases I have from them." He stumbled on, hating himself. "It's disgusting; I'm disgusting."

"Jude," Andy began, and as he spoke, he paused between every few words, and he could feel Andy picking his way across a mine-pocked lawn, so deliberately and slowly was he going. "You were a kid, a baby. Those things were done *to* you. You have nothing, *nothing* to blame yourself for, not ever, not in any universe."

Andy looked at him. "And even if you *hadn't* been a kid, even if you had just been some horny guy who wanted to fuck everything in sight and had ended up with a bunch of STDs, it *still* wouldn't be anything to be ashamed of." He sighed. "Can you try to believe me?"

He shook his head. "I don't know."

"I know," Andy said. They were quiet. "I wish you'd see a therapist, Jude," he added, and his voice was sad. He couldn't respond, and after a few minutes, Andy stood up. "Well," he said, sounding determined, "let's see them," and he took off his sweater and held out his arms.

He could tell by Andy's expression that it was worse than he had anticipated, and when he looked down and tried to view himself as something unfamiliar, he could see in flashes what Andy did: the gobs of bandages applied at intervals to the fresh cuts, the half-healed cuts, with their fragile stitchings of still-forming scar tissue, the one infected cut, which had developed a chunky cap of dried pus.

"So," Andy said after a long silence, after he'd almost finished his right arm, cleaning out the infected cut and painting antibiotic cream on the others, "what about your extreme weight loss?"

"I don't think it's extreme."

"Jude," said Andy, "twelve pounds in not quite eight weeks is extreme, and you didn't exactly have twelve pounds to spare to begin with."

"I'm just not hungry," he said, finally.

Andy didn't say anything else until he finished both his arms, and then sighed and sat down again and started scribbling on his pad. "I want you to eat three full meals a day, Jude," he said, "*plus* one of the things on this list. Every day. That's *in addition* to standard meals, do you understand me? Or I'm going to call your crew and make them sit with you every mealtime and watch you eat, and you don't want that, believe me." He ripped the page off the pad and handed it to him. "And then I want you back here next week. No excuses."

He looked at the list—PEANUT BUTTER SANDWICH. CHEESE SANDWICH. AVOCADO SANDWICH. 3 EGGS (WITH YOLKS!!!!). BANANA SMOOTHIE—and tucked it into his pants pocket.

"And the other thing I want you to do is this," said Andy. "When you wake up in the middle of the night and want to cut yourself, I want you to call me instead. I don't care what time it is, you call me, okay?" He nodded. "I mean it, Jude."

"I'm sorry, Andy," he said.

"I know you are," said Andy. "But you don't need to be sorry—not to me, anyway."

"To Harold," he said.

"No," Andy corrected. "Not to Harold, either. Just to yourself."

He went home and ate away at a banana until it turned to dirt in his mouth and then changed and continued washing the living-room windows, which he had begun the night before. He rubbed at them, inching the sofa closer so he could stand atop one of its arms, ignoring the twinges in his back as he climbed up and down, lugging the bucket of dirtied gray water slowly to the tub. After he'd finished the living room and Willem's room, he was in so much pain that he had to crawl to the bathroom, and after cutting himself, he rested, holding his arm above his head and wrapping the mat about him. When his phone rang, he sat up, disoriented, before groaningly moving to his bedroom—where the clock read three a.m.—and listening to a very cranky (but alert) Andy.

"I called too late," Andy guessed. He didn't say anything. "Listen, Jude," Andy continued, "you don't stop this and I really am going to have you committed. *And* I'll call Harold and tell him why. You can count on it." He paused. "And besides which," he added, "aren't you tired, Jude? You don't have to do this to yourself, you know. You don't need to."

He didn't know what it was—maybe it was just the calmness of Andy's voice, the steadiness with which he made his promise that made him realize that he was serious this time in a way he hadn't been before; or maybe it was just the realization that yes, he was tired, so tired that he was willing, finally, to accept someone else's orders—but over the next week, he did as he was told. He ate his meals, even as the food transformed itself by some strange alchemy to mud, to offal: he made himself chew and swallow, chew and swallow. They weren't big meals, but they were meals. Andy called every night at midnight, and Willem called every morning at six (he couldn't bring himself to ask, and Willem never volunteered, whether Andy had contacted him). The hours in between were the most difficult, and although he couldn't cease cutting himself entirely, he did limit it: two cuts, and he stopped. In the absence of cutting, he felt himself being tugged toward earlier punishments—before he had been taught to cut himself, there was a period in which he would toss himself against the wall outside the motel room he shared with Brother Luke again and again until he sagged, exhausted, to the ground, and his left side was permanently stained blue and purple and brown with bruises. He didn't do that now, but he remembered the sensation, the satisfying slam of his body against the wall, the awful pleasure of hurling himself against something so immovable.

On Friday he saw Andy, who wasn't approving (he hadn't gained any weight), but also didn't lecture him (nor had he lost any), and the next day he flew to Boston. He didn't tell anyone he was going, not even Harold. Julia, he knew, was at a conference in Costa Rica; but Harold, he knew, would be home.

Julia had given him a set of keys six years ago, when he was arriving for Thanksgiving at a time when both she and Harold happened to have department meetings, so he let himself into the house and poured a glass of water, looking out at the back garden as he drank. It was just before noon, and Harold would still be at his tennis game, so he went to the living room to wait for him. But he fell asleep, and when he woke, it was to Harold shaking his shoulder and urgently repeating his name.

"Harold," he said, sitting up, "I'm sorry, I'm sorry; I should've called."

"Jesus," Harold said, panting; he smelled cold and sharp. "Are you all right, Jude? What's wrong?"

"Nothing, nothing," he said, hearing before he said it how absurd his explanation was, "I just thought I'd stop by."

"Well," said Harold, momentarily silent. "It's good to see you." He sat in his chair and looked at him. "You've been something of a stranger these past few weeks."

"I know," he said. "I'm sorry."

Harold shrugged. "No apologies necessary. I'm just glad you're okay."

"Yes," he said. "I'm okay."

Harold tilted his head. "You don't look too good."

He smiled. "I've had the flu." He gazed up at the ceiling, as if his lines might be written there. "The forsythia's falling down, you know."

"I know. It's been a windy winter."

"I'll help you stake it, if you want."

Harold looked at him for a long moment then, his mouth slightly moving, as if he was both trying and not trying to speak. Finally he said, "Yeah. Let's go do that."

Outside it was abruptly, insultingly cold, and both of them began sniffling. He positioned the stake and Harold hammered it into the ground, although the earth was frozen and chipped up into pottery-like shards as he did. After they'd gotten it deep enough, Harold handed him lengths of twine, and he tied the center stalks of the bush to the stake, snugly enough so they'd be secure, but not so snug that they'd be constricted. He worked slowly, making sure the knots were tight, snapping off a few branches that were too bent to recover.

"Harold," he said, when he was halfway down the bush, "I wanted to talk to you about something, but—I don't know where to begin." *Stupid*, he told himself. *This is such a stupid idea. You were so stupid to think any of this could ever happen.* He opened his mouth to continue and then shut it, and then opened it again: he was a fish, dumbly blowing bubbles, and he wished he had never come, had never begun speaking.

"Jude," said Harold, "tell me. Whatever it is." He stopped. "Are you having second thoughts?"

"No," he said. "No, nothing like that." They were silent. "Are you?"

"No, of course not."

He finished the last tie and brought himself to his feet, Harold deliberately not helping him. "I don't want to tell you this," he said, and looked down at the forsythia, its bare twiggy ugliness. "But I have to because—because I don't want to be deceitful with you. But Harold—I think you think I'm one kind of person, and I'm not."

Harold was quiet. "What kind of person do I think you are?"

"A good person," he said. "Someone decent."

"Well," said Harold, "you're right. I do."

"But—I'm not," he said, and could feel his eyes grow hot, despite the cold. "I've done things that—that good people don't do," he continued, lamely. "And I just think you should know that about me. That I've done terrible things, things I'm ashamed of, and if you knew, you'd be ashamed to know me, much less be related to me."

"Jude," Harold said at last. "I can't imagine anything you might have done that would change the way I feel about you. I don't care what you did before. Or rather—I do care; I would love to hear about your life before we met. But I've always had the feeling, the very strong feeling, that you never wanted to discuss it." He stopped and waited. "Do you want to discuss it now? Do you want to tell me?"

He shook his head. He wanted to and didn't want to, both. "I can't," he said. Beneath the small of his back, he felt the first unfurlings of discomfort, a blackened seed spreading its thorned branches. *Not now,* he begged himself, *not now*, a plea as impossible as the plea he really meant: *Not now, not ever.*

"Well," Harold sighed, "in the absence of specifics, I won't be able to reassure you specifically, so I'm just going to give you a blanket, all-encompassing reassurance, which I hope you'll believe. Jude: whatever it is, whatever you did, I promise you, whether you someday tell me or not, that it will never make me regret wanting or having you as a member of my family." He took a deep breath, held his right hand before him. "Jude St. Francis, as your future parent, I hereby absolve you of— of everything for which you seek absolution."

And was this what he in fact wanted? Absolution? He looked at Harold's face, so familiar he could remember its every furrow when he closed his eyes, and which, despite the flourishes and formality of his declaration, was serious and unsmiling. Could he believe Harold? *The hardest thing is not finding the knowledge,* Brother Luke once said to him after he'd confessed he was having difficulty believing in God. *The hardest thing is believing it.* He felt he had failed once again: failed to confess properly, failed to determine in advance what he wanted to hear in response. Wouldn't it have been easier in a way if Harold had told him that he was right, that they should perhaps rethink the adoption? He would have been devastated, of course, but it would have been an old sensation, something he understood. In Harold's refusal to let him go lay a future he couldn't imagine, one in which someone might really want him for good, and that was a reality that he had never experienced before, for which he had no preparation, no signposts. Harold would lead and he would follow, until one day he would wake and Harold would be gone, and he would be left vulnerable and stranded in a foreign land, with no one there to guide him home.

Harold was waiting for his reply, but the pain was now unignorable, and he knew he had to rest. "Harold," he said. "I'm sorry. But I think—I think I'd better go lie down for a while."

"Go," said Harold, unoffended, "go."

In his room, he lies down atop the comforter and closes his eyes, but even after the episode ends, he's exhausted, and tells himself he'll nap for just a few minutes and then get up again and see what Harold has in the house: if he has brown sugar, he'll bake something—there was a bowl of persimmons in the kitchen, and maybe he'll make a persimmon cake.

But he doesn't wake up. Not when Harold comes to check on him in the next hour and places the back of his hand against his cheek and then drapes a blanket over him; not when Harold checks on him again, right before dinner. He sleeps through his phone ringing at midnight and again at six a.m., and through the house phone ringing at twelve thirty and then at six thirty, and Harold's conversations with first Andy and then Willem. He sleeps into the morning, and through lunch, and only wakes when he feels Harold's hand on his shoulder and hears Harold saying his name, telling him his flight's leaving in a few hours.

Before he wakes, he dreams of a man standing in a field. He can't see the man's features, but he is tall and thin, and he's helping another, older man hitch the hulk of a tractor carapace to the back of a truck. He knows he's in Montana from the whitened, curved-bowl vastness of the sky, and from the particular kind of cold there, which is completely without moisture and which feels somehow purer than cold he's felt anywhere else.

He still can't see the man's features, but he thinks he knows who he is, recognizes his long strides and his way of crossing his arms in front of him as he listens to the other man. "Cody," he calls out in his dream, and the man turns, but he's too far away, and so he can't quite tell if, under the brim of the man's baseball cap, they share the same face.

—

The fifteenth is a Friday, which he takes off from work. There had been some talk of a dinner party on Thursday night, but in the end, they settle on an early lunch the day of the ceremony (as JB calls it). Their court appointment is at ten, and after it's over, everyone will come back to the house to eat.

Harold had wanted to call a caterer, but he insisted he'd cook, and he spends the remains of Thursday evening in the kitchen. He does the baking that night—the chocolate-walnut cake Harold likes; the tarte tatin Julia likes; the sourdough bread they both like—and picks through ten pounds of crab and mixes the meat with egg and onion and parsley and bread crumbs and forms them into patties. He cleans the potatoes and gives the carrots a quick scrub, and chops the ends off the brussels sprouts, so that the next day all he'll have to do is toss them in oil and shove them into the oven. He shakes the cartons of figs into a bowl, which he'll roast and serve over ice cream topped with honey and balsamic vinaigrette. They are all of Harold and Julia's favorite dishes, and he is glad to make them, glad to have something to give them, however small. Throughout the evening, Harold and Julia wander in and out, and although he tells them not to, they wash dishes and pans as he dirties them, pour him glasses of water and wine, and ask if they can help him, even though he tells them they should relax. Finally they leave for bed, and although he promises them that he will as well, he instead stays up, the kitchen bright and silent around him, singing quietly, his hands moving to keep the mania at bay.

The past few days have been very difficult, some of the most difficult he can remember, so difficult that one night he even called Andy after their midnight check-in, and when Andy offered to meet him at a diner at two a.m., he accepted the offer and went, desperate to get himself out of the apartment, which suddenly seemed full of irresistible temptations: razors, of course, but also knives and scissors and matches, and staircases to throw himself down. He knows that if he goes to his room now, he won't be able to stop himself from heading directly to the bathroom, where he has long kept a bag, its contents identical to the one at Lispenard Street, taped to the sink's undercarriage: his arms ache with yearning, and he is determined not to give in. He has both dough and batter left over, and decides he'll make a tart with pine nuts and cranberries, and maybe a round flat cake glazed with slices of oranges and honey: by the time both are done baking, it will almost be daylight and he will be past danger and will have sucessfully saved himself.

Malcolm and JB will both be at the courthouse the next day; they're taking the morning flight. But Willem, who was supposed to be there, won't; he called the week before to say filming had been delayed, and he'll now be coming home on the eighteenth, not the fourteenth. He knows there's nothing to be done about this, but still, he mourns Willem's absence almost fiercely: a day like this without Willem won't be a day at all. "Call me the second it's over," Willem had said. "It's killing me I can't be there."

He did, however, invite Andy in one of their midnight conversations, which he grew to enjoy: in those talks, they discussed everyday things, calming things, normal things—the new Supreme Court justice nominee; the most recent health-care bill (he approved of it; Andy didn't); a biography of Rosalind Franklin they'd both read (he liked it;

Andy didn't); the apartment that Andy and Jane were renovating. He liked the novelty of hearing Andy say, with real outrage, "Jude, you've *got* to be fucking kidding me!," which he was used to hearing when being confronted about his cutting, or his amateurish bandaging skills, instead applied to his opinions about movies, and the mayor, and books, and even paint colors. Once he learned that Andy wouldn't use their talks as an occasion to reprimand him, or lecture him, he relaxed into them, and even managed to learn some more things about Andy himself: Andy spoke of his twin, Beckett, also a doctor, a heart surgeon, who lived in San Francisco and whose boyfriend Andy hated and was scheming to get Beckett to dump; and how Jane's parents were giving them their house on Shelter Island; and how Andy had been on the football team in high school, the very Americanness of which had made his parents uneasy; and how he had spent his junior year abroad in Siena, where he dated a girl from Lucca and gained twenty pounds. It wasn't that he and Andy never spoke of Andy's personal life—they did to some extent after every appointment—but on the phone he talked more, and he was able to pretend that Andy was only his friend and not his doctor, despite the fact that this illusion was belied by the call's very premise.

"Obviously, you shouldn't feel obligated to come," he added, hastily, after inviting Andy to the court date.

"I'd love to come," Andy said. "I was wondering when I'd be invited."

Then he felt bad. "I just didn't want you to feel you had to spend even more time with your weird patient who already makes your life so difficult," he said.

"You're not just my weird patient, Jude," Andy said. "You're also my weird friend." He paused. "Or at least, I hope you are."

He smiled into the phone. "Of course I am," he said. "I'm honored to be your weird friend."

And so Andy was coming as well: he'd fly back that afternoon, but Malcolm and JB would spend the night, and they'd all leave together on Saturday.

Upon arriving, he had been surprised, and then moved, to see how thoroughly Harold and Julia had cleaned the house, and how proud they were of the work they'd done. "Look!" one or the other kept saying, triumphantly pointing at a surface—a table, a chair, a corner of floor—that would normally have been obscured by stacks of books or journals, but which was now clear of all clutter. There were flowers everywhere—winter flowers: bunches of decorative cabbages and white-budded dogwood branches and paperwhite bulbs, with their sweet, faintly fecal fragrance—and the books in their cases had been straightened and even the nap on the sofa had been repaired.

"And look at *this*, Jude," Julia had said, linking her arm through his, and showing him the celadon-glazed dish on the hallway table, which had been broken for as long as he'd known them, the shards that had snapped off its side permanently nested in the bowl and furred with dust. But now it had been fixed, and washed and polished.

"Wow," he said when presented with each new thing, grinning idiotically, happy because they were so happy. He didn't care, he never had, whether their place was clean or not—they could've lived surrounded by Ionic columns of old *New York Times*, with colonies of rats squeaking plumply underfoot for all he cared—but he knew they thought he minded, and had mistaken his incessant, tedious cleaning of everything as a rebuke, as much as he'd tried, and tried, to assure them it wasn't. He cleaned now to stop himself, to distract himself, from doing other things, but when he was in college, he had cleaned for the others to express his gratitude: it was something he could do and had always done, and they gave him so much and he gave them so little. JB, who enjoyed living in squalor, never noticed. Malcolm, who had grown up with a housekeeper, always noticed and always thanked him. Only Willem hadn't liked it. "Stop it, Jude," he'd said one day, grabbing his wrist as he picked JB's dirty shirts off the floor, "you're not our maid." But he hadn't been able to stop, not then, and not now.

By the time he wipes off the countertops a final time, it's almost four thirty, and he staggers to his room, texts Willem not to call him, and falls into a brief, brutal sleep. When he wakes, he makes the bed and showers and dresses and returns to the kitchen, where Harold is standing at the counter, reading the paper and drinking coffee.

"Well," Harold says, looking up at him. "Don't you look handsome."

He shakes his head, reflexively, but the truth is that he'd bought a new tie, and had his hair cut the day before, and he feels, if not handsome, then at least neat and presentable, which he always tries to be. He rarely sees Harold in a suit, but he's wearing one as well, and the solemnity of the occasion makes him suddenly shy.

Harold smiles at him. "You were busy last night, clearly. Did you sleep at all?"

He smiles back. "Enough."

"Julia's getting ready," says Harold, "but I have something for you."

"For me?"

"Yes," says Harold, and picks up a small leather box, about the size of a baseball, from beside his coffee mug and holds it out to him. He opens it and inside is Harold's watch, with its round white face and sober, forthright numbers. The band has been replaced with a new black crocodile one.

"My father gave this to me when I turned thirty," says Harold, when he doesn't say anything. "It was his. And you *are* still thirty, so I at least haven't messed up the symmetry of this." He takes the box from him and removes the watch and reverses it so he can see the initials engraved on the back of the face: SS/HS/JSF. "Saul Stein," says Harold. "That was my father. And then HS for me, and JSF for you." He returns the watch to him.

He runs his thumbtip lightly over the initials. "I can't accept this, Harold," he says, finally.

"Sure you can," Harold says. "It's yours, Jude. I already bought a new one; you can't give it back."

He can feel Harold looking at him. "Thank you," he says, at last. "Thank you." He can't seem to say anything else.

"It's my pleasure," says Harold, and neither of them says anything for a few seconds, until he comes to himself and unclasps his watch and fastens Harold's—his, now—around his wrist, holding his arm up for Harold, who nods. "Nice," he says. "It looks good on you."

He's about to reply with something (what?), when he hears, and then sees, JB and Malcolm, both in suits as well.

"The door was unlocked," JB says, as Malcolm sighs. "Harold!" he hugs him, "Congratulations! It's a boy!"

"I'm sure Harold's never heard *that* one before," says Malcolm, waving hello at Julia, who's entering the kitchen.

Andy arrives next, and then Gillian; they'll meet Laurence at the courthouse.

The doorbell rings again. "Are we expecting someone else?" he asks Harold, who shrugs: "Can you get it, Jude?"

So he opens the door, and there is Willem. He stares at Willem for a second, and then, before he can tell himself to be calm, Willem springs at him like a civet cat and hugs him so hard that for a moment he fears he will tip over. "Are you surprised?" Willem says into his ear, and he can tell from his voice that he's smiling. It's the second time that morning he's unable to speak.

The court will be the third time. They take two cars, and in his (driven by Harold, with Malcolm in the front seat), Willem explains that his departure date actually had been changed; but when it was changed back again, he didn't tell him, only the others, so that his appearance would be a surprise. "Yeah, thanks for that, Willem," says Malcolm, "I had to monitor JB like the CIA to make sure he didn't say anything."

They go not to the family courts but to the appeals court on Pemberton Square. Inside Laurence's courtroom—Laurence unfamiliar in his robes: it is a day of everyone in costume—he and Harold and Julia make their promises to each other, Laurence smiling the entire time, and then there is a flurry of picture-taking, with everyone taking photos of everyone else in various arrangements and configurations. He is the only one who doesn't take any at all, as he's in every one.

He's standing with Harold and Julia, waiting for Malcolm to figure out his enormous, complicated camera, when JB calls his name, and all three of them look over, and JB takes the shot. "Got it," says JB. "Thanks."

"JB, this'd better not be for—" he begins, but then Malcolm announces he's ready, and the three of them swivel obediently toward him.

They're back at the house by noon, and soon people start arriving—Gillian and Laurence and James and Carey, and Julia's colleagues and Harold's, some of whom he hasn't seen since he had classes with them in law school. His old voice teacher comes, as does Dr. Li, his math professor, and Dr. Kashen, his master's adviser, and Allison, his former boss at Batter, and a friend of all of theirs from Hood Hall, Lionel, who teaches physics at Wellesley. People come and go all afternoon, going to and from classes, meetings, trials. He had initially been reluctant to have such a gathering, with so many people—wouldn't his acquisition of Harold and Julia as parents provoke, even encourage, questions about why he was parentless at all?—but as the hours pass, and no one asks any questions, no one demands to know why he needs a new set anyway, he finds himself forgetting his fears. He knows his telling other people about the adoption is a form of bragging, and that bragging has its own consequences, but he cannot help himself. *Just this once,* he implores whoever in the world is responsible for punishing him for his bad behavior. *Let me celebrate this thing that has happened to me just this once.*

There is no etiquette for such a party, and so their guests have invented their own: Malcolm's parents have sent a magnum of champagne and a case of super Tuscan from a vineyard they partly own outside of Montalcino. JB's mother sent him with a burlap sack of heirloom narcissus bulbs for Harold and Julia, and a card for him; his aunts have sent an orchid. The U.S. Attorney sends an enormous crate of fruit, with a card signed by Marshall and Citizen and Rhodes as well. People bring wine and flowers. Allison, who had years ago revealed him to Harold as the creator of the bacteria cookies, brings four dozen decorated with his original designs, which makes him blush and Julia shout with delight. The rest of the day is a binging on all things sweet: everything he does that day is perfect, everything he says comes out right. People reach for him and he doesn't move or shy away from them; they touch him and he lets them. His face hurts from smiling. Decades of approbation, of affection are stuffed into this one afternoon, and he gorges on it, reeling from the strangeness of it all. He overhears Andy arguing with Dr. Kashen about a massive new proposed landfill project in Gurgaon, watches Willem listen patiently to his old torts professor, eavesdrops on JB explaining to Dr. Li why the New York art scene is irretrievably fucked, spies Malcolm and Carey trying to extract the largest of the crab cakes without toppling the rest of the stack.

By the early evening, everyone has left, and it is just the six of them sprawled out in the living room: he and Harold and Julia and Malcolm and JB and Willem. The house is once again messy. Julia mentions dinner, but everyone—even he—has eaten too much, and no one, not even JB, wants to think about it. JB has given Harold and Julia a painting of him, saying, before he hands it over to them, "It's not based on a photo, just from sketches." The painting, which JB has done in watercolors and ink on a sheet of stiff paper, is of his face and neck, and is in a different style than he associates with JB's work: sparer and more gestural, in a somber, grayed palette. In it, his right hand is hovering over the base of his throat, as if he's about to grab it and throttle himself, and his mouth is slightly open, and his pupils are very large, like a cat's in gloom. It's undeniably him—he even recognizes the gesture as his own, although he can't, in the moment, remember what it's meant to signal, or what emotion it accompanies. The face is slightly larger than life-size, and all of them stare at it in silence.

"It's a really good piece," JB says at last, sounding pleased. "Let me know if you ever want to sell it, Harold," and finally, everyone laughs.

"JB, it's so, so beautiful—thank you so much," says Julia, and Harold echoes her. He is finding it difficult, as he always does when confronted with JB's pictures of him, to separate the beauty of the art itself from the distaste he feels for his own image, but he doesn't want to be ungracious, and so he repeats their praise.

"Wait, I have something, too," Willem says, heading for the bedroom, and returning with a wooden statue, about eighteen inches high, of a bearded man in hydrangea-blue robes, a curl of flames, like a cobra's hood, surrounding his reddish hair, his right arm held diagonally against his chest, his left by his side.

"Fuck's that dude?" asks JB.

"This dude," Willem replies, "is Saint Jude, also known as Judas Thaddeus." He puts him on the coffee table, turns him toward Julia and Harold. "I got him at a little antiques store in Bucharest," he tells them. "They said it's late nineteenth-century, but I don't know—I think he's probably just a village carving. Still, I liked him. He's handsome and stately, just like our Jude."

"I agree," says Harold, picking up the statue and holding it in his hands. He strokes the figure's pleated robe, his wreath of fire. "Why's his head on fire?"

"It's to symbolize that he was at Pentecost and received the holy spirit," he hears himself saying, the old knowledge never far, cluttering up his mind's cellar. "He was one of the apostles."

"How'd you know that?" Malcolm asks, and Willem, who's sitting next to him, touches his arm. "Of course you know," Willem says, quietly. "I always forget," and he feels a rush of gratitude for Willem, not for remembering, but for forgetting.

"The patron saint of lost causes," adds Julia, taking the statue from Harold, and the words come to him at once: *Pray for us, Saint Jude, helper and keeper of the hopeless, pray for us*—when he was a child, it was his final prayer of the night, and it wasn't until he was older that he would be ashamed of his name, of how it seemed to announce him to the world, and would wonder if the brothers had intended it as he was certain others saw it: as a mockery; as a diagnosis; as a prediction. And yet it also felt, at times, like it was all that was truly his, and although there had been moments he could have, even should have changed it, he never did. "Willem, thank you," Julia says. "I love him."

"Me too," says Harold. "Guys, this is all really sweet of you."

He, too, has brought a present for Harold and Julia, but as the day has passed, it's come to seem ever-smaller and more foolish. Years ago, Harold had mentioned that he and Julia had heard a series of Schubert's early lieder performed in Vienna when they were on their honeymoon. But Harold couldn't remember which ones they had loved, and so he had made up his own list, and augmented it with a few other songs he liked, mostly Bach and Mozart, and then rented a small sound booth and recorded a disc of himself singing them: every few months or so, Harold asks him to sing for them, but he's always too shy to do so. Now, though, the gift feels misguided and tinny, as well as shamefully boastful, and he is embarrassed by his own presumption. Yet he can't bring himself to throw it away. And so, when everyone is standing and stretching and saying their good nights, he slips away and wedges the disc, and the letters he's written each of them, between two books—a battered copy of *Common Sense* and a frayed edition of *White Noise*—on a low shelf, where they might sit, undiscovered, for decades.

Normally, Willem stays with JB in the upstairs study, as he's the only one who can tolerate JB's snoring, and Malcolm stays with him downstairs. But that evening, as everyone heads off for bed, Malcolm volunteers that he'll share with JB, so that he and Willem can catch up with each other.

"'Night, lovers," JB calls down the staircase at them.

As they get ready for bed, Willem tells him more stories from the set: about the lead actress, who perspired so much that her entire face had to be dusted with powder every two takes; about the lead actor, who played the devil, and who was constantly trying to curry favor with the grips by buying them beers and asking them who wanted to play football, but who then had a tantrum when he couldn't remember his lines; about the nine-year-old British actor playing the actress's son, who had approached Willem at the craft services table to tell him that he really shouldn't be eating crackers because they were empty calories, and wasn't he afraid of getting fat? Willem talks and talks, and he laughs as he brushes his teeth and washes his face.

But when the lights are turned off and they are both lying in the dark, he in the bed, Willem on the sofa (after an argument in which he tried to get Willem to take the bed himself), Willem says, gently, "The apartment's really fucking clean."

"I know," he winces. "I'm sorry."

"Don't be," Willem says. "But Jude—was it really awful?"

He understands then that Andy did tell Willem at least some of what had happened, and so he decides to answer honestly. "It wasn't great," he allows, and then, because he doesn't want Willem to feel guilty, "but it wasn't horrible."

They are both quiet. "I wish I could've been there," Willem says.

"You were," he assures him. "But Willem—I missed you."

Very quietly, Willem says, "I missed you, too."

"Thank you for coming," he says.

"Of course I was going to come, Judy," Willem says from across the room. "I would've no matter what."

He is silent, savoring this promise and committing it to memory so he can think about it in moments when he needs it most. "Do you think it went all right?" he asks.

"Are you serious?" Willem says, and he can hear him sit up. "Did you *see* Harold's face? He looked like the Green Party just elected its first president and the Second Amendment was eliminated and the Red Sox were canonized, all in the same day."

He laughs. "You really think so?"

"I know so. He was really, really happy, Jude. He loves you."

He smiles into the dark. He wants to hear Willem say such things over and over, an endless loop of promises and avowals, but he knows such wishes are self-indulgent, and so he changes the subject, and they talk of little things, nothings, until first Willem, and then he, fall asleep.

A week later, his giddiness has mellowed into something else: a contentment, a stillness. For the past week, his nights have been unbroken stretches of sleep in which he dreams not of the past but of the present: silly dreams about work, sunnily absurd dreams about his friends. It is the first complete week in the now almost two decades since he began cutting himself that he hasn't woken in the middle of the night, since he's felt no need for the razor. Maybe he is cured, he dares to think.

Maybe this is what he needed all along, and now that it's happened, he is better. He feels wonderful, like a different person: whole and healthy and calm. He is someone's son, and at times the knowledge of that is so overwhelming that he imagines it is manifesting itself physically, as if it's been written in something shining and gold across his chest.

He is back in their apartment. Willem is with him. He has brought back with him a second statue of Saint Jude, which they keep in the kitchen, but this Saint Jude is bigger and hollow and ceramic, with a slot chiseled into the back of his head, and they feed their change through it at the end of the day; when it's full, they decide, they'll go buy a really good bottle of wine and drink it, and then they'll begin again.

He doesn't know this now, but in the years to come he will, again and again, test Harold's claims of devotion, will throw himself against his promises to see how steadfast they are. He won't even be conscious that he's doing this. But he will do it anyway, because part of him will never believe Harold and Julia; as much as he wants to, as much as he thinks he does, he won't, and he will always be convinced that they will eventually tire of him, that they will one day regret their involvement with him. And so he will challenge them, because when their relationship inevitably ends, he will be able to look back and know for certain that he caused it, and not only that, but the specific incident that caused it, and he will never have to wonder, or worry, about what he did wrong, or what he could have done better. But that is in the future. For now, his happiness is flawless.

That first Saturday after he returns from Boston, he goes up to Felix's house as usual, where Mr. Baker has requested he come a few minutes early. They talk, briefly, and then he goes downstairs to find Felix, who is waiting for him in the music room, plinking at the piano keys.

"So, Felix," he says, in the break they take after piano and Latin but before German and math, "your father tells me you're going away to school next year."

"Yeah," says Felix, looking down at his feet. "In September. Dad went there, too."

"I heard," he says. "How do you feel about it?"

Felix shrugs. "I don't know," he says, at last. "Dad says you're going to catch me up this spring and summer."

"I will," he promises. "You're going to be so ready for that school that they won't know what hit them." Felix's head is still bent, but he sees the tops of his cheeks fatten a little and knows he's smiling, just a bit.

He doesn't know what makes him say what he does next: Is it empathy, as he hopes, or is it a boast, an alluding aloud to the improbable and wondrous turns his life has taken over the past month? "You know, Felix," he begins, "I never had friends, either, not for a very long time, not until I was much older than you." He can sense, rather than see, Felix become alert, can feel him listening. "I wanted them, too," he continues, going slowly now, because he wants to make sure his words come out right. "And I always wondered if I would ever find any, and how, and when." He traces his index finger across the dark walnut tabletop, up the spine of Felix's math textbook, down his cold glass of water. "And then I went to college, and I met people who, for whatever reason, decided to be my friends, and they taught me—everything, really. They made me, and make me, into someone better than I really am.

"You won't understand what I mean now, but someday you will: the only trick of friendship, I think, is to find people who are better than you are—not smarter, not cooler, but kinder, and more generous, and more forgiving—and then to appreciate them for what they can teach you, and to try to listen to them when they tell you something about yourself, no matter how bad—or good—it might be, and to trust them, which is the hardest thing of all. But the best, as well."

They're both quiet for a long time, listening to the click of the metronome, which is faulty and sometimes starts ticking spontaneously, even after he's stopped it. "You're going to make friends, Felix," he says, finally. "You will. You won't have to work as hard at finding them as you will at keeping them, but I promise, it'll be work worth doing. Far more worth doing than, say, Latin." And now Felix looks up at him and smiles, and he smiles back. "Okay?" he asks him.

"Okay," Felix says, still smiling.

"What do you want to do next, German or math?"

"Math," says Felix.

"Good choice," he says, and pulls Felix's math book over to him. "Let's pick up where we left off last time." And Felix turns to the page and they begin.

[III]

Vanities

1

THEIR NEXT-DOOR SUITEMATES their second year in Hood had been a trio of lesbians, all seniors, who had been in a band called Backfat and had for some reason taken a liking to JB (and, eventually, Jude, and then Willem, and finally, reluctantly, Malcolm). Now, fifteen years after the four of them had graduated, two of the lesbians had coupled up and were living in Brooklyn. Of the four of them, only JB talked to them regularly: Marta was a nonprofit labor lawyer, and Francesca was a set designer.

"Exciting news!" JB told them one Friday in October over dinner. "The Bitches of Bushwick called—Edie is in town!" Edie was the third in the lesbians' trio, a beefy, emotional Korean American who shuttled back and forth between San Francisco and New York, and seemed always to be preparing for one improbable job or another: the last time they had seen her, she was about to leave for Grasse to begin training to become a professional nose, and just eight months before that, she had finished a cooking course in Afghani cuisine.

"And why is this exciting news?" asked Malcolm, who had never quite forgiven the three of them for their inexplicable dislike of him.

"Well," said JB, and paused, grinning. "She's transitioning!"

"To a *man?*" asked Malcolm. "Give me a break, JB. She's never exhibited any gender dysphoric ideations for as long as we've known her!" A former coworker of Malcolm's had transitioned the year before and Malcolm had become a self-anointed expert on the subject, lecturing them about their intolerance and ignorance until JB had finally shouted at him, "Jesus, Malcolm, I'm far more trans than Dominic'll ever be!"

"Well, anyway, she is," JB continued, "and the Bitches are throwing her a party at their house, and we're all invited."

They groaned. "JB, I only have five weeks before I leave for London, and I have so much shit to get done," Willem protested. "I can't spend a night listening to Edie Kim complaining out in Bushwick."

"You can't *not* go!" shrieked JB. "They *specifically* asked for you! Francesca's inviting some girl who knows you from something or other and wants to see you again. If you don't go, they're all going to think you think you're too good for them now. And there's going to be a ton of other people we haven't seen in forever—"

"Yeah, and maybe there's a reason we haven't seen them," Jude said.

"—and besides, Willem, the pussy will be waiting for you whether you spend an hour in Brooklyn or not. And it's not like it's the end of the world. It's *Bushwick*. Judy'll drive us." Jude had bought a car the year before, and although it wasn't particularly fancy, JB loved to ride around in it.

"What? I'm not going," Jude said.

"Why not?"

"I'm in a wheelchair, JB, remember? And as I recall, Marta and Francesca's place doesn't have an elevator."

"Wrong place," JB replied triumphantly. "See how long it's been? They moved. Their new place definitely has one. A freight elevator, actually." He leaned back, drumming his fist on the table as the rest of them sat in a resigned silence. "And off we go!"

So the following Saturday they met at Jude's loft on Greene Street and he drove them to Bushwick, where he circled Marta and Francesca's block, looking for a parking space.

"There was a spot right back there," JB said after ten minutes.

"It was a loading zone," Jude told him.

"If you just put that handicapped sign up, we can park wherever we want," JB said.

"I don't like using it—you know that."

"If you're not going to use it, then what's the point of having a car?"

"Jude, I think that's a space," said Willem, ignoring JB.

"Seven blocks from the apartment," muttered JB.

"Shut up, JB," said Malcolm.

Once inside the party, they were each tugged by a different person to a separate corner of the room. Willem watched as Jude was pulled firmly away by Marta: *Help me,* Jude mouthed to him, and he smiled and gave him a little wave. *Courage,* he mouthed back, and Jude rolled his eyes. He knew how much Jude hadn't wanted to come, hadn't wanted to explain again and again why he was in a wheelchair, and yet Willem had begged him: "Don't make me go alone."

"You won't be alone. You'll be with JB and Malcolm."

"You know what I mean. Forty-five minutes and we're out of there. JB and Malcolm can find their own way back to the city if they want to stay longer."

"Fifteen minutes."

"Thirty."

"Fine."

Willem, meanwhile, had been ensnared by Edie Kim, who looked basically the same as she had when they were in college: a little rounder, maybe, but that was it. He hugged her. "Edie," he said, "congratulations."

"Thanks, Willem," said Edie. She smiled at him. "You look great. Really, really great." JB had always had a theory that Edie had a crush on him, but he'd never believed it. "I really loved *The Lacuna Detectives.* You were really great in it."

"Oh," he said. "Thanks." He had hated *The Lacuna Detectives.* He had despised the production of it so much—the story, which was fantastic, had concerned a pair of metaphysical detectives who entered the unconscious minds of amnesiacs, but the director had been so tyrannical that Willem's costar had quit two weeks into the shoot and had to be recast, and once a day, someone had run off the set crying—that he had never actually seen the film itself. "So," he said, trying to redirect the conversation, "when—"

"Why's Jude in a wheelchair?" Edie asked.

He sighed. When Jude had begun using the wheelchair regularly two months ago, the first time he'd had to in four years, since he was thirty-one, he had prepped them all on how to respond to this question. "It's not permanent," he said. "He just has an infection in his leg and it makes it painful for him to walk long distances."

"God, poor guy," said Edie. "Marta says he left the U.S. Attorney's and has a huge job at some corporate firm." JB had also always suspected Edie had a crush on Jude, which Willem thought was fairly plausible.

"Yeah, for a few years now," he said, eager to move the subject away from Jude, for whom he never liked to answer; he would have loved to talk about Jude, and he knew what he could and couldn't say about him, or on his behalf, but he didn't like the sly, confiding tone people took when asking about him, as if he might be cajoled or tricked into revealing what Jude himself wouldn't. (As if he ever would.) "Anyway, Edie, this is really exciting for you." He stopped. "I'm sorry—I should've asked—do you still want to be called Edie?"

Edie frowned. "Why wouldn't I?"

"Well—" He paused. "I didn't know how far into the process you were, and—"

"What process?"

"Um, the transition process?" He should've stopped when he saw Edie's befuddlement, but he didn't. "JB said you were transitioning?"

"Yeah, to Hong Kong," said Edie, still frowning. "I'm going to be a freelance vegan consultant for medium-size hospitality businesses. Wait a minute—you thought I was transitioning genders?"

"Oh god," he said, and two thoughts, separate but equally resonant, filled his mind: *I am going to kill JB.* And: *I can't wait to tell Jude about this conversation.* "Edie, I'm so, so sorry."

He remembered from college that Edie was tricky: little, little-kid things upset her (he once saw her sobbing because the top scoop of her ice cream cone had tumbled onto her new shoes), but big things (the death of her sister; her screaming, snowball-throwing breakup with her girlfriend, which had taken place in the Quad, and which everyone at Hood had leaned out of their windows to witness) seemed to leave her unfazed. He wasn't sure into which category his gaffe fell, and Edie herself appeared equally uncertain, her small mouth convoluting itself into shapes in confusion. Finally, though, she started laughing, and called across the room at someone—"Hannah! Hannah! Come here! You've got to hear this!"—and he exhaled, apologized to and congratulated her again, and made his escape.

He started across the room toward Jude. After years—decades, almost—of these parties, the two of them had worked out their own sign language, a pantomime whose every gesture meant the same thing— *save me*—albeit with varying levels of intensity. Usually, they were able to simply catch each other's eye across the room and telegraph their desperation, but at parties like this, where the loft was lit only by candles and the guests seemed to have multiplied themselves in the space of his short conversation with Edie, more expressive body language was often necessary. Grabbing the back of one's neck meant the other person should call him on his phone right away; fiddling with one's watchband meant "Come over here and replace me in this conversation, or at least join in"; and yanking down on the left earlobe meant "Get me out of this *right now*." He had seen, from the edge of his eye, that Jude had been pulling steadily on his earlobe for the past ten minutes, and he could now see that Marta had been joined by a grim-looking woman he vaguely remembered meeting (and disliking) at a previous party. The two of them were looming interrogatively over Jude in a way that made them appear proprietary and, in the candlelight, fierce, as if Jude were a child who had just been caught breaking a licorice-edged corner off their gingerbread house, and they were deciding whether to broil him with prunes or bake him with turnips.

He tried, he'd later tell Jude, he really did; but he was at one end of the room and Jude was at the other, and he kept getting stopped and tangled in conversations with people he hadn't seen in years and, more annoyingly, people he had seen just a few weeks ago. As he pressed forward, he waved at Malcolm and pointed in Jude's direction, but Malcolm gave him a helpless shrug and mouthed "What?" and he made a dismissive gesture back: *Never mind.*

I've got to get out of here, he thought, as he pushed through the crowd, but the truth was that he usually didn't mind these parties, not really; a large part of him even enjoyed them. He suspected the same might be true of Jude as well, though perhaps to a lesser extent— certainly he did fine for himself at parties, and people always wanted to talk to him, and although the two of them always complained to each other about JB and how he kept dragging them to these things and how tedious they were, they both knew they could simply refuse if they really wanted to, and they both rarely did—after all, where else would they get to use their semaphores, that language that had only two speakers in the whole world?

In recent years, as his life had moved further from college and the person he had been, he sometimes found it relaxing to see people from there. He teased JB about how he had never really graduated from

Hood, but in reality, he admired how JB had maintained so many of his, and their, relationships from then, and how he had somehow managed to contextualize so many of them. Despite his collection of friends from long ago, there was an insistent present tenseness to how JB saw and experienced life, and around him, even the most dedicated nostalgists found themselves less inclined to pick over the chaff and glitter of the past, and instead made themselves contend with whoever the person standing before them had become. He also appreciated how the people JB had chosen to remain friendly with were, largely, unimpressed with who he had become (as much as he could be said to have become any-one). Some of them behaved differently around him now—especially in the last year or so—but most of them were dedicated to lives and interests and pursuits that were so specific and, at times, marginal, that Willem's accomplishments were treated as neither more nor less impor-tant than their own. JB's friends were poets and performance artists and academics and modern dancers and philosophers—he had, Mal-colm once observed, befriended everyone at their college who was *least* likely to make money—and their lives were grants and residencies and fellowships and awards. Success, among JB's Hood Hall assortment, wasn't defined by your box-office numbers (as it was for his agent and manager) or your costars or your reviews (as it was by his grad-school classmates): it was defined simply and only by how good your work was, and whether you were proud of it. (People had actually said that to him at these parties: "Oh, I didn't see *Black Mercury 3081*. But were you proud of your work in it?" No, he hadn't been proud of it. He had played a brooding intergalactic scientist who was also a jujitsu warrior and who successfully and single-handedly defeated a gargantuan space monster. But he had been *satisfied* with it: he had worked hard and had taken his performance seriously, and that was all he ever hoped to do.) Sometimes he wondered whether he was being fooled, if this entire circle of JB's was a performance art piece in itself, one in which the competitions and concerns and ambitions of the real world—the world that sputtered along on money and greed and envy—were overlooked in favor of the pure pleasure of doing work. Sometimes this felt astringent to him, in the best way: he saw these parties, his time with the Hoodies, as something cleansing and restorative, something that returned him to who he once was, thrilled to get a part in the college production of *Noises Off*, making his roommates run lines with him every evening.

"A career mikva," said Jude, smiling, when he told him this.

"A free-market douche," he countered.

"An ambition enema."

"Ooh, that's good!"

But sometimes the parties—like tonight's—had the opposite effect. Sometimes he found himself resenting the others' definition of him, the reductiveness and immovability of it: he was, and forever would be, Willem Ragnarsson of Hood Hall, Suite Eight, someone bad at math and good with girls, an identity both simple and understandable, his persona drawn in two quick brushstrokes. They weren't wrong, necessarily—there was something depressing about being in an industry in which he was considered an intellectual simply because he didn't read certain magazines and websites and because he had gone to the college he had—but it made his life, which he knew was small anyway, feel smaller still.

And sometimes he sensed in his former peers' ignorance of his career something stubborn and willful and begrudging; last year, when his first truly big studio film had been released, he had been at a party in Red Hook and had been talking to a Hood hanger-on who was always at these gatherings, a man named Arthur who'd lived in the loser house, Dillingham Hall, and who now published an obscure but respected journal about digital cartography.

"So, Willem, what've you been doing lately?" Arthur asked, finally, after talking for ten minutes about the most recent issue of *The Histories*, which had featured a three-dimensional rendering of the Indochinese opium route from eighteen thirty-nine through eighteen forty-two.

He experienced, then, that moment of disorientation he occasionally had at these gatherings. Sometimes that very question was asked in a jokey, ironic way, as a congratulations, and he would smile and play along—"Oh, not much, still waiting at Ortolan. We're doing a great sablefish with tobiko these days"—but sometimes, people genuinely didn't know. The genuine not-knowing happened less and less frequently these days, and when it did, it was usually from someone who lived so far off the cultural grid that even the reading of *The New York Times* was treated as a seditious act or, more often, someone who was trying to communicate their disapproval—no, their dismissal—of him and his life and work by remaining determinedly ignorant of it.

He didn't know Arthur well enough to know into which category he fell (although he knew him well enough to not like him, the way he pressed so close into his space that he had literally backed into a wall), so he answered simply. "I'm acting."

"Really," said Arthur, blandly. "Anything I'd've heard of?"

This question—not the question itself, but Arthur's tone, its carelessness and derision—irritated him anew, but he didn't show it. "Well," he said slowly, "they're mostly indies. I did something last year called *The Kingdom of Frankincense*, and I'm leaving next month to shoot *The Unvanquished*, based on the novel?" Arthur looked blank. Willem sighed; he had won an award for *The Kingdom of Frankincense*. "And something I shot a couple of years ago's just been released: this thing called *Black Mercury 3081*."

"Sounds interesting," said Arthur, looking bored. "I don't think I've heard of it, though. Huh. I'll have to look it up. Well, good for you, Willem."

He hated the way certain people said "good for you, Willem," as if his job were some sort of spun-sugar fantasy, a fiction he fed himself and others, and not something that actually existed. He especially hated it that night, when not fifty yards away, framed clearly in the window just behind Arthur's head, happened to be a spotlit billboard mounted atop a building with his face on it—his scowling face, admittedly: he was, after all, fighting off an enormous mauve computer-generated alien— and BLACK MERCURY 3081: COMING SOON in two-foot-high letters. In those moments, he would be disappointed in the Hoodies. *They're no better than anyone else after all*, he would realize. *In the end, they're jealous and trying to make me feel bad. And I'm stupid, because I do feel bad.* Later, he would be irritated with himself: *This is what you wanted*, he would remind himself. *So why do you care what other people think?* But acting *was* caring what other people thought (sometimes it felt like that was all it was), and as much as he liked to think himself immune to other people's opinions—as if he was somehow above worrying about them—he clearly wasn't.

"I know it sounds so fucking petty," he told Jude after that party. He was embarrassed by how annoyed he was—he wouldn't have admitted it to anyone else.

"It doesn't sound petty at all," Jude had said. They were driving back to the city from Red Hook. "But Arthur's a jerk, Willem. He always has been. And years of studying Herodotus hasn't made him any less of one."

He smiled, reluctantly. "I don't know," he said. "Sometimes I feel there's something so . . . so pointless about what I do."

"How can you say that, Willem? You're an amazing actor; you really are. And you—"

"*Don't* say I bring joy to so many people."

"Actually, I wasn't going to say that. Your films aren't really the sorts of things that bring joy to anyone." (Willem had come to specialize in playing dark and complicated characters—often quietly violent, usually morally compromised—that inspired different degrees of sympathy. "Ragnarsson the Terrible," Harold called him.)

"Except aliens, of course."

"Right, except aliens. Although not even them—you kill them all in the end, don't you? But Willem, I love watching them, and so do so many other people. That's got to count for something, right? How many people get to say that, that they can actually remove someone from his daily life?" And when he didn't answer: "You know, maybe we should stop going to these parties; they're becoming unhealthy exercises in masochism and self-loathing for us both." Jude turned to him and grinned. "At least you're in the arts. *I* might as well be working for an arms dealer. Dorothy Wharton asked me tonight how it felt waking up each morning knowing I'd sacrificed yet another piece of my soul the day before."

Finally, he laughed. "No, she didn't."

"Yes, she did. It was like having a conversation with Harold."

"Yeah, if Harold was a white woman with dreadlocks."

Jude smiled. "As I said, like having a conversation with Harold."

But really, both of them knew why they kept attending these parties: because they had become one of the few opportunities the four of them had to be together, and at times they seemed to be their only opportunity to create memories the four of them could share, keeping their friendship alive by dropping bundles of kindling onto a barely smoldering black smudge of fire. It was their way of pretending everything was the same.

It also provided them an excuse to pretend that everything was fine with JB, when they all three knew that something wasn't. Willem couldn't quite identify what was wrong with him—JB could be, in his way, almost as evasive as Jude when it came to certain conversations—but he knew that JB was lonely, and unhappy, and uncertain, and that none of those sensations were familiar ones to him. He sensed that JB—who had so loved college, its structures and hierarchies and micro-societies that he had known how to navigate so well—was trying with every party to re-create the easy, thoughtless companionship they had once had, when their professional identities were still foggy to them and they were united by their aspirations instead of divided by their daily realities. So he organized these outings, and they all obediently fol-lowed as they had always done, giving him the small kindness of letting him be the leader, the one who decided for them, always.

He would have liked to have seen JB one-on-one, just the two of them, but these days, when he wasn't with his college friends, JB ran with a different crowd, one consisting mostly of art world hangers-on, who seemed to be only interested in doing lots of drugs and then hav-ing dirty sex, and it simply wasn't appealing to him. He was in New York less and less often—just eight months in the past three years—and when he *was* home, there were the twin and contradictory pressures to spend meaningful time with his friends and to do absolutely nothing at all.

Now, though, he kept moving toward Jude, who had at least been released by Marta and her grouchy friend and was talking to their friend Carolina (seeing this, he felt guilty anew, as he hadn't talked to Carolina in months and he knew she was angry with him), when Fran-cesca blocked his path to reintroduce him to a woman named Rachel with whom he had worked four years ago on a production of *Cloud 9*, for which she had been the assistant dramaturg. He was happy enough to see her again—he had liked her all those years ago; he had always thought she was pretty—but he knew, even as he was talking to her, that it would go no further than a conversation. After all, he hadn't been exaggerating: he started filming in five weeks. Now was not the time to get ensnared in something new and complicated, and he didn't really have the energy for a one-night hookup which, he knew, had a funny way of becoming as exhausting as something longer-term.

Ten minutes or so into his conversation with Rachel, his phone buzzed, and he apologized and checked the message from Jude: *Leav-*

ing. Don't want to interrupt your conversation with the future Mrs. Rag-narsson. See you at home.

"Shit," he said, and then to Rachel, "Sorry." Suddenly, the spell of the party ended, and he was desperate to leave. Their participation in these parties were a kind of theater that the four of them agreed to stage for themselves, but once one of the actors left the stage, there seemed little point in continuing. He said goodbye to Rachel, whose expression changed from perplexed to hostile once she realized he was truly leaving and she wasn't being invited to leave with him, and then to a group of other people—Marta, Francesca, JB, Malcolm, Edie, Carolina—at least half of whom seemed deeply annoyed with him. It took him another thirty minutes to extricate himself from the apartment, and on his way downstairs, he texted Jude back, hopefully, *You still here? Leaving now,* and then, when he didn't get a reply, *Taking train. Picking something up at the apt—see you soon.*

He took the L to Eighth Avenue and then walked the few blocks south to his apartment. Late October was his favorite time in the city, and he was always sad to miss it. He lived on the corner of Perry and West Fourth, in a third-floor unit whose windows were just level with the tops of the gingko trees; before he'd moved in, he'd had a vision that he would lie in bed late on the weekends and watch the tornado the yellow leaves made as they were shaken loose from their branches by the wind. But he never had.

He had no special feelings for the apartment, other than it was his and he had bought it, the first and biggest thing he had ever bought after paying off the last of his student loans. When he had begun looking, a year and a half ago, he had known only that he wanted to live downtown and that he needed a building with an elevator, so that Jude would be able to visit him.

"Isn't that a little codependent?" his girlfriend at the time, Philippa, had asked him, teasing but also not teasing.

"Is it?" he had asked, understanding what she meant but pretending not to.

"Willem," Philippa had said, laughing to conceal her irritation. "It is."

He had shrugged, unoffended. "I can't live somewhere he can't come visit," he said.

She sighed. "I know."

He knew that Philippa had nothing against Jude; she liked him, and Jude liked her as well, and had even one day gently told Willem that he thought he should spend more time with Philippa when he was in town. When he and Philippa had begun dating—she was a costume designer, mostly for theater—she had been amused, charmed even, by his friendships. She had seen them, he knew, as proof of his loyalty, and dependability, and consistency. But as they continued dating, as they got older, something changed, and the amount of time he spent with JB and Malcolm and, especially, Jude became evidence instead of his fundamental immaturity, his unwillingness to leave behind the comfort of one life—the life with them—for the uncertainties of another, with her. She never asked him to abandon them completely—indeed, one of the things he had loved about her was how close she was to her own group of friends, and that the two of them could spend a night with their own people, in their own restaurants, having their own conversations, and then meet at its end, two distinct evenings ending as a single shared one—but she wanted, finally, a kind of surrender from him, a dedication to her and their relationship that superseded the others.

Which he couldn't bring himself to do. But he felt he had given more to her than she recognized. In their last two years together, he hadn't gone to Harold and Julia's for Thanksgiving nor to the Irvines' at Christmas, so he could instead go to her parents' in Vermont; he had forgone his annual vacation with Jude; he had accompanied her to her friends' parties and weddings and dinners and shows, and had stayed with her when he was in town, watching as she sketched designs for a production of *The Tempest*, sharpening her expensive colored pencils while she slept and he, his mind still stuck in a different time zone, wandered through the apartment, starting and stopping books, opening and closing magazines, idly straightening the containers of pasta and cereal in the pantry. He had done all of this happily and without resentment. But it still hadn't been enough, and they had broken up, quietly and, he thought, well, the previous year, after almost four years together.

Mr. Irvine, hearing that they had broken up, shook his head (this had been at Flora's baby shower). "You boys are really turning into a bunch of Peter Pans," he said. "Willem, what are you? Thirty-six? I'm not sure what's going on with you lot. You're making money. You've achieved something. Don't you think you guys should stop clinging to one another and get serious about adulthood?"

But how was one to be an adult? Was couplehood truly the only appropriate option? (But then, a sole option was no option at all.) "Thousands of years of evolutionary and social development and this is our only choice?" he'd asked Harold when they were up in Truro this past summer, and Harold had laughed. "Look, Willem," he said, "I think you're doing just fine. I know I give you a hard time about settling down, and I agree with Malcolm's dad that couplehood is wonderful, but all you really have to do is just be a good person, which you already are, and enjoy your life. You're young. You have years and years to figure out what you want to do and how you want to live."

"And what if this *is* how I want to live?"

"Well, then, that's fine," said Harold. He smiled at Willem. "You boys are living every man's dream, you know. Probably even John Irvine's."

Lately, he had been wondering if codependence was such a bad thing. He took pleasure in his friendships, and it didn't hurt anyone, so who cared if it was codependent or not? And anyway, how was a friendship any more codependent than a relationship? Why was it admirable when you were twenty-seven but creepy when you were thirty-seven? Why wasn't friendship as good as a relationship? Why wasn't it even better? It was two people who remained together, day after day, bound not by sex or physical attraction or money or children or property, but only by the shared agreement to keep going, the mutual dedication to a union that could never be codified. Friendship was witnessing another's slow drip of miseries, and long bouts of boredom, and occasional triumphs. It was feeling honored by the privilege of getting to be present for another person's most dismal moments, and knowing that you could be dismal around him in return.

More troubling to him than his possible immaturity, though, were his capabilities as a friend. He had always taken pride in the fact that he was a good friend; friendship had always been important to him. But was he actually any good at it? There was the unresolved JB problem, for example; a good friend would have figured something out. And a good friend would certainly have figured out a better way to deal with Jude, instead of telling himself, chantlike, that there simply *was* no better way to deal with Jude, and if there was, if someone (Andy? Harold?

Anyone?) could figure out a plan, then he'd be happy to follow it. But even as he told himself this, he knew that he was just making excuses for himself.

Andy knew it, too. Five years ago, Andy had called him in Sofia and yelled at him. It was his first shoot; it had been very late at night, and from the moment he answered the phone and heard Andy say, "For someone who claims to be such a great friend, you sure as fuck haven't been around to prove it," he had been defensive, because he knew Andy was right.

"Wait a minute," he said, sitting upright, fury and fear clearing away any residual sleepiness.

"He's sitting at home fucking cutting himself to shreds, he's essentially all scar tissue now, he looks like a fucking skeleton, and where are you, Willem?" asked Andy. "And don't say 'I'm on a shoot.' Why aren't you checking in on him?"

"I call him every single day," he began, yelling himself.

"You *knew* this was going to be hard for him," Andy continued, talking over him. "You *knew* the adoption was going to make him feel more vulnerable. So why didn't you put any safeguards in place, Willem? Why aren't your other so-called friends doing anything?"

"Because he doesn't want them to know that he cuts himself, that's why! And I *didn't* know it was going to be this hard for him, Andy," he said. "He never tells me anything! How was I supposed to know?"

"Because! You're supposed to! Fucking use your brain, Willem!"

"Don't you fucking shout at me," he shouted. "You're just mad, Andy, because he's *your* patient and you can't fucking figure out a way to make him better and so you're blaming me."

He regretted it the moment he said it, and in that instant they were both silent, panting into their phones. "Andy," he began.

"Nope," said Andy. "You're right, Willem. I'm sorry. I'm sorry."

"No," he said, "I'm sorry." He was abruptly miserable, thinking of Jude in the ugly Lispenard Street bathroom. Before he had left, he had looked everywhere for Jude's razors—beneath the toilet tank lid; in the back of the medicine cabinet; even under the drawers in the cupboard, taking each out and examining them from all angles—but couldn't find them. But Andy was right—it *was* his responsibility. He should have done a better job. And he hadn't, so really, he had failed.

"No," said Andy. "I'm really sorry, Willem; it's totally inexcusable.

And you're right—I don't know what to do." He sounded tired. "It's just that he's had—he's had such a shitty life, Willem. And he trusts you."

"I know," he mumbled. "I know he does."

So they'd worked out a plan, and when he got back home, he'd monitored Jude more closely than he had before, a process that had proved singularly unrevealing. Indeed, in the month or so after the adoption, Jude was different than he'd seen him before. He couldn't exactly define how: except on rare occasions, he wasn't ever able to determine the days Jude was unhappy and the days he wasn't. It wasn't as if he normally moped around and was unemotive and then, suddenly, wasn't—his fundamental behavior and rhythms and gestures were the same as before. But something *had* changed, and for a brief period, he had the strange sensation that the Jude he knew had been replaced by another Jude, and that this other Jude, this changeling, was someone of whom he could ask anything, who might have funny stories about pets and friends and scrapes from childhood, who wore long sleeves only because he was cold and not because he was trying to hide something. He was determined to take Jude at his word as often and as much as he could: after all, he wasn't his doctor. He was his friend. His job was to treat him as he wanted to be treated, not as a subject to be spied on.

And so, after a certain point, his vigilance diminished, and eventually, that other Jude departed, back to the land of fairies and enchantments, and the Jude he knew reclaimed his space. But then, every once in a while, there would be troubling reminders that what he knew of Jude was only what Jude allowed him to know: he called Jude daily when he was away shooting, usually at a prearranged time, and one day last year he had called and they'd had a normal conversation, Jude sounding no different than he always did, and the two of them laughing at one of Willem's stories, when he heard in the background the clear and unmistakable intercom announcement of the sort one only hears at hospitals: "Paging Dr. Nesarian, Dr. Nesarian to OR Three."

"Jude?" he'd asked.

"Don't worry, Willem," he'd said. "I'm fine. I just have a slight infection; I think Andy's gone a little crazy."

"What kind of infection? Jesus, Jude!"

"A blood infection, but it's nothing. Honestly, Willem, if it was serious, I would've told you."

"No, you fucking wouldn't have, Jude. A blood infection *is* serious."

He was silent. "I would've, Willem."

"Does Harold know?"

"No," he said, sharply. "And you're not to tell him."

Exchanges like this left him stunned and bothered, and he spent the rest of the evening trying to remember the previous week's conversations, picking through them for clues that something might have been amiss and he might have simply, stupidly overlooked it. In more generous, wondering moments, he imagined Jude as a magician whose sole trick was concealment, but every year, he got better and better at it, so that now he had only to bring one wing of the silken cape he wore before his eyes and he would become instantly invisible, even to those who knew him best. But at other times, he bitterly resented this trick, the year-after-year exhaustion of keeping Jude's secrets and yet never being given anything in return but the meanest smidges of information, of not being allowed the opportunity to even try to help him, to publicly worry about him. This isn't fair, he would think in those moments. This isn't friendship. It's something, but it's not friendship. He felt he had been hustled into a game of complicity, one he never intended to play. Everything Jude communicated to them indicated that he didn't want to be helped. And yet he couldn't accept that. The question was how you ignored someone's request to be left alone—even if it meant jeopardizing the friendship. It was a wretched little koan: How can you help someone who won't be helped while realizing that if you *don't* try to help, then you're not being a friend at all? *Talk to me*, he sometimes wanted to shout at Jude. *Tell me things. Tell me what I need to do to make you talk to me.*

Once, at a party, he had overheard Jude tell someone that he told him, Willem, everything, and he had been both flattered and perplexed, because really: he knew nothing. It was sometimes incredible to him how much he cared about someone who refused to tell him any of the things friends shared with each other—how he had lived before they met, what he feared, what he craved, who he was attracted to, the mortifications and sadnesses of daily life. In the absence of talking to Jude himself, he often wished he could talk to Harold about Jude, and figure out how much he knew, and whether, if they—and Andy— braided together all their knowledge, they might be able to find some sort of solution. But this was dreaming: Jude would never forgive him, and instead of the connection he did have with him, he would have none at all.

Back in his apartment, he shuffled quickly through his mail—he rarely got anything of any interest: everything business-related went to his agent or lawyer; anything personal went to Jude's—found the copy of the script he'd forgotten there the week before when he stopped by the apartment after the gym, and left again; he didn't even take off his coat.

Since he'd bought the apartment a year ago, he'd spent a total of six weeks there. There was a futon in the bedroom, and the coffee table from Lispenard Street in the living room, and the scuffed Eames fiberglass chair that JB had found in the street, and his boxes of books. But that was it. In theory, Malcolm was meant to be renovating the space, converting the airless little study near the kitchen into a dining alcove and addressing a list of other issues as well, but Malcolm, as if sensing Willem's lack of interest, had made the apartment his last priority. He complained about this sometimes, but he knew it wasn't Malcolm's fault: after all, he hadn't answered Malcolm's e-mails about finishes or tiles or the dimensions of the built-in bookcase or banquette that Malcolm needed him to approve before he ordered the millwork. It was only recently that he'd had his lawyer's office send Malcolm the final paperwork he needed to begin construction, and the following week, they were finally going to sit down and he was going to make some decisions, and when he returned home in mid-January, the apartment would be, Malcolm promised him, if not totally transformed, then at least greatly improved.

In the meantime, he still more or less lived with Jude, into whose apartment on Greene Street he'd moved directly after he and Philippa had broken up. He used his unfinished apartment, and the promise he'd made to Andy, as the reasons for his apparently interminable occupancy of Jude's extra bedroom, but the fact was that he needed Jude's company and the constancy of his presence. When he was away in England, in Ireland, in California, in France, in Tangiers, in Algeria, in India, in the Philippines, in Canada, he needed to have an image of what was waiting for him back home in New York, and that image never included Perry Street. Home for him was Greene Street, and when he was far away and lonely, he thought of Greene Street, and his room there, and how on weekends, after Jude finished working, they would stay up late, talking, and he would feel time slow and expand, letting him believe the night might stretch out forever.

And now he was finally going home. He ran down the stairs and out the front door and onto Perry Street. The evening had turned cold, and he walked quickly, almost trotting, enjoying as he always did the pleasure of walking by himself, of feeling alone in a city of so many. It was one of the things he missed the most. On film sets, you were never alone. An assistant director walked you to your trailer and back to the set, even if the trailer and the set were fifty yards away. When he was getting used to sets, he was first startled, then amused, and then, finally, annoyed by the culture of actor infantilization that moviemaking seemed to encourage. He sometimes felt that he had been strapped, upright, to a dolly and was being wheeled from place to place: he was walked to the makeup department and then to the costume department. Then he was walked to the set, and then he was walked back to his trailer, and then, an hour or two later, he would be collected from the trailer and escorted to the set once again.

"Don't let me ever get used to this," he'd instruct Jude, begging him, almost. It was the concluding line to all his stories: about the lunches at which everyone segregated themselves by rank and caste— actors and the director at one table, cameramen at another, electricians at a third, the grips at a fourth, the costume department at a fifth—and you made small talk about your workouts, and restaurants you wanted to try, and diets you were on, and trainers, and cigarettes (how much you wanted one), and facials (how much you needed one); about the crew, who both hated the actors and yet were embarrassingly susceptible to even the slightest attention from them; about the cattiness of the hair and makeup team, who knew an almost bewildering amount of information about all the actors' lives, having learned to keep perfectly quiet and make themselves perfectly invisible as they adjusted hairpieces and dabbed on foundation and listened to actresses screaming at their boyfriends and actors whisperingly arranging late-night hookups on their phones, all while sitting in their chairs. It was on these sets that he realized he was more guarded than he'd always imagined himself, and also how easy, how tempting, it was to begin to believe that the life of the set—where everything was fetched for you, and where the sun could literally be made to shine on you—was actual life.

Once he had been standing on his mark as the cinematographer made a last adjustment, before coming over and cupping his head gently—"His hair!" barked the first assistant director, warningly—and tilting it an inch to the left, and then to the right, and then to the left again, as if he was positioning a vase on a mantel.

"Don't move, Willem," he'd cautioned, and he'd promised he wouldn't, barely breathing, but really he had wanted to break into giggles. He suddenly thought of his parents—whom, disconcertingly, he thought of more and more as he grew older—and of Hemming, and for half a second, he saw them standing just off the set to his left, just far enough out of range so he couldn't see their faces, whose expressions he wouldn't have been able to imagine anyway.

He liked telling Jude all of these things, making his days on set something funny and bright. This was not what he thought acting would be, but what had he known about what acting would be? He was always prepared, he was always on time, he was polite to everyone, he did what the cinematographer told him to do and argued with the director only when absolutely necessary. But even all these films later— twelve in the past five years, eight of them in the past two—and through all of their absurdities, he finds most surreal the minute before the camera begins rolling. He stands at his first mark; he stands at his second mark; the cameraman announces he's ready.

"Vanities!" shouts the first assistant director, and the vanities—hair, makeup, costume—hurry over to descend upon him as if he is carrion, plucking at his hair and straightening his shirt and tickling his eyelids with their soft brushes. It takes only thirty seconds or so, but in those thirty seconds, his lashes lowered so stray powder doesn't float into his eyes, other people's hands moving possessively over his body and head as if they're no longer his own, he has the strange sensation that he is gone, that he is suspended, and that his very life is an imagining. In those seconds, a whirl of images whips through his mind, too quickly and jumblingly to effectively identify each as it occurs to him: there is the scene he's about to shoot, of course, and the scene he'd shot earlier, but also all the things that occupy him, always, the things he sees and hears and remembers before he falls asleep at night—Hemming and JB and Malcolm and Harold and Julia. Jude.

Are you happy? he once asked Jude (they must have been drunk).

I don't think happiness is for me, Jude had said at last, as if Willem had been offering him a dish he didn't want to eat. *But it's for you, Willem.*

As Vanities tug and yank at him, it occurs to him that he should have asked Jude what he meant by that: why it was for him and not for Jude. But by the time he's finished shooting the scene, he won't remember the question, or the conversation that inspired it.

"Roll sound!" yells the first A.D., and Vanities scatter.

"Speed," the sound person answers, which means he's rolling.

"Roll camera," calls the cameraman, and then there's the announcement of the scene, and the clap.

And then he opens his eyes.

2

ONE SATURDAY MORNING shortly after he turns thirty-six, he opens his eyes and experiences that strange, lovely sensation he sometimes has, the one in which he realizes that his life is cloudless. He imagines Harold and Julia in Cambridge, the two of them moving dozily through the kitchen, pouring coffee into their stained and chipped mugs and shaking the dew off of the plastic newspaper bags, and, in the air, Willem flying toward him from Cape Town. He pictures Malcolm pressed against Sophie in bed in Brooklyn, and then, because he feels hopeful, JB safe and snoring in his bed on the Lower East Side. Here, on Greene Street, the radiator releases its sibilant sigh. The sheets smell like soap and sky. Above him is the tubular steel chandelier Malcolm installed a month ago. Beneath him is a gleaming black wood floor. The apartment—still impossible in its vastness and possibilities and potential—is silent, and his.

He points his toes toward the bottom of the bed and then flexes them toward his shins: nothing. He shifts his back against the mattress: nothing. He draws his knees toward his chest: nothing. Nothing hurts, nothing even threatens to hurt: his body is his again, something that will perform for him whatever he can imagine, without complaint or sabotage. He closes his eyes, not because he's tired but because it is a perfect moment, and he knows how to enjoy them.

These moments never last for long—sometimes, all he has to do is sit up, and he will be reminded, as if slapped across the face, that his body owns him, not the other way around—but in recent years, as things have gotten worse, he has worked very hard to give up the idea that he will ever improve, and has instead tried to concentrate on and be grateful for the minutes of reprieve, whenever and wherever his body chooses to bestow them. Finally he sits, slowly, and then stands, just as slowly. And still, he feels wonderful. A good day, he decides, and walks to the bathroom, past the wheelchair that sulks, a sullen ogre, in a corner of his bedroom.

He gets ready and then sits down with some papers from the office to wait. Generally, he spends most of Saturday at work—that at least hasn't changed from the days he used to take his walks: oh, his walks! Was that once him, someone who could trip, goatlike, to the Upper East Side and home again, all eleven miles on his own?—but today he's meeting Malcolm and taking him to his suitmaker's, because Malcolm is going to get married and needs to buy a suit.

They're not completely certain if Malcolm is actually getting married or not. They *think* he is. Over the past three years, he and Sophie have broken up and gotten back together, and broken up, and gotten back together. But in the past year, Malcolm has had conversations with Willem about weddings, and does Willem think they're an indulgence or not; and with JB about jewelry, and when women say they don't like diamonds, do they really mean it, or are they just testing the way it sounds; and with him about prenuptial agreements.

He had answered Malcolm's questions as best as he could, and then had given him the name of a classmate from law school, a matrimonial attorney. "Oh," Malcolm had said, moving backward, as if he had offered him the name of a professional assassin. "I'm not sure I need this yet, Jude."

"All right," he said, and withdrew the card, which Malcolm seemed unwilling to even touch. "Well, if and when you do, just ask."

And then, a month ago, Malcolm had asked if he could help him pick out a suit. "I don't even really have one, isn't that nuts?" he asked. "Don't you think I should have one? Don't you think I should start looking, I don't know, more grown-up or something? Don't you think it'd be good for business?"

"I think you look great, Mal," he said. "And I don't think you need any help on the business front. But if you want one, sure, I'm happy to help you."

"Thanks," said Malcolm. "I mean, I just think it's something I should have. You know, just in case something comes up." He paused. "I can't believe you have a suitmaker, by the way."

He smiled. "He's not *my* suitmaker," he said. "He's just someone who makes suits, and some of them happen to be mine."

"God," said Malcolm, "Harold really created a monster."

He laughed, obligingly. But he often feels as if a suit is the only thing that makes him look normal. For the months he was in a wheelchair, those suits were a way of reassuring his clients that he was competent and, simultaneously, of reassuring himself that he belonged with the others, that he could at least dress the way they did. He doesn't consider himself vain, but rather scrupulous: when he was a child, the boys from the home would occasionally play baseball games with the boys from the local school, who would taunt them, pinching their noses as they walked onto the field. "Take a bath!" they would shout. "You smell! You smell!" But they *did* bathe: they had mandatory showers every morning, pumping the greasy pink soap into their palms and onto washcloths and sloughing off their skin while one of the counselors walked back and forth before the row of showerheads, cracking one of the thin towels at the boys who were misbehaving, or shouting at the ones who weren't cleaning themselves with enough vigor. Even now, he has a horror of repulsing, by being unkempt, or dirty, or unsightly. "You'll always be ugly, but that doesn't mean you can't be neat," Father Gabriel used to tell him, and although Father Gabriel was wrong about many things, he knows he was right about this.

Malcolm arrives and hugs him hello and then begins, as he always does, surveying the space, telescoping his long neck and rotating in a slow circle around the room, his gaze like a lighthouse's beam, making little assessing noises as he does.

He answers Malcolm's question before he can ask it: "Next month, Mal."

"You said that three months ago."

"I know. But now I really mean it. Now I have the money. Or I will, at the end of this month."

"But we discussed this."

"I know. And Malcolm—it's so unbelievably generous of you. But I'm not going to not pay you."

He has lived in the apartment for more than four years now, and for four years, he's been unable to renovate it because he hasn't had the money, and he hasn't had the money because he was paying off the apartment. In the meantime, Malcolm has drawn up plans, and walled off the bedrooms, and helped him choose a sofa, which sits, a gray spacecraft, in the center of the living room, and fixed some minor problems, including the floors. "That's crazy," he had told Malcolm at the time. "You're going to have to redo it entirely once the renovation's done." But Malcolm had said he'd do it anyway; the floor dye was a new product he wanted to try, and until he was ready to begin work, Greene Street would be his laboratory, where he could do a little experimentation, if he didn't mind (and he didn't, of course). But otherwise the apartment is still very much as it was when he moved in: a long rectangle on the sixth floor of a building in southern SoHo, with windows at either end, one set facing west and the other facing east, as well as the entire southern wall, which looks over a parking lot. His room and bathroom are at the eastern-facing end, which looks onto the top of a stubby building on Mercer Street; Willem's rooms—or what he continues to think of as Willem's rooms—are at the western-facing end, which looks over Greene Street. There is a kitchen in the middle of the apartment, and a third bathroom. And in between the two suites of rooms are acres of space, the black floors shiny as piano keys.

It is still an unfamiliar feeling to have so much space, and a stranger one to be able to afford it. *But you can,* he has to remind himself sometimes, just as he does when he stands in the grocery store, wondering whether he should buy a tub of the black olives he likes, which are so salty they make his mouth pucker and his eyes water. When he first moved to the city, they were an indulgence, and he'd buy them just once a month, one glistening spoonful at a time. Every night he'd eat only one, sucking the meat slowly off the stone as he sat reading briefs. *You can buy them,* he tells himself. *You have the money.* But he still finds it difficult to remember.

The reason behind Greene Street, and the container of olives that are usually in the refrigerator, is his job at Rosen Pritchard and Klein, one of the city's most powerful and prestigious firms, where he is a litigator and, for a little more than a year now, a partner. Five years ago, he and Citizen and Rhodes had been working on a case concerning securities fraud at a large commercial bank called Thackery Smith, and shortly after the case had settled, he had been contacted by a man named Lucien Voigt, whom he knew was the chair of the litigation department at Rosen Pritchard and Klein, and who had represented Thackery Smith in their negotiations.

Voigt asked him to have a drink. He had been impressed by his work, especially in the courtroom, he said. And Thackery Smith had been as well. He had heard of him anyway—he and Judge Sullivan had been on law review together—and had researched him. Had he ever considered leaving the U.S. Attorney's Office and coming to the dark side?

He would have been lying if he said he hadn't. All around him, people were leaving. Citizen, he knew, was talking to an international firm in Washington, D.C. Rhodes was wondering whether he should go in-house at a bank. He himself had been approached by two other firms, and had turned them both down. They loved the U.S. Attorney's Office, all of them. But Citizen and Rhodes were older than he was, and Rhodes and his wife wanted to have a baby, and they needed to make money. Money, money: it was all they spoke of sometimes.

He, too, thought of money—it was impossible not to. Every time he came home from a party at one of JB's or Malcolm's friends' apartments, Lispenard Street seemed a little shabbier, a little less tolerable. Every time the elevator broke and he had to walk up the flights of stairs, and then rest on the floor in the hallway, his back against their front door, before he had the energy to let himself in, he dreamed of living somewhere functional and reliable. Every time he was standing at the top of the subway stairs, readying himself for the climb down, gripping the handrail and nearly breathing through his mouth with effort, he would wish he could take a taxi. And then there were other fears, bigger fears: in his very dark moments, he imagined himself as an old man, his skin stretched vellum-like over his ribs, still in Lispenard Street, pulling himself on his elbows to the bathroom because he was no longer able to walk. In this dream, he was alone—there was no Willem or JB or Malcolm or Andy, no Harold or Julia. He was an old, old man, and there was no one, and he was the only one left to take care of himself.

"How old are you?" asked Voigt.

"Thirty-one," he said.

"Thirty-one's young," said Voigt, "but you won't be young forever. Do you really want to grow old in the U.S. Attorney's Office? You know what they say about assistant prosecutors: Men whose best years are behind them." He talked about compensation, about an accelerated path to partnership. "Just tell me you'll think about it."

"I will," he said.

And he did. He didn't discuss it with Citizen or Rhodes—or Harold, because he knew what he'd say—but he did discuss it with Willem, and together they debated the obvious benefits of the job against the obvious drawbacks: the hours (but he never left work as it was, Willem argued), the tedium, the high probability he'd be working with assholes (but Citizen and Rhodes aside, he already worked with assholes, Willem argued). And, of course, the fact that he would now be defending the people he'd spent the past six years prosecuting: liars and crooks and thieves, the entitled and the powerful masquerading as victims. He wasn't like Harold or Citizen—he was practical; he knew that making a career as a lawyer meant sacrifices, either of money or of moralities, but it still troubled him, this forsaking of what he knew to be just. And for what? So he could insure he wouldn't become that old man, lonely and sick? It seemed the worst kind of selfishness, the worst kind of self-indulgence, to disavow what he knew was right simply because he was frightened, because he was scared of being uncomfortable and miserable.

Then, two weeks after his meeting with Voigt, he had come home one Friday night very late. He was exhausted; he'd had to use his wheelchair that day because the wound on his right leg hurt so much, and he was so relieved to get home, back to Lispenard Street, that he had felt himself go weak—in just a few minutes, he would be inside, and he would wrap a damp washcloth, hot and steamed from the microwave, around his calf and sit in the warmth. But when he tried the elevator button, he heard nothing but a grinding of gears, the faint winching noise the machine made when it was broken.

"No!" he shouted. "No!" His voice echoed in the lobby, and he smacked his palm against the elevator door again and again: "No, no, no!" He picked up his briefcase and threw it against the ground, and papers spun up from it. Around him, the building remained silent and unhelpful.

Finally he stopped, ashamed and angry, and gathered his papers back into his bag. He checked his watch: it was eleven. Willem was in a play, *Cloud 9*, but he knew he'd be off stage by then. But when he called him, Willem didn't pick up. And then he began to panic. Malcolm was on vacation in Greece. JB was at an artists' colony. Andy's daughter, Beatrice, had just been born the previous week: he couldn't call him. There were only so many people he would let help him, whom he felt at least semi-comfortable clinging to like a sloth, whom he would allow to drag him up the many flights.

But in that moment, he was irrationally, intensely desperate to get into the apartment. And so he stood, tucking his briefcase under his left arm and collapsing his wheelchair, which was too expensive to leave in the lobby, with his right. He began to work his way up the stairs, cleaving his left side to the wall, gripping the chair by one of its spokes. He moved slowly—he had to hop on his left leg, while trying to avoid putting any weight on his right, or letting the wheelchair bang against the wound. Up he went, pausing to rest every third step. There were a hundred and ten steps from the lobby to the fifth floor, and by the fiftieth, he was shaking so badly he had to stop and sit for half an hour. He called and texted Willem again and again. On the fourth call, he left the message he hoped he would never have to leave: "Willem, I really need help. Please call me. Please." He had a vision of Willem calling him right back, telling him he'd be right there, but he waited and waited and Willem didn't call, and finally he managed to stand again.

Somehow he made it inside. But he can't remember anything else from that night; when he woke the next day, Willem was asleep on the rug next to his bed, and Andy asleep on the chair they must have dragged into his room from the living room. He was thick-tongued, fogged, nauseated, and he knew that Andy must have given him an injection of pain medication, which he hated: he would feel disoriented and constipated for days.

When he woke again, Willem was gone, but Andy was awake, and staring at him.

"Jude, you've got to get the fuck out of this apartment," he said, quietly.

"I know," he said.

"Jude, what were you thinking?" Willem asked him later, after he had returned from the grocery store and Andy had helped him into the bathroom—he couldn't walk: Andy had had to carry him—and then put him back into bed, still in his clothes from the day before, and left. Willem had gone to a party after the show and hadn't heard his phone ring; when he had finally listened to his messages, he had rushed home and found him convulsing on the floor and had called Andy. "Why didn't you call Andy? Why didn't you go to a diner and wait for me? Why didn't you call Richard? Why didn't you call Philippa and make her find me? Why didn't you call Citizen, or Rhodes, or Eli, or Phaedra, or the Henry Youngs, or—"

"I don't know," he said, miserably. It was impossible to explain to the healthy the logic of the sick, and he didn't have the energy to try.

The following week, he contacted Lucien Voigt and finalized the terms of the job with him. And once he had signed the contract, he called Harold, who was silent for a long five seconds before taking a deep breath and beginning.

"I just don't get this, Jude," he said. "I don't. You've never struck me as a money-grubber. Are you? I mean, I guess you are. You had—you have—a great career at the U.S. Attorney's. You're doing work there that matters. And you're giving it all up to defend, who? Criminals. People so entitled, so certain they won't be caught that being caught—that very concern—doesn't even occur to them. People who think the laws are written for people who make less than nine figures a year. People who think the laws are applicable only by race, or by tax bracket."

He said nothing, just let Harold become more and more agitated, because he knew Harold was right. They had never explicitly discussed it, but he knew Harold had always assumed that he would make his career in public service. Over the years, Harold would talk with dismay and sorrow about talented former students he admired who had left jobs—at the U.S. Attorney's, at the Department of Justice, at public defender offices, at legal aid programs—to go to corporate firms. "A society cannot run as it should unless people with excellent legal minds make it their business to make it run," Harold often said, and he had always agreed with him. And he agreed with him still, which was why he couldn't defend himself now.

"Don't you have anything you want to say for yourself?" Harold asked him, finally.

"I'm sorry, Harold," he said. Harold said nothing. "You're so angry at me," he murmured.

"I'm not angry, Jude," Harold said. "I'm disappointed. Do you know how special you are? Do you know what a difference you could make if you stayed? You could be a judge if you wanted to—you could be a justice someday. But you're not going to be now. Now you're going to be another litigator in another corporate firm, and all the good work you could have done you'll instead be fighting against. It's just such a waste, Jude, such a waste."

He was silent again. He repeated Harold's words to himself: *Such a waste, such a waste.* Harold sighed. "So what is this about, really?" he asked. "Is it money? Is this what this is about? Why didn't you tell me you needed money, Jude? I could've given you some. Is this all about money? Tell me what you need, Jude, and I'm happy to help you out."

"Harold," he began, "that's so—that's so kind of you. But—I can't."

"Bullshit," said Harold, "you *won't*. I'm offering you a way to let you keep your job, Jude, to not have to take a job you're going to hate, for work you *will* hate—and that's not a maybe, that's a fact—with no expectations or strings attached. I'm telling you that I'm *happy* to give you money for this."

Oh, Harold, he thought. "Harold," he said, wretchedly, "the kind of money I need isn't the kind of money you have. I promise you."

Harold was silent, and when he spoke next, his tone was different. "Jude, are you in any kind of trouble? You can tell me, you know. Whatever it is, I'll help you."

"No," he said, but he wanted to cry. "No, Harold, I'm fine." He wrapped his right hand around his bandaged calf, with its steady, constant ache.

"Well," said Harold. "That's a relief. But Jude, what could you possibly need so much money for, besides an apartment, which Julia and I will help you buy, do you hear me?"

He sometimes found himself both frustrated and fascinated by Harold's lack of imagination: in Harold's mind, people had parents who were proud of them, and saved money only for apartments and vacations, and asked for things when they wanted them; he seemed to be curiously unaware of a universe in which those things might not be givens, in which not everyone shared the same past and future. But this was a highly ungenerous way to think, and it was rare—most of the time, he admired Harold's steadfast optimism, his inability or unwillingness to be cynical, to look for unhappiness or misery in every situation. He loved Harold's innocence, which was made more remarkable considering what he taught and what he had lost. And so how could he tell Harold that he had to consider wheelchairs, which needed to be replaced every few years, and which insurance didn't wholly cover? How could he tell him that Andy, who didn't take insurance, never charged him, had never charged him, but might want to someday, and if he did, he certainly wasn't not going to pay him? How could he tell him that this most recent time his wound had opened, Andy had mentioned hospitalization and, maybe, someday in the future, amputation? How could he tell him that if his leg was amputated, it would mean a hospital stay, and physical therapy, and prostheses? How could he tell him about the surgery he wanted on his back, the laser burning his carapace of scars down to nothing? How could he tell Harold of his deepest fears: his loneliness, of becoming the old man with a catheter and a bony, bare chest? How could he tell Harold that he dreamed not of marriage, or children, but that he would someday have enough money to pay someone to take care of him if he needed it, someone who would be kind to him and allow him privacy and dignity? And then, yes, there were the things he wanted: He wanted to live somewhere where the elevator worked. He wanted to take cabs when he wanted to. He wanted to find somewhere private to swim, because the motion stilled his back and because he wasn't able to take his walks any longer.

But he couldn't tell Harold any of this. He didn't want Harold to know just how flawed he was, what a piece of junk he'd acquired. And so he said nothing, and told Harold he had to go, and that he would talk to him later.

Even before he had talked to Harold, he had prepared himself to be resigned to his new job, nothing more, but to first his unease, and then his surprise, and then his delight, and then his slight disgust, he found that he enjoyed it. He'd had experience with pharmaceutical companies when he was a prosecutor, and so much of his initial caseload concerned that industry: he worked with a company that was opening an Asia-based subsidiary to develop an anticorruption policy, traveling back and forth to Tokyo with the senior partner on the case— this was a small, tidy, solvable job, and therefore unusual. The other cases were more complicated, and longer, at times infinitely long: he mostly worked on compiling a defense for another of the firm's clients, this a massive pharmaceutical conglomerate, against a False Claims Act charge. And three years into his life at Rosen Pritchard and Klein, when the investment management company Rhodes worked for was investigated for securities fraud, they came to him, and secured his partnership: he had trial experience, which most of the other associates didn't, but he had known he would need to bring in a client eventually, and the first client was always the hardest to find.

He would never have admitted it to Harold, but he actually liked directing investigations prompted by whistle-blowers, liked pressing up against the boundaries of the Foreign Corrupt Practices Act, liked being able to stretch the law, like a strip of elastic, just past its natural tension point, just to the point where it would snap back at you with a sting. By day he told himself it was an intellectual engagement, that his work was an expression of the plasticity of the law itself. But at night he would sometimes think of what Harold would say if he was honest with him about what he was doing, and would hear his words again: *Such a waste, such a waste.* What was he doing?, he would think in those moments. Had the job made him venal, or had he always been so and had just fancied himself otherwise?

It's all within the law, he would argue with the Harold-in-his-head.

Just because you can *do it doesn't mean you should,* Harold-in-his-head would shoot back at him.

And indeed, Harold hadn't been completely wrong, for he missed the U.S. Attorney's Office. He missed being righteous and surrounded by the passionate, the heated, the crusading. He missed Citizen, who had moved back to London, and Marshall, whom he occasionally met for drinks, and Rhodes, whom he saw more frequently but who was perpetually frazzled, and gray, and whom he had remembered as cheery and effervescent, someone who would play electrotango music and squire an imaginary woman around the room when they were at the office late and feeling punchy, just to get him and Citizen to look up from their computers and laugh. They were getting older, all of them. He liked Rosen Pritchard, he liked the people there, but he never sat with them late at night arguing about cases and talking about books: it wasn't that sort of office. The associates his age had unhappy girlfriends or boyfriends at home (or were themselves unhappy girlfriends or boyfriends); the ones older than he were getting married. In the rare moments they weren't discussing the work before them, they made small talk about engagements and pregnancies and real estate. They didn't discuss the law, not for fun or from fervor.

The firm encouraged its attorneys to do pro bono work, and he began volunteering with a nonprofit group that offered free legal advice to artists. The organization kept what they called "studio hours" every afternoon and evening, when artists could drop by and consult with a lawyer, and every Wednesday night he left work early, at seven, and sat in the group's creaky-floored SoHo offices on Broome Street for three hours, helping small publishers of radical treatises who wanted to establish themselves as nonprofit entities, and painters with intellectual property disputes, and dance groups, photographers, writers, and filmmakers with contracts that were either so extralegal (he was presented with one written in pencil on a paper towel) that they were meaningless or so needlessly complicated that the artists couldn't understand them—*he* could barely understand them—and yet had signed them anyway.

Harold didn't really approve of his volunteer work, either; he could tell he thought it frivolous. "Are any of these artists any *good?*" Harold asked. "Probably not," he said. But it wasn't for him to judge whether the artists were good or not—other people, plenty of other people, did that already. He was there only to offer the sort of practical help that so few of them had, as so many of them lived in a world that was deaf to practicalities. He knew it was romantic, but he admired them: he admired anyone who could live for year after year on only their fast-burning hopes, even as they grew older and more obscure with every day. And, just as romantically, he thought of his time with the organization as his salute to his friends, all of whom were living the sorts of lives he marveled at: he considered them such successes, and he was proud of them. Unlike him, they had had no clear path to follow, and yet they had plowed stubbornly ahead. They spent their days making beautiful things.

His friend Richard was on the board of the organization, and some Wednesdays he'd stop by on his way home—he had recently moved to SoHo—and sit and talk with him if he was between clients, or just give him a wave across the room if he was occupied. One night after studio hours, Richard invited him back to his apartment for a drink, and they walked west on Broome Street, past Centre, and Lafayette, and Crosby, and Broadway, and Mercer, before turning south on Greene. Richard lived in a narrow building, its stone gone the color of soot, with a towering garage door marking its first floor and, to its right, a metal door with a face-size glass window cut into its top. There was no lobby, but rather a gray, tiled-floor hallway lit by a series of three glowing bare bulbs dangling from cords. The hallway turned right and led to a cell-like industrial elevator, the size of their living room and Willem's bedroom at Lispenard Street combined, with a rattling cage door that shuddered shut at the press of a button, but which glided smoothly up through an exposed cinder-block shaft. At the third floor, it stopped, and Richard opened the cage and turned his key into the set of massive, forbidding steel doors before them, which opened into his apartment.

"God," he said, stepping into the space, as Richard flicked on some lights. The floors were whitewashed wood, and the walls were white as well. High above him, the ceiling winked and shone with scores of chandeliers—old, glass, new, steel—that were strung every three feet or so, at irregular heights, so that as they walked deeper into the loft, he could feel glass bugles skimming across the top of his head, and Richard, who was even taller than he was, had to duck so they wouldn't scrape his forehead. There were no dividing walls, but near the far end of the space was a shallow, freestanding box of glass as tall and wide as the front doors, and as he drew closer, he could see that within it was a gigantic honeycomb shaped like a graceful piece of fan coral. Beyond the glass box was a blanket-covered mattress, and before it was a shaggy white Berber rug, its mirrors twinkling in the lights, and a white woolen sofa and television, an odd island of domesticity in the midst of so much aridity. It was the largest apartment he had ever been in.

"It's not real," said Richard, watching him look at the honeycomb. "I made it from wax."

"It's spectacular," he said, and Richard nodded his thanks.

"Come on," he said, "I'll give you the tour."

He handed him a beer and then unbolted a door next to the refrigerator. "Emergency stairs," he said. "I love them. They're so—descent-into-hell looking, you know?"

"They are," he agreed, looking into the doorway, where the stairs seemed to vanish into the gloom. And then he stepped back, suddenly uneasy and yet feeling foolish for being so, and Richard, who hadn't seemed to notice, shut the door and bolted it.

They went down in the elevator to the second floor and into Richard's studio, and Richard showed him what he was working on. "I call them misrepresentations," he said, and let him hold what he had assumed was a white birch branch but was actually made from fired clay, and then a stone, round and smooth and lightweight, that had been whittled from ash and lathe-turned but that gave the suggestion of solidity and heft, and a bird skeleton made of hundreds of small porcelain pieces. Bisecting the space lengthwise was a row of seven glass boxes, smaller than the one upstairs with the wax honeycomb but each still as large as one of the casement windows, and each containing a jagged, crumbling mountain of a sickly dark yellow substance that appeared to be half rubber, half flesh. "These are real honeycombs, or they were," Richard explained. "I let the bees work on them for a while, and then I released them. Each one is named for how long they were occupied, for how long they were actually a home and a sanctuary."

They sat on the rolling leather desk chairs that Richard worked from and drank their beers and talked: about Richard's work, and about his next show, his second, that would open in six months, and about JB's new paintings.

"You haven't seen them, right?" Richard asked. "I stopped by his studio two weeks ago, and they're really beautiful, the best he's ever done." He smiled at him. "There're going to be a lot of you, you know."

"I know," he said, trying not to grimace. "So, Richard," he said, changing the subject, "how did you find this space? It's incredible."

"It's mine."

"Really? You own it? I'm impressed; that's so adult of you."

Richard laughed. "No, the building—it's mine." He explained: his grandparents had an import business, and when his father and his aunt were young, they had bought sixteen buildings downtown, all former factories, to store their wares: six in SoHo, six in TriBeCa, and four in Chinatown. When each of their four grandchildren turned thirty, they got one of the buildings. When they turned thirty-five—as Richard had the previous year—they got another. When they turned forty, they got a third. They would get the last when they turned fifty.

"Did you get to choose?" he asked, feeling that particular mix of giddiness and disbelief he did whenever he heard these kinds of stories: both that such wealth existed and could be discussed so casually, and that someone he had known for such a long time was in possession of it. They were reminders of how naïve and unsophisticated he somehow still was—he could never imagine such riches, he could never imagine people he knew *had* such riches. Even all these years later, even though his years in New York and, especially, his job had taught him differently, he couldn't help but imagine the rich not as Ezra or Richard or

Malcolm but as they were depicted in cartoons, in satires: older men, stamping out of cars with dark-tinted windows and fat-fingered and plush and shinily bald, with skinny brittle wives and large, polished-floor houses.

"No," Richard grinned, "they gave us the ones they thought would best suit our personalities. My grouchy cousin got a building on Franklin Street that was used to store vinegar."

He laughed. "What was this one used for?"

"I'll show you."

And so back in the elevator they went, up to the fourth floor, where Richard opened the door and turned on the lights, and they were confronted with pallets and pallets stacked high, almost to the ceiling, with what he thought were bricks. "But not *just* bricks," said Richard, "decorative terra-cotta bricks, imported from Umbria." He picked one up from an incomplete pallet and gave it to him, and he turned the brick, which was glazed with a thin, bright green finish, in his hand, running his palm over its blisters. "The fifth and sixth floors are full of them, too," said Richard, "they're in the process of selling them to a wholesaler in Chicago, and then those floors'll be clear." He smiled. "Now you see why I have such a good elevator in here."

They returned to Richard's apartment, back through the hanging garden of chandeliers, and Richard gave him another beer. "Listen," he said, "I need to talk to you about something important."

"Anything," he said, placing the bottle on the table and leaning forward.

"The tiles will probably be out of here by the end of the year," said Richard. "The fifth and sixth floors are set up exactly like this one—wet walls in the same place, three bathrooms—and the question is whether you'd want one of them."

"Richard," he said, "I'd love to. But how much are you charging?"

"I'm not talking about renting it, Jude," said Richard. "I'm talking about buying it." Richard had already talked to his father, who was his grandparents' lawyer: they'd convert the building into a co-op, and he'd buy a certain number of shares. The only thing Richard's family requested is that he or his heirs give them the right to buy the apartment back from him first if he ever decided to sell it. They would offer him a fair price, and he would pay Richard a monthly rent that would be applied toward his purchase. The Goldfarbs had done this before—

his grouchy cousin's girlfriend had bought a floor of the vinegar building a year ago—and it had worked out fine. Apparently, they got some
sort of tax break if they each converted one of their buildings into at
least a two-unit co-op, and so Richard's father was trying to get all of
the grandchildren to do so.

"Why are you doing this?" he asked Richard, quietly, once he had
recovered. "Why me?"

Richard shrugged. "It gets lonely here," he said. "Not that I'm going
to be stopping by all the time. But it'd be nice to know there's another
living being in this building sometimes. And you're the most responsible of my friends, not that there's a lot of competition for the title. And
I like your company. Also—" He stopped. "Promise you won't get mad."

"Oh god," he said. "But I promise."

"Willem told me about what happened, you know, when you were
trying to get upstairs last year and the elevator broke. It's not anything
to be embarrassed about, Jude. He's just worried about you. I told him
I was going to ask you about this anyway, and he thought—he thinks—
it's someplace you could live for a long time: forever. And the elevator
will never break here. And if it does, I'll be right downstairs. I mean—
obviously, you can buy somewhere else, but I hope you'll consider moving in here."

In that moment he feels not angry but exposed: not just to Richard but to Willem. He tries to hide as much as he can from Willem,
not because he doesn't trust him but because he doesn't want Willem to see him as less of a person, as someone who has to be looked
after and helped. He wants Willem, wants them all, to think of him as
someone reliable and hardy, someone they can come to with their problems, instead of him always having to turn to them. He is embarrassed,
thinking of the conversations that have been had about him—between
Willem and Andy, and between Willem and Harold (which he is certain happens more often than he fears), and now between Willem and
Richard—and saddened as well that Willem is spending so much time
worrying about him, that he is having to think of him the way he would
have had to think of Hemming, had Hemming lived: as someone who
needed care, as someone who needed decisions made for him. He sees
the image of himself as an old man again: Is it possible it is also Willem's vision, that the two of them share the same fear, that his ending
seems as inevitable to Willem as it does to himself?

He thinks, then, of a conversation he had once had with Willem and Philippa; Philippa was talking about how someday, when she and Willem were old, they'd take over her parents' house and orchards in southern Vermont. "I can see it now," she said. "The kids'll have moved back in with us, because they won't be able to make it in the real world, and *they'll* have six kids between them with names like Buster and Carrot and Vixen, who'll run around naked and won't be sent to school, and whom Willem and I will have to support until the end of time—"

"What will your kids do?" he asked, practical even in play.

"Oberon will make art installations using only food products, and Miranda will play a zither with yarn for strings," said Philippa, and he had smiled. "They'll stay in grad school forever, and Willem will have to keep working until he's so broken down that I have to push him onto the set in a wheelchair"—she stopped, blushing, but carried on after a hitch—"to pay for all their degrees and experiments. I'll have to give up costume design and start an organic applesauce company to pay all our debts and maintain the house, which'll be this huge, glorious wreck with termites everywhere, and we'll have a huge, scarred wooden table big enough to seat all twelve of us."

"Thirteen," said Willem, suddenly.

"Why thirteen?"

"Because—Jude'll be living with us, too."

"Oh, will I?" he asked lightly, but pleased, and relieved, to be included in Willem's vision of old age.

"Of course. You'll have the guest cottage, and every morning Buster will bring you your buckwheat waffles because you'll be too sick of us to join us at the main table, and then after breakfast I'll come hang out with you and hide from Oberon and Miranda, who're going to want me to make intelligent and supportive comments about their latest endeavors." Willem grinned at him, and he smiled back, though he could see that Philippa herself wasn't smiling any longer, but staring at the table. Then she looked up, and their eyes met for half a second, and she looked away, quickly.

It was shortly after that, he thought, that Philippa's attitude toward him changed. It wasn't obvious to anyone but him—perhaps not even to her—but where he used to come into the apartment and see her sketching at the table and the two of them were able to talk, companionably, as he drank a glass of water and looked at her drawings, she would now just nod at him and say, "Willem's at the store," or "He's coming back soon," even though he hadn't asked (she was always welcome at Lispenard Street, whether Willem was there or not), and he would linger a bit until it was clear she didn't want to speak, and then retreat to his room to work.

He understood why Philippa might resent him: Willem invited him everywhere with them, included him in everything, even in their retirement, even in Philippa's daydream of their old age. After that, he was careful to always decline Willem's invitations, even if it was to things that didn't involve his and Philippa's couplehood—if they were going to a party at Malcolm's to which he was also invited, he'd leave separately, and at Thanksgiving, he made sure to ask Philippa to Boston as well, though she hadn't come in the end. He had even tried to talk to Willem about what he sensed, to awaken him to what he was certain she was feeling.

"Do you not like her?" Willem had asked him, concerned.

"You know I like Philippa," he'd replied. "But I think—I think you should just hang out with her more alone, Willem, with just the two of you. It must get annoying for her to always have me around."

"Did she *say* that to you?"

"No, Willem, of course not. I'm just guessing. From my vast experience with women, you know."

Later, when Willem and Philippa broke up, he would feel as guilty as if he had been solely to blame. But even before that, he had wondered whether Willem, too, had come to realize that no serious girlfriend would tolerate his constant presence in Willem's life; he wondered whether Willem was trying to make alternative plans for him, so he *didn't* end up living in a cottage on the property he'd someday have with his wife, so he wouldn't be Willem's sad bachelor friend, a useless reminder of his forsaken, childish life. *I will be alone,* he decided. He wouldn't be the one to ruin Willem's chances for happiness: he *wanted* Willem to have the orchard and the termite-nibbled house and the grandchildren and the wife who was jealous of his company and attention. He wanted Willem to have everything he deserved, everything he desired. He wanted every day of his to be free of worries and obligations and responsibilities—even if that worry and obligation and responsibility was him.

The following week, Richard's father—a tall, smiling, pleasant man

he'd met at Richard's first show, three years ago—sent him the contract, which he had a law school classmate, a real estate lawyer, review
in tandem with him, and the building's engineering report, which he
gave to Malcolm. The price had almost nauseated him, but his classmate said he had to do it: "This is an unbelievable deal, Jude. You will
never, never, never find something that size in that neighborhood for
this amount of money." And after reviewing the report, and then the
space, Malcolm told him the same thing: Buy it.

So he did. And although he and the Goldfarbs had worked out a
leisurely ten-year payment schedule, an interest-free rent-to-own plan,
he was determined to pay the apartment off as soon as he could. Every
two weeks, he allotted half of his paycheck to the apartment, and the
other half to his savings and living expenses. He told Harold he had
moved during their weekly phone call ("Thank *Christ*," Harold said:
he had never liked Lispenard Street), but didn't tell him he had bought
a place, because he didn't want Harold to feel obligated to offer him
money for it. From Lispenard Street he brought only his mattress and
lamp and the table and a chair, all of which he arranged into one corner of the space. At nights, he would sometimes look up from his work
and think what a ludicrous decision this had been: How could he ever
fill so much room? How would it ever feel like his? He was reminded
of Boston, of Hereford Street, and how there, he had dreamed only of
a bedroom, of a door he might someday close. Even when he was in
Washington, clerking for Sullivan, he had slept in the living room of a
one-bedroom apartment he shared with a legislative assistant whom he
rarely saw—Lispenard Street had been the first time in his life that he'd
had a room, a real room with a real window, wholly to himself. But a
year after he moved into Greene Street, Malcolm installed the walls,
and the place began to feel a little more comfortable, and the year
after that, Willem moved in, and it felt more comfortable still. He saw
less of Richard than he thought he might—they were both traveling
frequently—but on Sunday evenings, he would sometimes go down to
his studio and help him with one of his projects, polishing a bunch of
small branches smooth with a leaf of sandpaper, or snipping the rachis
off the vane from a fluff of peacock feathers. Richard's studio was the
sort of place he would have loved as a child—everywhere were containers and bowls of marvelous things: twigs and stones and dried beetles
and feathers and tiny, bright-hued taxidermied birds and blocks in vari-

ous shapes made of some soft pale wood—and at times he wished he could be allowed to abandon his work and simply sit on the floor and play, which he had usually been too busy to do as a boy.

By the end of the third year, he had paid for the apartment, and had immediately begun saving for the renovation. This took less time than he'd thought it would, in part because of something that had happened with Andy. He'd gone uptown one day for his appointment, and Andy had walked in, looking grim and yet oddly triumphant.

"What?" he'd asked, and Andy had silently handed him a magazine article he'd sliced out of a journal. He read it: it was an academic report about how a recently developed semi-experimental laser surgery that had held great promise as a solution for damageless keloid removal was now proven to have adverse medium-term effects: although the keloids were eliminated, patients instead developed raw, burn-like wounds, and the skin beneath the scars became significantly more fragile, more susceptible to splitting and cracking, which resulted in blisters and infection.

"This is what you're thinking of doing, isn't it?" Andy asked him, as he sat holding the pages in his hand, unable to speak. "I *know* you, Judy. And I know you made an appointment at that quack Thompson's office. Don't deny it; they called for your chart. I didn't send it. Please don't do this, Jude. I'm serious. The last thing you need are open wounds on your back as well as your legs." And then, when he didn't say anything, "Talk to me."

He shook his head. Andy was right: he had been saving for this as well. Like his annual bonuses and most of his savings, all the money he'd made long ago from tutoring Felix had been given over to the apartment, but in recent months, as it was clear he was closing in on his final payments, he had begun saving anew for the surgery. He had it all worked out: he'd have the surgery and then he'd finish saving for the renovation. He had visions of it—his back made as smooth as the floors themselves, the thick, unbudgeable worm trail of scars vaporized in seconds, and with it, all evidence of his time in the home and in Philadelphia, the documentation of those years erased from his body. He tried so hard to forget, he tried every day, but as much as he tried, there it was to remind him, proof that what he pretended hadn't happened, actually had.

"Jude," Andy said, sitting next to him on the examining table. "I know you're disappointed. And I promise you that when there's a treatment available that's both effective and safe, I'll let you know. I know it bothers you; I'm always looking out for something for you. But right now there isn't anything, and I can't in good conscience let you do this to yourself." He was quiet; they both were. "I suppose I should have asked you this more frequently, Jude, but—do they hurt you? Do they cause you any discomfort? Does the skin feel tight?"

He nodded. "Look, Jude," Andy said after a pause. "There are some creams I can give you that'll help with that, but you're going to need someone to help massage them in nightly, or it's not going to be effective. Would you let someone do this for you? Willem? Richard?"

"I can't," he said, speaking to the magazine article in his hands.

"Well," said Andy. "I'll write you a scrip anyway, and I'll show you how to do it—don't worry, I asked an actual dermatologist, this isn't some method I've made up—but I can't say how efficacious it's going to be on your own." He slid off the table. "Will you open your gown for me and turn toward the wall?"

He did, and felt Andy's hands on his shoulders, and then moving slowly across his back. He thought Andy might say, as he sometimes did, "It's not so bad, Jude," or "You don't have anything to be self-conscious about," but this time he didn't, just trailed his hands across him, as if his palms were themselves lasers, something that was hovering over him and healing him, the skin beneath them turning healthy and unmarked. Finally Andy told him he could cover himself again, and he did, and turned back around. "I'm really sorry, Jude," Andy said, and this time, it was Andy who couldn't look at him.

"Do you want to grab something to eat?" Andy asked after the appointment was over, as he was putting his clothes back on, but he shook his head: "I should go back to the office." Andy was quiet then, but as he was leaving, he stopped him. "Jude," he said, "I really am sorry. I don't like being the one who has to destroy your hopes." He nodded—he knew Andy didn't—but in that moment, he couldn't stand being around him, and wanted only to get away.

However, he reminds himself—he is determined to be more realistic, to stop thinking he can make himself better—the fact that he can't get this surgery means he now has the money for Malcolm to begin the renovation in earnest. Over the years he has owned the apartment, he has witnessed Malcolm grow both bolder and more imaginative in his work, and so the plans he drew when he first bought the place have been changed and revised and improved upon multiple times: in them, he can see the development of what even he can recognize as an aesthetic confidence, a self-assured idiosyncrasy. Shortly before he began working at Rosen Pritchard and Klein, Malcolm had quit his job at Ratstar, and with two of his former colleagues and Sophie, an acquaintance of his from architecture school, had founded a firm called Bellcast; their first commission had been the renovation of the pied-à-terre of one of Malcolm's parents' friends. Bellcast did mostly residential work, but last year they had been awarded their first significant public commission, for a photography museum in Doha, and Malcolm—like Willem, like himself—was absent from the city more and more frequently.

"Never underestimate the importance of having rich parents, I guess," some asshole at one of JB's parties had grumbled, sourly, when he heard that Bellcast had been the runners-up in a competition to design a memorial in Los Angeles for Japanese Americans who had been interned in the war, and JB had started shouting at him before he and Willem had a chance; the two of them had smiled at each other over JB's head, proud of him for defending Malcolm so vehemently.

And so he has watched as, with each new revised blueprint for Greene Street, hallways have materialized and then vanished, and the kitchen has grown larger and then smaller, and bookcases have gone from stretching along the northern wall, which has no windows, to the southern wall, which does, and then back again. One of the renderings eliminated walls altogether—"It's a *loft*, Judy, and you should respect its integrity," Malcolm had argued with him, but he had been firm: he needed a bedroom; he needed a door he could close and lock—and in another, Malcolm had tried to block up the southern-facing windows entirely, which had been the reason he had chosen the sixth-floor unit to begin with, and which Malcolm later admitted had been an idiotic idea. But he enjoys watching Malcolm work, is touched that he has spent so much time—more than he himself has—thinking about how he might live. And now it is going to happen. Now he has enough saved for Malcolm to indulge even his most outlandish design fantasies. Now he has enough for every piece of furniture Malcolm has ever suggested he might get, for every carpet and vase.

These days, he argues with Malcolm about his most recent plans. The last time they reviewed the sketches, three months ago, he had noticed an element around the toilet in the master bathroom that he couldn't identify. "What's that?" he'd asked Malcolm.

"Grab bars," Malcolm said, briskly, as if by saying it quickly it would become less significant. "Judy, I know what you're going to say, but—" But he was already examining the blueprints more closely, peering at Malcolm's tiny notations in the bathroom, where he'd added steel bars in the shower and around the bathtub as well, and in the kitchen, where he'd lowered the height of some of the countertops.

"But I'm not even in a wheelchair," he'd said, dismayed.

"But Jude," Malcolm had begun, and then stopped. He knew what Malcolm wanted to say: *But you have been. And you will be again.* But he didn't. "These are standard ADA guidelines," he said instead.

"Mal," he'd said, chagrined by how upset he was. "I understand. But I don't want this to be some cripple's apartment."

"It won't be, Jude. It'll be yours. But don't you think, maybe, just as a precaution—"

"No, Malcolm. Get rid of them. I mean it."

"But don't you think, just as a matter of practicality—"

"*Now* you're interested in practicalities? The man who wanted me to live in a five-thousand-square-foot space with no walls?" He stopped. "I'm sorry, Mal."

"It's okay, Jude," Malcolm said. "I understand. I do."

Now, Malcolm stands before him, grinning. "I have something to show you," he says, waving the baton of rolled-up paper in his hand.

"Malcolm, thank you," he says. "But should we look at them later?" He'd had to schedule an appointment with the tailor; he doesn't want to be late.

"It'll be fast," Malcolm says, "and I'll leave them with you." He sits next to him and smooths out the sheaf of pages, giving him one end to hold, explaining things he's changed and tweaked. "Counters back up to standard height," says Malcolm, pointing at the kitchen. "No grab bars in the shower area, but I gave you this ledge that you can use as a seat, just in case. I swear it'll look nice. I kept the ones around the toilet—just think about it, okay? We'll install them last, and if you really, really hate them, we'll leave them off, but . . . but I'd do it, Judy." He nods, reluctantly. He won't know it then, but years later, he will be grateful that Malcolm has prepared for his future, even when he hadn't wanted to: he will notice that in his apartment, the passages are wider, that the bathroom and kitchen are oversize, so a wheelchair can make a full, clean revolution in them, that the doorways are generous, that wherever possible, the doors slide instead of swing, that there is no cabinetry under the master bathroom sink, that the highest-placed closet rods lower with the touch of a pneumatic button, that there is a bench-like seat in the bathtub, and, finally, that Malcolm won the fight about the grab bars around the toilet. He'll feel a sort of bitter wonderment that yet another person in his life—Andy, Willem, Richard, and now Malcolm—had foreseen his future, and knew how inevitable it was.

After their appointment, where Malcolm is measured for a navy suit and a dark gray one, and where Franklin, the tailor, greets him and asks why he hasn't seen him for two years—"I'm pretty sure that's my fault," Malcolm says, smiling—they have lunch. It's nice taking a Saturday off, he thinks, as they drink rosewater lemonade and eat za'atar-dusted roasted cauliflower at the crowded Israeli restaurant near Franklin's shop. Malcolm is excited to start work on the apartment, and he is, too. "This is such perfect timing," Malcolm keeps saying. "I'll have the office submit everything to the city on Monday, and by the time it's approved, I'll be done with Doha and be able to get started right away, and you can move into Willem's while it's being done." Malcolm has just finished the final pieces of work on Willem's apartment, which he has supervised more of than Willem has; by the end of the process, he was making decisions for Willem on paint colors. Malcolm did a beautiful job, he thinks; he won't mind at all staying there for the next year.

It is early when they finish lunch, and they linger on the sidewalk outside. For the past week it's been raining, but today the skies are blue and he is still feeling strong, and even a little restless, and he asks Malcolm if he wants to walk for a bit. He can see Malcolm hesitate, flicking his gaze up and down his body as if trying to determine how capable he is, but then he smiles and agrees, and the two of them start heading west, and then north, toward the Village. They pass the building on Mulberry Street that JB used to live in before he moved farther east, and they are quiet for a minute, both of them, he knows, thinking about JB and wondering what he's doing, and knowing but also not knowing why he hasn't answered their and Willem's calls, their texts, their e-mails. The three of them have had dozens of conversations with one another, with Richard, with Ali and the Henry Youngs about what to do, but with every attempt they have made to find JB, he has eluded them, or barred their way, or ignored them. "We just have to wait until it gets worse," Richard had said at one point, and he fears that Richard is correct. It is, sometimes, as if JB is no longer theirs at all, and they can do nothing but wait for the moment in which he will have a crisis only they can solve, and they will be able to parachute into his life once again.

"Okay, Malcolm, I've got to ask you," he says, as they walk up the stretch of Hudson Street that is deserted on the weekends, its sidewalks treeless and empty of people, "are you getting married to Sophie or not? We all want to know."

"God, Jude, I just don't know," Malcolm begins, but he sounds relieved, as if he's been waiting to be asked the question all along. Maybe he has. He lists the potential negatives (marriage is so conventional; it feels so permanent; he's not really interested in the idea of a wedding but fears Sophie is; his parents are going to try to get involved; something about spending the rest of his life with another architect depresses him; he and Sophie are cofounders of the firm—if something happens between them, what will happen to Bellcast?) and the positives, which also sound like negatives (if he doesn't propose, he thinks Sophie will leave; his parents have been bothering him about it nonstop and he'd like to shut them up; he really does love Sophie, and knows he won't be able to do better than her; he's thirty-eight, and feels he has to do *something*). As he listens to Malcolm, he tries not to smile: he has always liked this about Malcolm, how he can be so decisive on the page and in his designs, and yet in the rest of his life so in a dither, and so unself-conscious about sharing it. Malcolm has never been someone who pretended he was cooler, or more confident, or silkier than he actually is, and as they grow older, he appreciates and admires more and more his sweet guilelessness, his complete trust in his friends and their opinions.

"What do you think, Jude?" Malcolm asks at last. "I've actually really wanted to talk to you about this. Should we sit down somewhere? Do you have time? I know Willem's on his way back home."

He could be more like Malcolm, he thinks; he could ask his friends for help, he could be vulnerable around them. He has been before, after all; it just hasn't been by choice. But they have always been kind to him, they have never tried to make him feel self-conscious—shouldn't that teach him something? Maybe, for instance, he *will* ask Willem if he could help him with his back: if Willem is disgusted by his appearance, he'll never say anything. And Andy was right—it is too difficult to apply the creams by himself, and eventually he stopped, although he didn't throw any of them away, either.

He tries to think how he might begin the conversation with Willem, but he finds he can't move beyond the first word—*Willem*—even in his imaginings. And in that moment, he knows he won't be able to ask Willem after all: *Not because I don't trust you*, he says to Willem, with whom he will never have this conversation. *But because I can't bear to have you see me as I really am.* Now when he imagines himself as an old man, he is still alone, but on Greene Street, and in these wanderings, he sees Willem in a house somewhere green and tree-filled—the Adirondacks, the Berkshires—and Willem is happy, he is surrounded by people who love him, and maybe a few times a year he comes into the city to visit him on Greene Street, and they spend the afternoon together. In these dreams, he is always sitting down, so he's uncertain if he can still walk or not, but he knows that he is delighted to see Willem, always, and that at the end of all their meetings, he is able to tell him not to worry, that he can take care of himself, giving him that assurance like a benediction, pleased that he has had the strength to not spoil Willem's idyll with his needs, his loneliness, his wants.

But that, he reminds himself, is many years in the future. Right now there is Malcolm, and his hopeful, anxious face, waiting to hear his reply.

"He's not back until this evening," he tells Malcolm. "We've got all afternoon, Mal. I've got as much time as you need."

3

THE LAST TIME JB tried—really tried—to stop doing drugs, it was Fourth of July weekend. No one else was in the city. Malcolm was with Sophie visiting her parents in Hamburg. Jude was with Harold and Julia in Copenhagen. Willem was shooting in Cappadocia. Richard was in Wyoming, at an artists' colony. Asian Henry Young was in Reykjavík. Only he remained, and if he hadn't been so determined, he wouldn't have been in town, either. He'd have been in Beacon, where Richard had a house, or in Quogue, where Ezra had a house, or in Woodstock, where Ali had a house, or—well. There weren't that many other people who would give him their house nowadays, and besides, he wasn't talking to most of them because they were getting on his nerves. But he hated summer in New York. All fat people hated summer in New York: everything was always sticking to everything else, flesh to flesh, flesh to fabric. You never felt truly dry. And yet there he was, unlocking the door of his studio on the third floor of the white brick building in Kensington, glancing involuntarily toward the end of the hall, where Jackson's studio was, before he let himself in.

JB was not an addict. Yes, he did drugs. Yes, he did a lot of them. But he wasn't an addict. Other people were addicts. Jackson was an addict. So was Zane, and so was Hera. Massimo and Topher: also addicts. Sometimes it felt like he was the only one who hadn't slipped over the edge.

And yet he knew that a lot of people thought he had, which is why he was still in the city when he should be in the country: four days, no drugs, only work—and then no one would be able to say anything ever again.

Today, Friday, was day one. The air-conditioning unit in his studio was broken, so the first thing he did was open all the windows and then, once he had knocked, lightly, on Jackson's door to make sure he wasn't inside, the door as well. Normally he never opened the door, both because of Jackson and because of the noise. His studio was one of fourteen rooms on the third floor of a five-story building. The rooms were meant to be used only as studio space, but he guessed about twenty percent of the building's occupants actually lived there illegally. On the rare occasions he had arrived at his studio before ten in the morning, he would see people shuffling through the corridors in their boxers, and when he went to the bathroom at the end of the hall, there'd be someone in there taking a sponge bath in the sink or shaving or brushing his teeth, and he'd nod at them—"Whassup, man?"—and they'd nod back. Sadly, however, the overall effect was less collegiate and more institutional. This depressed him. JB could have found studio space elsewhere, better, more private studio space, but he'd taken this one because (he was embarrassed to admit) the building looked like a dormitory, and he hoped it might feel like college again. But it didn't.

The building was also supposed to be a "low noise density" site, whatever that meant, but along with the artists, a number of bands— ironic thrasher bands, ironic folk bands, ironic acoustic bands—had also rented studios there, which meant that the hallway was always jumbled with noise, all of the bands' instruments melding together to make one long whine of guitar feedback. The bands weren't supposed to be there, and once every few months, when the owner of the building, a Mr. Chen, stopped by for a surprise inspection, he would hear the shouts bouncing through the hallways, even through his closed door, each person's call of alarm echoed by the next, until the warning had saturated all five floors—"Chen!" "Chen!" "Chen!"—so by the time Mr. Chen stepped inside the front door, all was quiet, so unnaturally quiet that he imagined he could hear his next-door neighbor grinding his inks against his whetstone, and his other neighbor's spirograph skritching against canvas. And then Mr. Chen would get into his car and drive away, and the echoes would reverse themselves—"Clear!" "Clear!" "Clear!"—and the cacophony would rise up again, like a flock of screeching cicadas.

Once he was certain he was alone on the floor (god, where *was* everyone? Was he truly the last person left on earth?), he took off his shirt and then, after a moment, his pants, and began cleaning his studio, which he hadn't done in months. Back and forth he walked to the trash cans near the service elevator, stuffing them full of old pizza boxes and empty beer cans and scraps of paper with doodles on them and brushes whose bristles had gone strawlike because he hadn't cleaned them and palettes of watercolors that had turned to clay because he hadn't kept them moist.

Cleaning was boring; it was particularly boring while sober. He reflected, as he sometimes did, that none of the supposedly good things that were supposed to happen to you when you were on meth had happened to him. Other people he knew had grown gaunt, or had nonstop anonymous sex, or had binges in which they cleaned or organized their apartments or studios for hours. But he remained fat. His sex drive had vanished. His studio and apartment remained disasters. True, he was working remarkably long stretches—twelve, fourteen hours at a time— but he couldn't attribute that to the meth: he had always been a hard worker. When it came to painting or drawing, he had always had a long attention span.

After an hour or so of picking things up, the studio looked exactly the same as it had when he began, and he was craving a cigarette, which he didn't have, or a drink, which he also didn't have, and shouldn't have anyway, as it was still only noon. He knew he had a ball of gum in his jeans pocket, which he dug around for and found—it was slightly damp from the heat—and stuffed into his mouth, chewing it as he lay supine, his eyes closed, the cement floor cool beneath his back and thighs, pretending he was elsewhere, not in Brooklyn in July in the ninety-degree heat.

How am I feeling? he asked himself.

Okay, he answered himself.

The shrink he had started seeing had told him to ask himself that. "It's like a soundcheck," he'd said. "Just a way to check in with yourself: How am I feeling? Do I want to use? If I *do* want to use, *why* do I want to use? It's a way for you to communicate with yourself, to examine your impulses instead of simply giving in to them." What a moron, JB had thought. He still thought this. And yet, like many moronic things, he was unable to expunge the question from his memory. Now, at odd, unwelcome moments, he would find himself asking himself how he felt. Sometimes, the answer was, "Like I want to do drugs," and so he'd do them, if only to illustrate to his therapist just how moronic his method was. *See?* he'd say to Giles in his head, Giles who wasn't even a PhD, just an MSW. *So much for your self-examination theory. What else, Giles? What's next?*

Seeing Giles had not been JB's idea. Six months ago, in January, his mother and aunts had had a mini-intervention with him, which had begun with his mother sharing memories of what a bright and precocious boy JB had been, and look at him now, and then his aunt Christine, literally playing bad cop, yelling at him about how he was wasting all the opportunities that her sister had provided him and how he had become a huge pain in the ass, and then his aunt Silvia, who had always been the gentlest of the three, reminding him that he was so talented, and that they all wanted him back, and wouldn't he consider getting treatment? He had not been in the mood for an intervention, even one as low-key and cozy as theirs had been (his mother had provided his favorite cheesecake, which they all ate as they discussed his flaws), because, among other things, he was still angry at them. The month before, his grandmother had died, and his mother had taken a whole day to call him. She claimed it was because she couldn't find him and he wasn't picking up his phone, but he *knew* that the day she had died he had been sober, and his phone had been on all day, and so he wasn't sure why his mother was lying to him.

"JB, Grandma would have been heartbroken if she knew what you've become," his mother said to him.

"God, Ma, just fuck off," he'd said, wearily, sick of her wailing and quivering, and Christine had popped up and slapped him across the face.

After that, he'd agreed to go see Giles (some friend of a friend of Silvia's) as a way of apologizing to Christine and, of course, to his mother. Unfortunately, Giles truly was an idiot, and during their sessions (paid for by his mother: he wasn't going to waste his money on therapy, especially bad therapy), he would answer Giles's uninventive questions—*Why do you think you're so attracted to drugs, JB? What do you feel they give you? Why do you think your use of them has accelerated so much over the past few years? Why do you think you're not talking to Malcolm and Jude and Willem as much?*—with answers he knew would excite him. He would slip in mentions of his dead father, of the great emptiness and sense of loss his absence had inspired in him, of the shallowness of the art world, of his fears that he would never fulfill his promise, and watch Giles's pen bob ecstatically over his pad, and feel both disdain for stupid Giles as well as disgust for his own immaturity. Fucking with one's therapist—even if one's therapist truly deserved to be fucked with—was the sort of thing you did when you were nineteen, not when you were thirty-nine.

But although Giles was an idiot, JB did find himself thinking about his questions, because they were questions that he had asked himself as well. And although Giles posed each as a discrete quandary, he knew that in reality each one was inseparable from the last, and that if it had been grammatically and linguistically possible to ask all of them together in one big question, then that would be the truest expression of why he was where he was.

First, he'd say to Giles, he hadn't set out to like drugs as much as he did. That sounded like an obvious and even silly thing to say, but the truth was that JB knew people—mostly rich, mostly white, mostly boring, mostly unloved by their parents—who had in fact started taking drugs because they thought it might make them more interesting, or more frightening, or more commanding of attention, or simply because it made the time go faster. His friend Jackson, for example, was one of those people. But he was not. Of course, he had always done drugs—everyone had—but in college, and in his twenties, he had thought of drugs the way he thought of desserts, which he also loved: a consumable that had been forbidden to him as a child and which was now freely available. Doing drugs, like having post-dinner snacks of cereal so throat-singeingly sweet that the leftover milk in the bowl could be slurped down like sugarcane juice, was a privilege of adulthood, one he intended to enjoy.

Questions two and three: When and why had drugs become so important to him? He knew the answers to those as well. When he was thirty-two, he'd had his first show. Two things had happened after that show: The first was that he had become, genuinely, a star. There were articles written about him in the art press, and articles written about him in magazines and newspapers read by people who wouldn't know their Sue Williams from their Sue Coe. And the second was that his friendship with Jude and Willem had been ruined.

Perhaps "ruined" was too strong a word. But it had changed. He had done something bad—he could admit it—and Willem had taken Jude's side (and why should he have been surprised at all that Willem had taken Jude's side, because really, when he reviewed their entire friendship, there was the evidence: time after time after time of Willem always taking Jude's side), and although they both said they forgave him, something had shifted in their relationship. The two of them, Jude and Willem, had become their own unit, united against everyone, united against him (why had he never seen this before?): *We two form a multitude.* And yet he had always thought that *he* and Willem had been a unit.

But all right, they weren't. So who was he left with? Not Malcolm, because Malcolm had eventually started dating Sophie, and they made their own unit. And so who would be his partner, who would make his unit? No one, it often seemed. They had abandoned him.

And then, with each year, they abandoned him further. He had always known he would be the first among the four of them to be a success. This wasn't arrogance: he just knew it. He worked harder than Malcolm, he was more ambitious than Willem. (He didn't count Jude in this race, as Jude's profession was one that operated on an entirely different set of metrics, one that didn't much matter to him.) He was prepared to be the rich one, or the famous one, or the respected one, and he knew, even as he was dreaming about his riches and fame and respect, that he would remain friends with all of them, that he would never forsake them for anyone else, no matter how overwhelming the temptation might be. He loved them; they were his.

But he hadn't counted on *them* abandoning *him*, on them outgrowing him through their own accomplishments. Malcolm had his own business. Jude was doing whatever he did impressively enough so that when he was representing JB in a silly argument he'd had the previous spring with a collector he was trying to sue to reclaim an early painting that the collector had promised he could buy back and then reneged on, the collector's lawyer had raised his eyebrows when JB had told him to contact his lawyer, Jude St. Francis. "St. Francis?" asked the opposing lawyer. "How'd you get *him?*" He told Black Henry Young about this, who wasn't surprised. "Oh yeah," he said. "Jude's known for being icy, and vicious. He'll get it for you, JB, don't worry." This had startled him: *His* Jude? Someone who literally hadn't been able to lift his head and look him in the eye until their sophomore year? *Vicious?* He simply couldn't imagine it. "I know," said Black Henry Young, when he expressed his disbelief. "But he becomes someone else at work, JB; I saw him in court once and he was borderline frightening, just incredibly relentless. If I hadn't known him, I'd've thought he was a giant asshole." But Black Henry Young had turned out to be right—he got his painting back, and not only that, but he got a letter of apology from the collector as well.

And then, of course, there was Willem. The horrible, petty part of him had to admit that he had never, ever expected Willem to be as successful as he was. Not that he hadn't wanted it for him—he had just never thought it would happen. Willem, with his lack of competitive spirit; Willem, with his deliberateness; Willem, who in college had turned down a starring role in *Look Back in Anger* to go tend to his sick brother. On the one hand, he had understood it, and on the other hand—his brother hadn't been fatally ill, not then; even his own mother had told him not to come—he hadn't. Where once his friends had needed him—for color, for excitement—they no longer did. He didn't like to think of himself as someone who wanted his friends to be, well, not unsuccessful, but in thrall to him, but maybe he was.

The thing he hadn't realized about success was that success made people boring. Failure also made people boring, but in a different way: failing people were constantly striving for one thing—success. But successful people were also only striving to maintain their success. It was the difference between running and running in place, and although running was boring no matter what, at least the person running was moving, through different scenery and past different vistas. And yet here again, it seemed that Jude and Willem had something he didn't, something that was protecting them from the suffocating ennui of being successful, from the tedium of waking up and realizing that you were a success and that every day you had to keep doing whatever it was that made you a success, because once you stopped, you were no longer a success, you were becoming a failure. He sometimes thought that the real thing that distinguished him and Malcolm from Jude and Willem was not race or wealth, but Jude's and Willem's depthless capacity for wonderment: their childhoods had been so paltry, so gray, compared to his, that it seemed they were constantly being dazzled as adults. The June after they graduated, the Irvines had gotten them all tickets to

Paris, where, it emerged, they had an apartment—"a *tiny* apartment," Malcolm had clarified, defensively—in the seventh. He had been to Paris with his mother in junior high, and again with his class in high school, and between his sophomore and junior years of college, but it wasn't until he had seen Jude's and Willem's faces that he was able to most vividly realize not just the beauty of the city but its promise of enchantments. He envied this in them, this ability they had (though he realized that in Jude's case at least, it was a reward for a long and punitive childhood) to still be awestruck, the faith they maintained that life, adulthood, would keep presenting them with astonishing experiences, that their marvelous years were not behind them. He remembered too watching them try uni for the first time, and their reactions—like they were Helen Keller and were just comprehending that that cool splash on their hands had a name, and that they could know it—made him both impatient and intensely envious. What must it feel like to be an adult and still discovering the world's pleasures?

And that, he sometimes felt, was why he loved being high so much: not because it offered an escape from everyday life, as so many people thought, but because it made everyday life seem less everyday. For a brief period—briefer and briefer with each week—the world was splendid and unknown.

At other times, he wondered whether it was the world that had lost its color, or his friends themselves. When had everyone become so alike? Too often, it seemed that the last time people were so interesting had been college; grad school. And then they had, slowly but inevitably, become like everyone else. Take the members of Backfat: in school, they had marched topless, the three of them fat and luscious and jiggly, all the way down the Charles to protest cutbacks to Planned Parenthood (no one had been sure how the toplessness had been relevant, but whatever), and played amazing sets in the Hood Hall basement, and lit an effigy of an antifeminist state senator on fire in the Quad. But now Francesca and Marta were talking about having babies, and moving from their Bushwick loft into a Boerum Hill brownstone, and Edie was actually, actually starting a business for real this time, and last year, when he'd suggested they stage a Backfat reunion, they had all laughed, although he hadn't been joking. His persistent nostalgia depressed him, aged him, and yet he couldn't stop feeling that the most glorious years, the years when everything seemed drawn in fluorescents, were gone. Everyone had been so much more entertaining then. What had happened?

Age, he guessed. And with it: Jobs. Money. Children. The things to forestall death, the things to ensure one's relevance, the things to comfort and provide context and content. The march forward, one dictated by biology and convention, that not even the most irreverent mind could withstand.

But those were his peers. What he really wanted to know was when his *friends* had become so conventional, and why he hadn't noticed earlier. Malcolm had always been conventional, of course, but he had expected, somehow, more from Willem and Jude. He knew how awful this sounded (and so he never said it aloud), but he often thought that he had been cursed with a happy childhood. What if, instead, something actually interesting had happened to him? As it was, the only interesting thing that had happened to him was that he had attended a mostly white prep school, and that wasn't even interesting. Thank god he wasn't a writer, or he'd have had nothing to write about. And then there was someone like Jude, who *hadn't* grown up like everyone else, and *didn't* look like everyone else, and yet who JB knew was constantly trying to make himself exactly like everyone else. He would have taken Willem's looks, of course, but he would have killed something small and adorable to have looked like Jude, to have had a mysterious limp that was really more of a glide and to have the face and body that he did. But Jude spent most of his time trying to stand still and look down, as if by doing so, no one would notice he existed. This had been sad and yet somewhat understandable in college, when Jude had been so childlike and bony that it made JB's joints hurt to look at him, but these days, now that he'd grown into his looks, JB found it simply enraging, especially as Jude's self-consciousness often interfered with his own plans.

"Do you want to spend your life just being completely average and boring and typical?" he'd once asked Jude (this was during their second big fight, when he was trying to get Jude to pose nude, an argument he'd known even before he'd begun it that he had no chance at all of winning).

"Yes, JB," Jude had said, giving him that gaze he sometimes summoned, which was intimidating, even slightly scary, in its flat blankness. "That's in fact exactly what I want."

Sometimes he suspected that all Jude really wanted to do in life was hang out in Cambridge with Harold and Julia and play house with them. Last year, for example, JB had been invited on a cruise by one of his collectors, a hugely wealthy and important patron who had a yacht that plied the Greek islands and that was hung with modern master-pieces that any museum would have been happy to own—only they were installed in the bathroom of a boat.

Malcolm had been working on his project in Doha, or somewhere, but Willem and Jude had been in town, and he'd called Jude and asked him if he wanted to go: The collector would pay their way. He would send his plane. It would be five days on a yacht. He didn't know why he even needed to have a conversation. "Meet me at Teterboro," he should've just texted them. "Bring sunscreen."

But no, he had asked, and Jude had thanked him. And then Jude had said, "But that's over Thanksgiving."

"So?" he'd asked.

"JB, thank you so much for inviting me," Jude had said, as he listened in disbelief. "It sounds incredible. But I have to go to Harold and Julia's."

He had been gobsmacked by this. Of course, he too was very fond of Harold and Julia, and like the others, he too could see how good they were for Jude, and how he'd become slightly less haunted with their friendship, but come on! It was *Boston*. He could always see them. But Jude said no, and that was that. (And then, of course, because Jude said no, Willem had said no as well, and in the end, he had ended up with the two of them and Malcolm in Boston, seething at the scene around the table—parental stand-ins; friends of the parental stand-ins; lots of mediocre food; liberals having arguments with one another about Democratic politics that involved a lot of shouting about issues *they all agreed on*—that was so clichéd and generic that he wanted to scream and yet held such bizarre fascination for Jude and Willem.)

So which had come first: becoming close to Jackson or realizing how boring his friends were? He had met Jackson after the opening of his second show, which had come almost five years after his first. The show was called "Everyone I've Ever Known Everyone I've Ever Loved Everyone I've Ever Hated Everyone I've Ever Fucked" and was exactly that: a hundred and fifty fifteen-by-twenty-two-inch paintings on thin pieces of board of the faces of everyone he had ever known. The series had been inspired by a painting he had done of Jude and given to Harold and Julia on the day of Jude's adoption. (God, he loved that painting. He should have just kept it. Or he should have exchanged it: Harold and Julia would've been happy with a less-superior piece, as long as it was of Jude. The last time he had been in Cambridge, he had seriously considered stealing it, slipping it off its hook in the hallway and stuffing it into his duffel bag before he left.) Once again, "Everyone I've Ever Known" was a success, although it hadn't been the series he had wanted to do; the series he had wanted to do was the series he was working on now.

Jackson was another of the gallery's artists, and although JB had known of him, he had never actually met him before, and was surprised, after being introduced to him at the dinner after the opening, how much he had liked him, how unexpectedly funny he was, because Jackson was not the type of person he'd normally gravitate toward. For one thing, he hated, really hated Jackson's work: he made found sculptures, but of the most puerile and obvious sort, like a Barbie doll's legs glued to the bottom of a can of tuna fish. Oh god, he'd thought, the first time he'd seen that on the gallery's website. *He's* being represented by the same gallery as I am? He didn't even consider it art. He considered it provocation, although only a high-school student—no, a junior-high student—would consider it provocative. Jackson thought the pieces Kienholzian, which offended JB, and he didn't even like Kienholz.

For another, Jackson was rich: so rich that he had never worked a single day in his life. So rich that his gallerist had agreed to represent him (or so everyone said, and god, he hoped it was true) as a favor to Jackson's father. So rich that his shows sold out because, it was rumored, his mother—who had divorced Jackson's father, a manufacturer of some sort of essential widget of airplane machinery, when Jackson was young and married an inventor of some sort of essential widget of heart transplant surgeries—bought out all his shows and then auctioned the pieces, driving up the prices and then buying them back, inflating Jackson's sales record. Unlike other rich people he knew—including Malcolm and Richard and Ezra—Jackson only rarely pretended not to be rich. JB had always found the others' parsimoniousness put-on and irritating, but seeing Jackson once smack down a hundred-dollar bill for two candy bars when they were both high and giggly and starving at three in the morning, telling the cashier to keep the change, had sobered him. There was something obscene about how careless Jackson was with money, something that reminded JB that as much as he thought of himself otherwise, he too was boring, and conventional, and his mother's son.

For a third, Jackson wasn't even good-looking. He supposed he was straight—at any rate, there were always girls around, girls whom Jackson treated disdainfully and yet who drifted after him, lint-like, their faces smooth and empty—but he was the least sexy person JB had ever met. Jackson had very pale hair, almost white, and pimple-stippled skin, and teeth that were clearly once expensive-looking but had gone the color of dust and whose gaps were grouted with butter-yellow tartar, the sight of which repulsed JB.

His friends hated Jackson, and as it became clear that Jackson and his own group of friends—lonely rich girls like Hera and sort-of artists like Massimo and alleged art writers like Zane, many of them Jackson's classmates from the loser day school he'd gone to after failing out of every other private school in New York, including the one that JB had attended—were in his life to stay, they all tried to talk to him about Jackson.

"You're always going on about what a phony Ezra is," Willem had said. "But how, exactly, is Jackson any different than Ezra, other than being a total fucking asshole?"

And Jackson *was* an asshole, and around him, JB was an asshole as well. A few months ago, the fourth or fifth time he'd tried to stop doing drugs, he had called Jude one day. It was five in the afternoon, and he'd just woken up, and he felt so awful, so incredibly old and exhausted and just *done*—his skin slimy, his teeth furry, his eyes dry as wood—that he had wanted, for the first time, to be dead, to simply not have to keep going on and on and on. *Something has to change*, he told himself. *I have to stop hanging around with Jackson. I have to stop. Everything has to stop.* He missed his friends, he missed how innocent and clean they were, he missed being the most interesting among them, he missed never having to try around them.

So he had called Jude (naturally, Willem wasn't fucking in town, and Malcolm couldn't be trusted not to freak out) and asked him, begged him, to come over after work. He told him where, exactly, the rest of the crystal was (under the loose half-plank of wood under the right side of the bed), and where his pipe was, and asked him to flush it down the toilet, to get rid of it all.

"JB," Jude had said. "Listen to me. Go to that café on Clinton, okay? Take your sketch pad. Get yourself something to eat. I'm coming down as soon as I can, as soon as this meeting's over. And then I'll text you when I'm done and you can come home, all right?"

"Okay," he'd said. And he'd stood up, and taken a very long shower, hardly scrubbing himself, just standing under the water, and then had done exactly what Jude had instructed: He picked up his sketch pad and pencils. He went to the café. He ate some of a chicken club sandwich and drank some coffee. And he waited.

And while he was waiting, he saw, passing the window like a bipedal mongoose, with his dirty hair and delicate chin, Jackson. He watched Jackson walk by, his self-satisfied, rich-boy lope, that pleased half smile on his face that made JB want to hit him, as detached as if Jackson was just someone ugly he saw on the street, not someone ugly he saw almost every day. And then, just before he passed out of sight, Jackson turned, and looked in the window, directly at him, and smiled his ugly smile, and reversed direction and walked back toward the café and through the door, as if he had known all along that JB was there, as if he had materialized only to remind JB that JB was his now, that there would be no escaping from him, that JB was there to do what Jackson wanted him to do when Jackson wanted him to do it, and that his life would never be his own again. For the first time, he had been scared of Jackson, and panicked. *What has happened?* he wondered. He was Jean-Baptiste Marion, *he* made the plans, people followed *him*, not the other way around. Jackson would never let him go, he realized, and he was frightened. He was someone else's; he was owned now. How would he ever become un-owned? How could he ever return to who he was?

" 'Sup," said Jackson, unsurprised to see him, as unsurprised as if he had willed JB into being.

What could he say? " 'Sup," he said.

Then his phone rang: Jude, telling him that all was safe, and he could come back. "I've got to go," he said, standing, and as he left, Jackson followed him.

He watched Jude's expression change as he saw Jackson by his side. "JB," he said, calmly, "I'm glad to see you. Are you ready to go?"

"Go where?" he asked, stupidly.

"Back to my place," said Jude. "You said you'd help me reach that box I can't get?"

But he was so confused, still so muddled, that he hadn't under-stood. "What box?"

"The box on the closet shelf that I can't reach," Jude said, still ignoring Jackson. "I need your help; it's too difficult for me to climb the ladder on my own."

He should've known, then; Jude never made references to what he couldn't do. He was offering him a way out, and he was too stupid to recognize it.

But Jackson did. "I think your friend wants to get you away from me," he told JB, smirking. That was what Jackson always called them, even though he had met them all before: *Your friends. JB's friends.*

Jude looked at him. "You're right," he said, still in that calm, steady voice. "I do." And then, turning back to him, "JB—won't you come with me?"

Oh, he wanted to. But in that moment, he couldn't. He wouldn't know why, not ever, but he couldn't. He was powerless, so powerless that he couldn't even pretend otherwise. "I can't," he whispered to Jude.

"JB," said Jude, and took his arm and pulled him toward the curb, as Jackson watched them with his stupid, mocking smile. "Come with me. You don't have to stay here. Come with me, JB."

He had started crying then, not loudly, not steadily, but crying nonetheless. "JB," Jude said again, his voice low. "Come with me. You don't have to go back there."

But "I can't," he heard himself saying. "I can't. I want to go upstairs. I want to go home."

"Then I'll come in with you."

"No. No, Jude. I want to be alone. Thank you. But go home."

"JB," Jude began, but he turned from him and ran, jamming the key into the front door and running up the stairs, knowing Jude wouldn't be capable of following him, but with Jackson right behind him, laugh-ing his mean laugh, while Jude's calls—"JB! JB!"—trailed after him, until he was inside his apartment (Jude had cleaned while he was here: the sink was empty; the dishes were stacked in the rack, drying) and couldn't hear him any longer. He turned off his phone, on which Jude was calling him, and muted the front-door buzzer's intercom, on which Jude was ringing and ringing him.

And then Jackson had cut the lines of coke he had brought and they had snorted them, and the night had become the same night he'd had hundreds of times before: the same rhythms, the same despair, the same awful feeling of suspension.

"He *is* pretty, your friend," he heard Jackson say at some point late that evening. "But too bad about—" And he stood and did an imitation of Jude's walk, a lurching grotesquerie that looked nothing like it, his mouth slack like a cretin's, his hands bobbling in front of him. He had been too high to protest, too high to say anything at all, and so he had only blinked and watched Jackson hobble around the room, trying to speak words in Jude's defense, his eyes prickling with tears.

The next day he had awoken, late, facedown on the floor near the kitchen. He stepped around Jackson, who was also asleep on the floor, near his bookcases, and went into his room, where he saw that Jude had made his bed as well, and something about that made him want to cry again. He lifted the plank under the right side of the bed, cautiously, and stuck his hand inside the space: there was nothing there. And so he lay atop the comforter, bringing one end of it over himself completely, covering the top of his head the way he used to when he was a child.

As he tried to sleep, he made himself think of why he had fallen in with Jackson. It wasn't that he didn't know why; it was that he was ashamed to remember why. He had begun hanging out with Jackson to prove that he wasn't dependent on his friends, that he wasn't trapped by his life, that he could make and would make his own decisions, even if they were bad ones. By his age, you had met all the friends you would probably ever have. You had met your friends' friends. Life got smaller and smaller. Jackson was stupid and callow and cruel and not the sort of person he was supposed to value, who was supposed to be worth his time. He knew this. And that was why he kept at it: to dismay his friends, to show them that he wasn't bound by their expectations of him. It was stupid, stupid, stupid. It was hubris. And he was the only one who was suffering because of it.

"You can't *actually* like this guy," Willem had said to him once. And although he had known exactly what Willem meant, he had pretended not to, just to be a brat.

"Why *can't* I, Willem?" he'd asked. "He's fucking hilarious. He *actually* wants to do things. He's *actually* around when I need someone. Why can't I? Huh?"

It was the same with the drugs. Doing drugs wasn't hard core, it wasn't badass, it didn't make him more interesting. But it wasn't what he was supposed to do. These days, if you were serious about your art, you didn't do drugs. Indulgence, the very idea of it, had disappeared, was a thing of the Beats and AbExes and the Ops and the Pops. These days, *maybe* you'd smoke some pot. *Maybe*, every once in a while, if you were feeling very ironic, you might do a line of coke. But that was it. This was an age of discipline, of deprivation, not inspiration, and at any rate inspiration no longer meant drugs. No one he knew and respected— Richard, Ali, Asian Henry Young—did them: not drugs, not sugar, not caffeine, not salt, not meat, not gluten, not nicotine. They were artists-as-ascetics. In his more defiant moments, he tried to pretend to himself that doing drugs was so passé, so tired, that it had actually become cool again. But he knew this wasn't true. Just as he knew it wasn't really true that he enjoyed the sex parties that sometimes convened in Jackson's echoey apartment in Williamsburg, where shifting groups of soft skinny people groped blindly at one another, and where the first time a boy, too reedy and young and hairless to really be JB's type, told him he wanted JB to watch him suck away his own blood from a cut he'd give himself, he had wanted to laugh. But he hadn't, and had instead watched as the boy cut himself on his bicep and then twisted his neck to lap at the blood, like a kitten cleaning itself, and had felt a crush of sorrow. "Oh JB, I just want a nice white boy," his ex and now-friend Toby had once moaned to him, and he smiled a little, remembering it. He did, too. All he wanted was a nice white boy, not this sad salamander-like creature, so pale he was almost translucent, licking blood from himself in what had to be the least-erotic gesture in the world.

But of all the questions he was able to answer, there was one he was not: How was he to get out? How was he to stop? Here he was, literally trapped in his studio, literally peeking down the hallway to make sure Jackson wasn't approaching. How was he to escape Jackson? How was he to recover his life?

The night after he had made Jude get rid of his stash, he had finally called him back, and Jude had asked him over, and he had refused, and so Jude had come to him. He had sat and stared at the wall as Jude made him dinner, a shrimp risotto, handing him the plate and then leaning on the counter to watch him eat.

"Can I have more?" he asked when he was done with the first serv-ing, and Jude gave it to him. He hadn't realized how hungry he was, and his hand shook as he brought the spoon to his mouth. He thought of Sunday-night dinners at his mother's, which he hadn't gone to since his grandmother died.

"Aren't you going to lecture me?" he finally asked, but Jude shook his head.

After he ate, he sat on the sofa and watched television with the sound turned off, not really seeing anything but comforted by the flash and blur of images, and Jude had washed the dishes and then sat on the sofa near him, working on a brief.

One of Willem's movies was on television—the one in which he played a con man in a small Irish town, whose entire left cheek was webbed with scars—and he stopped on the channel, not watching it, but looking at Willem's face, his mouth moving silently. "I miss Willem," he'd said, and then realized how ungrateful he sounded. But Jude had put down his pen and looked at the screen. "I miss him, too," he said, and the two of them stared at their friend, so far away from them.

"Don't go," he'd said to Jude as he was falling asleep. "Don't leave me."

"I won't," Jude had said, and he knew Jude wouldn't.

When he woke early the next morning, he was still on the sofa, and the television was turned off, and he was under his duvet. And there was Jude, huddled into the cushions on the other end of the sectional, still asleep. Some part of him had always been insulted by Jude's unwillingness to divulge anything of himself to them, by his furtiveness and secretiveness, but in that moment he felt only gratitude toward and admiration for him, and had sat on the chair next to him, studying his face, which he so loved to paint, his sweep of complicated-colored hair that he could never see without remembering how much mixing, the number of shades it took to accurately represent it.

I can do this, he told Jude, silently. *I can do this.*

Except he clearly couldn't. He was in his studio, and it was still only one p.m., and he wanted to smoke so badly, so badly that in his head all he could see was the pipe, its glass frosted with leftover white powder, and it was only day one of his attempt not to do drugs, and already it was making—*he* was making—a mockery of him. Surrounding him were the only things he cared about, the paintings in his next series, "Seconds, Minutes, Hours, Days," for which he had followed Malcolm, Jude, and Willem around for an entire day, photographing everything they did, and then chose eight to ten images from each of their days to paint. He had decided to document a typical workday for each of them, all from the same month of the same year, and had labeled each painting with their name, location, and time of day he had shot the image.

Willem's series had been the most far-flung: he had gone to London, where Willem had been on location filming something called *Latecomers*, and the images he had chosen were a mix of Willem off and on the set. He had favorites from each person's take: for Willem, it was *Willem, London, October 8, 9:08 a.m.*, an image of him in the makeup artist's chair, staring at his reflection in the mirror, while the makeup artist held his chin up with the fingertips of her left hand and brushed powder onto his cheeks with her right. Willem's eyes were lowered, but it was still clear that he was looking at himself, and his hands were gripping the chair's wooden arms as if he was on a roller coaster and was afraid he'd fall off if he let go. Before him, the counter was cluttered with wood-shaving curls from freshly sharpened eyebrow pencils that looked like tatters of lace, and open makeup palettes whose every hue was a shade of red, all the reds you could imagine, and wads of tissue with more red smeared on them like blood. For Malcolm, he had taken a long shot of him late at night, sitting at his kitchen counter at home, making one of his imaginary buildings out of squares of rice paper. He liked *Malcolm, Brooklyn, October 23, 11:17 p.m.* not so much for its composition or color but for more personal reasons: in college, he had always made fun of Malcolm for those small structures he built and displayed on his windowsill, but really he had admired them and had liked watching Malcolm compose them—his breaths slowed, and he was completely silent, and his constant nervousness, which at times seemed almost physical, an appendage like a tail, fell away.

He worked on all of them out of sequence, but he couldn't quite get the colors the way he wanted them for Jude's installment, and so he had the fewest and least of these paintings done. As he'd gone through the photos, he'd noticed that each of his friends' days was defined, glossed, by a certain tonal consistency: he had been following Willem on the days he was shooting in what was supposed to be a large Belgravia flat, and the lighting had been particularly golden, like beeswax. Later, back in the apartment in Notting Hill that Willem was renting, he had taken pictures of him sitting and reading, and there, too, the light had been yellowish, although it was less like syrup and instead crisper, like the skin of a late-fall apple. By contrast, Malcolm's world was bluish: his sterile, white-marble-countertopped office on Twenty-second Street; the house he and Sophie had bought in Cobble Hill after they had gotten married. And Jude's was grayish, but a silvery gray, a shade particular to gelatin prints that was proving very difficult to reproduce with acrylics, although for Jude's he had thinned the colors considerably, trying to capture that shimmery light. Before he began, he had to first find a way to make gray seem bright, and clean, and it was frustrating, because all he wanted to do was paint, not fuss around with colors.

But getting frustrated with your paintings—and it was impossible not to think of your work as your colleague and co-participant, as if it was something that sometimes decided to be agreeable and collaborate with you, and sometimes decided to be truculent and unyielding, like a grouchy toddler—was just what happened. You had to just keep doing it, and doing it, and one day, you'd get it right.

And yet like his promise to himself—*You're not going to make it!* squealed the taunting, dancing imp in his head; *You're not going to make it!*—the paintings were making a mockery of him as well. For this series, he had decided he was going to paint a sequence of one of his days, too, and yet for almost three years, he had been unable to find a day worth documenting. He had tried—he had taken hundreds of pictures of himself over the course of dozens of days. But when he reviewed them, they all ended the same way: with him getting high. Or the images would stop in the early evening, and he'd know it was because he had gotten high, too high to keep taking pictures. And there were other things in those photographs that he didn't like, either: he didn't want to include Jackson in a documentation of his life, and yet Jackson was always there. He didn't like the goofy smile he saw on his face when he was on drugs, he didn't like seeing how his face changed from fat and hopeful to fat and avaricious as the day sank into night. This wasn't the version of himself he wanted to paint. But increasingly, he had begun to think this was the version of himself he *should* paint: this was, after all, his life. This was who he now was. Sometimes he would wake and it would be dark and he wouldn't know where he was or what time it was or what day it was. Days: even the very concept of a day had become a mockery. He could no longer accurately measure when one began or ended. *Help me,* he'd say aloud, in those moments. *Help me.* But he didn't know to whom he was addressing his plea, or what he expected to happen.

And now he was tired. He had tried. It was one thirty p.m. on Friday, the Friday of July Fourth weekend. He put on his clothes. He closed his studio's windows and locked the door and walked down the stairs of the silent building. "Chen," he said, his voice loud in the stairwell, pretending he was broadcasting a warning to his fellow artists, that he was communicating to someone who might need his help. "Chen, Chen, Chen." He was going home, he was going to smoke.

He woke to a horrible noise, the noise of machinery, of metal grinding against metal, and started screaming into his pillow to drown it out until he realized it was the buzzer, and then slowly brought himself to his feet, and slouched over to the door. "Jackson?" he asked, holding down the intercom button, and he heard how frightened he sounded, how tentative.

There was a pause. "No, it's us," said Malcolm. "Let us in." He did.

And then there they all were, Malcolm and Jude and Willem, as if they had come to see him perform a show. "Willem," he said. "You're supposed to be in Cappadocia."

"I just got back yesterday."

"But you're supposed to be gone until"—he knew this—"July sixth. That's when you said you'd be back."

"It's July seventh," Willem said, quietly.

He started to cry, then, but he was dehydrated and he didn't have any tears, just the sounds. July seventh: he had lost so many days. He couldn't remember anything.

"JB," said Jude, coming close to him, "we're going to get you out of this. Come with us. We're going to get you help."

"Okay," he said, still crying. "Okay, okay." He kept his blanket wrapped around him, he was so cold, but he allowed Malcolm to lead him to the sofa, and when Willem came over with a sweater, he held his arms up obediently, the way he had when he was a child and his mother had dressed him. "Where's Jackson?" he asked Willem.

"Jackson's not going to bother you," he heard Jude say, somewhere above him. "Don't worry, JB."

"Willem," he said, "when did you stop being my friend?"

"I've never stopped being your friend, JB," Willem said, and sat down next to him. "You know I love you."

He leaned against the sofa and closed his eyes; he could hear Jude and Malcolm talking to each other, quietly, and then Malcolm walking toward the other end of the apartment, where his bedroom was, and the plank of wood being lifted and then dropped back into place, and the flush of the toilet.

"We're ready," he heard Jude say, and he stood, and Willem stood with him, and Malcolm came over to him and put his arm across his back and they shuffled as a group toward the door, where he was gripped by a terror: if he went outside, he knew he would see Jackson, appearing as suddenly as he had that day in the café.

"I can't go," he said, stopping. "I don't want to go, don't make me go."

"JB," Willem began, and something about Willem's voice, about his very presence, made him in that moment irrationally furious, and he shook Malcolm's arm off of him and turned to face them, energy flooding his body. "You don't get a say in what I do, Willem," he said. "You're never here and you've never supported me and you never called me, and you don't get to come in making fun of me—poor, stupid, fucked-up JB, I'm Willem the Hero, I'm coming in to save the day—just because you want to, okay? So leave me the fuck alone."

"JB, I know you're upset," Willem said, "but no one's making fun of you, least of all me," but before he'd begun speaking, JB had seen Willem look over, quickly, and, it seemed, conspiratorially, at Jude, and for some reason this had made him even more livid. What had happened to the days when they all understood one another, when he and Willem had gone out every weekend, when they had returned the next day to share the night's stories with Malcolm and Jude, Jude who never went anywhere, who never shared stories of his own? How had it happened that he was the one who was all alone? Why had they left him for Jackson to pick over and destroy? Why hadn't they fought harder for him? Why had he ruined it all for himself? Why had they let him? He wanted to devastate them; he wanted them to feel as inhuman as he did.

"And you," he said, turning to Jude. "You like knowing how fucked up I am? You like always being the person who gets to learn everyone else's secrets, without ever telling us a single fucking thing? What do you think this is, Jude? You think you get to be a part of the club and you never have to say anything, you never have to tell us anything? Well, it doesn't fucking work like that, and we're all fucking sick of you."

"That's enough, JB," Willem said sharply, grabbing his shoulder, but he was strong suddenly, and he wrenched out of Willem's grasp, his feet unexpectedly nimble, dancing toward the bookcase like a boxer. He looked at Jude, who was standing in silence, his face very still and his eyes very large, almost as if he was waiting for him to continue, waiting for JB to hurt him further. The first time he had painted Jude's eyes, he had gone to a pet store to take photographs of a rough green snake because the colors were so similar. But in that moment they were darker, almost like a grass snake's, and he wished, ridiculously, that he had his paints, because he knew that if he had them, he'd be able to get the shade exactly right without even having to try.

"It doesn't work like that," he said to Jude again. And then, before he knew it, he was doing Jackson's imitation of Jude, the hideous parody, his mouth open as Jackson had done it, making an imbecile's moan, dragging his right leg behind him as if it were made of stone. "I'm Jude," he slurred. "I'm Jude St. Francis." For a few seconds, his was the only voice in the room, his movements the only movements, and in those seconds, he wanted to stop, but he couldn't stop. And then Willem had run at him, and the last thing he had seen was Willem drawing his fist back, and the last thing he had heard was the cracking of bone.

He woke and didn't know where he was. It was difficult to breathe. Something was on his nose, he realized. But when he tried to lift his hand to feel what it was, he couldn't. And then he had looked down and seen that his wrists were in restraints, and he knew he was in the hospital. He closed his eyes and remembered: Willem had hit him. Then he remembered why, and he shut his eyes very tightly, howling but not making a noise.

The moment passed and he opened his eyes again. He turned his head to the left, where an ugly blue curtain blocked his view of the door. And then he turned his head to the right, toward the early-morning light, and saw Jude, asleep in the chair next to his bed. The chair was too small for him to sleep in, and he had folded himself into a terrible-looking position: his knees drawn up to his chest, his cheek resting atop them, his arms wrapped around his calves.

You know you shouldn't sleep like that, Jude, he told him in his head. *Your back is going to hurt when you wake up.* But even if he could have reached his arm over to wake him, he wouldn't have.

Oh god, he thought. Oh god. What have I done?

I'm sorry, Jude, he said in his head, and this time he was able to cry properly, the tears running into his mouth, the mucus that he was unable to clean away bubbling over as well. But he was silent; he didn't make any noise. *I'm sorry, Jude, I'm so sorry,* he repeated to himself, and then he whispered the words aloud, but quietly, so quietly that he could hear only his lips opening and closing, nothing more. *Forgive me, Jude. Forgive me.*

Forgive me.
Forgive me.
Forgive me.

[IV]

The Axiom of Equality

1

THE NIGHT BEFORE he leaves for Boston for their friend Lionel's wedding, he gets a message from Dr. Li telling him that Dr. Kashen has died. "It was a heart attack; very fast," Dr. Li writes. The funeral is Friday afternoon.

The next morning he drives directly to the cemetery, and from the cemetery to Dr. Kashen's house, a two-story wooden structure in Newton where the professor used to host a year-end dinner for all of his current graduate students. It was understood that you weren't to discuss math at these parties. "You can talk about anything else," he'd tell them. "But we're not talking about math." Only at Dr. Kashen's parties would he be the least socially inept person in the room (he was also, not coincidentally, the least brilliant), and the professor would always make him start the conversation. "So, Jude," he'd say. "What are you interested in these days?" At least two of his fellow graduate students—both of them PhD candidates—had mild forms of autism, and he could see how hard they worked at making conversation, how hard they worked at their table manners, and prior to these dinners, he did some research into what was new in the worlds of online gaming (which one of them loved) and tennis (which the other loved), so he'd be able to ask them questions they could answer. Dr. Kashen wanted his students to someday be able to find jobs, and along with teaching them math, he also thought it his responsibility to socialize them, to teach them how to behave among others.

Sometimes Dr. Kashen's son, Leo, who was five or six years older than he, would be at dinner at well. He too had autism, but unlike Donald's and Mikhail's, his was instantly noticeable, and severe enough so that although he'd completed high school, he hadn't been able to attend more than a semester of college, and had only been able to get a job as a programmer for the phone company, where he sat in a small room day after day fixing screen after screen of code. He was Dr. Kashen's only child, and he still lived at home, along with Dr. Kashen's sister, who had moved in after his wife had died, years ago.

At the house, he speaks to Leo, who seems glazed, and mumbles, looking away from him as he does, and then to Dr. Kashen's sister, who was a math professor at Northeastern.

"Jude," she says, "it's lovely to see you. Thank you for coming." She holds his hand. "My brother always talked about you, you know."

"He was a wonderful teacher," he tells her. "He gave me so much. I'm so sorry."

"Yes," she says. "It was very sudden. And poor Leo"—they look at Leo, who is gazing at nothing—"I don't know how he's going to deal with this." She kisses him goodbye. "Thank you again."

Outside, it is fiercely cold, and the windshield is sticky with ice. He drives slowly to Harold and Julia's, letting himself in and calling their names.

"And here he is!" says Harold, materializing from the kitchen, wiping his hands on a dish towel. Harold hugs him, which he had begun doing at some point, and as uncomfortable as it makes him, he thinks it'll be more uncomfortable to try to explain why he'd like Harold to stop. "I'm so sorry about Kashen, Jude. I was shocked to hear it—I ran into him on the courts about two months back and he looked like he was in great shape."

"He was," he says, unwinding his scarf, as Harold takes his coat. "And not that old, either: seventy-four."

"Jesus," says Harold, who has just turned sixty-five. "There's a cheery thought. Go put your stuff in your room and come into the kitchen. Julia's tied up in a meeting but she'll be home in an hour or so."

He drops his bag in the guest room—"Jude's room," Harold and Julia call it; "your room"—and changes out of his suit and heads toward the kitchen, where Harold is peering into a pot on the stove, as if down a well. "I'm trying to make a bolognese," he says, without turning around, "but something's happening; it keeps separating, see?"

He looks. "How much olive oil did you use?"

"A lot."

"What's a lot?"

"A *lot*. Too much, obviously."

He smiles. "I'll fix it."

"Thank god," says Harold, stepping away from the stove. "I was hoping you'd say that."

Over dinner, they speak of Julia's favorite researcher, who she thinks might be trying to jump to another lab, and of the latest gossip circulating through the law school, and of the anthology of essays about *Brown versus Board of Education* that Harold is editing, and of one of Laurence's twin daughters, who is getting married, and then Harold says, grinning, "So, Jude, the big birthday's coming up."

"Three months away!" Julia chirps, and he groans. "What are you going to do?"

"Probably nothing," he says. He hasn't planned anything, and he has forbidden Willem from planning anything, either. Two years ago, he threw Willem a big party for his fortieth at Greene Street, and although the four of them had always said they'd go somewhere for each of their fortieth birthdays, it hasn't worked out that way. Willem had been in L.A. filming on his actual birthday, but after he had finished, they'd gone to Botswana on a safari. But it had been just the two of them: Malcolm had been working on a project in Beijing, and JB—well, Willem hadn't mentioned inviting JB, and he hadn't, either.

"You have to do *something*," says Harold. "We could have a dinner for you here, or in the city."

He smiles but shakes his head. "Forty's forty," he says. "It's just another year." As a child, though, he never thought he'd make it to forty: in the months after the injury, he would sometimes have dreams of himself as an adult, and although the dreams were very vague—he was never quite certain where he was living or what he was doing, though in those dreams he was usually walking, sometimes running—he was always young in them; his imagination refused to let him advance into middle age.

To change the subject, he tells them about Dr. Kashen's funeral, where Dr. Li gave a eulogy. "People who don't love math always accuse mathematicians of trying to make math complicated," Dr. Li had said. "But anyone who *does* love math knows it's really the opposite: math rewards simplicity, and mathematicians value it above all else. So it's no surprise that Walter's favorite axiom was also the most simple in the realm of mathematics: the axiom of the empty set.

"The axiom of the empty set is the axiom of zero. It states that there must be a concept of nothingness, that there must be the concept of zero: zero value, zero items. Math assumes there's a concept of nothingness, but is it proven? No. But it *must* exist.

"And if we are being philosophical—which we today are—we can say that life itself is the axiom of the empty set. It begins in zero and ends in zero. We know that both states exist, but we will not be conscious of either experience: they are states that are necessary parts of life, even as they cannot be experienced *as* life. We *assume* the concept of nothingness, but we cannot prove it. But it *must* exist. So I prefer to think that Walter has not died but has instead proven for himself the axiom of the empty set, that he has proven the concept of zero. I know nothing else would have made him happier. An elegant mind wants elegant endings, and Walter had the most elegant mind. So I wish him goodbye; I wish him the answer to the axiom he so loved."

They are all quiet for a while, contemplating this. "Please tell me that isn't *your* favorite axiom," Harold says suddenly, and he laughs. "No," he says. "It's not."

He sleeps in the next day, and that night he goes to the wedding, where because both of the grooms lived in Hood, he knows almost everyone. The non-Hood guests—Lionel's colleagues from Wellesley, and Sinclair's from Harvard, where he teaches European history—stand near one another as if for protection, looking bored and bemused. The wedding is loose-limbed and slightly chaotic—Lionel starts assigning his guests tasks as soon as they arrive, which most of them neglect: he is supposed to be making sure everyone signs the guest book; Willem is supposed to be helping people find their tables—and people walk around saying how, thanks to Lionel and Sinclair, thanks to this wedding, they won't have to go to their twentieth reunion this year. They are all here: Willem and his girlfriend, Robin; Malcolm and Sophie; and JB and his new boyfriend, whom he hasn't met, and he knows, even before checking their place cards, that they will all be assigned to the same table. "Jude!" people he hasn't seen in years say to him. "How are you? Where's JB? I just spoke to Willem! I just saw Malcolm!" And then, "Are you four all still as close as you were?"

"We all still talk," he says, "and they're doing great," which is the answer he and Willem had decided they'd give. He wonders what JB is saying, whether he is skimming over the truth, as he and Willem are, or whether he is lying outright, or whether, in a fit of JBish forthrightness, he is telling the truth: "No. We hardly ever speak anymore. I only really talk to Malcolm these days."

He hasn't seen JB in months and months. He hears of him, of course: through Malcolm, through Richard, through Black Henry Young. But he doesn't see him any longer, because even nearly three years later, he is unable to forgive him. He has tried and tried. He knows how intractable, how mean, how uncharitable he is being. But he can't. When he sees JB, he sees him doing his imitation of him, sees him confirming in that moment everything he has feared and thought he looks like, everything he has feared and thought other people think about him. But he had never thought his friends saw him like that; or at least, he never thought they would tell him. The accuracy of the imitation tears at him, but the fact that it was JB doing it devastates him. Late at night, when he can't sleep, the image he sometimes sees is JB dragging himself in a half-moon, his mouth agape and drooling, his hands held before him in claws: *I'm Jude. I'm Jude St. Francis.*

That night, after they had taken JB to the hospital and admitted him—JB had been stuporous and dribbling when they took him in, but then had recovered and become angry, violent, screaming wordlessly at them all, thrashing against the orderlies, wresting his body out of their arms until they had sedated him and dragged him, lolling, down the hallway—Malcolm had left in one taxi and he and Willem had gone home to Perry Street in another.

He hadn't been able to look at Willem in the cab, and without anything to distract him—no forms to fill out, no doctors to talk to—he had felt himself grow cold despite the hot, muggy night, and his hands begin to shake, and Willem had reached over and taken his right hand and held it in his left for the rest of the long, silent ride downtown.

He was there for JB's recovery. He decided he'd stay until he got better; he couldn't abandon JB then, not after all their time together. The three of them took shifts, and after work he'd sit by JB's hospital bed and read. Sometimes JB was awake, but most of the time he wasn't. He was detoxing, but the doctor had also discovered that JB had a kidney infection, and so he stayed on in the hospital's main ward, liquids dripping into his arm, his face slowly losing its bloat. When he was awake, JB would beg him for forgiveness, sometimes dramatically and pleadingly, and sometimes—when he was more lucid—quietly. These were the conversations he found most difficult.

"Jude, I'm so sorry," he'd say. "I was so messed up. Please tell me you forgive me. I was so awful. I love you, you know that. I would never want to hurt you, never."

"I know you were messed up, JB," he'd say. "I know."

"Then tell me you forgive me. Please, Jude."

He'd be silent. "It's going to be okay, JB," he'd say, but he couldn't make the words—*I forgive you*—leave his mouth. At night, alone, he would say them again and again: *I forgive you, I forgive you*. It would be so simple, he'd admonish himself. It would make JB feel better. *Say it*, he'd command himself as JB looked at him, the whites of his eyes smeary and yellowed. *Say it*. But he couldn't. He knew he was making JB feel worse; he knew it and was still unable to say it. The words were stones, held just under his tongue. He couldn't release them, he just couldn't.

Later, when JB called him nightly from rehab, strident and pedantic, he'd sat silently through his monologues on what a better person he'd become, and how he had realized he had no one to depend on but himself, and how he, Jude, needed to realize that there was more in life than just work, and to live every day in the moment and learn to love himself. He listened and breathed and said nothing. And then JB had come home and had had to readjust, and none of them heard very much from him at all for a few months. He had lost the lease on his apartment, and had moved back in with his mother while he reestablished his life.

But then one day he had called. It had been early February, almost seven months exactly after they had taken him to the hospital, and JB wanted to see him and talk. He suggested JB meet him at a café called Clementine that was near Willem's building, and as he inched his way past the tightly spaced tables to a seat against the back wall, he realized why he had chosen this place: because it was too small, and too cramped, for JB to do his impression of him, and recognizing that, he felt foolish and cowardly.

He hadn't seen JB in a long time, and JB leaned over the table and hugged him, lightly, carefully, before sitting down.

"You look great," he said.

"Thanks," said JB. "So do you."

For twenty minutes or so, they discussed JB's life: he had joined Crystal Meth Anonymous. He was going to live with his mother for another few months or so, and then decide what to do next. He was working again, on the same series he'd been working on before he went away.

"That's great, JB," he'd said. "I'm proud of you."

And then there was a silence, and they both stared at other people. A few tables away from him was a girl wearing a long gold necklace she kept winding and unwinding around her fingers. He watched her talk to her friend, wrapping and unwrapping her necklace, until she looked up at him and he looked away.

"Jude," JB began, "I wanted to tell you—completely sober—that I'm so sorry. It was horrible. It was—" He shook his head. "It was so cruel. I can't—" He stopped again, and there was a silence. "I'm sorry," he said. "I'm sorry."

"I know you are, JB," he said, and he felt a sort of sadness he'd never felt before. Other people had been cruel to him, had made him feel awful, but they hadn't been people he loved, they hadn't been people he had always hoped saw him as someone whole and undamaged. JB had been the first.

And yet JB had also been one of the first to be his friend. When he'd had the episode in college that had made his roommates take him to the hospital where he had met Andy, it had been JB, Andy later told him, who had carried him in, and JB who had demanded that he be seen first, who had made such an upset in the ER that he had been ejected—but not before a doctor had been summoned.

He could see JB's love for him in his paintings of him. He remembered one summer in Truro, watching JB sketch, and he had known from the expression on JB's face, his little smile, and the lingering, delicate way his large forearm moved over the page, that he was drawing something he treasured, something that was dear to him. "What're you drawing?" he'd asked, and JB had turned to him, and held up the notepad, and he had seen it was a picture of him, of his face.

Oh, JB, he thought. Oh, I will miss you.

"Can you forgive me, Jude?" JB asked, and looked at him.

He didn't have words, he could only shake his head. "I can't, JB," he

said, finally. "I can't. I can't look at you without seeing—" He stopped.
"I can't," he repeated. "I'm sorry, JB, I'm so sorry."

"Oh," said JB, and he swallowed. They sat there for a long time, not saying anything.

"I'll always want wonderful things for you," he said to JB, who nodded, slowly, not looking at him.

"Well," JB said, finally, and stood, and he stood as well, and held his hand out to JB, who looked at it as if it were something alien, something he'd never seen before, examining it, squinting at it. And then at last he took it, but instead of shaking it, he lowered his lips to it and held them there. And then JB returned his hand to him and bumbled, nearly ran, out of the café, bumping against the little tables—"Sorry, sorry"—as he went.

He still sees JB now and then, mostly at parties, always in groups, and the two of them are polite and cordial with each other. They make small talk, which is the most painful thing. JB has never tried to hug or kiss him again; he comes over to him with his hand already outstretched, and he takes it, and they shake. He sent JB flowers—but with only the briefest of notes—when "Seconds, Minutes, Hours, Days" opened, and although he skipped the opening, he had gone to the gallery the following Saturday, on his way up to work, where he had spent an hour moving slowly from one painting to the next. JB had planned on including himself in this series, but in the end he hadn't: there was just him, and Malcolm, and Willem. The paintings were beautiful, and as he looked at each, he thought not so much of the lives depicted in them, as of the life who created them—so many of these paintings were done when JB was at his most miserable, his most helpless, and yet they were self-assured, and subtle, and to see them was to imagine the empathy and tenderness and grace of the person who made them.

Malcolm has remained friends with JB, although he felt the need to apologize to him for this fact. "Oh no, Malcolm," he'd said, once Malcolm had confessed, asking him for his permission. "You should absolutely still be friends with him." He doesn't want JB to be abandoned by them all; he doesn't want Malcolm to feel he has to prove his loyalty to him by disavowing JB. He wants JB to have a friend who's known him since he was eighteen, since he was the funniest, brightest person in the school, and he and everyone else knew it.

But Willem has never spoken to JB again. Once JB returned from rehab, he called JB and said that he couldn't be friends with him any longer, and that JB knew why. And that had been the end. He had been surprised by this, and saddened, because he had always loved watching JB and Willem laugh together, and spar with each other, and loved having them tell him about their lives: they were both so fearless, so bold; they were his emissaries to a less inhibited, more joyful world. They had always known how to take pleasure from everything, and he had always admired that in them, and had been grateful that they had been willing to share it with him.

"You know, Willem," he said once, "I hope the reason you're not talking to JB isn't because of what happened with me."

"Of course it's because of what happened with you," Willem had said.

"But that's not a reason," he'd said.

"Of course it is," Willem had said. "There's no better reason than that."

He had never done it before, and so he had no real understanding of how slow, and sad, and difficult it was to end a friendship. Richard knows that he and JB and Willem and JB don't talk any longer, but he doesn't know why—or at least not from him. Now, years later, he no longer even blames JB; he simply cannot forget. He finds that some small but unignorable part of him is always wondering if JB will do it again; he finds he is scared of being left alone with him.

Two years ago, the first year JB didn't come up to Truro, Harold asked him if anything was the matter. "You never talk about him anymore," he said.

"Well," he began, not knowing how to continue. "We're not really— we're not really friends any longer, Harold."

"I'm sorry, Jude," Harold said after a silence, and he nodded. "Can you tell me what happened?"

"No," he said, concentrating on snapping the tops off the radishes. "It's a long story."

"Can it be repaired, do you think?"

He shook his head. "I don't think so."

Harold sighed. "I'm sorry, Jude," he repeated. "It must be bad." He was quiet. "I always loved seeing you four together, you know. You had something special."

He nodded, again. "I know," he said. "I agree. I miss him."

He misses JB still; he expects he always will. He especially misses JB at events like this wedding, where the four of them would once have spent the night talking and laughing about everyone else, enviable and near obnoxious in their shared pleasure, their pleasure in one another. But now there are JB and Willem, nodding at each other across the table, and Malcolm, talking very fast to try to obscure any tension, and the other three people at the table, whom the four of them—he will always think of them as the four of them; the four of us—start interrogating with inappropriate intensity, laughing loudly at their jokes, using them as unwitting human shields. He is seated next to JB's boyfriend— the nice white boy he had always wanted—who is in his twenties and has just gotten his nursing degree and is clearly besotted with JB. "What was JB like in college?" asks Oliver, and he says, "Very much the way he is today: funny, and sharp, and outrageous, and smart. And talented. He was always, always talented."

"Hmm," says Oliver thoughtfully, looking over at JB, who is listening to Sophie with what seems like exaggerated concentration. "I never think of JB as *funny*, really." And then he looks over at JB as well, wondering if Oliver has perhaps interpreted JB incorrectly or whether JB has, in fact, become someone else, someone he now wouldn't recognize as the person he knew for so many years.

At the end of the night, there are kisses and handshakes, and when Oliver—to whom JB has clearly told nothing—tells him they should get together, the three of them, because he's always wanted to get to know him, one of JB's oldest friends, he smiles and says something vague, and gives JB a wave before heading outside, where Willem is waiting for him.

"How was it for you?" Willem asks.

"Okay," he says, smiling back at him. He thinks these meetings with JB are even harder for Willem than they are for him. "You?"

"Okay," Willem says. His girlfriend drives up to the curb; they are staying at a hotel. "I'll call you tomorrow, all right?"

Back in Cambridge, he lets himself into the silent house and walks as softly as he can back to his bathroom, where he prises his bag from beneath the loose tile near the toilet and cuts himself until he feels absolutely empty, holding his arms over the bathtub, watching the porcelain stain itself crimson. As he always does after seeing JB, he wonders if he has made the right decision. He wonders if all of them—he, Willem, JB, Malcolm—will lie awake that night longer than usual, thinking of one another's faces and of conversations, good and bad, that they have had with one another over what had been more than twenty years of friendship.

Oh, he thinks, if I were a better person. If I were a more generous person. If I were a less self-involved person. If I were a braver person.

Then he stands, gripping the towel bar as he does; he has cut himself too much tonight, and he is faint. He goes over to the full-length mirror that is hung on the back of the bedroom's closet door. In his apartment on Greene Street, there are no full-length mirrors. "No mirrors," he told Malcolm. "I don't like them." But really, he doesn't want to be confronted with his image; he doesn't want to see his body, his face staring back at him.

But here at Harold and Julia's, there is a mirror, and he stands in front of it for a few seconds, contemplating himself, before adopting the hunched pose JB had that night. JB was right, he thinks. He was right. And that is why I can't forgive him.

Now he drops his mouth open. Now he hops in a little circle. Now he drags his leg behind him. His moans fill the air in the quiet, still house.

—

The first Saturday in May, he and Willem have what they've been calling the Last Supper at a tiny, very expensive sushi restaurant near his office on Fifty-sixth Street. The restaurant has only six seats, all at a wide, velvety cypress counter, and for the three hours they spend there, they are the only patrons.

Although they both knew how much the meal would cost, they're both stunned when they look at the check, and then both start laughing, though he's not sure if it's the absurdity of spending so much on a single dinner, or the fact that they have, or the fact that they can that is to blame.

"I'll get it," Willem says, but as he's reaching for his wallet, the waiter comes over to him with his credit card, which he'd given to him when Willem was in the bathroom.

"Goddammit, Jude," Willem says, and he grins.

"It's the Last Supper, Willem," he says. "You can get me a taco when you come back."

"*If* I come back," Willem says. It has been their running joke. "Jude, thank you. You weren't supposed to pay for this."

It's the first warm night of the year, and he tells Willem that if he really wants to thank him for dinner, he'll walk with him. "How far?" asks Willem, warily. "We're not going to walk all the way down to SoHo, Jude."

"Not far."

"It'd better not be," Willem says, "because I'm really tired." This is Willem's new strategy, and he is very fond of it: instead of telling him he can't do certain things because it's not good for his legs or back, Willem instead tries to make himself sound incapable in order to dissuade him. These days, Willem is always too tired to walk, or too achey, or too hot, or too cold. But he knows that these things are untrue. One Saturday afternoon after they'd gone to some galleries, Willem had told him he couldn't walk from Chelsea to Greene Street ("I'm too tired"), and so they had taken a cab instead. But then the next day at lunch, Robin had said, "Wasn't it a beautiful day yesterday? After Willem got home, we ran for—what, eight miles, right, Willem?—all the way up and down the highway."

"Oh, did you?" he asked her, looking at Willem, who smiled sheepishly at him.

"What can I say?" he said. "I unexpectedly got a second wind."

They start walking south, first veering east from Broadway so they won't have to cross through Times Square. Willem's hair has been colored dark for his next role, and he has a beard, so he's not instantly recognizable, but neither of them want to get stuck in a scrum of tourists.

This is the last time he will see Willem for what will likely be more than six months. On Tuesday, he leaves for Cyprus to begin work on *The Iliad* and *The Odyssey*; he will play Odysseus in both. The two films will be shot consecutively and released consecutively, but they will have the same cast and the same director, too. The shoot will take him all across southern Europe and northern Africa before moving to Australia, where some of the battle scenes are being shot, and because the pace is so intense and the distances he has to travel so far, it's unclear whether he'll have much time, if any, to come home on breaks. It is the most elaborate and ambitious shoot Willem has been on, and he is nervous. "It's going to be incredible, Willem," he reassures him.

"Or an incredible disaster," Willem says. He isn't glum, he never is, but he can tell Willem is anxious, and eager to do well, and worried that he will somehow disappoint. But he is worried before every film, and yet—as he reminds Willem—every one has turned out fine, better than fine. However, he thinks, this is one of the reasons that Willem will always have work, and good work: because he does take it seriously, because he does feel so responsible.

He, though, is dreading the next six months, especially because Willem has been so present for the last year and a half. First he was shooting a small project, one based in Brooklyn, that lasted just a few weeks. And then he was in a play, a production called *The Maldivian Dodo*, about two brothers, both ornithologists, one of whom is slowly tipping into an uncategorizable madness. The two of them had a late dinner every Thursday night for the entire run of the play, which he saw—as he has with all of Willem's plays—multiple times. On his third viewing, he spotted JB with Oliver, just a few rows ahead of him but on the left side of the theater, and throughout the show he kept glancing over at JB to see if he was laughing at or concentrating on the same lines, aware that this was the first of Willem's productions that the three of them hadn't seen together, as a group, at least once.

"So, listen," Willem says as they move down Fifth Avenue, which is empty of people, just bright-lit windows and stray bits of garbage twirling in the light, soft breeze—plastic bags, puffed up with air into jellyfish, and twists of newspaper—"I told Robin I'd talk to you about something."

He waits. He has been conscious of not making the same mistake with Robin and Willem that he made with Philippa and Willem—when Willem asks him to accompany them anywhere, he makes sure that he's cleared it with Robin first (finally Willem had told him to stop asking, that Robin knew how much he meant to him and she was fine with it, and if she wasn't fine with it, she'd have to get fine with it), and he has tried to present himself to Robin as someone independent and not likely to move in with them when he's old. (He's not sure exactly how to communicate this message, however, and so is therefore unsure if he's been successful or not.) But he likes Robin—she's a classics professor at Columbia who was hired to serve as a consultant on the films two years ago, and she has a spiky sense of humor that reminds him of JB, somehow.

"Okay," says Willem, and takes a deep breath, and he steadies himself. Oh no, he thinks. "Do you remember Robin's friend Clara?"

"Sure," he says. "The one I met at Clementine."

"Yes!" says Willem, triumphantly. "That's her!"

"God, Willem, give me some credit; it was just last week."

"I know, I know. Well, anyway, here's the thing—she's interested in you."

He is perplexed. "What do you mean?"

"She asked Robin if you were single." He pauses. "I told her I didn't think you were interested in seeing anyone, but I'd ask. So. I'm asking."

The idea is so preposterous that it takes him a while to understand what Willem's saying, and when he does, he stops, and laughs, embarrassed and disbelieving. "You've got to be kidding, Willem," he says. "That's ridiculous."

"Why is it ridiculous?" asks Willem, suddenly serious. "Jude, why?"

"Willem," he says, recovering himself. "It's very flattering. But—" He winces and laughs again. "It's absurd."

"What is?" Willem says, and he can feel the conversation turn. "That someone should be attracted to you? This isn't the first time this has happened, you know. You just can't see it because you won't let yourself."

He shakes his head. "Let's talk about something else, Willem."

"No," says Willem. "You're not getting out of this one, Jude. Why is it ridiculous? Why is it absurd?"

He is suddenly so uncomfortable that he actually does stop, right on the corner of Fifth and Forty-fifth, and starts scanning the avenue for a cab. But of course, there are no cabs.

As he considers how to respond, he thinks back to a time a few days after that night in JB's apartment, when he had asked Willem if JB had been correct, at least in some part: *Did* Willem resent him? Did he not tell them enough?

Willem had been silent for such a long time that he knew the answer even before he heard it. "Look, Jude," Willem had said, slowly, "JB was—JB was out of his mind. I could never be sick of you. You don't *owe* me your secrets." He paused. "But, yes, I do wish you'd share more of yourself with me. Not so I could have the information but so, maybe, I could be of some help." He stopped and looked at him. "That's all."

Since then, he has tried to tell Willem more things. But there are so many topics that he has never discussed with anyone since Ana, now twenty-five years ago, that he finds he literally doesn't have the language to do so. His past, his fears, what was done to him, what he has done to himself—they are subjects that can only be discussed in tongues he doesn't speak: Farsi, Urdu, Mandarin, Portuguese. Once, he tried to write some things down, thinking that it might be easier, but it wasn't—he is unclear how to explain himself to himself.

"You'll find your own way to discuss what happened to you," he remembers Ana saying. "You'll have to, if you ever want to be close to anyone." He wishes, as he often does, that he had let her talk to him, that he had let her teach him how to do it. His silence had begun as something protective, but over the years it has transformed into something near oppressive, something that manages him rather than the other way around. Now he cannot find a way out of it, even when he wants to. He imagines he is floating in a small bubble of water, encased on all sides by walls and ceilings and floors of ice, all many feet thick. He knows there is a way out, but he is unequipped; he has no tools to begin his work, and his hands scrabble uselessly against the ice's slick. He had thought that by not saying who he was, he was making himself more palatable, less strange. But now, what he doesn't say makes him stranger, an object of pity and even suspicion.

"Jude?" Willem prompts him. "Why is it absurd?"

He shakes his head. "It just is." He starts walking again.

For a block, they say nothing. Then Willem asks, "Jude, do you ever want to be with someone?"

"I never thought I would."

"But that's not what I asked."

"I don't know, Willem," he says, unable to look at Willem's face. "I guess I just don't think that sort of thing is for someone like me."

"What does that mean?"

He shakes his head again, not saying anything, but Willem persists. "Because you have some health problems? Is that why?"

Health problems, says something sour and sardonic inside him. *Now, that's a euphemism.* But he doesn't say this out loud. "Willem," he pleads. "I'm begging you to stop talking about this. We've had such a good night. It's our last night, and then I'm not going to see you. Can we please change the subject? Please?"

Willem doesn't say anything for another block, and he thinks the moment has passed, but then Willem says, "You know, when we first started going out, Robin asked me whether you were gay or straight and I had to tell her I didn't know." He pauses. "She was shocked. She kept saying, 'This is your best friend since you guys were teenagers and you don't know?' Philippa used to ask me about you as well. And I'd tell her the same thing I told Robin: that you're a private person and I've always tried to respect your privacy.

"But I guess this is the kind of stuff I wish you'd tell me, Jude. Not so I can do anything with the information, but just because it gives me a better sense of who you are. I mean, maybe you're neither. Maybe you're both. Maybe you're just not interested. It doesn't make a difference to me."

He doesn't, he can't say anything in response, and they walk another two blocks: Thirty-eighth Street, Thirty-seventh Street. He is conscious of his right foot dragging against the pavement the way it does when he is tired or dispirited, too tired or dispirited to make a greater effort, and is grateful that Willem is on his left, and therefore less likely to notice it.

"I worry sometimes that you've decided to convince yourself that you're somehow unattractive or unlovable, and that you've decided that certain experiences are off-limits for you. But they're not, Jude: anyone would be lucky to be with you," says Willem a block later. Enough of this, he thinks; he can tell by Willem's tone that he is building up to a longer speech and he is now actively anxious, his heart beating a funny rhythm.

"Willem," he says, turning to him. "I think I'd better take a taxi after all; I'm getting tired—I'd better get to bed."

"Jude, come on," says Willem, with enough impatience in his voice that he flinches. "Look, I'm sorry. But really, Jude. You can't just *leave* when I'm trying to talk to you about something important."

This stops him. "You're right," he says. "I'm sorry. And I'm grateful, Willem, I really am. But this is just too difficult for me to discuss."

"*Everything's* too difficult for you to discuss," says Willem, and he flinches again. Willem sighs. "I'm sorry. I always keep thinking that someday I'm going to talk to you, really talk to you, and then I never do, because I'm afraid you're going to shut down and then you won't talk to me at all." They are silent, and he is chastened, because he knows Willem is right—that is exactly what he'd do. A few years ago, Willem had tried to talk to him about his cutting. They had been walking then too, and after a certain point the conversation had become so intolerable that he had hailed a cab and frantically pulled himself in, leaving Willem standing on the sidewalk, calling his name in disbelief; he had cursed himself even as the car sped south. Willem had been furious; he had apologized; they had made up. But Willem has never initiated that conversation again, and neither has he. "But tell me this, Jude: Are you ever lonely?"

"No," he says, finally. A couple walks by, laughing, and he thinks of the beginning of their walk, when they too were laughing. How has he managed to ruin this night, the last time he will see Willem for months? "You don't need to worry about me, Willem. I'll always be fine. I'll always be able to take care of myself."

And then Willem sighs, and sags, and looks so defeated that he feels a twist of guilt. But he is also relieved, because he senses that Willem doesn't know how to continue the conversation, and he will soon be able to redirect him, and end the evening pleasantly, and escape. "You always say that."

"Because it's always true."

There is a long, long silence. They are standing in front of a Korean barbeque restaurant, and the air is dense and fragrant with steam and smoke and roasting meat. "Can I go?" he asks finally, and Willem nods. He goes to the curb and raises his arm, and a cab glides to his side.

Willem opens the door for him and then, as he's getting in, puts his arms around him and holds him, and he finally does the same. "I'm going to miss you," Willem says into the back of his neck. "Are you going to take care of yourself while I'm gone?"

"Yes," he says. "I promise." He steps back and looks at him. "Until November, then."

Willem makes a face that's not quite a smile. "November," he echoes.

In the cab, he finds he really is tired, and he leans his forehead against the greased window and closes his eyes. By the time he reaches home, he feels as leaden as a corpse, and in the apartment, he starts taking off his clothes—shoes, sweater, shirt, undershirt, pants—as soon as he's locked the door behind him, leaving them littering the floor in a trail as he makes his way to the bathroom. His hands tremor as he unsticks the bag from beneath the sink, and although he hadn't thought he'd need to cut himself that night—nothing that day or early evening had indicated he might—he is almost ravenous for it now. He has long ago run out of blank skin on his forearms, and he now recuts over old cuts, using the edge of the razor to saw through the tough, webby scar tissue: when the new cuts heal, they do so in warty furrows, and he is disgusted and dismayed and fascinated all at once by how severely he has deformed himself. Lately he has begun using the cream that Andy gave him for his back on his arms, and he thinks it helps, a bit: the skin feels looser, the scars a little softer and more supple.

The shower area Malcolm has created in this bathroom is enormous, so large he now sits within it when he's cutting, his legs stretched out before him, and after he's done, he's careful to wash away the blood because the floor is a great plain of marble, and as Malcolm has told him again and again, once you stain marble, there's nothing that can be done. And then he is in bed, light-headed but not quite sleepy, staring at the dark, mercury-like gleam the chandelier makes in the shadowy room.

"I'm lonely," he says aloud, and the silence of the apartment absorbs the words like blood soaking into cotton.

This loneliness is a recent discovery, and is different from the other lonelinesses he has experienced: it is not the childhood loneliness of not having parents; or of lying awake in a motel room with Brother Luke, trying not to move, not to rouse him, while the moon threw hard white stripes of light across the bed; or of the time he ran away from the home, the successful time, and spent the night wedged into the cleft of an oak tree's buckling roots that spread open like a pair of legs, making himself as small as he could. He had thought he was lonely then, but now he realizes that what he was feeling was not loneliness but fear. But now he has nothing to fear. Now he has protected himself: he has this apartment with its triple-locked doors, and he has money. He has parents, he has friends. He will never again have to do anything he doesn't want to for food, or transportation, or shelter, or escape.

He hadn't been lying to Willem: he is not meant for a relationship and has never thought he was. He has never envied his friends theirs—to do so would be akin to a cat coveting a dog's bark: it is something that would never occur to him to envy, because it is impossible, something that is simply alien to his very species. But recently, people have been behaving as if it is something he could have, or should want to have, and although he knows they mean it in part as a kindness, it feels like a taunt: they could be telling him he could be a decathlete and it would be as obtuse and as cruel.

He expects it from Malcolm and Harold; Malcolm because he is happy and sees a single path—his path—to happiness, and so therefore occasionally asks him if he can set him up with someone, or if he wants to find someone, and then is bewildered when he declines; Harold because he knows that the part of the parental role Harold most enjoys is inserting himself into his life and rooting about in it as best as he can. He has grown to enjoy this too, sometimes—he is touched that someone is interested enough in him to order him around, to be disappointed by the decisions he makes, to have expectations for him, to assume the responsibility of ownership of him. Two years ago, he and Harold were at a restaurant and Harold was giving him a lecture about how his job at Rosen Pritchard had made him essentially an accessory to corporate malfeasance, when they both realized that their waiter was standing above them, holding his pad before him.

"Pardon me," said the waiter. "Should I come back?"

"No, don't worry," Harold said, picking up his menu. "I'm just yelling at my son, but I can do that after we order." The waiter had given him a commiserating smile, and he had smiled back, thrilled to have been claimed as another's in public, to finally be a member of the tribe of sons and daughters. Later, Harold had resumed his rant, and he had pretended to be upset, but really, he had been happy the entire night, contentment saturating his every cell, smiling so much that Harold had finally asked him if he was drunk.

But now Harold too has started to ask him questions. "This is a terrific place," he said when he was in town the previous month for the birthday dinner he'd commanded Willem not to throw for him and which Willem had done anyway. Harold had stopped by the apartment the next day, and as he always did, rambled about it admiringly, saying the same things he always did: "This is a terrific place"; "It's so clean in here"; "Malcolm did such a good job"; and, lately, "It's massive, though, Jude. Don't you get lonely in here by yourself?"

"No, Harold," he said. "I like being alone."

Harold had grunted. "Willem seems happy," he said. "Robin seems like a nice girl."

"She is," he said, making Harold a cup of tea. "And I think he is happy."

"Jude, don't you want that for yourself?" Harold asked.

He sighed. "No, Harold, I'm fine."

"Well, what about me and Julia?" asked Harold. "We'd like to see you with someone."

"You know I want to make you and Julia happy," he said, trying to keep his voice level. "But I'm afraid I'm not going to be able to help you on this front. Here." He gave Harold his tea.

Sometimes he wonders whether this very idea of loneliness is something he would feel at all had he not been awakened to the fact that he *should* be feeling lonely, that there is something strange and unacceptable about the life he has. Always, there are people asking him if he misses what it had never occurred to him to want, never occurred to him he might have: Harold and Malcolm, of course, but also Richard, whose girlfriend, a fellow artist named India, has all but moved in with him, and people he sees less frequently as well—Citizen and Elijah and Phaedra and even Kerrigan, his old colleague from Judge Sullivan's chambers, who had looked him up a few months ago when he was in town with his husband. Some of them ask him with pity, and some ask him with suspicion: the first group feels sorry for him because they assume his singlehood is not his decision but a state imposed upon him; and the second group feels a kind of hostility for him, because they think that singlehood *is* his decision, a defiant violation of a fundamental law of adulthood.

Either way, being single at forty is different from being single at thirty, and with every year it becomes less understandable, less enviable, and more pathetic, more inappropriate. For the past five years, he has attended every partners' dinner alone, and a year ago, when he became an equity partner, he attended the partners' annual retreat alone as well. The week before the retreat, Lucien had come into his office one Friday night and sat down to review the week's business, as he often did. They talked about the retreat, which was going to be in Anguilla, and which the two of them genuinely dreaded, unlike the other partners, who pretended to dread it but actually (he and Lucien agreed) were looking forward to it.

"Is Meredith coming?" he asked.

"She is." There was a silence, and he knew what was coming next. "Are you bringing anyone?"

"No," he said.

Another silence, in which Lucien stared at the ceiling. "You've never brought anyone to one of these events, have you?" asked Lucien, his voice carefully casual.

"No," he said, and then, when Lucien didn't say anything, "Are you trying to tell me something, Lucien?"

"No, of course not," Lucien said, looking back at him. "This isn't the sort of firm where we keep track of those kinds of things, Jude, you know that."

He had felt a flush of anger and embarrassment. "Except it clearly is. If the management committee is saying something, Lucien, you have to tell me."

"Jude," said Lucien. "We're not. You know how much everyone here respects you. I just think—and this is not the firm talking, just me—that I'd like to see you settled down with someone."

"Okay, Lucien, thanks," he'd said, wearily. "I'll take that under advisement."

But as self-conscious as he is about appearing normal, he doesn't want a relationship for propriety's sake: he wants it because he has realized he is lonely. He is so lonely that he sometimes feels it physically, a sodden clump of dirty laundry pressing against his chest. He cannot unlearn the feeling. People make it sound so easy, as if the decision to want it is the most difficult part of the process. But he knows better: being in a relationship would mean exposing himself to someone, which he has still never done to anyone but Andy; it would mean the confrontation of his own body, which he has not seen unclothed in at least a decade—even in the shower he doesn't look at himself. And it would mean having sex with someone, which he hasn't done since he was fifteen, and which he dreads so completely that the thought of it makes his stomach fill with something waxy and cold. When he first started seeing Andy, Andy would occasionally ask him if he was sexually active, until he finally told Andy that he would tell him when and if it ever happened, and until then, Andy could stop asking him. So Andy never asked again, and he has never had to volunteer the information. Not having sex: it was one of the best things about being an adult.

But as much as he fears sex, he also wants to be touched, he wants to feel someone else's hands on him, although the thought of that too terrifies him. Sometimes he looks at his arms and is filled with a self-hatred so fiery that he can barely breathe: much of what his body has become has been beyond his control, but his arms have been all his doing, and he can only blame himself. When he had begun cutting himself, he cut on his legs—just the calves—and before he learned to be organized about how he applied them, he swiped the blade across the skin in haphazard strokes, so it looked as if he had been scratched by a crosshatch of grasses. No one ever noticed—no one ever looks at a person's calves. Even Brother Luke hadn't bothered him about them. But now, no one could not notice his arms, or his back, or his legs, which are striped with runnels where damaged tissue and muscle have been removed, and indentations the size of thumbprints, where the braces' screws had once been drilled through the flesh and into the bone, and satiny ponds of skin where he had sustained burns in the injury, and the places where his wounds have closed over, where the flesh now craters slightly, the area around them tinged a permanent dull bronze. When he has clothes on, he is one person, but without them, he is revealed as he really is, the years of rot manifested on his skin, his own flesh advertising his past, its depravities and corruptions.

Once, in Texas, one of his clients had been a man who was grotesque—so fat that his stomach had dropped into a pendant of flesh between his legs, and covered everywhere with floes of eczema, the skin so dry that when he moved, small ghostly strips of it floated from his arms and back and into the air. He had been sickened, seeing the man, and yet they all sickened him, and so in a way, this man was no better or worse than the others. As he had given the man a blow job, the man's stomach pressing against his neck, the man had cried, apologizing to him: *I'm sorry, I'm sorry*, he said, the tips of his fingers on the top of his head. The man had long fingernails, each as thick as bone, and he dragged them over his scalp, but gently, as if they were tines of a comb. And somehow, it is as if over the years he has become that man, and he knows that if anyone were to see him, they too would feel repulsed, nauseated by his deformities. He doesn't want someone to have to stand before the toilet retching, as he had done afterward, scooping handfuls of liquid soap into his mouth, gagging at the taste, trying to make himself clean again.

So he will never have to do anything he doesn't want to for food or shelter: he finally knows that. But what is he willing to do to feel less alone? Could he destroy everything he's built and protected so diligently for intimacy? How much humiliation is he ready to endure? He doesn't know; he is afraid of discovering the answer.

But increasingly, he is even more afraid that he will never have the chance to discover it at all. What does it mean to be a human, if he can never have this? And yet, he reminds himself, loneliness is not hunger, or deprivation, or illness: it is not fatal. Its eradication is not owed him. He has a better life than so many people, a better life than he had ever thought he would have. To wish for companionship along with everything else he has seems a kind of greed, a gross entitlement.

The weeks pass. Willem's schedule is erratic, and he calls him at odd hours: at one in the morning, at three in the afternoon. He sounds tired, but it isn't in Willem's nature to complain, and he doesn't. He tells him about the scenery, the archaeological sites they've been given permission to shoot in, the little mishaps on set. When Willem is away, he is increasingly inclined to stay indoors and do nothing, which he knows isn't healthy, and so he has been vigilant about filling his weekends with events, with parties and dinners. He goes to museum shows, and to plays with Black Henry Young and to galleries with Richard. Felix, whom he tutored so long ago, now helms a punk band called the Quiet Amerikans, and he makes Malcolm come with him to their show. He tells Willem about what he's seen and what he's read, about conversations with Harold and Julia, about Richard's latest project and his clients at the nonprofit, about Andy's daughter's birthday party and Phaedra's new job, about people he's talked to and what they've said.

"Five and a half more months," Willem says at the end of one conversation.

"Five and a half more," he repeats.

That Thursday he goes to dinner at Rhodes's new apartment, which is near Malcolm's parents' house, and which Rhodes had told him over drinks in December is the source of all his nightmares: he wakes at night with ledgers scrolling through his mind, the stuff of his life— tuition, mortgages, maintenances, taxes—reduced to terrifyingly large figures. "And this is *with* my parents' help," he'd said. "*And* Alex wants to have another kid. I'm forty-five, Jude, and I'm already beat; I'm going to be working until I'm eighty if we have a third."

Tonight, he is relieved to see, Rhodes seems more relaxed, his neck and cheeks pink. "Christ," Rhodes says, "how do you stay so thin year after year?" When they had met at the U.S. Attorney's Office, fifteen years ago, Rhodes had still looked like a lacrosse player, all muscle and sinew, but since joining the bank, he has thickened, grown abruptly old.

"I think the word you're looking for is 'scrawny,'" he tells Rhodes.

Rhodes laughs. "I don't think so," he says, "but I'd take scrawny at this point."

There are eleven people at dinner, and Rhodes has to retrieve his desk chair from his office, and the bench from Alex's dressing room. He remembers this about Rhodes's dinners: the food is always perfect, there are always flowers on the table, and yet something always goes wrong with the guest list and the seating—Alex invites someone she's just met and forgets to tell Rhodes, or Rhodes miscounts, and what is intended as a formal, organized event becomes instead chaotic and casual. "Shit!" Rhodes says, as he always does, but he's always the only one who minds.

Alex is seated to his left, and he talks to her about her job as the public relations director of a fashion label called Rothko, which she has just quit, to Rhodes's consternation. "Do you miss it yet?" he asks.

"Not yet," she says. "I know Rhodes isn't happy about it"—she smiles—"but he'll get over it. I just felt I should stay home while the kids are young."

He asks about the country house the two of them have bought in Connecticut (another source of Rhodes's nightmares), and she tells him about the renovation, which is grinding into its third summer, and he groans in sympathy. "Rhodes said you were looking somewhere in Columbia County," she says. "Did you end up buying?"

"Not yet," he says. It had been a choice: either the house, or he and Richard were going to renovate the ground floor, make the garage usable and add a gym and a small pool—one with a constant current, so you could swim in place in it—and in the end, he chose the renovation. Now he swims every morning in complete privacy; not even Richard enters the gym area when he's in it.

"We wanted to wait on the house, actually," Alex admits. "But really, we didn't have a choice—we wanted the kids to have a yard while they were little."

He nods; he has heard this story before, from Rhodes. Often, it feels as if he and Rhodes (and he and almost every one of his contemporaries at the firm) are living parallel versions of adulthood. Their world is governed by children, little despots whose needs—school and camp and activities and tutors—dictate every decision, and will for the next ten, fifteen, eighteen years. Having children has provided their adulthood with an instant and nonnegotiable sense of purpose and direction: they decide the length and location of that year's vacation; they determine if there will be any leftover money, and if so, how it might be spent; they give shape to a day, a week, a year, a life. Children are a kind of cartography, and all one has to do is obey the map they present to you on the day they are born.

But he and his friends have no children, and in their absence, the world sprawls before them, almost stifling in its possibilities. Without them, one's status as an adult is never secure; a childless adult creates adulthood for himself, and as exhilarating as it often is, it is also a state of perpetual insecurity, of perpetual doubt. Or it is to some people—certainly it is to Malcolm, who recently reviewed with him a list he'd made in favor of and against having children with Sophie, much as he had when he was deciding whether to marry Sophie in the first place, four years ago.

"I don't know, Mal," he said, after listening to Malcolm's list. "It sounds like the reasons for having them are because you feel you *should*, not because you really want them."

"*Of course* I feel I should," said Malcolm. "Don't you ever feel like we're all basically still living like children, Jude?"

"No," he said. And he never had: his life was as far from his childhood as he could imagine. "That's your dad talking, Mal. Your life won't be any less valid, or any less legitimate, if you don't have kids."

Malcolm had sighed. "Maybe," he said. "Maybe you're right." He'd smiled. "I mean, I don't really want them."

He smiled back. "Well," he said, "you can always wait. Maybe someday you can adopt a sad thirty-year-old."

"Maybe," Malcolm said again. "After all, I hear it *is* a trend in certain parts of the country."

Now Alex excuses herself to help Rhodes in the kitchen, who has been calling her name with mounting urgency—"Alex. Alex! *Alex!*"—

and he turns to the person on his right, whom he doesn't recognize from Rhodes's other parties, a dark-haired man with a nose that looks like it's been broken: it starts heading decisively in one direction before reversing directions, just as decisively, right below the bridge.

"Caleb Porter."

"Jude St. Francis."

"Let me guess: Catholic."

"Let *me* guess: not."

Caleb laughs. "You're right about that."

They talk, and Caleb tells him he's just moved to the city from London, where he's spent the past decade as the president of a fashion label, to take over as the new CEO at Rothko. "Alex very sweetly and spontaneously invited me yesterday, and I thought"—he shrugs—"why not? It's this, a good meal with nice people, or sitting in a hotel room looking desultorily at real estate listings." From the kitchen there is a timpani clatter of falling metal, and Rhodes swearing. Caleb looks at him, his eyebrows raised, and he smiles. "Don't worry," he reassures him. "This always happens."

Over the remainder of the meal, Rhodes makes attempts to corral his guests into a group conversation, but it doesn't work—the table is too wide, and he has unwisely seated friends near each other—and so he ends up talking to Caleb. He is forty-nine, and grew up in Marin County, and hasn't lived in New York since he was in his thirties. He too went to law school, although, he says, he's never used a day of what he learned at work.

"Never?" he asks. He is always skeptical when people say that; he is skeptical of people who claim law school was a colossal waste, a three-year mistake. Although he also recognizes that he is unusually sentimental about law school, which gave him not only his livelihood but, in many ways, his life.

Caleb thinks. "Well, maybe not *never*, but not in the way you'd expect," he finally says. He has a deep, careful, slow voice, at once soothing and, somehow, slightly menacing. "The thing that actually *has* ended up being useful is, of all things, civil procedure. Do you know anyone who's a designer?"

"No," he says. "But I have a lot of friends who're artists."

"Well, then. You know how differently they think—the better the artist, the higher the probability that they'll be completely unsuited for business. And they really are. I've worked at five houses in the past twenty-odd years, and what's fascinating is witnessing the patterns of behavior—the refusal to hew to deadlines, the inability to stay within budget, the near incompetence when it comes to managing a staff— that are so consistent you begin to wonder if lacking these qualities is something that's a prerequisite to having the job, or whether the job itself encourages these sorts of conceptual gaps. So what you have to do, in my position, is construct a system of governance within the company, and then make sure it's enforceable and punishable. I'm not quite sure how to explain it: you can't tell them that it's good business to do one thing or another—that means nothing to them, or at least to some of them, as much as they say they understand it—you have to instead present it as the bylaws of their own small universe, and convince them that if they don't follow these rules, their universe will collapse. As long as you can persuade them of this, you can get them to do what you need. It's completely maddening."

"So why do you keep working with them?"

"Because—they *do* think so differently. It's fascinating to watch. Some of them are essentially subliterate: you get notes from them and they can really barely construct a sentence. But then you watch them sketching, or draping, or just putting colors together, and it's . . . I don't know. It's wondrous. I can't explain it any better than that."

"No—I know exactly what you mean," he says, thinking of Richard, and JB, and Malcolm, and Willem. "It's as if you're being allowed entrée into a way of thinking you don't even have language to imagine, much less articulate."

"That's exactly right," Caleb says, and smiles at him for the first time.

The dinner winds down, and as everyone's drinking coffee, Caleb disentangles his legs from under the table. "I'm going to head off," he says. "I think I'm still on London time. But it was a pleasure meeting you."

"You, too," he says. "I really enjoyed it. And good luck establishing a system of civil governance within Rothko."

"Thanks, I'll need it," says Caleb, and then, as he's about to stand, he stops and says, "Would you like to have dinner sometime?"

For a moment, he is paralyzed. But then he rebukes himself: he has nothing to fear. Caleb has just moved back to the city—he knows how difficult it must be to find someone to talk to, how difficult it is to find friends when, in your absence, all your friends have started families and are strangers to you. It is talking, nothing more. "That'd be great," he says, and he and Caleb exchange cards.

"Don't get up," Caleb says, as he starts to rise. "I'll be in touch." He watches as Caleb—who is taller than he had thought, at least two inches taller than he is, with a powerful-looking back—rumbles his goodbyes to Alex and Rhodes and then leaves without turning around.

He gets a message from Caleb the following day, and they schedule a dinner for Thursday. Late in the afternoon, he calls Rhodes to thank him for dinner, and ask him about Caleb.

"I'm embarrassed to say I didn't even speak to him," Rhodes says. "Alex invited him very last minute. This is exactly what I'm talking about with these dinner parties: Why is she inviting someone who's taking over at a company she's just leaving?"

"So you don't know anything about him?"

"Nothing. Alex says he's well-respected and that Rothko fought hard to bring him back from London. But that's all I know. Why?" He can almost hear Rhodes smiling. "Don't tell me you're expanding your client base from the glamorous world of securities and pharma?"

"That's *exactly* what I'm doing, Rhodes," he says. "Thanks again. And tell Alex thanks as well."

Thursday arrives, and he meets Caleb at an izakaya in west Chelsea. After they've ordered, Caleb says, "You know, I was looking at you all through that dinner and trying to remember where I knew you from, and then I realized—it was a painting by Jean-Baptiste Marion. The creative director at my last company owned it—actually, he tried to make the company pay for it, but that's a different story. It's a really tight image of your face, and you're standing outside; you can see a streetlight behind you."

"Right," he says. This has happened to him a few times before, and he always finds it unsettling. "I know exactly the one you mean; it's from 'Seconds, Minutes, Hours, Days'—the third series."

"That's right," says Caleb, and smiles at him. "Are you and Marion close?"

"Not so much anymore," he says, and as always, it hurts him to admit it. "But we were college roommates—I've known him for years."

"It's a great series," Caleb says, and they talk about JB's other work, and Richard, whose work Caleb also knows, and Asian Henry Young; and about the paucity of decent Japanese restaurants in London; and about Caleb's sister, who lives in Monaco with her second husband and their huge brood of children; and about Caleb's parents, who died, after long illnesses, when he was in his thirties; and about the house in Bridgehampton that Caleb's law school classmate is letting him use this summer while he's in L.A. And then there is enough talk of Rosen Pritchard, and the financial mess that Rothko has been left in by the departing CEO to convince him that Caleb is looking not just for a friend but potentially for representation as well, and he starts thinking about who at the firm should be responsible for the company. He thinks: I should give this to Evelyn, who is one of the young partners the firm nearly lost the previous year to, in fact, a fashion house, where she would have been their in-house counsel. Evelyn would be good for this account—she is smart and she is interested in the industry, and it would be a good match.

He is thinking this when Caleb abruptly asks, "Are you single?" And then, laughing, "Why are you looking at me like that?"

"Sorry," he says, startled, but smiling back. "I am, yes. But—I was just having this very conversation with my friend."

"And what did your friend say?"

"He said—" he begins, but then stops, embarrassed, and confused by the sudden shift of topic, of tone. "Nothing," he says, and Caleb smiles, almost as if he has actually recounted the conversation, but doesn't press him. He thinks then how he will make this evening into a story to tell Willem, especially this most recent exchange. *You win, Willem,* he'll say to him, and if Willem tries to bring up the subject again, he decides he'll let him, and that this time, he won't evade his questions.

He pays and they walk outside, where it is raining, not heavily, but steadily enough so that there are no cabs, and the streets gleam like licorice. "I have a car waiting," Caleb says. "Can I drop you somewhere?"

"You don't mind?"

"Not at all."

The car takes them downtown, and by the time they've reached Greene Street it's pouring, so hard that they can no longer discern shapes through the window, just colors, spangles of red and yellow lights, the city reduced to the honking of horns and the clatter of rain against the roof of the car, so loud that they can barely hear each other over the din. They stop and he's about to get out when Caleb tells him to wait, he has an umbrella and will walk him into the building, and before he can object, Caleb is getting out and unsnapping an umbrella, and the two of them huddle beneath it and into the lobby, the door thudding shut behind him, leaving them standing in the darkened entryway.

"This is a hell of a lobby," Caleb says, dryly, looking up at the bare bulb. "Although it *does* have a sort of end-of-empire chic," and he laughs, and Caleb smiles. "Does Rosen Pritchard know you're living in a place like this?" he asks, and then, before he can answer, Caleb leans in and kisses him, very hard, so that his back is pressed against the door, and Caleb's arms make a cage around him.

In that moment, he goes blank, the world, his very self, erasing themselves. It has been a long, long time since anyone has kissed him, and he remembers the sense of helplessness he felt whenever it happened, and how Brother Luke used to tell him to just open his mouth and relax and do nothing, and now—out of habit and memory, and the inability to do anything else—that is what he does, and waits for it to be over, counting the seconds and trying to breathe through his nose.

Finally, Caleb steps back and looks at him, and after a while, he looks back. And then Caleb does it again, this time holding his face between his hands, and he has that sensation he always had when he was a child and was being kissed, that his body was not his own, that every gesture he made was predetermined, reflex after reflex after reflex, and that he could do nothing but succumb to whatever might happen to him next.

Caleb stops a second time and steps back again, looking at him and raising his eyebrows the way he had at Rhodes's dinner, waiting for him to say something.

"I thought you were looking for legal representation," he says at last, and the words are so idiotic that he can feel his face get hot.

But Caleb doesn't laugh. "No," he says. There is another long silence, and it is Caleb who speaks next. "Aren't you going to invite me up?" he asks.

"I don't know," he says, and he wishes, suddenly, for Willem, although this is not the sort of problem that Willem has helped him with before, and in fact, probably not the sort of problem that Willem would even consider a problem at all. He knows what a stolid, careful person he is, and although that stolidity and sense of caution guarantee he will never be the most interesting, or provocative, or glittery person in any gathering, in any room, they have protected him so far, they have given him an adulthood free of sordidness and filth. But sometimes he wonders whether he has insulated himself so much that he has neglected some essential part of being human: maybe he *is* ready to be with someone. Maybe enough time has passed so it will be different. Maybe he is wrong, maybe Willem is right: maybe this isn't an experience that is forbidden to him forever. Maybe he is less disgusting than he thinks. Maybe he really is capable of this. Maybe he won't be hurt after all. Caleb seems, in that moment, to have been conjured, djinn-like, the offspring of his worst fears and greatest hopes, and dropped into his life as a test: On one side is everything he knows, the patterns of his existence as regular and banal as the steady plink of a dripping faucet, where he is alone but safe, and shielded from everything that could hurt him. On the other side are waves, tumult, rainstorms, excitement: everything he cannot control, everything potentially awful and ecstatic, everything he has lived his adult life trying to avoid, everything whose absence bleeds his life of color. Inside him, the creature hesitates, perching on its hind legs, pawing the air as if feeling for answers.

Don't do it, don't fool yourself, no matter what you tell yourself, you know what you are, says one voice.

Take a chance, says the other voice. *You're lonely. You have to try.* This is the voice he always ignores.

This may never happen again, the voice adds, and this stops him.

It will end badly, says the first voice, and then both voices fall silent, waiting to see what he will do.

He doesn't know what to do; he doesn't know what will happen. He has to find out. Everything he has learned tells him to leave; everything he has wished for tells him to stay. *Be brave,* he tells himself. *Be brave for once.*

And so he looks back at Caleb. "Let's go," he says, and although he is already frightened, he begins the long walk down the narrow hallway toward the elevator as if he is not, and along with the scrape of his right foot against the cement, he hears the tap of Caleb's footsteps, and the explosions of rain pinging off the fire escape, and the thrum of his own anxious heart.

———

A year ago, he had begun working on a defense for a gigantic pharmaceutical company called Malgrave and Baskett whose board of directors was being sued by a group of their shareholders for malfeasance, incompetence, and neglect of their fiduciary duties. "Gee," Lucien had said, sarcastically, "I wonder why they'd think that?"

He had sighed. "I know," he said. Malgrave and Baskett was a disaster, and everyone knew it. Over the previous few years, before they had come to Rosen Pritchard, the company had had to contend with two whistle-blower lawsuits (one alleging that a manufacturing facility was dangerously out of date, the other that a different facility was producing contaminated products), had been served with subpoenas in connection with an investigation into an elaborate kickback scheme involving a chain of nursing homes, and had been alleged to be illegally marketing one of their bestselling drugs, which was approved only for treatment of schizophrenics, to Alzheimer's patients.

And so he had spent the last eleven months interviewing fifty of Malgrave and Baskett's current and former directors and officers and compiling a report to answer the lawsuit's claims. He had fifteen other lawyers on his team; one night he overheard some of them referring to the company as Malpractice and Bastard.

"Don't you dare let the client hear you say that," he scolded them. It was late, two in the morning; he knew they were tired. If he had been Lucien, he would have yelled at them, but he was tired too. The previous week, another of the associates on the case, a young woman, had stood up from her desk at three a.m., looked around her, and collapsed. He had called an ambulance and sent everyone home for the night, as long as they returned by nine a.m.; he had stayed an hour longer and then had gone home himself.

"You let them *go home* and you stayed here?" asked Lucien the next day. "You're getting soft, St. Francis. Thank god you don't act like this when you're at trial or we'd never get anywhere. If only opposing counsel knew what a pushover they were actually dealing with."

"So does this mean the firm isn't going to send poor Emma Gersh any flowers?"

"Oh, we already sent them," said Lucien, getting up and wandering out of his office. "'Emma: Get better, get back here soon. Or else. Love from your family at Rosen Pritchard.'"

He loved going to trial, he loved arguing and speaking in a courtroom—you never got to do it enough—but his goal with Malgrave and Baskett was to get the lawsuit tossed by a judge before it entered the grinding, tedious drone years of investigation and discovery. He wrote the motion to dismiss, and in early September, the district court judge threw out the suit.

"I'm proud of you," Lucien says that night. "Malpractice and Bastard don't know how fucking lucky they are; that suit was as solid as they come."

"Well, there's a lot that Malpractice and Bastard don't seem to know," he says.

"True. But I guess you can be complete cretins as long as you have enough sense to hire the right lawyer." He stands. "Are you going anywhere this weekend?"

"No."

"Well, do something relaxing. Go outside. Have a meal. You don't look too good."

"Good night, Lucien!"

"Okay, okay. Good night. And congratulations—really. This is a big one."

He stays at the office for another two hours, tidying and sorting papers, attempting to batten down the constant detritus. He feels no sense of relief, or victory, after these outcomes: just a tiredness, but a simple, well-earned tiredness, as if he has completed a day's worth of physical labor. Eleven months: interviews, research, more interviews, fact-checking, writing, rewriting—and then, in an instant, it is over, and another case will take its place.

Finally he goes home, where he is suddenly so exhausted that he stops on the way to his bedroom to sit on the sofa, and wakes an hour later, disoriented and parched. He hasn't seen or talked to most of his friends in the past few months—even his conversations with Willem have been briefer than usual. Part of this is attributable to Malpractice and Bastard, and the frantic preparations they had demanded; but the other part is attributable to his ongoing confusion over Caleb, about whom he has not told Willem. This weekend, though, Caleb is in Bridgehampton, and he is glad of the time alone.

He still doesn't know how he feels about Caleb, even three months later. He is not altogether certain that Caleb even likes him. Or rather: he knows he enjoys talking to him, but there are times when he catches Caleb looking at him with an expression that borders on disgust. "You're really handsome," Caleb once said, his voice perplexed, taking his chin between his fingers and turning his face toward him. "But—" And although he didn't finish, he could sense what Caleb wanted to say: But something's wrong. But you still repel me. But I don't understand why I don't like you, not really.

He knows Caleb hates his walk, for example. A few weeks after they had started seeing each other, Caleb was sitting on the sofa and he had gone to get a bottle of wine, and as he was walking back, he noticed Caleb staring at him so intently that he had grown nervous. He poured the wine, and they drank, and then Caleb said, "You know, when I met you, we were sitting down, so I didn't know you had a limp."

"That's true," he said, reminding himself that this was not something for which he had to apologize: he hadn't entrapped Caleb; he hadn't intended to deceive him. He took a breath and tried to sound light, mildly curious. "Would you not have wanted to go out with me if you'd known?"

"I don't know," Caleb said, after a silence. "I don't know." He had wanted to vanish, then, to close his eyes and reel back time, back to before he had ever met Caleb. He would have turned down Rhodes's invitation; he would have kept living his little life; he would have never known the difference.

But as much as Caleb hates his walk, he loathes his wheelchair. The first time Caleb had come over in daylight, he had given him a tour of the apartment. He was proud of the apartment, and every day he was grateful to be in it, and disbelieving that it was his. Malcolm had kept Willem's suite—as they called it—where it had been, but had enlarged it and added an office at its northern edge, close to the elevator. And then there was the long open space, with a piano, and a living-room area facing south, and a table that Malcolm had designed on the northern side, the side without windows, and behind it, a bookcase that covered the entire wall until the kitchen, hung with art by his friends, and friends of friends, and other pieces that he had bought over the years. The whole eastern end of the apartment was his: you crossed from the bedroom, on the north side, through the closet and into the bathroom, which had windows that looked east and south. Although he mostly kept the shades in the apartment lowered, you could open them all at once and the space would feel like a rectangle of pure light, the veil between you and the outside world mesmerizingly thin. He often feels as if the apartment is a falsehood: it suggests that the person within it is someone open, and vital, and generous with his answers, and he of course is not that person. Lispenard Street, with its half-obscured alcoves and dark warrens and walls that had been painted over so many times that you could feel ridges and blisters where moths and bugs had been entombed in its layers, was a much more accurate reflection of who he is.

For Caleb's visit, he had let the place shimmer with sunlight, and he could tell Caleb was impressed. They walked slowly through it, Caleb looking at the art and asking about different pieces: where he had gotten them, who had made them, noting the ones he recognized.

And then they came to the bedroom, and he was showing Caleb the piece at the far end of the room—a painting of Willem in the makeup chair he had bought from "Seconds, Minutes, Hours, Days"—when Caleb asked, "Whose wheelchair is that?"

He looked where Caleb was looking. "Mine," he said, after a pause.

"But why?" Caleb had asked him, looking confused. "You can walk."

He didn't know what to say. "Sometimes I need it," he said, finally. "Rarely. I don't use it that often."

"Good," said Caleb. "See that you don't."

He was startled. Was this an expression of concern, or was it a threat? But before he could figure out what he should feel, or what he should answer, Caleb had turned, and was heading into his closet, and he followed him, continuing his tour.

A month after that, he had met Caleb late one night outside his office in the far western borderland of the Meatpacking District. Caleb too worked long hours; it was early July and Rothko would present their spring line in eight weeks. He had driven to work that day, but it was a dry night, and so he got out of the car and sat in his chair under a streetlamp until Caleb came down, talking to someone else. He knew Caleb had seen him—he had raised his hand in his direction and Caleb had given him a barely perceptible nod: neither of them were demonstrative people—and watched Caleb until he finished his conversation and the other man had begun walking east.

"Hi," he said, as Caleb came over to him.

"Why are you in your wheelchair?" Caleb demanded.

For a moment, he couldn't speak, and when he did, he stammered. "I had to use it today," he finally said.

Caleb sighed, and rubbed at his eyes. "I thought you didn't use it."

"I don't," he said, so ashamed that he could feel himself start to sweat. "Not really. I only use it when I absolutely have to."

Caleb nodded, but continued pinching the bridge of his nose. He wouldn't look at him. "Look," he said at last, "I don't think we should have dinner after all. You're obviously not feeling well, and I'm tired. I've got to get some sleep."

"Oh," he said, dismayed. "That's all right. I understand."

"Okay, good," said Caleb. "I'll call you later." He watched Caleb move down the street with his long strides until he disappeared around the corner, and then had gotten into his car and driven home and cut himself until he was bleeding so much that he couldn't grip the razor properly.

The next day was Friday, and he didn't hear from Caleb at all. Well, he thought. That's that. And it was fine: Caleb didn't like the fact that he was in a wheelchair. Neither did he. He couldn't resent Caleb for not being able to accept what he himself couldn't accept.

But then, on Saturday morning, Caleb called just as he was coming back upstairs from the pool. "I'm sorry about Thursday night," Caleb said. "I know it must seem heartless and bizarre to you, this—aversion I have to your wheelchair."

He sat down in one of the chairs around the dining-room table. "It doesn't seem bizarre at all," he said.

"I told you my parents were sick for much of my adult life," Caleb said. "My father had multiple sclerosis, and my mother—no one knew what she had. She got sick when I was in college and never got better. She had face pains, headaches: she was in a sort of constant low-grade discomfort, and although I don't doubt it was real, what bothered me so much is that she never seemed to *want* to try to get better. She just gave up, as did he. Everywhere you looked there was evidence of their surrender to illness: first canes, then walkers, then wheelchairs, then scooters, and vials of pills and tissues and the perpetual scent of pain creams and gels and who knows what else."

He stopped. "I want to keep seeing you," he said, at last. "But—but I can't be around these accessories to weakness, to disease. I just can't. I hate it. It embarrasses me. It makes me feel—not depressed, but furious, like I need to fight against it." He paused again. "I just didn't know that's who you were when I met you," he said at last. "I thought I could be okay with it. But I'm not sure I can. Can you understand that?"

He swallowed; he wanted to cry. But he could understand it; he felt exactly as Caleb did. "I can," he said.

And yet improbably, they had continued after all. He is astonished, still, by the speed and thoroughness with which Caleb insinuated himself into his life. It was like something out of a fairy tale: a woman living on the edge of a dark forest hears a knock and opens the door of her cottage. And although it is just for a moment, and although she sees no one, in those seconds, dozens of demons and wraiths have slipped past her and into her house, and she will never be able to rid herself of them, ever. Sometimes this was how it felt. Was this the way it was for other people? He doesn't know; he is too afraid to ask. He finds himself replaying old conversations he has had or overheard with people talking about their relationships, trying to gauge the normalcy of his against theirs, looking for clues about how he should conduct himself.

And then there is the sex, which is worse than he had imagined: he had forgotten just how painful it was, how debasing, how repulsive, how much he disliked it. He hates the postures, the positions it demands, each of them degrading because they leave him so helpless and weak; he hates the tastes of it and the smells of it. But mostly, he hates the sounds of it: the meaty smack of flesh hitting flesh, the wounded-animal moans and grunts, the things said to him that were perhaps meant to be arousing but he can only interpret as diminishing. Part of him, he realizes, had always thought it would be better as an adult, as if somehow the mere fact of age would transform the experience into something glorious and enjoyable. In college, in his twenties, in his thirties, he would listen to people talk about it with such pleasure, such delight, and he would think: *That's* what you're so excited about? *Really?* That's not how I remember it at all. And yet he cannot be the one who's correct, and everyone else—millennia of people—wrong. So clearly there is something he doesn't understand about sex. Clearly he is doing something incorrectly.

That first night they had come upstairs, he had known what Caleb had expected. "We have to go slowly," he told him. "It's been a long time."

Caleb looked at him in the dark; he hadn't turned on the light. "How long?" he asked.

"Long," was all he could say.

And for a while, Caleb was patient. But then he wasn't. There came a night in which Caleb tried to remove his clothes, and he had pulled out of his grasp. "I can't," he said. "Caleb—I can't. I don't want you to see what I look like." It had taken everything he had to say this, and he was so scared he was cold.

"Why?" Caleb had asked.

"I have scars," he said. "On my back and legs, and on my arms. They're bad; I don't want you to see them."

He hadn't known, really, what Caleb would say. Would he say: I'm sure they're not so bad? And then would he have to take his clothes off after all? Or would he say: Let's see, and then he would take his clothes off, and Caleb would get up and leave? He saw Caleb hesitate.

"You won't like them," he added. "They're disgusting."

And that had seemed to decide something for Caleb. "Well," he said, "I don't need to see all of your body, right? Just the relevant parts." And for that night, he had lain there, half dressed and half not, waiting for it to be over and more humiliated than if Caleb had demanded he take his clothes off after all.

But despite these disappointments, things have also not been horrible with Caleb, either. He likes Caleb's slow, thoughtful way of speaking, the way he talks about the designers he's worked with, his understanding of color and his appreciation of art. He likes that he can discuss his work—about Malpractice and Bastard—and that Caleb will not only understand the challenges his cases present for him but will find them interesting as well. He likes how closely Caleb listens to his stories, and how his questions show how closely he's been paying attention. He likes how Caleb admires Willem's and Richard's and Malcolm's work, and lets him talk about them as much as he wants. He likes how, when he is leaving, Caleb will put his hands on either side of his face and hold them there for a moment in a sort of silent blessing. He likes Caleb's solidity, his physical strength: he likes watching him move, likes how, like Willem, he is so easy in his own body. He likes how Caleb will sometimes in sleep sling an arm possessively across his chest. He likes waking with Caleb next to him. He likes how Caleb is slightly strange, how he carries a faint threat of danger: he is different from the people he has sought out his entire adult life, people he has determined will never hurt him, people defined by their kindnesses. When he is with Caleb, he feels simultaneously more and less human.

The first time Caleb hit him, he was both surprised and not. This was at the end of July, and he had gone over to Caleb's at midnight, after leaving the office. He had used his wheelchair that day—lately, something had been going wrong with his feet; he didn't know what it was, but he could barely feel them, and had the dislocating sense that he would topple over if he tried to walk—but at Caleb's, he had left the chair in the car and had instead walked very slowly to the front door, lifting each foot unnaturally high as he went so he wouldn't trip.

He knew from the moment he entered the apartment that he shouldn't have come—he could see that Caleb was in a terrible mood and could feel how the very air was hot and stagnant with his anger. Caleb had finally moved into a building in the Flower District, but he hadn't unpacked much, and he was edgy and tense, his teeth squeaking against themselves as he tightened his jaw. But he had brought food, and he moved his way slowly over to the counter to set it down, talking brightly to try to distract Caleb from his gait, trying, desperately, to make things better.

"Why are you walking like that?" Caleb interrupted him.

He hated admitting to Caleb that something else was wrong with him; he couldn't bring himself to do it once again. "Am I walking strangely?" he asked.

"Yeah—you look like Frankenstein's monster."

"I'm sorry," he said. *Leave*, said the voice inside him. *Leave now.* "I wasn't aware of it."

"Well, stop it. It looks ridiculous."

"All right," he said, quietly, and spooned some curry into a bowl for Caleb. "Here," he said, but as he was heading toward Caleb, trying to walk normally, he tripped, his right foot over his left, and dropped the bowl, the green curry splattering against the carpet.

Later, he will remember how Caleb didn't say anything, just whirled around and struck him with the back of his hand, and he had fallen back, his head bouncing against the carpeted floor. "Just get out of here, Jude," he heard Caleb say, not even yelling, even before his vision returned. "Get out; I can't look at you right now." And so he had, bringing himself to his feet and walking his ridiculous monster's walk out of the apartment, leaving Caleb to clean up the mess he had made.

The next day his face began to turn colors, the area around his left eye shading into improbably lovely tones: violets and ambers and bottle greens. By the end of the week, when he went uptown for his appointment with Andy, his cheek was the color of moss, and his eye was swollen nearly shut, the upper lid a puffed, tender, shiny red.

"Jesus Christ, Jude," said Andy, when he saw him. "What the fuck happened to you?"

"Wheelchair tennis," he said, and even grinned, a grin he had practiced in the mirror the night before, his cheek twitching with pain. He had researched everything: where the matches were played, and how frequently, and how many people were in the club. He had made up a story, recited it to himself and to people at the office until it sounded natural, even comic: a forehand from the opposing player, who had played in college, he not turning quickly enough, the thwack the ball had made when it hit his face.

He told all this to Andy as Andy listened, shaking his head. "Well," he said. "I'm glad you're trying something new. But Christ, Jude. Is this such a good idea?"

"You're the one who's always telling me to stay off my feet," he reminded Andy.

"I know, I know," said Andy. "But you have the pool; isn't that enough? And at any rate, you should've come to me after this happened."

"It's just a bruise, Andy," he said.

"It's a pretty fucking bad bruise, Jude. I mean, Jesus."

"Well, anyway," he said, trying to sound unconcerned, even a little defiant. "I need to talk to you about my feet."

"Tell me."

"It's such a strange sensation; they feel like they're encased in cement coffins. I can't feel where they are in space—I can't control them. I lift one leg up and when I put it back down, I can feel in my calf that I've placed the foot, but I can't feel it in the foot itself."

"Oh, Jude," Andy said. "It's a sign of nerve damage." He sighed. "The good news, besides the fact that you've been spared it all this time, is that it's not going to be a permanent condition. The bad news is that I can't tell you when it'll end, or when it might start again. And the other bad news is that the only thing we can do—besides wait—is treat it with pain medication, which I know you won't take." He paused. "Jude, I know you don't like the way they make you feel," Andy said, "but there are some better ones on the market now than when you were twenty, or even thirty. Do you want to try? At least let me give you something mild for your face: Isn't it killing you?"

"It's not so bad," he lied. But he did accept a prescription from Andy in the end.

"And stay off your feet," Andy said, after he had examined his face. "And stay off the courts, too, for god's sake." And, as he was leaving, "And don't think we're not going to discuss your cutting!" because he was cutting himself more since he had begun seeing Caleb.

Back on Greene Street, he parked in the short driveway preceding the building's garage and was fitting his key into the front door when he heard someone call his name, and then saw Caleb climbing out of his car. He was in his wheelchair, and he tried to get inside quickly. But Caleb was faster than he, and grabbed the door as it was closing, and then the two of them were in the lobby again, alone.

"You shouldn't be here," he said to Caleb, at whom he couldn't look.

"Jude, listen," Caleb said. "I'm so sorry. I really am. I was just— it's been a terrible time at work, everything's such shit there—I'd have come over earlier this week, but it's been so bad that I couldn't even get away—and I completely took it out on you. I'm really sorry." He crouched beside him. "Jude. Look at me." He sighed. "I'm so sorry." He took his face in his hands and turned it toward him. "Your poor face," he said quietly.

He still can't quite understand why he let Caleb come up that night. If he is to admit it to himself, he feels there was something inevitable, even, in a small way, a relief, about Caleb's hitting him: all along, he had been waiting for some sort of punishment for his arrogance, for thinking he could have what everyone else has, and here—at last—it was. *This is what you get*, said the voice inside his head. *This is what you get for pretending to be someone you know you're not, for thinking you're as good as other people.* He remembers how JB had been so terrified of Jackson, and how he had understood his fear, how he had understood how you could get trapped by another human being, how what seemed so easy—the act of walking away from them—could feel so difficult. He feels about Caleb the way he once felt about Brother Luke: someone in whom he had, rashly, entrusted himself, someone in whom he had placed such hopes, someone he hoped could save him. But even when it became clear that they would not, even when his hopes turned rancid, he was unable to disentangle himself from them, he was unable to leave. There is a sort of symmetry to his pairing with Caleb that makes sense: they are the damaged and the damager, the sliding heap of garbage and the jackal sniffing through it. They exist only to themselves—he has met no one in Caleb's life, and he has not introduced Caleb to anyone in his. They both know that something about what they are doing is shameful. They are bound to each other by their mutual disgust and discomfort: Caleb tolerates his body, and he tolerates Caleb's revulsion.

He has always known that if he wanted to be with someone, he would have to make an exchange. And Caleb, he knows, is the best he will ever be able to find. At least Caleb isn't misshapen, isn't a sadist. Nothing being done to him now is something that hasn't been done to him before—he reminds himself of this again and again.

One weekend at the end of September, he drives out to Caleb's friend's house in Bridgehampton, which Caleb is now occupying until early October. Rothko's presentation went well, and Caleb has been more relaxed, affectionate, even. He has only hit him once more, a punch to the sternum that sent him skidding across the floor, but had apologized directly afterward. But other than that, things have been unremarkable: Caleb spends Wednesday and Thursday nights at Greene Street and then drives out to the beach on Fridays. He goes to the office early and stays late. After his success with Malpractice and Bastard, he had thought he might have a respite, even a short one, but he hasn't—a new client, an investment firm being investigated for securities fraud, has come in, and even now, he feels guilty about skipping a Saturday at work.

His guilt aside, that Saturday is perfect, and they spend most of the day outdoors, both of them working. In the evening, Caleb grills them steaks. As he does, he sings, and he stops working to listen to him, and knows that they are both happy, and that for a moment, all of their ambivalence about each other is dust, something impermanent and weightless. That night, they go to bed early, and Caleb doesn't make him have sex, and he sleeps deeply, better than he has in weeks.

But the next morning, he can tell even before he is fully conscious that the pain in his feet is back. It had vanished, completely and unpredictably, two weeks ago, but now it's returned, and as he stands, he can also tell it's gotten worse: it is as if his legs end at his ankles, and his feet are simultaneously inanimate and vividly painful. To walk, he must look down at them; he needs visual confirmation that he is lifting one, and visual confirmation that he is placing it down again.

He takes ten steps, but each one takes a greater and greater effort—the movement is so difficult, takes so much mental energy, that he is nauseated, and sits down again on the edge of the bed. *Don't let Caleb see you like this,* he warns himself, before remembering: Caleb is out running, as he does every morning. He is alone in the house.

He has some time, then. He drags himself to the bathroom on his arms and into the shower. He thinks of the spare wheelchair in his car. Surely Caleb will have no objections to him getting it, especially if he can present himself as basically healthy, and this as just a small setback, a day-long inconvenience. He was planning on driving back to the city very early the next morning, but he could leave earlier if he needs to, although he would rather not—yesterday had been so nice. Maybe today can be as well.

He is dressed and waiting on the sofa in the living room, pretending to read a brief, when Caleb returns. He can't tell what kind of mood he's in, but he's generally mild after his runs, even indulgent.

"I sliced some of the leftover steak," he tells him. "Do you want me to make you eggs?"

"No, I can do it," Caleb says.

"How was your run?"

"Good. Great."

"Caleb," he says, trying to keep his tone light, "listen—I've been having this problem with my feet; it's just some side effects from nerve damage that comes and goes, but it makes it really difficult for me to walk. Do you mind if I get the wheelchair from my car?"

Caleb doesn't say anything for a minute, just finishes drinking his bottle of water. "You *can* still walk, though, right?"

He forces himself to look back at Caleb. "Well—technically, yes. But—"

"Jude," says Caleb, "I know your doctor probably disagrees, but I have to say I think there's something a little—weak, I guess, about your always going to the easiest solution. I think you have to just endure some things, you know? This is what I meant with my parents: it was always such a succumbing to their every pain, their every twinge.

"So I think you should tough it out. I think if you *can* walk, you should. I just don't think you should get into this habit of babying yourself when you're capable of doing better."

"Oh," he says. "Right. I understand." He feels a profound shame, as if he has just asked for something filthy and illicit.

"I'm going to shower," says Caleb, after a silence, and leaves.

For the rest of the day, he tries to move very little, and Caleb, as if not wanting to find reason to get angry with him, doesn't ask him to do anything. Caleb makes lunch, which they both eat on the sofa, both working on their computers. The kitchen and living room are one large sunlit space, with full-length windows that open onto the lawn over- looking the beach, and when Caleb is in the kitchen making dinner, he takes advantage of his turned back to inch, wormlike, to the hallway bathroom. He wants to go to the bedroom to get more aspirin out of his bag, but it's too far, and he instead waits in the doorway on his knees until Caleb turns toward the stove again before crawling back to the sofa, where he has spent the entire day.

"Dinner," Caleb announces, and he takes a breath and brings him- self to his feet, which are cinder blocks, they are so heavy and clunky, and, watching them, begins to make his way to the table. It feels like it takes minutes, hours, to walk to his chair, and at one point he looks up and sees Caleb, his jaw moving, watching him with what looks like hate.

"Hurry up," Caleb says.

They eat in silence. He can barely stand it. The scrape of the knife against the plate: unbearable. The crunch of Caleb biting down, unnecessarily hard, on a green bean: unbearable. The feel of food in his mouth, all of it becoming a fleshy nameless beast: unbearable.

"Caleb," he begins, very quietly, but Caleb doesn't answer him, just pushes back his chair and stands and goes to the sink.

"Bring me your plate," Caleb says, and then watches him. He stands, slowly, and begins his trek to the sink, eyeing each footfall before he begins a new step.

He will wonder, later, if he forced the moment, if he could have in fact made the twenty steps without falling had he just concentrated harder. But that isn't what happens. He moves his right foot just half a second before his left one has landed, and he falls, and the plate falls before him, the china shattering on the floor. And then, moving as swiftly as if he'd anticipated it, there is Caleb, yanking him up by his hair and punching him in the face with his fist, so hard that he is air-borne, and when he lands, he does so against the table, knocking the base of his skull against its edge. His fall makes the bottle of wine jump off the surface, the liquid glugging onto the floor, and Caleb makes a roar, and snatches at the bottle by its throat and hits him on the back of his neck with it.

"Caleb," he gasps, "please, please." He was never one to beg for mercy, not even as a child, but he has become that person, somehow. When he was a child, his life meant little to him; he wishes, now, that that were still true. "Please," he says. "Caleb, please forgive me—I'm sorry, I'm sorry."

But Caleb, he knows, is no longer human. He is a wolf, he is a coy-ote. He is muscle and rage. And he is nothing to Caleb, he is prey, he is disposable. He is being dragged to the edge of the sofa, he knows what will happen next. But he continues to ask, anyway. "Please, Caleb," he says. "Please don't. Caleb, please."

When he regains consciousness, he is on the floor near the back of the sofa, and the house is silent. "Hello?" he calls, hating the quaver in his voice, but he doesn't hear anything. He doesn't need to—he knows, somehow, that he is alone.

He sits up. He pulls up his underwear and pants and flexes his fingers, his hands, brings his knees to his chest and back down again, moves his shoulders back and forward, turns his neck from left to right. There is something sticky on the back of his neck, but when he exam-ines it, he's relieved to see it's not blood but wine. Everything hurts, but nothing is broken.

He crawls to the bedroom. He quickly cleans himself off in the bathroom and gathers his things and puts them in his bag. He scuttles to the door. For an instant he is afraid that his car will have disappeared, and he will be stranded, but it is there, next to Caleb's, waiting for him. He checks his watch: it is midnight.

He moves his way across the lawn on his hands and knees, his bag slung painfully over one shoulder, the two hundred feet between the door and the car transforming themselves into miles. He wants to stop, he is so tired, but he knows he must not.

In the car, he doesn't look at his reflection in the mirror; he starts the engine and drives away. But about half an hour later, once he knows he is far enough from the house to be safe, he begins to shake, so badly that the car swerves beneath him, and he pulls off the road to wait, leaning his forehead against the steering wheel.

He waits for ten minutes, twenty. And then he turns, although the very movement is a punishment, and finds his phone in his bag. He dials Willem's number and waits.

"Jude!" says Willem, sounding surprised. "I was just going to call you."

"Hi, Willem," he says, and hopes his voice sounds normal. "I guess I read your thoughts."

They talk for a few minutes, and then Willem asks, "Are you okay?"

"Of course," he says.

"You sound a little strange."

Willem, he wants to say. *Willem, I wish you were here.* But instead he says, "Sorry. I just have a headache."

They talk some more, and as they're about to hang up, Willem says, "You're sure you're okay."

"Yes," he says. "I'm fine."

"Okay," says Willem. "Okay." And then, "Five more weeks."

"Five more." He wishes for Willem so intensely he can barely breathe.

After they hang up, he waits for another ten minutes, until he finally stops shaking, and then he starts the car again and drives the rest of the way home.

The next day, he makes himself look at his reflection in the bathroom mirror and nearly cries out in shame and shock and misery. He is so deformed, so astoundingly ugly—even for him, it is extraordinary. He makes himself as presentable as he can; he puts on his favorite suit. Caleb had kicked him in his side, and every movement, every breath, is painful. Before he leaves the house, he makes an appointment with the dentist because he can feel that one of his upper teeth has been knocked loose, and an appointment at Andy's for that evening.

He goes to work. "This is not a good look for you, St. Francis," one of the other senior partners, whom he likes a lot, says at the morning management committee meeting, and everyone laughs.

He forces a smile. "I'm afraid you're right," he says. "And I'm sure you'll all be disappointed when I announce that my days as a potential Paralympic tennis champion are, sadly, over."

"Well, *I'm* not sad," says Lucien, as everyone around the table groans in mock disappointment. "You get plenty of aggression out in court. I think that should be your sole combat sport from now on."

That night at his appointment, Andy swears at him. "What'd I say about tennis, Jude?" he asks.

"I know," he says. "But never again, Andy, I promise."

"What's this?" Andy asks, placing his fingers on the back of his neck.

He sighs, theatrically. "I turned, and there was an incident with a nasty backhand." He waits for Andy to say something, but he doesn't, only smears some antibiotic cream on his neck and then bandages it.

The next day, Andy calls him at his office. "I need to talk to you in person," he says. "It's important. Can you meet me somewhere?"

He's alarmed. "Is everything okay?" he asks. "Are you all right, Andy?"

"I'm fine," Andy says. "But I need to see you."

He takes an early dinner break and they meet near his office, at a bar whose regular customers are the Japanese bankers who work in the tower next to Rosen Pritchard's. Andy is already there when he arrives, and he places his palm, gently, on the unmarked side of his face.

"I ordered you a beer," Andy says.

They drink in silence and then Andy says, "Jude, I wanted to see your face when I asked you this. But are you—are you hurting yourself?"

"What?" he asks, surprised.

"These tennis accidents," Andy says, "are they actually—something else? Are you throwing yourself down stairs or against walls, or something?" He takes a breath. "I know you used to do that when you were a kid. Are you doing it again?"

"No, Andy," he says. "No. I'm not doing this to myself. I swear to you. I swear on—on Harold and Julia. I swear on Willem."

"Okay," Andy says, exhaling. "I mean, that's a relief. It's a relief to know you're just being a bonehead and not following doctor's orders, which, of course, is nothing new. And, apparently, that you're a terrible tennis player." He smiles, and he makes himself smile back.

Andy orders them more beers, and for a while, they are quiet. "Do you know, Jude," Andy says, slowly, "that over the years I have wondered and wondered what to do about you? No, don't say anything—let me finish. I would—I do—lie awake at night asking myself if I'm making the right decisions about you: there've been so many times when I was so close to having you committed, to calling Harold or Willem and telling them that we needed to get together and have you taken to a hospital. I've talked to classmates of mine who are shrinks and told them about you, about this patient I'm very close to, and asked them what they would do in my position. I've listened to all their advice. I've listened to *my* shrink's advice. But no one can ever tell me for certain what the right answer is.

"I've tortured myself about this. But I've always felt—you're so high-functioning in so many ways, and you've achieved this weird but undeniably successful equilibrium in your life, that I felt that, I don't know, I just shouldn't upset it. You know? So I've let you go on cutting yourself year after year, and every year, every time I see you, I wonder if I'm doing the right thing by letting you do so, and how and if I should be pushing harder to get you help, to make you stop doing this to yourself."

"I'm sorry, Andy," he whispers.

"No, Jude," Andy says. "It's not your fault. You're the patient. I'm supposed to figure out what's best for you, and I feel—I don't know if I have. So when you came in with bruises, the first thing I thought was that I had made the wrong decision after all. You know?" Andy looks at him, and he is surprised once more to see Andy swipe, quickly, at his eyes. "All these years," says Andy, after a pause, and they are both quiet again.

"Andy," he says, wanting to cry himself. "I swear to you I'm not doing anything else to myself. Just the cutting."

"Just the cutting!" Andy repeats, and makes a strange squawk of laughter. "Well, I suppose—given the context—I have to be grateful for that. 'Just the cutting.' You know how messed up that is, right, that that should be such a relief to me?"

"I know," he says.

Tuesday turns to Wednesday, and then to Thursday; his face feels worse, and then better, and then worse again. He had worried that Caleb might call him or, worse, materialize at his apartment, but the days pass and he doesn't: maybe he has stayed out in Bridgehampton. Maybe he has gotten run over by a car. He finds, oddly, that he feels nothing—not fear, not hate, not anything. The worst has happened, and now he is free. He has had a relationship, and it was awful, and now he will never need to have one again, because he has proven himself incapable of being in one. His time with Caleb has confirmed everything he feared people would think of him, of his body, and his next task is to learn to accept that, and to do so without sorrow. He knows he will still probably feel lonely in the future, but now he has something to answer that loneliness; now he knows for certain that loneliness is the preferable state to whatever it was—terror, shame, disgust, dismay, giddiness, excitement, yearning, loathing—he felt with Caleb.

That Friday he sees Harold, who is in town for a conference at Columbia. He had already written Harold to warn him of his injury, but it doesn't stop Harold from overreacting, exclaiming and fussing over him and asking him dozens of times if he is actually all right.

They have met at one of Harold's favorite restaurants, where the beef comes from cows that the chef has named and raised himself on a farm upstate, and the vegetables are grown on the roof of the building, and they are talking and eating their entrées—he is careful to only chew on the right side of his mouth, and to avoid letting any food come in contact with his new tooth—when he senses someone standing near their table, and when he looks up, it is Caleb, and although he had convinced himself he feels nothing, he is immediately, overwhelmingly terrified.

He had never seen Caleb drunk in their time together, but he can tell instantly that he is, and in a dangerous mood. "Your secretary told me where you were," Caleb says to him. "You must be Harold," he says, and extends his hand to Harold, who shakes it, looking bewildered.

"Jude?" Harold asks him, but he can't speak.

"Caleb Porter," says Caleb, and slides into the semicircular booth, pressing against his side. "Your son and I are dating."

Harold looks at Caleb, and then at him, and opens his mouth, speechless for the first time since he has known him.

"Let me ask you something," Caleb says to Harold, leaning in as if delivering a confidence, and he stares at Caleb's face, his vulpine hand-someness, his dark, glinting eyes. "Be honest. Don't you ever wish you had a normal son, not a cripple?"

For a moment, no one says anything, and he can feel something, a current, sizzle in the air. "Who the fuck are you?" hisses Harold, and then he watches Harold's face change, his features contorting so quickly and violently from shock to disgust to anger that he looks, for an instant, inhuman, a ghoul in Harold's clothing. And then his expression changes again, and he watches something harden in Harold's face, as if his very muscles are ossifying before him.

"You did this to him," he says to Caleb, very slowly. And then to him, in dismay, "It wasn't tennis, was it, Jude. This man did this to you."

"Harold, don't," he begins to say, but Caleb has grabbed his wrist, and is gripping it so hard that he feels it might be breaking. "You little liar," he says to him. "You're a cripple and a liar and a bad fuck. And you're right—you're disgusting. I couldn't even look at you, not ever."

"Get the fuck out of here," says Harold, biting down on each word. They are all of them speaking in whispers, but the conversation feels so loud, and the rest of the restaurant so silent, that he is certain everyone can hear them.

"Harold, don't," he begs him. "Stop, please."

But Harold doesn't listen to him. "I'm going to call the police," he says, and Caleb slides out of the booth and stands, and Harold stands as well. "Get out of here right now," Harold repeats, and now everyone really is looking in their direction, and he is so mortified that he feels sick.

"Harold," he pleads.

He can tell from Caleb's swaying motion that he is really very drunk, and when he pushes at Harold's shoulder, Harold is about to push back when he finds his voice, finally, and shouts Harold's name, and Harold turns to him and lowers his arm. Caleb gives him his small smile, then, and turns and leaves, shoving past some of the waiters who have silently gathered around him.

Harold stands there for a moment, staring at the door, and then begins to follow Caleb, and he calls Harold's name again, desperate, and Harold comes back to him.

"Jude—" Harold begins, but he shakes his head. He is so angry, so furious, that his humiliation has almost been eclipsed by his rage.

Around them, he can hear people's conversations resuming. He hails their waiter and gives him his credit card, which is returned to him in what feels like seconds. He doesn't have his wheelchair today, for which he is enormously, bitterly grateful, and in those moments he is leaving the restaurant, he feels he has never been so nimble, has never moved so quickly or decisively.

Outside, it is pouring. His car is parked a block away, and he shuffles down the sidewalk, Harold silent at his side. He is so livid he wishes he could not give Harold a ride at all, but they are on the east side, near Avenue A, and Harold will never be able to find a cab in the rain.

"Jude—" Harold says once they're in the car, but he interrupts him, keeping his eyes on the road before him. "I was *begging* you not to say anything, Harold," he says. "And you did anyway. Why did you do that, Harold? You think my life is a joke? You think my problems are just an opportunity for you to grandstand?" He doesn't even know what he means, doesn't know what he's trying to say.

"No, Jude, of course not," says Harold, his voice gentle. "I'm sorry—I just lost it."

This sobers him for some reason, and for a few blocks they are silent, listening to the sluice of the wipers.

"Were you really going out with him?" Harold asks.

He gives a single, terse nod. "But not anymore?" Harold asks, and he shakes his head. "Good," Harold mutters. And then, very softly, "Did he hit you?"

He has to wait and control himself before he can answer. "Only a few times," he says.

"Oh, Jude," says Harold, in a voice he has never heard Harold use before.

"Let me ask you something, though," Harold says, as they edge down Fifteenth Street, past Sixth Avenue. "Jude—why were you going out with someone who would treat you like that?"

He doesn't answer for another block, trying to think of what he could say, how he could articulate his reasons in a way Harold would understand. "I was lonely," he says, finally.

"Jude," Harold says, and stops. "I understand that," he says. "But why him?"

"Harold," he says, and he hears how awful, how wretched, he sounds, "when you look like I do, you have to take what you can get."

They are quiet again, and then Harold says, "Stop the car."

"What?" he says. "I can't. There are people behind me."

"Stop the damn car, Jude," Harold repeats, and when he doesn't, Harold reaches over and grabs the wheel and pulls it sharply to the right, into an empty space in front of a fire hydrant. The car behind passes them, its horn bleating a long, warning note.

"Jesus, Harold!" he yells. "What the hell are you trying to do? You nearly got us into an accident!"

"Listen to me, Jude," says Harold slowly, and reaches for him, but he pulls himself back against the window, away from Harold's hands. "You are the most beautiful person I have ever met—ever."

"Harold," he says, "stop, stop. Please stop."

"Look at me, Jude," says Harold, but he can't. "You are. It breaks my heart that you can't see this."

"Harold," he says, and he is almost moaning, "please, please. If you care about me, you'll stop."

"Jude," says Harold, and reaches for him again, but he flinches, and brings his hands up to protect himself. Out of the edge of his eye, he can see Harold lower his hand, slowly.

He finally puts his hands back on the steering wheel, but they are shaking too badly for him to start the ignition, and he tucks them under his thighs, waiting. "Oh god," he hears himself repeating, "oh god."

"Jude," Harold says again.

"Leave me alone, Harold," he says, and now his teeth are chattering as well, and it is difficult for him to speak. "Please."

They sit there in silence for minutes. He concentrates on the sound of the rain, the traffic light turning red and green and orange, and the count of his breaths. Finally his shaking stops, and he starts the car and drives west, and north, up to Harold's building.

"Come stay in the apartment tonight," Harold says, turning to him, but he shakes his head, staring straight ahead. "At least come up and have a cup of tea and wait until you feel a little better," but he shakes his head again. "Jude," Harold says, "I'm really sorry—for everything, for all of it." He nods, but still can't say anything. "Will you call me if you need anything?" Harold persists, and he nods again. And then Harold reaches his hand up, slowly, as if he is a feral animal, and strokes the back of his head, twice, before getting out, closing the door softly behind him.

He takes the West Side Highway home. He is so sore, so depleted: but now his humiliations are complete. He has been punished enough, he thinks, even for him. He will go home, and cut himself, and then he will begin forgetting: this night in particular, but also the past four months.

At Greene Street he parks in the garage and rides the elevator up past the silent floors, clinging to the cage-door mesh; he is so tired that he will slump to the ground if he doesn't. Richard is away for the fall at a residency in Rome, and the building is sepulchral around him.

He steps into his darkened apartment and is feeling for the light switch when something clots him, hard, on the swollen side of his face, and even in the dark he can see his new tooth project itself into the air.

It is Caleb, of course, and he can hear and smell his breath even before Caleb flicks the master switch and the apartment is illuminated, dazzlingly, into something brighter than day, and he looks up and sees Caleb above him, peering down at him. Even drunk, he is composed, and now some of his drunkenness has been clarified by rage, and his gaze is steady and focused. He feels Caleb grab him by his hair, feels him hit him on the right side of his face, the good one, feels his head snapping backward in response.

Caleb still hasn't said anything, and now he drags him to the sofa, the only sounds Caleb's steady breaths and his frantic gulps. He pushes his face into the cushions and holds his head down with one hand, while with the other, he begins pulling off his clothes. He begins to panic, then, and struggle, but Caleb presses one arm against the back of his neck, which paralyzes him, and he is unable to move; he can feel himself become exposed to the air piece by piece—his back, his arms, the backs of his legs—and when everything's been removed, Caleb yanks him to his feet again and pushes him away, but he falls, and lands on his back.

"Get up," says Caleb. "Right now."

He does; his nose is discharging something, blood or mucus, that is making it difficult for him to breathe. He stands; he has never felt more naked, more exposed in his life. When he was a child, and things were happening to him, he used to be able to leave his body, to go somewhere else. He would pretend he was something inanimate—a curtain rod, a ceiling fan—a dispassionate, unfeeling witness to the scene occurring beneath him. He would watch himself and feel nothing: not pity, not anger, nothing. But now, although he tries, he finds he cannot remove himself. He is in this apartment, his apartment, standing before a man who detests him, and he knows this is the beginning, not the end, of a long night, one he has no choice but to wait through and endure. He will not be able to control this night, he will not be able to stop it.

"My god," Caleb says, after looking at him for a few long moments; it is the first time he has ever seen him wholly naked. "My god, you really are deformed. You really are."

For some reason, it is this, this pronouncement, that brings them both back to themselves, and he finds himself, for the first time in decades, crying. "Please," he says. "Please, Caleb, I'm sorry." But Caleb has already grabbed him by the back of his neck and is hurrying him, half dragging him, toward the front door. Into the elevator they go, and down the flights, and then he is being dragged out of the elevator and marched down the hallway toward the lobby. By now he is hysterical, pleading with Caleb, asking him again and again what he's doing, what he's going to do to him. At the front door, Caleb lifts him, and for a moment his face is fitted into the tiny dirty glass window that looks out onto Greene Street, and then Caleb is opening the door and he is being pushed out, naked, into the street.

"No!" he shouts, half inside, half outside. "Caleb, please!" He is pulled between a crazed hope and a desperate fear that someone will walk by. But it is raining too hard; no one will walk by. The rain drums a wild pattern on his face.

"Beg me," says Caleb, raising his voice over the rain, and he does, pleading with him. "Beg me to stay," Caleb demands. "Apologize to me," and he does, again and again, his mouth filling with his own blood, his own tears.

Finally he is brought inside, and is dragged back to the elevator, where Caleb says things to him, and he apologizes and apologizes, repeating Caleb's words back to him as he instructs: *I'm repulsive. I'm disgusting. I'm worthless. I'm sorry, I'm sorry.*

In the apartment, Caleb lets go of his neck, and he falls, his legs unsteady beneath him, and Caleb kicks him in the stomach so hard that he vomits, and then again in his back, and he slides over Malcolm's lovely, clean floors and into the vomit. His beautiful apartment, he thinks, where he has always been safe. This is happening to him in his beautiful apartment, surrounded by his beautiful things, things that have been given to him in friendship, things that he has bought with money he has earned. His beautiful apartment, with its doors that lock, where he was meant to be protected from broken elevators and the degradation of pulling himself upstairs on his arms, where he was meant to always feel human and whole.

Then he is being lifted again, and moved, but it is difficult to see where he's being taken: one eye is already swollen shut, and the other is blurry. His vision keeps blinking in and out.

But then he realizes that Caleb is taking him to the door that leads to the emergency stairs. It is the one element of the old loft that Malcolm kept: both because he had to and because he liked how bluntly utilitarian it was, how unapologetically ugly. Now Caleb unslides the bolt, and he finds himself standing at the top of the dark, steep staircase. "So descent-into-hell looking," he remembers Richard saying. One side of him is gluey with vomit; he can feel other liquids—he cannot think about what they are—moving down other parts of him: his face, his neck, his thighs.

He is whimpering from pain and fear, clutching the edge of the doorframe, when he hears, rather than sees, Caleb move back and run at him, and then his foot is kicking him in his back, and he is flying into the black of the staircase.

As he soars, he thinks, suddenly, of Dr. Kashen. Or not of Dr. Kashen, necessarily, but the question he had asked him when he was applying to be his advisee: *What's your favorite axiom?* (The nerd pickup line, CM had once called it.)

"The axiom of equality," he'd said, and Kashen had nodded, approvingly. "That's a good one," he'd said.

The axiom of equality states that x always equals x: it assumes that if you have a conceptual thing named x, that it must always be equivalent to itself, that it has a uniqueness about it, that it is in possession of something so irreducible that we must assume it is absolutely, unchangeably equivalent to itself for all time, that its very elementalness can never be altered. But it is impossible to prove. Always, absolutes, nevers: these are the words, as much as numbers, that make up the world of mathematics. Not everyone liked the axiom of equality—Dr. Li had once called it coy and twee, a fan dance of an axiom—but he had always appreciated how elusive it was, how the beauty of the equation itself would always be frustrated by the attempts to prove it. It was the kind of axiom

that could drive you mad, that could consume you, that could easily
become an entire life.

But now he knows for certain how true the axiom is, because he
himself—his very life—has proven it. The person I was will always be
the person I am, he realizes. The context may have changed: he may be
in this apartment, and he may have a job that he enjoys and that pays
him well, and he may have parents and friends he loves. He may be
respected; in court, he may even be feared. But fundamentally, he is
the same person, a person who inspires disgust, a person meant to be
hated. And in that microsecond that he finds himself suspended in the
air, between the ecstasy of being aloft and the anticipation of his landing, which he knows will be terrible, he knows that x will always equal
x, no matter what he does, or how many years he moves away from the
monastery, from Brother Luke, no matter how much he earns or how
hard he tries to forget. It is the last thing he thinks as his shoulder cracks
down upon the concrete, and the world, for an instant, jerks blessedly
away from beneath him: $x = x$, he thinks. $x = x$, $x = x$.

2

WHEN JACOB WAS very small, maybe six months old or so, Liesl came down with pneumonia. Like most healthy people, she was a terrible sick person: grouchy and petulant and, mostly, stunned by the unfamiliar place in which she now found herself. "I don't get sick," she kept saying, as if some mistake had been made, as if what had been given her had been meant for someone else.

Because Jacob was a sickly baby—not in any dramatic way, but he had already had two colds in his short life, and even before I knew what his smile looked like, I knew what his cough sounded like: a surprisingly mature hack—we decided that it would be better if Liesl spent the next few days at Sally's to rest and get better, and I stayed at home with Jacob.

I thought myself basically competent with my son, but over the course of the weekend, I must have called my father twenty times to ask him about the various little mysteries that kept presenting themselves, or to confirm with him what I knew I knew but which, in my fluster, I had forgotten: He was making strange noises that sounded like hiccups but were too irregular to actually be hiccups—what were they? His stool was a little runny—was that a sign of anything? He liked to sleep on his stomach, but Liesl said that he should be on his back, and yet I had always heard that he'd be perfectly fine on his stomach—would he be? Of course, I could've looked all of this up, but I wanted definitive answers, and I wanted to hear them from my father, who had not just the right answers but the right way of delivering them. It comforted me to hear his voice. "Don't worry," he said at the end of every call. "You're doing just fine. You know how to do this." He made me believe I did.

After Jacob got sick, I called my father less: I couldn't bear to talk to him. The questions I now had for him—how would I get through this?; what would I do, afterward?; how could I watch my child die?—were ones I couldn't even bring myself to ask, and ones I knew would make him cry to try to answer.

He had just turned four when we noticed that something was wrong. Every morning, Liesl would take him to nursery school, and every afternoon, after my last class, I would pick him up. He had a serious face, and so people thought that he was a more somber kid than he really was: at home, though, he ran around, up and down the staircase, and I ran after him, and when I was lying on the couch reading, he would come flopping down on top of me. Liesl too became playful around him, and sometimes the two of them would run through the house, shrieking and squealing, and it was my favorite noise, my favorite kind of clatter.

It was October when he began getting tired. I picked him up one day, and all of the other children, all of his friends, were in a jumble, talking and jumping, and then I looked for my son and saw him in a far corner of the room, curled on his mat, sleeping. One of the teachers was sitting near him, and when she saw me, she waved me over. "I think he might be coming down with something," she said. "He's been a little listless for the past day or so, and he was so tired after lunch that we just let him sleep." We loved this school: other schools made the kids try to read, or have lessons, but this school, which was favored by the university's professors, was what I thought school should be for a four-year-old—all they seemed to do was listen to people reading them books, and make various crafts, and go on field trips to the zoo.

I had to carry him out to the car, but when we got home, he woke and was fine, and ate the snack I made him, and listened to me read to him before we built the day's centerpiece together. For his birthday, Sally had gotten him a set of beautiful wooden blocks that were carved into geode-like shapes and could be stacked very high and into all sorts of interesting forms; every day we built a new construction in the center of the table, and when Liesl got home, Jacob would explain to her what we'd been building—a dinosaur, a spaceman's tower—and Liesl would take a picture of it.

That night I told Liesl what Jacob's teacher had said, and the next day, Liesl took him to the doctor, who said he seemed perfectly normal, that nothing seemed out of the ordinary. Still, we watched him over the next few days: Was he more energetic or less? Was he sleeping longer than usual, eating less than usual? We didn't know. But we were frightened: there is nothing more terrifying than a listless child. The very word seems, now, a euphemism for a terrible fate.

And then, suddenly, things began to accelerate. We went to my parents' over Thanksgiving and were having dinner when Jacob began seizing. One moment he was present, and the next he was rigid, his body becoming a plank, sliding off the chair and beneath the table, his eyeballs rolling upward, his throat making a strange, hollow clicking noise. It lasted only ten seconds or so, but it was awful, so awful I can still hear that horrible clicking noise, still see the horrible stillness of his head, his legs marching back and forth in the air.

My father ran and called a friend of his at New York Presbyterian and we rushed there, and Jacob was admitted, and the four of us stayed in his room overnight—my father and Adele lying on their coats on the floor, Liesl and I sitting on either side of the bed, unable to look at each other.

Once he had stabilized, we went home, where Liesl had called Jacob's pediatrician, another med-school classmate of hers, to make appointments with the best neurologist, the best geneticist, the best immunologist—we didn't know what it was, but whatever it was, she wanted to make sure Jacob had the best. And then began the months of going from one doctor to the next, of having Jacob's blood drawn and brain scanned and reflexes tested and eyes peered into and hearing examined. The whole process was so invasive, so frustrating—I had never known there were so many ways to say "I don't know" until I met these doctors—and at times I would think of how difficult, how impossible it must be for parents who didn't have the connections we did, who didn't have Liesl's scientific literacy and knowledge. But that literacy didn't make it easier to see Jacob cry when he was pricked with needles, so many times that one vein, the one in his left arm, began to collapse, and all those connections didn't prevent him from getting sicker and sicker, from seizing more and more, and he would shake and froth, and emit a growl, something primal and frightening and far too low-pitched for a four-year-old, as his head knocked from side to side and his hands gnarled themselves.

By the time we had our diagnosis—an extremely rare neurodegenerative disease called Nishihara syndrome, one so rare that it wasn't even included on batteries of genetic tests—he was almost blind. That was February. By June, when he turned five, he rarely spoke. By August, we didn't think he could hear any longer.

He seized more and more. We tried one drug after the next; we tried them in combinations. Liesl had a friend who was a neurologist who told us about a new drug that hadn't been approved in the States yet but was available in Canada; that Friday, Liesl and Sally drove up to Montreal and back, all in twelve hours. For a while the drug worked, although it gave him a terrible rash, and whenever we touched his skin he would open his mouth and scream, although no sound came out, and tears would run out of his eyes. "I'm sorry, buddy," I would plead with him, even though I knew he couldn't hear me, "I'm sorry, I'm sorry."

I could barely concentrate at work. I was only teaching part-time that year; it was my second year at the university, my third semester. I would walk through campus and overhear conversations—someone talking about splitting up with her boyfriend, someone talking about a bad grade he got on a test, someone talking about his sprained ankle— and would feel rage. You stupid, petty, selfish, self-absorbed people, I wanted to say. You hateful people, I hate you. Your problems aren't problems. My son is dying. At times my loathing was so profound I would get sick. Laurence was teaching at the university then as well, and he would pick up my classes when I had to take Jacob to the hospital. We had a home health-care worker, but we took him to every appointment so we could keep track of how fast he was leaving us. In September, his doctor looked at us after he had examined him. "Not long now," he said, and he was very gentle, and that was the worst part.

Laurence came over every Wednesday and Saturday night; Gillian came every Tuesday and Thursday; Sally came every Monday and Sunday; another friend of Liesl's, Nathan, came every Friday. When they were there, they would cook or clean, and Liesl and I would sit with Jacob and talk to him. He had stopped growing sometime in the last year, and his arms and legs had gone soft from lack of use: they were floppy, boneless even, and you had to make sure that when you held him, you held his limbs close to you, or they would simply dangle off of him and he would look dead. He had stopped opening his eyes at all in early September, although sometimes they would leak fluids: tears, or a clumpy, yellowish mucus. Only his face remained plump, and that was because he was on such massive doses of steroids. One drug or another had left him with an eczematic rash on his cheeks, candied-red and sandpapery, that was always hot and rough to the touch.

My father and Adele moved in with us in mid-September, and I couldn't look at him. I knew he knew what it was like to see children dying; I knew how much it hurt him that it was my child. I felt as if I had failed: I felt that I was being punished for not wanting Jacob more passionately when he had been given to us. I felt that if I had been less ambivalent about having children, this never would have happened; I felt that I was being reminded of how foolish and stupid I'd been to not recognize what a gift I'd been given, a gift that so many people yearned for and yet I had been willing to send back. I was ashamed—I would never be the father my father was, and I hated that he was here witnessing my failings.

Before Jacob had been born, I had asked my father one night if he had any words of wisdom for me. I had been joking, but he took it seriously, as he took all questions I asked him. "Hmm," he said. "Well, the hardest thing about being a parent is recalibration. The better you are at it, the better you will be."

At the time, I had pretty much ignored this advice, but as Jacob got sicker and sicker, I thought of it more and more frequently, and realized how correct he was. We all say we want our kids to be happy, only happy, and healthy, but we don't want that. We want them to be like we are, or better than we are. We as humans are very unimaginative in that sense. We aren't equipped for the possibility that they might be worse. But I guess that would be asking too much. It must be an evolutionary stopgap—if we were all so specifically, vividly aware of what might go horribly wrong, we would none of us have children at all.

When we first realized that Jacob was sick, that there was something wrong with him, we both tried very hard to recalibrate, and quickly. We had never *said* that we wanted him to go to college, for example; we simply assumed he would, and to graduate school as well, because we both had. But that first night we spent in the hospital, after his first seizure, Liesl, who was always a planner, who had a brilliant ability to see five steps, ten steps, ahead, said, "No matter what this is, he can still live a long and healthy life, you know. There are great schools we can send him to. There are places where he can be taught to be independent." I had snapped at her: I had accused her of writing him off so quickly, so easily. Later, I felt ashamed about this. Later, I admired her: I admired how rapidly, how fluidly, she was adjusting to the fact that the child she thought she would have was not the child she did have. I admired how she knew, well before I did, that the point of a child is not what you hope he will accomplish in your name but the pleasure that he will bring you, whatever form it comes in, even if it is a form that is barely recognizable as pleasure at all—and, more important, the pleasure you will be privileged to bring him. For the rest of Jacob's life, I lagged one step behind Liesl: I kept dreaming he would get better, that he would return to what he had been; she, however, thought only about the life he could have given the current realities of his situation. Maybe he could go to a special school. Okay, he couldn't go to school at all, but maybe he could be in a playgroup. Okay, he wouldn't be able to be in a playgroup, but maybe he would be able to live a long life anyway. Okay, he wouldn't live a long life, but maybe he could live a short happy life. Okay, he couldn't live a short happy life, but maybe he could live a short life with dignity: we could give him that, and she would hope for nothing else for him.

I was thirty-two when he was born, thirty-six when he was diagnosed, thirty-seven when he died. It was November tenth, just less than a year after his first seizure. We had a service at the university, and even in my deadened state, I saw all the people—our parents, our friends and colleagues, and Jacob's friends, first graders now, and their parents—who had come, and had cried.

My parents went home to New York. Liesl and I eventually went back to work. For months, we barely spoke. We couldn't even touch each other. Part of it was exhaustion, but we were also ashamed: of our mutual failure, of the unfair but unshakable feeling that each of us could have done better, that the other person hadn't quite risen to the occasion. A year after Jacob died, we had our first conversation about whether we should have another child, and although it began politely, it ended awfully, in recriminations: about how I had never wanted Jacob in the first place, about how she had never wanted him, about how I had failed, about how she had. We stopped talking; we apologized. We tried again. But every discussion ended the same way. They were not conversations from which it was possible to recover, and eventually, we separated.

It amazes me now how thoroughly we stopped communicating. The divorce was very clean, very easy—perhaps too clean, too easy. It made me wonder what had brought us together before Jacob—had we not had him, how and for what would we have stayed together? It was only later that I was able to remember why I had loved Liesl, what I had seen and admired in her. But at the time, we were like two people who'd had a single mission, difficult and draining, and now the mission was over, and it was time for us to part and return to our regular lives.

For many years, we didn't speak—not out of acrimony, but out of something else. She moved to Portland. Shortly after I met Julia, I ran into Sally—she had moved as well, to Los Angeles—who was in town visiting her parents and who told me that Liesl had remarried. I told Sally to send her my best, and Sally said she would.

Sometimes I would look her up: she was teaching at the medical school at the University of Oregon. Once I had a student who looked so much like what we had always imagined Jacob would look like that I nearly called her. But I never did.

And then, one day, she called me. It had been sixteen years. She was in town for a conference, and asked if I wanted to have lunch. It was strange, both foreign and instantly familiar, to hear her voice again, that voice with which I'd had thousands of conversations, about things both important and mundane. That voice I had heard sing to Jacob as he juddered in her arms, that voice I had heard say "This is the best one yet!" as she took a picture of the day's tower of blocks.

We met at a restaurant near the medical college's campus that had specialized in what it had called "upscale hummus" when she was a resident and which we had considered a special treat. Now it was a place that specialized in artisanal meatballs, but it still smelled, interestingly, of hummus.

We saw each other; she looked as I had remembered her. We hugged and sat. For a while we spoke of work, of Sally and her new girlfriend, of Laurence and Gillian. She told me about her husband, an epidemiologist, and I told her about Julia. She'd had another child, a girl, when she was forty-three. She showed me a picture. She was beautiful, the girl, and looked just like Liesl. I told her so, and she smiled. "And you?" she asked. "Did you ever have another?"

I did, I said. I had just adopted one of my former students. I could see she was surprised, but she smiled, and congratulated me, and asked me about him, and how it had happened, and I told her.

"That's great, Harold," she said, after I'd finished. And then, "You love him a lot."

"I do," I said.

I would like to tell you that it was the beginning of a sort of second-stage friendship for us, that we stayed in touch and that every year, we would talk about Jacob, what he could have been. But it wasn't, though not in a bad way. I did tell her, in that meeting, about that student of mine who had so unnerved me, and she said that she understood exactly what I meant, and that she too had had students—or had simply passed young men in the street—whom she thought she recognized from somewhere, only to realize later that she had imagined they might be our son, alive and well and away from us, no longer ours, but walking freely through the world, unaware that we might have been searching for him all this time.

I hugged her goodbye; I wished her well. I told her I cared about her. She said all the same things. Neither of us offered to stay in touch with the other; both of us, I like to think, had too much respect for the other to do so.

But over the years, at odd moments, I would hear from her. I would get an e-mail that read only "Another sighting," and I would know what she meant, because I sent her those e-mails, too: "Harvard Square, appx 25-y-o, 6'2", skinny, reeking of pot." When her daughter graduated from college, she sent me an announcement, and then another for her daughter's wedding, and a third when her first grandchild was born.

I love Julia. She was a scientist too, but she was always so different from Liesl—cheery where Liesl was composed, expressive where Liesl was interior, innocent in her delights and enthusiasms. But as much as I love her, for many years a part of me couldn't stop feeling that I had something deeper, something more profound with Liesl. We had made someone together, and we had watched him die together. Sometimes I felt that there was something physical connecting us, a long rope that stretched between Boston and Portland: when she tugged on her end, I felt it on mine. Wherever she went, wherever I went, there it would be, that shining twined string that stretched and pulled but never broke, our every movement reminding us of what we would never have again.

——

After Julia and I decided we were going to adopt him, about six months before we actually asked him, I told Laurence. I knew Laurence liked him a great deal, and respected him, and thought he was good for me, and I also knew that Laurence—being Laurence—would be wary.

He was. We had a long talk. "You know how much I like him," he said, "but really, Harold, how much do you *actually* know about this kid?"

"Not much," I said. But I knew he wasn't Laurence's worst possible scenario: I knew he wasn't a thief, that he wasn't going to come kill me and Julia in our bed at night. Laurence knew this, too.

Of course, I also knew, without knowing for certain, without any real evidence, that something had gone very wrong for him at some point. That first time you were all up in Truro, I came down to the kitchen late one night and found JB sitting at the table, drawing. I always thought JB was a different person when he was alone, when he was certain he didn't have to perform, and I sat and looked at what he was sketching—pictures of all of you—and asked him about what he was studying in grad school, and he told me about people whose work he admired, three-fourths of whom were unknown to me.

As I was leaving to go upstairs, JB called my name, and I came back. "Listen," he said. He sounded embarrassed. "I don't want to be rude or anything, but you should lay off asking him so many questions."

I sat down again. "Why?"

He was uncomfortable, but determined. "He doesn't have any parents," he said. "I don't know the circumstances, but he won't even discuss it with us. Not with me, anyway." He stopped. "I think something terrible happened to him when he was a kid."

"What kind of terrible?" I asked.

He shook his head. "We're not really certain, but we think it must be really bad physical abuse. Haven't you noticed he never takes off his clothes, or how he never lets anyone touch him? I think someone must have beat him, or—" He stopped. He was loved, he was protected; he didn't have the courage to conjure what might have followed that *or*, and neither did I. But I had noticed, of course—I hadn't been asking to make him uncomfortable, but even when I saw that it *did* make him uncomfortable, I hadn't been able to stop.

"Harold," Julia would say after he left at night, "you're making him uneasy."

"I know, I know," I'd say. I knew nothing good lay behind his silence, and as much as I didn't want to hear what the story was, I wanted to hear it as well.

About a month before the adoption went through, he turned up at the house one weekend, very unexpectedly: I came in from my tennis game, and there he was on the couch, asleep. He had come to talk to me, he had come to try to confess something to me. But in the end, he couldn't.

That night Andy called me in a panic looking for him, and when I asked Andy why he was calling him at midnight anyway, he quickly turned vague. "He's been having a really hard time," he said.

"Because of the adoption?" I asked.

"I can't really say," he said, primly—as you know, doctor-patient confidentiality was something Andy adhered to irregularly but with great dedication when he did. And then you called, and made up your own vague stories.

The next day, I asked Laurence if he could find out if he had any juvenile records in his name. I knew it was unlikely that he'd discover anything, and even if he did, the records would be sealed.

I had meant what I told him that weekend: whatever he had done didn't matter to me. I knew him. Who he had become was the person who mattered to me. I told him that who he was before made no difference to me. But of course, this was naïve: I adopted the person he was, but along with that came the person he had been, and I didn't know who that person was. Later, I would regret that I hadn't made it clearer to him that that person, whoever he was, was someone I wanted as well. Later, I would wonder, incessantly, what it would have been like for him if I had found him twenty years before I did, when he was a baby. Or if not twenty, then ten, or even five. Who would he have been, and who would I have been?

Laurence's search turned up nothing, and I was relieved and disappointed. The adoption happened; it was a wonderful day, one of the best. I never regretted it. But being his parent was never easy. He had all sorts of rules he'd constructed for himself over the decades, based on lessons someone must have taught him—what he wasn't entitled to; what he mustn't enjoy; what he mustn't hope or wish for; what he mustn't covet—and it took some years to figure out what these rules were, and longer still to figure out how to try to convince him of their falsehood. But this was very difficult: they were rules by which he had survived his life, they were rules that made the world explicable to him. He was terrifically disciplined—he was in everything—and discipline, like vigilance, is a near-impossible quality to get someone to abandon.

Equally difficult was my (and your) attempts to get him to abandon certain ideas about himself: about how he looked, and what he deserved, and what he was worth, and who he was. I have still never met anyone as neatly or severely bifurcated as he: someone who could be so utterly confident in some realms and so utterly despondent in others. I remember watching him in court once and feeling both awed and chilled. He was defending one of those pharmaceutical companies in whose care and protection he had made his name in a federal whistle-blower suit. It was a big suit, a major suit—it is on dozens of syllabi now—but he was very, very calm; I have rarely seen a litigator so calm. On the stand was the whistle-blower in question, a middle-aged woman, and he was so relentless, so dogged, so pointed, that the courtroom was silent, watching him. He never raised his voice, he was never sarcastic, but I could see that he relished it, that this very act, catching that witness in her inconsistencies—which were slight, very slight, so slight another lawyer might have missed them—was nourishing to him, that he found pleasure in it. He was a gentle person (though not to himself), gentle in manners and voice, and yet in the courtroom that gentleness burned itself away and left behind something brutal and cold. This was about seven months after the incident with Caleb, five months before the incident to follow, and as I watched him reciting the witness's own statements back to her, never glancing down at the notepad before him, his face still and handsome and self-assured, I kept seeing him in the car that terrible night, when he had turned from me and had protected his head with his hands when I reached out to touch the side of his face, as if I were another person who would try to hurt him. His very existence was twinned: there was who he was at work and who he was outside of it; there was who he was then and who he had been; there was who he was in court and who he had been in the car, so alone with himself that I had been frightened.

That night, uptown, I had paced in circles, thinking about what I had learned about him, what I had seen, how hard I had fought to keep from howling when I heard him say the things he had—worse than Caleb, worse than what Caleb had said, was hearing that he believed it, that he was so wrong about himself. I suppose I had always known he felt this way, but hearing him say it so baldly was even worse than I could have imagined. I will never forget him saying "when you look like I do, you have to take what you can get." I will never forget the despair and anger and hopelessness I felt when I heard him say that. I will never forget his face when he saw Caleb, when Caleb sat down next to him, and I was too slow to understand what was happening. How can you call yourself a parent if your child feels this way about himself? That was something I would never be able to recalibrate. I suppose—having never parented an adult myself—that I had never known how much was actually involved. I didn't resent having to do it: I felt only stupid and inadequate that I hadn't realized it earlier. After all, I had been an adult with a parent, and I had turned to my father constantly.

I called Julia, who was in Santa Fe at a conference about new diseases, and told her what had happened, and she gave a long, sad sigh. "Harold," she began, and then stopped. We'd had conversations about what his life had been before us, and although both of us were wrong, her guesses would turn out to be more accurate than mine, although at the time I had thought them ridiculous, impossible.

"I know," I said.

"You have to call him."

But I had been. I called and called and the phone rang and rang.

That night I lay awake alternately worrying and having the kinds of fantasies men have: guns, hit men, vengeance. I had waking dreams in which I called Gillian's cousin, who was a detective in New York, and had Caleb Porter arrested. I had dreams in which I called you, and you and Andy and I staked out his apartment and killed him.

The next morning I left early, before eight, and bought bagels and orange juice and went down to Greene Street. It was a gray day, soggy and humid, and I rang the buzzer three times, each for several seconds, before stepping back toward the curb, squinting up at the sixth floor.

I was about to buzz again when I heard his voice coming over the speaker: "Hello?"

"It's me," I said. "Can I come up?" There was no response. "I want to apologize," I said. "I need to see you. I brought bagels."

There was another silence. "Hello?" I asked.

"Harold," he said, and I noticed his voice sounded funny. Muffled, as if his mouth had grown an extra set of teeth and he was speaking around them. "If I let you up, do you promise you won't get angry and start yelling?"

I was quiet then, myself. I didn't know what this meant. "Yes," I said, and after a second or two, the door clicked open.

I stepped off the elevator, and for a minute, I saw nothing, just that lovely apartment with its walls of light. And then I heard my name and looked down and saw him.

I nearly dropped the bagels. I felt my limbs turn to stone. He was sitting on the ground, but leaning on his right hand for support, and as I knelt beside him, he turned his head away and held his left hand before his face as if to shield himself.

"He took the spare set of keys," he said, and his face was so swollen that his lips barely had room to move. "I came home last night and he was here." He turned toward me then, and his face was an animal skinned and turned inside out and left in the heat, its organs melting together into a pudding of flesh: all I could see of his eyes were their long line of lashes, a smudge of black against his cheeks, which were a horrible blue, the blue of decay, of mold. I thought he might have been crying then, but he didn't cry. "I'm sorry, Harold, I'm so sorry."

I made sure I wasn't going to start shouting—not at him, just shouting to express something I couldn't say—before I spoke to him. "We're going to get you better," I said. "We're going to call the police, and then—"

"No," he said. "Not the police."

"We have to," I said. "Jude. You have to."

"No," he said. "I won't report it. I can't"—he took a breath—"I can't take the humiliation. I can't."

"All right," I said, thinking that I would discuss this with him later. "But what if he comes back?"

He shook his head, just slightly. "He won't," he said, in his new mumbly voice.

I was beginning to feel light-headed from the effort of suppressing the need to run out and find Caleb and kill him, from the effort of accepting that someone had done this to him, from seeing him, someone who was so dignified, who made certain to always be composed and neat, so beaten, so helpless. "Where's your chair?" I asked him.

He made a sound like a bleat, and said something so quietly I had to ask him to repeat it, though I could see how much pain it caused him to speak. "Down the stairs," he finally said, and this time, I was certain he was crying, although he couldn't even open his eyes enough for tears. He began to shake.

I was shaking myself by this point. I left him there, sitting on the floor, and went to retrieve his wheelchair, which had been thrown down the stairs so hard that it had bounced off the far wall and was halfway down to the fourth floor. On the way back to him, I noticed the floor was tacky with something, and saw too a large bright splash of vomit near the dining-room table, congealed into paste.

"Put your arm around my neck," I told him, and he did, and as I lifted him, he cried out, and I apologized and settled him in his chair. As I did, I noticed that the back of his shirt—he was wearing one of those gray thermal-weave sweatshirts he liked to sleep in—was bloody, with new and old blood, and the back of his pants were bloody as well.

I stepped away from him and called Andy, told him I had an emergency. I was lucky: Andy had stayed in the city that weekend, and he would meet us at his office in twenty minutes.

I drove us there. I helped him out of the car—he seemed unwilling to use his left arm, and when I had him stand, he held his right leg aloft, so that it wouldn't touch the ground, and made a strange noise, a bird's noise, as I wrapped my arm around his chest to lower him into the chair—and when Andy opened the door and saw him, I thought he was going to throw up.

"Jude," Andy said once he could speak, crouching beside him, but he didn't respond.

Once we'd installed him in an examination room, we spoke in the receptionist's area. I told him about Caleb. I told him what I thought had happened. I told him what I thought was wrong: that I thought he had broken his left arm, that something was wrong with his right leg, that he was bleeding and where, that the floors had blood on them. I told him he wouldn't report it to the police.

"Okay," Andy said. He was in shock, I could see. He kept swallowing. "Okay, okay." He stopped and rubbed at his eyes. "Will you wait here for a little while?"

He came out from the examining room forty minutes later. "I'm going to take him to the hospital to get some X-rays," he said. "I'm pretty sure his left wrist is broken, and some of his ribs. And if his leg is—" He stopped. "If it is, this is really going to be a problem," he said. He seemed to have forgotten I was in the room. Then he recalled himself. "You should go," he said. "I'll call you when I'm almost done."

"I'll stay," I said.

"Don't, Harold," he said, and then, more gently, "you have to call his office; there's no way he can go into work this week." He paused. "He said—he said you should tell them he was in a car accident."

As I was leaving, he said, quietly, "He told me he was playing tennis."

"I know," I said. I felt bad for us, then, for being so stupid. "He told me that, too."

I went back to Greene Street with his keys. For a long time, many minutes, I just stood there in the doorway, looking at the space. Some of the cloud cover had parted, but it didn't take much sun—even with the shades drawn—to make that apartment feel light. I had always thought it a hopeful place, with its high ceilings, its cleanliness, its visibility, its promise of transparency.

This was his apartment, and so of course there were lots of cleaning products, and I started cleaning. I mopped the floors; the sticky areas were dried blood. It was difficult to distinguish because the floors were so dark, but I could smell it, a dense, wild scent that the nose instantly recognizes. He had clearly tried to clean the bathroom, but here too there were swipes of blood on the marble, dried into the rusty pinks of sunsets; these were difficult to remove, but I did the best I could. I looked in the trash cans—for evidence, I suppose, but there was nothing: they had all been cleaned and emptied. His clothes from the night before were scattered near the living-room sofa. The shirt was so ripped, clawed at almost, that I threw it away; the suit I took to be dry-cleaned. Otherwise, the apartment was very tidy. I had entered the bedroom with dread, expecting to find lamps broken, clothes strewn about, but it was so unruffled that you might have thought that no one lived there at all, that it was a model house, an advertisement for an enviable life. The person who lived here would have parties, and would be carefree and sure of himself, and at night he would raise the shades and he and his friends would dance, and people passing by on Greene Street, on Mercer, would look up at that box of light floating in the sky, and imagine its inhabitants above unhappiness, or fear, or any concerns at all.

I e-mailed Lucien, whom I'd met once, and who was a friend of a friend of Laurence's, actually, and said there had been a terrible car accident, and that Jude was in the hospital. I went to the grocery store and bought things that would be easy for him to eat: soups, puddings, juices. I looked up Caleb Porter's address, and repeated it to myself—Fifty West Twenty-ninth Street, apartment 17J—until I had it memorized. I called the locksmith and said it was an emergency and that I needed to have all the locks changed: front door, elevator, apartment door. I opened the windows to let the damp air carry away the fragrance of blood, of disinfectant. I left a message with the law school secretary saying there was a family emergency and I wouldn't be able to teach that week. I left messages for a couple of my colleagues asking if they could cover for me. I thought about calling my old law school friend, who worked at the D.A.'s office. I would explain what had happened; I wouldn't use his name. I would ask how we could have Caleb Porter arrested.

"But you're saying the victim won't report it?" Avi would say.

"Well, yes," I'd have to admit.

"Can he be convinced?"

"I don't think so," I'd have to admit.

"Well, Harold," Avi would say, perplexed and irritated. "I don't know what to tell you, then. You know as well as I do that I can't do anything if the victim won't speak." I remembered thinking, as I very rarely thought, what a flimsy thing the law was, so dependent on contingencies, a system of so little comfort, of so little use to those who needed its protections the most.

And then I went into his bathroom and felt under the sink and found his bag of razors and cotton pads and threw it down the incinerator. I hated that bag, I hated that I knew I would find it.

Seven years before, he had come to the house in Truro in early

May. It had been a spontaneous visit: I was up there trying to write, there were cheap tickets, I told him he should come, and to my sur- prise—he never left the offices of Rosen Pritchard, even then—he did. He was happy that day, and so was I. I left him chopping a head of purple cabbage in the kitchen and took the plumber upstairs, where he was installing a new toilet in our bathroom, and then on his way out asked him if he could come take a look at the sink in the downstairs bathroom, the one in Jude's room, which had been leaking.

He did, tightened something, changed something else, and then, as he was emerging from the cabinet, handed something to me. "This was taped under the basin," he said.

"What is it?" I asked, taking the package from him.

He shrugged. "Dunno. But it was stuck there pretty good, with duct tape." He repacked his things as I stood there dumbly, staring at the bag, and gave me a wave and left; I heard him say goodbye to Jude as he walked out, whistling.

I looked at the bag. It was a regular, pint-size clear plastic bag, and inside it was a stack of ten razor blades, and individually packaged alcohol wipes, and pieces of gauze, folded into springy squares, and bandages. I stood there, holding this bag, and I knew what it was for, even though I had never seen proof of it, and had indeed never seen anything like it. But I knew.

I went to the kitchen, and there he was, washing off a bowlful of fingerlings, still happy. He was even humming something, very softly, which he did only when he was very contented, like how a cat purrs to itself when it's alone in the sun. "You should've told me you needed help installing the toilet," he said, not looking up. "I could have done it for you and saved you a bill." He knew how to do all those things: plumbing, electrical work, carpentry, gardening. We once went to Lau- rence's so he could explain to Laurence how, exactly, he could safely unearth the young crabapple tree from one corner of his backyard and successfully move it to another, one that got more sun.

For a while I stood there watching him. I felt so many things at once that together, they combined to make nothing, a numbness, an absence of feeling caused by a surplus of feeling. Finally I said his name, and he looked up. "What's this?" I asked him, and held the bag in front of him.

He went very still, one hand suspended above the bowl, and I remember watching how little droplets of water beaded and dripped off the ends of his fingertips, as if he had slashed himself with a knife and was bleeding water. He opened his mouth, and shut it.

"I'm sorry, Harold," he said, very softly. He lowered his hand, and dried it, slowly, on the dish towel.

That made me angry. "I'm not asking you to apologize, Jude," I told him. "I'm asking you what this is. And don't say 'It's a bag with razors in it.' What is this? Why did you tape it beneath your sink?"

He stared at me for a long time with that look he had—I know you know the one—where you can see him receding even as he looks at you, where you can see the gates within him closing and locking themselves, the bridges being cranked above the moat. "You know what it's for," he finally said, still very quietly.

"I want to hear you say it," I told him.

"I just need it," he said.

"Tell me what you do with these," I said, and watched him.

He looked down into the bowl of potatoes. "Sometimes I need to cut myself," he said, finally. "I'm sorry, Harold."

And suddenly I was panicked, and my panic made me irrational. "What the fuck does that mean?" I asked him—I may have even shouted it.

He was moving backward now, toward the sink, as if I might lunge at him and he wanted some distance. "I don't know," he said. "I'm sorry, Harold."

"How often is sometimes?" I asked.

He too was panicking now, I could see. "I don't know," he said. "It varies."

"Well, estimate. Give me a ballpark."

"I don't know," he said, desperate, "I don't know. A few times a week, I guess."

"A few times a *week*!" I said, and then stopped. Suddenly I had to get out of there. I took my coat from the chair and crammed the bag into its inside pocket. "You'd better be here when I get back," I told him, and left. (He was a bolter: whenever he thought Julia or I were displeased with him, he would try as quickly as he could to get out of our sight, as if he were an offending object that needed to be removed.)

I walked downstairs, toward the beach, and then through the dunes, feeling the sort of rage that comes with the realization of one's gross inadequacy, of knowing for certain that you are at fault. It was the first time I realized that as much as he was two people around us, so were we two people around him: we saw of him what we wanted, and allowed ourselves not to see anything else. We were so ill-equipped. Most people are easy: their unhappinesses are our unhappinesses, their sorrows are understandable, their bouts of self-loathing are fast-moving and negotiable. But his were not. We didn't know how to help him because we lacked the imagination needed to diagnose the problems. But this is making excuses.

By the time I returned to the house it was almost dark, and I could see, through the window, his outline moving about in the kitchen. I sat on a chair on the porch and wished Julia were there, that she wasn't in England with her father.

The back door opened. "Dinner," he said, quietly, and I got up to go inside.

He'd made one of my favorite meals: the sea bass I had bought the day before, poached, and potatoes roasted the way he knew I liked them, with lots of thyme and carrots, and a cabbage salad that I knew would have the mustard-seed dressing I liked. But I didn't have an appetite for any of it. He served me, and then himself, and sat.

"This looks wonderful," I told him. "Thank you for making it." He nodded. We both looked at our plates, at his lovely meal that neither of us would eat.

"Jude," I said, "I have to apologize. I'm really sorry—I never should have run out on you like that."

"It's all right," he said, "I understand."

"No," I told him. "It was wrong of me. I was just so upset."

He looked back down. "Do you know why I was upset?" I asked him.

"Because," he began, "because I brought that into your house."

"No," I said. "That's not why. Jude, this house isn't just my house, or Julia's: it's yours, too. I want you to feel you can bring anything you'd have at home here.

"I'm upset because you're doing this terrible thing to yourself." He didn't look up. "Do your friends know you do this? Does Andy?"

He nodded, slightly. "Willem knows," he said, in a low voice. "And Andy."

"And what does Andy say about this?" I asked, thinking, Goddammit, Andy.

"He says—he says I should see a therapist."

"And have you?" He shook his head, and I felt rage build up in me again. "Why not?" I asked him, but he didn't say anything. "Is there a bag like this in Cambridge?" I said, and after a silence, he looked up at me and nodded again.

"Jude," I said, "why do you do this to yourself?"

For a long time, he was quiet, and I was quiet too. I listened to the sea. Finally, he said, "A few reasons."

"Like what?"

"Sometimes it's because I feel so awful, or ashamed, and I need to make physical what I feel," he began, and glanced at me before looking down again. "And sometimes it's because I feel so many things and I need to feel nothing at all—it helps clear them away. And sometimes it's because I feel happy, and I have to remind myself that I shouldn't."

"Why?" I asked him once I could speak again, but he only shook his head and didn't answer, and I too went silent.

He took a breath. "Look," he said, suddenly, decisively, looking at me directly, "if you want to dissolve the adoption, I'll understand."

I was so stunned that I was angry—that hadn't even occurred to me. I was about to bark something back when I looked at him, at how he was trying to be brave, and saw that he was terrified: He really did think this was something I might want to do. He really would understand if I said I did. He was expecting it. Later, I realized that in those years just after the adoption, he was always wondering how permanent it was, always wondering what he would eventually do that would make me disown him.

"I would never," I said, as firmly as I could.

That night, I tried to talk to him. He was ashamed of what he did, I could see that, but he genuinely couldn't understand why I cared so much, why it so upset you and me and Andy. "It's not fatal," he kept saying, as if that were the concern, "I know how to control it." He wouldn't see a shrink, but he couldn't tell me why. He hated doing it, I could tell, but he also couldn't conceive of a life without it. "I need it," he kept saying. "I need it. It makes things right." But surely, I told him, there was a time in your life when you *didn't* have it?, and he shook his head. "I need it," he repeated. "It helps me, Harold, you have to believe me on this one."

"*Why* do you need it?" I asked.

He shook his head. "It helps me control my life," he said, finally.

At the end, there was nothing more I could say. "I'm keeping this," I said, holding the bag up, and he winced, and nodded. "Jude," I said, and he looked back at me. "If I throw this away, are you going to make another one?"

He was very quiet, then, looking at his plate. "Yes," he said.

I threw it out anyway, of course, stuffing it deep into a garbage bag that I carried to the Dumpster at the end of the road. We cleaned the kitchen in silence—we were both exhausted, and neither of us had eaten anything—and then he went to bed, and I did as well. In those days I was still trying to be respectful of his personal space, or I'd have grabbed him and held him, but I didn't.

But as I was lying awake in bed, I thought of him, his long fingers craving the slice of the razor between them, and went downstairs to the kitchen. I got the big mixing bowl from the drawer beneath the oven, and began loading it with everything sharp I could find: knives and scissors and corkscrews and lobster picks. And then I took it with me to the living room, where I sat in my chair, the one facing the sea, clasping the bowl in my arms.

I woke to a creaking. The kitchen floorboards were noisy, and I sat up in the dark, willing myself to stay silent, and listened to his walk, the distinctive soft stamp of his left foot followed by the swish of his right, and then a drawer opening and, a few seconds later, shutting. Then another drawer, then another, until he had opened and shut every drawer, every cupboard. He hadn't turned on the light—there was moonlight enough—and I could envision him standing in the newly blunt world of the kitchen, understanding that I'd taken everything from him: I had even taken the forks. I sat, holding my breath, listening to the silence from the kitchen. For a moment it was almost as if we were having a conversation, a conversation without words or sight. And then, finally, I heard him turn and his footsteps retreating, back to his room.

When I got home to Cambridge the next night, I went to his bathroom and found another bag, a double of the Truro one, and threw it away. But I never found another of those bags again in either Cambridge or Truro. He must have found some other place to hide them, someplace I never discovered, because he couldn't have carried those blades back and forth on the plane. But whenever I was at Greene Street, I would find an opportunity to sneak off to his bathroom. Here, he kept the bag in his same old hiding place, and every time, I would steal it, and shove it into my pocket, and then throw it away after I left. He must have known I did this, of course, but we never discussed it. Every time it would be replaced. Until he learned he had to hide it from you as well, there was not a single time I checked that I failed to find it. Still, I never stopped checking: whenever I was at the apartment, or later, the house upstate, or the flat in London, I would go to his bathroom and look for that bag. I never found it again. Malcolm's bathrooms were so simple, so clean-lined, and yet even in them he had found somewhere to conceal it, somewhere I would never again discover.

Over the years, I tried to talk about it with him. The day after I found the first bag, I called Andy and started yelling at him, and Andy, uncharacteristically, let me. "I know," he said. "I know." And then: "Harold, I'm not asking sarcastically or rhetorically. I want you to tell me: What should I do?" And of course, I didn't know what to tell him.

You were the one who got furthest with him. But I know you blamed yourself. I blamed myself, too. Because I did something worse than accepting it: I tolerated it. I chose to forget he was doing this, because it was too difficult to find a solution, and because I wanted to enjoy him as the person he wanted us to see, even though I knew better. I told myself that I was letting him keep his dignity, while choosing to forget that for thousands of nights, he sacrificed it. I would rebuke him and try to reason with him, even though I knew those methods didn't work, and even knowing that, I didn't try something else: something more radical, something that might alienate me from him. I knew I was being a coward, because I never told Julia about that bag, I never told her what I had learned about him that night in Truro. Eventually she found out, and it was one of the very few times I'd seen her so angry. "How could you let this keep happening?" she asked me. "How could you let this go on for this long?" She never said she held me directly responsible, but I knew she did, and how could she not? I did, too.

And now here I was in his apartment, where a few hours ago, while I was lying awake, he was being beaten. I sat down on the sofa with my phone in my hand to wait for Andy's call, telling me that he was ready to be returned to me, that he was ready to be released into my care. I opened the shade across from me and sat back down and stared into the steely sky until each cloud blurred into the next, until finally I could see nothing at all, only a haze of gray as the day slowly slurred into night.

———

Andy called at six that evening, nine hours after I'd dropped him off, and met me at the door. "He's asleep in the examining room," he said. And then: "Broken left wrist, four broken ribs, thank *Christ* no broken bones in his legs. No concussion, thank god. Fractured coccyx. Dislocated shoulder, which I reset. Bruising all up and down his back and torso; he was kicked, clearly. But no internal bleeding. His face looks worse than it is: his eyes and nose are fine, no breaks, and I iced the bruising, which you have to do, too—regularly.

"Lacerations on his legs. This is what I'm worried about. I've written you a scrip for antibiotics; I'm going to start him on a low dosage as a preventative measure, but if he mentions feeling hot, or chilled, you have to let me know right away—the last thing he needs is an infection there. His back is stripped—"

"What do you mean, 'stripped'?" I asked him.

He looked impatient. "Flayed," he said. "He was whipped, probably with a belt, but he wouldn't tell me. I bandaged them, but I'm giving you this antibiotic ointment and you're going to need to keep the wounds cleaned and change the dressings starting tomorrow. He's not going to want to let you, but it's too fucking bad. I wrote down all the instructions in here."

He handed me a plastic bag; I looked inside: bottles of pills, rolls of bandages, tubes of cream. "These," said Andy, plucking something out, "are painkillers, and he hates them. But he's going to need them; make him take a pill every twelve hours: once in the morning, once at night. They're going to make him woozy, so don't let him outside on his own, don't let him lift anything. They're also going to make him nauseated, but you have to make him eat: something simple, like rice and broth. Try to make him stay in his chair; he's not going to want to move around much anyway.

"I called his dentist and made an appointment for Monday at nine;

he's lost a couple of teeth. The most important thing is that he sleeps as much as he can; I'll stop by tomorrow afternoon and every night this week. Do *not* let him go to work, although—I don't think he'll want to."

He stopped as abruptly as he'd started, and we stood there in silence. "I can't fucking believe this," Andy said, finally. "That fucking asshole. I want to find that fuck and kill him."

"I know," I said. "Me too."

He shook his head. "He wouldn't let me report it," he said. "I begged him."

"I know," I said. "Me too."

It was a shock anew to see him, and he shook his head when I tried to help him into the chair, and so we stood and watched as he lowered himself into the seat, still in his same clothes, the blood now dried into rusty continents. "Thank you, Andy," he said, very quietly. "I'm sorry," and Andy placed his palm on the back of his head and said nothing.

By the time we got back to Greene Street, it was dark. His wheelchair was, as you know, one of those very lightweight, elegant ones, one so aggressive about its user's self-sufficiency that there were no handles on it, because it was assumed that the person in it would never allow himself the indignity of being pushed by another. You had to grab the top of the backrest, which was very low, and guide the chair that way. I stopped in the entryway to turn on the lights, and we both blinked.

"You cleaned," he said.

"Well, yes," I said. "Not as good a job as you would've done, I'm afraid."

"Thank you," he said.

"Of course," I said. We were quiet. "Why don't I help you get changed and then you can have something to eat?"

He shook his head. "No, thank you. But I'm not hungry. And I can do it myself." Now he was subdued, controlled: the person I had seen earlier was gone, caged once more in his labyrinth in some little-opened cellar. He was always polite, but when he was trying to protect himself or assert his competency, he became more so: polite and slightly remote, as if he was an explorer among a dangerous tribe, and was being careful not to find himself too involved in their goings-on.

I sighed, inwardly, and took him to his room; I told him I'd be here if he needed me, and he nodded. I sat on the floor outside the closed door and waited: I could hear the faucets turning on and off, and then his steps, and then a long period of silence, and then the sigh of the bed as he sat on it.

When I went in, he was under the covers, and I sat down next to him, on the edge of the bed. "Are you sure you don't want to eat anything?" I asked.

"Yes," he said, and after a pause, he looked at me. He could open his eyes now, and against the white of the sheets, he was the loamy, fecund colors of camouflage: the jungle-green of his eyes, and the streaky gold-and-brown of his hair, and his face, less blue than it had been this morning and now a dark shimmery bronze. "Harold, I'm so sorry," he said. "I'm sorry I yelled at you last night, and I'm sorry I cause so many problems for you. I'm sorry that—"

"Jude," I interrupted him, "you don't need to be sorry. *I'm* sorry. I wish I could make this better for you."

He closed his eyes, and opened them, and looked away from me. "I'm so ashamed," he said, softly.

I stroked his hair, then, and he let me. "You don't have to be," I said. "You didn't do anything wrong." I wanted to cry, but I thought he might, and if he wanted to, I would try not to. "You know that, right?" I asked him. "You know this wasn't your fault, you know you didn't deserve this?" He said nothing, so I kept asking, and asking, until finally he gave a small nod. "You know that guy is a fucking asshole, right?" I asked him, and he turned his face away. "You know you're not to blame, right?" I asked him. "You know that this says nothing about you and what you're worth?"

"Harold," he said. "Please." And I stopped, although really, I should have kept going.

For a while we said nothing. "Can I ask you a question?" I said, and after a second or two, he nodded again. I didn't even know what I was going to say until I was saying it, and as I was saying it, I didn't know where it had come from, other than I suppose it was something I had always known and had never wanted to ask, because I dreaded his answer: I knew what it would be, and I didn't want to hear it. "Were you sexually abused as a child?"

I could sense, rather than see, him stiffen, and under my hand, I could feel him shudder. He still hadn't looked at me, and now he rolled to his left side, moving his bandaged arm to the pillow next to him. "Jesus, Harold," he said, finally.

I withdrew my hand. "How old were you when it happened?" I asked.

There was a pause, and then he pushed his face into the pillow. "Harold," he said, "I'm really tired. I need to sleep."

I put my hand on his shoulder, which jumped, but I held on. Beneath my palm I could feel his muscles tense, could feel that shiver running through him. "It's okay," I told him. "You don't have anything to be ashamed of," I said. "It's not your fault, Jude, do you understand me?" But he was pretending to be asleep, though I could still feel that vibration, everything in his body alert and alarmed.

I sat there for a while longer, watching him hold himself rigid. Finally I left, closing the door behind me.

I stayed for the rest of the week. You called him that night, and I answered his phone and lied to you, said something useless about an accident, heard the worry in your voice and wanted so badly to tell you the truth. The next day, you called again and I listened outside his door as he lied to you as well: "A car accident. No. No, not serious. What? I was up at Richard's house for the weekend. I nodded off and hit a tree. I don't know; I was tired—I've been working a lot. No, a rental. Because mine's in the shop. It's not a big deal. No, I'm going to be fine. No, you know Harold—he's just overreacting. I promise. I swear. No, he's in Rome until the end of next month. Willem: I promise. It's fine! Okay. I know. Okay. I promise; I will. You too. Bye."

Mostly, he was meek, tractable. He ate his soup every morning, he took his pills. They made him logy. Every morning he was in his study, working, but by eleven he was on the couch, sleeping. He slept through lunch, and all afternoon, and I only woke him for dinner. You called him every night. Julia called him, too: I always tried to eavesdrop, but couldn't hear much of their conversations, only that he didn't say much, which meant Julia must have been saying a great deal. Malcolm came over several times, and the Henry Youngs and Elijah and Rhodes visited as well. JB sent over a drawing of an iris; I had never known him to draw flowers before. He fought me, as Andy had predicted, on the dressings on his legs and back, which he wouldn't, no matter how I pleaded with and shouted at him, let me see. He let Andy, and I heard Andy say to him, "You're going to need to come uptown every other day and let me change these. I mean it."

"Fine," he snapped.

Lucien came to see him, but he was asleep in his study. "Don't wake him," he said, and then, peeking in at him, "Jesus." We talked for a bit, and he told me about how admired he was at the firm, which is something you never get tired of hearing about your child, whether he is four and in preschool and excels with clay, or is forty and in a white-shoe firm and excels in the protection of corporate criminals. "I'd say you must be proud of him, but I think I know your politics too well for that." He grinned. He liked Jude quite a bit, I could tell, and I found myself feeling slightly jealous, and then stingy for feeling jealous at all.

"No," I said. "I *am* proud of him." I felt bad then, for my years of scolding him about Rosen Pritchard, the one place where he felt safe, the one place he felt truly weightless, the one place where his fears and insecurities banished themselves.

By the following Monday, the day before I left, he looked better: his cheeks were the color of mustard, but the swelling had subsided, and you could see the bones of his face again. It seemed to hurt him a little less to breathe, a little less to speak, and his voice was less breathy, more like itself. Andy had let him halve his morning pain dosage, and he was more alert, though not exactly livelier. We played a game of chess, which he won.

"I'll be back on Thursday evening," I told him over dinner. I only had classes on Tuesdays, Wednesdays, and Thursdays that semester.

"No," he said, "you don't have to. Thank you, Harold, but really— I'll be fine."

"I already bought the ticket," I said. "And anyway, Jude—you don't always have to say no, you know. Remember? Acceptance?" He didn't say anything else.

So what else can I tell you? He went back to work that Wednesday, despite Andy's suggestion he stay home through the end of the week. And despite his threats, Andy came over every night to change his dressings and inspect his legs. Julia returned, and every weekend in October, she or I would go to New York and stay with him at Greene Street. Malcolm stayed with him during the week. He didn't like it, I could tell, but we decided we didn't care what he liked, not in this matter.

He got better. His legs didn't get infected. Neither did his back. He was lucky, Andy kept saying. He regained the weight he had lost. By the time you came home, in early November, he was almost healed. By Thanksgiving, which we had that year at the apartment in New York so he wouldn't have to travel, his cast had been removed and he was walking again. I watched him closely over dinner, watched him talking with Laurence and laughing with one of Laurence's daughters, but couldn't stop thinking of him that night, his face when Caleb grabbed his wrist, his expression of pain and shame and fear. I thought of the day I had learned he was using a wheelchair at all: it was shortly after I had found the bag in Truro and was in the city for a conference, and he had come into the restaurant in his chair, and I had been shocked. "Why did you never tell me?" I asked, and he had pretended to be surprised, acted like he thought he had. "No," I said, "you hadn't," and finally he had told me that he hadn't wanted me to see him that way, as someone weak and helpless. "I would never think of you that way," I'd told him, and although I didn't think I did, it *did* change how I thought of him; it made me remember that what I knew of him was just a tiny fraction of who he was.

It sometimes seemed as if that week had been a haunting, one that only Andy and I had witnessed. In the months that followed, someone would occasionally joke about it: his poor driving, his Wimbledon ambitions, and he would laugh back, make some self-deprecating comment. He could never look at me in those moments; I was a reminder of what had really happened, a reminder of what he saw as his degradation.

But later, I would recognize how that incident had taken something large from him, how it had changed him: into someone else, or maybe into someone he had once been. I would see the months before Caleb as a period in which he was healthier than he'd been: he had allowed me to hug him when I saw him, and when I touched him—putting an arm around him as I passed him in the kitchen—he would let me; his hand would go on chopping the carrots before him in the same steady rhythm. It had taken twenty years for that to happen. But after Caleb, he regressed. At Thanksgiving, I had gone toward him to embrace him, but he had quickly stepped to the left—just a bit, just enough so that my arms closed around air, and there had been a second in which we looked at each other, and I knew that whatever I had been allowed just a few months ago I would be no longer: I knew I would have to start all over. I knew that he had decided that Caleb was right, that he was disgusting, that he had, somehow, deserved what had happened to him. And that was the worst thing, the most reprehensible thing. He had decided to believe Caleb, to believe him over us, because Caleb confirmed what he had always thought and always been taught, and it is always easier to believe what you already think than to try to change your mind.

Later, when things got bad, I would wonder what I could have said or done. Sometimes I would think that there was nothing I could have said—there was something that might have helped, but none of us saying it could have convinced him. I still had those fantasies: the gun, the posse, Fifty West Twenty-ninth Street, apartment 17J. But this time we wouldn't shoot. We would take Caleb Porter by each arm, lead him down to the car, drive him to Greene Street, drag him upstairs. We would tell him what to say, and warn him that we would be just outside the door, waiting in the elevator, the pistol cocked and pointed at his back. And from behind the door, we'd listen to what he said: *I didn't mean any of it. I was completely wrong. The things I did, but more than that, the things I said, they were meant for someone else. Believe me, because you believed me before: you are beautiful and perfect, and I never meant what I said. I was wrong, I was mistaken, no one could ever have been more wrong than I was.*

3

EVERY AFTERNOON AT four, after the last of his classes and before the first of his chores, he had a free period of an hour, but on Wednesdays, he was given two hours. Once, he had spent those afternoons reading or exploring the grounds, but recently, ever since Brother Luke had told him he could, he had spent them all at the greenhouse. If Luke was there, he would help the brother water the plants, memorizing their names—*Miltonia spectabilis, Alocasia amazonica, Asystasia gangetica*—so he could repeat them back to the brother and be praised. "I think the *Heliconia vellerigera*'s grown," he'd say, petting its furred bracts, and Brother Luke would look at him and shake his head. "Unbelievable," he'd say. "My goodness, what a great memory you have," and he'd smile to himself, proud to have impressed the brother.

If Brother Luke wasn't there, he instead passed the time playing with his things. The brother had shown him how if he moved aside a stack of plastic planters in the far corner of the room, there was a small grate, and if you removed the grate, there was a small hole beneath, big enough to hold a plastic garbage bag of his possessions. So he had unearthed his twigs and stones from under the tree and moved his haul to the greenhouse, where it was warm and humid, and where he could examine his objects without losing feeling in his hands. Over the months, Luke had added to his collection: he gave him a wafer of sea glass that the brother said was the color of his eyes, and a metal whistle that had a round little ball within it that jangled like a bell when you shook it, and a small cloth doll of a man wearing a woolen burgundy top and a belt trimmed with tiny turquoise-colored beads that the brother said had been made by a Navajo Indian, and had been his when he was a boy. Two months ago, he had opened his bag and discovered that Luke had left him a candy cane, and although it had been February, he had been thrilled: he had always wanted to taste a candy cane, and he broke it into sections, sucking each into a spear point before biting down on it, gnashing the sugar into his molars.

The brother had told him that the next day he had to make sure to come right away, as soon as classes ended, because he had a surprise for him. All day he had been antsy and distracted, and although two of the brothers had hit him—Michael, across the face; Peter, across the backside—he had barely noticed. Only Brother David's warning, that he would be made to do extra chores instead of having his free hours if he didn't start concentrating, made him focus, and somehow, he finished the day.

As soon as he was outside, out of view of the monastery building, he ran. It was spring, and he couldn't help but feel happy: he loved the cherry trees, with their froth of pink blossoms, and the tulips, their glossed, improbable colors, and the new grass, soft and tender beneath him. Sometimes, when he was alone, he would take the Navajo doll and a twig he had found that was shaped like a person outside and sit on the grass and play with them. He made up voices for them both, whispering to himself, because Brother Michael had said that boys didn't play with dolls, and that he was getting too old to play, anyway.

He wondered if Brother Luke was watching him run. One Wednesday, Brother Luke had said, "I saw you running up here today," and as he was opening his mouth to apologize, the brother had continued, "Boy, what a great runner you are! You're so fast!" and he had been literally speechless, until the brother, laughing, told him he should close his mouth.

When he stepped inside the greenhouse, there was no one there. "Hello?" he called out. "Brother Luke?"

"In here," he heard, and he turned toward the little room that was appended to the greenhouse, the one stocked with the supplies of fertilizer and bottles of ionized water and a hanging rack of clippers and shears and gardening scissors and the floor stacked with bags of mulch. He liked this room, with its woodsy, mossy smell, and he went toward it eagerly and knocked.

When he walked in, he was at first disoriented. The room was dark and still, but for a small flame that Brother Luke was bent over on the floor. "Come closer," said the brother, and he did.

"Closer," the brother said, and laughed. "Jude, it's okay."

So he went closer, and the brother held something up and said "Surprise!" and he saw it was a muffin, a muffin with a lit wooden match thrust into its center.

"What is it?" he asked.

"It's your birthday, right?" asked the brother. "And this is your birthday cake. Go on, make a wish; blow out the candle."

"It's for me?" he asked, as the flame guttered.

"Yes, it's for you," said the brother. "Hurry, make a wish."

He had never had a birthday cake before, but he had read about them and he knew what to do. He shut his eyes and wished, and then opened them and blew out the match, and the room went completely dark.

"Congratulations," Luke said, and turned on the light. He handed him the muffin, and when he tried to offer the brother some of it, Luke shook his head: "It's yours." He ate the muffin, which had little blueberries and which he thought was the best thing he had ever tasted, so sweet and cakey, and the brother watched him and smiled.

"And I have something else for you," said Luke, and reached behind him, and handed him a package, a large flat box wrapped in newspaper and tied with string. "Go on, open it," Luke said, and he did, removing the newspaper carefully so it could be reused. The box was plain faded cardboard, and when he opened it, he found it contained an assortment of round pieces of wood. Each piece was notched on both ends, and Brother Luke showed him how the pieces could be slotted within one another to build boxes, and then how he could lay twigs across the top to make a sort of roof. Many years later, when he was in college, he would see a box of these logs in the window of a toy store, and would realize that his gift had been missing parts: a red-peaked triangular structure to build a roof, and the flat green planks that lay across it. But in the moment, it had left him mute with joy, until he had remembered his manners and thanked the brother again and again.

"You're welcome," said Luke. "After all, you don't turn eight every day, do you?"

"No," he admitted, smiling wildly at the gift, and for the rest of his free period, he had built houses and boxes with the pieces while Brother Luke watched him, sometimes reaching over to tuck his hair behind his ears.

He spent every minute he could with the brother in the greenhouse. With Luke, he was a different person. To the other brothers, he was a burden, a collection of problems and deficiencies, and every day brought a new detailing of what was wrong with him: he was too dreamy, too emotional, too energetic, too fanciful, too curious, too impatient, too skinny, too playful. He should be more grateful, more graceful, more controlled, more respectful, more patient, more dexterous, more disciplined, more reverent. But to Brother Luke, he was smart, he was quick, he was clever, he was lively. Brother Luke never told him he asked too many questions, or told him that there were certain things he would have to wait to know until he grew up. The first time Brother Luke tickled him, he had gasped and then laughed, uncontrollably, and Brother Luke had laughed with him, the two of them tussling on the floor beneath the orchids. "You have such a lovely laugh," Brother Luke said, and "What a great smile you have, Jude," and "What a joyful person you are," until it was as if the greenhouse was someplace bewitched, somewhere that transformed him into the boy Brother Luke saw, someone funny and bright, someone people wanted to be around, someone better and different than he actually was.

When things were bad with the other brothers, he imagined himself in the greenhouse, playing with his things or talking to Brother Luke, and repeated back to himself the things Brother Luke said to him. Sometimes things were so bad he wasn't able to go to dinner, but the next day, he would always find something in his room that Brother Luke had left him: a flower, or a red leaf, or a particularly bulbous acorn, which he had begun collecting and storing under the grate.

The other brothers had noticed he was spending all his time with Brother Luke and, he sensed, disapproved. "Be careful around Luke," warned Brother Pavel of all people, Brother Pavel who hit him and yelled at him. "He's not who you think he is." But he ignored him. They were none of them who they said they were.

One day he went to the greenhouse late. It had been a very hard week; he had been beaten very badly; it hurt him to walk. He had been visited by both Father Gabriel and Brother Matthew the previous evening, and every muscle hurt. It was a Friday; Brother Michael had unexpectedly released him early that day, and he had thought he might go play with his logs. As he always did after those sessions, he wanted to be alone—he wanted to sit in that warm space with his toys and pretend he was far away.

No one was in the greenhouse when he arrived, and he lifted the grate and took out his Indian doll and the box of logs, but even as he was playing with them, he found himself crying. He was trying to cry less—it always made him feel worse, and the brothers hated it and punished him for it—but he couldn't help himself. He had at least learned to cry silently, and so he did, although the problem with crying silently was that it hurt, and it took all your concentration, and eventually he had to put his toys down. He stayed until the first bell rang, and then put his things away and ran back downhill toward the kitchen, where he would peel carrots and potatoes and chop celery for the night's meal.

And then, for reasons he was never able to determine, not even when he was an adult, things suddenly became very bad. The beatings got worse, the sessions got worse, the lectures got worse. He wasn't sure what he had done; to himself, he seemed the same as he always had. But it was as if the brothers' collective patience with him were reaching some sort of end. Even Brothers David and Peter, who loaned him books, as many as he wanted, seemed less inclined to speak to him. "Go away, Jude," said Brother David, when he came to talk to him about a book of Greek myths the brother had given him. "I don't want to look at you now."

Increasingly he was becoming convinced that they were going to get rid of him, and he was terrified, because the monastery was the only home he had ever had. How would he survive, what would he do, in the outside world, which the brothers had told him was full of dangers and temptations? He could work, he knew that; he knew how to garden, and how to cook, and how to clean: maybe he could get a job doing one of those things. Maybe someone else might take him in. If that happened, he reassured himself, he would be better. He wouldn't make any of the mistakes he had made with the brothers.

"Do you know how much it costs to take care of you?" Brother Michael had asked him one day. "I don't think we ever thought we'd have you around for this long." He hadn't known what to say to either of those statements, and so had sat staring dumbly at the desk. "You should apologize," Brother Michael told him.

"I'm sorry," he whispered.

Now he was so tired that he didn't have strength even to go to the greenhouse. Now after his classes he went down to a corner of the cellar, where Brother Pavel had told him there were rats but Brother Matthew said there weren't, and climbed onto one of the wire storage units where boxes of oil and pasta and sacks of flour were stored, and rested, waiting until the bell rang and he had to go back upstairs. At dinners, he avoided Brother Luke, and when the brother smiled at him, he turned away. He knew for certain now that he wasn't the boy Brother Luke thought he was—joyful? funny?—and he was ashamed of himself, of how he had deceived Luke, somehow.

He had been avoiding Luke for a little more than a week when one day he went down to his hiding place and saw the brother there, waiting for him. He looked for somewhere to hide, but there was nowhere, and instead he began to cry, turning his face to the wall and apologizing as he did.

"Jude, it's all right," said Brother Luke, and stood near him, patting him on the back. "It's all right, it's all right." The brother sat on the cellar steps. "Come here, come sit next to me," he said, but he shook his head, too embarrassed to do so. "Then at least sit down," said Luke, and he did, leaning against the wall. Luke stood, then, and began looking through the boxes on one of the high shelves, until he retrieved something from one and held it out to him: a glass bottle of apple juice.

"I can't," he said, instantly. He wasn't supposed to be in the cellar at all: he entered it through the small window on the side and then climbed down the wire shelves. Brother Pavel was in charge of the stores and counted them every week; if something was missing, he'd be blamed. He always was.

"Don't worry, Jude," said the brother. "I'll replace it. Go on—take it," and finally, after some coaxing, he did. The juice was sweet as syrup, and he was torn between sipping it, to make it last, and gulping it, in case the brother changed his mind and it was taken from him.

After he had finished, they sat in silence, and then the brother said, in a low voice, "Jude—what they do to you: it's not right. They shouldn't be doing that to you; they shouldn't be hurting you," and he almost started crying again. "I would never hurt you, Jude, you know that, don't you?" and he was able to look at Luke, at his long, kind, worried face, with his short gray beard and his glasses that made his eyes look even larger, and nod.

"I know, Brother Luke," he said.

Brother Luke was quiet for a long time before he spoke next. "Do you know, Jude, that before I came here, to the monastery, I had a son? You remind me so much of him. I loved him so much. But he died, and then I came here."

He didn't know what to say, but he didn't have to say anything, it seemed, because Brother Luke kept talking.

"I look at you sometimes, and I think: you don't deserve to have these things happen to you. You deserve to be with someone else, someone—" And then Brother Luke stopped again, because he had begun to cry again. "Jude," he said, surprised.

"Don't," he sobbed, "please, Brother Luke—don't let them send me away; I'll be better, I promise, I promise. Don't let them send me away."

"Jude," said the brother, and sat down next to him, pulling him into his body. "No one's sending you away. I promise; no one's going to send you away." Finally he was able to calm himself again, and the two of them sat silent for a long time. "All I meant to say was that you deserve to be with someone who loves you. Like me. If you were with me, I'd never hurt you. We'd have such a wonderful time."

"What would we do?" he asked, finally.

"Well," said Luke, slowly, "we could go camping. Have you ever been camping?"

He hadn't, of course, and Luke told him about it: the tent, the fire, the smell and snap of burning pine, the marshmallows impaled on sticks, the owls' hoots.

The next day he returned to the greenhouse, and over the following weeks and months, Luke would tell him about all the things they might do together, on their own: they would go to the beach, and to the city, and to a fair. He would have pizza, and hamburgers, and corn on the cob, and ice cream. He would learn how to play baseball, and how to fish, and they would live in a little cabin, just the two of them, like father and son, and all morning long they would read, and all afternoon they would play. They would have a garden where they would grow all their vegetables, and flowers, too, and yes, maybe they'd have a greenhouse someday as well. They would do everything together, go everywhere together, and they would be like best friends, only better.

He was intoxicated by Luke's stories, and when things were awful, he thought of them: the garden where they'd grow pumpkins and squash, the creek that ran behind the house where they'd catch perch, the cabin—a larger version of the ones he built with his logs—where Luke promised him he would have a real bed, and where even on the coldest of nights, they would always be warm, and where they could bake muffins every week.

One afternoon—it was early January, and so cold that they had to wrap all the greenhouse plants in burlap despite the heaters—they had been working in silence. He could always tell when Luke wanted to talk about their house and when he didn't, and he knew that today was one of his quiet days, when the brother seemed elsewhere. Brother Luke was never unkind when he was in these moods, only quiet, but the kind of quiet he knew to avoid. But he yearned for one of Luke's stories; he needed it. It had been such an awful day, the kind of day in which he had wanted to die, and he wanted to hear Luke tell him about their cabin, and about all the things they would do there when they were alone. In their cabin, there would be no Brother Matthew or Father Gabriel or Brother Peter. No one would shout at him or hurt him. It would be like living all the time in the greenhouse, an enchantment without end.

He was reminding himself not to speak when Brother Luke spoke to him. "Jude," he said, "I'm very sad today."

"Why, Brother Luke?"

"Well," said Brother Luke, and paused. "You know how much I care for you, right? But lately I've been feeling that you don't care for me."

This was terrible to hear, and for a moment he couldn't speak. "That's not true!" he told the brother.

But Brother Luke shook his head. "I keep talking to you about our house in the forest," he said, "but I don't get the feeling that you really want to go there. To you, they're just stories, like fairy tales."

He shook his head. "No, Brother Luke. They're real to me, too." He wished he could tell Brother Luke just how real they were, just how much he needed them, how much they had helped him. Brother Luke looked so upset, but finally he was able to convince him that he wanted that life, too, that he wanted to live with Brother Luke and no one else, that he would do whatever he needed to in order to have it. And finally, finally, the brother had smiled, and crouched and hugged him, moving his arms up and down his back. "Thank you, Jude, thank you," he said, and he, so happy to have made Brother Luke so happy, thanked him back.

And then Brother Luke looked at him, suddenly serious. He had been thinking about it a lot, he said, and he thought it was time for them to build their cabin; it was time that they go away together. But he, Luke, wouldn't do it alone: Was Jude going to come with him? Did he give him his word? Did he want to be with Brother Luke the way Brother Luke wanted to be with him, just the two of them in their small and perfect world? And of course he did—of course he did.

So there was a plan. They would leave in two months, before Easter; he would celebrate his ninth birthday in their cabin. Brother Luke would take care of everything—all he needed to do was be a good boy, and study hard, and not cause any problems. And, most important, say nothing. If they found out what they were doing, Brother Luke said, then he would be sent away, away from the monastery, to make his way on his own, and Brother Luke wouldn't be able to help him then. He promised.

The next two months were terrible and wonderful at the same time. Terrible because they passed so slowly. Wonderful because he had a secret, one that made his life better, because it meant his life in the monastery had an end. Every day he woke up eager, because it meant he was one day closer to being with Brother Luke. Every time one of the brothers was with him, he would remember that soon he would be far away from them, and it would be a little less bad. Every time he was beaten or yelled at, he would imagine himself in the cabin, and it would give him the fortitude—a word Brother Luke had taught him—to withstand it.

He had begged Brother Luke to let him help with the preparations, and Brother Luke had told him to gather a sample of every flower and leaf from all the different kinds of plants on the monastery grounds. And so in the afternoons he prowled the property with his Bible, pressing leaves and petals between its pages. He spent less time in the greenhouse, but whenever he saw Luke, the brother would give him one of

his somber winks, and he would smile to himself, their secret something warm and delicious.

The night finally arrived, and he was nervous. Brother Matthew
was with him in the early evening, right after dinner, but eventually
he left, and he was alone. And then there was Brother Luke, holding
his finger pressed to his lips, and he nodded. He helped Luke load
his books and underwear into the paper bag he held open, and then
they were tiptoeing down the hallway, and down the stairs, and then
through the darkened building and into the night.

"There's just a short walk to the car," Luke whispered to him, and
then, when he stopped, "Jude, what's wrong?"

"My bag," he said, "my bag from the greenhouse."

And then Luke smiled his kind smile, and put his hand on his
head. "I put it in the car already," he said, and he smiled back, so grateful to Luke for remembering.

The air was cold, but he hardly noticed. On and on they walked,
down the monastery's long graveled driveway, and past the wooden
gates, and up the hill that led to the main road, and then down the
main road itself, the night so silent it hummed. As they walked, Brother
Luke pointed out different constellations and he named them, he got
them all right, and Luke murmured in admiration and stroked the
back of his head. "You're so smart," he said. "I'm so glad I picked you,
Jude."

Now they were on the road, which he had only been on a few times
in his life—to go to the doctor, or to the dentist—although now it was
empty, and little animals, muskrats and possums, gamboled before
them. Then they were at the car, a long maroon station wagon piebald
with rust, its backseat filled with boxes and black trash bags and some
of Luke's favorite plants—the *Cattleya schilleriana*, with its ugly speckled petals; the *Hylocereus undatus*, with its sleepy drooping head of a
blossom—in their dark-green plastic nests.

It was strange to see Brother Luke in a car, stranger than being in
the car itself. But stranger than that was the feeling he had, that everything had been worth it, that all his miseries were going to end, that
he was going to a life that would be as good as, perhaps better than,
anything he had read about in books.

"Are you ready to go?" Brother Luke whispered to him, and grinned.

"I am," he whispered back. And Brother Luke turned the key in the ignition.

—

There were two ways of forgetting. For many years, he had envisioned (unimaginatively) a vault, and at the end of the day, he would gather the images and sequences and words that he didn't want to think about again and open the heavy steel door only enough to hurry them inside, closing it quickly and tightly. But this method wasn't effective: the memories seeped out anyway. The important thing, he came to realize, was to eliminate them, not just to store them.

So he had invented some solutions. For small memories—little slights, insults—you relived them again and again until they were neutralized, until they became near meaningless with repetition, or until you could believe that they were something that had happened to someone else and you had just heard about it. For larger memories, you held the scene in your head like a film strip, and then you began to erase it, frame by frame. Neither method was easy: you couldn't stop in the middle of your erasing and examine what you were looking at, for example; you couldn't start scrolling through parts of it and hope you wouldn't get ensnared in the details of what had happened, because you of course would. You had to work at it every night, until it was completely gone.

Though they never disappeared completely, of course. But they were at least more distant—they weren't things that followed you, wraithlike, tugging at you for attention, jumping in front of you when you ignored them, demanding so much of your time and effort that it became impossible to think of anything else. In fallow periods—the moments before you fell asleep; the minutes before you were landing after an overnight flight, when you weren't awake enough to do work and weren't tired enough to sleep—they would reassert themselves, and so it was best to imagine, then, a screen of white, huge and light-lit and still, and hold it in your mind like a shield.

In the weeks following the beating, he worked on forgetting Caleb. Before going to bed, he went to the door of his apartment and, feeling foolish, tried forcing his old set of keys into the locks to assure himself that they didn't fit, that he really was once again safe. He set, and reset, the alarm system he'd had installed, which was so sensitive that even passing shadows triggered a flurry of beeps. And then he lay awake, his eyes open in the dark room, concentrating on forgetting. But it was so difficult—there were so many memories from those months that stabbed him that he was overwhelmed. He heard Caleb's voice saying things to him, he saw the expression on Caleb's face as he had stared at his unclothed body, he felt the horrid blank airlessness of his fall down the staircase, and he crunched himself into a knot and put his hands over his ears and closed his eyes. Finally he would get up and go to his office at the other end of the apartment and work. He had a big case coming up, and he was grateful for it; his days were so occupied that he had little time to think of anything else. For a while he was hardly going home at all, just two hours to sleep and an hour to shower and change, until one evening he'd had an episode at work, a bad one, the first time he ever had. The night janitor had found him on the floor, and had called the building's security department, who had called the firm's chairman, a man named Peterson Tremain, who had called Lucien, who was the only one he had told what to do in case something like this should happen: Lucien had called Andy, and then both he and the chairman had come into the office and waited with him for Andy to arrive. He had seen them, seen their feet, and even as he had gasped and writhed on the ground, he had tried to find the energy to beg them to leave, to reassure them that he was fine, that he just needed to be left alone. But they hadn't left, and Lucien had wiped the vomit from his mouth, tenderly, and then sat on the floor near his head and held his hand and he had been so embarrassed he had almost cried. Later, he had told them again and again that it was nothing, that this happened all the time, but they had made him take the rest of the week off, and the following Monday, Lucien had told him that they were making him go home at a reasonable hour: midnight on the weekdays, nine p.m. on the weekends.

"Lucien," he'd said, frustrated, "this is ridiculous. I'm not a child."

"Believe me, Jude," Lucien had said. "I told the rest of the management committee I thought we should ride you like you were an Arabian at the Preakness, but for some strange reason, they're worried about your health. Also, the case. For some reason, they think if you get sick, we won't win the case." He had fought and fought with Lucien, but it hadn't made a difference: at midnight, his office lights abruptly clicked off, and he had at last resigned himself to going home when he had been told.

Since the Caleb incident, he had barely been able to talk to Harold; even seeing him was a kind of torture. This made Harold and Julia's visits—which were increasingly frequent—challenging. He was mortified that Harold had seen him like that: when he thought of it, Harold seeing his bloody pants, Harold asking him about his childhood (How obvious was he? Could people actually tell by talking to him what had happened to him so many years ago? And if so, how could he better conceal it?), he was so sharply nauseated that he had to stop what he was doing and wait for the moment to pass. He could feel Harold trying to treat him the same as he had, but something had shifted. No longer did Harold harass him about Rosen Pritchard; no longer did he ask him what it was like to abet corporate malfeasance. And he certainly never mentioned the possibility that he might settle down with someone. Now his questions were about how he felt: How was he? How was he feeling? How were his legs? Had he been tiring himself out? Had he been using the chair a lot? Did he need help with anything? He always answered the exact same way: fine, fine, fine; no, no, no.

And then there was Andy, who had abruptly reinitiated his nightly phone calls. Now he called at one a.m. every night, and during their appointments—which Andy had increased to every other week—he was un-Andyish, quiet and polite, which made him anxious. He examined his legs, he counted his cuts, he asked all the questions he always did, he checked his reflexes. And every time he got home, when he was emptying his pockets of change, he found that Andy had slipped in a card for a doctor, a psychologist named Sam Loehmann, and on it had written FIRST VISIT'S ON ME. There was always one of these cards, each time with a different note: DO IT FOR ME, JUDE, or ONE TIME. THAT'S IT. They were like annoying fortune cookies, and he always threw them away. He was touched by the gesture but also weary of it, of its pointlessness; it was the same feeling he had whenever he had to replace the bag under the sink after Harold's visits. He'd go to the corner of his closet where he kept a box filled with hundreds of alcohol wipes and bandages, stacks and stacks of gauze, and dozens of packets of razors, and make a new bag, and tape it back in its proper place. People had always decided how his body would be used, and although he knew that Harold and Andy were trying to help him, the childish, obdurate part of him resisted: *he* would decide. He had such little control of his body anyway—how could they begrudge him this?

He told himself he was fine, that he had recovered, that he had regained his equilibrium, but really, he knew something was wrong, that he had been changed, that he was slipping. Willem was home, and even though he hadn't been there to witness what had happened, even though he didn't know about Caleb, about his humiliation—he had made certain of this, telling Harold and Julia and Andy that he'd never speak to them again if they said anything to anyone—he was still somehow ashamed to be seen by him. "Jude, I'm so sorry," Willem had said when he had returned and seen his cast. "Are you sure you're okay?" But the cast was nothing, the cast was the least shameful part, and for a minute, he had been tempted to tell Willem the truth, to collapse against him the way he never had and start crying, to confess everything to Willem and ask him to make him feel better, to tell him that he still loved him in spite of who he was. But he didn't, of course. He had already written Willem a long e-mail full of elaborate lies detailing his car accident, and the first night they were reunited, they had stayed up so late talking about everything but that e-mail that Willem had slept over, the two of them falling asleep on the living-room sofa.

But he kept his life moving along. He got up, he went to work. He simultaneously craved company, so he wouldn't think of Caleb, and dreaded it, because Caleb had reminded him how inhuman he was, how deficient, how disgusting, and he was too embarrassed to be around other people, normal people. He thought of his days the way he thought of taking steps when he was experiencing the pain and numbness in his feet: he would get through one, and then the next, and then the next, and eventually things would get better. Eventually he would learn how to fold those months into his life and accept them and keep going. He always had.

The court case came, and he won. It was a huge win, Lucien kept telling him, and he knew it was, but mostly he felt panic: *Now* what was he going to do? He had a new client, a bank, but the work there was of the long, tedious, fact-gathering sort, not the kind of frantic work that required twenty-hour days. He would be at home, by himself, with nothing but the Caleb incident to occupy his mind. Tremain congratulated him, and he knew he should be happy, but when he asked the chairman for more work, Tremain had laughed. "No, St. Francis," he said. "You're going on vacation. That's an order."

He didn't go on vacation. He promised first Lucien, and then Tremain, he would, but that he couldn't at the moment. But it was as he had feared: he would be at home, making himself dinner, or at a movie with Willem, and suddenly a scene from his months with Caleb would appear. And then there would be a scene from the home, and a scene from his years with Brother Luke, and then a scene from his months with Dr. Traylor, and then a scene from the injury, the headlights' white glare, his head jerking to the side. And then his mind would fill with images, banshees demanding his attention, snatching and tearing at him with their long, needley fingers. Caleb had unleashed something within him, and he was unable to coax the beasts back into their dungeon—he was made aware of how much time he actually spent controlling his memories, how much concentration it took, how fragile his command over them had been all along.

"Are you all right?" Willem asked him one night. They had seen a play, which he had barely registered, and then had gone out to dinner, where he had half listened to Willem, hoping he was making the correct responses as he moved his food around his plate and tried to act normal.

"Yes," he said.

Things were getting worse; he knew it and didn't know how to make it better. It was eight months after the incident, and every day he thought about it more, not less. He felt sometimes as if his months with Caleb were a pack of hyenas, and every day they chased him, and every day he spent all his energy running from them, trying to escape being devoured by their snapping, foaming jaws. All the things that had helped in the past—the concentrating; the cutting—weren't helping now. He cut himself more and more, but the memories wouldn't disappear. Every morning he swam, and every night he swam again, for miles, until he had energy enough only to shower and climb into bed. As he swam, he chanted to himself: he conjugated Latin verbs, he recited proofs, he quoted back to himself decisions that he had studied in law school. His mind was his, he told himself. He would control this; he wouldn't be controlled.

"I have an idea," Willem said at the end of another meal in which he had failed to say much of anything. He had responded a second or two too late to everything Willem had said, and after a while, they were both quiet. "We should take a vacation together. We should go on that trip to Morocco we were supposed to take two years ago. We can do it as soon as I get back. What do you think, Jude? It'll be fall, then—it'll be beautiful." It was late June: nine months after the incident. Willem was leaving again at the beginning of August for a shoot in Sri Lanka; he wouldn't be back until the beginning of October.

As Willem spoke, he was thinking of how Caleb had called him deformed, and only Willem's silence had reminded him it was his turn to respond. "Sure, Willem," he said. "That sounds great."

The restaurant was in the Flatiron District, and after they paid, they walked for a while, neither of them saying anything, when suddenly, he saw Caleb coming toward them, and in his panic, he grabbed Willem and yanked him into the doorway of a building, startling them both with his strength and swiftness.

"Jude," Willem said, alarmed, "what are you doing?"

"Don't say anything," he whispered to Willem. "Just stay here and don't turn around," and Willem did, facing the door with him.

He counted the seconds until he was certain Caleb must have passed, and then looked cautiously out toward the sidewalk and saw that it hadn't been Caleb at all, just another tall, dark-haired man, but not Caleb, and he had exhaled, feeling defeated and stupid and relieved all at once. He noticed then that he still had Willem's shirt bunched in his hand, and he released it. "Sorry," he said. "Sorry, Willem."

"Jude, what happened?" Willem asked, trying to look him in the eyes. "What was that?"

"Nothing," he said. "I just thought I saw someone I didn't want to see."

"Who?"

"No one. This lawyer on a case I'm working on. He's a prick; I hate dealing with him."

Willem looked at him. "No," he said, at last. "It wasn't another lawyer. It was someone else, someone you're scared of." There was a pause. Willem looked down the street, and then back at him. "You're frightened," he said, his voice wondering. "Who was it, Jude?"

He shook his head, trying to think of a lie he could tell Willem. He was always lying to Willem: big lies, small lies. Their entire relationship was a lie—Willem thought he was one person, and really, he wasn't. Only Caleb knew the truth. Only Caleb knew what he was.

"I told you," he said, at last. "This other lawyer."

"No, it wasn't."

"Yes, it was." Two women walked by them, and as they passed, he heard one of them whisper excitedly to the other, "That was Willem Ragnarsson!" He closed his eyes.

"Listen," Willem said, quietly, "what's going on with you?"

"Nothing," he said. "I'm tired. I need to go home."

"Fine," Willem said. He hailed a cab, and helped him in, and then got in himself. "Greene and Broome," he said to the driver.

In the cab, his hands began to shake. This had been happening more and more, and he didn't know how to stop it. It had started when he was a child, but it had happened only in extreme circumstances— when he was trying not to cry, or when he was in extraordinary pain but knew that he couldn't make a sound. But now it happened at strange moments: only cutting helped, but sometimes the shaking was so severe that he had difficulty controlling the razor. He crossed his arms against himself and hoped Willem wouldn't notice.

At the front door, he tried to get rid of Willem, but Willem wouldn't leave. "I want to be alone," he told him.

"I understand," Willem said. "We'll be alone together." They had stood there, facing each other, until he had finally turned to the door, but he couldn't fit the key into the lock because he was shaking so badly, and Willem took the keys from him and opened the door.

"What the hell is going on with you?" Willem asked as soon as they were in the apartment.

"Nothing," he said, "nothing," and now his teeth were chattering, which was something that had never accompanied the shaking when he was young but now happened almost every time.

Willem stepped close to him, but he turned his face away. "Something happened while I was away," Willem said, tentatively. "I don't know what it is, but something happened. Something's wrong. You've been acting strangely ever since I got home from *The Odyssey*. I don't know why." He stopped, and put his hands on his shoulders. "Tell me, Jude," he said. "Tell me what it is. Tell me and we'll figure out how to make it better."

"No," he whispered. "I can't, Willem, I can't." There was a long silence. "I want to go to bed," he said, and Willem released him, and he went to the bathroom.

When he came out, Willem was wearing one of his T-shirts, and was lofting the duvet from the guest room over the sofa in his bedroom, the sofa under the painting of Willem in the makeup chair. "What're you doing?" he asked.

"I'm staying here tonight," Willem said.

He sighed, but Willem started talking before he could. "You have three choices, Jude," he said. "One, I call Andy and tell him I think there's something really going wrong with you and I take you up to his office for an evaluation. Two, I call Harold, who freaks out and calls Andy. Or three, you let me stay here and monitor you because you won't talk to me, you won't fucking tell me anything, and you never seem to understand that you at least owe your friends the opportunity to *try* to help you—you at *least* owe me that." His voice cracked. "So what's it going to be?"

Oh Willem, he thought. You don't know how badly I want to tell you. "I'm sorry, Willem," he said, instead.

"Fine, you're sorry," said Willem. "Go to bed. Do you still have extra toothbrushes in the same place?"

"Yes," he said.

The next night he came home late from work, and found Willem lying on the sofa in his room again, reading. "How was your day?" he asked, not lowering his book.

"Fine," he said. He waited to see if Willem was going to explain himself, but he didn't, and eventually he went to the bathroom. In the closet, he passed Willem's duffel bag, which was unzipped and filled with enough clothes that it was clear he was going to stay for a while.

He felt pathetic admitting it to himself, but having Willem there— not just in his apartment, but in his room—helped. They didn't speak much, but his very presence steadied and refocused him. He thought less of Caleb; he thought less of everything. It was as if the necessity of proving himself normal to Willem really did make him more normal. Just being around someone he knew would never harm him, not ever, was soothing, and he was able to quiet his mind, and sleep. As grateful as he was, though, he was also disgusted at himself, by how dependent he was, how weak. Was there no end to his needs? How many people had helped him over the years, and why had they? Why had he let them? A better friend would have told Willem to go home, told him he would be fine on his own. But he didn't do this. He let Willem spend the few remaining weeks he had in New York sleeping on his sofa like a dog.

At least he didn't have to worry about upsetting Robin, as Willem and Robin had broken up toward the end of the *Odyssey* shoot, when Robin discovered that Willem had cheated on her with one of the costume assistants. "And I didn't even really like her," Willem had told him in one of their phone calls. "I did it for the worst reason of all—because I was bored."

He had considered this. "No," he said, "the worst reason of all would've been because you were trying to be cruel. Yours was just the *stupidest* reason of all."

There had been a pause, and then Willem had started laughing. "Thanks for that, Jude," he said. "Thanks for making me feel both better and worse."

Willem stayed with him until the very day he had to leave for Colombo. He was playing the eldest son of a faded Dutch merchant family in Sri Lanka in the early nineteen-forties, and had grown a thick mustache that curled up at its tips; when Willem hugged him, he felt it brushing against his ear. For a moment, he wanted to break down and beg Willem not to leave. *Don't go,* he wanted to tell him. *Stay here with me. I'm scared to be alone.* He knew that if he did say this, Willem would: or he would at least try. But he would never say this. He knew it would be impossible for Willem to delay the shoot, and he knew that Willem would feel guilty for his inability to do so. Instead, he tightened his hold on Willem, which was something he rarely did—he rarely showed Willem any physical affection—and he could feel that Willem was surprised, but then he increased his pressure as well, and the two of them stood there, wrapped around each other, for a long time. He remembered thinking that he wasn't wearing enough layers to really let Willem hug him this closely, that Willem would be able to feel the scars on his back through his shirt, but in the moment it was more important to simply be near him; he had the sense that this was the last time this would happen, the last time he would see Willem. He had this fear every time Willem went away, but it was keener this time, less theoretical; it felt more like a real departure.

After Willem left, things were fine for a few days. But then they got bad again. The hyenas returned, more numerous and famished than before, more vigilant in their hunt. And then everything else returned as well: years and years and years of memories he had thought he had controlled and defanged, all crowding him once again, yelping and leaping before his face, unignorable in their sounds, indefatigable in their clamor for his attention. He woke gasping for air: he woke with the names of people he had sworn he would never think of again on his tongue. He replayed the night with Caleb again and again, obsessively, the memory slowing so that the seconds he was standing naked in the rain on Greene Street stretched into hours, so that his flight down the stairs took days, so that Caleb's raping him in the shower, in the elevator, took weeks. He had visions of taking an ice pick and jamming it through his ear, into his brain, to stop the memories. He dreamed of slamming his head against the wall until it split and cracked and the gray meat tumbled out with a wet, bloody thunk. He had fantasies of emptying a container of gasoline over himself and then striking a match, of his mind being gobbled by fire. He bought a set of X-ACTO blades and held three of them in his palm and made a fist around them and watched the blood drip from his hand into the sink as he screamed into the quiet apartment.

He asked Lucien for more work and was given it, but it wasn't enough. He tried to volunteer for more hours at the artists' nonprofit, but they didn't have any additional shifts to give him. He tried to volunteer at a place where Rhodes had once done some pro bono work, an immigrants' rights organization, but they said they were really looking for Mandarin and Arabic speakers at the moment and didn't want to waste his time. He cut himself more and more; he began cutting around the scars themselves, so that he could actually remove wedges of flesh, each piece topped with a silvery sheen of scar tissue, but it didn't help, not enough. At night, he prayed to a god he didn't believe in, and hadn't for years: *Help me, help me, help me,* he pleaded. He was losing himself; this had to stop. He couldn't keep running forever.

It was August; the city was empty. Malcolm was in Sweden on holiday with Sophie; Richard was in Capri; Rhodes was in Maine; Andy was on Shelter Island ("Remember," he'd said before he left, as he always said before a long vacation, "I'm just two hours away; you need me, and I catch the next ferry back"). He couldn't bear to be around Harold, whom he couldn't see without being reminded of his debasement; he called and told him he had too much work to go to Truro. Instead he spontaneously bought a ticket to Paris and spent the long, lonely Labor Day weekend there, wandering the streets by himself. He didn't contact anyone he knew there—not Citizen, who was working for a French bank, or Isidore, his upstairs neighbor from Hereford Street, who was teaching there, or Phaedra, who had taken a job as the director of a satellite of a New York gallery—they wouldn't have been in the city anyway.

He was tired, he was so tired. It was taking so much energy to hold the beasts off. He sometimes had an image of himself surrendering to them, and they would cover him with their claws and beaks and talons and peck and pinch and pluck away at him until he was nothing, and he would let them.

After he returned from Paris, he had a dream in which he was running across a cracked reddish plain of earth. Behind him was a dark cloud, and although he was fast, the cloud was faster. As it drew closer, he heard a buzzing, and realized it was a swarm of insects, terrible and oily and noisy, with pincerlike protuberances jutting out from beneath their eyes. He knew that if he stopped, he would die, and yet even in the dream he knew he couldn't go on for much longer; at some point, he had stopped being able to run and had started hobbling instead, reality asserting itself even in his dreams. And then he heard a voice, one unfamiliar but calm and authoritative, speak to him. *Stop*, it said. *You can end this. You don't have to do this.* It was such a relief to hear those words, and he stopped, abruptly, and faced the cloud, which was seconds, feet away from him, exhausted and waiting for it to be over.

He woke, frightened, because he knew what the words meant, and they both terrified and comforted him. Now, as he moved through his days, he heard that voice in his head, and he was reminded that he could, in fact, stop. He didn't, in fact, have to keep going.

He had considered killing himself before, of course; when he was in the home, and in Philadelphia, and after Ana had died. But something had always stopped him, although now, he couldn't remember what that thing had been. Now as he ran from the hyenas, he argued with himself: Why was he doing this? He was so tired; he so wanted to stop. Knowing that he didn't have to keep going was a solace to him, somehow; it reminded him that he had options, it reminded him that even though his subconscious wouldn't obey his conscious, it didn't mean he wasn't still in control.

Almost as an experiment, he began thinking of what it would mean for him to leave: in January, after his most lucrative year at the firm yet, he had updated his will, so that was in order. He would need to write a letter to Willem, a letter to Harold, a letter to Julia; he would also want to write something to Lucien, to Richard, to Malcolm. To Andy. To JB, forgiving him. Then he could go. Every day, he thought about it, and thinking about it made things easier. Thinking about it gave him fortitude.

And then, at some point, it was no longer an experiment. He couldn't remember how he had decided, but after he had, he felt lighter, freer, less tormented. The hyenas were still chasing him, but now he could see, very far in the distance, a house with an open door, and he knew that once he had reached that house, he would be safe, and everything that pursued him would fall away. They didn't like it, of course—they could see the door as well, they knew he was about to elude them—and every day the hunt got worse, the army of things chasing him stronger and louder and more insistent. His brain was vomiting memories, they were flooding everything else—he thought of people and sensations and incidents he hadn't thought of in years. Tastes appeared on his tongue as if by alchemy; he smelled fragrances he hadn't smelled in decades. His system was compromised; he would drown in his memories; he had to do something. He had tried—all his life, he had tried. He had tried to be someone different, he had tried to be someone better, he had tried to make himself clean. But it hadn't worked. Once he had decided, he was fascinated by his own hopefulness, by how he could have saved himself years of sorrow by just ending it—he could have been his own savior. No law said he had to keep on living; his life was still his own to do with what he pleased. How had he not realized this in all these years? The choice now seemed obvious; the only question was why it had taken him so long.

He talked to Harold; he could tell by the relief in Harold's voice that he must be sounding more normal. He talked to Willem. "You sound better," Willem said, and he could hear the relief in Willem's voice as well.

"I am," he said. He felt a pull of regret after talking to both of them, but he was determined. He was no good for them, anyway; he was only an extravagant collection of problems, nothing more. Unless he stopped himself, he would consume them with his needs. He would take and take and take from them until he had chewed away their every bit of flesh; they could answer every difficulty he posed to them and he would still find new ways to destroy them. For a while, they would mourn him, because they were good people, the best, and he was sorry for that—but eventually they would see that their lives were better without him in it. They would see how much time he had stolen from them; they would understand what a thief he had been, how he had suckled away all their energy and attention, how he had exsanguinated them. He hoped they would forgive him; he hoped they would see that this was his apology to them. He was releasing them—he loved them most of all, and this was what you did for people you loved: you gave them their freedom.

The day came: a Monday at the end of September. The night before he had realized that it was almost exactly a year after the beating, although he hadn't planned it that way. He left work early that evening. He had spent the weekend organizing his projects; he had written Lucien a memo detailing the status of everything he had been working on. At home, he lined up his letters on the dining-room table, and a copy of his will. He had left a message with Richard's studio manager that the toilet in the master bathroom kept running and asked if Richard could let in the plumber the following day at nine—both Richard and Willem had a set of keys to his apartment—because he would be away on business.

He took off his suit jacket and tie and shoes and watch and went to the bathroom. He sat in the shower area with his sleeves pushed up. He had a glass of scotch, which he sipped at to steady himself, and a box cutter, which he knew would be easier to hold than a razor. He knew what he needed to do: three straight vertical lines, as deep and long as he could make them, following the veins up both arms. And then he would lie down and wait.

He waited for a while, crying a bit, because he was tired and frightened and because he was ready to go, he was ready to leave. Finally he rubbed his eyes and began. He started with his left arm. He made the first cut, which was more painful than he had thought it would be, and he cried out. Then he made the second. He took another drink of the scotch. The blood was viscous, more gelatinous than liquid, and a brilliant, shimmering oil-black. Already his pants were soaked with it, already his grip was loosening. He made the third.

When he was done with both arms, he slumped against the back of the shower wall. He wished, absurdly, for a pillow. He was warm from the scotch, and from his own blood, which lapped at him as it pooled around his legs—his insides meeting his outsides, the inner bathing the outer. He closed his eyes. Behind him, the hyenas howled, furious at him. Before him stood the house with its open door. He wasn't close yet, but he was closer than he'd been: close enough to see that inside, there was a bed where he could rest, where he could lie down and sleep after his long run, where he would, for the first time in his life, be safe.

———

After they crossed into Nebraska, Brother Luke stopped at the edge of a wheat field and beckoned him out of the car. It was still dark, but he could hear the birds stirring, hear them talk back to a sun they couldn't yet see. He took the brother's hand and they skulked from the car and to a large tree, where Luke explained that the other brothers would be looking for them, and they would have to change their appearance. He took off the hated tunic, and put on the clothes Brother Luke held out for him: a sweatshirt with a hood and a pair of jeans. Before he did, though, he stood still as Luke cut off his hair with an electric razor. The brothers rarely cut his hair, and it was long, past his ears, and Brother Luke made sad noises as he removed it. "Your beautiful hair," he said, and carefully wrapped the length of it in his tunic and then stuffed it into a garbage bag. "You look like every other boy now, Jude. But later, when we're safe, you can grow it back, all right?" and he nodded, although really, he liked the idea of looking like every other boy. And then Brother Luke changed clothes himself, and he turned away to give the brother privacy. "You can look, Jude," said Luke, laughing, but he shook his head. When he turned back, the brother was unrecognizable, in a plaid shirt and jeans of his own, and he smiled at him before shaving off his beard, the silvery bristles falling from him like splinters of metal. There were baseball caps for both of them, although the inside of Brother Luke's was fitted with a yellowish wig, which covered his balding head completely. There were pairs of glasses for both of them as well: his were black and round and fitted with just glass, not real lenses, but Brother Luke's were square and large and brown and had the same thick lenses as his real glasses, which he put into the bag. He could take them off when they were safe, Brother Luke told him.

They were on their way to Texas, which is where they'd build their cabin. He had always imagined Texas as flat land, just dust and sky and road, which Brother Luke said was mostly true, but there were parts of the state—like in east Texas, where he was from—that were forested with spruce and cedars.

It took them nineteen hours to reach Texas. It would have been less time, but at one point Brother Luke pulled off the side of the highway and said he needed to nap for a while, and the two of them slept for several hours. Brother Luke had packed them something to eat as well—peanut butter sandwiches—and in Oklahoma they stopped again in the parking lot of a rest stop to eat them.

The Texas of his mind had, with just a few descriptions from Brother Luke, transformed from a landscape of tumbleweeds and sod into one of pines, so tall and fragrant that they cottoned out all other sound, all other life, so when Brother Luke announced that they were now, officially, in Texas, he looked out the window, disappointed.

"Where are the forests?" he asked.

Brother Luke laughed. "Patience, Jude."

They would need to stay in a motel for a few days, Brother Luke explained, both to make sure the other brothers weren't following them and so he could begin scouting for the perfect place to build their cabin. The motel was called The Golden Hand, and their room had two beds—real beds—and Brother Luke let him choose which one he wanted. He took the one near the bathroom, and Brother Luke took the one near the window, with a view of their car. "Why don't you take a shower, and I'm going to go to the store and get us some supplies," said the brother, and he was suddenly frightened. "What's wrong, Jude?"

"Are you going to come back?" he asked, hating how scared he sounded.

"Of course I'll come back, Jude," said the brother, hugging him. "Of course I will."

When he did, he had a loaf of sliced bread, and a jar of peanut butter, and a hand of bananas, and a quart of milk, and a bag of almonds, and some onions and peppers and chicken breasts. That evening, Brother Luke set up the small hibachi he'd brought in the parking lot and they grilled the onions and peppers and chicken, and Brother Luke gave him a glass of milk.

Brother Luke established their routine. They woke early, before the sun was up, and Brother Luke made himself a pot of coffee with the coffeemaker he'd brought, and then they drove into town, to the high school's track, where Luke let him run around for an hour as he sat in the bleachers, drinking his coffee and watching him. Then they returned to the motel room, where the brother gave him lessons. Brother Luke had been a math professor before he came to the monastery, but he had wanted to work with children, and so he had later taught sixth grade. But he knew about other subjects as well: history and books and music and languages. He knew so much more than the other brothers, and he wondered why Luke had never taught him when they lived at the monastery. They ate lunch—peanut butter sandwiches again—and then had more classes until three p.m., when he was allowed outside again to run around the parking lot, or to take a walk with the brother down the highway. The motel faced the interstate, and the whoosh of the passing cars provided a constant soundtrack. "It's like living by the sea," Brother Luke always said.

After this, Brother Luke made a third pot of coffee and then drove off to look for locations where they'd build their cabin, and he stayed behind in their motel room. The brother always locked him into the room for his safety. "Don't open the door for anyone, do you hear me?" asked the brother. "Not for anyone. I have a key and I'll let myself in. And don't open the curtains; I don't want anyone to see you're in here alone. There are dangerous people out there in the world; I don't want you to get hurt." It was for this same reason that he wasn't to use Brother Luke's computer, which he took with him anyway whenever he left the room. "You don't know who's out there," Brother Luke would say. "I want you to be safe, Jude. Promise me." He promised.

He would lie on his bed and read. The television was forbidden to him: Luke would feel it when he came back to the room, to see if it was warm, and he didn't want to displease him, he didn't want to get in trouble. Brother Luke had brought a piano keyboard in his car, and he practiced on it; the brother was never mean to him, but he did take lessons seriously. As the sky grew dark, though, he would find himself sitting on the edge of Brother Luke's bed, pinching back the curtain and scanning the parking lot for Brother Luke's car; some part of him was always worried that Brother Luke wouldn't return for him after all, that he was growing tired of him, that he would be left alone. There was so much he didn't know about the world, and the world was a scary place. He tried to remind himself that there were things he could do, that he knew how to work, that maybe he could get a job cleaning the motel, but he was always anxious until he saw the station wagon pulling toward him, and then he would be relieved, and would promise himself that he would do better the next day, that he would never give Brother Luke a reason to not return to him.

One evening the brother came back to the room looking tired. A few days ago, he had returned excited: he had found the perfect piece of land, he said. He described a clearing surrounded by cedars and pines, a little stream nearby busy with fish, the air so cool and quiet that you could hear every pinecone as it fell to the soft ground. He had even shown him a picture, all dark greens and shadows, and had explained where their cabin would go, and how he could help build it, and where they would make a sleeping loft, a secret fort, just for him.

"What's wrong, Brother Luke?" he asked him, after the brother had been silent so long that he could no longer stand it.

"Oh, Jude," said the brother, "I've failed." He told him how he had tried and tried to buy the land, but he just didn't have the money. "I'm sorry, Jude, I'm sorry," he said, and then, to his amazement, the brother began to cry.

He had never before seen an adult cry. "Maybe you could teach again, Brother Luke," he said, trying to comfort him. "I like you. If I were a kid, I'd like to be taught by you," and the brother smiled a bit at him and stroked his hair and said it didn't work like that, that he'd have to get licensed by the state, and it was a long and complicated process.

He thought and thought. And then he remembered: "Brother Luke," he said, "I could help—I could get a job. I could help earn money."

"No, Jude," said the brother. "I can't let you do that."

"But I want to," he said. He remembered Brother Michael telling him how much he cost for the monastery to maintain, and felt guilty and frightened, both. Brother Luke had done so much for him, and he had done nothing in return. He not only wanted to help earn money; he had to.

At last he was able to convince the brother, who hugged him. "You really are one in a million, you know that?" Luke asked him. "You really are special." And he smiled into the brother's sweater.

The next day they had classes as usual, and then the brother left again, this time, he said, to find him a good job: something he could do that would help them earn money so they could buy the land and build the cabin. And this time Luke returned smiling, excited even, and seeing this, he was excited as well.

"Jude," said the brother, "I met someone who wants to give you some work; he's waiting right outside and you can start now."

He smiled back at the brother. "What am I going to do?" he asked. At the monastery, he had been taught to sweep, and dust, and mop. He could wax a floor so well that even Brother Matthew had been impressed. He knew how to polish silver, and brass, and wood. He knew how to clean between tiles and how to scrub a toilet. He knew how to clean leaves out of gutters and clean and reset a mousetrap. He knew how to wash windows and do laundry by hand. He knew how to iron, he knew how to sew on buttons, he knew how to make stitches so even and fine that they looked as if they had been done by machine.

He knew how to cook. He could only make a dozen or so dishes from start to finish, but he knew how to clean and peel potatoes, carrots, rutabaga. He could chop hills of onions and never cry. He could debone a fish and knew how to pluck and clean a chicken. He knew how to make dough, he knew how to make bread. He knew how to whip egg whites until they transformed from liquid to solid to something better than solid: something like air given form.

And he knew how to garden. He knew which plants craved sun and which shied from it. He knew how to determine whether a plant was parched or drowning in too much water. He knew when a tree or bush needed to be repotted, and when it was hardy enough to be transferred into the earth. He knew which plants needed to be protected from cold, and how to protect them. He knew how to make a clipping and how to make the clipping grow. He knew how to mix fertilizer, how to add eggshells into the soil for extra protein, how to crush an aphid without destroying the leaf it was perched on. He could do all of these things, although he was hoping he would get to garden, because he wanted to work outside, and on his morning runs, he could feel that summer was coming, and on their drives to the track, he had seen fields in bloom with wildflowers, and he wanted to be among them.

Brother Luke knelt by him. "You're going to do what you did with Father Gabriel and a couple of the brothers," he said, and then, slowly, he understood what Luke was saying, and he stepped back toward the bed, everything within him seizing with fear. "Jude, it's going to be different now," Luke said, before he could say anything. "It'll be over so fast, I promise you. And you're so good at it. And I'll be waiting in the bathroom to make sure nothing goes wrong, all right?" He stroked his hair. "Come here," he said, and held him. "You are a wonderful kid," he said. "It's because of you and what you're doing that we're going to have our cabin, all right?" Brother Luke had talked and talked, and finally, he had nodded.

The man had come in (many years later, his would be one of the very few of their faces he would remember, and sometimes, he would see men on the street and they would look familiar, and he would think: How do I know him? Is he someone I was in court with? Was he the opposing counsel on that case last year? And then he would remember: he looks like the first of them, the first of the clients) and Luke had gone to the bathroom, which was just behind his bed, and he and the man had had sex and then the man had left.

That night he was very quiet, and Luke was gentle and tender with him. He had even brought him a cookie—a gingersnap—and he had tried to smile at Luke, and tried to eat it, but he couldn't, and when Luke wasn't looking, he wrapped it in a piece of paper and threw it away. The next day he hadn't wanted to go to the track in the morning, but Luke had said he'd feel better with some exercise, and so they had gone and he had tried to run, but it was too painful and he had eventually sat down and waited until Luke said they could leave.

Now their routine was different: they still had classes in the mornings and afternoons, but now, some evenings, Brother Luke brought back men, his clients. Sometimes there was just one; sometimes there were several. The men brought their own towels and their own sheets, which they fitted over the bed before they began and unpeeled and took with them when they left.

He tried very hard not to cry at night, but when he did, Brother Luke would come sit with him and rub his back and comfort him.

"How many more until we can get the cabin?" he asked, but Luke just shook his head, sadly. "I won't know for a while," he said. "But you're doing such a good job, Jude. You're so good at it. It's nothing to be ashamed of." But he knew there *was* something shameful about it. No one had ever told him there was, but he knew anyway. He knew what he was doing was wrong.

And then, after a few months—and many motels; they moved every ten days or so, all around east Texas, and with every move, Luke took him to the forest, which really was beautiful, and to the clearing where they'd have their cabin—things changed again. He was lying in his bed one night (a night during a week in which there had been no clients. "A little vacation," Luke had said, smiling. "Everyone needs a break, especially someone who works as hard as you do") when Luke asked, "Jude, do you love me?"

He hesitated. Four months ago, he would've said yes immediately, proudly and unthinkingly. But now—*did* he love Brother Luke? He often wondered about this. He wanted to. The brother had never hurt him, or hit him, or said anything mean to him. He took care of him. He was always waiting just behind the wall to make sure nothing bad happened to him. The week before, a client had tried to make him do something Brother Luke said he never had to do if he didn't want to, and he had been struggling and trying to cry out, but there had been a pillow over his face and he knew his noises were muffled. He was frantic, almost sobbing, when suddenly the pillow had been lifted from his face, and the man's weight from his body, and Brother Luke was telling the man to get out of the room, in a tone he had never before heard from the brother but which had frightened and impressed him.

And yet something else told him that he shouldn't love Brother Luke, that the brother had done something to him that was wrong. But he hadn't. He had volunteered for this, after all; it was for the cabin in the woods, where he would have his own sleeping loft, that he was doing this. And so he told the brother he did.

He was momentarily happy when he saw the smile on the brother's face, as if he had presented him with the cabin itself. "Oh, Jude," he said, "that is the greatest gift I could ever get. Do you know how much I love you? I love you more than I love my own self. I think of you like my own son," and he had smiled back, then, because sometimes, he had privately thought of Luke as his father, and he as Luke's son. "Your dad said you're nine, but you look older," one of the clients had said to him, suspiciously, before they had begun, and he had answered what Luke had told him to say—"I'm tall for my age"—both pleased and oddly not-pleased that the client had thought Luke was his father.

Then Brother Luke had explained to him that when two people loved each other as much as they did, that they slept in the same bed, and were naked with each other. He hadn't known what to say to this, but before he could think of what it might be, Brother Luke was moving into bed with him and taking off his clothes and then kissing him. He had never kissed before—Brother Luke didn't let the clients do it with him—and he didn't like it, didn't like the wetness and the force of it. "Relax," the brother told him. "Just relax, Jude," and he tried to as much as he could.

The first time the brother had sex with him, he told him it would be different than with the clients. "Because we're in love," he'd said, and he had believed him, and when it had felt the same after all—as painful, as difficult, as uncomfortable, as shameful—he assumed he was doing something wrong, especially because the brother was so happy afterward. "Wasn't that nice?" the brother asked him, "didn't it feel different?," and he had agreed, too embarrassed to admit that it had been no different at all, that it had been just as awful as it had been with the client the day before.

Brother Luke usually didn't have sex with him if he'd seen clients earlier in the evening, but they always slept in the same bed, and they always kissed. Now one bed was used for the clients, and the other was theirs. He grew to hate the taste of Luke's mouth, its old-coffee tang, his tongue something slippery and skinned trying to burrow inside of him. Late at night, as the brother lay next to him asleep, pressing him against the wall with his weight, he would sometimes cry, silently, praying to be taken away, anywhere, anywhere else. He no longer thought of the cabin: he now dreamed of the monastery, and thought of how stupid he'd been to leave. It had been better there after all. When they were out in the mornings and would pass people, Brother Luke would tell him to lower his eyes, because his eyes were distinctive and if the brothers were looking for them, they would give them away. But sometimes he wanted to raise his eyes, as if they could by their very color and shape telegraph a message across miles and states to the brothers: *Here I am. Help me. Please take me back.* Nothing was his any longer: not his eyes, not his mouth, not even his name, which Brother Luke only called him in private. Around everyone else, he was Joey. "And this is Joey," Brother Luke would say, and he would rise from the bed and wait, his head bent, as the client inspected him.

He cherished his lessons, because they were the one time Brother Luke didn't touch him, and in those hours, the brother was who he remembered, the person he had trusted and followed. But then the lessons would end for the day, and every evening would conclude the same as the evening before.

He grew more and more silent. "Where's my smiley boy?" the brother would ask him, and he would try to smile back at him. "It's okay to enjoy it," the brother would say, sometimes, and he would nod, and the brother would smile at him and rub his back. "You like it, don't you?" he would ask, and wink, and he would nod at him, mutely. "I can tell," Luke would say, still smiling, proud of him. "You were made for this, Jude." Some of the clients would say that to him as well—*You were born for this*—and as much as he hated it, he also knew that they were right. He was born for this. He had been born, and left, and found, and used as he had been intended to be used.

In later years, he would try to remember when exactly it was that he must have realized that the cabin was never going to be built, that the life he had dreamed of would never be his. When he had begun, he had kept track of the number of clients he had seen, thinking that when he reached a certain number—forty? fifty?—he would surely be done, he would surely be allowed to stop. But then the number grew larger and larger, until one day he had looked at it and realized how large it was and had started crying, so scared and sick of what he had done that he had stopped counting. So was it when he reached that number? Or was it when they left Texas altogether, Luke promising him that the forests were better in Washington State anyway, and they drove west, through New Mexico and Arizona, and then north, stopping for weeks in little towns, staying in little motels that were the twins of that very first motel they had ever stayed in, and that no matter where they stopped, there were always men, and on the nights there weren't men, there was Brother Luke, who seemed to crave him the way he himself had never craved anything? Was it when he realized that he hated his weeks off even more than the normal weeks, because the return to his regular life was so much more terrible than if he had never had a vacation at all? Was it when he began noticing the inconsistencies in Brother Luke's stories: how sometimes it wasn't his son but a nephew, who hadn't died but had in fact moved away, and Brother Luke never saw him again; or how sometimes, he stopped teaching because he had felt the calling to join the monastery, and sometimes it was because he was weary from having to constantly negotiate with the school's principal, who clearly didn't care for children the way the brother did; or how in some stories, he had grown up in east Texas, but in others, he had spent his childhood in Carmel, or Laramie, or Eugene?

Or was it the day that they were passing through Utah to Idaho, on their way to Washington? They rarely ventured into actual towns—their America was denuded of trees, of flowers, theirs was just long stretches of roadway, the only green thing Brother Luke's lone surviving cattleya, which continued to live and leaf, though not bud—but this time they had, because Brother Luke had a doctor friend in one of the towns, and he wanted him to be examined because it was clear he had picked up some sort of disease from one of the clients, despite the precautions Brother Luke made them take. He didn't know the name of the town, but he was startled at the signs of normalcy, of life around him, and he stared out of his window in silence, looking at these scenes that he had always imagined but rarely saw: women standing on the street with strollers, talking and laughing with one another; a jogger panting by; families with dogs; a world made of not just men but also of children and women. Normally on these drives he would close his eyes—he slept all the time now, waiting for each day to end—but this day, he felt unusually alert, as if the world was trying to tell him something, and all he had to do was listen to its message.

Brother Luke was trying to read the map and drive at the same time, and finally he pulled over, studying the map and muttering. Luke had stopped across the street from a baseball field, and he watched as, if at once, it began to fill with people: women, mostly, and then, running and shouting, boys. The boys wore uniforms, white with red stripes, but despite that, they all looked different—different hair, different eyes, different skin. Some were skinny, like he was, and some were fat. He had never seen so many boys his own age at one time, and he looked and looked at them. And then he noticed that although they were different, they were actually the same: they were all smiling, and laughing, excited to be outside, in the dry, hot air, the sun bright above them, their mothers unloading cans of soda and bottles of water and juice from plastic carrying containers.

"Aha! We're back on track!" he heard Luke saying, and heard him fold up the map. But before he started the engine again, he felt Luke follow his gaze, and for a moment the two of them sat staring at the boys in silence, until at last Luke stroked his hair. "I love you, Jude," he said, and after a moment, he replied as he always did—"I love you, too, Brother Luke"—and they drove away.

He was the same as those boys, but he was really not: he was different. He would never be one of them. He would never be someone who would run across a field while his mother called after him to come have a snack before he played so he wouldn't get tired. He would never have his bed in the cabin. He would never be clean again. The boys were playing on the field, and he was driving with Brother Luke to the doctor, the kind of doctor he knew from his previous visits to other doctors would be somehow wrong, somehow not a good person. He was as far away from them as he was from the monastery. He was so far gone from himself, from who he had hoped to be, that it was as if he was no longer a boy at all but something else entirely. This was his life now, and there was nothing he could do about it.

At the doctor's office, Luke leaned over and held him. "We're going to have fun tonight, just you and me," he said, and he nodded, because there was nothing else he could do. "Let's go," said Luke, releasing him, and he got out of the car, and followed Brother Luke across the parking lot and toward the brown door that was already opening to let them inside.

—

The first memory: a hospital room. He knew it was a hospital room even before he opened his eyes because he could smell it, because its quality of silence—a silence that wasn't really silent—was familiar. Next to him: Willem, asleep in a chair. Then he had been confused—why was Willem here? He was supposed to be away, somewhere. He remembered: Sri Lanka. But he wasn't. He was here. How strange, he thought. I wonder why he's here? That was the first memory.

The second memory: the same hospital room. He turned and saw Andy sitting on the side of his bed, Andy, unshaven and awful-looking, giving him a strange, unconvincing smile. He felt Andy squeeze his hand—he hadn't realized he had a hand until he felt Andy squeeze it—and had tried to squeeze back, but couldn't. Andy had looked up at someone. "Nerve damage?" he heard Andy ask. "Maybe," said this other person, the person he couldn't see, "but if we're lucky, it's more likely it's—" And he had closed his eyes and fallen back asleep. That was the second memory.

The third and fourth and fifth and sixth memories weren't really memories at all: they were people's faces, their hands, their voices, leaning into his face, holding his hand, talking to him—they were Harold and Julia and Richard and Lucien. Same for the seventh and eighth: Malcolm, JB.

The ninth memory was Willem again, sitting next to him, telling him he was so sorry, but he had to leave. Just for a little while, and then he'd be back. He was crying, and he wasn't sure why, but it didn't seem so unusual—they all cried, they cried and apologized to him, which he found perplexing, as none of them had done anything wrong: he knew that much, at least. He tried to tell Willem not to cry, that he was fine, but his tongue was so thick in his mouth, a great useless slab, and he couldn't make it operate. Willem was already holding one of his hands, but he didn't have the energy to lift the other so he could put it on Willem's arm and reassure him, and finally he had given up.

In the tenth memory, he was still in the hospital, but in a different room, and he was still so tired. His arms ached. He had two foam balls, one cupped in each palm, and he was supposed to squeeze them for five seconds and then release them for five. Then squeeze them for five, and release them for five. He couldn't remember who had told him this, or who had given him the balls, but he did so anyway, although whenever he did, his arms hurt more, a burning, raw pain, and he couldn't do more than three or four repetitions before he was exhausted and had to stop.

And then one night he had awoken, swimming up through layers of dreams he couldn't remember, and had realized where he was, and why. He had gone back to sleep then, but the next day he turned his head and saw a man sitting in a chair next to his bed: he didn't know who the man was, but he had seen him before. He would come and sit and stare at him and sometimes he would talk to him, but he could never concentrate on what the man was saying, and would eventually close his eyes.

"I'm in a mental institution," he told the man now, and his voice sounded wrong to him, reedy and hoarse.

The man smiled. "You're in the psychiatric wing of a hospital, yes," he said. "Do you remember me?"

"No," he said, "but I recognize you."

"I'm Dr. Solomon. I'm a psychiatrist here at the hospital." There was a silence. "Do you know why you're here?"

He closed his eyes and nodded. "Where's Willem?" he asked. "Where's Harold?"

"Willem had to go back to Sri Lanka to finish shooting," said the doctor. "He'll be back"—he heard the sound of paper flipping—"October ninth. So in ten days. Harold's coming at noon; it's when he's been coming, do you remember?" He shook his head. "Jude," the doctor said, "can you tell me why you're here?"

"Because," he began, swallowing. "Because of what I did in the shower."

There was another silence. "That's right," said the doctor, softly. "Jude, can you tell me why—" But that was all he heard, because he had fallen asleep again.

The next time he woke, the man was gone, but Harold was in his place. "Harold," he said, in his strange new voice, and Harold, who had been sitting with his elbows on his thighs and his face in his hands, looked up as suddenly as if he'd shouted.

"Jude," he said, and sat next to him on the bed. He took the ball out of his right hand and replaced it with his own hand.

He thought that Harold looked terrible. "I'm sorry, Harold," he said, and Harold began to cry. "Don't cry," he told him, "please don't cry," and Harold got up and went to the bathroom and he could hear him blowing his nose.

That night, once he was alone, he cried as well: not because of what he had done but because he hadn't been successful, because he had lived after all.

His mind grew a little clearer with every day. Every day, he was awake a little longer. Mostly, he felt nothing. People came to see him and cried and he looked at them and could register only the strangeness of their faces, the way everyone looked the same when they cried, their noses hoggy, rarely used muscles pulling their mouths in unnatural directions, into unnatural shapes.

He thought of nothing, his mind was a clean sheet of paper. He learned little pieces of what had happened: how Richard's studio manager had thought the plumber was coming at nine that night, not nine the following morning (even in his haze, he wondered how anyone could think a plumber would come at nine in the evening); how Richard had found him and called an ambulance and had ridden with him to the hospital; how Richard had called Andy and Harold and Willem; how Willem had flown back from Colombo to be with him. He did feel sorry that it had been Richard who'd had to discover him—that was always the part of the plan that had made him uncomfortable, although at the time he had remembered thinking that Richard had a high tolerance for blood, having once made sculptures with it, and so was the least likely among his friends to be traumatized—and had apologized to Richard, who had stroked the back of his hand and told him it was fine, it was okay.

Dr. Solomon came every day and tried to talk to him, but he didn't have much to say. Most of the time, people didn't talk to him at all. They came and sat and did work of their own, or spoke to him without seeming to expect a reply, which he appreciated. Lucien came often, usually with a gift, once with a large card that everyone in the office had signed—"I'm sure this is just the thing to make you feel better," he'd said, dryly, "but here it is, anyway"—and Malcolm made him one of his imaginary houses, its windows crisp vellum, which he placed on his bedside table. Willem called him every morning and every night. Harold read *The Hobbit* to him, which he had never read, and when Harold couldn't come, Julia came, and picked up where Harold had left off: those were his favorite visits. Andy arrived every evening, after visiting hours had ended, and had dinner with him; he was concerned that he wasn't eating enough, and brought him a serving of whatever he was having. He brought him a container of beef barley soup, but his hands were still too weak to hold the spoon, and Andy had to feed him, one slow spoonful after the next. Once, this would have embarrassed him, but now he simply didn't care: he opened his mouth and accepted the food, which was flavorless, and chewed and swallowed.

"I want to go home," he told Andy one evening, as he watched Andy eat his turkey club sandwich.

Andy finished his bite and looked at him. "Oh, do you?"

"Yes," he said. He couldn't think of anything else to say. "I want to leave." He thought Andy would say something sarcastic, but he only nodded, slowly. "Okay," he said. "Okay. I'll talk to Solomon." He grimaced. "Eat your sandwich."

The next day Dr. Solomon said, "I hear you want to go home."

"I feel like I've been here a long time," he said.

Dr. Solomon was quiet. "You *have* been here a little while," he said. "But given your history of self-injury and the seriousness of your attempt, your doctor—Andy—and parents thought it was for the best."

He thought about this. "So if my attempt had been less serious, I could have gone home earlier?" It seemed too logical to be an effective policy.

The doctor smiled. "Probably," he said. "But I'm not completely opposed to letting you go home, Jude, although I think we have to put some protective measures in place." He stopped. "It troubles me, however, that you've been so unwilling to discuss why you made the attempt in the first place. Dr. Contractor—I'm sorry: Andy—tells me that you've always resisted therapy, can you tell me why?" He said nothing, and neither did the doctor. "Your father tells me that you were in an abusive relationship last year, and that it's had long-term reverberations," said the doctor, and he felt himself go cold. But he willed himself not to answer, and closed his eyes, and finally he could hear Dr. Solomon get up to leave. "I'll be back tomorrow, Jude," he said as he left.

Eventually, once it was clear that he wasn't going to speak to any of them and that he was in no state to hurt himself again, they let him go, with stipulations: He was to be released into Julia and Harold's care. It was strongly recommended that he remain on a milder course of the drugs that he'd been given in the hospital. It was very strongly recommended that he see a therapist twice a week. He was to see Andy once a week. He was to take a sabbatical from work, which had already been arranged. He agreed to everything. He signed his name—the pen wobbly in his grip—on the discharge papers, under Andy's and Dr. Solomon's and Harold's.

Harold and Julia took him to Truro, where Willem was already waiting for him. Every night he slept, extravagantly, and during the day he and Willem walked slowly down the hill to the ocean. It was early October and too cold to get into the water, but they would sit on the sand and look out at the horizon line, and sometimes Willem would talk to him and sometimes he wouldn't. He dreamed that the sea had turned into a solid block of ice, its waves frozen in mid-crest, and that Willem was at a far shore, beckoning to him, and he was making his way slowly across its wide expanse to him, his hands and face numb from the wind.

They ate dinner early, because he went to bed so early. The meals were always something simple, easy to digest, and if there was meat, one of the three of them would cut it up for him in advance so he wouldn't have to try to wield a knife. Harold poured him a glass of milk every dinner, as if he was a child, and he drank it. He wasn't allowed to leave the table until he had eaten at least half of what was on his plate, and he wasn't allowed to serve himself, either. He was too tired to fight this; he did the best he could.

He was always cold, and sometimes he woke in the middle of the night, shivering despite the covers heaped on top of him, and he would lie there, watching Willem, who was sharing his room, breathing on the couch opposite him, watching clouds drift across the slice of moon he could see between the edge of the window frame and the blind, until he was able to sleep again.

Sometimes he thought about what he had done and felt that same sorrow he had felt in the hospital: the sorrow that he had failed, that he was still alive. And sometimes he thought about it and felt dread: now everyone really would treat him differently. Now he really was a freak, a bigger freak than he'd been before. Now he would have to begin anew in his attempts to convince people he was normal. He thought of the office, the one place where what he had been hadn't mattered. But now there would always be another, competing story about him. Now he wouldn't just be the youngest equity partner in the firm's history (as Tremain sometimes introduced him); now he would be the partner who had tried to kill himself. They must be furious with him, he thought. He thought of his work there, and wondered who was handling it. They probably didn't even need him to come back. Who would want to work with him again? Who would trust him again?

And it wasn't just Rosen Pritchard who would see him differently—it was everyone. All the autonomy he had spent years accumulating, trying to prove to everyone that he deserved: now it was gone. Now he couldn't even cut his own food. The day before, Willem had had to help him tie his shoes. "It'll get better, Judy," he said to him, "it'll get better. The doctor said it's just going to take time." In the mornings, Harold or Willem had to shave him because his hands were still too unsteady; he looked at his unfamiliar face in the mirror as they dragged the razor down his cheeks and under his chin. He had taught himself to shave in Philadelphia when he was living with the Douglasses, but Willem had retaught him their freshman year, alarmed, he later told him, by his tentative, hacking movements, as if he was clearing brush with a scythe. "Good at calculus, bad at shaving," he'd said then, and had smiled at him so he wouldn't feel more self-conscious.

Then he would tell himself, *You can always try again*, and just thinking that made him feel stronger, although perversely, he was somehow less inclined to try again. He was too exhausted. Trying again meant preparation. It meant finding something sharp, finding some time alone, and he was never alone. Of course, he knew there were other methods, but he remained stubbornly fixated on the one he had chosen, even though it hadn't worked.

Mostly, though, he felt nothing. Harold and Julia and Willem asked him what he wanted for breakfast, but the choices were impossible and overwhelming—pancakes? Waffles? Cereal? Eggs? What kind of eggs? Soft-boiled? Hard? Scrambled? Sunny-side? Fried? Over easy? Poached?—and he'd shake his head, and they eventually stopped asking. They stopped asking his opinion on anything, which he found restful. After lunch (also absurdly early), he napped on the living-room sofa in front of the fire, falling asleep to the sound of their murmurs, the slosh of water as they did the dishes. In the afternoons, Harold read to him; sometimes Willem and Julia stayed to listen as well.

After ten days or so, he and Willem went home to Greene Street. He had been dreading his return, but when he went to his bathroom, the marble was clean and stainless. "Malcolm," said Willem, before he had to ask. "He finished last week. It's all new." Willem helped him into bed, and gave him a manila envelope with his name on it, which he opened after Willem left. Inside were the letters he had written everyone, still sealed, and the sealed copy of his will, and a note from Richard: "I thought you would want these. Love, R." He slid them back into the envelope, his hands shaking; the next day he put them in his safe.

The next morning he woke very early, creeping past Willem sleeping on the sofa at the far end of his bedroom, and walked through the apartment. Someone had put flowers in every room, or branches of maple leaves, or bowls of squashes. The space smelled delicious, like apples and cedar. He went to his study, where someone had stacked his mail on his desk, and where Malcolm's little paper house sat atop a stack of books. He saw unopened envelopes from JB, from Asian Henry Young, from India, from Ali, and knew they had made drawings for him. He walked past the dining-room table, letting his fingers skim along the spines of the books lined up on their shelves; he wandered into the kitchen and opened the refrigerator and saw that it was filled with things he liked. Richard had started working more with ceramics, and at the center of the dining table was a large, amorphous piece, the glaze rough and pleasant under his palms, painted with white thread-like veins. Next to it stood his and Willem's Saint Jude statue, which Willem had taken with him when he moved to Perry Street, but which had now found its way back to him.

The days slipped by and he let them. In the morning he swam, and he and Willem ate breakfast. The physical therapist came and had him practice squeezing rubber balls, short lengths of rope, toothpicks, pens. Sometimes he had to pick up multiple objects with one hand, holding them between his fingers, which was difficult. His hands shook more than ever, and he felt sharp prickles vibrating through his fingers, but she told him not to worry, that it was his muscles repairing themselves, his nerves resetting themselves. He had lunch, he napped. While he napped, Richard came to watch him and Willem went out to run errands and go downstairs to the gym and, he hoped, do something interesting and indulgent that didn't involve him and his problems. People came to see him in the afternoon: all the same people, and new people, too. They stayed an hour and then Willem made them leave. Malcolm came with JB and the four of them had an awkward, polite conversation about things they had done when they were in college, but he was glad to see JB, and thought he might like to see him again when he was less cloudy-headed, so he could apologize to him and tell him he forgave him. As he was leaving, JB told him, quietly, "It'll get better, Judy. Trust me, I know," and then added, "At least you didn't hurt anyone in the process," and he felt guilty, because he knew he had. Andy came at the end of the day and examined him; he unwrapped his bandages and cleaned the area around his stitches. He still hadn't looked at his stitches—he couldn't bring himself to—and when Andy was cleaning them, he looked elsewhere or closed his eyes. After Andy left, they ate dinner, and after dinner, after the boutiques and few remaining galleries had shuttered for the night and the neighborhood was deserted, they walked, making a neat square around SoHo—east to Lafayette, north to Houston, west to Sixth, south to Grand, east to Greene—before returning home. It was a short walk, but it left him exhausted, and he once fell on the way to the bedroom, his legs simply sliding out from beneath him. Julia and Harold took the train down on Thursdays and spent all day Friday and Saturday with him, and part of Sunday as well.

Every morning, Willem asked him, "Do you want to talk to Dr. Loehmann today?" And every morning he answered, "Not yet, Willem. Soon, I promise."

By the end of October, he was feeling stronger, less shaky. He was managing to stay awake for longer stretches at a time. He could lie on his back and hold a book up without it trembling so badly that he had to roll over onto his stomach so he could prop it against a pillow. He could butter his own bread, and he could wear shirts with buttons again because he was able to slip the button into its hole.

"What're you reading?" he asked Willem one afternoon, sitting next to him on the living-room couch.

"A play I'm thinking of doing," Willem said, putting the pages down.

He looked at a point beyond Willem's head. "Are you going away again?" It was monstrously selfish to ask, but he couldn't stop himself.

"No," said Willem, after a silence. "I thought I'd stick around New York for a while, if that's okay with you."

He smiled at the couch's cushions. "It's fine with me," he said, and looked up to see Willem smiling at him. "It's nice to see you smile again," was all he said, and went back to reading.

In November he realized that he had done nothing to celebrate Willem's forty-third birthday in late August, and mentioned it to him. "Well, technically, you get a pass, because I wasn't here," said Willem.

"But sure, I'll let you make it up to me. Let's see." He thought. "Are you ready to go out into the world? Do you want to have dinner? An early dinner?"

"Sure," he said, and they went the next week to a little Japanese place in the East Village that served pressed sushi and where they'd been going for years. He ordered his own food, although he had been nervous, worried that he was somehow choosing incorrectly, but Willem was patient and waited as he deliberated, and when he had decided, he'd nodded at him. "Good choice," he said. As they ate, they spoke of their friends, and the play Willem had decided he was going to do, and the novel he was reading: anything but him.

"I think we should go to Morocco," he said as they walked slowly home, and Willem looked at him.

"I'll look into it," Willem said, and took his arm to move him out of the path of a bicyclist who was zooming down the street.

"I want to get you something for your birthday," he said, a few blocks later. Really, he wanted to get Willem something to thank him, and to try to express what he couldn't say to him: a gift that would properly convey years of gratitude and love. After their earlier conversation about the play, he had remembered that Willem had, in fact, committed the previous year to a project that would be shooting in Russia in early January. But when he mentioned this to him, Willem had shrugged. "Oh, that?" he'd asked. "Didn't work out. It's fine. I didn't really want to do it anyway." He had been suspicious, though, and when he had looked online, there were reports that Willem had pulled out of the film for personal reasons; another actor had been cast instead. He had stared at the screen then, the story blurring before him, but when he had asked Willem about it, Willem had shrugged again. "That's what you say when you realize you and the director really aren't on the same page and no one wants to lose face," he said. But he knew that Willem wasn't telling him the truth.

"You don't need to get me anything," Willem said, as he knew he would, and he said (as he always did), "I know I don't need to, but I want to." And then he added, also as he always did, "A better friend would know what to get you and wouldn't have to ask for suggestions."

"A better friend would," Willem agreed, as *he* always did, and he smiled, because it felt like one of their normal conversations.

More days passed. Willem moved back into his suite at the other end of the apartment. Lucien called him a few times to ask him about one thing or another, apologizing as he did, but he was happy to get his calls, and happy that Lucien now began their conversations by complaining about a client or a colleague instead of asking how he was. Aside from Tremain and Lucien and one or two other people, no one at the firm knew the real reason he'd been absent: they, like his clients, had been told he was recovering from emergency spinal cord surgery. He knew that when he returned to Rosen Pritchard, Lucien would immediately restart him on his normal caseload; there would be no talk of giving him an easy transition, no speculation about his ability to handle the stress, and he was grateful for that. He stopped taking his drugs, which he realized were making him feel dopey, and after they had left his system, he was amazed by how clear he felt—even his vision was different, as if a plate-glass window had been wiped clean of all grease and smears and he was finally getting to admire the brilliant green lawn beyond it, the pear trees with their yellow fruit.

But he also realized that the drugs had been protecting him, and without them, the hyenas returned, less numerous and more sluggish, but still circling him, still following him, less motivated in their pursuit but still there, his unwanted but dogged companions. Other memories came back to him as well, the same old ones, but new ones too, and he was made much more sharply aware of how severely he had inconvenienced everyone, of how much he had asked from people, of how he had taken what he would never, ever be able to repay. And then there was the voice, which whispered to him at odd moments, *You can try again, you can try again,* and he tried to ignore it, because at some point—in the same, undefinable way that he had decided to kill himself in the first place—he had decided he would work on getting better, and he didn't want to be reminded that he could try again, that being alive, as ignominious and absurd as it often was, wasn't his only option.

Thanksgiving came, which they once again had at Harold and Julia's apartment on West End Avenue, and which was once again a small group: Laurence and Gillian (their daughters had gone to their husbands' families' houses for the holiday), him, Willem, Richard and India, Malcolm and Sophie. At the meal, he could feel everyone trying not to pay too much attention to him, and when Willem mentioned the trip they were taking to Morocco in the middle of December, Harold was so relaxed, so incurious, that he knew that he must have already thoroughly discussed it with Willem (and, probably, Andy) in advance, and given his permission.

"When do you go back to Rosen Pritchard?" asked Laurence, as if he'd been away on holiday.

"January third," he said.

"So soon!" said Gillian.

He smiled back at her. "Not soon enough," he said. He meant it; he was ready to try to be normal again, to make another attempt at being alive.

He and Willem left early, and that evening he cut himself for the second time since he was released from the hospital. This was another thing the drugs had dampened: his need to cut, to feel that bright, startling slap of pain. The first time he did it, he was shocked by how much it hurt, and had actually wondered why he had been doing this to himself for so long—what had he been thinking? But then he felt everything within him slow, felt himself relax, felt his memories dim, and had remembered how it helped him, remembered why he had begun doing it at all. The scars from his attempt were three vertical lines on both arms, from the base of his palm to just below the inside of his elbow, and they hadn't healed well; it looked as if he had shoved pencils just beneath the skin. They had a strange, pearly shine, almost as if the skin had been burned, and now he made a fist, watching them tighten in response.

That night he woke screaming, which had been happening as he readjusted to life, to an existence with dreams; on the drugs, there were no dreams, not really, or if there were, they were so strange and pointless and meandering that he soon forgot them. But in this dream he was in one of the motel rooms, and there was a group of men, and they were grabbing at him, and he was desperate, trying to fight them. But they kept multiplying, and he knew he would lose, he knew he would be destroyed.

One of the men kept calling his name, and then put his hand on his cheek, and for some reason that made him more terrified, and he pushed his hand away, and then the man poured water on him and he woke, gasping, to see Willem next to him, his face pale, holding a glass in his hand. "I'm sorry, I'm sorry," Willem said, "I couldn't get you out of it, Jude, I'm sorry. I'm going to get you a towel," and came back with a towel and the glass filled with water, but he was shaking too badly to hold it. He apologized again and again to Willem, who shook his head and told him not to worry, that it was all right, that it was just a dream. Willem got him a new shirt, and turned around as he changed and then took the wet one to the bathroom.

"Who's Brother Luke?" asked Willem, as they sat there together in silence and waited for his breathing to return to normal. And then, when he didn't answer, "You kept screaming 'Help me, Brother Luke, help me.'" He was quiet. "Who is he, Jude? Was he someone from the monastery?"

"I can't, Willem," he said, and he yearned for Ana. *Ask me one more time, Ana*, he said to her, *and I'll tell you. Teach me how to do it. This time I'll listen. This time I'll talk.*

That weekend they went to Richard's house upstate and took a long walk through the woods that backed the property. Later, he successfully completed the first meal he'd cooked since he was released. He made Willem's favorite, lamb chops, and although he'd needed Willem's help carving the chop itself—he still wasn't agile enough to do it on his own—he did everything else by himself. That night he woke again, screaming, and again there was Willem (though without the glass of water this time), and him asking about Brother Luke, and why he kept begging for his help, and again, he wasn't able to answer.

The next day he was tired, and his arms ached, and his body ached as well, and on their walk, he said very little, and Willem didn't say much himself. In the afternoon they reviewed their plans for Morocco: they would begin in Fez, and then drive through the desert, where they'd stay near Ouarzazate, and end in Marrakech. On their way back, they'd stop in Paris to visit Citizen and a friend of Willem's for a few days; they'd be home just before the new year.

As they were eating dinner, Willem said, "You know, I thought of what you could give me for my birthday."

"Oh?" he said, relieved to be able to concentrate on something he could give Willem, rather than having to ask Willem for yet more help, thinking of all the time he had stolen from him. "Let's hear it."

"Well," said Willem, "it's kind of a big thing."

"Anything," he said. "I mean it," and Willem gave him a look he couldn't quite interpret. "Really," he assured him. "Anything."

Willem put down his lamb sandwich and took a breath. "Okay," he said. "What I really want for my birthday is for you to tell me who

Brother Luke is. And not just who he is, but what your—your relationship with him was, and why you think you keep calling out his name at
night." He looked at him. "I want you to be honest, and thorough, and
tell me the whole story. That's what I want."

There was a long silence. He realized he still had a mouthful of
food, and he somehow swallowed it, and put down his sandwich as well,
which he was still holding aloft. "Willem," he said at last, because he
knew that Willem was serious, and that he wouldn't be able to dissuade
him, to convince him to wish for something else, "part of me *does* want
to tell you. But if I do—" He stopped. "But if I do, I'm afraid you're going
to be disgusted by me. Wait," he said, as Willem began to speak. He
looked at Willem's face. "I promise you I will. I promise you. But—but
you're going to have to give me some time. I've never really discussed it
before, and I need to figure out how to say the words."

"Okay," Willem said at last. "Well." He paused. "How about if we
work up to it, then? I ask you about something easier, and you answer
that, and you'll see that it's not so bad, talking about it? And if it is, we'll
discuss that, too."

He inhaled; exhaled. *This is Willem*, he reminded himself. *He
would never hurt you, not ever. It's time. It's time.* "Okay," he said, finally.
"Okay. Ask me."

He could see Willem leaning back in his chair and staring at him,
trying to determine which to choose of the hundreds of questions that
one friend should be able to ask another and yet he had never been
allowed to do. Tears came to his eyes, then, for how lopsided he had
let their friendship become, and for how long Willem had stayed with
him, year after year, even when he had fled from him, even when he
had asked him for help with problems whose origins he wouldn't reveal.
In his new life, he promised himself, he would be less demanding of his
friends; he would be more generous. Whatever they wanted, he would
give them. If Willem wanted information, he could have it, and it was
up to him to figure out how to give it to him. He would be hurt again
and again—everyone was—but if he was going to try, if he was going
to be alive, he had to be tougher, he had to prepare himself, he had to
accept that this was part of the bargain of life itself.

"Okay, I've got one," Willem said, and he sat up straighter, readying
himself. "How did you get the scar on the back of your hand?"

He blinked, surprised. He wasn't sure what the question was going to be, but now that it had come, he was relieved. He rarely thought of the scar these days, and now he looked at it, its taffeta gleam, and as he ran his fingertips across it, he thought of how this scar led to so many other problems, and then to Brother Luke, and then to the home, and to Philadelphia, to all of it.

But what in life wasn't connected to some greater, sadder story? All Willem was asking for was this one story; he didn't need to drag everything else behind it, a huge ugly snarl of difficulties.

He thought about how he could start, and plotted what he'd say in his head before he opened his mouth. Finally, he was ready. "I was always a greedy kid," he began, and across the table, he watched Willem lean forward on his elbows, as for the first time in their friendship, he was the listener, and he was being told a story.

—

He was ten, he was eleven. His hair grew long again, longer even than it had been at the monastery. He grew taller, and Brother Luke took him to a thrift store, where you could buy a sack of clothes and pay by the pound. "Slow down!" Brother Luke would joke with him, pushing down on the top of his head as if he were squashing him back to a smaller size. "You're growing up too fast for me!"

He slept all the time now. In his lessons, he was awake, but as the day turned to late afternoon, he would feel something descend upon him, and would begin yawning, unable to keep his eyes open. At first Brother Luke joked about this as well—"My sleepyhead," he said, "my dreamer"—but one night, he sat down with him after the client had left. For months, years, he had struggled with the clients, more out of reflex than because he thought he was capable of making them stop, but recently, he had begun to simply lie there, inert, waiting for whatever was going to happen to be over. "I know you're tired," Brother Luke had said. "It's normal; you're growing. It's tiring work, growing. And I know you work hard. But Jude, when you're with your clients, you have to show a little life; they're paying to be with you, you know—you have to show them you're enjoying it." When he said nothing, the brother added, "Of course, I know it's not *enjoyable* for you, not the way it is with just us, but you have to show a little energy, all right?" He leaned over, tucked his hair behind his ear. "All right?" He nodded.

It was also around then that he began throwing himself into walls. The motel they were staying in—this was in Washington—had a second floor, and once he had gone upstairs to refill their bucket of ice. It had been a wet, slippery day, and as he was walking back, he had tripped and fallen, bouncing the entire way downstairs. Brother Luke had heard the noise his fall made and had run out. Nothing had been broken, but he had been scraped and was bleeding, and Brother Luke had canceled the appointment he had for that evening. That night, the brother had been careful with him, and had brought him tea, but he had felt more alive than he had in weeks. Something about the fall, the freshness of the pain, had been restorative. It was honest pain, clean pain, a pain without shame or filth, and it was a different sensation than he had felt in years. The next week, he went to get ice again, but this time, on his way back to the room, he stopped in the little triangle of space beneath the stairwell, and before he was conscious of what he was doing, he was tossing himself against the brick wall, and as he did so, he imagined he was knocking out of himself every piece of dirt, every trace of liquid, every memory of the past few years. He was resetting himself; he was returning himself to something pure; he was punishing himself for what he had done. After that, he felt better, energized, as if he had run a very long race and then had vomited, and he had been able to return to the room.

Eventually, however, Brother Luke realized what he was doing, and there had been another talk. "I understand you get frustrated," Brother Luke said, "but Jude, what you're doing isn't good for you. I'm worried about you. And the clients don't like seeing you all bruised." They were silent. A month ago, after a very bad night—there had been a group of men, and after they had left, he had sobbed, wailed, coming as close to a tantrum as he had in years, while Luke sat next to him and rubbed his sore stomach and held a pillow over his mouth to muffle the sound—he had begged Luke to let him stop. And the brother had cried and said he would, that there was nothing more he'd like than for it to be just the two of them, but he had long ago spent all his money taking care of him. "I don't regret it for an instant, Jude," said the brother, "but we don't have any money now. You're all I've got. I'm so sorry. But I'm really saving now; eventually, you'll be able to stop, I promise."

"When?" he had sobbed.

"Soon," said Luke, "soon. A year. I promise," and he had nodded, although he had long since learned that the brother's promises were meaningless.

But then the brother said that he would teach him a secret, something that would help him relieve his frustrations, and the next day he had taught him to cut himself, and had given him a bag already packed with razors and alcohol wipes and cotton and bandages. "You'll have to experiment to see what feels best," the brother had said, and had shown him how to clean and bandage the cut once he had finished. "So this is yours," he said, giving him the bag. "You let me know when you need more supplies, and I'll get them for you." He had at first missed the theatrics, the force and weight, of his falls and his slams, but he soon grew to appreciate the secrecy, the control of the cuts. Brother Luke was right: the cutting was better. When he did it, it was as if he was draining away the poison, the filth, the rage inside him. It was as if his old dream of leeches had come to life and had the same effect, the effect he had always hoped it would. He wished he was made of metal, of plastic: something that could be hosed down and scrubbed clean. He had a vision of himself being pumped full of water and detergent and bleach and then blasted dry, everything inside him made hygienic again. Now, after the final client of the night had left, he took Brother Luke's place in the bathroom, and until he heard the brother telling him it was time to come to bed, his body was his to do with what he chose.

He was so dependent on Luke: for his food, for his protection, and now for his razors. When he needed to be taken to the doctor because he was sick—he got infections from the clients, no matter how hard Brother Luke tried, and sometimes he didn't properly clean his cuts and they became infected as well—Brother Luke took him, and got him the antibiotics he needed. He grew accustomed to Brother Luke's body, his mouth, his hands: he didn't like them, but he no longer jolted when Luke began to kiss him, and when the brother put his arms around him, he obediently returned the embrace. He knew there was no one else who would ever treat him as well as Luke did: even when he did something wrong, Luke never yelled at him, and even after all these years, he had still never hit him. Earlier, he had thought he might someday have a client who would be better, who might want to take him away, but now he knew that would never be the case. Once, he had started getting undressed before the client was ready, and the man had slapped his face and snapped at him. "Jesus," he'd said, "slow down, you little slut. How many times have you done this, anyway?" And as he always did whenever the clients hit him, Luke had come out of the bathroom to yell at the man, and had made the man promise to behave better if he was going to stay. The clients called him names: he was a slut, a whore, filthy, disgusting, a nympho (he had to look that one up), a slave, garbage, trash, dirty, worthless, a nothing. But Luke never said any of those things to him. He was perfect, said Luke, he was smart, he was good at what he did and there was nothing wrong with what he did.

The brother still talked of their being together, although now he talked of a house on the sea, somewhere in central California, and would describe the stony beaches, the noisy birds, the storm-colored water. They would be together, the two of them, like a married couple. No longer were they father and son; now they were equals. When he turned sixteen, they would get married. They would go on a honeymoon to France and Germany, where he could finally use his languages around real French and Germans, and to Italy and Spain, where Brother Luke had lived for two years: once as a student, once the year after he graduated college. They would buy him a piano so he could play and sing. "Other people won't want you if they knew how many clients you'd been with," the Brother said. "And they'd be silly to not want you. But I'll always want you, even if you've been with ten thousand clients." He would retire when he was sixteen, Brother Luke said, and he had cried then, quietly, because he had been counting the days until he was twelve, when Brother Luke had promised he could stop.

Sometimes Luke apologized for what he had to do: when the client was cruel, when he was in pain, when he bled or was bruised. And sometimes Luke acted as if he enjoyed it. "Well, that was a good one," he'd say, after one of the men left. "I could tell you liked that one, am I right? Don't deny it, Jude! I heard you enjoying yourself. Well, it's good. It's good to enjoy your work."

He turned twelve. They were now in Oregon, working their way toward California, Luke said. He had grown again; Brother Luke predicted he would be six foot one, six foot two when he stopped—still shorter than Brother Luke, but not by much. His voice was changing. He wasn't a child anymore, and this made finding clients more difficult. Now there were fewer individual clients and more groups. He hated the groups, but Luke said that was the best he could do. He looked too old for his age: clients thought he was thirteen or fourteen, and at this age, Luke said, every year counted.

It was fall; September twentieth. They were in Montana, because Luke thought he would like to see the night sky there, the stars as bright as electrical lights. There was nothing strange about that day. Two days earlier, he'd had a large group, and it had been so awful that Luke had not only canceled his clients for the day after but had let him sleep alone for both nights, the bed completely his. That evening, though, life had returned to normal. Luke joined him in bed, and began kissing him. And then, as they were having sex, there was a banging at their door, so loud and insistent and sudden that he had almost bitten down on Brother Luke's tongue. "Police," he could hear, "open up. Open up right now."

Brother Luke had clamped his hand over his mouth. "Don't say a word," he hissed.

"Police," shouted the voice again. "Edgar Wilmot, we have a warrant for your arrest. Open the door right now."

He was confused: Who was Edgar Wilmot? Was he a client? He was about to tell Brother Luke that they had made a mistake when he looked up and saw his face and realized that they were looking for Brother Luke.

Brother Luke pulled out of him and motioned for him to stay in the bed. "Don't move," he whispered. "I'll be right back." And then he ran into the bathroom; he could hear the door lock click.

"No," he'd whispered wildly, as Luke left him. "Don't leave me, Brother Luke, don't leave me alone." But the brother had left anyway.

And then everything seemed to move very slowly and very fast, both at the same time. He hadn't moved, he had been too petrified, but then there was the splintering of wood, and the room was filled with men holding flashlights high by their heads, so that he couldn't see their faces. One of them came over to him and said something to him—he couldn't hear for the noise, for his panic—and pulled up his underwear and helped him to his feet. "You're safe now," someone told him.

He heard one of the men swear, and shout from the bathroom, "Get an ambulance right now," and he wrestled free from the man who was holding him and ducked under another man's arm and made three fast leaps to the bathroom, where he had seen Brother Luke with an extension cord around his neck, hanging from the hook in the center of the bathroom ceiling, his mouth open, his eyes shut, his face as gray as his beard. He had screamed, then, screamed and screamed, and then he was being dragged from the room, screaming Brother Luke's name again and again.

He remembers little of what followed. He was questioned again and again; he was taken to a doctor at a hospital who examined him and asked him how many times he had been raped, but he hadn't been able to answer him: *Had* he been raped? He had agreed to this, to all of this; it had been his decision, and he had made it. "How many times have you had sex?" the doctor asked instead, and he said, "With Brother Luke, or with the others?" and the doctor had said, "What others?" And after he had finished telling him, the doctor had turned away from him and put his face in his hands and then looked back at him and had opened his mouth to say something, but nothing came out. And then he knew for certain that what he had been doing was wrong, and he felt so ashamed, so dirty that he had wanted to die.

They took him to the home. They brought him his things: his books, the Navajo doll, the stones and twigs and acorns and the Bible with its pressed flowers he had carried with him from the monastery, his clothes that the other boys made fun of. At the home, they knew what he was, they knew what he had done, they knew he was ruined already, and so he wasn't surprised when some of the counselors began doing to him what people had been doing to him for years. Somehow, the other boys also knew what he was. They called him names, the same names the clients had called him; they left him alone. When he approached a group of them, they would get up and run away.

They hadn't brought him his bag with razors, and so he had learned to improvise: he stole an aluminum can lid from the trash and sterilized it over the gas flame one afternoon when he was on kitchen duty and used that, stuffing it under his mattress. He stole a new lid every week.

He thought of Brother Luke every day. At the school, he skipped four grades; they allowed him to attend classes in math, in piano, in English literature, in French and German at the community college. His teachers asked him who had taught him what he knew, and he said his father had. "He did a good job," his English teacher told him. "He must have been an excellent teacher," and he had been unable to respond, and she had eventually moved on to the next student. At night, when he was with the counselors, he pretended that Brother Luke was standing right behind the wall, waiting to spring out in case things got too awful, which meant that everything that was happening to him were things Brother Luke knew he could bear.

After he had come to trust Ana, he told her a few things about Brother Luke. But he was unwilling to tell her everything. He told no one. He had been a fool to follow Luke, he knew that. Luke had lied to him, he had done terrible things to him. But he wanted to believe that, through everything, in spite of everything, Luke really had loved him, that that part had been real: not a perversion, not a rationalization, but real. He didn't think he could take Ana saying, as she said of the others, "He was a monster, Jude. They say they love you, but they say that so they can manipulate you, don't you see? This is what pedophiles do; this is how they prey on children." As an adult, he was still unable to decide what he thought about Luke. Yes, he was bad. But was he worse than the other brothers? Had he *really* made the wrong decision? Would it *really* have been better if he had stayed at the monastery? Would he have been more or less damaged by his time there? Luke's legacies were in everything he did, in everything he was: his love of reading, of music, of math, of gardening, of languages—those were Luke. His cutting, his hatred, his shame, his fears, his diseases, his inability to have a normal sex life, to be a normal person—those were Luke, too. Luke had taught him how to find pleasure in life, and he had removed pleasure absolutely.

He was careful never to say his name aloud, but sometimes he thought it, and no matter how old he got, no matter how many years had passed, there would appear Luke's face, smiling, conjured in an instant. He thought of Luke when the two of them were falling in love, when he was being seduced and had been too much of a child, too naïve, too lonely and desperate for affection to know it. He was running to the greenhouse, he was opening the door, the heat and smell of flowers were surrounding him like a cape. It was the last time he had been so simply happy, the last time he had known such uncomplicated joy. "And here's my beautiful boy!" Luke would cry. "Oh, Jude—I'm so happy to see you."

[V]

The Happy Years

1

THERE HAD BEEN a day, about a month after he turned thirty-eight, when Willem realized he was famous. Initially, this had fazed him less than he would have imagined, in part because he had always considered himself sort of famous—he and JB, that is. He'd be out downtown with someone, Jude or someone else, and somebody would come over to say hello to Jude, and Jude would introduce him: "Aaron, do you know Willem?" And Aaron would say, "Of course. Willem Ragnarsson. Everyone knows Willem," but it wouldn't be because of his work—it would be because Aaron's former roommate's sister had dated him at Yale, or he had two years ago done a reading for Aaron's friend's brother's friend who was a playwright, or because Aaron, who was an artist, had once been in a group show with JB and Asian Henry Young, and he'd met Willem at the after-party. New York City, for much of his adulthood, had simply been an extension of college, where everyone had known him and JB, and the entire infrastructure of which sometimes seemed to have been lifted out of Boston and plunked down within a few blocks' radius in lower Manhattan and outer Brooklyn. The four of them talked to the same—well, if not the same people, the same *types* of people at least, that they had in college, and in that realm of artists and actors and musicians, of course he was known, because he always had been. It wasn't such a vast world; everyone knew everyone else.

Of the four of them, only Jude, and to some degree Malcolm, had experience living in another world, the real world, the one populated with people who did the necessary stuff of life: making laws, and teaching, and healing people, and solving problems, and handling money, and selling and buying things (the bigger surprise, he always thought, was not that *he* knew Aaron but that Jude did). Just before he turned thirty-seven, he had taken a role in a quiet film titled *The Sycamore Court* in which he played a small-town Southern lawyer who was finally coming out of the closet. He'd taken the part to work with the actor playing his father, who was someone he admired and who in the film was taciturn and casually vituperative, a man disapproving of his own son and made unkind by his own disappointments. As part of his research, he had Jude explain to him what, exactly, he did all day, and as he listened, he found himself feeling slightly sad that Jude, whom he considered brilliant, brilliant in ways he would never understand, was spending his life doing work that sounded so crushingly dull, the intellectual equivalent of housework: cleaning and sorting and washing and tidying, only to move on to the next house and have to begin all over. He didn't say this, of course, and on one Saturday he met Jude at Rosen Pritchard and looked through his folders and papers and wandered around the office as Jude wrote.

"Well, what do you think?" Jude asked, and leaned back in his chair and grinned at him, and he smiled back and said, "Pretty impressive," because it was, in its own way, and Jude had laughed. "I know what you're thinking, Willem," he'd said. "It's okay. Harold thinks it, too. 'Such a waste,'" he said in Harold's voice. "'Such a waste, Jude.'"

"That's not what I'm thinking," he protested, although really, he had been: Jude was always bemoaning his own lack of imagination, his own unswervable sense of practicality, but Willem had never seen him that way. And it did seem a waste: not that he was at a corporate firm but that he was in law at all, when really, he thought, a mind like Jude's should be doing something else. What, he didn't know, but it wasn't this. He knew it was ridiculous, but he had never truly believed that Jude's attending law school would actually result in his becoming a lawyer: he had always imagined that at some point he'd give it up and do something else, like be a math professor, or a voice teacher, or (although he had recognized the irony, even then) a psychologist, because he was such a good listener and always so comforting to his friends. He didn't know why he clung to this idea of Jude, even after it was clear that he loved what he did and excelled at it.

The Sycamore Court had been an unexpected hit and had won Willem the best reviews he'd ever had, and award nominations, and its release, paired with a larger, flashier film that he had shot two years earlier but had been delayed in postproduction, had created a certain moment that even he recognized would transform his career. He had always chosen his roles wisely—if he could be said to have superior talent in anything, he always thought it was that: his taste for parts—but until that year, there had never been a time in which he felt that he was truly secure, that he could talk about films he'd like to do when he was in his fifties or sixties. Jude had always told him that he had an overdeveloped sense of circumspection about his career, that he was far better along than he thought, but it had never felt that way; he knew he was respected by his peers and by critics, but a part of him always feared that it would end abruptly and without warning. He was a practical person in the least practical of careers, and after every job he booked, he would tell his friends he would never book another, that this was certain to be the last, partly as a way of staving off his fears—if he acknowledged the possibility, it was less likely to happen—and partly to give voice to them, because they were real.

Only later, when he and Jude were alone, would he allow himself to truly worry aloud. "What if I never work again?" he would ask Jude.

"That won't happen," Jude would say.

"But what if it *does?*"

"Well," said Jude, seriously, "in the extraordinarily unlikely event that you never act again, then you'll do something else. And while you figure it out, you'll move in with me."

He knew, of course, that he would work again: he had to believe it. Every actor did. Acting was a form of grifting, and once you stopped believing you could, so did everyone else. But he still liked having Jude reassure him; he liked knowing he had somewhere to go just in case it really did end. Once in a while, when he was feeling particularly, uncharacteristically self-pitying, he would think of what he *would* do if it ended: he thought he might work with disabled children. He would be good at it, and he would enjoy it. He could see himself walking home from an elementary school he imagined might be on the Lower East Side, west to SoHo, toward Greene Street. His apartment would be gone, of course, sold to pay for his master's program in education (in this dream, all the millions he'd earned, all the millions he had never spent, had somehow vanished), and he would be living in Jude's apartment, as if the past two decades had never happened at all.

But after *The Sycamore Court*, these mopey fantasies had diminished in frequency, and he spent the latter half of his thirty-seventh year feeling closer to confidence than he ever had before. Something had shifted; something had cemented; somewhere his name had been tapped into stone. He would always have work; he could rest for a bit if he wanted to.

It was September, and he was coming back from a shoot and about to embark upon a European publicity tour; he had one day in the city, just one, and Jude told him he'd take him anywhere he wanted. They'd see each other, they'd have lunch, and then he'd get back into the car and go straight to the airport for the flight to London. It had been so long since he had been in New York, and he really wanted to go somewhere cheap and downtown and homey, like the Vietnamese noodle place they had gone to when they were in their twenties, but he instead picked a French restaurant known for its seafood in midtown so Jude wouldn't have to travel far.

The restaurant was filled with businessmen, the kinds of people who telegraphed their wealth and power with the cut of their suits and the subtlety of their watches: you had to be wealthy and powerful yourself in order to understand what was being communicated. To everyone else, they were men in gray suits, indistinguishable from one another. The hostess brought him to Jude, who was there already, waiting, and when Jude stood, he reached over and hugged him very close, which he knew Jude didn't like but which he had recently decided he would start doing anyway. They stood there, holding each other, surrounded on either side by gray-suited men, until he released Jude and they sat.

"Did I embarrass you enough?" he asked him, and Jude smiled and shook his head.

There were so many things to discuss in so little time that Jude had actually written an agenda on the back of a receipt, which he had laughed at when he had seen it but which they ended up following fairly closely. Between Topic Five (Malcolm's wedding: What were they going to say in their toasts?) and Topic Six (the progression of the Greene Street apartment, which was being gutted), he had gotten up to go to the bathroom, and as he walked back to the table, he had the unsettling feeling that he was being watched. He was of course used to being appraised and inspected, but there was something different about the quality of this attention, its intensity and hush, and for the first time in a long time, he was self-conscious, aware of the fact that he was wearing jeans and not a suit, and that he clearly didn't belong. He became aware, in fact, that everyone was wearing a suit, and he was the only one not.

"I think I'm wearing the wrong thing," he said quietly to Jude as he sat back down. "Everyone's staring."

"They're not staring at you because of what you're wearing," Jude said. "They're staring at you because you're famous."

He shook his head. "To you and literally dozens of other people, maybe."

"No, Willem," Jude had said. "You are." He smiled at him. "Why do you think they didn't make you wear a jacket? They don't let just anyone waltz in here who's not in corporate mufti. And why do you think they keep bringing over all these appetizers? It's not because of me, I guarantee you." Now he laughed. "Why did you choose this place anyway? I thought you were going to pick somewhere downtown."

He groaned. "I heard the crudo was good. And what do you mean: Is there a dress code here?"

Jude smiled again and was about to answer when one of the discreet gray-suited men came over to them and, vividly embarrassed, apologized for interrupting them. "I just wanted to say that I loved *The Sycamore Court*," he said. "I'm a big fan." Willem thanked him, and the man, who was older, in his fifties, was about to say something else when he saw Jude and blinked, clearly recognizing him, and stared at him for a bit, obviously recategorizing Jude in his head, refiling what he knew about him. He opened his mouth and shut it and then apologized again as he left, Jude smiling serenely at him the entire time.

"Well, well," said Jude, after the man had hurried away. "That was the head of the litigation department of one of the biggest firms in the city. And, apparently, an admirer of yours." He grinned at Willem. "*Now* are you convinced you're famous?"

"If the benchmark for fame is being recognized by twentysomething female RISD graduates and aging closet cases, then yes," he said, and the two of them started snickering, childishly, until they were both able to compose themselves again.

Jude looked at him. "Only you could be on magazine covers and not think you're famous," he said, fondly. But Willem wasn't anywhere real when those magazine covers came out; he was on set. On set, everyone acted like they were famous.

"It's different," he told Jude. "I can't explain it." But later, in the car to the airport, he realized what the difference was. Yes, he was used to being looked at. But he was only really used to being looked at by certain kinds of people in certain kinds of rooms—people who wanted to sleep with him, or who wanted to talk to him because it might help their own careers, or people for whom the simple fact that he was recognizable was enough to trigger something hungry and frantic in them, to crave being in his presence. He wasn't, however, accustomed to being looked at by people who had other things to do, who had bigger and more important matters to worry about than an actor in New York. Actors in New York: they were everywhere. The only time men with power ever looked at him was at premieres, when he was being presented to the studio head and they were shaking his hand and making small talk even as he could see them examining him, calculating how well he'd tested and how much they'd paid for him and how much the film would have to earn in order for them to look at him more closely.

Perversely, though, as this began happening more and more—he would enter a room, a restaurant, a building, and would feel, just for a second, a slight collective pause—he also began realizing that he could turn his own visibility on and off. If he walked into a restaurant expecting to be recognized, he always was. And if he walked in expecting not to be, he rarely was. He was never able to determine what, exactly, beyond his simply willing it, made the difference. But it worked; it was why, six years after that lunch, he was able to walk through much of SoHo in plain sight, more or less, after he moved in with Jude.

He had been at Greene Street since Jude got home from his suicide attempt, and as the months passed, he found that he was migrating more and more of his things—first his clothes, then his laptop, then his boxes of books and his favorite woolen blanket that he liked to wrap about himself and shuffle around in as he made his morning coffee: his life was so itinerant that there really wasn't much else he needed or owned—to his old bedroom. A year later, he was living there still. He'd woken late one morning and made himself some coffee (he'd had to bring his coffeemaker as well, because Jude didn't have one), and had meandered sleepily about the apartment, noticing as if for the first time that somehow his books were now on Jude's shelves, and the pieces of art he'd brought over were hanging on Jude's walls. When had this happened? He couldn't quite remember, but it felt right; it felt right that he should be back here.

Even Mr. Irvine agreed. Willem had seen him at Malcolm's house the previous spring for Malcolm's birthday and Mr. Irvine had said, "I hear you've moved back in with Jude," and he said he had, preparing himself for a lecture on their eternal adolescence: he was going to be forty-four, after all; Jude was nearly forty-two. But "You're a good friend, Willem," Mr. Irvine had said. "I'm glad you boys are taking care of each other." He had been deeply rattled by Jude's attempt; they all had, of course, but Mr. Irvine had always liked Jude the best of all of them, and they all knew it.

"Well, thanks, Mr. Irvine," he'd said, surprised. "I'm glad, too."

In the first, raw weeks after Jude had gotten out of the hospital, Willem used to go into his room at odd hours to give himself confirmation that Jude was there, and alive. Back then, Jude slept constantly, and he would sometimes sit on the end of his bed, staring at him and feeling a sort of horrible wonder that he was still with them at all. He would think: If Richard had found him just twenty minutes later, Jude would have been dead. About a month after Jude had been released, Willem had been at the drugstore and had seen a box cutter hanging on the rack—such a medieval, cruel instrument, it seemed—and had almost burst into tears: Andy had told him that the emergency room surgeon had said Jude's had been the deepest, most decisive self-inflicted incisions he had ever seen in his career. He had always known that Jude was troubled, but he was awestruck, almost, by how little he knew him, by the depths of his determination to harm himself.

He felt that he had in some ways learned more about Jude in the past year than he had in the past twenty-six, and each new thing he learned was awful: Jude's stories were the kinds of stories that he was unequipped to answer, because so many of them were unanswerable. The story of the scar on the back of his hand—that had been the one that had begun it—had been so terrible that Willem had stayed up that night, unable to sleep, and had seriously contemplated calling Harold, just to be able to have someone else share the story with him, to be speechless alongside him.

The next day he couldn't stop himself from staring at Jude's hand, and Jude had finally drawn his sleeve over it. "You're making me self-conscious," he said.

"I'm sorry," he'd said.

Jude had sighed. "Willem, I'm not going to tell you these stories if you're going to react like this," he said, finally. "It's okay, it really is. It was a long time ago. I never think about it." He paused. "I don't want you to look at me differently if I tell you these things."

He'd taken a deep breath. "No," he said. "You're right. You're right." And so now when he listened to these stories of Jude's, he was careful not to say anything, to make small, nonjudgmental noises, as if all his friends had been whipped with a belt soaked in vinegar until they had passed out or been made to eat their own vomit off the floor, as if those were normal rites of childhood. But despite these stories, he still knew nothing: He still didn't know who Brother Luke was. He still didn't know anything except isolated stories about the monastery, or the home. He still didn't know how Jude had made it to Philadelphia or what had happened to him there. And he still didn't know the story about the injury. But if Jude was beginning with the easier stories, he now knew enough to know that those stories, if he ever heard them, would be horrific. He almost didn't want to know.

The stories had been part of a compromise when Jude had made it clear that he wouldn't go to Dr. Loehmann. Andy had been stopping by most Friday nights, and he came over one evening shortly after Jude had returned to Rosen Pritchard. As Andy examined Jude in his bedroom, Willem made everyone drinks, which they had on the sofa, the lights low and the sky outside grainy with snow.

"Sam Loehmann says you haven't called him," Andy said. "Jude— this is bullshit. You've got to call him. This was part of the deal."

"Andy, I've told you," Jude said, "I'm not going." Willem was pleased, then, to hear that Jude's stubbornness had returned, even though he disagreed with him. Two months ago, when they had been in Morocco, he had looked up from his plate at dinner to see Jude staring at the dishes of mezze before him, unable to serve himself any of them. "Jude?" he'd asked, and Jude had looked at him, his face fearful. "I don't know how to begin," he'd said, quietly, and so Willem had reached over and spooned a little from each dish onto Jude's plate, and told him to start with the scoop of stewed eggplant at the top and eat his way clockwise through the rest of it.

"You have to do *something*," Andy said. He could tell Andy was trying to remain calm, and failing, and that too he found heartening: a sign of a certain return to normalcy. "Willem thinks so too, right, Willem? You can't just keep going on like this! You've had a major trauma in your life! You have to start discussing things with someone!"

"Fine," said Jude, looking tired. "I'll tell Willem."

"Willem's not a health-care professional!" said Andy. "He's an actor!" And at that, Jude had looked at him and the two of them had started laughing, so hard that they had to put their drinks down, and Andy had finally stood and said that they were both so immature he didn't know why he bothered and had left, Jude trying to call after him—"Andy! We're sorry! Don't leave!"—but laughing too hard to be intelligible. It was the first time in months—the first time since even before the attempt—that he had heard Jude laugh.

Later, when they had recovered, Jude had said, "I thought I might, you know, Willem—start telling you things sometimes. But *do* you mind? Is it going to be a burden?" And he had said of course it wouldn't be, that he wanted to know. He had always wanted to know, but he didn't say this; he knew it would sound like criticism.

But as much as he was able to convince himself that Jude had returned to himself, he was also able to recognize that he had been changed. Some of these changes were, he thought, good ones: the talking, for example. And some of them were sad ones: although his hands were much stronger, and although it was less and less frequent, they still shook occasionally, and he knew Jude was embarrassed by it. And he was more skittish than ever about being touched, especially, Willem noticed, by Harold; a month ago, when Harold had visited, Jude had practically danced out of the way to keep Harold from hugging him. He had felt bad for Harold, seeing the expression on his face, and so had gone over and hugged him himself. "You know he can't help it," he told Harold quietly, and Harold had kissed him on the cheek. "You're a sweet man, Willem," he'd said.

Now it was October, thirteen months after the attempt. During the evening he was at the theater; two months after his run ended in December, he'd start shooting his first project since he returned from

Sri Lanka, an adaptation of *Uncle Vanya* that he was excited about and was being filmed in the Hudson Valley: he'd be able to come home every night.

Not that the location was a coincidence. "Keep me in New York," he'd instructed his manager and his agent after he'd dropped out of the film in Russia the previous fall.

"For how long?" asked Kit, his agent.

"I don't know," he'd said. "At least the next year."

"Willem," Kit had said, after a silence, "I understand how close you and Jude are. But don't you think you should take advantage of the momentum you have? You could do whatever you wanted." He was referring to *The Iliad* and *The Odyssey*, which had both been enormous successes, proof, Kit liked to point out, that he could do anything he wanted now. "From what I know of Jude, he'd say the same thing." And then, when he didn't say anything, "It's not like this is your wife, or kid, or something. This is your friend."

"You mean 'just your friend,'" he'd said, testily. Kit was Kit; he thought like an agent, and he trusted how Kit thought—he had been with him since the beginning of his career; he tried not to fight with him. And Kit had always guided him well. "No fat, no filler," he liked to brag about Willem's career, reviewing the history of his roles. They both knew that Kit was far more ambitious for him than he was—he always had been. And yet it had been Kit who'd gotten him on the first flight out of Sri Lanka after Richard had called him; Kit who'd had the producers shut down production for seven days so he could fly to New York and back.

"I don't mean to offend you, Willem," Kit had said, carefully. "I know you love him. But come on. If he were the love of your life, I'd understand. But this seems extreme to me, to inhibit your career like this."

And yet he sometimes wondered if he could ever love anyone as much as he loved Jude. It was the fact of him, of course, but also the utter comfort of life with him, of having someone who had known him for so long and who could be relied upon to always take him as exactly who he was on that particular day. His work, his very life, was one of disguises and charades. Everything about him and his context was constantly changing: his hair, his body, where he would sleep that night. He often felt he was made of something liquid, something that was being continually poured from bright-colored bottle to bright-colored bottle, with a little being lost or left behind with each transfer. But his friendship with Jude made him feel that there was something real and immutable about who he was, that despite his life of guises, there was something elemental about him, something that Jude saw even when he could not, as if Jude's very witness of him made him real.

In graduate school he'd had a teacher who had told him that the best actors are the most boring people. A strong sense of self was detrimental, because an actor had to let the self disappear; he had to let himself be subsumed by a character. "If you want to be a personality, be a pop star," his teacher had said.

He had understood the wisdom of this, and still did, but really, the self was what they all craved, because the more you acted, the further and further you drifted from who you thought you were, and the harder and harder it was to find your way back. Was it any wonder that so many of his peers were such wrecks? They made their money, their lives, their identities by impersonating others—was it a surprise, then, that they needed one set, one stage after the next, to give their lives shape? Without them, what and who were they? And so they took up religions, and girlfriends, and causes to give them something that could be their own: they never slept, they never stopped, they were terrified to be alone, to have to ask themselves who they were. ("When an actor talks and there's no one to hear him, is he still an actor?" his friend Roman had once asked. He sometimes wondered.)

But to Jude, he wasn't an actor: he was his friend, and that identity supplanted everything else. It was a role he had inhabited for so long that it had become, indelibly, who he was. To Jude, he was no more primarily an actor than Jude was primarily a lawyer—it was never the first or second or third way that either of them would describe the other. It was Jude who remembered who he had been before he had made a life pretending to be other people: someone with a brother, someone with parents, someone to whom everything and everyone seemed so impressive and beguiling. He knew other actors who didn't want anyone to remember them as they'd been, as someone so determined to be someone else, but he wasn't that person. He *wanted* to be reminded of who he was; he wanted to be around someone for whom his career would never be the most interesting thing about him.

And if he was to be honest, he loved what came with Jude as well: Harold and Julia. Jude's adoption had been the first time he had ever felt envious of anything Jude had. He *admired* a lot of what Jude had—his intelligence and thoughtfulness and resourcefulness—but he had never been jealous of him. But watching Harold and Julia with him, watching how they watched him even when he wasn't looking at them, he had felt a kind of emptiness: he was parentless, and while most of the time he didn't think about this at all, he felt that, for as remote as his parents had been, they had at least been something that had anchored him to his life. Without any family, he was a scrap of paper floating through the air, being picked up and tossed aloft with every gust. He and Jude had been united in this.

Of course, he knew this envy was ridiculous, and beyond mean: he had grown up with parents, and Jude hadn't. And he knew that Harold and Julia felt an affection for him as well, as much as he did for them. They had both seen every one of his films, and both sent him long and detailed reviews of them, always praising his performance and making intelligent comments about his costars and the cinematography. (The only one they had never seen—or at least never commented on—was *The Prince of Cinnamon*, which was the film he had been shooting when Jude had tried to kill himself. He had never seen it himself.) They read every article about him—like his reviews, he avoided these articles—and bought a copy of every magazine that featured him. On his birthday, they would call and ask him what he was going to do to celebrate, and Harold would remind him of how old he was getting. At Christmas, they always sent him something—a book, along with a jokey little gift, or a clever toy that he would keep in his pocket to fiddle with as he talked on the phone or sat in the makeup chair. At Thanksgiving, he and Harold would sit in the living room watching the game, while Julia kept Jude company in the kitchen.

"We're running low on chips," Harold would say.

"I know," he'd say.

"Why don't you go get more?" Harold would say.

"*You're* the host," he'd remind Harold.

"*You're* the guest."

"Yeah, exactly."

"Call Jude and get him to bring us more."

"You call him!"

"No, *you* call him."

"Fine," he'd say. "Jude! Harold wants more chips!"

"You're such a confabulator, Willem," Harold would say, as Jude came in to refill the bowl. "Jude, this was completely Willem's idea."

But mostly, he knew that Harold and Julia loved him because he loved Jude; he knew they trusted him to take care of Jude—that was who he was to them, and he didn't mind it. He was proud of it.

Lately, however, he had been feeling differently about Jude, and he wasn't sure what to do about it. They had been sitting on the sofa late one Friday night—he just home from the theater, Jude just home from the office—and talking, talking about nothing in particular, when he had almost leaned over and kissed him. But he had stopped himself, and the moment had passed. But since then, he had been revisited by that impulse again: twice, three times, four times.

It was beginning to worry him. Not because Jude was a man: he'd had sex with men before, everyone he knew had, and in college, he and JB had drunkenly made out one night out of boredom and curiosity (an experience that had been, to their mutual relief, entirely unsatisfying: "It's really interesting how someone so good-looking can be such a turnoff," had been JB's exact words to him). And not because he hadn't always felt a sort of low-key hum of attraction for Jude, the way he felt for more or less all his friends. It was because he knew that if he tried anything, he would have to be certain about it, because he sensed, powerfully, that Jude, who was casual about nothing, certainly wouldn't be casual about sex.

Jude's sex life, his sexuality, had been a subject of ongoing fascination for everyone who knew him, and certainly for Willem's girlfriends. Occasionally, it had come up among the three of them—he and Malcolm and JB—when Jude wasn't around: Was he having sex? Had he ever? With whom? They had all seen people looking at him at parties, or flirting with him, and in every case, Jude had remained oblivious.

"That girl was all over you," he'd say to Jude as they walked home from one party or another.

"What girl?" Jude would say.

They talked about it with one another because Jude had made it clear he wouldn't discuss it with any of them: when the topic was raised, he would give them one of his stares and then change the subject with a declarativeness that was impossible to misinterpret.

"Has he ever spent the night away from home?" asked JB (this was when he and Jude were living on Lispenard Street).

"Guys," he'd say (the conversation made him uncomfortable), "I don't think we should be talking about this."

"Willem!" JB would say. "Don't be such a pussy! You're not betraying any confidences. Just tell us: yes or no. Has he ever?"

He'd sigh. "No," he'd say.

There would be a silence. "Maybe he's asexual," Malcolm would say, after a while.

"No, that's you, Mal."

"Fuck off, JB."

"Do you think he's a virgin?" JB would ask.

"No," he'd say. He didn't know why he knew this, but he was certain he wasn't.

"It's such a waste," JB would say, and he and Malcolm would look at each other, knowing what was coming next. "His looks've been wasted on him. *I* should've gotten his looks. *I* would've had a good time with them, at least."

After a while, they grew to accept it as part of who Jude was; they added the subject to the list of things they knew not to discuss. Year after year passed and he dated no one, they saw him with no one. "Maybe he's living some hot double life," Richard once suggested, and Willem had shrugged. "Maybe," he said. But really, although he had no proof of this, he knew that Jude wasn't. It was in this same, proof-less way that he assumed Jude was probably gay (though maybe not), and probably hadn't ever had a relationship (though he really hoped he was wrong about this). And as much as Jude claimed otherwise, Willem wasn't ever convinced that he wasn't lonely, that he didn't, in some small dark part of himself, want to be with someone. He remembered Lionel and Sinclair's wedding, where it had been Malcolm with Sophie and he with Robin and JB—though they hadn't been speaking then—with Oliver, and Jude with no one. And although Jude hadn't seemed bothered by this, Willem had looked at him across the table and had felt sad for him. He didn't want Jude to get old alone; he wanted him to be with someone who would take care of him and be attracted to him. JB was right: it *was* a waste.

And so was this what this was, this attraction? Was it fear and sympathy that had morphed itself into a more palatable shape? Was he convincing himself he was attracted to Jude because he couldn't stand to see him alone? He didn't *think* so. But he didn't know.

The person he would've once discussed this with was JB, but he couldn't speak to JB about this, even though they were friends again, or at least working toward friendship. After they had returned from Morocco, Jude had called JB and the two of them had gone out for dinner, and a month later, Willem and JB had gone out on their own. Oddly, though, he found it much more difficult to forgive JB than Jude had, and their first meeting had been a disaster—JB showily, exaggeratedly blithe; he seething—until they had left the restaurant and started yelling at each other. There they had stood on deserted Pell Street—it had been snowing, lightly, and no one else was out—accusing each other of condescension and cruelty; irrationality and self-absorption; self-righteousness and narcissism; martyrdom and cluelessness.

"You think *anyone* hates themselves as much as I do?" JB had shouted at him. (His fourth show, the one that documented his time on drugs and with Jackson, had been titled "The Narcissist's Guide to Self-Hatred," and JB had referenced it several times during their dinner as proof that he had punished himself mightily and publicly and had now been reformed.)

"Yeah, JB, I do," he'd shouted back at him. "I think Jude hates himself far more than you could ever hate *yourself*, and I think you knew that and you made him hate himself even more."

"You think I don't know that?" JB had yelled. "You think I don't fucking hate myself for that?"

"I don't think you hate yourself *enough* for it, no," he'd yelled back. "*Why* did you do that, JB? Why did you do that to *him*, of all people?"

And then, to his surprise, JB had sunk, defeated, to the curb. "Why didn't you ever love me the way you love him, Willem?" he asked.

He sighed. "Oh, JB," he said, and sat down next to him on the chilled pavement. "You never needed me as much as he did." It wasn't the only reason, he knew, but it was part of it. No one else in his life needed him. People *wanted* him—for sex, for their projects, for his friendship, even—but only Jude needed him. Only to Jude was he essential.

"You know, Willem," said JB, after a silence, "maybe he doesn't need you as much as you think he does."

He had thought about this for a while. "No," he said, finally, "I think he does."

Now JB sighed. "Actually," he had said, "I think you're right."

After that, things had, strangely, improved. But as much as he was—

cautiously—learning to enjoy JB again, he wasn't sure he was ready to discuss this particular topic with him. He wasn't sure he wanted to hear JB's jokes about how he had already fucked everything with two X chromosomes and so was now moving on to the Ys, or about his abandonment of heteronormative standards, or, worst of all, about how this attraction he thought he was feeling for Jude was really something else: a misplaced guilt for the suicide attempt, or a form of patronization, or simple, misdirected boredom.

So he did nothing and said nothing. As the months passed, he dated, casually, and he examined his feelings as he did. *This is crazy*, he told himself. *This is not a good idea.* Both were true. It would be so much easier if he didn't have these feelings at all. *And so what if he did?* he argued with himself. Everyone had feelings that they knew better than to act upon because they knew that doing so would make life so much more complicated. He had whole pages of dialogue with himself, imagining the lines—his and JB's, both spoken by him—typeset on white paper.

But still, the feelings persisted. They went to Cambridge for Thanksgiving, the first time in two years that they'd done so. He and Jude shared his room because Julia's brother was visiting from Oxford and had the upstairs bedroom. That night, he lay awake on the bedroom sofa, watching Jude sleep. How easy would it be, he thought, to simply climb into bed next to him and fall asleep himself? There was something about it that seemed almost preordained, and the absurdity was not in the fact of it but in his resistance to the fact of it.

They had taken the car to Cambridge, and Jude drove them home so he could sleep. "Willem," Jude said as they were about to enter the city, "I want to ask you about something." He looked at him. "Are you okay? Is something on your mind?"

"Sure," he said. "I'm fine."

"You've seemed really—pensive, I guess," Jude said. He was quiet. "You know, it's been a huge gift having you live with me. And not just live with me, but—everything. I don't know what I would have done without you. But I know it must be draining for you. And I just want you to know: if you want to move back home, I'll be fine. I promise. I'm not going to hurt myself." He had been staring at the road as he spoke, but now he turned to him. "I don't know how I got so lucky," he said.

He didn't know what to say for a while. "Do you *want* me to move home?" he asked.

Jude was silent. "Of course not," he said, very quietly. "But I want you to be happy, and you haven't seemed very happy recently."

He sighed. "I'm sorry," he said. "I've been distracted, you're right. But it's certainly not because I'm living with you. I love living with you." He tried to think of the right, the perfect next thing to add, but he couldn't. "I'm sorry," he said again.

"Don't be," Jude said. "But if you want to talk about any of it, ever, you always can."

"I know," he said. "Thanks." They were quiet the rest of the way home.

And then it was December. His run finished. They went to India on holiday, the four of them: the first trip they'd taken as a unit in years. In February, he began filming *Uncle Vanya*. The set was the kind he trea-sured and sought but only rarely found—he had worked with everyone before, and they all liked and respected one another, and the director was shaggy and mild and gentle, and the adaptation, which had been done by a novelist Jude admired, was beautiful and simple, and the dialogue was a pleasure to get to speak.

When Willem was young, he had been in a play called *The House on Thistle Lane*, which had been about a family that was packing up and leaving a house in St. Louis that had been owned by the father's family for generations, but which they could no longer afford to main-tain. But instead of a set, they had staged the play on one floor of a dilapidated brownstone in Harlem, and the audience had been allowed to wander between the rooms as long as they remained outside a roped-off area; depending on where you stood to watch, you saw the actors, and the space itself, from different perspectives. He had played the eldest, most damaged son, and had spent most of the first act mute and in the dining room, wrapping dishes in pieces of newspaper. He had developed a nervous tic for the son, who couldn't imagine leaving his childhood house, and as the character's parents fought in the living room, he would put down the plates and press himself into the far cor-ner of the dining room near the kitchen and peel off the wallpaper in shreds. Although most of that act took place in the living room, there would always be a few audience members who would remain in his room, watching him, watching him scraping off the paper—a blue so dark it was almost black, and printed with pale pink cabbage roses—and rolling it between his fingers and dropping it to the floor, so that every night, one corner would become littered with little cigars of wallpaper, as if he were a mouse inexpertly building its tiny nest. It had been an exhausting play, but he had loved it: the intimacy of the audience, the unlikeliness of the stage, the small, detailed physicality of the role.

This production felt very much like that play. The house, a Gilded Age mansion on the Hudson, was grand but creaky and shabby—the kind of house his ex-girlfriend Philippa had once imagined they'd live in when they were married and ancient—and the director used only three rooms: the dining room, the living room, and the sunporch. Instead of an audience, they had the crew, who followed them as they moved through the space. But although he relished the work, part of him also recognized that *Uncle Vanya* was not exactly the most helpful thing he could be doing at the moment. On set, he was Dr. Astrov, but once he was back at Greene Street, he was Sonya, and Sonya—as much as he loved the play and always had, as much as he loved and pitied poor Sonya herself—was not a role he had ever thought he might perform, under any circumstance. When he had told the others about the film, JB had said, "So it's a gender-blind cast, then," and he'd said, "What do you mean?" and JB had said, "Well, you're obviously Elena, right?" and everyone had laughed, especially him. This was what he loved about JB, he had thought; he was always smarter than even he knew. "He's far too old to play Elena," Jude had added, affectionately, and everyone had laughed again.

Vanya was an efficient shoot, just thirty-six days, and was over by the last week in March. One day shortly after it had ended, he met an old friend and former girlfriend of his, Cressy, for lunch in TriBeCa, and as he walked back to Greene Street in the light, dry snow, he was reminded of how much he enjoyed the city in the late winter, when the weather was suspended between one season and the next, and when Jude cooked every weekend, and when you could walk the streets for hours and never see anyone but a few lone people taking their dogs out for a stroll.

He was heading north on Church Street and had just crossed Reade when he glanced into a café on his right and saw Andy sitting at a table in the corner, reading. "Willem!" said Andy, as he approached him. "What're you doing here?"

"I just had lunch with a friend and I'm walking home," he said. "What're *you* doing here? You're so far downtown."

"You two and your walks," Andy said, shaking his head. "George is at a birthday party a few blocks from here, and I'm waiting until I have to go pick him up."

"How old is George now?"

"Nine."

"God, already?"

"I know."

"Do you want some company?" he asked. "Or do you want to be alone?"

"No," said Andy. He tucked a napkin into his book to mark his place. "Stay. Please." And so he sat.

They talked for a while of, of course, Jude, who was on a business trip in Mumbai, and *Uncle Vanya* ("I just remember Astrov as being an unbelievable tool," Andy said), and his next project, which began shooting in Brooklyn at the end of April, and Andy's wife, Jane, who was expanding her practice, and their children: George, who had just been diagnosed with asthma, and Beatrice, who wanted to go to boarding school the following year.

And then, before he could stop himself—not that he felt any particular need to try—he was telling Andy about his feelings for Jude, and how he wasn't sure what they meant or what to do about them. He talked and talked, and Andy listened, his face expressionless. There was no one else in the café but the two of them, and outside, the snow fell faster and thicker, and he felt, despite his anxiety, deeply calm, and glad he was telling somebody, and that that somebody was a person who knew him and Jude both, and had for many years. "I know this seems strange," he said. "And I've thought about what it could be, Andy, I really have. But part of me wonders if it was always meant to be this way; I mean, I've dated and dated for decades now, and maybe the reason it's never worked out is because it was never meant to, because I was supposed to be with him all along. Or maybe I'm telling myself this. Or maybe it's simple curiosity. But I don't think it is; I think I know myself better than that." He sighed. "What do you think I should do?"

Andy was quiet for a while. "First," he said, "I don't think it's strange, Willem. I think it makes sense in a lot of ways. You two have always had something different, something unusual. So—I always wondered, despite your girlfriends."

"Selfishly, I think it'd be wonderful: for you, but especially for him. I think if you wanted to be in a relationship with him, it'd be the greatest, most restorative gift he could ever get."

"But Willem, if you do this, you should go in prepared to make some sort of commitment to him, and to being with him, because you're right: you're not going to be able to just fool around and then get out of it. And I think you should know that it's going to be very, very hard. You're going to have to get him to trust you all over again, and to see you in a different way. I don't think I'm betraying anything when I say that it's going to be very tough for him to be intimate with you, and you're going to have to be really patient with him."

They were both silent. "So if I do it, I should do so thinking it's going to be forever," he told Andy, and Andy looked at him for a few seconds and then smiled.

"Well," Andy said, "there are worse life sentences."

"True," he said.

He went back to Greene Street. April arrived, and Jude returned home. They celebrated Jude's birthday—"Forty-three," Harold sighed, "I vaguely remember forty-three"—and he began shooting his next project. An old friend of his, a woman he'd known since graduate school, was starring in the production as well—he was playing a corrupt detective, and she was playing his wife—and they slept together a few times. Everything marched along as it always had. He worked; he came home to Greene Street; he thought about what Andy had said.

And then one Saturday morning he woke very early, just as the sky was brightening. It was late May, and the weather was unpredictable: some days it felt like March, other days, like July. Ninety feet away from him lay Jude. And suddenly his timidity, his confusion, his dithering seemed silly. He was home, and home was Jude. He loved him; he was meant to be with him; he would never hurt him—he trusted himself with that much. And so what was there to fear?

He remembered a conversation he'd had with Robin when he had been preparing to shoot *The Odyssey* and was rereading it and *The Iliad*, neither of which he had looked at since he was a freshman in college.

This was when they had first begun dating, and were both still trying to impress each other, when a sort of giddiness was derived from deferring to the other's expertise. "What're the most overrated lines from the poem?" he'd asked, and Robin had rolled her eyes and recited: "'We have still not reached the end of our trials. One more labor lies in store—boundless, laden with danger, great and long, and I must brave it out from start to finish.'" She made some retching noises. "So obvious. And somehow, that's been co-opted by every losing football team in the country as their pregame rallying cry," she added, and he'd laughed. She looked at him, slyly. "*You* played football," she said. "I'll bet those're your favorite lines as well."

"Absolutely not," he'd said, in mock outrage. This was part of their game that wasn't always a game: he was the dumb actor, the dumber jock, and she was the smart girl who went out with him and taught him what he didn't know.

"Then tell me what they are," she'd challenged him, and after he did, she'd looked at him, intently. "Hmm," she said. "Interesting."

Now he got out of bed and wrapped his blanket around himself, yawning. That evening, he'd talk to Jude. He didn't know where he was going, but he knew he would be safe; he would keep them both safe. He went to the kitchen to make himself coffee, and as he did, he whispered the lines back to himself, those lines he thought of whenever he was coming home, coming back to Greene Street after a long time away— "And tell me this: I must be absolutely sure. This place I've reached, is it truly Ithaca?"—as all around him, the apartment filled with light.

—

Every morning he gets up and swims two miles, and then comes back upstairs and sits down and has breakfast and reads the papers. His friends make fun of him for this—for the fact that he actually prepares a meal instead of buying something on the way to work; for the fact that he actually still gets the papers delivered, in paper form—but the ritual of it has always calmed him: even in the home, it was the one time when the counselors were too mild, the other boys too sleepy to bother him. He would sit in the corner of the dining area and read and eat his breakfast, and for those minutes he would be left alone.

He is an efficient reader, and he skims first through *The Wall Street*

Journal, and then the *Financial Times*, before beginning with *The New York Times*, which he reads front to back, when he sees the headline in Obituaries: "Caleb Porter, 52, Fashion Executive." Immediately, his mouthful of scrambled eggs and spinach turns to cardboard and glue, and he swallows hard, feeling sick, feeling every nerve ending thrumming alive. He has to read the article three times before he can make sense of any of the facts: pancreatic cancer. "Very fast," said his colleague and longtime friend. Under his stewardship, emerging fashion label Rothko saw aggressive expansion into the Asian and Middle Eastern markets, as well as the opening of their first New York City boutique. Died at his home in Manhattan. Survived by his sister, Michaela Porter de Soto of Monte Carlo, six nieces and nephews, and his partner, Nicholas Lane, also a fashion executive.

He is still for a moment, staring at the page until the words rearrange themselves into an abstraction of gray before his eyes, and then he hobbles as fast as he can to the bathroom near the kitchen, where he vomits up everything he's just eaten, gagging over the toilet until he's coughing up long strands of saliva. He lowers the toilet seat and sits, resting his face in his hands, until he feels better. He wishes, desperately, for his razors, but he has always been careful not to cut himself during the day, partly because it feels wrong and partly because he knows he has to impose limits upon himself, however artificial, or he'd be cutting himself all day. Lately, he has been trying very hard not to cut himself at all. But tonight, he thinks, he will grant himself an exception. It is seven a.m. In around fifteen hours, he'll be home again. All he has to do is make it through the day.

He puts his plate in the dishwasher and walks quietly through the bedroom and into the bathroom, where he showers and shaves and then gets dressed in the closet, first making sure that the door between the closet and the bedroom is completely closed. At this point, he has added a new step to his morning routine: now, if he were to do what he has been for the past month, he would open the door and walk over to the bed, where he'd perch on its left side and put his hand on Willem's arm, and Willem would open his eyes and smile at him.

"I'm off," he'd say, smiling back, and Willem would shake his head. "Don't go," Willem would say, and he'd say, "I have to," and Willem would say, "Five minutes," and he'd say, "Five." And then Willem would lift his end of the blanket and he'd crawl beneath it, with Willem pressed against his back, and he would close his eyes and wait for Willem to wrap his arms around him and wish he could stay forever. And then, ten or fifteen minutes later, he would at last, reluctantly, get up, and kiss Willem somewhere near, but not on, his mouth—he is still having trouble with this, even four months later—and leave for the day.

This morning, however, he skips this step. He instead pauses at the dining-room table to write Willem a note explaining that he had to leave early and didn't want to wake him, and then, as he's walking to the door, he comes back and grabs the *Times* off the table and takes it with him. He knows how irrational it is, but he doesn't want Willem to see Caleb's name, or picture, or any evidence of him. Willem still doesn't know about what Caleb did to him, and he doesn't want him to. He doesn't even want him to be aware of Caleb's very existence—or, he realizes, his once-existence, for Caleb no longer exists. Beneath his arm, the paper feels almost alive with heat, Caleb's name a dark knot of poison cradled inside its pages.

He decides to drive to work so he'll be able to be alone for a little while, but before he leaves the garage, he takes out the paper and reads the article one more time before folding it up again and shoving it into his briefcase. And then suddenly, he is crying, frantic, breathy sobs, the kind that come from his diaphragm, and as he leans his head on the steering wheel, trying to regain control, he is finally able to admit to himself how plainly, profoundly relieved he is, and how frightened he has been for the past three years, and how humiliated and ashamed he is still. He retrieves the paper, hating himself, and reads the obituary again, stopping at "and by his partner, Nicholas Lane, also a fashion executive." He wonders: Did Caleb do to Nicholas Lane what he did to him, or is Nicholas—as he must be—someone undeserving of such treatment? He hopes that Nicholas never experienced what he had, but he's also certain he hasn't, and the knowledge of that makes him cry harder. That had been one of Harold's arguments when he was trying to get him to report the attack; that Caleb was dangerous, and that by reporting him, by having him arrested, he would be protecting other people from him. But he had known that wasn't true: Caleb wouldn't do to other people what he did to him. He hadn't hit and hated him because he hit and hated other people; he had hit and hated him because of who *he* was, not because of who Caleb was.

Finally, he's able to compose himself, and he wipes his eyes and blows his nose. The crying: another leftover from his time with Caleb. For years and years he was able to control it, and now—ever since that night—it seems he is always crying, or on the verge of it, or actively trying to stop himself from doing it. It's as if all his progress from the past few decades has been erased, and he is again that boy in Brother Luke's care, so teary and helpless and vulnerable.

He's about to start the car when his hands begin shaking. Now he knows he can do nothing but wait, and he folds them in his lap and tries to make his breaths deep and regular, which sometimes helps. By the time his phone rings a few minutes later, they've slowed somewhat, and he hopes he sounds normal as he answers. "Hi, Harold," he says.

"Jude," says Harold. His voice is flattened, somehow. "Have you read the *Times* today?"

Immediately, the shaking intensifies. "Yes," he says.

"Pancreatic cancer is a terrible way to go," says Harold. He sounds grimly satisfied. "Good. I'm glad." There's a pause. "Are you all right?"

"Yes," he says, "yes, I'm fine."

"The connection keeps cutting out," says Harold, but he knows it's not: it's because he's shaking so badly that he can't hold the phone steady.

"Sorry," he says. "I'm in the garage. Look, Harold, I'd better get up to work. Thanks for calling."

"Okay." Harold sighs. "You'll call me if you want to talk, right?"

"Yes," he says. "Thanks."

It's a busy day, for which he's grateful, and he tries to give himself no time to think about anything but work. Late in the morning, he gets a text from Andy—*Assume you've seen that the asshole is dead. Pancreatic cancer = major suffering. You okay?*—and writes back to assure him he's fine, and over lunch he reads the obituary one last time before stuffing the entire paper into the shredder and turning back to his computer.

In the afternoon he gets a text from Willem saying that the director he's meeting with about his next project has pushed back their dinner, so he doesn't think he'll be home before eleven, and he is relieved. At nine, he tells his associates he's leaving early, and then drives home and goes directly to the bathroom, shucking his jacket and rolling up his sleeves and unstrapping his watch as he goes; he's almost hyperventilating with desire by the time he makes the first cut. It has been nearly two months since he's made more than two cuts in a single sitting, but now he abandons his self-discipline and cuts and cuts and cuts, until finally his breathing slows and he feels the old, comforting emptiness settle inside him. After he's done, he cleans up and washes his face and goes to the kitchen, where he reheats some soup he'd made the weekend before and has his first real meal of the day, and then brushes his teeth and collapses into bed. He is weak from the cutting, but he knows if he rests for a few minutes, he'll be fine. The goal is to be normal by the time Willem comes home, to not give him anything to worry about, to not do anything else to upset this impossible and delirious dream he's been living in for the past eighteen weeks.

When Willem had told him of his feelings, he had been so discomfited, so disbelieving, that it was only the fact that it was Willem saying it that convinced him it wasn't some terrible joke: his faith in Willem was more powerful than the absurdity of what Willem was suggesting.

But only barely. "What are you saying?" he asked Willem for the tenth time.

"I'm saying I'm attracted to you," Willem said, patiently. And then, when he didn't say anything, "Judy—I don't think it's all that odd, really. Haven't you ever felt that way about me, in all these years?"

"No," he said instantly, and Willem had laughed. But he hadn't been joking. He would never, ever have been so presumptuous as to even picture himself with Willem. Besides, he wasn't what he had ever imagined for Willem: he had imagined someone beautiful (and female) and intelligent for Willem, someone who would know how fortunate she was, someone who would make him feel fortunate as well. He knew this was—like so many of his imaginings about adult relationships— somewhat gauzy and naïve, but that didn't mean it couldn't happen. *He* was certainly not the kind of person Willem should be with; for Willem to be with him over the theoretical fantasy woman he'd conjured for him was an unbelievable tumble.

The next day, he presented Willem with a list of twenty reasons why he shouldn't want to be with him. As he handed it to him, he could see that Willem was amused, slightly, but then he started to read it and his expression changed, and he retreated to his study so he wouldn't have to watch him.

After a while, Willem knocked. "Can I come in?" he asked, and he told him he could.

"I'm looking at point number two," said Willem, seriously. "I hate to tell you this, Jude, but we have the same body." He looked at him. "You're an inch taller, but can I remind you that we can wear each other's clothes?"

He sighed. "Willem," he said, "you know what I mean."

"Jude," Willem said, "I understand that this is strange for you, and unexpected. If you really don't want this, I'll back off and leave you alone and I promise things won't change between us." He stopped. "But if you're trying to convince me not to be with you because you're scared and self-conscious—well, I understand that. But I don't think it's a good enough reason not to try. We'll go as slowly as you want, I promise."

He was quiet. "Can I think about it?" he asked, and Willem nodded. "Of course," he said, and left him alone, sliding the door shut behind him.

He sat in his office in silence for a long time, thinking. After Caleb, he had sworn he would never again do this to himself. He knew Willem would never do anything bad to him, and yet his imagination was limited: he was incapable of conceiving of a relationship that wouldn't end with his being hit, with his being kicked down the stairs, with his being made to do things he had told himself he would never have to do again. Wasn't it possible, he asked himself, that he could push even someone as good as Willem to that inevitability? Wasn't it foregone that he would inspire a kind of hatred from even Willem? Was he so greedy for companionship that he would ignore the lessons that history—his own history—had taught him?

But then there was another voice inside him, arguing back. *You're crazy if you turn this opportunity down,* said the voice. *This is the one person you have always trusted. Willem isn't Caleb; he would never do that, not ever.*

And so, finally, he had gone to the kitchen, where Willem was making dinner. "Okay," he said. "Let's do it."

Willem had looked at him and smiled. "Come here," he said, and he did, and Willem kissed him. He had been scared, and panicky, and once again he had thought of Brother Luke, and he had opened his eyes to remind himself that this was Willem after all, not someone to fear. But just as he was relaxing into it, he had seen Caleb's face flashing through his mind like a pulse, and he pulled away from Willem, choking, rubbing his hand across his mouth. "I'm sorry," he said, pivoting away from him. "I'm sorry. I'm not very good at this, Willem."

"What do you mean?" Willem had asked, turning him back around. "You're great at it," and he had felt himself sag with relief that Willem wasn't angry at him.

Since then, he has been constantly pitting what he knows of Willem against what he expects of someone—anyone—who has any physical desire for him. It is as if he somehow expects that the Willem he has known will be replaced by another; as if there will be a different Willem for what is a different relationship. In the first few weeks, he was terrified that he might upset or disappoint Willem in some way, that he might drive him toward anger. He had waited for days, summoning his courage, to tell Willem that he couldn't tolerate the taste of coffee in his mouth (although he didn't explain to him why: Brother Luke, his awful, muscular tongue, the grain of coffee grounds that had permanently furred his gumline. This had been one of the things he had appreciated about Caleb: that he hadn't drunk coffee). He apologized and apologized until Willem told him to stop. "Jude, it's fine," he said. "I should've realized: really. I just won't drink it."

"But you love coffee," he said.

Willem had smiled. "I enjoy it, yes," he said, "but I don't *need* it." He smiled again. "My dentist will be thrilled."

Also in that first month, he had talked to Willem about sex. They had these conversations at night, in bed, when it was easier to say things. He had always associated night with cutting, but now it was becoming about something else—those talks with Willem in a darkened room, when he was less self-conscious about touching him, and where he could see every one of Willem's features and yet was also able to pretend that Willem couldn't see his.

"Do you want to have sex someday?" he asked him one night, and even as he was saying it, he heard how stupid he sounded.

But Willem didn't laugh at him. "Yes," he said, "I'd like to."

He nodded. Willem waited. "It's going to take me a while," he said, at last.

"That's okay," Willem said. "I'll wait."

"But what if it takes me months?"

"Then it'll take months," Willem said.

He thought about that. "What if it takes longer?" he asked, quietly.

Willem had reached over and touched the side of his face. "Then it will," he said.

They were quiet for a long time. "What're you going to do in the meantime?" he asked, and Willem laughed. "I do have *some* self-control, Jude," he said, smiling at him. "I know this comes as a shock to you, but I *can* go for stretches without having sex."

"I didn't mean anything," he began, remorseful, but Willem grabbed him and kissed him, noisily, on the cheek. "I'm kidding," he said. "It's okay, Jude. You'll take as long as you need."

And so they still haven't had sex, and sometimes he is even able to convince himself that maybe they never will. But in the meantime, he has grown to enjoy, to crave even, Willem's physicality, his affection, which is so easy and natural and spontaneous that it makes him feel easier and more spontaneous as well. Willem sleeps on the left side of the bed, and he on the right, and the first night they slept in the same bed, he turned to his right on his side, the way he always did, and Willem pressed up against him, tucking his right arm under his neck and then across his shoulders, and his left arm around his stomach, moving his legs between his legs. He was surprised by this, but once he overcame his initial discomfort, he found he liked it, that it was like being swaddled.

One night in June, however, Willem didn't do it, and he worried he had done something wrong. The next morning—early mornings were the other time they talked about things that seemed too tender, too difficult, to be said in the daylight—he asked Willem if he was upset with him, and Willem, looking surprised, said no, of course not.

"I just wondered," he began, stammering, "because last night you didn't—" But he couldn't finish the sentence; he was too embarrassed.

But then he could see Willem's expression clear, and he rolled into him and wrapped his arms around him. "This?" he asked, and he nodded. "It was just because it was so hot last night," Willem said, and he waited for Willem to laugh at him, but he didn't. "That's the only reason, Judy." Since then, Willem has held him in the same way every night, even through July, when not even the air-conditioning could erase the heaviness from the air, and when they both woke damp with sweat. This, he realizes, is what he wanted from a relationship all along. This is what he meant when he hoped he might someday be touched. Sometimes Caleb had hugged him, briefly, and he always had to resist the impulse to ask him to do it again, and for longer. But now, here it is: all the physical contact that he knows exists between healthy people who love each other and are having sex, without the dreaded sex itself.

He cannot bring himself to initiate contact with Willem, nor ask for it, but he waits for it, for every time that Willem grabs his arm as he passes him in the living room and pulls him close to kiss him, or comes up behind him as he stands at the stove and puts his arms around him in the same position—chest, stomach—that he does in bed. He has always admired how physical JB and Willem are, both with each other and with everyone around them; he knew they knew not to do it with him, and as grateful as he was for their carefulness with him, it sometimes made him wistful: he sometimes wished they would disobey him, that they would lay claim to him with the same friendly confidence they did with everyone else. But they never did.

It took him three months, until the end of August, to finally take off his clothes in front of Willem. Every night he came to bed in his long-sleeve T-shirt and sweatpants, and every night Willem came to bed in his underwear. "Is this uncomfortable for you?" Willem asked, and he shook his head, even though it was—uncomfortable, but not entirely unwelcome. Every day the month before, he promised himself: he would take off his clothes and be done with it. He would do it that night, because he had to do it at some point. But that was as far as his imagination would let him proceed; he couldn't think about what Willem's reaction might be, or what he might do the following day. And then night would come, and they would be in bed, and his resolve would fail him.

One night, Willem reached beneath his shirt and put his hands on his back, and he yanked himself away so forcefully that he fell off the bed. "I'm sorry," he told Willem, "I'm sorry," and he climbed back in, keeping himself just at the edge of the mattress.

They were quiet, the two of them. He lay on his back and stared at the chandelier. "You know, Jude," Willem said at last. "I *have* seen you without your shirt on."

He looked at Willem, who took a breath. "At the hospital," he said. "They were changing your dressings, and giving you a bath."

His eyes turned hot, and he looked back up at the ceiling. "How much did you see?" he asked.

"I didn't see everything," Willem reassured him. "But I know you have scars on your back. And I've seen your arms before." Willem waited, and then, when he didn't say anything, sighed. "Jude, I promise you it's not what you think it is."

"I'm afraid you're going to be disgusted by me," he was finally able to say. Caleb's words floated back to him: *You really are deformed; you really are.* "I don't suppose I could just never take my clothes off at all, right?" he asked, trying to laugh, to turn it into a joke.

"Well, no," Willem said. "Because I think—although it's not going to feel like it, initially—it'll be a good thing for you, Judy."

And so the next night, he did it. As soon as Willem came to bed, he undressed quickly, under the covers, and then flung the blanket away and rolled onto his side, so his back was facing Willem. He kept his eyes shut the entire time, but when he felt Willem place his palm on his back, just between his shoulder blades, he began to cry, savagely, the kind of bitter, angry weeping he hadn't done in years, tucking into himself with shame. He kept remembering the night with Caleb, the last time he had been so exposed, the last time he had cried this hard, and he knew that Willem would only understand part of the reason he was so upset, that he didn't know that the shame of this very moment—of being naked, of being at another's mercy—was almost as great as his shame for what he had revealed. He heard, more from the tone than the words themselves, that Willem was being kind to him, that he was dismayed and was trying to make him feel better, but he was so distraught that he couldn't even comprehend what Willem was saying. He tried to get out of the bed so he could go to the bathroom and cut himself, but Willem caught him and held him so tightly that he couldn't move, and eventually he somehow calmed himself.

When he woke the following morning—late: it was a Sunday—Willem was staring at him. He looked tired. "How are you?" he asked.

The night returned to him. "Willem," he said, "I'm so, so sorry. I'm so sorry. I don't know what happened." He realized, then, that he still wasn't wearing any clothes, and he put his arms beneath the sheet, and pulled the blanket up to his chin.

"No, Jude," Willem said. "*I'm* sorry. I didn't know it was going to be so traumatic for you." He reached over and stroked his hair. They were quiet. "That was the first time I've ever seen you cry, you know."

"Well," he said, swallowing. "For some reason it's not as successful a seduction method as I'd hoped," and smiled at Willem, a little, and Willem smiled back.

They lay in bed that morning and talked. Willem asked him about certain scars, and he told him. He explained how he had gotten the scars on his back: about the day he had been caught trying to run away from the home; the beating that had followed; the resulting infection, the way his back had wept pus for days, the bubbles of blisters that had formed around the stray splinters from the broom handle that had embedded themselves into his flesh; what he had been left with when it was all over. Willem asked him when he was last naked before anyone and he lied and told him that—except for Andy—it had been when he was fifteen. And then Willem said various kind and unbelievable things about his body, which he chose to ignore, because he knew they weren't true.

"Willem, if you want out, I understand," he said. It had been his idea not to tell anyone that their friendship might be changing into something else, and although he had told Willem it would give them space, and privacy, to figure out how to be with each other, he had also thought it would give Willem time to reconsider, opportunities to change his mind without fear of everyone else's opinions. Of course, with this decision he cannot help but hear the echoes of his last relationship, which had also been conducted in secrecy, and he had to remind himself that this one was different; it was different unless he made it the same.

"Jude, of course I don't," Willem said. "Of course not."

Willem was running his fingertip over his eyebrow, which for some reason he found a comforting gesture: it was affectionate without being in the least sexual. "I just feel like I'm going to be this series of nasty surprises for you," he said at last, and Willem shook his head. "Surprises, maybe," he said. "But not nasty ones."

And so every night, he tries to remove his clothes. Sometimes he can do it; other times, he can't. Sometimes he can allow Willem to touch him on his back and arms, and other times, he can't. But he has been unable to be naked before Willem in the daytime, or even in light, or to do any of the things that he knows from movies and eavesdropping on other people that couples are supposed to do around each other: he cannot get dressed in front of Willem, or shower with him, which he'd had to do with Brother Luke, and which he had hated.

His own self-consciousness has not, however, proven contagious, and he is fascinated by how often, and how matter-of-factly, Willem is naked. In the morning, he pulls back Willem's side of the blanket and studies Willem's sleeping form with a clinical rigor, noting how perfect it is, and then remembers, with a strange queasy giddiness, that he is the one seeing it, that it is being bestowed upon him.

Sometimes, the improbability of what has happened wallops him, and he is stilled. His first relationship (can it be called a relationship?): Brother Luke. His second: Caleb Porter. And his third: Willem Ragnarsson, his dearest friend, the best person he knows, a person who could have virtually anyone he wanted, man or woman, and yet for some bizarre set of reasons—a warped curiosity? madness? pity? idiocy?—has settled on him. He has a dream one night of Willem and Harold sitting together at a table, their heads bent over a piece of paper, Harold adding up figures on a calculator, and he knows, without being told, that Harold is paying Willem to be with him. In the dream, he feels humiliation along with a kind of gratitude: that Harold should be so generous, that Willem should play along. When he wakes, he is about to say something to Willem when logic reasserts itself, and he has to remind himself that Willem certainly doesn't need the money, that he has plenty of his own, that however perplexing and unknowable Willem's reasons are for being with him, for choosing him, that he has not been coerced, that he has made the decision freely.

That night he reads in bed as he waits for Willem to come home, but falls asleep anyway and wakes to Willem's hand on the side of his face.

"You're home," he says, and smiles at him, and Willem smiles back.

They lie awake in the dark talking about Willem's dinner with the director, and the shoot, which begins in late January in Texas. The film, Duets, is based on a novel he likes, and follows a closeted lesbian and a closeted gay man, both music teachers at a small-town high school, through a twenty-five-year marriage that spans the nineteen-sixties through the nineteen-eighties. "I'm going to need your help," Willem tells him. "I really, really have to brush up on my piano playing. And I am going to be singing in it, after all. They're getting me a coach, but will you practice with me?"

"Of course," he says. "And you don't need to worry: you have a beautiful voice, Willem."

"It's thin."

"It's sweet."

Willem laughs, and squeezes his hand. "Tell Kit that," he says. "He's already freaking out." He sighs. "How was your day?" he asks.

"Fine," he says.

They begin to kiss, which he still has to do with his eyes open, to remind himself that it is Willem he is kissing, not Brother Luke, and he is doing well until he remembers the first night he had come back to the apartment with Caleb, and Caleb's pressing him against the wall, and everything that followed, and he pulls himself abruptly away from Willem, turning his face from him. "I'm sorry," he says. "I'm sorry." He has not taken off his clothes tonight, and now he pulls his sleeves down over his hands. Beside him, Willem waits, and into the silence, he hears himself saying, "Someone I know died yesterday."

"Oh, Jude," says Willem. "I'm so sorry. Who was it?"

He is silent for a long time, trying to speak the words. "Someone I was in a relationship with," he says at last, and his tongue feels clumsy in his mouth. He can feel Willem's focus intensify, can feel him move an inch or two closer to him.

"I didn't know you were in a relationship," says Willem, quietly. He clears his throat. "When?"

"When you were shooting *The Odyssey*," he says, just as quietly, and again, he feels the air change. *Something happened while I was away*, he remembers Willem saying. *Something's wrong.* He knows Willem is remembering the same conversation.

"Well," says Willem, after a long pause. "Tell me. Who was the lucky person?"

He can barely breathe now, but he keeps going. "It was a man," he begins, and although he's not looking at Willem—he's concentrating on the chandelier—he can feel him nod, encouragingly, willing him to continue. But he can't; Willem will have to prompt him, and he does.

"Tell me about him," Willem says. "How long did you go out for?"

"Four months," he says.

"And why did it end?"

He thinks of how to answer this. "He didn't like me very much," he says at last.

He can feel Willem's anger before he hears it. "So he was a moron," Willem says, his voice tight.

"No," he says. "He was a very smart guy." He opens his mouth to say something else—what, he doesn't know—but he can't continue, and he shuts it, and the two of them lie there in silence.

Finally, Willem prompts him again. "Then what happened?" he asks.

He waits, and Willem waits with him. He can hear them breathing in tandem, and it is as if they are bringing all the air from the room, from the apartment, from the world, into their lungs and then releasing it, just the two of them, all by themselves. He counts their breaths: five, ten, fifteen. At twenty, he says, "If I tell you, Willem, do you promise you won't get mad?" and he feels Willem shift again.

"I promise," Willem says, his voice low.

He takes a deep breath. "Do you remember the car accident I was in?"

"Yes," says Willem. He sounds uncertain, strangled. His breathing is quick. "I do."

"It wasn't a car accident," he says, and as if on cue, his hands begin to shake, and he plunges them beneath the covers.

"What do you mean?" Willem asks, but he remains silent, and eventually he feels, rather than sees, Willem realize what he's saying. And then Willem is flopping onto his side, facing him, and reaching beneath the covers for his hands. "Jude," Willem says, "did someone do that to you? Did someone"—he can't say the words—"did someone beat you?"

He nods, barely, thankful that he's not crying, although he feels like he's going to explode: he imagines bits of flesh bursting like shrapnel from his skeleton, smacking themselves against the wall, dangling from the chandelier, bloodying the sheets.

"Oh god," Willem says, and drops his hands, and he watches as Willem hurries out of bed.

"Willem," he calls after him, and then gets up and follows him into the bathroom, where Willem is bent over the sink, breathing hard, but when he tries to touch his shoulder, Willem shrugs his hand off.

He goes back to their room and waits on the edge of the bed, and when Willem comes out, he can tell he's been crying.

For several long minutes they sit next to each other, their arms touching, but not saying anything. "Was there an obituary?" Willem asks, finally, and he nods. "Show me," Willem says, and they go to the computer in his study and he stands back and watches Willem read it. He watches as Willem reads it twice, three times. And then Willem stands and holds him, very tightly, and he holds Willem back.

"Why didn't you tell me?" Willem says into his ear.

"It wouldn't have made a difference," he says, and Willem steps back and looks at him, holding him by the shoulders.

He can see Willem trying to control himself, and he watches as he holds his long mouth firm, his jaw muscles moving against themselves. "I want you to tell me everything," Willem says. He takes his hand and walks him to the sofa in his study and sits him down. "I'm going to make myself a drink in the kitchen, and then I'm coming back," Willem says. He looks at him. "I'll make you one, too." He can do nothing but nod.

As he waits, he thinks of Caleb. He never heard from Caleb after that night, but every few months, he would look him up. There he was, for anyone to see: pictures of Caleb smiling at parties, at openings, at shows. An article about Rothko's first freestanding boutique, with Caleb talking about the challenges a young label encounters when trying to break out in a crowded market. A magazine piece about the reemergence of the Flower District, with a quote from Caleb about living in a neighborhood that, despite its hotels and boutiques, still felt appealingly rough-edged. Now, he thinks: Did Caleb ever look him up as well? Did he show a picture of him to Nicholas? Did he say, "I once went out with him; he was grotesque"? Did he demonstrate to Nicholas—whom he imagines as blond and neat and confident—how he had walked, did they laugh with each other about how terrible, how lifeless, he had been in bed? Did he say, "He disgusted me"? Or did he say nothing at all? Did Caleb forget him, or at least choose never to consider him—was he a mistake, a brief sordid moment, an aberration to be wrapped in plastic and shoved to the far corner of Caleb's mind, with broken toys from childhood and long-ago embarrassments? He wishes he too could forget, that he too could choose never to consider Caleb again. Always, he wonders why and how he has let four months— months increasingly distant from him—so affect him, so alter his life. But then, he might as well ask—as he often does—why he has let the first fifteen years of his life so dictate the past twenty-eight. He has been lucky beyond measure; he has an adulthood that people dream about: Why, then, does he insist on revisiting and replaying events that happened so long ago? Why can he not simply take pleasure in his present?

Why must he so honor his past? Why does it become more vivid, not less, the further he moves from it?

Willem returns with two glasses of ice and whiskey. He has put on a shirt. For a while, they sit on the sofa, sipping at their drinks, and he feels his veins fill with warmth. "I'm going to tell you," he says to Willem, and Willem nods, but before he does, he leans over and kisses Willem. It is the first time in his life that he has ever initiated a kiss, and he hopes that with it he is conveying to Willem everything he cannot say, not even in the dark, not even in the early-morning gray: everything he is ashamed of, everything he is grateful for. This time, he keeps his eyes closed, imagining that soon, he too will be able to go wherever people go when they kiss, when they have sex: that land he has never visited, that place he wants to see, that world he hopes is not forbidden to him forever.

—

When Kit was in town, they met either for lunch or dinner or at the agency's New York offices, but when he came to the city in early December, Willem suggested they meet instead at Greene Street. "I'll make you lunch," he told Kit.

"Why?" asked Kit, instantly wary: although the two of them were close in their own way, they weren't friends, and Willem had never invited him over to Greene Street before.

"I need to talk to you about something," he said, and he could hear Kit making his breaths long and slow.

"Okay," said Kit. He knew better than to ask what that something might be, and whether something was wrong; he just assumed it. "I need to talk to you about something" was not, in Kit's universe, a prelude to good news.

He knew this, of course, and although he could have reassured Kit, the slightly diabolical part of him decided not to. "Okay!" he said, brightly. "See you next week!" On the other hand, he thought after he hung up, maybe his refusal to reassure Kit wasn't just childishness: *he* thought what he had to tell Kit—that he and Jude were now together—wasn't bad news, but he wasn't sure Kit would see it the same way.

They had decided to tell just a few people about their relationship. First they told Harold and Julia, which was the most rewarding and enjoyable reveal, although Jude had been very nervous for some reason. This had been just a couple of weeks ago, at Thanksgiving, and they had both been so happy, so excited, and they had both hugged him and Harold had cried, a little, while Jude sat on the sofa and watched the three of them, a small smile on his face.

Then they told Richard, who hadn't been as surprised as they'd anticipated. "I think this is a fantastic idea," he'd said, firmly, as if they'd announced they were investing in a piece of property together. He hugged them both. "Good job," he said. "Good job, Willem," and he knew what Richard was trying to communicate to him: the same thing he had tried to communicate to Richard when he told him, years ago, that Jude needed somewhere safe to live, when really, he was asking Richard to look over Jude when he could not.

Then they told Malcolm and JB, separately. First, Malcolm, who they thought would either be shocked or sanguine, and who had turned out to be the latter. "I'm so happy for you guys," he said, beaming at them both. "This is so great. I love the idea of you two together." He asked them how it had happened, and how long ago, and, teasingly, what they'd discovered about the other that they hadn't known before. (The two of them had glanced at each other then—if only Malcolm knew!—and had said nothing, which Malcolm had smiled at, as if it was evidence of a rich cache of sordid secrets that he would someday unearth.) And then he'd sighed. "I'm just sad about one thing, though," he'd said, and they had asked him what it was. "Your apartment, Willem," he said. "It's so beautiful. It must be so lonely by itself." Somehow, they had managed not to laugh, and he had reassured Malcolm that he was actually renting it to a friend of his, an actor from Spain who had been shooting a project in Manhattan and had decided to stay on for another year or so.

JB was trickier, as they'd known he would be: they knew he would feel betrayed, and neglected, and possessive, and that all of these feelings would be exacerbated by the fact that he and Oliver had recently split up after more than four years. They took him out to dinner, where there was less of a chance (though, as Jude pointed out, no guarantee) that he would make a scene, and Jude—around whom JB was still slightly careful and to whom JB was less likely to say something inappropriate—delivered the news. They watched as JB put his fork down and put his head in his hands. "I feel sick," he said, and they waited until he looked up and said, "But I'm really happy for you guys," before they exhaled. JB forked into his burrata. "I mean, I'm pissed that you didn't tell me earlier, but happy." The entrées came, and JB stabbed at his sea bass. "I mean, I'm actually *really* pissed. But. I. Am. Happy." By the time dessert arrived, it was clear that JB—who was frantically spooning up his guava soufflé—was highly agitated, and they kicked each other under the table, half on the verge of hysterics, half genuinely concerned that JB might erupt right there in the restaurant.

After dinner they stood outside and Willem and JB had a smoke and they discussed JB's upcoming show, his fifth, and his students at Yale, where JB had been teaching for the past few years: a momentary truce that was ruined by some girl coming up to him ("Can I get a picture with you?"), at which JB made a sound that was somewhere between a snort and a groan. Later, back at Greene Street, he and Jude did laugh: at JB's befuddlement, at his attempts at graciousness, which had clearly cost him, at his consistent and consistently applied self-absorption. "Poor JB," Jude said. "I thought his head was going to blow off." He sighed. "But I understand it. He's always been in love with you, Willem."

"Not like that," he said.

Jude looked at him. "*Now* who can't see themselves for who they are?" he asked, because that was what Willem was always telling him: that Jude's vision, his version of himself was singular to the point of being delusional.

He sighed, too. "I should call him," he said.

"Leave him alone tonight," Jude said. "He'll call you when he's ready."

And so he had. That Sunday, JB had come over to Greene Street, and Jude had let him in and then had excused himself, saying he had work to do, and closed himself in his study so Willem and JB could be alone. For the next two hours, Willem had sat and listened as JB delivered a disorganized roundelay whose many accusations and questions were punctuated by his refrain of "But I really am happy for you." JB was angry: that Willem hadn't told him earlier, that he hadn't even consulted him, that they had told Malcolm and Richard—Richard!— before him. JB was upset: Willem could tell him the truth; he'd always liked Jude more, hadn't he? Why couldn't he just admit it? Also, had he always felt this way? Were his years of fucking women just some colossal lie that Willem had created to distract them? JB was jealous: he got the attraction to Jude, he did, and he knew it was illogical and maybe a tiny bit self-involved, but it wouldn't be truthful if he didn't tell Willem that part of him was miffed that Willem had picked Jude and not him.

"JB," he said, again and again, "it was very organic. I didn't tell you because I needed time to figure it out in my own head. And as for being attracted to you, what can I say? I'm not. And you aren't attracted to me, either! We made out once, remember? You said it was a huge turnoff for you, remember?"

JB ignored all this, however. "I still don't understand why you told Malcolm and Richard first," he said, sullenly, to which Willem had no response. "Anyway," JB said, after a silence, "I really am happy for you two. I am."

He sighed. "Thank you, JB," he said. "That means a lot." They were both quiet again.

"JB," said Jude, coming out of his study, looking surprised that JB was still there. "Do you want to stay for dinner?"

"What're you having?"

"Cod. And I'll roast some potatoes the way you like them."

"I guess," JB said, sulkily, and Willem grinned at Jude over JB's head.

He joined Jude in the kitchen and began making a salad, and JB slumped to the dining-room table and started flipping through a novel Jude had left there. "I read this," he called over to him. "Do you want to know what happens in the end?"

"No, JB," said Jude. "I'm only halfway through."

"The minister character dies after all."

"JB!"

After that, JB's mood seemed to improve. Even his final salvos were somewhat listless, as if he were delivering them out of obligation rather than true depth of feeling. "In ten years, I'll bet you two will have made the full transition to lesbiandom. I predict cats," was one, and "Watching you two in the kitchen is like watching a slightly more racially ambiguous version of that John Currin painting. Do you know what I'm talking about? Look it up," was another.

"Are you going to come out or keep it quiet?" JB asked over dinner.

"I'm not sending out a press release, if that's what you mean," Willem said. "But I'm not going to hide it, either."

"I think it's a mistake," Jude added, quickly. Willem didn't bother answering; they had been having this argument for a month.

After dinner, he and JB lounged on the sofa and drank tea and Jude loaded the dishwasher. By this time, JB seemed almost appeased, and he recalled that this was the arc of most dinners with JB, even back at Lispenard Street: he began the evening as something sharp and tart, and ended it as something soothed and gentled.

"How's the sex?" JB asked him.

"Amazing," he said, immediately.

JB looked glum. "Dammit," he said.

But of course, this was a lie. He had no idea if the sex was amazing, because they hadn't had sex. The previous Friday, Andy had come over, and they'd told him, and Andy had stood and hugged them both very solemnly, as if he was Jude's father and they had told him that they had just gotten engaged. Willem had walked him to the door, and as they were waiting for the elevator, Andy said to him, quietly, "How's it going?"

He paused. "Okay," he said at last, and Andy, as if he could discern everything he wasn't saying, squeezed his shoulder. "I know it's not easy, Willem," he said. "But you must be doing something right—I've never seen him more relaxed or happier, not ever." He looked as if he wanted to say something else, but what could he say? He couldn't say, Call me if you want to talk about him, or Let me know if there's anything I can help you with, and so instead he left, giving Willem a little salute as the elevator sank out of sight.

That night, after JB had gone home, he thought of the conversation he and Andy had had in the café that day, and how even as Andy had been warning him how difficult it would be, he hadn't fully believed him. In retrospect, he was glad he hadn't: because believing Andy might have intimidated him, because he might have been too scared to try.

He turned and looked at Jude, who was asleep. This was one of the nights he'd taken off his clothes, and he was lying on his back, one of his arms crooked near his head, and Willem, as he often did, ran his fingers down the inside of this arm, its scars rendering it into a miserable terrain, a place of mountains and valleys singed by fire. Sometimes, when he was certain Jude was very deeply asleep, he would switch on the light near his side of the bed and study his body more closely, because Jude refused to let himself be examined in daylight. He would uncover him and move his palms over his arms, his legs, his back, feeling the texture of the skin change from rough to glossy, marveling at all the permutations flesh could take, at all the ways the body healed itself, even when attempts had been made to destroy it. He had once shot a film on the Big Island of Hawaii, and on their day off, he and the rest of the cast had trekked across the lava fields, watching the land change from rock as porous and dry as petrified bone into a gleaming black landscape, the lava frozen into exuberant swirls of frosting. Jude's skin was as diverse, as wondrous, and in places so unlike skin as he had felt or understood it that it too seemed something otherworldly and futuristic, a prototype of what flesh might look like ten thousand years from now.

"You're repulsed," Jude had said, quietly, the second time he had taken his clothes off, and he had shaken his head. And he hadn't been: Jude had always been so secretive, so protective of his body that to see it for real was somehow anticlimactic; it was so normal, finally, so less dramatic than what he had imagined. But the scars were difficult for him to see not because they were aesthetically offensive, but because each one was evidence of something withstood or inflicted. Jude's arms were for that reason the part of his body that upset him the most. At nights, as Jude slept, he would turn them over in his hands, counting the cuts, trying to imagine himself in a state in which he would willingly inflict pain on himself, in which he would actively try to erode his own being. Sometimes there were new cuts—he always knew when Jude had cut himself, because he slept in his shirt on those nights, and he would have to push up his sleeves as he slept and feel for the bandages—and he would wonder when Jude had made them, and why he hadn't noticed. When he had moved in with Jude after the suicide attempt, Harold had told him where Jude hid his bag of razors, and he, like Harold, had begun throwing them away. But then they had disappeared entirely, and he couldn't figure out where Jude was keeping them.

Other times, he would feel not curiosity, but awe: he was so much more damaged than Willem had comprehended. *How could I have not known this?* he would ask himself. *How could I not have seen this?*

And then there was the matter of sex. He knew Andy had warned him about sex, but Jude's fear of and antipathy toward it disturbed and occasionally frightened him. One night toward the end of November, after they'd been together six months, he had reached his hands down Jude's underwear and Jude had made a strange, strangled noise, the kind of noise an animal makes when it's being caught in another animal's jaws, and had jerked himself away with such violence that he had cracked his head against his nightstand. "I'm sorry," they had apologized to each other, "I'm sorry." And that was the first moment that Willem, too, had felt a certain fear. All along he had assumed that Jude was shy, profoundly so, but that eventually, he would abandon some of his self-consciousness, that he would feel comfortable enough to have sex. But in that moment, he realized that what he had thought was a reluctance to have sex was actually a terror of it: that Jude would perhaps never be comfortable, that if and when they did eventually have sex, it would be because Jude decided he had to or Willem decided he had to force him. Neither option appealed to him. People had always given themselves to him; he had never had to wait, never had to try to convince someone that he wasn't dangerous, that he wasn't going to hurt them. *What am I going to do?* he asked himself. He wasn't smart enough to figure this out on his own—and yet there was no one else he could ask. And then there was the fact that with every week, his desire grew sharper and less ignorable, his determination greater. It had been a long time since he had wanted to have sex with anyone so keenly, and the fact that it was someone he loved made the waiting both more unbearable and more absurd.

As Jude slept that night, he watched him. Maybe I made a mistake, he thought.

Aloud, he said, "I didn't know it was going to be this complicated." Next to him, Jude breathed, ignorant of Willem's treachery.

And then the morning arrived and he was reminded why he had decided to pursue this relationship to begin with, his own naïveté and arrogance aside. It was early, but he had woken anyway, and he watched as, through the half-open closet door, Jude got dressed. This had been a recent development, and Willem knew how difficult it was for him. He saw how hard Jude tried; he saw how everything he and everyone he knew took for granted—getting dressed in front of someone; getting undressed in front of someone—were things Jude had to practice again and again: he saw how determined he was, he saw how brave he was being. And this reminded him that he, too, had to keep trying. Both of them were uncertain; both of them were trying as much as they could; both of them would doubt themselves, would progress and recede. But they would both keep trying, because they trusted the other, and because the other person was the only other person who would ever be worth such hardships, such difficulties, such insecurities and exposure.

When he opened his eyes again, Jude was sitting on the edge of the bed and smiling at him, and he was filled with affection for him: for how beautiful he was, for how dear he was, for how easy it was to love him. "Don't go," he said.

"I have to," Jude said.

"Five minutes," he said.

"Five," Jude said, and slid beneath the covers, and Willem wrapped his arms around him, careful not to wrinkle his suit, and closed his eyes. And this too he loved: he loved knowing that in those moments, he was making Jude happy, loved knowing that Jude wanted affection and that he was the person who was allowed to provide it. Was this arrogance? Was this pride? Was this self-congratulation? He didn't think so; he didn't care. That night, he told Jude that he thought they should tell Harold and Julia that they were together when they went up for Thanksgiving that week. "Are you sure, Willem?" Jude had asked him, looking worried, and he knew that Jude was really asking if he was sure about the relationship itself: he was always holding the door open for him, letting him know he could leave. "I want you to really think about this, especially before we tell them." He didn't need to say it, but Willem knew, once again, what the consequences would be if they told Harold and Julia and, later, he changed his mind: they would forgive him, but things would never be the same. They would always, always pick Jude over him. He knew this: it was the way it should be.

"I'm positive," he'd said, and so they had.

He thought of this conversation as he poured Kit a glass of water and carried the plate of sandwiches to the table. "What is this?" Kit asked, looking suspiciously at the sandwiches.

"Grilled peasant bread with Vermont cheddar and figs," he said. "And escarole salad with pears and jamón."

Kit sighed. "You know I'm trying not to eat bread, Willem," he said, although he didn't know. Kit bit into a sandwich. "Good," he said, reluctantly. "Okay," he continued, putting it down, "tell me."

And so he did, and added that while he wasn't planning on

announcing the relationship, he wasn't going to pretend otherwise about it, either, and Kit groaned. "Fuck," he said. "Fuck. I thought it might be this. I don't know why, I just did. Fuck, Willem." He put his forehead down on the table. "I need a minute," Kit said to the table. "Have you told Emil?"

"Yeah," he said. Emil was Willem's manager. Kit and Emil worked with each other best when they were united against Willem. When they agreed, they liked each other. When they didn't, they didn't.

"And what did he say?"

"He said, 'God, Willem, I'm so happy that you've finally committed to someone you truly love and feel comfortable around, and I couldn't be happier for you as your friend and longtime supporter.'" (What Emil had actually said was, "Christ, Willem. Are you *sure*? Did you talk to Kit yet? What did he say?")

Kit lifted his head and glared at him (he didn't have much of a sense of humor). "Willem, I *am* happy for you," he said. "I care about you. But have you thought about what's going to happen to your career? Have you thought about how you're going to be typecast? You don't know what it's like being a gay actor in this business."

"I don't really think of myself as gay, though," he began, and Kit rolled his eyes. "Don't be so naïve, Willem," he said. "Once you've touched a dick, you're gay."

"Said with subtlety and grace, as always."

"Whatever, Willem; you can't afford to be cavalier about this."

"I'm not, Kit," he said. "But I'm not a leading man."

"You keep saying that! But you are, whether you like it or not. You're just acting like your career is going to keep going on the same trajectory it's been on—do you not remember what happened to Carl?" Carl was a client of a colleague of Kit's, and one of the biggest movie stars of the previous decade. Then he had been forced out of the closet, and his career had faded. Ironically, it was Carl's obsolescence, his sudden unpopularity, that had encouraged the rise of Willem's own career—at least two roles that Willem had gotten were ones that would once have gone, reflexively, to Carl. "Now, look: you're far more talented than Carl, and more diversified as well. And it's a different climate now than when Carl came out—domestically, at least. But I'd be doing you a disservice if I didn't tell you to prepare for a certain chill. You're private as it is: Can't you just keep this under wraps?"

He didn't reply, just reached for another sandwich, and Kit studied him. "What does Jude think?"

"He thinks I'm going to end up performing in a Kander and Ebb revue on a cruise ship to Alaska," he admitted.

Kit snorted. "Somewhere between how Jude thinks and how you think is how you need to think, Willem," he said. "After everything we've built together," he added, mournfully.

He sighed, too. The first time Jude had met Kit, almost fifteen years ago, he'd turned to Willem afterward and said, smiling, "He's your Andy." And over the years, he had come to realize how true this was. Not only did Kit and Andy actually, creepily know each other—they were in the same class, and had lived in the same dorm their freshman year—but they both liked to present themselves as, to some extent, Willem's and Jude's creators. They were their defenders and their guardians, but they also tried, at every opportunity, to determine the shape and form of their lives.

"I thought you'd be a little more supportive of this, Kit," he said, sadly.

"Why? Because I'm gay? Being a gay agent is far different than being a gay actor of your stature, Willem," said Kit. He grunted. "Well, at least someone's going to be happy about this. Noel"—the director of *Duets*—"will be fucking thrilled. This is going to be great publicity for his little project. I hope you like doing gay movies, Willem, because that's what you might end up doing *for the rest of your life*."

"I don't really think of *Duets* as a gay movie," he said, and then, before Kit could roll his eyes and start lecturing him again, "and if that's how it ends up, that's fine." He told Kit what he had told Jude: "I'll always have work; don't worry."

("But what if your film work dries up?" Jude had asked.

"Then I'll do plays. Or I'll work in Europe: I've always wanted to do more work in Sweden. Jude, I promise you, I will always, always work."

Jude had been silent, then. They had been lying in bed; it had been late. "Willem, I really won't mind—not at all—if you want to keep this quiet," he said.

"But I don't want to," he said. He didn't. He didn't have the energy for it, the sense of planning for it, the endurance for it. He knew a couple of other actors—older, much more commercial than he—who actually were gay and yet were married to women, and he saw how hollow, how fabricated, their lives were. He didn't want that life for himself: he didn't want to step off the set and still feel he was in character. When he was home, he wanted to feel he was truly at home.

"I'm just afraid you're going to resent me," Jude admitted, his voice low.

"I'll never resent you," he promised him.)

Now, he listened to Kit's gloomy predictions for another hour, and then, finally, when it was clear that Willem wouldn't change his mind, Kit seemed to change his. "Willem, it'll be fine," he said, determinedly, as if Willem had been the one who was concerned all along. "If anyone can do this, you can. We're going to make this work for you. It's going to be fine." Kit tilted his head, looking at him. "Are you guys going to get married?"

"Jesus, Kit," he said, "you were just trying to break us up."

"No, I wasn't, Willem. I wasn't. I was just trying to get you to keep your mouth shut, that's all." He sighed again, but resignedly this time. "I hope Jude appreciates the sacrifice you're making for him."

"It's not a sacrifice," he protested, and Kit cut his eyes at him. "Not now," he said, "but it may be."

Jude came home early that night. "How'd it go?" he asked Willem, looking closely at him.

"Fine," he said, staunchly. "It went fine."

"Willem—" Jude began, and he stopped him.

"Jude," he said, "it's done. It's going to be fine, I swear to you."

Kit's office managed to keep the story quiet for two weeks, and by the time the first article was published, he and Jude were on a plane to Hong Kong to see Charlie Ma, Jude's old roommate from Hereford Street, and from there to Vietnam, Cambodia, and Laos. He tried not to check his messages while he was on vacation, but Kit had gotten a call from a writer at *New York* magazine, and so he knew there would be a story. He was in Hanoi when the piece was published: Kit forwarded it to him without comment, and he skimmed it, quickly, when Jude was in the bathroom. "Ragnarsson is on vacation and was unavailable for comment, but his representative confirmed the actor's relationship with Jude St. Francis, a highly regarded and prominent litigator with the powerhouse firm of Rosen Pritchard and Klein and a close friend since they were roommates their freshman year of college," he read, and "Ragnarsson is the highest-profile actor by far to ever willingly declare himself in a gay relationship," followed, obituary-like, with a recapping of his films and various quotes from various agents and publicists congratulating him on his bravery while simultaneously predicting the almost-certain diminishment of his career, and nice quotes from actors and directors he knew promising his revelation wouldn't change a thing, and a concluding quote from an unnamed studio executive who said that his strength had never been as a romantic lead anyway, and so he'd probably be fine. At the end of the story, there was a link to a picture of him with Jude at the opening of Richard's show at the Whitney in September.

When Jude came out, he handed him the phone and watched him read the article as well. "Oh, Willem," he said, and then, later, looking stricken, "My name's in here," and for the first time, it occurred to him that Jude may have wanted him to keep quiet as much for his own privacy as for Willem's.

"Don't you think you should ask Jude first if I can confirm his identity?" Kit had asked him when they were deciding what he'd say to the reporter on Willem's behalf.

"No, it's fine," he'd said. "He won't mind."

Kit had been quiet. "He might, Willem."

But he really hadn't thought he would. Now, though, he wondered if he had been arrogant. *What*, he asked himself, *just because you're okay with it, you thought he would be, too?*

"Willem, I'm sorry," Jude said, and although he knew that he should reassure Jude, who was probably feeling guilty, and apologize to him as well, he wasn't in the mood for it, not then.

"I'm going for a run," he announced, and although he wasn't looking at him, he could feel Jude nod.

It was so early that outside, the city was still quiet and still cool, the air a dirtied white, with only a few cars gliding down the streets. The hotel was near the old French opera house, which he ran around, and then back to the hotel and toward the colonial-era district, past vendors squatted near large, flat, woven-bamboo baskets piled with tiny, bright green limes, and stacks of cut herbs that smelled of lemon and roses and peppercorns. As the streets grew threadlike, he slowed to a walk, and turned down an alley that was crowded with stall after stall of small, improvised restaurants, just a woman standing behind a kettle roiling with soup or oil, and four or five plastic stools on which customers sat, eating quickly before hurrying back to the mouth of the alley, where they got on their bikes and pedaled away. He stopped at the far end of the alley, waiting to let a man cycle past him, the basket strapped to the back of his seat loaded with spears of baguettes, their hot, steamed-milk fragrance filling his nostrils, and then headed down another alley, this one busy with vendors crouched over more bundles of herbs, and black hills of mangosteens, and metal trays of silvery-pink fish, so fresh that he could hear them gulping, could see their eyes rolling desperately back in their sockets. Above him, necklaces of cages were strung like lanterns, each containing a vibrant, chirping bird. He had a little cash with him, and he bought Jude one of the herb bouquets; it looked like rosemary but smelled pleasantly soapy, and although he didn't know what it was, he thought Jude might.

He was so naïve, he thought as he made his slow way back to the hotel: about his career, about Jude. Why did he always think he knew what he was doing? Why did he think he could do whatever he wanted and everything would work out the way he imagined it? Was it a failure of creativity, or arrogance, or (as he assumed) simple stupidity? People, people he trusted and respected, were always warning him—Kit, about his career; Andy, about Jude; Jude, about himself—and yet he always ignored them. For the first time, he wondered if Kit was right, if Jude was right, if he would never work again, or at least not the kind of work he enjoyed. Would he resent Jude? He didn't think so; he hoped not. But he had never thought he would have to find out, not really.

But greater than that fear was the one he was rarely able to ask himself: What if the things he was making Jude do weren't good for him after all? The day before, they had taken a shower together for the first time, and Jude had been so silent afterward, so deep inside one of his fugue states, his eyes so flat and blank, that Willem had been momentarily frightened. He hadn't wanted to do it, but Willem had coerced him, and in the shower, Jude had been rigid and grim, and Willem had been able to tell from the set of Jude's mouth that he was enduring it, that he was waiting for it to be over. But he hadn't let him get out of the shower; he had made him stay. He had behaved (unintentionally, but who cared) like Caleb—he had made Jude do something he didn't want to, and Jude had done it because he had told him to do it. "It'll be good for you," he'd said, and remembering this—although he had believed it—he felt almost nauseated. No one had ever trusted him as unquestioningly as Jude did. But he had no idea what he was doing.

"Willem's not a health-care professional," he remembered Andy saying. "He's an actor." And although both he and Jude had laughed at the time, he wasn't sure Andy was wrong. Who was he to try to direct Jude's mental health? "Don't trust me so much," he wanted to say to Jude. But how could he? Wasn't this what he had wanted from Jude, from this relationship? To be so indispensable to another person that that person couldn't even comprehend his life without him? And now he had it, and the demands of the position terrified him. He had asked for responsibility without understanding completely how much damage he could do. Was he able to do this? He thought of Jude's horror of sex and knew that behind that horror lay another, one he had always surmised but had never inquired about: So what was he supposed to do? He wished there was someone who could tell him definitively if he was doing a good job or not; he wished he had someone guiding him in this relationship the way Kit guided him in his career, telling him when to take a risk and when to retreat, when to play Willem the Hero and when to be Ragnarsson the Terrible.

Oh, what am I doing? he chanted to himself as his feet smacked against the road, as he ran past men and women and children readying themselves for the day, past buildings as narrow as closets, past little shops selling stiff, brick-like pillows made of plaited straw, past a small boy cradling an imperious-looking lizard to his chest, *What am I doing, oh what am I doing?*

By the time he returned to the hotel an hour later, the sky was shading from white to a delicious, minty pale blue. The travel agent had booked them a suite with two beds, as always (he hadn't remembered to have his assistant correct this), and Jude was lying on the one they had both slept in the night before, dressed for the day, reading, and when Willem came in, he stood and came over and hugged him.

"I'm all sweaty," he mumbled, but Jude didn't let go.

"It's okay," Jude said. He stepped back and looked at him, holding him by the arms. "It's going to be fine, Willem," he said, in the same firm, declarative way Willem sometimes heard him speak to clients on the phone. "It really is. I'll always take care of you, you know that, right?"

He smiled. "I know," he said, and what comforted him was not so much the reassurance itself, but that Jude seemed so confident, so competent, so certain that he, too, had something to offer. It reminded Willem that their relationship wasn't a rescue mission after all, but an extension of their friendship, in which he had saved Jude and, just as often, Jude had saved him. For every time he had gotten to help Jude when he was in pain, or defend him against people asking too many questions, Jude had been there to listen to him worrying about his work, or to talk him out of his misery after he hadn't gotten a part, or to (for three consecutive months, humiliatingly) pay his college loans when a job had fallen through and he didn't have enough money to cover them himself. And yet somehow in the past seven months he had decided that he was going to repair Jude, that he was going to fix him, when really, he didn't need fixing. Jude had always taken him at face value; he needed to try to do the same for him.

"I ordered breakfast," Jude said. "I thought you might want some privacy. Do you want to take a shower?"

"Thanks," he said, "but I think I'll wait until after we eat." He took a breath. He could feel his anxiety fade; he could feel himself returning to who he was. "But would you sing with me?" Every morning for the past two months, they had been singing with each other in preparation for *Duets*. In the film, his character and the character's wife led an annual Christmas pageant, and both he and the actress playing his wife would be performing their own vocals. The director had sent him a list of songs to work on, and Jude had been practicing with him: Jude took the melody, and he took the harmony.

"Sure," Jude said. "Our usual?" For the past week, they'd been working on "Adeste Fideles," which he would have to sing a cappella, and for the past week, he'd been pitching sharp at the exact same point, at "*Venite adoremus*," right in the first stanza. He'd wince every time he did it, hearing the error, and Jude would shake his head at him and keep going, and he'd follow him until the end. "You're overthinking it," Jude would say. "When you go sharp, it's because you're concentrating too hard on staying on key; just don't think about it, Willem, and you'll get it."

That morning, though, he felt certain he'd get it right. He gave Jude the bunch of herbs, which he was still holding, and Jude thanked him, pinching its little purple flowers between his fingers to release its perfume. "I think it's a kind of perilla," he said, and held his fingers up for Willem to smell.

"Nice," he said, and they smiled at each other.

And so Jude began, and he followed, and he made it through without going sharp. And at the end of the song, just after the last note, Jude immediately began singing the next song on the list, "For Unto Us a Child Is Born," and after that, "Good King Wenceslas," and again and again, Willem followed. His voice wasn't as full as Jude's, but he could tell in those moments that it was good enough, that it was maybe better than good enough: he could tell it sounded better with Jude's, and he closed his eyes and let himself appreciate it.

They were still singing when the doorbell chimed with their breakfast, but as he was standing, Jude put his hand on his wrist, and they remained there, Jude sitting, he standing, until they had sung the last words of the song, and only after they had finished did he go to answer the door. Around him, the room was redolent of the unknown herb he'd found, green and fresh and yet somehow familiar, like something he hadn't known he had liked until it had appeared, suddenly and unexpectedly, in his life.

2

THE FIRST TIME Willem left him—this was some twenty months ago, two Januarys ago—everything went wrong. Within two weeks of Willem's departure to Texas to begin filming *Duets*, he'd had three episodes with his back (including one at the office, and another, this one at home, that had lasted a full two hours). The pain in his feet returned. A cut (from what, he had no idea) opened up on his right calf. And yet it had all been fine. "You're so damn *cheerful* about all of this," Andy had said, when he was forced to make his second appointment with him in a week. "I'm suspicious."

"Oh, well," he'd said, even though he could hardly speak because the pain was so intense. "It happens, right?" That night, though, as he lay in bed, he thanked his body for keeping itself in check, for controlling itself for so long. For those months he secretly thought of as his and Willem's courtship, he hadn't used his wheelchair once. His episodes had been seldom, and brief, and never in Willem's presence. He knew it was silly—Willem knew what was wrong with him, he had seen him at his worst—but he was grateful that as the two of them were beginning to view each other in a different way, he had been allowed a period of reinvention, a spell of being able to impersonate an able-bodied person. So when he was returned to his normal state, he didn't tell Willem about what had been happening to him—he was so bored by the subject that he couldn't imagine anyone else wouldn't be as well—and by the time Willem came home in March, he was more or less better, walking again, the wound once again mostly under control.

Since that first time, Willem has been gone for extended periods four additional times—twice for shooting, twice for publicity tours—and each time, sometimes the very day Willem left, his body had broken itself somehow. But he had appreciated its sense of timing, its courtesy: it was as if his body, before his mind, had decided for him that he should pursue this relationship, and had done its part by removing as many obstacles and embarrassments as possible.

Now it is mid-September, and Willem is preparing to leave again. As has become their ritual—ever since the Last Supper, a lifetime ago—they spend the Saturday before Willem's departure having dinner somewhere extravagant and then the rest of the night talking. Sunday they sleep late into the morning, and Sunday afternoon, they review practicalities: things to be done while Willem is away, outstanding matters to be resolved, decisions to be made. Ever since their relationship has changed from what it had been into what it now is, their conversations have become both more intimate and more mundane, and that final weekend is always a perfect, condensed reflection of that: Saturday is for fears and secrets and confessions and remembrances; Sunday is for logistics, the daily mapmaking that keeps their life together inching along.

He likes both types of conversations with Willem, but he appreciates the mundane ones more than he'd imagined he would. He had always felt bound to Willem by the big things—love; trust—but he likes being bound to him by the small things as well: bills and taxes and dental checkups. He is always reminded of a visit to Harold and Julia's he'd made years ago, when he had come down with a terrible cold and had wound up spending most of the weekend on the living-room sofa, wrapped in a blanket and sliding in and out of sleep. That Saturday evening, they had watched a movie together, and at one point, Harold and Julia had begun talking about the Truro house's kitchen renovation. He half dozed, listening to their quiet talk, which had been so dull that he couldn't follow any of the details but had also filled him with a great sense of peace: it had seemed to him the ideal expression of an adult relationship, to have someone with whom you could discuss the mechanics of a shared existence.

"So I left a message with the tree guy and told him you're going to call this week, right?" Willem asks. They are in the bedroom, doing the last of Willem's packing.

"Right," he says. "I wrote myself a note to call him tomorrow."

"And I told Mal you'd go up with him to the site next weekend, you know."

"I know," he says. "I have it in my schedule."

Willem has been dropping stacks of clothes into his bag as he talks, but now he stops and looks at him. "I feel bad," he says. "I'm leaving you with so much stuff."

"Don't," he says. "It's not a problem, I swear." Most of the scheduling in their lives is handled by Willem's assistant, by his secretaries: but they are managing the details of the house upstate themselves. They never discussed how this happened, but he senses it's important for them both to be able to participate in the creation and witness of this place they are building together, the first place they will have built together since Lispenard Street.

Willem sighs. "But you're so busy," he says.

"Don't worry," he says. "Really, Willem. I can handle it," although Willem continues to look worried.

That night, they lie awake. For as long as he has known Willem, he has always had the same feeling the day before he leaves, when even as he speaks to Willem he is already anticipating how much he'll miss him when he's gone. Now that they are actually, physically together, that feeling has, curiously, intensified; now he is so used to Willem's presence that his absence feels more profound, more debilitating. "You know what else we have to talk about," Willem says, and when he doesn't say anything, Willem pushes down his sleeve and holds his left wrist, loosely, in his hand. "I want you to promise me," Willem says.

"I swear," he says. "I will." Next to him, Willem releases his arm and rolls onto his back, and they are quiet.

"We're both tired," Willem yawns, and they are: in less than two years, Willem has been reclassified as gay; Lucien has retired from the firm and he has taken over as the chair of the litigation department; and they are building a house in the country, eighty minutes north of the city. When they are together on the weekends—and when Willem is home, he too tries to be, going into the office even earlier on the weekdays so he doesn't have to stay as late on Saturdays—they sometimes spend the early evening simply lying together on the sofa in the living room, not speaking, as around them the light leaves the room. Sometimes they go out, but far less frequently than they used to.

"The transition to lesbiandom took much less time than I antici-pated," JB observed one evening when they had him and his new boy-friend, Fredrik, over for dinner, along with Malcolm and Sophie and Richard and India and Andy and Jane.

"Give them a break, JB," said Richard, mildly, as everyone else laughed, but he didn't think Willem minded, and he certainly didn't himself. After all, what did he care about anything but Willem?

For a while he waits to see if Willem will say anything else. He won-ders if he will have to have sex; he is still mostly unable to determine when Willem wants to and when he doesn't—when an embrace will become something more invasive and unwanted—but he is always pre-pared for it to happen. It is—and he hates admitting this, hates thinking it, would never say it aloud—one of the very few things he anticipates about Willem's departures: for those weeks or months that he is away, there is no sex, and he can finally relax.

They have been having sex for eighteen months now (he realizes he has to make himself stop counting, as if his sexual life is a prison term, and he is working toward its completion), and Willem had waited for him for almost ten. During those months, he had been intensely aware that there was a clock somewhere counting itself down, and that although he didn't know how much time he had left, he did know that as patient as Willem was, he wouldn't be patient forever. Months before, when he had overheard Willem lie to JB about how amazing their sex life was, he had vowed to himself that he would tell Willem he was ready that night. But he had been too frightened, and had allowed himself to let the moment pass. A little more than a month after that, when they were on holiday in Southeast Asia, he once again promised himself he'd try, and once again, he had done nothing.

And then it was January, and Willem had left for Texas to film *Duets*, and he had spent the weeks alone readying himself, and the night after Willem came home—he was still astonished that Willem had come back to him at all; astonished and ecstatic, so happy he had wanted to lean his head out the window and scream for no other reason but the improbability of it all—he had told Willem that he was ready.

Willem had looked at him. "Are you sure?" he'd asked him.

He wasn't, of course. But he knew that if he wanted to be with Wil-lem, he would have to do it eventually. "Yes," he said.

"Do you want to, really?" Willem asked next, still looking at him.

What was this, he wondered: Was this a challenge? Or was this a real question? It was better to be safe, he thought. So "Yes," he said. "Of course I do," and he knew by Willem's smile that he'd chosen the correct answer.

But first he'd had to tell Willem about his diseases. "When you have sex in the future, you'd better make sure you always disclose beforehand," one of the doctors in Philadelphia had told him, years ago. "You don't want to be responsible for passing these on to someone else." The doctor had been stern, and he had never forgotten the shame he had felt, nor the fear that he might share his filth with another. And so he had written down a speech for himself and recited it until he had it memorized, but the actual telling had been much more difficult than he had expected, and he had spoken so quietly that he'd had to repeat himself, which was somehow even worse. He had given this talk only once before, to Caleb, who had been silent and then had said in his low voice, "Jude St. Francis. A slut after all," and he had made himself smile and agree. "College," he had managed to say, and Caleb had smiled back at him, slightly.

Willem too had been silent, watching him, and had asked, "When did you get these, Jude?" and then, "I'm so sorry."

They had been lying next to each other, Willem on his side, facing him, he on his back. "I had a lost year in D.C.," he said at last, although that hadn't been true, of course. But telling the truth would mean a longer conversation, and he wasn't ready to have that conversation, not yet.

"Jude, I'm sorry," Willem had said, and had reached for him. "Will you tell me about it?"

"No," he'd said, stubbornly. "I think we should do it. Now." He had already prepared himself. Another day of waiting wasn't going to change things, and he would only lose his nerve.

So they had. A large part of him had hoped, expected even, that things would be different with Willem, that he would, finally, enjoy the process. But once it had begun, he could feel every bad old sensation returning. He tried to direct his attention to how this time was clearly better: how Willem was more gentle than Caleb had been, how he didn't get impatient with him, how it was, after all, Willem, someone he loved. But when it was over, there was the same shame, the same nausea, the same desire to hurt himself, to scoop out his insides and hurl them against the wall with a bloody thwack.

"Was it okay?" Willem asked, quietly, and he turned and looked at Willem's face, which he loved so much.

"Yes," he said. Maybe, he thought, it would be better the next time. And then, the next time, when it had been the same, he thought it might be better the time after that. Every time, he hoped things would be different. Every time, he told himself it would be. The sorrow he felt when he realized that even Willem couldn't save him, that he was irredeemable, that this experience was forever ruined for him, was one of the greatest of his life.

Eventually, he made some rules for himself. First, he would never refuse Willem, ever. If this was what Willem wanted, he could have it, and he would never turn him away. Willem had sacrificed so much to be with him, and had brought him such peace, that he was determined to try to thank him however he could. Second, he would try—as Brother Luke had once asked him—to show a little life, a little enthusiasm. Toward the end of his time with Caleb, he had begun reverting to what he had done all his life: Caleb would turn him over, and pull down his pants, and he would lie there and wait. Now, with Willem, he tried to remember Brother Luke's commands, which he had always obeyed—*Roll over; Now make some noise; Now tell me you like it*—and incorporate them when he could, so he would seem like an active participant. He hoped his competency would somehow conceal his lack of enthusiasm, and as Willem slept, he made himself remember the lessons that Brother Luke taught him, lessons he had spent his adulthood trying to forget. He knew Willem was surprised by his fluency: he, who had always remained silent when the others had bragged about what they'd done in bed, or what they hoped to; he, who could and did tolerate every conversation his friends had about the subject but had never engaged in them himself.

The third rule was that he would initiate sex once for every three times Willem did, so it didn't seem so uneven. And fourth, whatever Willem wanted him to do, he would do. *This is Willem,* he would remind himself, again and again. *This is someone who would never intentionally hurt you. Whatever he asks you to do is within reason.*

But then he would see Brother Luke's face before him. *You trusted him, too,* the voice nagged him. *You thought he was protecting you, too.*

How dare you, he would argue with the voice. *How dare you compare Willem to Brother Luke.*

What's the difference? the voice snapped back. *They both want the same thing from you. You're the same thing to them in the end.*

Eventually his fear of the process diminished, though not his dread. He had always known that Willem enjoyed sex, but he had been surprised and dismayed that he seemed to enjoy it so much with him. He knew how unfair he was being, but he found himself respecting Willem less for this, and hating himself more for those feelings.

He tried to focus on what had improved about the experience since Caleb. Although it was still painful, it was less painful than it had been with anyone else, and surely that was a good thing. It was still uncomfortable, although again, less so. And it was still shameful, although with Willem, he was able to comfort himself with the knowledge that he was giving at least a small bit of pleasure to the person he cared about most, and that knowledge helped sustain him every time.

He told Willem that he had lost the ability to have erections because of the car injury, but that wasn't true. According to Andy (this was years ago), there was no physical reason why he couldn't have them. But at any rate, he couldn't, and hadn't for years, not since he was in college, and even then, they had been rare and uncontrollable. Willem asked if there was something he could do—a shot, a pill—but he told him that he was allergic to one of the ingredients in those shots and pills, and that it didn't make a difference to him.

Caleb hadn't been so bothered by this inability of his, but Willem was. "Isn't there *something* we can do to help you?" he asked, again and again. "Have you talked to Andy? Should we try something different?" until finally he snapped at Willem to stop asking him, that he was making him feel like a freak.

"I'm sorry, Jude; I didn't mean to," Willem said after a silence. "I just want you to enjoy this."

"I am," he said. He hated lying so much to Willem, but what was the alternative? The alternative meant losing him, meant being alone forever.

Sometimes, often, he cursed himself, and how limited he was, but at other times, he was kinder: he recognized how much his mind had protected his body, how it had shut down his sexual drive in order to shelter him, how it had calcified every part of him that had caused him such pain. But usually, he knew he was wrong. He knew his resentment of Willem was wrong. He knew his impatience with Willem's affection for foreplay—that long, embarrassing period of throat-clearing that preceded every interaction, the small physical gestures of intimacy that he knew were Willem's way of experimenting with the depths of his own ability for arousal—was wrong. But sex in his experience was something to be gotten through as quickly as possible, with an efficiency and brusqueness that bordered on the brutal, and when he sensed Willem was trying to prolong their encounters he began offering direction with a sort of decisiveness that he later realized Willem must mistake for zeal. And then he would hear Brother Luke's triumphant declaration in his head—*I could hear you enjoying yourself*—and cringe. *I don't*, he had always wanted to say, and he wanted to say it now: *I don't*. But he didn't dare. They were in a relationship. People in relationships had sex. If he wanted to keep Willem, he had to fulfill his side of the bargain, and his dislike for his duties didn't change this.

Still, he didn't give up. He promised himself he would work on repairing himself, for Willem's sake if not his own. He bought—surreptitiously, his face prickling as he placed the order—three self-help books on sex and read them while Willem was on one of his publicity tours, and when Willem returned, he tried to use what he had learned, but the results had been the same. He bought magazines meant for women with articles about being better in bed, and studied them carefully. He even ordered a book about how victims of sexual abuse—a term he hated and didn't apply to himself—dealt with sex, which he read furtively one night, locking his study door so Willem wouldn't discover him. But after about a year, he decided to alter his ambitions: *he* might not ever be able to enjoy sex, but that didn't mean he couldn't make it more enjoyable for Willem, both as an expression of gratitude and, more selfishly, a way to keep him close. So he fought past his feelings of shame; he concentrated on Willem.

Now that he was having sex again, he realized how much he had been surrounded by it all these years, and how completely he had managed to banish thoughts of it from his waking life. For decades, he had shied from discussions of sex, but now he listened to them wherever he encountered them: he eavesdropped on his colleagues, on women in restaurants, on men walking past him on the street, all talking about sex, about when they were having it, about how they wanted it more (no one wanted it less, it seemed). It was as if he was back in college, his peers once again his unwitting teachers: always, he was alert for information, for lessons on how to be. He watched talk shows on television, many of which seemed to be about how couples eventually stop having sex; the guests were married people who hadn't had sex in months, occasionally in years. He would study these shows, but none of them ever gave him the information he wanted: How long into the relationship did the sex last? How much longer would he have to wait until this happened to him and Willem, too? He looked at the couples: Were they happy? (Obviously not; they were on talk shows telling strangers about their sex lives and asking for help.) But they seemed happy, didn't they, or a version of happy at least, that man and woman who hadn't had sex in three years and yet, through the touch of the man's hand on the woman's arm, obviously still had affection for each other, obviously stayed together for reasons more important than sex. On planes, he watched romantic comedies, farces about married people not having sex. All the movies with young people were about wanting sex; all the movies with old people were about wanting sex. He would watch these films and feel defeated. When did you get to *stop* wanting to have sex? At times he would appreciate the irony of this: Willem, the ideal partner in every way, who still wanted to have sex, and he, the unideal partner in every way, who didn't. He, the cripple, who didn't, and Willem, who somehow wanted him anyway. And still, Willem was his own version of happiness; he was a version of happiness he never thought he'd have.

He assured Willem that if he missed having sex with women, he should, and that he wouldn't mind. But "I don't," Willem said. "I want to have sex with you." Another person would have been moved by this, and he was too, but he also despaired: When would this end? And then, inevitably: What if it never did? What if he was never allowed to stop? He was reminded of the years in the motel rooms, although even then he'd had a date to anticipate, however false: sixteen. When he turned sixteen, he would be able to stop. Now he was forty-five, and it was as if he was eleven once again, waiting for the day when someone—once Brother Luke, now (unfair, unfair) Willem—would tell him "That's it. You've fulfilled your duty. No more." He wished someone would tell him that he was still a full human being despite his feelings; that there was nothing wrong with who he was. Surely there was someone, *some-*

one in the world who felt as he did? Surely his hatred for the act was not a deficiency to be corrected but a simple matter of preference?

One night, he and Willem were lying in bed—both of them tired from their respective days—and Willem had begun talking, abruptly, of an old friend he'd had lunch with, a woman named Molly he'd met once or twice over the years, and who, Willem said, had been having a difficult time; now, after decades, she had finally told her mother that her father, who had died the year before, had sexually abused her.

"That's terrible," he said, automatically. "Poor Molly."

"Yes," said Willem, and there was a silence. "I just told her that she had nothing to be ashamed of, that she hadn't done anything wrong."

He could feel himself getting hot. "You were right," he said at last, and yawned, extravagantly. "Good night, Willem."

For a minute or two, they were quiet. "Jude," Willem said, gently. "Are you ever going to tell me about it?"

What could he say, he thought, as he held himself still. Why was Willem asking about this now? He thought he had been doing such a good job being normal—but maybe he hadn't. He would have to try harder. He never had told Willem about what had happened to him with Brother Luke, but along with being unable to speak of it, part of him knew he didn't need to: in the past two years, Willem had tried to approach the subject through various directions—through stories of friends and acquaintances, some named, some not (he had to assume some of these people were creations, as surely no one person could have such a vast collection of sexually abused friends), through stories about pedophilia he read in magazines, through various discourses on the nature of shame, and how it was often unearned. After each speech, Willem would stop, and wait, as if he were mentally extending a hand and asking him to dance. But he never took Willem's hand. Each time, he would remain silent, or change the subject, or simply pretend Willem had never spoken at all. He didn't know how Willem had come to learn this about him; he didn't want to know. Obviously the person he thought he was presenting wasn't the person Willem—or Harold—saw.

"Why are you asking me this?" he asked.

Willem shifted. "Because," he said, and then stopped. "Because," he continued, "I should've made you talk about this a long time ago." He stopped again. "Certainly before we started having sex."

He closed his eyes. "Am I not doing a good enough job?" he asked, quietly, and regretted the question as soon as he said it: it was something he would have asked Brother Luke, and Willem was not Brother Luke.

He could tell from Willem's silence that he was taken aback by the question as well. "No," he said. "I mean, yes. But Jude—I know something happened to you. I wish you'd tell me. I wish you'd let me help you."

"It's over, Willem," he said at last. "It was a long time ago. I don't need help."

There was another silence. "Was Brother Luke the person who hurt you?" Willem asked, and then, when he was quiet, the seconds ticking past, "Do you like having sex, Jude?"

If he spoke, he would cry, and so he didn't speak. The word *no*, so short, so easy to say, a child's sound, a noise more than a word, a sharp exhalation of air: all he had to do was part his lips, and the word would come out, and—and what? Willem would leave, and take everything with him. I can endure this, he would think when they had sex, I can endure this. He could endure it for every morning he woke next to Willem, for every affection Willem gave him, for the comfort of his company. When Willem was watching television in the living room and he was walking by, Willem would reach out his hand and he would take it, and they would remain there, Willem watching the screen and sitting, he standing, their hands in each other's, and finally he would let go and continue moving. He needed Willem's presence; every day since Willem had moved back in with him, he had experienced that same feeling of calm he had when Willem had stayed with him before he left to shoot *The Prince of Cinnamon*. Willem was his ballast, and he clung to him, even though he was always aware of how selfish he was being. If he truly loved Willem, he knew, he would leave him. He would allow Willem—he would force him, if he had to—to find someone better to love, someone who would enjoy having sex with him, someone who actually desired him, someone with fewer problems, someone with greater charms. Willem was good for him, but he was bad for Willem.

"Do *you* like having sex with me?" he asked when he could finally speak.

"Yes," said Willem, immediately. "I love it. But do *you* like it?"

He swallowed, counted to three. "Yes," he said, quietly, furious at himself and relieved as well. He had won himself more time: of Willem's presence, but also of sex. What, he wonders, if he had said no?

And so on they went. But in compensation for the sex, there is the cutting, which he has been doing more and more: to help ease the feelings of shame, and to rebuke himself for his feelings of resentment. For so long, he had been so disciplined: once a week, two cuts each time, no more. But in the past six months, he has broken his rules again and again, and now he is cutting himself as much as he had when he was with Caleb, as much as he had in the weeks before the adoption.

His accelerated cutting was the topic of their first truly awful fight, not only as a couple but ever, in their entire twenty-nine years of friendship. Sometimes the cutting has no place in their relationship. And sometimes it *is* their relationship, their every conversation, the thing they are discussing even when they're not saying anything. He never knows when he'll come to bed in his long-sleeved T-shirt and Willem will say nothing, or when Willem will begin interrogating him. He has explained to Willem so many times that he needs it, that it helps him, that he is unable to stop, but Willem cannot or will not comprehend him.

"Don't you understand why this upsets me so much?" Willem asks him.

"No, Willem," he says. "I know what I'm doing. You have to trust me."

"I *do* trust you, Jude," Willem says. "But trust is not the issue here. The issue is you hurting yourself." And then the conversation deadends itself.

Or there is the conversation that leads to Willem saying, "Jude, how would you feel if I did this to myself?" and him saying, "It's not the same thing, Willem," and Willem saying, "Why?" and him saying, "Because, Willem—it's *you*. You don't deserve it," and Willem saying, "And you *do*?" and him being unable to answer, or at least not able to provide an answer that Willem would find adequate.

About a month before the fight, they'd had a different fight. Willem had, of course, noticed that he was cutting himself more, but he hadn't known why, only that he was, and one night, after he was certain Willem was asleep, he was creeping toward the bathroom, when suddenly, Willem had grabbed him hard around the wrist, and he had gasped from fright. "Jesus, Willem," he'd said. "You scared me."

"Where are you going, Jude?" Willem had asked, his voice tense.

He'd tried to pull his arm free, but Willem's grip was too strong. "I have to go to the bathroom," he said. "Let go, Willem, I'm serious." They had stared at each other in the dark until finally Willem had released him, and then had gotten out of bed as well.

"Let's go, then," he'd said. "I'm going to watch you."

They had quarreled, then, hissing at each other, each of them furious at the other, each of them feeling betrayed, he accusing Willem of treating him like a child, Willem accusing him of keeping secrets from him, each as close as they had ever been to yelling at the other. It had ended with him wrenching out of Willem's grasp and trying to run toward his study so he could lock himself in and cut himself with a pair of scissors, but in his panic he had stumbled and fallen and split his lip, and Willem had hurried over with a bag of ice and they had sat there on the living-room floor, halfway between their bedroom and his study, their arms around each other, apologizing.

"I can't have you doing this to yourself," Willem had said the next day.

"I can't not," he said, after a long silence. *You don't want to see me without it*, he wanted to tell Willem, as well as: *I don't know how I'd make my way through life without it.* But he didn't. He was never able to explain to Willem what the cutting did for him in a way he'd understand: how it was a form of punishment and also of cleansing, how it allowed him to drain everything toxic and spoiled from himself, how it kept him from being irrationally angry at others, at everyone, how it kept him from shouting, from violence, how it made him feel like his body, his life, was truly his and no one else's. Certainly he could never have sex without it. Sometimes he wondered: If Brother Luke hadn't given it to him as a solution, who would he have become? Someone who hurt other people, he thought; someone who tried to make everyone feel as terrible as he did; someone even worse than the person he was.

Willem had been silent for even longer. "Try," he said. "For me, Judy. Try."

And he did. For the next few weeks, when he woke in the night, or after they'd had sex and he was waiting for Willem to fall asleep so he could go to the bathroom, he instead made himself lie still, his hands in fists, counting his breaths, the back of his neck perspiring, his mouth dry. He pictured one of the motels' stairwells, and throwing himself against it, the thud he would make, how satisfyingly tiring it would be, how much it would hurt. He both wished Willem knew how hard he was trying and was grateful that he didn't.

But sometimes this wasn't enough, and on those nights, he would skulk down to the ground floor, where he would swim, trying to exhaust himself. In the mornings, Willem demanded to look at his arms, and they had fought over that as well, but in the end it had been easier to just let Willem look. "Happy?" he barked at him, jerking his arms back from Willem's hands, rolling his sleeves back down and buttoning the cuffs, unable to look at him.

"Jude," Willem said, after a pause, "come lie down next to me before you go," but he shook his head and left, and all day he had regretted it, and with every passing day that Willem didn't ask him again, he hated himself more. Their new morning ritual was Willem examining his arms, and every time, sitting next to Willem in bed as Willem looked for evidence of cuts, he felt his frustration and humiliation increase.

One night a month after he had promised Willem he would try harder, he had known that he was in trouble, that there would be nothing he could do to quell his desires. It had been an unexpectedly, peculiarly memory-rich day, one in which the curtain that separated his past from his present had been oddly gauzy. All evening he had seen, as if in peripheral vision, fragments of scenes drifting before him, and over dinner he had fought to stay rooted, to not let himself wander into that frightening, familiar shadow world of memories. That night was the first night he had almost told Willem he didn't want to have sex, but in the end he had managed not to, and they had.

Afterward, he was exhausted. He always struggled to remain present when they were having sex, to not let himself float away. When he was a child and had learned that he could leave himself, the clients had complained to Brother Luke. "His eyes look dead," they had said; they hadn't liked it. Caleb had said the same thing to him. "Wake up," he'd once said, tapping him on the side of his face. "Where are you?" And so he worked to stay engaged, even though it made the experience more vivid. That night he lay there, watching Willem asleep on his stomach, his arms tucked under his pillow, his face more severe in sleep than it was in wakefulness. He waited, counting to three hundred, and then three hundred again, until an hour had passed. He snapped on the light next to his side of the bed and tried to read, but all he could see was the razor, and all he could feel was his arms tingling with need, as if he had not veins but circuitry, fizzing and blipping with electricity.

"Willem," he whispered, and when Willem didn't answer, he placed his hand on Willem's neck, and when Willem didn't move, he finally got out of bed and walked as softly as he could into their closet, where he retrieved his bag, which he had learned to store in the interior pocket of one of his winter coats, and then out of the room and across the apartment to the bathroom at the opposite end, where he closed the door. Here too there was a large shower, and he sat down inside of it and took off his shirt and leaned his back against the cool stone. His forearms were now so thickened from scar tissue that from a distance, they appeared to have been dipped in plaster, and you could barely distinguish where he had made the cuts in his suicide attempt: he had cut between and around each stripe, layering the cuts, camouflaging the scars. Lately he had begun concentrating more on his upper arms (not the biceps, which were also scarred, but the triceps, which were somehow less satisfying; he liked to see the cuts as he made them without twisting his neck), but now he made long, careful cuts down his left tricep, counting the seconds it took to make each one—one, two, three—against his breaths.

Down he cut, four times on his left, and three times on his right, and as he was making the fourth, his hands fluttery from that delicious weakness, he had looked up and had seen Willem in the doorway, watching him. In all his decades of cutting himself, he had never been witnessed in the act itself, and he stopped, abruptly, the violation as shocking as if he had been slugged.

Willem didn't say anything, but as he walked toward him, he cowered, pressing himself against the shower wall, mortified and terrified, waiting for what might happen. He watched Willem crouch, and gently remove the razor from his hand, and for a moment they remained in those positions, both of them staring at the razor. And then Willem stood and, without preamble or warning, sliced the razor across his own chest.

He snapped alive, then. "No!" he shouted, and tried to get up, but he didn't have the strength, and he fell back. "Willem, no!"

"Fuck!" Willem yelled. "Fuck!" But he made a second cut anyway, right under the first.

"Stop it, Willem!" he shouted, almost in tears. "Willem, stop it! You're hurting yourself!"

"Oh, yeah?" asked Willem, and he could tell by how bright Willem's eyes were that he was almost crying himself. "You see what it feels like, Jude?" And he made a third cut, cursing again.

"Willem," he moaned, and lunged for his feet, but Willem stepped out of his way. "Please stop. Please, Willem."

He had begged and begged, but it was only after the sixth cut that Willem stopped, slumping down against the opposite wall. "Fuck," he said, quietly, bending over at the waist and wrapping his arms around himself. "Fuck, that hurts." He scooted over to Willem with his bag to help clean him up, but Willem moved away from him. "Leave me alone, Jude," he said.

"But you need to bandage them," he said.

"Bandage your own goddamn arms," Willem said, still not looking at him. "This isn't some fucked-up ritual we're going to share, you know: bandaging each other's self-inflicted cuts."

He shrank back. "I wasn't trying to suggest that," he said, but Willem didn't answer him, and finally, he did clean off his cuts, and then slid the bag over toward Willem, who at last did the same, wincing as he did.

They sat there in silence for a long, long time, Willem still bent over, he watching Willem. "I'm sorry, Willem," he said.

"Jesus, Jude," Willem said, a while later. "This really hurts." He finally looked at him. "How can you stand this?"

He shrugged. "You get used to it," he said, and Willem shook his head.

"Oh, Jude," Willem said, and he saw that Willem was crying, silently. "Are you even happy with me?"

He felt something in him break and fall. "Willem," he began, and then started again. "You've made me happier than I've ever been in my life."

Willem made a sound that he later realized was a laugh. "Then why are you cutting yourself so much?" he asked. "Why has it gotten so bad?"

"I don't know," he said, softly. He swallowed. "I guess I'm afraid you're going to leave." It wasn't the entire story—the entire story he couldn't say—but it was part of it.

"Why am I going to leave?" Willem asked, and then, when he couldn't answer, "So is this a test, then? Are you trying to see how far you can push me and whether I'll stay with you?" He looked up, wiping his eyes. "Is that it?"

He shook his head. "Maybe," he said, to the marble floor. "I mean, not consciously. But—maybe. I don't know."

Willem sighed. "I don't know what I can say to convince you I'm not going to leave, that you don't need to test me," he said. They were quiet again, and then Willem took a deep breath. "Jude," he said, "do you think you should maybe go back to the hospital for a while? Just to, I don't know, sort things out?"

"No," he said, his throat tightening with panic. "Willem, no—you won't make me, will you?"

Willem looked at him. "No," he said. "No, I won't make you." He paused. "But I wish I could."

Somehow, the night ended, and somehow, the next day began. He was so tired he was tipsy, but he went to work. Their fight had never ended in any conclusive way—there were no promises extracted, there were no ultimatums given—but for the next few days, Willem didn't speak to him. Or rather: Willem spoke, but he spoke about nothing. "Have a good day," he'd say when he left in the morning, and "How was your day?" when he came home at night.

"Fine," he'd say. He knew Willem was wondering what to do and how he felt about the situation, and he tried to be as unobtrusive as possible in the meantime. At night they lay in bed, and where they usually talked, they were both quiet, and their silence was like a third creature in bed between them, huge and furred and ferocious when prodded.

On the fourth night, he couldn't tolerate it any longer, and after lying there for an hour or so, both of them silent, he rolled over the creature and wrapped his arms around Willem. "Willem," he whispered, "I love you. Forgive me." Willem didn't answer him, but he plowed on. "I'm trying," he told him. "I really am. I slipped up; I'll try harder." Willem still didn't say anything, and he held him tighter. "Please, Willem," he said. "I know it bothers you. Please give me another chance. Please don't be mad at me."

He could feel Willem sigh. "I'm not mad at you, Jude," he said. "And I know you're trying. I just wish you didn't have to try; I wish this weren't something you had to fight against so hard."

Now it was his turn to be quiet. "Me too," he said, at last.

Since that night, he has tried different methods: the swimming, of course, but also baking, late at night. He makes sure there's always flour in the kitchen, and sugar, and eggs and yeast, and as he waits for whatever's in the oven to finish, he sits at the dining-room table working, and by the time the bread or cake or cookies (which he has Willem's assistant send to Harold and Julia) are done, it's almost daylight, and he slips back into bed for an hour or two of sleep before his alarm wakes him. For the rest of the day, his eyes burn with exhaustion. He knows that Willem doesn't like his late-night baking, but he also knows he prefers it to the alternative, which is why he says nothing. Cleaning is no longer an option: since moving to Greene Street, he has had a housekeeper, a Mrs. Zhou, who now comes four times a week and is depressingly thorough, so thorough that he is sometimes tempted to dirty things up intentionally, only so he can clean them. But he knows this is silly, and so he doesn't.

"Let's try something," Willem says one evening. "When you wake up and want to cut yourself, you wake me up, too, all right? Whatever time it is." He looks at him. "Let's try it, okay? Just humor me."

So he does, mostly because he is curious to see what Willem will do. One night, very late, he rubs Willem's shoulder and when Willem opens his eyes, he apologizes to him. But Willem shakes his head, and then moves on top of him, and holds him so tightly that he finds it difficult to breathe. "You hold me back," Willem tells him. "Pretend we're falling and we're clinging together from fear."

He holds Willem so close that he can feel muscles from his back to his fingertips come alive, so close that he can feel Willem's heart beating against his, can feel his rib cage against his, and his stomach deflating and inflating with air. "Harder," Willem tells him, and he does until his arms grow first fatigued and then numb, until his body is sagging with tiredness, until he feels that he really is falling: first through the mattress, and then the bed frame, and then the floor itself, until he is sinking in slow motion through all the floors of the building, which yield and swallow him like jelly. Down he goes through the fifth floor, where Richard's family is now storing stacks of Moroccan tiles, down through the fourth floor, which is empty, down through Richard and India's apartment, and Richard's studio, and then to the ground floor, and into the pool, and then down and down, farther and farther, past the subway tunnels, past bedrock and silt, through underground lakes and oceans of oil, through layers of fossils and shale, until he is drifting into the fire at the earth's core. And the entire time, Willem is wrapped around him, and as they enter the fire, they aren't burned but melted into one being, their legs and chests and arms and heads fusing into one. When he wakes the next morning, Willem is no longer on top of him but beside him, but they are still intertwined, and he feels slightly drugged, and relieved, for he has not only not cut himself but he has slept, deeply, two things he hasn't done in months. That morning he feels fresh-scrubbed and cleansed, as if he is being given yet another opportunity to live his life correctly.

But of course he can't wake Willem up whenever he feels he needs him; he limits himself to once every ten days. The other six or seven bad nights in those ten-day periods he gets through on his own: swimming, baking, cooking. He needs physical work to stave off the craving—Richard has given him a key to his studio, and some nights he heads downstairs in his pajamas, where Richard has left him a task that is both helpfully, mindlessly repetitive and at the same time utterly mysterious: he sorts bird vertebrae by sizes one week, and separates a stack of gleaming and faintly greasy ferret pelts by color another. These tasks remind him of how, years ago, the four of them would spend their weekends untangling hair for JB, and he wishes he could tell Willem about them, but he can't, of course. He has made Richard promise not to say anything to Willem either, but he knows Richard isn't exactly comfortable with the situation—he has noticed that he is never given jobs that involve razors or scissors or paring knives, which is significant considering how much of Richard's work demands sharp edges.

One night, he peers into an old coffee can that has been left out on Richard's desk and sees that it is full of blades: small angled ones, large wedge-shaped ones, and plain rectangles of the sort he prefers. He dips his hand cautiously into the can, scoops up a loose fistful of the blades, watches them pour from his palm. He takes one of the rect- angular blades and slips it into his pants pocket, but when he's finally ready to leave for the night—so exhausted that the floor tilts beneath him—he returns it gently to the can before he goes. In those hours he is awake and prowling through the building, he sometimes feels he is a demon who has disguised himself as a human, and only at night is it safe to shed the costume he must wear by daylight, and indulge his true nature.

And then it is Tuesday, a day that feels like summer, and Willem's last in the city. He leaves for work early that morning but comes home at lunchtime so he can say goodbye.

"I'm going to miss you," he tells Willem, as he always does.

"I'm going to miss you more," Willem says, as he always does, and then, also as he always does, "Are you going to take care of yourself?"

"Yes," he says, not letting go of him. "I promise." He feels Willem sigh.

"Remember you can always call me, no matter what time it is," Willem tells him, and he nods.

"Go," he says. "I'll be fine," and Willem sighs again, and goes.

He hates to have Willem leave, but he is excited, too: for selfish reasons, and also because he is relieved, and happy, that Willem is working so much. After they had returned from Vietnam that January, just before he left to film *Duets*, Willem had been alternately anxious and bluffly confident, and although he tried not to speak of his insecurities, he knew how worried Willem was. He knew Willem worried that his first movie after the announcement of their relationship was, no matter how much he protested otherwise, a gay movie. He knew Willem worried when the director of a science-fiction thriller he wanted to do didn't call him back as quickly as he had thought he might (though he had in the end, and everything had worked out the way he had hoped). He knew Willem worried about the seemingly endless series of articles, the ceaseless requests for interviews, the speculations and television segments, the gossip columns and the editorials, about his revelation that had greeted them on their return to the States, and which, as Kit told them, they were powerless to control or stop: they would simply have to wait until people grew bored of the subject, and that might take months. (Willem didn't read stories about himself in general, but there were just so many of them: when they turned on the television, when they went online, when they opened the paper, there they were—stories about Willem, and what he now represented.) When they spoke on the phone—Willem in Texas, he at Greene Street—he could feel Willem trying not to talk too much about how nervous he was and knew it was because Willem didn't want him to feel guilty. "Tell me, Willem," he finally said. "I promise I'm not going to blame myself. I swear." And after he had repeated this every day for a week, Willem did at last tell him, and although he *did* feel guilty—he cut himself after every one of these conversations—he didn't ask Willem for reassurances, he didn't make Willem feel worse than he already did; he only listened and tried to be as soothing as he could. *Good*, he'd praise himself after they'd hung up, after every time he'd kept his mouth closed against his own fears. *Good job.* Later, he'd burrow the tip of the razor into one of his scars, flicking the tissue upward with the razor's corner until he had cut down to the soft flesh beneath.

He thinks it a good sign that the film Willem is shooting in London now is, as Kit would say, a gay film. "Normally I'd say not to," Kit told Willem. "But it's too good a script to pass up." The film is titled *The Poisoned Apple*, and is about the last few years of Alan Turing's life, after he was arrested for indecency and was chemically castrated. He idolized Turing, of course—all mathematicians did—and had been moved almost to tears by the script. "You have to do it, Willem," he had said.

"I don't know," Willem had said, smiling, *"another* gay movie?"

"*Duets* did really well," he reminded Willem—and it had: better than anyone had thought it would—but it was a lazy sort of argument, because he knew Willem had already decided to do the film, and he was proud of him, and childishly excited to see him in it, the way he was about all of Willem's movies.

The Saturday after Willem leaves, Malcolm meets him at the apartment and he drives the two of them north, to just outside Garrison, where they are building a house. Willem had bought the land—seventy acres, with its own lake and its own forest—three years ago, and for three years it had sat empty. Malcolm had drawn plans, and Willem had approved them, but he had never actually told Malcolm he could begin. But one morning, about eighteen months ago, he had found Willem at the dining-room table, looking at Malcolm's drawings.

Willem held out his hand to him, not lifting his eyes from the papers, and he took it and allowed Willem to pull him to his side. "I think we should do this," Willem said.

And so they had met with Malcolm again, and Malcolm had drawn new plans: the original house had been two stories, a modernist saltbox, but the new house was a single level and mostly glass. He had offered to pay for it, but Willem had refused. They argued back and forth, Willem pointing out that he wasn't contributing anything toward the maintenance of Greene Street, and he pointing out that he didn't care. "Jude," Willem said at last, "we've never fought about money. Let's not start now." And he knew Willem was right: their friendship had never been measured by money. They had never talked about money when they hadn't had any—he had always considered whatever he earned Willem's as well—and now that they had it, he felt the same way.

Eight months ago, when Malcolm was breaking ground, he and Willem had gone up to the property and had wandered around it. He had been feeling unusually well that day, and had even allowed Willem to hold his hand as they walked down the gentle hill that sloped from where the house would sit, and then left, toward the forest that held the lake in its embrace. The forest was denser than they had imagined, the ground so thick with pine needles that their every footfall sank, as if the earth beneath them was made of something rubbery and squashy and pumped half full of air. It was difficult terrain for him, and he grasped Willem's hand in earnest, but when Willem asked him if he wanted to stop, he shook his head. About twenty minutes later, when they were almost halfway around the lake, they came to a clearing that looked like something out of a fairy tale, the sky above them all dark green fir tops, the floor beneath them that same soft pelt of the trees' leavings. They stopped then, looking around them, quiet until Willem said, "We should just build it here," and he smiled, but inside him something wrenched, a feeling like his entire nervous system was being tugged out of his navel, because he was remembering that other forest he had once thought he'd live in, and was realizing that he was to finally have it after all: a house in the woods, with water nearby, and someone who loved him. And then he shuddered, a tremor that rippled its way through his body, and Willem looked at him. "Are you cold?" he asked. "No," he said, "but let's keep walking," and so they had.

Since then, he has avoided the woods, but he loves coming up to the site, and is enjoying working with Malcolm again. He or Willem go up every other weekend, though he knows Malcolm prefers it when he goes, because Willem is largely uninterested in the details of the project. He trusts Malcolm, but Malcolm doesn't want trust: he wants someone to show the silvery, stripey marble he's found from a small quarry outside Izmir and argue about how much of it is too much; and to make smell the cypress from Gifu that he's sourced for the bathroom tub; and to examine the objects—hammers; wrenches; pliers—he's embedded like trilobites in the poured concrete floors. Aside from the house and the garage, there is an outdoor pool and, in the barn, an indoor pool: the house will be done in a little more than three months, the pool and barn by the following spring.

Now he walks through the house with Malcolm, running his hands over its surfaces, listening to Malcolm instruct the contractor on everything that needs fixing. As always, he is impressed watching Malcolm at work: he never tires of watching any of his friends at work, but Malcolm's transformation has been the most gratifying to witness, more so than even Willem's. In these moments, he remembers how carefully and meticulously Malcolm built his imaginary houses, and with such seriousness; once, when they were sophomores, JB had (accidentally, he claimed later) set one on fire when he was high, and Malcolm had been so angry and hurt that he had almost started crying. He had followed Malcolm as he ran out of Hood, and had sat with him on the library steps in the cold. "I know it's silly," Malcolm had said after he'd calmed down. "But they mean something to me."

"I know," he'd said. He had always loved Malcolm's houses; he still has the first one Malcolm ever made him all those years ago, for his seventeenth birthday. "It's not silly." He knew what the houses meant to Malcolm: they were an assertion of control, a reminder that for all the uncertainties of his life, there was one thing that he could manipulate perfectly, that would always express what he was unable to in words. "What does *Malcolm* have to worry about?" JB would ask them when Malcolm was anxious about something, but he knew: he was worried because to be alive was to worry. Life was scary; it was unknowable. Even Malcolm's money wouldn't immunize him completely. Life would happen to him, and he would have to try to answer it, just like the rest of them. They all—Malcolm with his houses, Willem with his girlfriends, JB with his paints, he with his razors—sought comfort, something that was theirs alone, something to hold off the terrifying largeness, the impossibility, of the world, of the relentlessness of its minutes, its hours, its days.

These days, Malcolm works on fewer and fewer residences; in fact, they see far less of him than they once did. Bellcast now has offices in London and Hong Kong, and although Malcolm handles most of the

American business—he is now planning a new wing of the museum at their old college—he is increasingly scarce. But he has overseen their house himself, and he has never missed or rescheduled one of their appointments. As they leave the property, he puts his hand on Malcolm's shoulder. "Mal," he says, "I can't thank you enough," and Malcolm smiles. "This is my favorite project, Jude," he says. "For my favorite people."

Back in the city, he drops Malcolm off in Cobble Hill and then drives over the bridge and north, to his office. This is the final piece of pleasure he finds in Willem's absences: because it means he can stay at work later, and longer. Without Lucien, work is simultaneously more and less enjoyable—less, because although he still sees Lucien, who has retired to a life of, as he says, pretending to enjoy golf in Connecticut, he misses talking to him daily, misses Lucien's attempts to appall and provoke him; more, because he has found that he enjoys chairing the department, that he enjoys being on the firm's compensation committee, deciding how the company's profits will be divvied up each year. "Who knew you were such a powermonger, Jude?" Lucien asked him when he admitted this, and he had protested: it wasn't that, he told Lucien—it was that he took satisfaction in seeing what had actually been brought in each year, how his hours and days at the office—his and everyone else's—had translated themselves into numbers, and then those numbers into cash, and then that cash into the stuff of his colleagues' lives: their houses and tuitions and vacations and cars. (He didn't tell Lucien this part. Lucien would think he was being romantic, and there would be a wry, ironic lecture on his tendency toward sentimentalism.)

Rosen Pritchard had always been important to him, but after Caleb it had become essential. In his life at the firm, he was assessed only by the business he secured, by the work he did: there, he had no past, he had no deficiencies. His life there began with where he had gone to law school and what he had done there; it ended with each day's accomplishments, with each year's tallies of billable hours, with each new client he could attract. At Rosen Pritchard, there was no room for Brother Luke, or Caleb, or Dr. Traylor, or the monastery, or the home; they were irrelevant, they were extraneous details, they had nothing to do with the person he had created for himself. There, he wasn't someone who cowered in the bathroom, cutting himself, but instead a series of numbers: one number to signify how much money he brought in, and another for the number of hours he billed; a third representing how many people he oversaw, a fourth for how much he rewarded them. It was something he had never been able to explain to his friends, who marveled at and pitied him for how much he worked; he could never tell them that it was at that office, surrounded by work and people he knew they found almost stultifyingly dull, that he felt at his most human, his most dignified and invulnerable.

Willem comes home twice during the course of the shoot for long weekends; but one weekend he is sick with a stomach flu, and the next Willem is sick with bronchitis. But both times—as he feels every time he hears Willem walk into the apartment, calling his name—he must remind himself that this is his life, and that in this life, Willem is coming home to him. In those moments, he feels that his dislike of sex is miserly, that he must be misremembering how bad it is, and that even if he isn't, he has simply to try harder, that he has to pity himself less. *Toughen up*, he scolds himself as he kisses Willem goodbye at the end of these weekends. *Don't you dare ruin this. Don't you dare complain about what you don't even deserve.*

And then one night, less than a month before Willem is due to come home for good, he wakes and believes he is in the trailer of a massive semitruck, and that the bed beneath him is a dirtied blue quilt folded in half, and that his every bone is being jounced as the truck trundles its way down the highway. Oh no, he thinks, oh no, and he gets up and hurries to the piano and begins playing as many Bach partitas as he can remember, out of sequence and too loud and too fast. He is reminded of a fable Brother Luke had once told him during one of their piano lessons of an old woman in a house who played her lute faster and faster so the imps outside her door would dance themselves into a sludge. Brother Luke had told him this story to illustrate a point—he needed to pick up his tempo—but he had always liked the image, and sometimes, when he feels a memory encroaching, just a single one, easy to control and dismiss, he sings or plays until it goes away, the music a shield between him and it.

He was in his first year of law school when his life began appearing to him as memories. He would be doing something everyday—cooking dinner, filing books at the library, frosting a cake at Batter, looking up an article for Harold—and suddenly, a scene would appear before him, a dumb show meant only for him. In those years, the memories were tableaux, not narratives, and he would see a single one repeatedly for days: a diorama of Brother Luke on top of him, or one of the counselors from the home, who used to grab him as he walked by, or a client emptying his change from his pants pockets and setting it in the dish on the nightstand that Brother Luke had placed there for that purpose. And sometimes the memories were briefer and vaguer still: a client's blue sock patterned with horse heads that he had worn even in bed; the first meal in Philadelphia that Dr. Traylor had ever given him (a burger; a paper sleeve of French fries); a peachy woolen pillow in his room at Dr. Traylor's house that he could never look at without thinking of torn flesh. When these memories announced themselves, he would find himself disoriented: it always took him a moment to remember that these scenes were not only from his life, but his life itself. In those days, he would let them interrupt him, and there would be times in which he would come out of his spell and would find his hand still wrapped around the plastic cone of frosting poised over the cookie before him, or still holding the book half on, half off the shelf. It was then that he began comprehending how much of his life he had learned to simply erase, even days after it had happened, and also that somehow, somewhere, he had lost that ability. He knew it was the price of enjoying life, that if he was to be alert to the things he now found pleasure in, he would have to accept its cost as well. Because as assaultive as his memories were, his life coming back to him in pieces, he knew he would endure them if it meant he could also have friends, if he kept being granted the ability to take comfort in others.

He thought of it as a slight parting of worlds, in which something buried wisped up from the loamy, turned earth and hovered before him, waiting for him to recognize it and claim it as his own. Their very reappearance was defiant: *Here we are*, they seemed to say to him. *Did you really think we would let you abandon us? Did you really think we wouldn't come back?* Eventually, he was also made to recognize how much he had edited—edited and reconfigured, refashioned into something easier to accept—from even the past few years: the film he had seen his junior year of two detectives coming to tell a student at college that the man who had hurt him had died in prison hadn't been a film at all—it had been his life, and he had been the student, and he had stood there in the Quad outside of Hood, and the two detectives were the people who had found him and arrested Dr. Traylor in the field that night, and they had taken him to the hospital and had made sure Dr. Traylor had gone to prison, and they had come to find him to tell him in person that he had nothing to fear again. "Pretty fancy stuff," one of the detectives had said, looking around him at the beautiful campus, at its old brick buildings where you could go and be absolutely safe. "We're proud of you, Jude." But he had fuzzed this memory, he had changed it to the detective simply saying "We're proud of you," and had left off his name, just as he had left out the panic he now remembered he had vividly felt despite their news, the dread that later someone would ask him who those people were that he had been talking to, the almost nauseous wrongness of his past life intruding so physically on his present.

Eventually he had learned how to manage the memories. He couldn't stop them—after they had begun, they had never ended—but he had grown more adept at anticipating their arrival. He became able to diagnose it, that moment or day in which he could tell that something was going to visit him, and he would have to figure out how it wanted to be addressed: Did it want confrontation, or soothing, or simply attention? He would determine what sort of hospitality it wanted, and then he would determine how to make it leave, to retreat back to that other place.

A small memory he could contain, but as the days go by and he waits for Willem, he recognizes that this is a long eel of a memory, slippery and uncatchable, and it whipsaws its way through him, its tail slapping against his organs so that he feels the memory as something alive and wounding, feels its meaty, powerful smack against his intestines, his heart, his lungs. Sometimes they were like this, and these were the hardest to lasso and corral, and with every day it seems to grow inside him, until he feels himself stuffed not with blood and muscle and water and bone but with the memory itself, expanding balloon-like to inflate his very fingertips. After Caleb, he had realized that there were some memories he was simply not going to be able to control, and so his only recourse was to wait until they had tired themselves out, until they swam back into the dark of his subconscious and left him alone again.

And so he waits, letting the memory—the nearly two weeks he had spent in trucks, trying to get from Montana to Boston—occupy him, as if his very mind, his body, is a motel, and this memory his sole guest. His challenge in this period is to fulfill his promise to Willem, to not cut himself, and so he creates a strict and consuming schedule for the hours between midnight and four a.m., which are the most danger-ous. On Saturday he makes a list of what he will do each night for the next few weeks, rotating swimming with cooking and piano-playing and baking and work at Richard's and sorting through all of his and Willem's old clothes and pruning the bookcases and resewing the loose buttons on Willem's shirt that he was going to have Mrs. Zhou do but is perfectly capable of doing himself and cleaning out the detritus that has accumulated in the drawer near the stove: twist ties and sticky rubber bands and safety pins and matchbooks. He makes pints of chicken stock and ground-lamb meatballs for Willem's return and freezes them, and bakes loaves of bread for Richard to take to the food kitchen where they are both on the board and whose finances he helps administer. After feeding the starter, he sits at the table and reads novels, old favorites of his, the words and plots and characters comforting and lived-in and unchanged. He wishes he had a pet—a dumb, grateful dog, panting and smiling; a frigid cat, glaring judgmentally at him through her slit-ted orange eyes—some other breathing thing in the apartment that he could speak to, the sound of whose soft padding footsteps would bring him back to himself. He works all night, and just before he drops off to sleep, he cuts himself—once on the left arm, once on the right—and when he wakes, he is tired but proud of himself for making it through intact.

But then it is two weeks before Willem is to come home, and just as the memory is fading, checking out of him until the next time it comes to visit, the hyenas return. Or perhaps return is the wrong word, because once Caleb introduced them into his life, they have never left. Now, however, they don't chase him, because they know they don't need to: his life is a vast savanna, and he is surrounded by them. They lie splayed in the yellow grass, drape themselves lazily over the baobab trees' low branches that spread from their trunks like tentacles, and stare at him with their keen yellow eyes. They are always there, and after he and Willem began having sex, they multiplied, and on bad days, or on days when he was particularly dreading it, they multiply fur-ther. On those days, he can feel their whiskers twitch as he moves slowly through their territory, he can feel their careless derision: he knows he is theirs, and they know it, too.

And although he craves the vacations from sex that Willem's work provides him, he knows too that he ought not to, for the reentry into that world is always difficult; it had been that way when he was a child, too, when the only thing worse than the rhythms of sex had been readjusting to the rhythms of sex. "I can't wait to come home and see you," Willem says when they next speak, and although there is nothing leering in his tone, although he hasn't mentioned sex at all, he knows from past experience that Willem will want to have it the night of his return, and that he will want to have it more times than usual for the remainder of his first week back home, and that he will especially want to have it because both of them had taken turns being sick on his two furloughs and so nothing had happened either time.

"Me too," he says.

"How's the cutting?" Willem asks, lightly, as if he's asking about how Julia's maple trees are faring, or how the weather is. He always asks this at the end of their conversations, as if the subject is something he's only mildly interested in and is inquiring about to be polite.

"Fine," he says, as he always does. "Only twice this week," he adds, and this is true.

"Good, Judy," Willem says. "Thank god. I know it's hard. But I'm proud of you." He always sounds so relieved in these moments, as if he is expecting to hear—which he probably is—some other answer entirely: *Not well, Willem. I cut myself so much last night that my arm fell off entirely. I don't want you to be surprised when you see me.* He feels a mix of genuine pride, then, both that Willem should trust him so much and that he is actually getting to tell him the truth, and an enervating, bone-deep sorrow, that Willem should have to ask him at all, that this should be something that they are actually proud of. Other people are proud of their boyfriends' talents or looks or athleticism; Willem, however, gets to be proud that his boyfriend has managed to pass another night without slicing himself with a razor.

And then, finally, there comes an evening in which he knows that his efforts will not satisfy him any longer: he needs to cut himself, extensively and severely. The hyenas are beginning to make little howls, sharp yelps that seem to come from some other creature within them, and he knows that they will be quieted only by his pain. He considers what to do: Willem will be home in a week. If he cuts himself now, the cuts won't heal properly before he returns, and Willem will be angry. But if he *doesn't* do something—then he doesn't know. He has to, he has to. He has waited too long, he realizes; he has thought he could see himself through; he has been unrealistic.

He gets up from bed and walks through the empty apartment, into the quiet kitchen. The night's schedule—cookies for Harold; organize Willem's sweaters; Richard's studio—glows whitely from the counter, ignored but beckoning, pleading to be heeded, the salvation it offers as flimsy as the paper it's printed on. For a moment he stands, unable to move, and then slowly, reluctantly, he walks to the door above the staircase and unbolts it, and then, after another moment's pause, swings it open.

He hasn't opened this door since the night with Caleb, and now he leans into its mouth, looking down into its black, clutching its frame as he had on that night, wondering if he can bring himself to do it. He knows this will appease the hyenas. But there is something so degrading about it, so extreme, so sick, that he knows that if he were to do it, he will have crossed some line, that he will, in fact, have become someone who needs to be hospitalized. Finally, finally, he unsticks himself from the frame, his hands shaking, and slams the door shut, slams the bolt back into its slot, and stumps away from it.

At work the next day, he goes downstairs with another of the partners, Sanjay, and a client so the client can smoke. They have a few clients who smoke, and when they go downstairs, he goes with them, and they continue their meeting on the sidewalk. Lucien had a theory that smokers are most comfortable, and relaxed, while smoking, and therefore easier to manipulate in the moment, and although he had laughed when Lucien had told him that, he knows he's probably correct.

He is in his wheelchair that day because his feet are throbbing, although he hates to have the clients see him so impaired. "Believe me, Jude," Lucien had said when he had worried aloud about this to him years ago, "the clients think you're the same ball-crushing asshole whether you're sitting down or standing up, so for god's sake, stay in your chair." Outside it is cold and dry, which makes his feet hurt a little less for some reason, and as the three of them talk, he finds himself staring, hypnotized, at the small orange flame at the tip of the client's cigarette, which winks at him, growing duller and brighter, as the client exhales and inhales. Suddenly, he knows what he is going to do, but that revelation is followed almost instantly by a blunt punch to his abdomen, because he knows that he is going to betray Willem, and not only is he going to betray him but he is going to lie to him as well.

That day is a Friday, and as he drives to Andy's, he works out his plan, excited and relieved to have a solution. Andy is in one of his cheerful, combative moods, and he allows himself to be distracted by him, by his brisk energy. Somewhere along the way, he and Andy have begun speaking of his legs the way one would of a troublesome and wayward relative who is nonetheless impossible to abandon and in need of constant care. "The old bastards," Andy calls them, and the first time he did, he had begun laughing at the accuracy of the nickname, with its suggestion of exasperation that always threatened to overshadow the underlying and reluctant fondness.

"How're the old bastards?" Andy asks him now, and he smiles and says, "Lazy and sucking up all my resources, as usual."

But his mind is also full of what he is about to do, and when Andy asks him, "And what does your better half have to say for himself these days?" he snaps at him: "What do you mean by that?" and Andy stops and looks at him, curiously. "Nothing," he says. "I just wanted to know how Willem's doing."

Willem, he thinks, and simply hearing his name said aloud fills him with anguish. "He's great," he says, quietly.

At the end of the appointment, as always, Andy examines his arms, and this time, as he has for the last few times, grunts his approval. "You've really cut back," he says. "No pun intended."

"You know me—always trying to better myself," he says, keeping his tone jocular, but Andy looks him in the eyes. "I know," he says, softly. "I know it must be hard, Jude. But I'm glad, I really am."

Over dinner, Andy complains about his brother's new boyfriend, whom he hates. "Andy," he tells him, "you can't hate *all* of Beckett's boyfriends."

"I know, I know," Andy says. "It's just that he's such a lightweight, and Beckett could do so much better. I did tell you he pronounced Proust as Prowst, right?"

"Several times," he says, smiling to himself. He had met this new reviled boyfriend of Beckett's—a sweet, jovial aspiring landscape architect—at a dinner party at Andy's three months ago. "But Andy—I thought he was nice. And he loves Beckett. And anyway, are you really going to sit around having conversations about Proust with him?"

Andy sighs. "You sound like Jane," he says, grouchily.

"Well," he says, smiling again. "Maybe you should listen to Jane." He laughs, then, feeling lighter than he has in weeks, and not just because of Andy's sulky expression. "There are worse crimes than not being fully conversant with *Swann's Way*, you know."

As he drives home, he thinks of his plan, but then realizes he will have to wait, because he is going to claim that he has burned himself in a cooking accident, and if something goes wrong and he has to see Andy, Andy will ask him why he was cooking on the same night they were eating dinner. Tomorrow, then, he thinks; I'll do it tomorrow. That way, he can write an e-mail to Willem tonight in which he'll mention that he's going to try to make the fried plantains JB likes: a semi-spontaneous decision that will go terribly wrong.

You do know that this is how mentally ill people make their plans, says the dry and belittling voice inside him. *You do know that this planning is something only a sick person would do.*

Stop it, he tells it. *Stop it. The fact that I know this is sick means I'm not.* At that, the voice hoots with laughter: at his defensiveness, at his six-year-old's illogic, at his revulsion for the word "sick," his fear that it might attach itself to him. But even the voice, its mocking, swaggering distaste for him, isn't enough to stop him.

The next evening he changes into a short-sleeve T-shirt, one of Willem's, and goes to the kitchen. He arranges everything he needs: the olive oil; a long wooden match. He places his left forearm in the sink, as if it's a bird to be plucked, and chooses an area a few inches above where his palm begins, before taking the paper towel he's wet with oil and rubbing it onto his skin in an apricot-sized circle. He stares for a few seconds at the gleaming grease stain, and then he takes a breath and strikes the match against the side of its box and holds the flame to his skin until he catches on fire.

The pain is—what is the pain? Ever since the injury, there has not been a single day in which he is not in some sort of pain. Sometimes the pain is infrequent, or mild, or intermittent. But it is always there. "You have to be careful," Andy is always telling him. "You've gotten so inured to it that you've lost the ability to recognize when it's a sign of

something worse. So even if it's only a five or a six, if it looks like *this*"—
they had been speaking about one of the wounds on his legs around
which he had noticed that the skin was turning a poisonous blackish
gray, the color of rot—"then you have to imagine that for most people it
would be a nine or a ten, and you have to, *have to* come see me. Okay?"

But this pain is a pain he has not felt in decades, and he screams
and screams. Voices, faces, scraps of memories, odd associations whir
through his mind: the smell of smoking olive oil leads him to a memory
of a meal of roasted *funghi* he and Willem had had in Perugia, which
leads him to a Tintoretto exhibit that he and Malcolm had seen in their
twenties at the Frick, which leads him to a boy in the home everyone
called Frick, but he never knew why, as the boy's name was Jed, which
leads him to the nights in the barn, which leads him to a bale of hay in
an empty, fog-smeared meadow outside Sonoma against which he and
Brother Luke had once had sex, which leads him to, and to, and to, and
to, and to. He smells burning meat, and he breaks out of his trance
and looks wildly at the stove, as if he has left something there, a slab of
steak seething to itself in a pan, but there is nothing, and he realizes he
is smelling himself, his own arm cooking beneath him, and this makes
him turn on the faucet at last and the water splashing against the burn,
the oily smoke rising from it, makes him scream again. And then he is
reaching, again wildly, with his right arm, his left still lying useless in
the sink, an amputation in a kidney-shaped metal bowl, and he is grabbing the container of sea salt from the cupboard above the stove, and he
is sobbing, rubbing a handful of the sharp-edged crystals into the burn,
which reactivates the pain into something whiter than white, and it is as
if he is staring into the sun and he is blinded.

When he wakes, he is on the floor, his head against the cupboard
beneath the sink. His limbs are jerking; he is feverish, but he is cold,
and he presses himself against the cupboard as if it is something soft,
as if it will consume him. Behind his closed eyelids he sees the hyenas,
licking their snouts as if they have literally fed upon him. *Happy?* he
asks them. *Are you happy?* They cannot answer, of course, but they are
dazed and satiated; he can see their vigilance waning, their large eyes
shutting contentedly.

The next day he has a fever. It takes him an hour to get from the
kitchen to his bed; his feet are too sore, and he cannot pull himself on
his arms. He doesn't sleep so much as move in and out of conscious-

ness, the pain sloshing through him like a tide, sometimes receding enough to let him wake, sometimes consuming him beneath a grayed, filthy wave. Late that night he rouses himself enough to look at his arm, where there is a large crisped circle, black and venomous, as if it is a piece of land where he has been practicing a terrifying occult ritual: witch-burning, perhaps. Animal sacrifice. A summoning of spirits. It looks not like skin at all (and indeed, it no longer is) but like something that never was skin: like wood, like paper, like tarmac, all burned to ash.

By Monday, he knows it will become infected. At lunchtime he changes the bandage he had applied the night before, and as he eases it off, his skin tears as well, and he stuffs his pocket square into his mouth so he won't scream out loud. But things are falling out of his arm, clots with the consistency of blood but the color of coal, and he sits on the floor of his bathroom, rocking himself back and forth, his stomach heaving forth old food and acids, his arm heaving forth its own disease, its own excretia.

The next day the pain is worse, and he leaves work early to go see Andy. "My god," Andy says, seeing the wound, and for once, he is silent, utterly, which terrifies him.

"Can you fix it?" he whispers, because until that point, he had never thought himself capable of hurting himself in a way that couldn't be fixed. He has, suddenly, a vision of Andy telling him he will lose the arm altogether, and the next thing he thinks is: What will I tell Willem?

But "Yes," Andy says. "I'll do what I can, and then you need to go to the hospital. Lie back." He does, and lets Andy irrigate the wound and clean and dress it, lets Andy apologize to him when he cries out.

He is there for an hour, and when he is finally able to sit—Andy has given him a shot to numb the area—the two of them are silent.

"Are you going to tell me how you got a third-degree burn in such a perfect circle?" Andy asks him at last, and he ignores Andy's chilly sarcasm, and instead recites to him his prepared story: the plantains, the grease fire.

Then there is another silence, this one different in a way he cannot explain but does not like. And then Andy says, very quietly, "You're lying, Jude."

"What do you mean?" he asks, his throat suddenly dry despite the orange juice he has been drinking.

"You're lying," Andy repeats, still in that same quiet voice, and he slides off the examining table, the bottle of juice slipping from his grasp and shattering on the floor, and moves for the door.

"Stop," Andy says, and he is cold, and furious. "Jude, you fucking tell me now. *What did you do?*"

"I told you," he says, "I told you."

"No," Andy says. "You tell me what you did, Jude. You say the words. *Say them.* I want to hear you say them."

"*I told you,*" he shouts, and he feels so terrible, his brain thumping against his skull, his feet thrust full of smoldering iron ingots, his arm with its simmering cauldron burned into it. "Let me go, Andy. *Let me go.*"

"No," Andy says, and he too is shouting. "Jude, you—you—" He stops, and he stops as well, and they both wait to hear what Andy will say. "You're sick, Jude," he says, in a low, frantic voice. "You're crazy. This is crazy behavior. This is behavior that could and should get you locked away for years. You're sick, you're sick and you're crazy and you need help."

"Don't you *dare* call me crazy," he yells, "don't you *dare*. I'm not, *I'm not.*"

But Andy ignores him. "Willem gets back on Friday, right?" he asks, although he knows the answer already. "You have one week from tonight to tell him, Jude. One week. And after that, I'm telling him myself."

"You can't *legally* do that, Andy," he shouts, and everything spins before him. "I'll sue you for so much that you won't even—"

"Better check your recent case law, *counselor,*" Andy hisses back at him. "*Rodriguez versus Mehta.* Two years ago. If a patient who's been involuntarily committed attempts serious self-injury again, the patient's doctor has the right—no, the *obligation*—to inform the patient's partner or next of kin, whether that patient has fucking given consent or not."

He is struck silent then, reeling from pain and fear and the shock of what Andy has just told him. The two of them are still standing in the examining room, that room he has visited so many, so many times, but he can feel his legs pleating beneath him, can feel the misery overtake him, can feel his anger ebb. "Andy," he says, and he can hear the beg in his voice, "please don't tell him. Please don't. If you tell him, he'll leave me." As he says it, he knows it is true. He doesn't know why Willem will leave him—whether it will be because of what he has done or because he has lied about it—but he knows he is correct. Willem will leave him, even though he has done what he has done so he can keep having sex, because if he stops having sex, he knows Willem will leave him anyway.

"Not this time, Jude," says Andy, and although he isn't yelling any longer, his voice is grim and determined. "I'm not covering for you this time. You have one week."

"It's not his business, though," he says, desperately. "It's my own."

"That's the thing, though, Jude," Andy says. "It *is* his business. That's what being in a goddamned relationship is—don't you understand that yet? Don't you get that you just can't do what you want? Don't you get that when you hurt yourself, you're hurting him as well?"

"No," he says, shaking his head, gripping the side of the examining table with his right hand to try to remain upright. "No. I do this to myself so I *won't* hurt him. I'm doing it to spare him."

"No," Andy says. "If you ruin this, Jude—if you keep lying to someone who loves you, who *really* loves you, who has only ever wanted to see you exactly as you are—then you *will* only have yourself to blame. It *will* be your fault. And it'll be your fault not because of who you are or what's been done to you or the diseases you have or what you think you look like, but because of how you behave, because you won't trust Willem enough to talk to him honestly, to extend to him the same sort of generosity and faith that he has always, *always* extended to you. I know you think you're sparing him, but you're not. You're selfish. You're selfish and you're stubborn and you're proud and you're going to ruin the best thing that has happened to you. Don't you understand that?"

He is speechless for the second time that evening, and it is only when he begins, finally, to fall, so tired is he, that Andy reaches out and grabs him around his waist and the conversation ends.

He spends the next three nights in the hospital, at Andy's insistence. During the day, he goes to work, and then he comes back in the evening and Andy readmits him. There are two plastic bags dangling above him, one for each arm. One, he knows, has only glucose in it. The second has something else, something that makes the pain furry and gentle and that makes sleep something inky and still, like the dark blue skies in a Japanese woodblock print of winter, all snow and a silent traveler wearing a woven-straw hat beneath.

It is Friday. He returns home. Willem will be arriving at around ten that night, and although Mrs. Zhou has already cleaned, he wants to make certain there is no evidence, that he has hidden every clue, although without context, the clues—salt, matches, olive oil, paper towels—are not clues at all, they are symbols of their life together, they are things they both reach for daily.

He still hasn't decided what he will do. He has until the following Sunday—he has begged nine extra days from Andy, has convinced him that because of the holidays, because they are driving to Boston next Wednesday for Thanksgiving, that he needs the time—to either tell Willem, or (although he doesn't say this) to convince Andy to change his mind. Both scenarios seem equally impossible. But he will try anyway. One of the problems with having slept so much these past few nights is that he has had very little time to think about how he can negotiate this situation. He feels he has become a spectacle to himself, with all the beings who inhabit him—the ferret-like creature; the hyenas; the voices—watching to see what he will do, so they can judge him and scoff at him and tell him he's wrong.

He sits down on the living-room sofa to wait, and when he opens his eyes, Willem is sitting next to him, smiling at him and saying his name, and he puts his arms around him, careful not to let his left arm exert any pressure, and for that one moment, everything seems both possible—and indescribably difficult.

How could I go on without this? he asks himself.

And then: *What am I going to do?*

Nine days, the voice inside him nags. *Nine days.* But he ignores it.

"Willem," he says aloud, from within the huddle of Willem's arms. "You're home, you're home." He gives a long exhalation of air; hopes Willem doesn't hear its shudder. "Willem," he says again and again, letting his name fill his mouth. "Willem, Willem—you don't know how much I missed you."

—

The best part about going away is coming home. Who said that? Not him, but it might as well have been, he thinks as he moves through the apartment. It is noon: a Tuesday, and tomorrow they will drive to Boston.

If you love home—and even if you don't—there is nothing quite as cozy, as comfortable, as delightful, as that first week back. That week, even the things that would irritate you—the alarm waahing from some car at three in the morning; the pigeons who come to clutter and cluck on the windowsill behind your bed when you're trying to sleep in— seem instead reminders of your own permanence, of how life, your life, will always graciously allow you to step back inside of it, no matter how far you have gone away from it or how long you have left it.

Also that week, the things you like anyway seem, in their very exis- tence, to be worthy of celebration: the candied-walnut vendor on Crosby Street who always returns your wave as you jog past him; the falafel sandwich with extra pickled radish from the truck down the block that you woke up craving one night in London; the apartment itself, with its sunlight that lopes from one end to the other in the course of a day, with your things and food and bed and shower and smells.

And, of course, there is the person you come back to: his face and body and voice and scent and touch, his way of waiting until you fin- ish whatever you're saying, no matter how lengthy, before he speaks, the way his smile moves so slowly across his face that it reminds you of moonrise, how clearly he has missed you and how clearly happy he is to have you back. Then there are the things, if you are particularly lucky, that this person has done for you while you're away: how in the pantry, in the freezer, in the refrigerator will be all the food you like to eat, the scotch you like to drink. There will be the sweater you thought you lost the previous year at the theater, clean and folded and back on its shelf. There will be the shirt with its dangling buttons, but the buttons will be sewn back in place. There will be your mail stacked on one side of his desk; there will be a contract for an advertising campaign you're going to do in Germany for an Austrian beer, with his notes in the margin to discuss with your lawyer. And there will be no mention of it, and you will know that it was done with genuine pleasure, and you will know that part of the reason—a small part, but a part—you love being in this apartment and in this relationship is because this other person is always making a home for you, and that when you tell him this, he won't be offended but pleased, and you'll be glad, because you meant it with gratitude. And in these moments—almost a week back home—you will wonder why you leave so often, and you will wonder whether, after the next year's obligations are fulfilled, you ought not just stay here for a period, where you belong.

But you will also know—as he knows—that part of your constant leaving is reactive. After his relationship with Jude was made public, while he and Kit and Emil were waiting to see what would happen next, he had experienced that same insecurity that had visited him as a younger man: What if he never worked again? What if this was it? And although things had, he could now see, continued with almost no discernible hitch at all, it had taken him a year to be reassured that his circumstances hadn't changed, that he was still as he had been, desirable to some directors and not to others ("Bullshit," Kit had said, and he was grateful for him; "anyone would want to work with you"), and at any rate, the same actor, no better or worse, that he had been before.

But if he was allowed to be the same actor, he was not allowed to be the same person, and in the months after he was declared gay—and never refuted it; he didn't have a publicist to issue these sorts of denials and avowals—he found himself in possession of more identities than he'd had in a very long time. For much of his adult life, he had been placed in circumstances that required the shedding of selves: no longer was he a brother; no longer was he a son. But with a single revelation, he had now become a gay man; a gay actor; a high-profile gay actor; a high-profile, nonparticipating gay actor; and, finally, a high-profile traitorous gay actor. A year or so ago he had gone to dinner with a director named Max whom he'd known for many years, and over dinner Max had tried to get him to give a speech at a gala dinner benefiting a gay-rights organization at which he would announce himself as gay. Willem had always supported this organization, and he told Max that although he would be pleased to present an award or sponsor a table—as he had every year for the past decade—he wouldn't come out, because he didn't believe there was anything to come out of: he wasn't gay.

"Willem," Max said, "you're in a relationship, a serious relationship, with a man. That is the very *definition* of gay."

"I'm not in a relationship with a man," he said, hearing how absurd the words were, "I'm in a relationship with Jude."

"Oh my god," Max muttered.

He'd sighed. Max was sixteen years older than he; he had come of age in a time when identity politics were your very identity, and he understood Max's—and the other people who pecked at and pleaded with him to come out, and then accused him of self-loathing, and cowardice, and hypocrisy, and denial, when he didn't—arguments; he understood that he had come to represent something he had never

asked to represent; he understood that whether he wanted this representation or not was almost incidental. But he still couldn't do it.

Jude had told him that he and Caleb had told no one in their lives
about the other, and although Jude's secretiveness had been motivated
by shame (and Caleb's, Willem could only hope, by at least some small
glint of guilt), he too felt that his relationship with Jude existed to no
one but themselves: it seemed something sacred, and fought-for, and
unique to them. Of course, this was ridiculous, but it was the way he
felt—to be an actor in his position was to be, in many ways, a possession, to be fought over and argued about and criticized by anyone who
wanted to say something, anything, about his abilities or appearance or
performance. But his relationship was different: in it, he played a role
for one other person, and that person was his only audience, and no one
else ever saw it, no matter how much they thought they might.

His relationship also felt sacred because he had just recently—in
the last six months or so—felt he had gotten the rhythm of it. The person he thought he knew had turned out to be, in some ways, not the
person before him, and it had taken him time to figure out how many
facets he had yet to see: it was as if the shape he had all along thought
was a pentagram was in reality a dodecahedron, many sided and many
fractaled and much more complicated to measure. Despite this, he had
never considered leaving: he stayed, unquestioningly, out of love, out
of loyalty, out of curiosity. But it hadn't been easy. In truth, it had been
at times aggressively difficult, and in some ways remained so. When
he had promised himself that he wouldn't try to repair Jude, he had
forgotten that to solve someone is to *want* to repair them: to diagnose a
problem and then not try to fix that problem seemed not only neglect-
ful but immoral.

The primary issue was sex: their sexual life, and Jude's attitude
about it. Toward the end of the ten-month period in which he and Jude
had been together and he had been waiting for him to be ready (the
longest sustained period of celibacy he had endured since he was fifteen, and which he had accomplished as partly a challenge to himself,
the way other people stopped eating bread or pasta because their boyfriends or girlfriends had stopped eating them as well), he had begun to
seriously worry about where this was all going, and about whether sex
was something Jude was simply not capable of. Somehow he knew, and
had always known, that Jude had been abused, that something awful

(maybe several things awful) had happened to him, but to his shame, he was unable to find the words to discuss it with him. He told himself that even if he *could* find the words, Jude wouldn't talk about it until he was ready, but the truth, Willem knew, was that he was too much of a coward, and that cowardice was really the only reason for his inaction. But then he had come home from Texas, and they'd had sex after all, and he had been relieved, and relieved too that he had enjoyed it as much as he had, that there had been nothing strained or unnatural about it, and when it turned out that Jude was much more sexually dextrous than he had assumed he would be, he allowed himself to be relieved a third time. He couldn't bring himself, however, to determine *why* Jude was so experienced: Had Richard been right, and had Jude been leading some sort of double life all this time? It seemed too tidy an explanation. And yet the alternative—that this was knowledge Jude had accumulated before they had met, which meant these would have been lessons learned in childhood—was overwhelming to him. And so, to his great guilt, he said nothing. He chose to believe the theory that made his life less complicated.

One night, though, he'd had a dream that he and Jude had just had sex (which they had) and that Jude was next to him and crying, trying to stay silent and failing, and he knew, even in the dream, why he was crying: because he hated what he was doing; he hated what Willem was making him do. The next night he had asked Jude, outright: *Do you like this?* And he had waited, not knowing what the answer would be, until Jude had said yes, and then he had been relieved yet again: that the fiction could continue, that their equilibrium would remain unchanged, that he wouldn't have to have a conversation that he didn't know how to begin, much less lead. He had an image of a little boat, a dinghy, rocking wildly on the waves, but then righting itself again and sailing placidly on, even though the waters beneath it were black and filled with monsters and floes of seaweed that threatened with every current to pull the poor small boat beneath the ocean's surface, where it would glug out of sight and be lost.

But every so often, too sporadically and randomly to track, there would be moments when he would see Jude's face as he pushed into him, or, after, would feel his silence, so black and total that it was almost gaseous, and he would know that Jude had lied to him: that he had asked him a question to which only one answer was acceptable, and

Jude had given him that answer, but that he hadn't meant it. And then he would argue with himself, trying to justify his behavior, and reproving himself for it as well. But when he was being very honest, he knew there was a problem.

Though he couldn't quite articulate what the problem was: after all, Jude always seemed to want to have sex whenever he did. (Though wasn't that suspicious in itself?) But he had never met anyone who was so opposed to foreplay, who didn't want to even discuss sex, who never said the very word. "This is embarrassing, Willem," Jude would say whenever he tried. "Let's just do it." He felt, often, as if their sessions together were being timed, and that his job was to perform as quickly and thoroughly as he could and then never talk about it. He was less concerned with Jude's lack of erections than he was with the curious sensation he sometimes experienced—too indefinable and contradictory to even name it with language—that with every encounter they had, he was drawing closer to Jude, even as Jude pulled further from him. Jude said all the right things; he made all the right sounds; he was affectionate and willing: but still, Willem knew something, *something* was wrong. He found it bewildering; people had always enjoyed having sex with him—so what was happening here? Perversely, it made him want to have it more, if only so he could find some answers, even if he also dreaded them.

And in the same way he knew there was a problem with their sex life, he also knew—knew without knowing, without ever being told—that Jude's cutting was related to the sex. This realization would always make him shiver, as would his old, careworn way of excusing himself—*Willem Ragnarsson, what do you think you're doing? You're too dumb to figure this out*—from further exploration, from plunging an arm into the snake- and centipede-squirming muck of Jude's past to find that many-paged book, sheathed in yellowed plastic, that would explain someone he had thought he had fundamentally understood. And then he would think how none of them—not he, not Malcolm, not JB or Richard or even Harold—had been brave enough to try. They had found other reasons to keep themselves from having to dirty their hands. Andy was the only person who could say otherwise.

And yet it was easy for him to pretend, to ignore what he knew, because most of the time, pretending was easy: because they were friends, because they liked being around each other, because he loved

Jude, because they had a life together, because he was attracted to him, because he desired him. But there was the Jude he knew in the day-light, and even in the dusk and dawn, and then there was the Jude who possessed his friend for a few hours each night, and that Jude, he some-times feared, was the real Jude: the one who haunted their apartment alone, the one whom he had watched draw the razor so slowly down his arm, his eyes wide with agony, the one whom he could never reach, no matter how many reassurances he made, no matter how many threats he levied. It sometimes seemed as if it was that Jude who truly directed their relationship, and when he was present, no one, not even Willem, could dispel him. And still, he remained stubborn: he would banish him, through the intensity and the force and the determination of his love. He knew this was childish, but all stubborn acts are childish acts. Here, stubbornness was his only weapon. Patience; stubbornness; love: he had to believe these would be enough. He had to believe that they would be stronger than any habit of Jude's, no matter how long or dili-gently practiced.

Sometimes he was given progress reports of sorts from Andy and Harold, both of whom thanked him whenever they saw him, which he found unnecessary but reassuring, because it meant that the changes *he* thought he saw in Jude—a heightened sense of demonstrativeness; a certain diminishment of physical self-consciousness—weren't things he was imagining after all. But he also felt keenly alone, alone with his new suspicions about Jude and the depths of his difficulties, alone with the knowledge that he was unable or unwilling to properly address those difficulties. A few times he had been very close to contacting Andy and asking him what to do, asking him whether he was making the right decisions. But he hadn't.

Instead, he allowed his native optimism to obscure his fears, to make their relationship into something essentially joyous and sunny. Often he was struck by the sensation—which he had experienced at Lispenard Street as well—that they were playing house, that he was living some boyhood fantasy of running away from the world and its rules with his best friend and living in some unsuitable but perfectly commodious structure (a train car; a tree house) that wasn't meant to be a home but had become one because of its occupants' shared con-viction to make it so. Mr. Irvine hadn't been entirely wrong, he would think on those days when life felt like an extended slumber party, one they'd been having for almost three decades, one that gave him the thrilling feeling that they had gotten away with something large, something they were meant to have abandoned long ago: you went to parties and when someone said something ridiculous, you'd look across the table, and he'd look back at you, expressionless, with just the barest hint of a raised eyebrow, and you'd have to hurriedly drink some water to keep from spewing out your mouthful of food with laughter, and then back at your apartment—your ridiculously beautiful apartment, which you both appreciated an almost embarrassing amount, for reasons you never had to explain to the other—you would recap the entire awful dinner, laughing so much that you began to equate happiness with pain. Or you got to discuss your problems every night with someone smarter and more thoughtful than you, or talk about the continued awe and discomfort you both felt, all these years later, about having money, absurd, comic-book-villain money, or drive up to his parents' house, one of you plugging into the car's stereo an outlandish playlist, with which you would both sing along, loudly, being extravagantly silly as adults the way you never were as children. As you got older, you realized that really, there were very few people you truly wanted to be around for more than a few days at a time, and yet here you were with someone you wanted to be around for years, even when he was at his most opaque and confusing. So: happy. Yes, he was happy. He didn't have to think about it, not really. He was, he knew, a simple person, the simplest of people, and yet he had ended up with the most complicated of people.

"All I want," he'd said to Jude one night, trying to explain the satisfaction that at that moment was burbling inside him, like water in a bright blue kettle, "is work I enjoy, and a place to live, and someone who loves me. See? Simple."

Jude had laughed, sadly. "Willem," he said, "that's all I want, too."

"But you have that," he'd said, quietly, and Jude was quiet, too.

"Yes," he said, at last. "You're right." But he hadn't sounded convinced.

That Tuesday night, they are lying next to each other, half talking and half not in one of the meandering almost-conversations they have when they both want to stay awake but are both falling asleep, when

Jude says his name with a sort of seriousness that makes him open his eyes. "What is it?" he asks him, and Jude's face is so still, so sober, that he is frightened. "Jude?" he says. "Tell me."

"Willem, you know I've been trying not to cut myself," he says, and Willem nods at him and waits. "And I'm going to keep trying," Jude continues. "But sometimes—sometimes I might not be able to control myself."

"I know," he says. "I know you're trying. I know how hard it is for you."

Jude turns from him then, and Willem rolls over and wraps his arms around him. "I just want you to understand if I make a mistake," Jude says, and his voice is muffled.

"Of course I will," he says. "Jude—of course I will." There is a long silence, and he waits to see if Jude will say anything else. He is thin, with a marathon runner's long muscles, but in the past six months, he has become thinner still, almost as thin as when he was released from the hospital, and Willem holds him a little tighter. "You've lost more weight," he tells him.

"Work," Jude says, and they are quiet again.

"I think you should eat more," he says. He had to gain weight to play Turing, and although he's lost some of it, he feels massive beside Jude, something puffed and expansive. "Andy's going to think I'm not doing a good job taking care of you and he's going to yell at me," he adds, and Jude makes a sound he thinks is a laugh.

The next morning, the day before Thanksgiving, they are both cheery—they both like driving—and load their bag and the boxes of cookies and pies and breads that Jude has baked for Harold and Julia into the car and set off early, the car bouncing east over the cobble-stoned streets of SoHo, and then whooshing up the FDR Drive, singing along to the *Duets* soundtrack. Outside Worcester they stop at a gas station and Jude goes in to buy them mints and water. He waits in the car, leafing through the paper, and when Jude's phone rings, he reaches over and sees who it is and answers it.

"Have you told Willem yet?" he hears Andy's voice saying even before he can say hello. "You have three more days after today, Jude, and then I'm telling him myself. I mean it."

"Andy?" he says, and there is a sudden, sharp silence.

"Willem," Andy says. "Fuck." In the background, he can hear a

small child's delighted voice trill out—"Uncle Andy said a bad word!"—
and then Andy swears again, and he can hear a door sliding shut.
"Why're you answering Jude's phone?" Andy asks. "Where is he?"

"We're driving up to Harold and Julia's," he says. "He's getting water."
On the other end, there is silence. "Tell me what, Andy?" he asks.

"Willem," Andy says, and stops. "I can't. I told him I'd let him do it."

"Well, he hasn't said anything to me," he says, and he can feel
himself fill with strata of emotions: fear layered upon irritation layered
upon fear layered upon curiosity layered upon fear. "Andy, you'd better
tell me," he says. Something in him starts to panic. "Is it bad?" he asks.
And then he begins to plead: "Andy, don't do this to me."

He hears Andy breathing, slowly. "Willem," he says, quietly. "Ask
him how he really got the burn on his arm. I have to go."

"Andy!" he yells. "*Andy!*" But he's gone.

He twists his head and looks out the window and sees Jude walking toward him. The burn, he thinks: What about the burn? Jude had
gotten it when he tried to make the fried plantains JB likes. "Fucking
JB," he'd said, seeing the bandage wrapped around Jude's arm. "Always
fucking everything up," and Jude had laughed. "Seriously, though,"
he'd said, "are you okay, Judy?" And Jude had said he was: he had gone
to Andy's, and they had done a graft with some artificial skin-like material. They'd had an argument, then, that Jude hadn't told him how serious the burn was—from Jude's e-mail, he had assumed it was a singe,
certainly not something worthy of a skin graft—and another one this
morning when Jude insisted on driving, even though his arm was still
clearly hurting him, but: What about the burn? And then, suddenly,
he realizes that there is only one way to interpret Andy's words, and he
has to quickly lower his head because he is as dizzy as if someone had
just hit him.

"Sorry," Jude says, easing back into the car. "The line took forever."
He shakes the mints out of the bag, and then turns and sees him. "Willem?" he asks. "What's wrong? You look terrible."

"Andy called," he says, and he watches Jude's face, watches it
become stony and scared. "Jude," he says, and his own voice sounds far
away, as if he's speaking from the depths of a gulch, "how did you get
the burn on your arm?" But Jude won't answer him, just stares at him.
This isn't happening, he tells himself.

But of course it is. "Jude," he repeats, "how did you get the burn on your arm?" But Jude only keeps staring at him, his lips closed, and he asks again, and again. Finally, "*Jude!*" he shouts, astonished by his own fury, and Jude ducks his head. "Jude! Tell me! *Tell me right now!*"

And then Jude says something so quietly he can't hear him. "*Louder,*" he shouts at him. "*I can't hear you.*"

"I burned myself," Jude says at last, very softly.

"How?" he asks, wildly, and once again, Jude's answer is delivered in such a low voice that he misses most of it, but he can still distinguish certain words: *olive oil—match—fire.*

"Why?" he yells, desperately. "*Why* did you do this, Jude?" He is so angry—at himself, at Jude—that for the first time since he has known him, he wants to hit him, he can see his fist smashing into Jude's nose, into his cheek. He wants to see his face shattered, and he wants to be the one to do it.

"I was trying not to cut myself," Jude says, tinily, and this makes him newly livid.

"So it's my fault?" he asks. "You're doing this to punish me?"

"No," Jude pleads with him, "no, Willem, no—I just—"

But he interrupts him. "Why have you never told me who Brother Luke is?" he hears himself ask.

He can tell that Jude is startled. "What?" he asks.

"You promised me you would," he says. "Remember? It was my *birthday present.*" The final words sound more sarcastic than he intended. "Tell me," he says. "Tell me right now."

"I can't, Willem," Jude says. "Please. Please."

He sees that Jude is in agony, and still he pushes. "You've had four years to figure out how to do it," he says, and as Jude moves to put the keys in the ignition, he reaches over and snatches them from him. "I think that's enough of a grace period. Tell me right now," and then, when there is still no reaction, he shouts at Jude again: "*Tell me.*"

"He was one of the brothers at the monastery," Jude whispers.

"And?" he screams at him. *I am so stupid,* he thinks, even as he yells. *I am so, so, so stupid. I am so gullible.* And then, simultaneously: *He's scared of me. I'm yelling at someone I love and making him scared of me.* He suddenly remembers yelling at Andy all those years ago: *You're mad because you can't figure out how to make him better and so you're taking it out on me.* Oh god, he thinks. Oh god. Why am I doing this?

"And I ran away with him," Jude says, his voice so faint now that Willem has to lean in to hear him.

"And?" he says, but he can see that Jude is about to cry, and suddenly, he stops, and leans back, exhausted and disgusted with himself, and suddenly frightened as well: What if the next question he asks is the question that finally opens the gates, and everything he has ever wanted to know about Jude, everything he has never wanted to confront, comes surging out at last? They sit there for a long time, the car filling with their shaky breaths. He can feel his fingertips turning numb. "Let's go," he finally says.

"Where?" Jude asks, and Willem looks at him.

"We only have an hour to Boston," he says. "And they're expecting us," and Jude nods, and wipes his face with his handkerchief, and takes the keys from him, and drives them slowly out of the gas station.

As they move down the highway, he has a sudden vision of what it really means to set yourself on fire. He thinks of the campfires he had built as a Boy Scout, the tepee of twigs you'd arrange around a knot of newspaper, the way the shimmering flames made the air around them wobbly, their awful beauty. And then he thinks of Jude doing that to his own skin, imagines orange chewing through his flesh, and he is sick. "Pull over," he gasps to Jude, and Jude screeches off the road and he leans out of the car and vomits until he has nothing more to expel.

"Willem," he hears Jude saying, and the sound of his voice enrages him and devastates him, both.

They are silent for the rest of the drive, and when Jude pulls the car bumpily into Harold and Julia's driveway, there is a brief moment in which they look at each other, and it is as if he is looking at someone he has never seen before. He looks at Jude and sees a handsome man with long hands and legs and a beautiful face, the kind of face you look at and keep looking at, and if he were meeting this man at a party or at a restaurant, he would talk to him, because it would be an excuse to keep looking at him, and he would never think that this man would be someone who cut himself so much that the skin on his arms no longer felt like skin, but cartilage, or that he once dated someone who beat him so hard he could have died, or that one night he rubbed his skin with oil so that the flame he touched to his own body would burn brighter and faster, and that he had gotten this idea from someone who had once done this very thing to him, years ago, when he was a child and had done nothing worse than take something shiny and irresistible from a loathed and loathsome guardian's desk.

He opens his mouth to say something when they hear Harold and Julia calling out their welcomes to them, and they both blink and turn and get out of the car, fixing their mouths into smiles as they do. As he kisses Julia, he can hear Harold, behind him, saying to Jude, "Are you okay? Are you sure? You look a little off," and then Jude's murmured assent.

He goes to the bedroom with their bag, and Jude goes directly to the kitchen. He takes out their toothbrushes and electric razors and puts them in the bathroom, and then he lies down on the bed.

He sleeps all afternoon; he is too overwhelmed to do anything else. Dinner is just the four of them, and he looks in the mirror, quickly practicing his laugh, before he joins the others in the dining room. Over dinner, Jude is very quiet, but Willem tries to talk and listen as if everything is normal, though it is difficult, as his mind is full of what he has learned.

Even through his rage and despair, he registers that Jude has almost nothing on his plate, but when Harold says, "Jude, you have to eat more; you've gotten way too skinny. Right, Willem?" and looks to him for the support and cajoling he would normally, reflexively offer, he instead shrugs. "Jude's an adult," he says, his voice odd to him. "He knows what's best for him," and out of the corner of his eyes, he sees Julia and Harold exchange glances with each other, and Jude look down at his plate. "I ate a lot when I was cooking," he says, and they all know this is untrue, because Jude never snacks while he's cooking, and doesn't let anyone else do so, either: "The Snack Stasi," JB calls him. He watches Jude absentmindedly cup his hand around his sweatered arm right where the burn would be, and then he looks up, and sees Willem staring, and drops his hand and looks back down again.

Somehow they get through dinner, and as he and Julia do the dishes, he keeps the conversation topical and light. After, they go to the living room, where Harold is waiting for him to watch the previous weekend's game, which he has recorded. At the entryway to the room, he pauses: normally, he would join Jude and squash in beside him on the oversize, overstuffed chair that has been squished in next to what they call Harold's Chair, but tonight he cannot sit next to Jude—he can barely look at him. And yet if he doesn't, Julia and Harold will know for certain that something is seriously wrong between them. But as he hesitates, Jude stands and, as if anticipating his quandary, announces that he's tired and is going to bed. "Are you sure?" Harold asks. "The evening's just beginning." But Jude says he is, and kisses Julia good night and waves vaguely in Harold and Willem's direction, and once again, he sees Julia and Harold look at each other.

Julia eventually leaves as well—she has never understood the appeal of American football—and after she goes, Harold pauses the game and looks over at him. "Is everything okay with you two?" he asks, and Willem nods. Later, when he too is going to bed, Harold reaches out his hand for his own as he passes him. "You know, Willem," he says, squeezing his palm, "Jude's not the only one we love," and he nods again, his vision blurring, and tells Harold good night and leaves.

Their bedroom is silent, and for a while he stands, staring at Jude's form beneath the blanket. Willem can tell he's not actually asleep—he is too still to actually be sleeping—but is pretending to be, and finally, he undresses, folding his clothes over the back of the chair near the dresser. When he slips into bed, he can tell Jude is still awake, and the two of them lie there for a long time on their opposite sides of the bed, both of them afraid of what he, Willem, might say.

He sleeps, though, and when he wakes, the room is more silent still, a real silence this time, and out of habit, he rolls toward Jude's side of the bed, and opens his eyes when he realizes that Jude isn't there, and that in fact his side of the bed is cool.

He sits. He stands. He hears a small sound, too small to even be named as sound, and then he turns and sees the bathroom door, closed. But all is dark. He goes to the door anyway, and fiercely turns the knob, slams it open, and the towel that's been jammed under the door to blot out the light trails after it like a train. And there, leaning against the bathtub, is Jude, as he knew he would be, fully dressed, his eyes huge and terrified.

"Where is it?" he spits at him, although he wants to moan, he wants to cry: at his failing, at this horrible, grotesque play that is being performed night after night after night, for which he is the only, accidental audience, because even when there is no audience, the play is staged anyway to an empty house, its sole performer so diligent and dedicated that nothing can prevent him from practicing his craft.

"I'm not," Jude says, and Willem knows he's lying.

"Where is it, Jude?" he asks, and he crouches before him, seizes his hands: nothing. But he knows he has been cutting himself: he knows it from how large his eyes are, from how gray his lips are, from how his hands are shaking.

"I'm not, Willem, I'm not," Jude says—they are speaking in whispers so they won't wake Julia and Harold, one flight above them—and then, before he can think, he is tearing at Jude, trying to pull his clothes away from him, and Jude is fighting him but he can't use his left arm at all and isn't at his strongest anyway, and they are screaming at each other with no sound. He is on top of Jude, then, working his knees into his shoulders the way a fightmaster on a set once taught him to do, a method he knows both paralyzes and hurts, and then he is stripping Jude's clothes off and Jude is frantic beneath him, threatening and then begging him to stop. He thinks, dully, that anyone watching them would think this was a rape, but he isn't trying to rape, he reminds himself: he is trying to find the razor. And then he hears it, the ping of metal on tile, and he grabs the edge of it between his fingers and throws it behind him, and then goes back to undressing him, yanking his clothes away with a brutal efficiency that surprises him even as he does it, but it isn't until he pulls down Jude's underwear that he sees the cuts: six of them, in neat parallel horizontal stripes, high on his left thigh, and he releases Jude and scuttles away from him as if he is diseased.

"You—are—crazy," he says, flatly and slowly, after his initial shock has lessened somewhat. "You're crazy, Jude. To cut yourself on your legs, of all places. You *know* what can happen; you *know* you can get infected there. What the *hell* are you thinking?" He is gasping with exertion, with misery. "You're sick," he says, and he is recognizing, again as if Jude is a stranger, how thin he really is, and wondering why he hadn't noticed before. "You're sick. You need to be hospitalized. You need—"

"Stop trying to *fix* me, Willem," Jude spits back at him. "What am I to you? Why are you with me anyway? I'm not your *goddamned* charity project. I was doing just fine without you."

"Oh yeah?" he asks. "Sorry if I'm not living up to being the ideal boyfriend, Jude. I know you prefer your relationships heavy on the sadism, right? Maybe if I kicked you down the stairs a few times I'd be living up to your standards?" He sees Jude move back from him then, pressing himself hard against the tub, sees something in his eyes flatten and close.

"I'm not *Hemming*, Willem," Jude hisses at him. "I'm not going to be the cripple you get to save for the one you couldn't."

He rocks back on his heels then, stands, backs away, scooping up the razor as he does and then throwing it as hard as he can at Jude's face, Jude bringing his arms up to shield himself, the razor bouncing off his palm. "Fine," he pants. "Fucking cut yourself to ribbons for all I care. You love the cutting more than you love me, anyway." He leaves, wishing he could slam the door behind him, banging off the light switch as he goes.

Back in the bedroom, he grabs his pillows and one of the blankets from the bed and flings himself down on the sofa. If he could leave altogether, he would, but Harold and Julia's presence stops him, so he doesn't. He turns facedown and screams, really screams, into the pillow, hitting his fists and kicking his legs against the cushions like a child having a tantrum, his rage mingling with a regret so complete that he is breathless. He is thinking many things, but he cannot articulate or distinguish any of them, and three successive fantasies spool quickly through his mind: he will get in the car and escape and never talk to Jude again; he will go back into the bathroom and hold him until he acquiesces, until he can heal him; he will call Andy now, right now, and have Jude committed first thing in the morning. But he does none of those things, just beats and kicks uselessly, as if he is swimming in place.

At last, he stops, and lies still, and finally, after what feels like a very long time, he hears Jude creep into the room, as soft and slow as something beaten, a dog perhaps, some unloved creature who lives only to be abused, and then the creak of the bed as he climbs into it.

The long ugly night lurches on, and he sleeps, a shallow, furtive slumber, and when he wakes, it isn't quite daylight, but he pulls on his clothes and running shoes and goes outside, wrung dry with exhaustion, trying not to think of anything. As he runs, tears, whether from the cold or from everything, intermittently cloud his vision, and he rubs his eyes angrily, keeps going, making himself go faster, inhaling the wind in large, punishing gulps, feeling its ache in his lungs. When he returns, he goes back to their room, where Jude is still lying on his side, curled into himself, and for a second he imagines, with a jolt of horror, that he is dead, and is about to speak his name when Jude shifts a bit in his sleep, and he instead goes to the bathroom and showers, packs his running clothes into their bag, dresses for the day, and goes to the kitchen, shutting the bedroom door quietly behind him. There in the kitchen is Harold, who offers him a cup of coffee as he always does, and as always since he began his relationship with Jude, he shakes his head, although right now just the smell of coffee—its woody, barky warmth—makes him almost ravenous. Harold doesn't know why he's stopped drinking it, only that he has, and is always, as he says, trying to lead him back down the road to temptation, and although normally he would joke around with him, this morning he doesn't. He can't even look at Harold, he is so ashamed. And he is resentful as well: of Harold's unspoken but, he senses, unshakable expectation that he will always know what to do about Jude; the disappointment, the disdain he knows Harold would feel for him if he knew what he had said and done in the nighttime.

"You don't look great," Harold tells him.

"I'm not," he says. "Harold, I'm really sorry. Kit texted late last night, and this director I thought I was going to meet up with this week is leaving town tonight; I have to get back to the city today."

"Oh no, Willem, really?" Harold begins, and then Jude walks in, and Harold says, "Willem says you guys have to go back to the city this morning."

"You can stay," he says to Jude, but doesn't lift his eyes from the toast he's buttering. "Keep the car. But I need to get back."

"No," says Jude, after a short silence. "I should get back, too."

"What the hell kind of Thanksgiving is this? You guys just eat and run? What am I going to do with all that turkey?" Harold says, but his theatrical outrage is muted, and Willem can feel him looking at both of them in turn, trying to figure out what's happening, what's gone wrong.

He waits for Jude to get ready, trying to make small talk with Julia and ignore Harold's unspoken questions. He goes to the car first to make it clear he's driving, and as he's saying goodbye, Harold looks at him and opens his mouth, and then shuts it, and hugs him instead. "Drive safely," he says.

In the car he seethes, keeps accelerating and then reminding himself to slow down. It's not even eight in the morning, and it's Thanksgiving Day, and the highway is empty. Next to him, Jude is turned away from him, his face against the glass: Willem still hasn't looked at him, doesn't know what expression he wears, can't see the smudges under his eyes that Andy had told him in the hospital were a telltale sign that Jude has been cutting himself too much. His anger quickens and recedes by the mile: sometimes he sees Jude lying to him—he is always lying to him, he realizes—and the fury fills him like hot oil. And sometimes he thinks of what he said, and the way he behaved, and the entire situation, that the person he loves is so terrible to himself, and feels such a sense of remorse that he has to grip the steering wheel to make himself focus. He thinks: Is he right? *Do* I see him as Hemming? And then he thinks: No. That's Jude's delusion, because he can't understand why anyone would want to be with him. It's not the truth. But the explanation doesn't comfort him, and indeed makes him more wretched.

Just past New Haven, he stops. Normally, the passage through New Haven is the opportunity for him to recount their favorite stories from when he and JB were roommates in grad school: The time he was made to help JB and Asian Henry Young mount their guerrilla exhibition of swaying carcasses of meat outside of the medical college. The time JB cut off all his dreads and left them in the sink until Willem finally cleaned them up two weeks later. The time he and JB danced to techno music for forty straight minutes so JB's friend Greig, a video artist, could record them. "Tell me the one when JB filled Richard's tub with tadpoles," Jude would say, grinning in anticipation. "Tell me the one about the time you dated that lesbian." "Tell me the one when JB crashed that feminist orgy." But today neither of them says anything, and they roll past New Haven in silence.

He gets out of the car to gas up and go to the bathroom. "I'm not stopping again," he tells Jude, who hasn't moved, but Jude only shakes his head, and Willem slams the door shut, his anger returning.

They are at Greene Street before noon, and they get out of the car in silence, into the elevator in silence, into the apartment in silence. He takes their bag to the bedroom; behind him, he can hear Jude sit down and begin playing something on the piano—Schumann, he recognizes, Fantasy in C: a pretty vigorous number for someone who's so wan and helpless, he thinks sourly—and realizes he has to get out of the apartment.

He doesn't even take his coat off, just heads back into the living room with his keys. "I'm going out," he says, but Jude doesn't stop playing. "Do you hear me?" he shouts. "I'm leaving."

Then Jude looks up, stops playing. "When are you coming back?" he asks, quietly, and Willem feels his resolve weaken.

But then he remembers how angry he is. "I don't know," he says. "Don't wait up." He punches the button for the elevator. There is a pause, and then Jude resumes playing.

And then he is out in the world, and all the stores are closed, and SoHo is quiet. He walks to the West Side Highway, walks up it in silence, his sunglasses on, his scarf, which he bought in Jaipur (a gray for Jude, a blue for him), and which is of such soft cashmere that it snags on even the slightest of stubble, wrapped around his stubbly neck. He walks and walks; later, he won't even remember what he thought about, if he thought about anything. When he is hungry, he veers east to buy a slice of pizza, which he eats on the street, hardly tasting it, before returning to the highway. This is my world, he thinks, as he stands at the river and looks across it toward New Jersey. This is my little world, and I don't know what to do in it. He feels trapped, and yet how can he feel trapped when he can't even negotiate the small place he occupies? How can he hope for more when he can't comprehend what he thought he did?

Nightfall is abrupt and brief, and the wind more intense, and still he walks. He wants warmth, food, a room with people laughing. But he can't bear to go into a restaurant, not by himself on Thanksgiving, not in the mood he's in: he'll be recognized, and he doesn't have the energy for the small talk, the bonhomie, the graciousness, that such encounters will necessitate. His friends have always teased him about his invisibility claim, his idea that he can somehow manipulate his own visibility, his own recognizability, but he had really believed it, even when evidence kept disproving him. Now he sees this belief as yet more proof of his self-deception, his way of constantly pretending that the world will align itself to his vision of it: That Jude will get better because he wants him to. That he understands him because he likes to think he does. That he can walk through SoHo and no one will know who he is. But really, he is a prisoner: of his job, of his relationship, and mostly, of his own willful naïveté.

Finally he buys a sandwich and catches a taxi south to Perry Street, to his apartment that is barely his anymore: in a few weeks, in fact, it no longer will be, because he has sold it to Miguel, his friend from

Spain, who is spending more time in the States. But tonight, it still is, and he lets himself in, cautiously, as if the apartment may have deteriorated, may have started breeding monsters, since he was last there. It is early, but he takes off his clothes anyway, and picks Miguel's clothes off Miguel's chaise longue and takes Miguel's blanket off Miguel's bed and lies down on the chaise, letting the helplessness and tumult of the day—only a day, and so much has happened!—descend, and cries.

As he's crying, his phone rings, and he gets up, thinking it might be Jude, but it's not: it's Andy.

"Andy," he cries, "I fucked up, I really fucked up. I did something horrible."

"Willem," Andy says gently. "I'm sure it's not as bad as you think it is. I'm sure you're being too hard on yourself."

So he tells Andy, haltingly, explaining what has happened, and after he is finished, Andy is silent. "Oh, Willem," he sighs, but he doesn't sound angry, only sad. "Okay. It *is* as bad as you think it is," and for some reason, this makes him laugh a little, but then also moan.

"What should I do?" he asks, and Andy sighs again.

"If you want to stay with him, I'd go home and talk to him," he says, slowly. "And if you *don't* want to stay with him—I'd go home and talk to him anyway." He pauses. "Willem, I'm really sorry."

"I know," he says. And then, as Andy's saying goodbye, he stops him. "Andy," he says, "tell me honestly: Is he mentally ill?"

There's a very long silence, until Andy says, "I don't think so, Willem. Or rather: I don't think there's anything chemically wrong with him. I think his craziness is all man-made." He is silent. "Make him talk to you, Willem," he says. "If he talks to you, I think you'll—I think you'll understand why he is the way he is." And suddenly, he needs to get home, and he is dressing and hurrying out the door, hailing a cab and getting into it, getting out and getting into the elevator, opening the door and letting himself into the apartment, which is silent, disconcertingly silent. On the way over, he had a sudden image, one that felt like a premonition, that Jude had died, that he had killed himself, and he runs through the apartment shouting his name.

"Willem?" he hears, and he runs through their bedroom, with their bed still made, and then sees Jude in the far left corner of their closet, curled up on the ground, facing the wall. But he doesn't think about why he's there, he just drops to the floor next to him. He doesn't know if he has permission to touch him, but he does so anyway, wrapping his arms around him. "I'm sorry," he says to the back of Jude's head. "I'm so sorry, I'm so sorry. I didn't mean what I said—I would be distraught if you hurt yourself. I *am* distraught." He exhales. "And I never, ever should have gotten physical with you. Jude, I'm so sorry."

"I'm sorry, too," Jude whispers, and they are silent. "I'm sorry about what I said. I'm sorry I lied to you, Willem."

They are quiet for a long time. "Do you remember the time you told me you were afraid that you were a series of nasty surprises for me?" he asks him, and Jude nods, slightly. "You aren't," he tells him. "You aren't. But being with you is like being in this fantastic landscape," he continues, slowly. "You think it's one thing, a forest, and then suddenly it changes, and it's a meadow, or a jungle, or cliffs of ice. And they're all beautiful, but they're strange as well, and you don't have a map, and you don't understand how you got from one terrain to the next so abruptly, and you don't know when the next transition will arrive, and you don't have any of the equipment you need. And so you keep walking through, and trying to adjust as you go, but you don't really know what you're doing, and often you make mistakes, bad mistakes. That's sometimes what it feels like."

They're silent. "So basically," Jude says at last, "basically, you're saying I'm New Zealand."

It takes him a second to realize Jude is joking, and when he does he begins to laugh, unhingedly, with relief and sorrow, and he turns Jude toward him and kisses him. "Yes," he says. "Yes, you're New Zealand."

Then they are quiet again, and serious, but at least they are looking at each other.

"Are you going to leave?" Jude asks, so quietly that Willem can barely hear him.

He opens his mouth; shuts it. Oddly, even with everything he has thought and not thought over the last day and night, he has not considered leaving, and now he thinks about it. "No," he says. And then, "I don't think so," and he watches Jude shut his eyes and then open them, and nod. "Jude," he says, and the words come to his mouth as he says them, and as he speaks, he knows he is doing the right thing, "I do think you need help—help I don't know how to give you." He takes a breath. "I either want you to voluntarily commit yourself, or I want you to start seeing Dr. Loehmann twice a week." He watches Jude for a long time; he can't tell what he's thinking.

"And what if I don't want to do either?" Jude asks. "Are you going to leave?"

He shakes his head. "Jude, I love you," he says. "But I can't—I can't condone this kind of behavior. I won't be able to stick around and watch you do this to yourself if I thought you'd interpret my presence as some sort of tacit approval. So. Yes. I guess I would."

Again they are quiet, and Jude turns over and lies on his back. "If I tell you what happened to me," he begins, falteringly, "if I tell you everything I can't discuss—if I tell you, Willem, do I still have to go?"

He looks at him, shakes his head again. "Oh, Jude," he says. "Yes. Yes, you still have to. But I hope you'll tell me anyway, I really do. Whatever it is; whatever it is."

They are quiet once more, and this time, their quiet turns to sleep, and the two of them fit into each other and sleep and sleep until Willem hears Jude's voice speaking to him, and then he wakes, and he listens as Jude talks. It will take hours, because Jude is sometimes unable to continue, and Willem will wait and hold him so tightly that Jude won't be able to breathe. Twice he will try to wrench himself away, and Willem will pin him to the ground and hold him there until he calms himself. Because they are in the closet, they won't know what time it is, only that there has been a day that has arrived and departed, because they will have seen flat carpets of sun unroll themselves into the closet's doorways from the bedroom, from the bathroom. He will listen to stories that are unimaginable, that are abominable; he will excuse himself, three times, to go to the bathroom and study his face in the mirror and remind himself that he has only to find the courage to listen, although he will want to cover his ears and cover Jude's mouth to make the stories cease. He will study the back of Jude's head, because Jude can't face him, and imagine the person he thinks he knows collapsing into rubble, clouds of dust gusting around him, as nearby, teams of artisans try to rebuild him in another material, in another shape, as a different person than the person who had stood for years and years. On and on and on the stories will go, and in their path will lie squalor: blood and bones and dirt and disease and misery. After Jude has finished telling him about his time with Brother Luke, Willem will ask him, again, if he enjoys having sex at all, even a little, even occasionally, and he will wait the many long minutes until Jude says he doesn't, that he hates it, that he always has, and he will nod, devastated, but relieved to have the real answer. And then he will ask him, not even knowing where the question has been hiding, if he's even attracted to men, and Jude will tell him, after a silence, that he's not certain, that he had always had sex with men, and so assumed he always would. "Are you interested in having sex with women?" he'll ask him, and he'll watch as, after another long silence, Jude shakes his head. "No," he'll say. "It's too late for me, Willem," and he will tell him it's not, that there are things they can do to help him, but Jude will shake his head again. "No," he'll say. "No, Willem, I've had enough. No more," and he will realize, as if slapped, the truth of this, and will stop. They will sleep again, and this time, his dreams will be terrible. He will dream he is one of the men in the motel rooms, he will realize that he has behaved like one of them; he will wake with nightmares, and it will be Jude who has to calm him. Finally they will heave themselves from the floor—it will be Saturday afternoon, and they will have been lying in the closet since Thursday night—and shower and eat something, something hot and comforting, and then they will go directly from the kitchen into the study, where he will listen as Jude leaves a message for Dr. Loehmann, whose card Willem has kept in his wallet all these years and produces, magician-like, within seconds, and from there to bed, and they will lie there, looking at each other, each afraid to ask the other: he to ask Jude to finish his story; Jude to ask him when he is leaving, because his leaving now seems an inevitability, a matter of logistics.

On and on they stare, until Jude's face becomes almost meaningless as a face to him: it is a series of colors, of planes, of shapes that have been arranged in such a way to give other people pleasure, but to give its owner nothing. He doesn't know what he is going to do. He is dizzy with what he has heard, with comprehending the enormity of his misconceptions, with stretching his understanding past what is imaginable, with the knowledge that all of his carefully maintained edifices are now destroyed beyond repair.

But for now, they are in their bed, in their room, in their apartment, and he reaches over and takes Jude's hand, holds it gently in his own.

"You've told me about how you got to Montana," he hears himself saying. "So tell me: What happened next?"

—

It was a time he rarely thought about, his flight to Philadelphia, because it was a period in which he had been so afloat from himself that even as he had lived his life, it had felt dreamlike and not quite real; there had been times in those weeks when he had opened his eyes and was genuinely unable to discern whether what had just happened had actually happened, or whether he had imagined it. It had been a useful skill, this persistent and unshatterable somnambulism, and it had protected him, but then that ability, like his ability to forget, had abandoned him as well and he was never to acquire it again.

He had first noticed this suspension at the home. At nights, he would sometimes be awakened by one of the counselors, and he would follow them down to the office where one of them was always on duty, and he would do whatever they wanted. After they were done, he would be escorted back to his room—a small space with a bunk bed that he shared with a mentally disabled boy, slow and fat and frightened-looking and prone to rages, whom he knew the counselors also sometimes took with them at night—and locked in again. There were a few of them the counselors used, but aside from his roommate, he didn't know who the other boys were, only that they existed. He was nearly mute in those sessions, and as he knelt or squatted or lay, he thought of a round clock face, its second hand gliding impassively around it, counting the revolutions until it ended. But he never begged, he never pled. He never bargained or made promises or cried. He didn't have the energy; he didn't have the conviction—not any longer, not anymore.

It was a few months after his weekend with the Learys that he tried to run away. He had classes at the community college on Mondays, Tuesdays, Wednesdays, and Fridays, and on those days, one of the counselors would wait for him in the parking lot and drive him back to the home. He dreaded the end of classes, he dreaded the ride home: he never knew which counselor would be waiting for him, and when he reached the parking lot and saw who it was, his footsteps would sometimes slow, but it was as if he was a magnet, something controlled by ions, not will, and into the car he would be drawn.

But one afternoon—this was in March, shortly before he turned fourteen—he had turned the corner and had seen the counselor, a man named Rodger who was the cruelest, the most demanding, the most vicious of them all, and he had stopped. For the first time in a long time, something in him resisted, and instead of continuing toward Rodger, he had crept backward down the hallway, and then, once he was certain he was safely out of sight, he had run.

He hadn't prepared for this, he had no plan, but some hidden, fiery part of him had, it seemed, been making observations as the rest of his mind sat cocooned in its thick, cottony slumber, and he found himself running toward the science lab, which was being renovated, and then under a curtain of blue plastic tarp that shielded one exposed side of the building, and then worming into the eighteen inches of space that separated the decaying interior wall from the new cement exterior that they were building around it. There was just enough room for him to wedge himself in, and he burrowed himself as deep into the space as he could, carefully working himself into a horizontal position, making sure his feet weren't visible.

As he lay there, he tried to decide what he could do next. Rodger would wait for him and then, when he didn't appear, they would eventually look for him. But if he could last here for the night, if he could wait until everything was silent around him, then he could escape. This was as far as he could think, although he was cognizant enough to realize that his chances were poor: he had no food, no money, and although it was only five in the afternoon, it was already very cold. He could feel his back and legs and palms, all the parts pressed against the stone, numbing themselves, could feel his nerves turning to thousands of pinpricks. But he could also feel, for the first time in months, his mind coming alert, could feel, for the first time in years, the giddy thrill of being able to make a decision, however poor or ill-conceived or unlikely. Suddenly, the pinpricks felt like not a punishment but a celebration, like hundreds of miniature fireworks exploding within him and for him, as if his body were reminding him of who he was and of what he still owned: himself.

He lasted two hours before the security guard's dog found him and he was dragged out by his feet, his palms scraping against the cement blocks he clung to even then, by this time so cold that he tripped as he walked, that his fingers were too iced to open the car door, and as soon as he was inside, Rodger had turned around and hit him in the face, and the blood from his nose was thick and hot and reassuring and the taste of it on his lips oddly nourishing, like soup, as if his body were something miraculous and self-healing, determined to save itself.

That evening they had taken him to the barn, where they sometimes took him at night, and beat him so badly that he had blacked out almost immediately after it had begun. He had been hospitalized that night, and then again a few weeks later, when the wounds had gotten infected. For those weeks, he had been left alone, and although they had been told at the hospital that he was a delinquent, that he was troubled, that he was a problem and a liar, the nurses were kind to him: there was one, an older woman, who had sat by his bed and held a glass of apple juice with a straw in it so he could sip from it without lifting his head (he'd had to lie on his side so they could clean his back and drain the wounds).

"I don't care what you did," she told him one night, after she had changed his bandages. "No one deserves this. Do you hear me, young man?"

Then help me, he wanted to say. *Please help me.* But he didn't. He was too ashamed.

She sat next to him again and put her hand on his forehead. "Try to behave yourself, all right?" she had said, but her voice had been gentle. "I don't want to see you back here."

Help me, he wanted to say again, as she left the room. *Please. Please.* But he couldn't. He never saw her again.

Later, as an adult, he would wonder if he had invented this nurse, if he had conjured her out of desperation, a simulacrum of kindness that was almost as good as the real thing. He would argue with himself: If she had existed, truly existed, wouldn't she have told someone about him? Wouldn't someone have been sent to help him? But his memories from this period were something slightly blur-edged and unreliable, and as the years went by, he was to come to realize that he was, always, trying to make his life, his childhood, into something more acceptable, something more normal. He would startle himself from a dream about the counselors, and would try to comfort himself: *There were only two of them who used you,* he would tell himself. *Maybe three. The others didn't. They weren't all cruel to you.* And then he would try, for days, to remember how many there had actually been: Was it two? Or was it three? For years, he couldn't understand why this was so important to him, why it mattered to him so much, why he was always trying to argue against his own memories, to spend so much time debating the details of what had happened. And then he realized that it was because he thought that if he could convince himself that it was less awful than he remembered, then he could also convince himself that he was less damaged, that he was closer to healthy, than he feared he was.

Finally he was sent back to the home, and the first time he had seen his back, he had recoiled, moving so quickly away from the bathroom mirror that he had slipped and fallen on a section of wet tile. In those initial weeks after the beating, when the scar tissue was still forming, it had made a puffed mound of flesh on his back, and at lunch he would sit alone and the older boys would whip damp pellets of napkin at it, trying to get them to ping off of it as against a target, cheering when they hit him. Until that point, he had never thought too specifically about his appearance. He knew he was ugly. He knew he was ruined. He knew he was diseased. But he had never considered himself grotesque. But now he was. There seemed to be an inevitability to this, to his life: that every year he would become worse—more disgusting, more depraved. Every year, his right to humanness diminished; every year, he became less and less of a person. But he didn't care any longer; he couldn't allow himself to.

It was difficult to live without caring, however, and he found himself curiously unable to forget Brother Luke's promise, that when he was sixteen, his old life would stop and his new life would begin. He knew, he did, that Brother Luke had been lying, but he couldn't stop thinking about it. Sixteen, he would think to himself at night. Sixteen. When I am sixteen, this will end.

He had asked Brother Luke, once, what their life would be like after he turned sixteen. "You'll go to college," Luke had said, immediately, and he had thrilled to this. He had asked where he would go, and Luke had named the college he had attended as well (although when he had gotten to that college after all, he had looked up Brother Luke—Edgar Wilmot—and had realized there was no record of him having ever attended the school, and he had been relieved, relieved to not have something in common with the brother, although it was he who had let him imagine that he might someday be there). "I'll move to Boston, too," Luke said. "And we'll be married, so we'll live in an apartment off campus." Sometimes they discussed this: the courses he would take, the things Brother Luke had done when he was at college, the places they would travel to after he graduated. "Maybe we'll have a son together one day," Luke said once, and he had stiffened, for he knew without Luke saying so that Luke would do to this phantom son of theirs what had been done to him, and he remembered thinking that that would never happen, that he would never let this ghost child, this child who didn't exist, ever exist, that he would never let another child be around Luke. He remembered thinking that he would protect this son of theirs, and for a brief, awful moment, he wished he would never turn sixteen at all, because he knew that once he did, Luke would need someone else, and that he couldn't let that happen.

But now Luke was dead. The phantom child was safe. He could safely turn sixteen. He could turn sixteen and be safe.

The months passed. His back healed. Now a security guard waited for him after his classes and walked him to the parking lot to wait for the counselor on duty. One day at the end of the fall semester, his math professor talked to him after class had ended: Had he thought about college yet? He could help him; he could help him get there—he could go somewhere excellent, somewhere top-flight. And oh, he wanted to go, he wanted to get away, he wanted to go to college. He was tugged, in those days, between trying to resign himself to the fact that his life would forever more be what it was, and the hope, small and stupid and stubborn as it was, that it could be something else. The balance—between resignation and hope—shifted by the day, by the hour, sometimes by the minute. He was always, always trying to decide how he should be—if his thoughts should be of acceptance or of escape. In that moment he had looked at his professor, but as he was about to answer—Yes; yes, help me—something stopped him. The professor had always been kind to him, but wasn't there something about that kindness that made him resemble Brother Luke? What if the professor's offer of help cost him? He argued with himself as the professor waited for his answer. One more time won't hurt you, said the desperate part of him, the part that wanted to leave, the part that was counting every day until sixteen, the part the other part of him jeered at. It's one more time. He's another client. Now is not the time to start getting proud.

But in the end, he had ignored that voice—he was so tired, he was so sore, he was so exhausted from being disappointed—and had shaken his head. "College isn't for me," he told the professor, his voice thin from the strain of lying. "Thank you. But I don't need your help."

"I think you're making a big mistake, Jude," said his professor, after a silence. "Promise me you'll reconsider?" and he had reached out and touched his arm, and he had jerked away, and the professor had looked at him, strangely, and he had turned and fled the room, the hallway blurring into planes of beige.

That night he was taken to the barn. The barn was no longer a working barn, but a place to store the shop class's and the auto repair class's projects—in the stalls were half-assembled carburetors, and hulls of half-repaired trucks, and half-sanded rocking chairs that the home sold for money. He was in the stall with the rocking chairs, and as one of the counselors seesawed into him, he left himself and flew above the stalls, to the rafters of the barn, where he paused, looking at the scene below him, the machinery and furniture like alien sculpture, the floor dusty with dirt and the stray pieces of hay, reminders of the barn's original life that they never seemed able to fully erase, at the two people making a strange eight-legged creature, one silent, one noisy and grunting and thrusting and alive. And then he was flying out of the round window cut high into the wall, and over the home, over its fields that were so beautiful and green and yellow with wild mustard in the summer, and now, in December, were still beautiful in their own way, a shimmering expanse of lunar white, the snow so fresh and new that no one had yet trampled it. He flew above this all, and across landscapes he had read about but had never seen, across mountains so clean that they made him feel clean just to contemplate them, over lakes as big as oceans, until he was floating above Boston, and circling down and down to that series of buildings that trimmed the side of the river, an expansive ring of structures punctuated by squares of green, where he would go and be remade, and where his life would begin, where he could pretend that everything that had come before had been someone else's life, or a series of mistakes, never to be discussed, never to be examined.

When he came back to himself, the counselor was on top of him, asleep. His name was Colin, and he was often drunk, as he was tonight, his hot yeasty breath puffing against his face. He was naked; Colin was wearing a sweater but nothing else, and for a while he lay there under

Colin's weight, breathing too, waiting for him to wake so he could be returned to his bedroom and cut himself.

And then, unthinkingly, almost as if he was a marionette, his limbs moving without thought, he was wriggling out from beneath Colin, quiet and quick, and hurrying his clothes back on, and then, again before he knew it, grabbing Colin's puffed coat from the hook on the inside of the stall and shrugging it on. Colin was much larger than he was, fatter and more muscular, but he was almost as tall, and it was less wieldy than it looked. And then he was grabbing Colin's jeans from the ground, and snatching out his wallet, and then the money within it—he didn't count how much it was, but he could tell by how thin a sheaf it was that it wasn't much—and shoving that into his own jeans pocket, and then he was running. He had always been a good runner, swift and silent and certain—watching him at the track, Brother Luke had always said he must be part Mohican—and now he ran out of the barn, its doors open to the sparkling, hushed night, looking about him as he left, and then, seeing no one, toward the field behind the home's dormitory.

It was half a mile from the dormitory to the road, and although he would normally have been in pain after what happened in the barn, that night he felt no pain, only elation, a sense of hyper-wakefulness that seemed to have been conjured particularly for this night, for this adventure. At the edge of the property he dropped to the ground and rolled carefully under the barbed wire, wrapping Colin's jacket sleeves around his hands and then holding the coils of wire above him so he could scoot beneath them. Once he was safely free, his elation only intensified, and he ran and ran in the direction he knew was east, toward Boston, away from the home, from the West, from everything. He knew he would eventually have to leave this road, which was narrow and mostly dirt, and move toward the highway, where he would be more exposed but also more anonymous, and he moved quickly down the hill that led toward the black dense woods that separated the road from the interstate. Running on grass was more difficult, but he did so anyway, keeping close to the edge of the forest so that if a car passed, he could duck within it and hide behind a tree.

As an adult, as a crippled adult, and then as a crippled adult who was truly crippled, as someone who could no longer even walk, as someone for whom running was a magic trick, as impossible as flying, he would look back on that night with awe: how fleet he had been, how fast, how tireless, how lucky. He would wonder how long he had run that night—at least two hours, he thought, maybe three—although at the time he hadn't thought about that at all, only that he needed to get as far as he could from the home. The sun began to appear in the sky, and he ran into the woods, which were the source of many of the younger boys' fears, and which were so crowded and lightless that even he was frightened, and he was not frightened in general by nature, but he had gone as deep into them as he could, both because he had to go through the woods to reach the interstate and because he knew that the deeper he hid within them, the less likely he was to be discovered, and finally he had chosen a large tree, one of the largest, as if its size offered some promise of reassurance, as if it would guard and protect him, and had tucked himself between its roots and slept.

When he woke it was dark again, although whether it was late afternoon or late evening or early morning he wasn't certain. He began moving his way through the trees again, humming to comfort himself and to announce himself to whatever might be waiting for him, to show them he was unafraid, and by the time he had been spat out by the woods on the other side, it was still dark, so he knew it was in fact nighttime, and he had slept all day, and that knowledge made him feel stronger and more energetic. *Sleep is more important than food*, he remonstrated himself, because he was very hungry, and then to his legs: *Move*. And he did, running again uphill toward the interstate.

He had realized at some point in the forest that there was only one way he would be able to get to Boston, and so he stood by the side of the road, and when the first truck stopped for him and he climbed aboard, he knew what he would have to do when the truck stopped, and he did it. He did it again and again and again; sometimes the drivers gave him food or money, and sometimes they didn't. They all had little nests they had made for themselves in the trailers of their trucks, and they lay there, and sometimes after it was over, they would drive him a little farther, and he would sleep, the world moving beneath him in a perpetual earthquake. At filling stations he would buy things to eat and would wait around, and eventually someone would choose him— someone always did—and he would climb into the truck.

"Where're you headed?" they would ask him.

"Boston," he would say. "My uncle's there."

Sometimes he felt the shame of what he was doing so intensely he wanted to vomit: he knew he would never be able to claim to himself that he had been coerced; he'd had sex with these men freely, he had let them do whatever they wanted, he had performed enthusiastically and well. And sometimes he was unsentimental: he was doing what he had to do. There was no other way. This was his skill, his one great skill, and he was using it to get somewhere better. He was using himself to save himself.

Sometimes the men would want him for longer and they would get a motel room, and he would imagine Brother Luke waiting in the bathroom for him. Sometimes they would talk to him—I have a son your age, they'd say; I have a daughter your age—and he would lie there and listen. Sometimes they would watch television until they were ready to go again. Some of them were cruel to him; some of them made him fear he would be killed, or hurt so badly he wouldn't be able to escape, and in those moments he would be terrified, and he would wish, desperately, for Brother Luke, for the monastery, for the nurse who had been so kind to him. But most of them were neither cruel nor kind. They were clients, and he was giving them what they wanted.

Years later, when he was able to review these weeks more objectively, he would be dumbstruck by how stupid he had been, by how small his oculus: Why hadn't he simply escaped? Why hadn't he taken the money he had earned and bought a bus ticket? He would try and try to remember how much he had earned, and although he knew it hadn't been much, he thought that it might have been enough for a ticket somewhere, *anywhere*, even if not Boston. But then, it simply hadn't occurred to him. It was as if the entire store of resourcefulness he had possessed, every piece of courage, had been spent on his flight from the home, and once on his own, he had simply let his life be dictated to him by others, following one man after the next, the way he had been taught to do. And of all the ways in which he changed himself as an adult, it would be this, this idea that he could create at least some part of his own future, that would be the most difficult lesson to learn, as well as the most rewarding.

Once there had been a man who had smelled so terribly and had been so sweatily large that he had almost changed his mind, but although the sex had been horrific, the man had been gentle with him afterward, had bought him a sandwich and a soda and had asked him real questions about himself and had listened carefully to his made-up answers. He had stayed with the man for two nights, and as he drove, the man had listened to bluegrass music and had sung along: he had had a lovely voice, low and clear, and he had taught him the words, and he had found himself singing along with this man, the road smooth beneath them. "God, you have a nice voice, Joey," the man had said, and he had—how weak he was, how pathetic!—allowed himself to be warmed by this comment, had gobbled up this affection as a rat would a piece of molding bread. On the second day, the man had asked him if he wanted to stay with him; they were in Ohio, and unfortunately he wasn't going any farther east, he was headed south now, but if he wanted to stay with him, he would be delighted, he would make sure he was taken care of. He had declined the man's offer, and the man had nodded, as if he had expected he would, and given him a fold of money and kissed him, the first of them who had. "Good luck to you, Joey," he said, and later, after the man had left, he had counted the money and realized it was more than he thought, it was more than he'd made in his previous ten days altogether. Later, when the next man was brutish, when he was violent and rough, he had wished he had gone with the other man: suddenly, Boston seemed less important than tenderness, than someone who would protect him and be good to him. He lamented his poor choices, how he seemed unable to appreciate the people who were actually decent to him: he thought again of Brother Luke, how Luke had never hit him or yelled at him; how he had never called him names.

Somewhere he had gotten sick, but he didn't know if it was from his time on the road or from the home. He made the men use condoms, but a few of them had said they would and then hadn't, and he had struggled and shouted but there had been nothing he could do. He knew, from past experience, that he would need a doctor. He stank; he was in so much pain he could barely walk. On the outskirts of Philadelphia he decided he'd take a break—he had to. He had torn a small hole in the sleeve of Colin's jacket and had rolled his money into a tube and shoved it inside and then closed the hole with a safety pin he had found in one of the motel rooms. He climbed out of the last truck, although at the time he hadn't known it would be the last truck; at the time he had thought: one more. One more and I'll make it to Boston. He hated that he had to stop now when he was so close, but he knew he needed help; he had waited as long as he could.

The driver had stopped at a filling station near Philadelphia—he didn't want to drive into the city. There, he made his slow way to the bathroom; he tried to clean himself. The illness made him tired; he had a fever. The last thing he remembered from that day—it had been late January, he thought; still cold, and now with a wet, stinging wind that seemed to slap against him—was walking to the edge of the gas station, where there had been a small tree, barren and unloved and alone, and sitting down against it, resting his back in Colin's now-filthy jacket against its spindly, unconvincing trunk, and shutting his eyes, hoping that if he slept for a while, he might feel at least a little stronger.

When he woke he knew he was in the backseat of a car, and the car was moving, and there was Schubert playing, and he allowed himself to be comforted by that, because it was something he knew, something familiar in such unfamiliarity, in a strange car being driven by a stranger, a stranger he was too weak to sit up and examine, through a strange landscape to an unknown destination. When he woke again he was in a room, a living room, and he looked around him: at the sofa he was on, the coffee table in front of it, two armchairs, a stone fireplace, all in shades of brown. He stood, still dizzy but less dizzy, and as he did, he noticed there was a man standing in a doorway, watching him, a man a little shorter than he, and thin, but with a sloping stomach and fertile, swelling hips. He had glasses that had black plastic bracketing their top half but were clear glass beneath, and a tonsure of hair trimmed very short and soft, like a mink's coat.

"Come to the kitchen and have something to eat," the man said in a quiet toneless voice, and he did, walking slowly after him and into a kitchen that, except for its tiles and walls, was also brown: brown table, brown cupboards, brown chairs. He sat in the chair at the foot of the table, and the man put a plate before him with a hamburger and a slide of fries, a glass filled with milk. "I normally don't get fast food," the man said, and looked at him.

He wasn't sure what to say. "Thank you," he said, and the man nodded. "Eat," he said, and he did, and the man sat at the head of the table and watched him. Normally this would have made him self-conscious, but he was too hungry to care this time.

When he was finished he sat back and thanked the man again, and the man nodded again, and there was a silence.

"You're a prostitute," the man said, and he flushed, and looked down at the table, at its shined brown wood.

"Yes," he admitted.

The man made a little noise, a little snuffle. "How long have you been a prostitute?" he asked, but he couldn't answer him and was silent. "Well?" the man asked. "Two years? Five years? Ten years? Your whole life?" He was impatient, or almost impatient, but his voice was soft, and he wasn't yelling.

"Five years," he said, and the man made the same small noise again.

"You have a venereal disease," the man said, "I can smell it on you," and he cringed, and bent his head, and nodded.

The man sighed. "Well," he said, "you're in luck, because I'm a doctor, and I happen to have some antibiotics in the house." He got up and padded over to one of the cupboards, and came back with an orange plastic bottle, and took out a pill. "Take this," he said, and he did. "Finish your milk," the man said, and he did, and then the man left the room and he waited until he came back. "Well?" the man said. "Follow me."

He did, his legs stringy beneath him, and followed the man to a door across from the living room, which the man unlocked and held open for him. He hesitated, and the man made an impatient clucking noise. "Go on," he said. "It's a bedroom," and he shut his eyes, weary, and then opened them again. He began preparing himself for the man to be cruel; the quiet ones always were.

When he reached the doorway, he saw that it led to a basement, and there was a set of wooden steps, steep like a ladder, that he would have to descend, and he paused once more, wary, and the man made his strange insect-like sound again and shoved him, not hard, against the small of his back, and he stumbled down the stairs.

He had been expecting a dungeon, slippery and leaking and dank, but it really was a bedroom, with a mattress made up with a blanket and sheets, and a blue circular rug beneath it, and lining the left-hand wall, bookcases of the same unfinished wood the staircase had been made from, with books on them. The space was bright-lit in that aggressive, relentless way he remembered from hospitals and police stations, and there was a small window, about the size of a dictionary, cut high into the far wall.

"I put out some clothes for you," the man said, and he saw that folded on the mattress was a shirt and a pair of sweatpants, and a towel and toothbrush as well. "The bathroom's there," the man said, pointing to the far right-hand corner of the room.

And then he began to leave. "Wait," he called after the man, and the man stopped his climb and looked at him, and he began, under the man's gaze, to unbutton his shirt. Something changed in the man's face, then, and he climbed another few steps. "You're sick," he said. "You have to get better first," and then he left the room, the door clicking shut after him.

He slept that night, both from lack of anything else to do and from exhaustion. The next morning he woke and smelled food, and he groaned to his feet and walked slowly up the stairs, where he found a plastic tray with a plate of eggs, poached, and two lengths of bacon, a roll, a glass of milk, a banana, and another of the white pills. He was too wobbly to bring it down without falling, so he sat there, on one of the unfinished wooden steps, and ate the food and swallowed the pill. After resting, he stood to open the door and take the tray to the kitchen, but the knob wouldn't turn because the door was locked. There was a small square cut into the bottom of the door, a cat door, he assumed, although he hadn't seen a cat, and he held back its curtain of rubber and poked his head out. "Hello?" he called. He realized he didn't know the man's name, which wasn't unusual—he never knew their names. "Sir? Hello?" But there was no answer, and he could tell from the way the house was silent that he was alone.

He should have felt panic, he should have felt fear, but he felt neither, only a crush of tiredness, and he left the tray at the top of the stairs and worked his way slowly down again, and then into bed, where he slept once more.

He dozed for that entire day, and when he woke, the man was standing above him again, watching him, and he sat up, abruptly. "Dinner," the man said, and he followed him upstairs, still in his borrowed clothes, which were too wide in the waist and too short in the sleeves and legs, because when he had looked for his own clothes, they were missing. My money, he thought, but he was too addled to think beyond that.

Once again he sat in the brown kitchen, and the man brought him his pill, and a plate with brown meat loaf, and a slop of mashed potatoes, and broccoli, and another plate for himself, and they began to eat in silence. Silence didn't make him nervous—usually, he was grateful for it—but this man's silence was closer to inwardness, the way a cat will be silent and watching, watching, watching so fixedly that you don't know what it sees, and then suddenly it will jump, and trap something beneath its paw.

"What kind of doctor are you?" he asked, tentatively, and the man looked at him.

"A psychiatrist," the doctor said. "Do you know what that is?"

"Yes," he said.

The man made his noise again. "Do you like being a prostitute?" he asked, and he felt, unaccountably, tears in his eyes, but then he blinked and they were gone.

"No," he said.

"Then why do you do it?" the man asked, and he shook his head. "Speak," the man said.

"I don't know," he said, and the man made a huffing noise. "It's what I know how to do," he said at last.

"Are you good at it?" the man asked, and once again, he felt that sting, and he was quiet for a long time.

"Yes," he said, and it was the worst admission he had ever made, the hardest word for him to say.

After they were done, the doctor escorted him once again to the door, and gave him the same little shove inside. "Wait," he said to the man, as he was closing the door. "My name's Joey," and when the man said nothing, only stared at him, "what's yours?"

The man kept looking at him, but now he was, he thought, almost smiling, or at least he was about to make some sort of expression. But then he didn't. "Dr. Traylor," the man said, and then pulled the door quickly shut behind him, as if that very information was a bird that might fly away if it too were not trapped inside with him.

The next day he felt less sore, less febrile. When he stood, though, he realized he was still weak, and he swayed and grabbed at the air and in the end, he didn't fall. He moved toward the bookshelves, examining the books, which were paperbacks, swollen and buckling from heat and moisture and smelling sweetly of mildew. He found a copy of *Emma*, which he had been reading in class at the college before he ran away, and carried the book slowly up the stairs with him, where he found the place he'd left off and read as he ate his breakfast and took his pill. This time there was a sandwich as well, wrapped in a paper towel, with the word "Lunch" written on the towel in small letters. After he had eaten, he went downstairs with the book and sandwich and lay in bed, and he was reminded of how much he had missed reading, of how grateful he was for this opportunity to leave behind his life.

He slept again; woke again. By evening, he was very tired, and some of the pain had returned, and when Dr. Traylor held open the door for him, it took him a long time to mount the stairs. At dinner, he didn't say anything, and neither did Dr. Traylor, but when he offered to help Dr. Traylor with the dishes or the cooking, Dr. Traylor had looked at him. "You're sick," he said.

"I'm better," he said. "I can help you in the kitchen if you want."

"No, I mean—you're sick," Dr. Traylor said. "You're diseased. I can't have a diseased person touching my food," and he had looked down, humiliated.

There was a silence. "Where are your parents?" Dr. Traylor asked, and he shook his head again. "*Speak*," Dr. Traylor said, and this time he was impatient, although he still hadn't raised his voice.

"I don't know," he stammered, "I never had any."

"How did you become a prostitute?" Dr. Traylor asked. "Did you start yourself, or did someone help you do it?"

He swallowed, feeling the food in his stomach turning to paste. "Someone helped me," he whispered.

There was a silence. "You don't like it when I call you a prostitute," the man said, and he managed, this time, to raise his head and look at him. "No," he said. "I understand," the man said. "But that *is* what you are, isn't it? Although I could call you something else, if you like: a whore, maybe." He was quiet again. "Is that better?"

"No," he whispered again.

"So," the man said, "a prostitute it is, then, right?" and looked at him, and finally, he nodded.

That night in the bedroom, he looked for something to cut himself with, but there was nothing sharp in the room, nothing at all; even the books had only soft bloated pages. So he pressed his fingernails into his calves as hard as he could, bent over and wincing from the effort and discomfort, and finally he was able to puncture the skin, and then work his nail back and forth in the cut to make it wider. He was only able to make three incisions in his right leg, and then he was too tired, and he fell asleep again.

The third morning he felt demonstrably better: stronger, more alert. He ate his breakfast and read his book, and then he moved the tray aside and stuck his head through the flapped cutout and tried and tried to fit his shoulders through it. But no matter what angle he tried, he was simply too large and the opening too small and at last he had to stop.

After he had rested, he poked his head through the hole again. He had a direct view of the living room to his left, and the kitchen area to his right, and he looked and looked as if for clues. The house was very tidy; he could tell from how tidy it was that Dr. Traylor lived alone. If he craned his neck, he could see, on the far left, a staircase leading to a second story, and just beyond that, the front door, but he couldn't see how many locks it had. Mainly, though, the house was defined by its silence: there was no ticking of clocks, no sound of cars or people outside. It could have been a house zooming through space, so quiet was it. The only noise was the refrigerator, purring its intermittent whir, but when it stopped, the silence was absolute.

But as featureless as the house was, he was also fascinated by it: it was only the third house he had ever been in. The second had been the Learys'. The first house had been a client's, a very important client, Brother Luke had told him, outside Salt Lake City, who had paid extra because he didn't want to come to the motel room. That house had been enormous, all sandstone and glass, and Brother Luke had come with him, and had secreted himself in the bathroom—a bathroom as big as one of their motel rooms—off the bedroom where he and the client had had sex. Later, as an adult, he would fetishize houses, especially his own house, although even before he had Greene Street, or Lantern House, or the flat in London, he would treat himself every few months to a magazine about homes, about people who spent their lives making pretty places even prettier, and he would turn the pages slowly, studying every picture. His friends laughed at him for this, but he didn't care: he dreamed of the day he'd have someplace of his own, with things that were absolutely his.

That night Dr. Traylor let him out again, and again it was the kitchen, and the meal, and the two of them eating in silence. "I feel better now," he ventured, and then, when Dr. Traylor didn't say anything, "if you want to do something." He was realistic enough to know that he wasn't going to be allowed to leave without repaying Dr. Traylor in some way; he was hopeful enough to think that he might be allowed to leave at all.

But Dr. Traylor shook his head. "You may feel better, but you're still diseased," he said. "The antibiotics take ten days to eliminate the infection." He took a fish bone, so fine it was transluscent, out of his mouth, placed it on the edge of his plate. "Don't tell me this is the first venereal disease you've ever had," he said, looking up at him, and he flushed again.

That night he thought about what to do. He was almost strong enough to run, he thought. At the next dinner, he would follow Dr. Traylor, and then when his back was turned, he would run to the door and outside and look for help. There were some problems with this plan—he still didn't have his clothes; he didn't have any shoes—but he knew that there was something wrong with this house, that there was something wrong with Dr. Traylor, that he had to get out.

He tried to conserve his energy the next day. He was too twitchy to read, and he had to keep himself from pacing the floor. He saved that day's sandwich and stuffed it into the pocket of the borrowed sweatpants so he would have something to eat if he had to hide for a long period. In the other pocket he shoved the plastic bag that lined the trash can in the bathroom—he thought he could tear it in half and make shoes for himself once he was safely out of Dr. Traylor's reach. And then he waited.

But that night he wasn't let out of the room at all. From his perch near the flap, he could see the living room lights turning on, he could smell food cooking. "Dr. Traylor?" he called. "Hello?" But there was silence except for the sound of meat frying in a pan, the evening's news on the television. "Dr. Traylor!" he called. "Please, please!" But nothing happened, and after calling and calling, he was spent, and slumped back down the stairs.

That night he had a dream that on the upper floor of the house was a series of other bedrooms, all with low beds and round tufted rugs beneath them, and that each bed held a boy: some of the boys were older, because they had been in the house for a long time, and some were younger. None of them knew that the others existed; none of them could hear one another. He realized that he didn't know the physical dimensions of the house, and in the dream the house became a sky-scraper, filled with hundreds of rooms, of cells, each containing a dif-ferent boy, each waiting for Dr. Traylor to let him out. He woke, then, gasping, and ran to the top of the stairs, but when he pushed against the flap, it didn't move. He lifted it up and saw that the hole had been closed with a piece of gray plastic, and as hard as he pushed against it, it wouldn't budge.

He didn't know what to do. He tried to stay up the rest of the night, but he fell asleep, and when he woke, there was the tray with his break-fast and his lunch and two pills: one for the morning, one for evening. He pinched the pills between his fingers and considered them—if he didn't take them, he wouldn't get better, and Dr. Traylor wouldn't touch him unless he was well. But if he didn't take them, then he wouldn't get better, and he knew from prior experience how awful he would feel, how almost unimaginably filthy he would be, as if his entire self, inside and out, had been sprayed with excrement. He began to rock himself, then. *What do I do*, he asked, *what do I do?* He thought of the fat truck driver, the one who had been kind to him. *Help me*, he begged him, *help me*.

Brother Luke, he pled, *help me, help me*.

Once again, he thought: I have made the wrong decision. I have left somewhere where I at least had the outdoors, and school, and where I knew what was going to happen to me. And now I have none of those things.

You're so stupid, the voice inside him said, *you're so stupid*.

For six more days it went on like this: his food would appear some-time when he was sleeping. He took the pills; he couldn't not.

On the tenth day, the door opened, and Dr. Traylor was standing there. He was so alarmed, so surprised, that he hadn't been prepared, but before he could stand, Dr. Traylor had closed the door and was coming toward him. Over one shoulder he held an iron fire poker, loosely, as one would a baseball bat, and as he came toward him, he was terrified by it: What did it mean? What would be done to him with it?

"Take off your clothes," Dr. Traylor said, still in his same bland voice, and he did, and Dr. Traylor swung the poker off his shoulder and he ducked, reflexively, lifting his arms over his head. He heard the doctor make his small wet noise. And then Dr. Traylor unbelted his pants and stood before him. "Take them down," he said, and he did, but before he was able to begin, Dr. Traylor nudged him in the neck with the poker. "You try anything," he said, "biting, *anything*, and I will beat you in the head with this until you become a vegetable, do you understand me?"

He nodded, too petrified to say anything. "*Speak*," Dr. Traylor yelled, and he startled.

"Yes," he gulped. "Yes, I understand."

He was scared of Dr. Traylor, of course; he was scared of all of them. But it had never occurred to him to fight with the clients, had never occurred to him to challenge them. They were powerful and he was not. And Brother Luke had trained him too well. He was too obedient. He was, as Dr. Traylor had made him admit, a good prostitute.

Every day was like this, and although the sex was no worse than what he'd had before, he remained convinced that it was a prelude, that it would eventually get very bad, very strange. He had heard stories from Brother Luke—he had seen videos—about things people did to one another: objects they used, props and weapons. A few times he had experienced these things himself. But he knew that in many ways he was lucky: he had been spared. The terror of what might be ahead of him was, in many ways, worse than the terror of the sex itself. At night he would imagine what he didn't know to imagine and begin gasping with panic, his clothes—a different set of clothes now, but still not his clothes—becoming clammy with perspiration.

At the end of one session, he asked Dr. Traylor if he could leave. "Please," he said. "Please." But Dr. Traylor said that he had given him ten days of hospitality, and that he needed to repay those ten days. "And then can I go?" he asked, but the doctor was already walking out the door.

On the sixth day of his repayment he thought of a plan. There was a second or two—just that—in which Dr. Traylor tucked the fire poker under his left arm and unbelted his pants with his right hand. If he could time it correctly, he could hit the doctor in the face with a book, and try to run out. He would have to be very quick; he would have to be very agile.

He scanned the books on their shelves, wishing yet again that some of them were hardcovers, not these thick bricks of paperbacks. A small one, he knew, would feel more like a slap, would be more wieldy, and so finally he chose a copy of *Dubliners*: it was thin enough for him to grip, pliable enough to crack against a face. He tucked it under his mattress, and then realized he didn't even need to bother with the deception; he could just leave it by his side. So he did, and waited.

And then there was Dr. Traylor and the fire poker, and as he began to unbelt his pants, he sprang up and smacked the doctor as hard as he could across his face, and he heard and felt the doctor screaming and the fire poker falling to the cement floor with a clang, and the doctor's hand grabbing at his ankle, but he kicked away and stumbled up the stairs, tugged open the door, and ran. At the front door he saw a mess of locks, and he nearly sobbed, his fingers clumsy, throwing the bolts this way and that, and then he was outside and running, running faster than he ever had. *You can do it, you can do it,* screamed the voice in his head, encouraging for once, and then, more urgently, *Faster, faster, faster.* As he had gotten better, Dr. Traylor's meals for him had gotten smaller and smaller, which meant that he was always weak, always tired, but now he was vividly alert and he was running, shouting for help as he did. But even as he ran and shouted, he could see that no one would hear his calls: there was no other house in sight, and although he had expected there might be trees, there weren't, just flat blank stretches of land, with nothing to hide behind. And then he felt how cold it was, and how things were embedding themselves into the soles of his feet, but still he ran.

And then behind him he heard another pair of footsteps slapping against the pavement, and a familiar jangling noise, and he knew it was Dr. Traylor. He didn't even shout at him, he didn't even threaten, but as he turned his head to see how close the doctor was—and he was very close, just a few yards behind him—he tripped and fell, his cheek banging against the road.

After he had fallen, all of his energy deserted him, a flock of birds rising noisily and swiftly flying away, and he saw that the jangling noise was Dr. Traylor's unbuckled belt, which he was sliding out from his pants and then using to beat him, and he huddled into himself as he was hit and hit and hit. All that time, the doctor said nothing, and all he could hear were Dr. Traylor's breaths, his gasps from exertion as he brought the belt down harder and harder on his back, his legs, his neck.

Back at the house, the beating continued, and over the next days, the next weeks, he was beat more. Not regularly—he never knew when it might happen next—but often enough so that coupled with his lack of food, he was always dizzy, he was always weak: he felt he would never have the strength to run again. As he feared, the sex also got worse, and he was made to do things that he was never able to talk about, not to anyone, not even to himself, and again, although it wasn't always terrifying, it was often enough so that he lived in a constant half daze of fear, so that he knew that he would die in Dr. Traylor's house. One night he had a dream of himself as a man, a real adult, but he was still in the basement and waiting for Dr. Traylor, and he knew in the dream that something had happened to him, that he had lost his mind, that he was like his roommate in the home, and he woke and prayed that he might die soon. During the daytime, as he slept, he dreamed of Brother Luke, and when he woke from those dreams he realized how much Luke had always protected him, how well he had treated him, how kind he had been to him. He had limped to the top of the wooden staircase then, and thrown himself down it, and then had pulled himself up and had done it again.

And then one day (Three months later? Four? Later, Ana would tell him that Dr. Traylor had said it was twelve weeks after he had found him at the gas station), Dr. Traylor said, "I'm tired of you. You're dirty and you disgust me and I want you to leave."

He couldn't believe it. But then he remembered to speak. "Okay," he said, "okay. I'll leave now."

"No," said Dr. Traylor, "you'll leave how I want you to leave."

For several days, nothing happened, and he assumed that this too had been a lie, and he was grateful that he hadn't gotten too excited, that he was finally able to recognize a lie when he was told it. Dr. Traylor had begun to serve him his meals on a fold of the day's newspaper, and one day he looked at the date and realized it was his birthday. "I am fifteen," he announced to the quiet room, and hearing himself say those words—the hopes, the fantasies, the impossibilities that only he knew lay behind them—he was sick. But he didn't cry: his ability to not cry was his only accomplishment, the only thing he could take pride in.

And then one night Dr. Traylor came downstairs with his fire poker. "Get up," he said, and jabbed him in the back with the poker as he fumblingly climbed the stairs, falling to his knees and getting up again and tripping again and standing again. He was prodded all the way to the front door, which was ajar, just slightly, and then outside, into the night. It was still cold, and still wet, but even through his fear he could recognize that the weather was changing, that even as time had suspended itself for him, it had not for the rest of the world, in which the seasons had marched on uncaringly; he could smell the air turning green. Next to him was a bare bush with a black branch, but at its very tip it was sprouting buboes of pale lilac, and he stared at it frantically, trying to seize a picture of it and hold it in his mind, before he was poked forward.

At the car Dr. Traylor held open the trunk and jabbed him again with the fire poker, and he could hear himself making sounds like sobs, but he wasn't crying, and he climbed inside, although he was so weak that Dr. Traylor had to help him, pinching the sleeve of his shirt between his fingers so he wouldn't have to actually touch him.

They drove. The trunk was clean and large, and he rolled about in it, feeling them go around corners and up hills and down hills, and then along long stretches of plain, even road. And then the car swerved left and he was being bounced along some uneven surface and then the car stopped.

For a while, three minutes—he counted—nothing happened, and he listened and listened but he could hear nothing, just his own breaths, his own heart.

The trunk opened, and Dr. Traylor helped him out, plucking his shirt, and shoved him to the front of the car with the fire poker. "Stay there," he said, and he did, shivering, watching the doctor get back into the car, roll down the window, lean out at him. "Run," the doctor said, and when he stood there, frozen, "you like running so much, right? So run." And Dr. Traylor started the engine and finally, he woke and ran.

They were in a field, a large barren square of dirt where there would in a few weeks be grass but now there was nothing, just patches of shallow ice that broke under his bare feet like pottery, and small white pebbles that glowed like stars. The field dipped in the middle, just slightly, and on his right was the road. He couldn't see how big the road was, only that there was one, but there were no cars passing. To his left the field was fenced with wire, but it was farther away, and he couldn't see what lay beyond the wire.

He ran, the car just behind him. At first it actually felt good to be running, to be outdoors, to be away from that house: even this, the ice under his feet like glass, the wind smacking against his face, the tap of the fender as it nudged against the back of his legs, even all this was better than that house, that room with its cinder-block walls and window so small it was no window at all.

He ran. Dr. Traylor followed him, and sometimes he would accelerate, and he would run faster. But he couldn't run like he used to run, and he fell, and fell again. Each time he fell, the car would slow, and Dr. Traylor would call out—not angrily, not even loudly—"Get up. Get up and run; get up and run or we're going back to the house," and he would make himself stand and run again.

He ran. He didn't know then that this was the last time in his life that he would ever run, and much later he would wonder: If I had known that, would I have been able to run faster? But of course it was an impossible question, a non-question, an axiom with no solution. He fell again and again, and on the twelfth time, he was moving his mouth, trying to say something, but nothing would come out. "Get up," he heard the man say. "Get up. The next time you fall will be the last," and he got up again.

By this time he was no longer running, he was walking and stumbling, he was crawling from the car and the car was bumping against him harder and harder. Make this stop, he thought, make this stop. He remembered—who had told him this? one of the brothers, but which one?—a story of a piteous little boy, a boy, he had been told, in much worse circumstances than he was in, who after being so good for so long (another way in which he and the boy had been different), prayed one night to God to take him: I'm ready, the boy said in the story, I'm ready, and an angel, terrible and golden-winged, with eyes that burned with fire, appeared and wrapped his wings around the boy and the boy turned to cinders and was gone, released from this world.

I'm ready, he said, I'm ready, and he waited for the angel with his awful, fearsome beauty to come save him.

The last time he fell, he couldn't get up again. "Get up!" he heard Dr. Traylor yell. "Get up!" But he couldn't. And then he heard the engine start again, and he felt the headlights coming toward him, two streams of fire like the angel's eyes, and he turned his head to the side and waited, and the car came toward him and then over him and it was done.

And that was the end. After that, he became an adult. As he lay in the hospital, Ana sitting by his side, he made promises to himself. He evaluated the mistakes he had made. He never had known whom to trust: he had followed anyone who had shown him any kindness. After, though, he decided that he would change this. No longer would he trust people so quickly. No longer would he have sex. No longer would he expect to be saved.

"It'll never be this bad," Ana used to say to him in the hospital. "Things'll never be this bad again," and although he knew she meant the pain, he also liked to think she meant his life in general: that with every year, things would get better. And she had been right: things did get better. And Brother Luke had been right as well, because when he was sixteen, his life changed. A year after Dr. Traylor, he was in the college he had dreamed of; with every day he didn't have sex, he was becoming cleaner and cleaner. His life became more improbable by the year. Every year, his own good fortunes multiplied and intensified, and he was astonished again and again by the things and generosities that were bequeathed to him, by the people who entered his life, people so different from the people he had known that they seemed to be another species altogether: How, after all, could Dr. Traylor and Willem both be named the same sort of being? How could Father Gabriel and Andy? How could Brother Luke and Harold? Did what existed in the first group also exist in the second, and if so, how had that second group chosen otherwise, how had they chosen what to become? Things had not just corrected themselves; they had reversed themselves, to an almost absurd degree. He had gone from nothing to an embarrassing bounty. He would remember, then, Harold's claim that life compensated for its losses, and he would realize the truth of that, although sometimes it would seem like life had not just compensated for itself but had done so extravagantly, as if his very life was begging him to forgive it, as if it were piling riches upon him, smothering him in all things beautiful and wonderful and hoped-for so he wouldn't resent it, so he would allow it to keep moving him forward. And so, as the years went by, he broke his promises to himself again and again. He *did* end up following people who were kind to him. He *did* trust people again. He *did* have sex again. He *did* hope to be saved. And he was right to do so: not every time, of course, but most of the time. He ignored what the past had taught him and more often than he should have been, he was rewarded for it. He regretted none of it, not even the sex, because he had had it with hope, and to make someone else happy, someone who had given him everything.

One night shortly after he and Willem had become a couple, they had been at a dinner party at Richard's, a raucous, casual affair of just people they loved and people they liked—JB and Malcolm and Black Henry Young and Asian Henry Young and Phaedra and Ali and all of their boyfriends and girlfriends, their husbands and wives. He was in the kitchen helping Richard prepare dessert, and JB came in—he was a little drunk—and put his arm around his neck and kissed him on the cheek. "Well, Judy," he said, "you really ended up with it all in the end, didn't you? The career, the money, the apartment, the man. How'd you get so lucky?" JB had grinned at him, and he had grinned back. He was glad Willem wasn't there to overhear that comment, because he knew Willem would get testy at what he saw as JB's jealousy, at his conviction that everyone else had, and had had, life easier than he did, that he, Jude, was blessed in a way that no one else was.

But he didn't see it like this. He knew it was in part JB's way of being ironic, of congratulating him for fortune that they both knew was, yes, excessive but also deeply appreciated. And if he was to be honest, he was also flattered by JB's jealousy: to JB, he wasn't a cripple who was being cosmically repaid for a lousy run; he was JB's equal, someone in whom JB saw only the things to envy and never the things to pity. And besides, JB was right: How *did* he get so lucky? How *did* he end up with everything he had? He was never to know; he was always to wonder.

"I don't know, JB," he said, handing him the first slice of cake and smiling at him, as from the dining room, he could hear Willem's voice saying something, and then a blast of laughter from everyone else, a sound of pure delight. "But you know, I've been lucky all my life."

3

THE WOMAN'S NAME is Claudine and she is a friend of a friend of an acquaintance, a jewelry designer, which is something of a deviation for him, as he usually only sleeps with people in the industry, who are more accustomed to, more forgiving of, temporary arrangements.

She is thirty-three, with long dark hair that lightens at its tips, and very small hands, hands like a child's, on which she wears rings that she has made, dark with gold and glinting with stones; before they have sex, she takes them off last, as if these rings, not her underwear, are what conceal the most private parts of her.

They have been sleeping together—not seeing each other, because he sees no one—for almost two months, which again is a deviation for him, and he knows he will have to end it soon. He had told her when they had begun that it was only sex, that he was in love with someone else, and that he couldn't spend the night, not ever, and she had seemed fine with that; she had said she was fine with it, anyway, and that she was in love with someone else herself. But he has seen no evidence of another man in her apartment, and whenever he texts, she is always available. Another warning sign: he will have to end it.

Now he kisses her on her forehead, sits up. "I have to go," he says.

"No," she says. "Stay. Just a little longer."

"I can't," he says.

"Five minutes," she says.

"Five," he agrees, and lies back down. But after five minutes he kisses her again on the side of the face. "I really do have to go," he tells her, and she makes a noise, one of protest and resignation, and turns over onto her side.

He goes to her bathroom, showers and rinses out his mouth, comes back and kisses her again. "I'll text you," he says, disgusted by how he has been reduced to a vocabulary consisting almost entirely of clichés. "Thank you for letting me come over."

At home, he walks silently through the darkened apartment, and in the bedroom he takes off his clothes, gets into bed with a groan, rolls over and wraps his arms around Jude, who wakes and turns to him. "Willem," he says, "you're home," and Willem kisses him to cover the guilt and sorrow he always feels when he hears the relief and happiness in Jude's voice.

"Of course," he says. He always comes home; he has never not. "I'm sorry it's so late."

It is a hot night, humid and still, and yet he presses against Jude as if he is trying to warm himself, threading their legs together. Tomorrow, he tells himself, he will end it with Claudine.

They have never discussed it, but he knows Jude knows he is having sex with other people. He has even given Willem his permission. This was after that terrible Thanksgiving, when after years of obfuscation, Jude was revealed to him completely, the shreds of cloud that had always obscured him from view abruptly wiped away. For many days, he hadn't known what to do (other than run back into therapy himself; he had called his shrink the day after Jude had made his first appointment with Dr. Loehmann), and whenever he looked at Jude, scraps of his narrative would return to him, and he would study him covertly, wondering how he had gotten from where he had been to where he was, wondering how he had become the person he had when everything in his life had argued that he shouldn't be. The awe he had felt for him, then, the despair and horror, was something one felt for idols, not for other humans, at least no other humans he knew.

"I know how you feel, Willem," Andy had said in one of their secret conversations, "but he doesn't want you to admire him; he wants you to see him as he is. He wants you to tell him that his life, as inconceivable as it is, is still a life." He paused. "Do you know what I mean?"

"I do know," he said.

In the first bleary days after Jude's story, he could feel Jude being very quiet around him, as if he was trying not to call attention to himself, as if he didn't want to remind Willem of what he now knew. One night a week or so later, they were eating a muted dinner at the apartment, and Jude had said, softly, "You can't even look at me anymore." He had looked up then and had seen his pale, frightened face, and had dragged his chair close to Jude's and sat there, looking at him.

"I'm sorry," he murmured. "I'm afraid I'm going to say something stupid."

"Willem," Jude said, and was quiet. "I think I turned out pretty normal, all things considered, don't you?" and Willem had heard the strain, and the hope, in his voice.

"No," he said, and Jude winced. "I think you turned out extraordinary, all things considered or not," and finally, Jude smiled.

That night, they had discussed what they were going to do. "I'm afraid you're stuck with me," he began, and when he saw how relieved Jude was, he cursed himself for not making it clearer earlier that he was going to stay. Then he gathered himself and they talked about physical matters: how far he could go, what Jude didn't want to do.

"We can do whatever you want, Willem," Jude said.

"But you don't like it," he'd said.

"But I owe it to you," Jude had said.

"No," he told him. "It shouldn't feel like something you owe me; and besides, you don't owe it to me." He stopped. "If it's not arousing for you, it's not for me, either," he added, although, to his shame, he *did* still want to have sex with Jude. He wouldn't, not anymore, not if Jude didn't want to, but it didn't mean he would be able to suddenly stop craving it.

"But you've sacrificed so much to be with me," Jude said after a silence.

"Like what?" he asked, curious.

"Normalcy," Jude said. "Social acceptability. Ease of life. Coffee, even. I can't add sex to that list."

They had talked and talked, and he had finally managed to convince him, had managed to get Jude to define what he actually liked. (It hadn't been much.) "But what are you going to do?" Jude asked him.

"Oh, I'll be fine," he said, not really knowing himself.

"You know, Willem," Jude had said, "you should obviously sleep with whomever you want. I just"—he fumbled—"I know this is selfish, but I just don't want to hear about it."

"It's not selfish," he said, reaching across the bed for him. "And I wouldn't do that, not ever."

That was eight months ago, and in those eight months, things had gotten better: not, Willem thought, his former version of better, in which he pretended everything was fine and ignored all inconvenient evidence or suspicions that suggested otherwise, but actually better. He could tell Jude really was more relaxed: he was less inhibited physically, he was more affectionate, and he was both of those things because he knew that Willem had released him from what he thought were his obligations. He was cutting himself far less frequently. Now he didn't need Harold or Andy to confirm for him that Jude was better: now he knew it to be true. The only difficulty was that he did still desire Jude, and at times he had to remind himself not to go any further, that he was getting close to the boundaries of what Jude could tolerate, and he would make himself stop. In those moments he would be angry, not at Jude or even at himself—he had never felt guilty about wanting to have sex, and he didn't feel guilty about wanting to have it now—but at life, at how it had conspired to make Jude afraid of something that he had always associated with nothing but pleasure.

He was careful about who he chose to sleep with: he picked people (women, really: they had almost all been women) who he either sensed or knew, from previous experience, were truly only interested in him for sex and were going to be discreet. Often, they were confused, and he didn't blame them. "Aren't you in a relationship with a man?" they would ask, and he would tell them that he was, but that they had an open relationship. "So are you not really gay?" they would ask, and he would say, "No, not fundamentally." The younger women were more accepting of this: they'd had boyfriends (or had boyfriends) who had slept with other men as well; they had slept with other women. "Oh," they'd say, and that would usually be it—if they had other concerns, other questions, they didn't ask. These younger women—actresses, makeup assistants, costume assistants—also didn't want a relationship with him; often, they didn't want a relationship at all. Sometimes the women asked him questions about Jude—how they had met, what he was like—and he answered them, and felt wistful, and missed him.

But he was vigilant about not letting this life intrude on his life at home. Once there had been a blind item in a gossip column— forwarded to him by Kit—that was clearly about him, and after debating whether to say something to Jude or not, he had in the end decided not to; Jude would never see the story, and there was no reason to make what Jude knew was happening in theory something he was forced to confront in reality.

JB, however, *had* seen the item (he supposed other people he knew had seen it as well, but JB was the only one to actually mention it to him), and had asked him if it was true. "I didn't know you guys had an open relationship," he said, more curious than accusatory.

"Oh yeah," he said, casually. "Right from the start."

It saddened him, of course, that his sex life and his home life should have to be two distinct realms, but he was old enough now to know that within every relationship was something unfulfilled and disappointing, something that had to be sought elsewhere. His friend Roman, for example, was married to a woman who, while beautiful and loyal, was famously unintelligent: she didn't understand the films Roman was in, and when you talked to her, you found yourself consciously recalibrating the velocity and complexity and content of your conversation, because she so often looked confused when the talk turned to politics, or finance, or literature, or art, or food, or architecture, or the environment. He knew that Roman was aware of this deficiency, in both Lisa and in his relationship. "Ah, well," he had once said to Willem, unprompted, "if I want good conversation, I can talk to my friends, right?" Roman had been among the first of his friends to get married, and at the time, he had been fascinated by and disbelieving of his choice. But now he knew: you always sacrificed something. The question was what you sacrificed. He knew that to some people—JB; Roman, probably—his own sacrifice would be unthinkable. It would have been once to him as well.

He thought frequently these days of a play he had done in graduate school, by a beetley, plodding woman in the playwriting division who had gone on to have great success as a writer of spy movies but who in graduate school had tried to write Pinteresque dramas about unhappy married couples. *If This Were a Movie* was about an unhappy married couple—he was a professor of classical music; she was a librettist—who lived in New York. Because the couple was in their forties (at the time, a gray-colored land, impossibly far and unimaginably grim), they were devoid of humor and in a constant state of yearning for their younger selves, back when life had actually seemed so full of promise and hope, back when they had been romantic, back when life itself had been a romance. He had played the husband, and while he had long ago realized that it had been, really, an awful play (it had included lines like "This isn't *Tosca*, you know! This is *life*!"), he had never forgotten the final monologue he had delivered in the second act, when the wife announces that she wants to leave, that she doesn't feel fulfilled in their marriage, that she's convinced that someone better awaits her:

> SETH: But don't you understand, Amy? You're wrong.
> Relationships never provide you with *everything*. They provide
> you with *some* things. You take all the things you want from
> a person—sexual chemistry, let's say, or good conversation, or
> financial support, or intellectual compatibility, or niceness,
> or loyalty—and you get to pick three of those things. *Three—*
> that's it. Maybe four, if you're very lucky. The rest you have
> to look for elsewhere. It's only in the movies that you find
> someone who gives you all of those things. But this isn't the
> movies. In the real world, you have to identify which three
> qualities you want to spend the rest of your life with, and then
> you look for those qualities in another person. That's real life.
> Don't you see it's a trap? If you keep trying to find everything,
> you'll wind up with nothing.
> AMY: [crying] So what did you pick?
> SETH: I don't know. [beat] I don't know.

At the time, he hadn't believed these words, because at the time, everything really did seem possible: he was twenty-three, and everyone was young and attractive and smart and glamorous. Everyone thought they would be friends for decades, forever. But for most people, of course, that hadn't happened. As you got older, you realized that the qualities you valued in the people you slept with or dated weren't necessarily the ones you wanted to live with, or be with, or plod through your days with. If you were smart, and if you were lucky, you learned this and accepted this. You figured out what was most important to you and you looked for it, and you learned to be realistic. They all chose differently: Roman had chosen beauty, sweetness, pliability; Malcolm, he thought, had chosen reliability, and competence (Sophie was intimidatingly efficient), and aesthetic compatibility. And he? He had chosen friendship. Conversation. Kindness. Intelligence. When he was in his thirties, he had looked at certain people's relationships and asked the question that had (and continued to) fuel countless dinner-party conversations: What's going on there? Now, though, as an almost-forty-eight-year-old, he saw people's relationships as reflections of their keenest yet most inarticulable desires, their hopes and insecurities taking shape physically, in the form of another person. Now he looked at couples—in restaurants, on the street, at parties—and wondered: Why are you together? What did you identify as essential to you? What's missing in you that you want someone else to provide? He now viewed a successful relationship as one in which both people had recognized the best of what the other person had to offer and had chosen to value it as well.

And perhaps not coincidentally, he also found himself doubting therapy—its promises, its premises—for the first time. He had never before questioned that therapy was, at worst, a benign treatment: when he was younger, he had even considered it a form of luxury, this right to speak about his life, essentially uninterrupted, for fifty minutes proof that he had somehow become someone whose life deserved such lengthy consideration, such an indulgent listener. But now, he was conscious of his own impatience with what he had begun to see as the sinister pedantry of therapy, its suggestion that life was somehow reparable, that there existed a societal norm and that the patient was being guided toward conforming to it.

"You seem to be holding back, Willem," said Idriss—his shrink now for years—and he was quiet. Therapy, therapists, promised a rigorous lack of judgment (but wasn't that an impossibility, to talk to a person and not be judged?), and yet behind every question was a nudge, one that pushed you gently but inexorably toward a recognition of some flaw, toward solving a problem you hadn't known existed. Over the years, he'd had friends who had been convinced that their childhoods were happy, that their parents were basically loving, until therapy had awakened them to the fact that they had not been, that they were not. He didn't want that to happen to him; he didn't want to be told that his contentment wasn't contentment after all but delusion.

"And how do you feel about the fact that Jude doesn't ever want to have sex?" Idriss had asked.

"I don't know," he'd said. But he did know, and he said it: "I wish he wanted to, for his sake. I feel sad that he's missing one of life's greatest experiences. But I think he's earned the right not to." Across from him, Idriss was silent. The truth was, he didn't want Idriss to try to diagnose what was wrong with his relationship. He didn't want to be told how to repair it. He didn't want to try to make Jude, or himself, do something neither of them wanted to because they were supposed to. Their relationship was, he felt, singular but workable: he didn't want to be taught otherwise. He sometimes wondered if it was simple lack of creativity—his and Jude's—that had made them both think that their relationship had to include sex at all. But it had seemed, then, the only way to express a deeper level of feeling. The word "friend" was so vague, so undescriptive and unsatisfying—how could he use the same term to describe what Jude was to him that he used for India or the Henry Youngs? And so they had chosen another, more familiar form of relationship, one that hadn't worked. But now they were inventing their own type of relationship, one that wasn't officially recognized by history or immortalized in poetry or song, but which felt truer and less constraining.

He didn't, however, mention his growing skepticism about therapy to Jude, because some part of him did still believe in it for people who were truly ill, and Jude—he was finally able to admit to himself—was truly ill. He knew that Jude hated going to the therapist; after the first few sessions he had come home so quiet, so withdrawn, that Willem had to remind himself that he was making Jude go for his own good.

Finally he couldn't stand it any longer. "How's it been with Dr. Loehmann?" he asked one night about a month after Jude had begun.

Jude sighed. "Willem," he said, "how much longer do you want me to go?"

"I don't know," he said. "I hadn't really thought about it."

Jude had studied him. "So you were thinking I'd go forever," he said.

"Well," he said. (He actually had been thinking that.) "Is it really so awful?" He paused. "Is it Loehmann? Should we get you someone else?"

"No, it's not Loehmann," Jude said. "It's the process itself."

He sighed, too. "Look," he said. "I know this is hard for you. I know it is. But—give it a year, Jude, okay? A year. And try hard. And then we'll see." Jude had promised.

And then in the spring he had been away, filming, and he and Jude had been talking one night when Jude said, "Willem, in the interest of full disclosure, I have something I have to tell you."

"Okay," he said, gripping the phone tighter. He had been in London, shooting *Henry & Edith*. He was playing—twelve years too early and sixty pounds too thin, Kit pointed out, but who was counting?—Henry James, at the beginning of his friendship with Edith Wharton. The film was actually something of a road-trip movie, shot mostly in France and southern England, and he was working his way through his final scenes.

"I'm not proud of this," he heard Jude say. "But I've missed my last four sessions with Dr. Loehmann. Or rather—I've been going, but not going."

"What do you mean?" he asked.

"Well, I go," Jude said, "but then—then I sit outside in the car and read through the session, and then when the session's over, I drive back to the office."

He was quiet, and so was Jude, and then they both started laughing. "What're you reading?" he asked when he could finally speak again.

"*On Narcissism*," Jude admitted, and they both started laughing again, so hard that Willem had to sit down.

"Jude—" he began at last, and Jude interrupted him. "I know, Willem," he said, "I know. I'll go back. It was stupid. I just couldn't bring myself to go in these past few times; I'm not sure why."

When he hung up, he was still smiling, and when he heard Idriss's voice in his head—"And Willem, what do you think about the fact that Jude isn't going when he said he would?"—he waved his hand before his face, as if fanning the words away. Jude's lying; his own self-deceptions—both, he realized, were forms of self-protection, practiced since childhood, habits that had helped them make the world into something more digestible than it sometimes was. But now Jude was trying to lie less, and he was trying to accept that there were certain things that would never conform to his idea of how life should be, no matter how intensely he hoped or pretended they might. And so really, he knew that therapy would be of limited use to Jude. He knew Jude would keep cutting himself. He knew he would never be able to cure him. The person he loved was sick, and would always be sick, and his responsibility was not to make him better but to make him less sick.

He was never to make Idriss understand this shift in perspective; some-times, he could hardly understand it himself.

That night he'd had a woman over, the deputy production designer, and as they lay there, he answered all the same questions: he explained how he had met Jude; he explained who he was, or at least the version of who he was that he had created for answers such as these.

"This is a lovely space," said Isabel, and he glanced at her, a little suspiciously; JB, upon seeing the flat, had said it looked like it had been raped by the Grand Bazaar, and Isabel, he had heard the director of photography proclaim, had excellent taste. "Really," she said, seeing his face. "It's pretty."

"Thanks," he said. He owned the flat—he and Jude. They had bought it only two months ago, when it had become evident that both of them would be doing more work in London. He had been in charge of finding something, and because it had been his responsibility, he had deliberately chosen quiet, deeply dull Marylebone—not for its sober prettiness or convenience but because of the neighborhood's surplus of doctors. "Ah," Jude had said, studying the directory of the building's tenants as they waited for the estate agent to show them the apartment Willem had settled on, "look at what's downstairs from the unit: an orthopedic surgeon's clinic." He looked at Willem, raised an eyebrow. "That's an interesting coincidence, isn't it?"

He had smiled. "Isn't it?" he asked. But beneath their joking was something that neither of them had been able to discuss, not just in their relationship but almost in their friendship as a whole—that at some point, they didn't know when but that it would happen, Jude would get worse. What that might mean, specifically, Willem wasn't certain, but as part of his new dedication to honesty, he was trying to prepare himself, themselves, for a future he couldn't predict, for a future in which Jude might not be able to walk, might not be able to stand. And so finally, the fourth-floor Harley Street space had been the only possible option; of all the flats he had seen, this had been the one that had best approximated Greene Street: a single-story apartment with large doors and wide hallways, big square rooms, and bathrooms that could be converted to accommodate a wheelchair (the downstairs orthopedist's office had been the final, unignorable argument that this apartment should be theirs). They bought the flat; he had moved into it all the rugs and lamps and blankets that he had spent his working life accumulating and that had been packed in boxes in the Greene Street basement; and before he returned to New York after the shoot ended, one of Malcolm's young former associates who had moved back to London to work in Bellcast's satellite office would begin renovating it.

Oh, he thought whenever he looked at the plans for Harley Street, it was so difficult, it was so sad sometimes, living in reality. He had been reminded of this the last time he had met with the architect, when he had asked Vikram why they weren't retaining the old wood-framed windows in the kitchen that overlooked the brick patio, with its views of the rooftops of Weymouth Mews beyond it. "Shouldn't we keep them?" he'd wondered. "They're so beautiful."

"They *are* beautiful," Vikram agreed, "but these windows are actually very difficult to open from a sitting position—they demand a good amount of lift from the legs." He realized then that Vikram had taken seriously what he had instructed him to do in their initial conversation: to assume that eventually one of the people who lived in the apartment might have a very limited range of motion.

"Oh," he'd said, and had blinked his eyes, rapidly. "Right. Thanks. Thanks."

"Of course," Vikram had said. "I promise you, Willem, it's going to feel like home for both of you." He had a soft, gentle voice, and Willem had been unsure whether the sorrow he had felt in that moment was from the kindness of what Vikram said, or the kindness with which he said it.

He remembers this now, back in New York. It is the end of July; he has convinced Jude to take a day off, and they have driven to their house upstate. For weeks, Jude had been tired and unusually weak, but then, suddenly, he hadn't been, and it was on days like this—the sky above them vivid with blue, the air hot and dry, the fields around their house buttery with clumps of yarrow and cowslip, the stones around the pool cool beneath his feet, Jude singing to himself in the kitchen as he made lemonade for Julia and Harold, who had come to stay with them—that Willem found himself slipping back into his old habit of pretending. On these days, he succumbed to a sort of enchantment, a state in which his life seemed both unimprovable and, paradoxically, perfectly fixable: Of course Jude wouldn't get worse. Of course he could be repaired. Of course Willem would be the person to repair him. Of course this was possible; of course this was probable. Days like this seemed to have no nights, and if there were no nights, there was no cutting, there was no sadness, there was nothing to dismay.

"You're dreaming of miracles, Willem," Idriss would say if he knew what he was thinking, and he knew he was. But then again, he would think, what about his life—and about Jude's life, too—wasn't it a miracle? He should have stayed in Wyoming, he should have been a ranch hand himself. Jude should have wound up—where? In prison, or in a hospital, or dead, or worse. But they hadn't. Wasn't it a miracle that someone who was basically unexceptional could live a life in which he made millions pretending to be other people, that in that life that person would fly from city to city, would spend his days having his every need fulfilled, working in artificial contexts in which he was treated like the potentate of a small, corrupt country? Wasn't it a miracle to be adopted at thirty, to find people who loved you so much that they wanted to call you their own? Wasn't it a miracle to have survived the unsurvivable? Wasn't friendship its own miracle, the finding of another person who made the entire lonely world seem somehow less lonely? Wasn't this house, this beauty, this comfort, this life a miracle? And so who could blame him for hoping for one more, for hoping that despite knowing better, that despite biology, and time, and history, that they would be the exception, that what happened to other people with Jude's sort of injury wouldn't happen to him, that even with all that Jude had overcome, he might overcome just one more thing?

He is sitting by the pool and talking to Harold and Julia when abruptly, he feels that strange hollowing in his stomach that he occasionally experiences even when he and Jude are in the same house: the sensation of missing him, an odd sharp desire to see him. And although he would never say it to him, this is the way in which Jude reminds him of Hemming—that awareness that sometimes touches him, as lightly as wings, that the people he loves are more temporal, somehow, than others, that he has borrowed them, and that someday they will be reclaimed from him. "Don't go," he had told Hemming in their phone calls, back when Hemming was dying. "Don't leave me, Hemming," even though the nurses who were holding the receiver to Hemming's ear hundreds of miles away had instructed him to tell Hemming exactly the opposite: that it was all right for him to leave; that Willem was releasing him. But he couldn't.

And he hadn't been able to either when Jude was in the hospital, so delirious from the drugs that his eyes had skittered back and forth with a rapidity that had frightened him almost more than anything else. "Let me go, Willem," Jude had begged him then, "let me go."

"I can't, Jude," he had cried. "I can't do that."

Now he shakes his head to clear the memory. "I'm going to go check on him," he tells Harold and Julia, but then he hears the glass door slide open, and all three of them turn and look up the sloping hill to see Jude holding a tray of drinks, and all three of them stand to go help him. But there is a moment before they begin heading uphill and Jude begins walking toward them in which they all hold their positions, and it reminds him of a set, in which every scene can be redone, every mistake can be corrected, every sorrow reshot. And in that moment, they are on one edge of the frame, and Jude is on the other, but they are all smiling at one another, and the world seems to hold nothing but sweetness.

—

The last time in his life he would walk on his own—really walk: not just edging along the wall from one room to the next; not shuffling down the hallways of Rosen Pritchard; not inching his way through the lobby to the garage, sinking into the car seat with a groan of relief—had been their Christmas vacation. He was forty-six. They were in Bhutan: a good choice, he would later realize, for his final sustained spell of walking (although of course he hadn't known that at the time), because it was a country in which everyone walked. The people they met there, including an old acquaintance of theirs from college, Karma, who was now the minister of forestry, spoke of walking not in terms of kilometers but in terms of hours. "Oh yes," Karma had said, "when my father was growing up, he used to walk four hours to visit his aunt on the weekends. And then he would walk four hours back home." He and Willem had marveled at this, although later, they had also agreed: the countryside was so pretty, a series of swooping, treed parabolas, the sky above a thin clear blue, that time spent walking here must move more quickly and pleasantly than time spent walking anywhere else.

He hadn't felt at his best on that trip, although at least he was mobile. In the months before, he had been feeling weaker, but not in any truly specifiable way, not in any way that seemed to suggest some greater problem. He simply lost energy faster; he was achey instead of sore, a dull, constant thud of pain that followed him into sleep and was there to greet him when he woke. It was the difference, he told Andy, between a month speckled by thundershowers and a month in which it rained daily: not heavily but ceaselessly, a kind of dreary, enervating discomfort. In October, he'd had to use his wheelchair every day, which had been the most consecutive days he had ever been dependent on it. In November, although he had been well enough to make Thanksgiving dinner at Harold's, he had been in too much pain to actually sit at the table to eat it, and he had spent the evening in his bedroom, lying as still as he could, semi-aware of Harold and Willem and Julia coming in to check on him, semi-aware of his apologizing for ruining the holiday for them, semi-aware of the muted conversation among the three of them and Laurence and Gillian, James and Carey, that he half heard coming from the dining room. After that, Willem had wanted to cancel their trip, but he had insisted, and he was glad he had—for he felt there was something restorative about the beauty of the landscape, about the cleanliness and quiet of the mountains, about getting to see Willem surrounded by streams and trees, which was always where he looked most comfortable.

It was a good vacation, but by the end, he was ready to leave. One of the reasons he had been able to convince Willem that they could go on this trip at all was because his friend Elijah, who now ran a hedge fund that he represented, was going on holiday to Nepal with his family, and they caught flights both from and back to New York on his plane. He had worried that Elijah might be in a talkative mood, but he hadn't been, and he had slept, gratefully, almost the entire way home, his feet and back blazing with pain.

The day after they returned to Greene Street he couldn't lift himself out of bed. He was in such distress that his body seemed to be one long exposed nerve, frayed at either end; he had the sense that if he were to be touched with a drop of water, his entire being would sizzle and hiss in response. He was rarely so exhausted, so sore that he couldn't even sit up, and he could tell that Willem—around whom he made a particular effort, so he wouldn't worry—was alarmed, and he had to plead with him not to call Andy. "All right," Willem had said, reluctantly, "but if you're not better by tomorrow, I'm calling him." He nodded, and Willem sighed. "Dammit, Jude," he said, "I *knew* we shouldn't've gone."

But the next day, he was better: better enough to get out of bed, at least. He couldn't walk; all day, his legs and feet and back felt as if they were being driven through with iron bolts, but he made himself smile and talk and move about, though when Willem left the room or turned away from him, he could feel his face drooping with fatigue.

And then that was how it was, and they both grew used to it: although he now needed his wheelchair daily, he tried to walk every day for as much as he could, even if it was just to the bathroom, and he was careful about conserving his energy. When he was cooking, he made certain he had everything assembled on the counter in front of him before he started so he wouldn't have to keep going back and forth to the refrigerator; he turned down invitations to dinners, parties, openings, fund-raisers, telling people, telling Willem that he had too much work to attend them, but really he came home and wheeled his way slowly across the apartment, the punishingly large apartment, stopping to rest when he needed to, dozing in bed so he'd have enough life in him to talk to Willem when he returned.

At the end of January he finally went to see Andy, who listened to him and then examined him, carefully. "There's nothing *wrong* with you, as such," he said when he was finished. "You're just getting older."

"Oh," he said, and they were both quiet, for what was there for them to say? "Well," he said, at last, "maybe I'll get so weak that I'll be able to convince Willem I don't have the energy to go to Loehmann any longer," because one night that fall he had—stupidly, drunkenly, romantically even—promised Willem he'd see Dr. Loehmann for another nine months.

Andy had sighed but had smiled, too. "You're such a brat," he said.

Now, though, he thinks back on this period fondly, for in every other way that mattered, that winter was a glorious time. In December, Willem had been nominated for a major award for his work in *The Poisoned Apple*; in January, he won it. Then he was nominated again, for an even bigger and more prestigious award, and again, he won. He had been in London on business the night Willem won, but had set his alarm for two a.m. so he could wake and watch the ceremony online; when Willem's name was called, he shouted out loud, watched Willem, beaming, kiss Julia—whom he had brought as his date—and bound up the stairs to the stage, listened as he thanked the filmmakers, the studio, Emil, Kit, Alan Turing himself, Roman and Cressy and Richard and Malcolm and JB, and "my in-laws, Julia Altman and Harold Stein, for always making me feel like I was their son as well, and, finally and most important, Jude St. Francis, my best friend and the love of my life, for everything." He'd had to stop himself from crying then, and when he got through to Willem half an hour later, he had to stop himself again. "I'm so proud of you, Willem," he said. "I knew you would win, I knew it."

"You always think that," Willem laughed, and he laughed too, because Willem was right: he always did. He always thought Willem deserved to win awards for whatever he was nominated for; on the occasions he didn't, he was genuinely perplexed—politics and preferences aside, how could the judges, the voters, deny what was so obviously a superior performance, a superior actor, a superior person?

In his meetings the next morning—in which he had to stop himself from not crying, but smiling, dopily and incessantly—his colleagues congratulated him and asked him again why he hadn't gone to the ceremony, and he had shaken his head. "Those things aren't for me," he said, and they weren't; of all the awards shows, all the premieres, all the parties that Willem went to for work, he had attended only two or three. This past year, when Willem was being interviewed by a serious, literary magazine for a long profile, he vanished whenever he knew the writer would be present. He knew Willem wasn't offended by this, that he attributed his scarcity to his sense of privacy. And while this was true, it wasn't the only reason.

Once, shortly after they had become a couple, there had been a picture of them that had run with a *Times* story about Willem and the first installment he had completed in a spy movie trilogy. The photo had been taken at the opening of JB's fifth, long-delayed show, "Frog and Toad," which had been exclusively images of the two of them, but very blurred, and much more abstract than JB's previous work. (They hadn't quite known what to think of the series title, though JB had claimed it was affectionate. "Arnold Lobel?" he had screeched at them when they asked him about it. "*Hello?!*" But neither he nor Willem had read Lobel's books as children, and they'd had to go out and buy them to make sense of the reference.) Curiously, it had been this show, even more than the initial *New York* magazine story about Willem's new life, that had made their relationship real for their colleagues and peers, despite the fact that most of the paintings had been made from photographs taken before they had become a couple.

It was also this show that would mark, as JB later said, his ascendancy: they knew that despite his sales, his reviews, his fellowships and accolades, he was tormented that Richard had had a mid-career museum retrospective (as had Asian Henry Young), and he hadn't. But after "Frog and Toad," something shifted for JB, the way that *The Sycamore Court* had shifted things for Willem, the way that the Doha museum had shifted things for Malcolm, even the way—if he was to be boastful—that the Malgrave and Baskett suit had shifted things for him. It was only when he stepped outside his firmament of friends that he realized that that shift, that shift they had all hoped for and received, was rarer and more precious than they even knew. Of all of them, only JB had been certain that he *deserved* that shift, that it was absolutely going to happen for him; he and Malcolm and Willem had had no such certainty, and so when it was given to them, they were befuddled. But although JB had had to wait the longest for his life to change, he was calm when it finally did—something in him seemed to become defanged; he became, for the first time since they had known him, mellowed, and the constant prickly humor that fizzed off of him like static was demagnetized and quieted. He was glad for JB; he was glad he now had the kind of recognition he wanted, the kind of recognition he thought JB should have received after "Seconds, Minutes, Hours, Days."

"The question is which one of us is the frog and which is the toad," Willem had said after they'd first seen the show, in JB's studio, and read the kindhearted books to each other late that night, laughing helplessly as they did.

He'd smiled; they had been lying in bed. "Obviously, I'm the toad," he said.

"No," Willem said, "I think you're the frog; your eyes are the same color as his skin."

Willem sounded so serious that he grinned. "*That's* your evidence?" he asked. "And so what do you have in common with the toad?"

"I think I actually have a jacket like the one he has," Willem said, and they began laughing again.

But really, he knew: he *was* the toad, and seeing the picture in the *Times* of the two of them together had reminded him of this. He wasn't so bothered by this for his own sake—he was trying to care less about his own anxieties—but for Willem's, because he was aware of how mismatched, how distorted a couple they made, and he was embarrassed for him, and worried that his mere presence might be somehow harmful to Willem. And so he tried to stay away from him in public. He had always thought that Willem was capable of making him better, but over the years he feared: If Willem could make him better, didn't that also mean that he could make Willem sick? And in the same way, if Willem could make him into someone less difficult to regard, couldn't he also make Willem into something ugly? He knew this wasn't logical, but he thought it anyway, and sometimes as they were getting ready to go out, he glimpsed himself in the bathroom mirror, his stupid, pleased expression, as absurd and grotesque as a monkey dressed in expensive clothes, and would want to punch the glass with his fist.

But the other reason he was worried about being seen with Willem was because of the exposure it entailed. Ever since his first day of college, he had feared that someday someone from his past—a client; one of the boys from the home—would try to contact him, would try to extort something from him for their silence. "No one will, Jude," Ana had assured him. "I promise. To do so would be to admit how they know you." But he was always afraid, and over the years, there had been a few ghosts who had announced themselves. The first arrived shortly after he'd started at Rosen Pritchard: just a postcard, from someone who claimed he had known him from the home—someone with the unhelpfully indistinct name of Rob Wilson, someone he didn't remember—and for a week, he had panicked, barely able to sleep, his mind scrolling through scenarios that seemed as terrifying as they were inevitable. What if this Rob Wilson contacted Harold, contacted his colleagues at the firm, and told them who he was, told them about the things he had done? But he made himself not react, not do what he wanted to do—write a near-hysterical cease-and-desist letter that would prove nothing but his own existence, and the existence of his past—and he never heard from Rob Wilson again.

But after a few pictures of him with Willem had appeared in the press, he received two more letters and an e-mail, all sent to his work. One of the letters and the e-mail were again from men who claimed they had been at the home with him, but once again, he hadn't recognized their names, and he never responded, and they never contacted him again. But the second letter had contained a copy of a photograph, black-and-white, of an undressed boy on a bed, and of such low quality that he couldn't tell if it was him or not. And with this letter, he had done what he had been told to do all those years ago, when he was a child in a hospital bed in Philadelphia, should any of the clients figure out who he was and try to establish communication with him: he had put the letter in an envelope and had sent it to the FBI. They always knew where he was, that office, and every four or five years an agent would appear at his workplace to show him pictures, to ask him if he remembered one man or another, men who were decades later still being uncovered as Dr. Traylor's, Brother Luke's, friends and fellow criminals. He rarely had advance warning before these visits, and over the years he had learned what he needed to do in the days afterward in order to neutralize them, how he needed to surround himself with people, with events, with noise and clamor, with evidence of the life he now inhabited.

In this period, the one in which he had received and disposed of the letter, he had felt vividly ashamed and intensely alone—this had been before he had told Willem about his childhood, and he had never given Andy enough context so that he would appreciate the terror that he was experiencing—and after, he had finally made himself hire an investigative agency (though not the one that Rosen Pritchard used) to uncover everything they could about him. The investigation had taken a month, but at its end, there was nothing conclusive, or at least nothing that could conclusively identify him as who he had been. It was only then that he allowed himself to relax, to believe, finally, that Ana had been right, to accept that, for the most part, his past had been erased so completely that it was as if it had never existed. The people who knew the most about it, who had witnessed and made it—Brother Luke; Dr. Traylor; even Ana—were dead, and the dead can speak to no one. *You're safe*, he would remind himself. And although he was, it didn't mean he wasn't still cautious; it didn't mean that he should want to have his photograph in magazines and newspapers.

He accepted that this was what his life with Willem would be, of course, but sometimes he wished it could be different, that he could be less circumspect about claiming Willem in public the way Willem had claimed him. In idle moments, he played the clip of Willem making his speech over and over, feeling that same giddiness he had when Harold had first named him as his son to another person. *This has really happened,* he had thought at the time. *This isn't something I've made up.* And now, the same delirium: he really was Willem's. He had said so himself.

In March, at the end of awards season, he and Richard had thrown Willem a party at Greene Street. A large shipment of carved-teak doorways and benches had just been moved out of the fifth floor, and Richard had strung the ceiling with ropes of lights and had lined every wall with glass jars containing candles. Richard's studio manager had brought two of their largest worktables upstairs, and he had called the caterers and a bartender. They had invited everyone they could think of: all of their friends in common, and all of Willem's as well. Harold and Julia, James and Carey, Laurence and Gillian, Lionel and Sinclair had come down from Boston; Kit had come out from L.A., Carolina from Yountville, Phaedra and Citizen from Paris, Willem's friends Cressy and Susannah from London, Miguel from Madrid. He made himself stand and walk through that party, at which people he knew only from Willem's stories—directors and actors and playwrights—approached him and said they'd been hearing about him for years, and that it was so nice to finally meet him, that they'd been thinking that Willem had invented him, and although he had laughed, he had been sad as well, as if he should have ignored his fears and involved himself more in Willem's life.

So many people there hadn't seen one another in so many years that it was a very busy party, the kind of party they had gone to when they were young, with people shouting at one another over the music that one of Richard's assistants, an amateur DJ, was playing, and a few hours into it he was exhausted, and leaned against the northern wall of the space to watch everyone dance. In the middle of the scrum he could see Willem dancing with Julia, and he smiled, watching them, before noticing that Harold was standing on the other side of the room, watching them as well, smiling as well. Harold saw him, then, and raised his glass to him, and he raised his in return, and then watched as Harold worked his way toward him.

"Good party," Harold shouted into his ear.

"It's mostly Richard's doing," he shouted back, but as he was about to say something else, the music became louder, and he and Harold looked at each other and laughed and shrugged. For a while they simply stood, both of them smiling, watching the dancers heave and blur before them. He was tired, he was in pain, but it didn't matter; his tiredness felt like something sweet and warm, his pain was familiar and expected, and in those moments he was aware that he was capable of joyfulness, that life was honeyed. Then the music turned, grew dreamy and slow, and Harold yelled that he was going to reclaim Julia from Willem's clutches.

"Go," he told him, but before Harold left him, something made him reach out and put his arms around him, which was the first time he had voluntarily touched Harold since the incident with Caleb. He could see that Harold was stunned, and then delighted, and he felt guilt course through him, and moved away as quickly as he could, shooing Harold onto the dance floor as he did.

There was a nest of cotton-stuffed burlap sacks in one of the corners, which Richard had put down for people to lounge against, and he was headed toward them when Willem appeared, and grabbed his hand. "Come dance with me," he said.

"Willem," he admonished him, smiling, "you know I can't dance."

Willem looked at him then, appraisingly. "Come with me," he said, and he followed Willem toward the east end of the loft, and to the bathroom, where Willem pulled him inside and closed and locked the door behind them, placing his drink on the edge of the sink. They could still hear the music—a song that had been popular when they were in college, embarrassing and yet somehow moving in its unapologetic sentimentalism, in its syrup and sincerity—but in the bathroom it was dampened, as if it was being piped in from some far-off valley. "Put your arms around me," Willem told him, and he did. "Move your right foot back when I move my left one toward it," he said next, and he did.

For a while they moved slowly and clumsily, looking at each other, silent. "See?" Willem said, quietly. "You're dancing."

"I'm not good at it," he mumbled, embarrassed.

"You're perfect at it," Willem said, and although his feet were by this point so sore that he was beginning to perspire from the discipline it was taking not to scream, he kept moving, but so minimally that toward the end of the song they were only swaying, their feet not leaving the ground, Willem holding him so he wouldn't fall.

When they emerged from the bathroom, there was a whooping from the groups of people nearest to them, and he blushed—the last, the final, time he'd had sex with Willem had been almost sixteen months ago—but Willem grinned and raised his arm as if he was a prizefighter who had just won a bout.

And then it was April, and his forty-seventh birthday, and then it was May, and he developed a wound on each calf, and Willem left for Istanbul to shoot the second installment in his spy trilogy. He had told Willem about the wounds—he was trying to tell him things as they happened, even things he didn't consider that important—and Willem had been upset.

But he hadn't been concerned. How many of these wounds had he had over the years? Tens; dozens. The only thing that had changed was the amount of time he spent trying to resolve them. Now he went to Andy's office twice a week—every Tuesday lunchtime and Friday evening—once for debriding and once for a wound vacuum treatment, which Andy's nurse performed. Andy had always thought that his skin was too fragile for that treatment, in which a piece of sterile foam was fitted above the open sore and a nozzle moved above it that sucked the dead and dying tissues into the foam like a sponge, but in recent years he had tolerated it well, and it had proven more successful than simply debriding alone.

As he had grown older, the wounds—their frequency, their severity, their size, the level of discomfort that attended them—had grown steadily worse. Long gone, decades gone, were the days in which he was able to walk any great distance when he had them. (The memory of strolling from Chinatown to the Upper East Side—albeit painfully— with one of these wounds was so strange and remote that it didn't even seem to belong to him, but to somebody else.) When he was younger, it might take a few weeks for one to heal. But now it took months. Of all the things that were wrong with him, he was the most dispassionate about these sores; and yet he was never able to accustom himself to their very appearance. And although of course he wasn't scared of blood, the sight of pus, of rot, of his body's desperate attempt to heal itself by trying to kill part of itself still unsettled him even all these years later.

By the time Willem came home for good, he wasn't better. There were now four wounds on his calves, the most he had ever had at one time, and although he was still trying to walk daily, it was sometimes difficult enough to simply stand, and he was vigilant about parsing his efforts, about determining when he was trying to walk because he thought he could, and when he was trying to walk to prove to himself that he was still capable of it. He could feel he had lost weight, he could feel he had gotten weaker—he could no longer even swim every morning—but he knew it for sure once he saw Willem's face. "Judy," Willem had said, quietly, and had knelt next to him on the sofa. "I wish you had told me." But in a funny way, there had been nothing to tell: this was who he was. And besides his legs, his feet, his back, he felt fine. He felt—though he hesitated to say this about himself: it seemed so bold a statement—mentally healthy. He was back to cutting himself only once a week. He heard himself whistling as he removed his pants at night, examining the area around the bandages to make sure none of them were leaking fluids. People got used to anything their bodies gave them; he was no exception. If your body was well, you expected it to perform for you, excellently, consistently. If your body was not, your expectations were different. Or this, at least, was what he was trying to accept.

Shortly after he returned at the end of July, Willem gave him permission to terminate his mostly silent relationship with Dr. Loehmann— but only because he genuinely didn't have the time any longer. Four hours of his week were now spent at doctors' offices—two with Andy, two with Loehmann—and he needed to reclaim two of those hours so he could go twice a week to the hospital, where he took off his pants and flipped his tie over his shoulder and was slid into a hyperbaric chamber, a glass coffin where he lay and did work and hoped that the concentrated oxygen that was being piped in all around him might help hasten his healing. He had felt guilty about his eighteen months with Dr. Loehmann, in which he had revealed almost nothing, had spent most of his time childishly protecting his privacy, trying not to say anything, wasting both his and the doctor's time. But one of the few subjects they *had* discussed was his legs—not how they had been damaged but the logistics of caring for them—and in his final session, Dr. Loehmann had asked what would happen if he didn't get better.

"Amputation, I guess," he had said, trying to sound casual, although of course he wasn't casual, and there was nothing to guess: he knew that as surely as he would someday die, he would do so without his legs.

He just had to hope it wouldn't be soon. *Please*, he would sometimes beg his legs as he lay in the glass chamber. *Please. Give me just a few more years. Give me another decade. Let me get through my forties, my fifties, intact. I'll take care of you, I promise.*

By late summer, his new bout of sicknesses, of treatments had become so commonplace to him that he hadn't realized how affected Willem might be by them. Early that August, they were discussing what to do (something? nothing?) for Willem's forty-ninth birthday, and Willem had said he thought they should just do something low-key this year.

"Well, we'll do something big next year, for your fiftieth," he said. "If I'm still alive by then, that is," and it wasn't until he heard Willem's silence that he had looked up from the stove and seen Willem's expression and had recognized his mistake. "Willem, I'm sorry," he said, turning off the burner and making his slow, painful way over to him. "I'm sorry."

"You can't joke like that, Jude," Willem said, and he put his arms around him.

"I know," he said. "Forgive me. I was being stupid. Of course I'm going to be around next year."

"And for many years to come."

"And for many years to come."

Now it is September, and he is lying on the examining table in Andy's office, his wounds uncovered and still split open like pomegranates, and at nights he is lying in bed next to Willem. He is often conscious of the unlikeliness of their relationship, and often guilty at his unwillingness to fulfill one of the core duties of couplehood. Every once in a while, he thinks he will try again, and then, just as he is trying to say the words to Willem, he stops, and another opportunity quietly slides away. But his guilt, as great as it is, cannot overwhelm his sense of relief, nor his sense of gratitude: that he should have been able to keep Willem despite his inabilities is a miracle, and he tries, in every other way he can, to always communicate to Willem how thankful he is.

He wakes one night sweating so profusely that the sheets beneath him feel as if they've been dragged through a puddle, and in his haze, he stands before he realizes he can't, and falls. Willem wakes, then, and fetches him the thermometer, standing over him as he holds it under his tongue. "One hundred and two," he says, examining it, and places his palm on his forehead. "But you're freezing." He looks at him, worried. "I'm going to call Andy."

"Don't call Andy," he says, and despite the fever, the chills, the sweating, he feels normal; he doesn't feel sick. "I just need some aspirin." So Willem gets it, brings him a shirt, strips and remakes the bed, and they fall asleep again, Willem wrapped around him.

The next night he wakes again with a fever, again with chills, again with sweating. "There's something going around the office," he tells Willem this time. "Some forty-eight-hour bug. I must've caught it." Again he takes aspirin; again it helps; again he goes back to sleep.

The day after that is a Friday and he goes to Andy to have his wounds cleaned, but he doesn't mention the fever, which disappears by daylight. That night Willem is away, having dinner with Roman, and he goes to bed early, swallowing some aspirin before he does. He sleeps so deeply that he doesn't even hear Willem come in, but when he wakes the following morning, he is so sweaty that it looks as if he's been standing under the shower, and his limbs are numb and shaky. Beside him, Willem gently snores, and he sits, slowly, running his hands through his wet hair.

He really is better that Saturday. He goes to work. Willem goes to meet a director for lunch. Before he leaves the offices for the evening, he texts Willem and tells him to ask Richard and India if they want to meet for sushi on the Upper East Side, at a little restaurant he and Andy sometimes go to after their appointments. He and Willem have two favorite sushi places near Greene Street, but both of them have flights of descending stairs, and so they have been unable to go for months because the steps are too difficult for him. That night he eats well, and even as the fatigue punches him midway through the meal, he is conscious that he is enjoying himself, that he is grateful to be in this small, warm place, with its yellow-lit lanterns above him and the wooden geta-like slab atop which are laid tongues of mackerel sashimi—Willem's favorite—before him. At one point he leans against Willem's side, from exhaustion and affection, but isn't even aware he's done so until he feels Willem move his arm and put it around him.

Later, he wakes in their bed, disoriented, and sees Harold sitting next to him, staring at him. "Harold," he says, "what're you doing here?" But Harold doesn't speak, just lunges at him, and he realizes with a sickening lurch that Harold is trying to take his clothes off. *No, he tells himself. Not Harold. This can't be.* This is one of his deepest, ugliest, most secret fears, and now it is coming true. But then his old instincts awaken: Harold is another client, and he will fight him away. He yells, then, twisting himself, pinwheeling his arms and what he can of his legs, trying to intimidate, to fluster this silent, determined Harold before him, screaming for Brother Luke's help.

And then, suddenly, Harold vanishes and is replaced by Willem, his face near his, saying something he can't understand. But behind Willem's head he sees Harold's again, his strange, grim expression, and he resumes his fight. Above him, he can hear words, can hear that Willem is talking to someone, can register, even through his own fright, Willem's fright as well. "Willem," he calls out. "He's trying to hurt me; don't let him hurt me, Willem. Help me. Help me. Help me—please."

Then there is nothing—a stretch of blackened time—and when he wakes again, he is in the hospital. "Willem," he announces to the room, and there, immediately, is Willem, sitting at the edge of his bed, taking his hand. There is a length of plastic tubing snaking out of the back of this hand, and out of the other as well. "Careful," Willem tells him, "the IVs."

For a while they are silent, and Willem strokes his forehead. "He was trying to attack me," he finally confesses to Willem, stumbling as he speaks. "I never thought Harold would do that to me, not ever."

He can see Willem stiffen. "No, Jude," he says. "Harold wasn't there. You were delirious from the fever; it didn't happen."

He is relieved and terrified to hear this. Relieved to hear that it wasn't true; terrified because it seemed so real, so actual. Terrified because what does it say about him, about how he thinks and what his fears are, that he should even imagine this about Harold? How cruel can his own mind be to try to convince him to turn against someone he has struggled so hard to trust, someone who has only ever shown him kindness? He can feel tears in his eyes, but he has to ask Willem: "He wouldn't do that to me, would he, Willem?"

"No," says Willem, and his voice is strained. "Never, Jude. Harold would never, ever do that to you, not for anything."

When he wakes again, he realizes he doesn't know what day it is, and when Willem tells him it's Monday, he panics. "Work," he says, "I have to go."

"No fucking way," Willem says, sharply. "I called them, Jude. You're not going anywhere, not until Andy figures out what's going on."

Harold and Julia arrive later, and he makes himself return Harold's embrace, although he cannot look at him. Over Harold's shoulder, he sees Willem, who nods at him reassuringly.

They are all together when Andy comes in. "Osteomyelitis," he says to him, quietly. "A bone infection." He explains what will happen: he will have to stay in the hospital for at least a week—"A *week!*" he exclaims, and the four of them start shouting at him before he has a chance to protest further—or possibly two, until they get the fever under control. The antibiotics will be dispensed through a central line, but the remaining ten to eleven weeks of treatment will be given to him on an outpatient basis. Every day, a nurse will come administer the IV drip: the treatment will take an hour, and he is not to miss a single one of these. When he tries, again, to protest, Andy stops him. "Jude," he says. "This is serious. I mean it. I don't fucking care about Rosen Pritchard. You want to keep your legs, you do this and you follow my instructions, do you understand me?"

Around him, the others are silent. "Yes," he says, at last.

A nurse comes to prep him so Andy can administer the central venous catheter, which will be inserted into the subclavian vein, directly beneath his right collarbone. "This is a tricky vein to access because it's so deep," the nurse says, pulling down the neck of his gown and cleaning a square of his skin. "But you're lucky to have Dr. Contractor. He's very good with needles; he never misses." He isn't worried, but he knows Willem is, and he holds Willem's hand as Andy first pierces his skin with the cold metal needle and then threads the coil of guide wire into him. "Don't look," he tells Willem. "It's okay." And so Willem stares instead at his face, which he tries to keep still and composed until Andy is finished and is taping the catheter's length of slender plastic tubing to his chest.

He sleeps. He had thought he might be able to work from the hospital, but he is more exhausted than he thought he would be, cloudier, and after talking to the chairs of the various committees and some of his colleagues, he doesn't have the strength to do anything else.

Harold and Julia leave—they have classes and office hours—but except for Richard and a few people from work, they don't tell anyone he's hospitalized; he won't be there for long, and Willem has decided he needs sleep more than he needs visitors. He is still febrile, but less so, and there have been no further episodes of delirium. And strangely, for all that is happening, he feels, if not optimistic, then at least calm. Everyone around him is so sober, so thin-lipped, that he feels determined to defy them somehow, to defy the severity of the situation they keep telling him he's in.

He can't remember when he and Willem started referring to the hospital as the Hotel Contractor, in honor of Andy, but it seems they always have. "Watch out," Willem would say to him even back at Lispenard Street, when he was hacking at a piece of steak some enraptured sous-chef at Ortolan had sneaked Willem at the end of his shift, "that cleaver's really sharp, and if you chop off a thumb, we'll have to go to the Hotel Contractor." Or once, when he was hospitalized for a skin infection, he had sent Willem (away somewhere, shooting) a text reading "At Hotel Contractor. Not a big deal, but didn't want you to hear through M or JB." Now, though, when he tries to make Hotel Contractor jokes—complaining about the Hotel's increasingly poor food and beverage services; about its poor quality of linens—Willem doesn't respond.

"This isn't funny, Jude," he snaps on Friday evening, as they wait for Harold and Julia to arrive with dinner. "I wish you'd fucking stop kidding around." He is quiet then, and they look at each other. "I was so scared," Willem says, in a low voice. "You were so sick and I didn't know what was going to happen, and I was so scared."

"Willem," he says, gently, "I know. I'm so grateful for you." He hurries on before Willem can tell him he doesn't need him to be grateful, he needs him to take the situation seriously. "I'm going to listen to Andy, I promise. I promise you I'm taking this seriously. And I promise you I'm not in any discomfort. I feel fine. It's going to be fine."

After ten days, Andy is satisfied that the fever has been eliminated, and he is discharged and sent home for two days to rest; he is back at the office on Friday. He had always resisted having a driver—he liked to drive himself; he liked the independence, the solitude—but now Willem's assistant has hired a driver for him, a small, serious man named Mr. Ahmed, and on his way to and from the office, he sleeps. Mr. Ahmed also picks up his nurse, a woman named Patrizia who rarely speaks but is very gentle, and every day at one p.m., she meets him at Rosen Pritchard. His office there is all glass and looks out onto the floor, and he lowers the shades for privacy and takes off his jacket and tie and shirt, and lies down on the sofa in his undershirt and covers himself with a blanket, and Patrizia cleans the catheter and checks the skin around it to make sure there are no signs of infection—no swelling, no redness—and then inserts the IV and waits as the medicine drips into the catheter and slides into his veins. As they wait, he works and she reads a nursing journal or knits. Soon this too becomes normal: every Friday he sees Andy, who debrides his wounds and then examines him, sending him to the hospital after their session for X-rays so he can track the infection and make sure it isn't spreading.

They cannot go away on the weekends because he needs to have his treatment, but in early October, after four weeks of antibiotics, Andy announces that he's been talking to Willem, and if he doesn't mind, he and Jane are going to come up to stay with them in Garrison for the weekend, and he'll administer the drip himself.

It is wonderful, and rare, being out of the city, being back at their house, and the four of them enjoy one another's company. He even feels well enough to give Andy an abbreviated tour of the property, which Andy has visited only in springtime or summer, but which is different in autumn: raw, sad, lovely, the barn's roof plastered with fallen yellow gingko leaves that make it look as if it's been laid with sheets of gold leaf.

Over dinner that Saturday night, Andy asks him, "You do realize we've now known each other for thirty years, right?"

"I do," he smiles. He has in fact bought Andy something—a safari vacation for him and his family, to go on whenever he wants—for their anniversary, although he hasn't told him about it yet.

"Thirty years of being disobeyed," Andy moans, and the rest of them laugh. "Thirty years of dispensing priceless medical advice gleaned from years of experience and training at top institutions, only to have it ignored by a *corporate litigator*, who's decided his understanding of human biology is superior to my own."

After they've stopped laughing, Jane says, "But you know, Andy, if it weren't for Jude, I never would have married you." To him, she says, "In medical school, I always thought Andy was sort of a self-absorbed douche bag, Jude; he was so arrogant, so borderline callow"—"What!" Andy says, feigning injury—"that I assumed he was going to be one of those typical surgeons—you know, 'not always right, but always certain.'

But then I heard him talk about you, how much he loved and respected you, and I thought there might be something more to him. And I was right."

"You were," he tells her, after they all laugh again. "You were right," and they all look at Andy, who gets embarrassed and pours himself another glass of wine.

The week after that, Willem begins rehearsals for his new film. A month ago, when he got sick, he had backed out of the project, and then it had been delayed to wait for him, and now things are stable enough that he has signed on again. He doesn't understand why Willem had backed out in the first place—the film is a remake of *Desperate Characters*, and most of the filming will be done just across the river, in Brooklyn Heights—but he is relieved to have Willem at work again and not hovering over him, looking worried and asking him if he's sure he has the energy to do any of the very basic things (going to the grocery store; making a meal; staying late at work) that he wants to do.

In early November he goes back into the hospital with another fever, but only stays for two nights before he's released again. Patrizia draws his blood every week, but Andy has told him that he'll have to be patient; bone infections take a long time to eradicate, and he probably won't have a sense of whether he's been healed for good or not until the end of the twelve-week cycle. But otherwise, everything trudges on: He goes to work. He goes to have his treatments in the hyperbaric chamber. He goes to have his wounds vacuum-treated. He goes to have them debrided. One of the side effects from the antibiotics is diarrhea; another is nausea. He is losing weight at a rate even he can tell is problematic; he has eight of his shirts and two of his suits retailored. Andy prescribes him high-calorie drinks meant for malnourished children, and he swallows them five times a day, gulping water afterward to erase their chalky, tongue-coating flavor. Except for the hours he keeps at the office, he is conscious of being more obedient than he ever has been, of heeding every one of Andy's warnings, of following his every piece of advice. He is still trying not to think of how this episode might end, trying not to worry himself, but in dark, quiet moments, he replays what Andy said to him on one of his recent checkups: "Heart: perfect. Lungs: perfect. Vision, hearing, cholesterol, prostate, blood sugar, blood pressure, lipids, kidney function, liver function, thyroid function: all perfect. Your body's equipped to work as hard as it can for you, Jude;

make sure you let it." He knows that isn't the complete measure of who he is—circulation, for example: not perfect; reflexes: not perfect; anything south of his groin: compromised—but he tries to take comfort in Andy's reassurances, to remind himself that things could be worse, that he is, essentially, still a healthy person, still a lucky person.

Late November. Willem finishes *Desperate Characters*. They have Thanksgiving at Harold and Julia's uptown, and although they have been coming into the city every other weekend to see him, he can sense them both trying very hard not to say anything about his appearance, not to bother him about how little he's eating at dinner. Thanksgiving week also marks his final week of antibiotic treatments, and he submits to another round of blood work and X-rays before Andy tells him he can stop. He says goodbye to Patrizia for what he hopes is the last time; he gives her a gift to thank her for her care.

Although his wounds have shrunk, they haven't shrunk as much as Andy had hoped, and on his recommendation, they stay in Garrison for Christmas. They promise Andy it will be a quiet week; everyone else will be out of town anyway, so it will be only the two of them and Harold and Julia.

"Your two goals are: sleeping and eating," says Andy, who is going to visit Beckett in San Francisco for the holidays. "I want to see you five pounds heavier by the first Friday in January."

"Five pounds is a lot," he says.

"Five," Andy repeats. "And then ideally, fifteen more after that."

On Christmas itself, a year to the day he and Willem had walked along the spine of a low, wavy mountainside in Punakha, one that took them behind the king's hunting lodge, a simple wooden structure that looked like it might be full of Chaucerian pilgrims, not the royal family, he tells Harold he wants to take a walk. Julia and Willem have gone horseback riding at an acquaintance's nearby ranch, and he is feeling stronger than he has in a long time.

"I don't know, Jude," says Harold, warily.

"Come on, Harold," he says. "Just to the first bench." Malcolm has placed three benches along the path he has hacked through the forest to the house's rear; one is located about a third of a way around the lake; the second at the halfway point; and the third at the two-thirds point. "We'll go slowly, and I'll take my cane." It has been years since he has had to use a cane—not since he was a teenager—but now he needs it for any distance longer than fifty yards or so. Finally, Harold agrees, and he grabs his scarf and coat before Harold can change his mind.

Once they are outdoors, his euphoria increases. He loves this house: he loves how it looks, he loves its quiet, and most of all, he loves that it is his and Willem's, as far from Lispenard Street as imaginable, but as much theirs as that place was, something they made together and share. The house, which faces a second, different forest, is a series of glass cubes, and preceding it is a long driveway that switchbacks through the woods, so at certain angles you can see only swatches of it, and at other angles it disappears completely. At night, when it is lit, it glows like a lantern, which was what Malcolm had named it in his monograph: Lantern House. The back of the house looks out onto a wide lawn and beyond it, a lake. At the bottom of the lawn is a pool, which is lined with slabs of slate so that the water is always cold and clear, even on the hottest days, and in the barn there is an indoor pool and a living room; every wall of the barn can be lifted up and away from the structure, so that the entire interior is exposed to the outdoors, to the tree peonies and lilac bushes that bloom around it in the early spring; to the panicles of wisteria that drip from its roof in the early summer. To the right of the house is a field that paints itself red with poppies in July; to the left is another through which he and Willem scattered thousands of wildflower seeds: cosmos and daisies and foxglove and Queen Anne's lace. One weekend shortly after they had moved in, they spent two days making their way through the forests before and behind the house, planting lilies of the valley near the mossy hillocks around the oak and elm trees, and sowing mint seeds throughout. They knew Malcolm didn't approve of their landscaping efforts—he thought them sentimental and trite—and although they knew Malcolm was probably right, they also didn't really care. In spring and summer, when the air was fragrant, they often thought of Lispenard Street, its aggressive ugliness, and of how then they wouldn't even have had the visual imagination to conjure a place like this, where the beauty was so uncomplicated, so undeniable that it seemed at times an illusion.

He and Harold set off toward the forest, where the rough walkway means that it is easier for him to navigate than it had been when construction began. Even so, he has to concentrate, for the path is only cleared once a season, and in the months between it becomes cluttered with saplings and ferns and twigs and tree matter.

They aren't quite halfway to the first bench when he knows he has made a mistake. His legs began throbbing as soon as they finished walking down the lawn, and now his feet are throbbing as well, and each step is agonizing. But he doesn't say anything, just grips his cane more tightly, trying to re-center the discomfort, and pushes forward, clenching his teeth and squaring his jaw. By the time they reach the bench—really, a dark-gray limestone boulder—he is dizzy, and they sit for a long time, talking and looking out onto the lake, which is silvery in the cold air.

"It's chilly," Harold says eventually, and it is; he can feel the cool of the stone through his pants. "We should get you back to the house."

"Okay," he swallows, and stands, and immediately, he feels a hot stake of pain being thrust upward through his feet and gasps, but Harold doesn't notice.

They are only thirty steps into the forest when he stops Harold. "Harold," he says, "I need—I need—" But he can't finish.

"Jude," Harold says, and he can tell Harold is worried. He takes his left arm, slings it around his neck, and holds his hand in his own. "Lean on me as much as you can," Harold says, putting his other arm around his waist, and he nods. "Ready?" He nods again.

He's able to take twenty more steps—such slow steps, his feet tangling in the mulch—before he simply can't move any more. "I can't, Harold," he says, and by this time he can barely speak, the pain is so extreme, so unlike anything he has felt in such a long time. Not since he was in the hospital in Philadelphia have his legs, his back, his feet hurt so profoundly, and he lets go of Harold and falls to the forest floor.

"Oh god, Jude," Harold says, and bends over him, helping him to sit up against a tree, and he thinks how stupid, how selfish, he is. Harold is seventy-two. He should not be asking a seventy-two-year-old man, even an admirably healthy seventy-two-year-old man, for physical assistance. He cannot open his eyes because the world is torquing itself around him, but he hears Harold take out his phone, hears him try to call Willem, but the forest is so dense that the reception is poor, and Harold curses. "Jude," he hears Harold say, but his voice is very faint, "I'm going to have to go back to the house and get your wheelchair. I'm so sorry. I'm going to be right back." He nods, barely, and feels Harold button his coat closed, feels him push his hands into his coat's pockets, feels him wrap something around his legs—Harold's own coat, he realizes. "I'll be right back," Harold says. "I'll be right back." He hears Harold's feet running away from him, the crunch of the sticks and leaves as they snap and crumple beneath him.

He turns his head to the side and the ground beneath him shifts, dangerously, and he vomits, coughing up everything he has eaten that day, feels it slide off of his lips and drool down his cheek. Then he feels a bit better, and he leans his head against the tree again. He is reminded of his time in the forest when he was running away from the home, how he had hoped the trees might protect him, and now he hopes for it again. He takes his hand out of his pocket, feels for his cane, and squeezes it as hard as he can. Behind his eyelids, bright spangled drops of light burst into confetti, and then blink out into oily smears. He concentrates on the sound of his breath, and on his legs, which he imagines as large lumpen shards of wood into which have been drilled dozens of long metal screws, each as thick as a thumb. He pictures the screws being drawn out in reverse, each one rotating slowly out of him and landing with a ringing clang on a cement floor. He vomits again. He is so cold. He can feel himself begin to spasm.

And then he hears someone running toward him, and he can smell it is Willem—his sweet sandalwood scent—before he hears his voice. Willem gathers him, and when he lifts him, everything sways again, and he thinks he is going to be sick, but he isn't, and he puts his right arm around Willem's neck and turns his vomity face into his shoulder and lets himself be carried. He can hear Willem panting—he may weigh less than Willem, but they are still the same height, and he knows how unwieldy he must be, his cane, still in his hand, banging against Willem's thighs, his calves knocking against Willem's rib cage—and is grateful when he feels himself being lowered into his chair, hears Willem's and Harold's voices above him. He bends over, resting his forehead on his knees, and is pushed back out of the forest and up the hill to the house, and once inside, he is lifted into bed. Someone takes off his shoes, and he screams out and is apologized to; someones wipes his face; someone wraps his hands around a hot-water bottle; someone wraps his legs with blankets. Above him, he can hear Willem being angry—"Why did you fucking go along with this? You *know* he can't fucking do this!"—and Harold's apologetic, miserable replies: "I know,

Willem. I'm so sorry. It was moronic. But he wanted to go so badly." He tries to speak, to defend Harold, to tell Willem it was his fault, that he made Harold come with him, but he can't.

"Open your mouth," Willem says, and he feels a pill, bitter as metal, being placed on his tongue. He feels a glass of water being tipped toward his lips. "Swallow," Willem says, and he does, and soon after, the world ceases to exist.

When he wakes, he turns and sees Willem in bed with him, staring at him. "I'm so sorry," he whispers, but Willem doesn't say anything. He reaches over and runs his hand through Willem's hair. "Willem," he says, "it wasn't Harold's fault. I made him do it."

Willem snorts. "Obviously," he says. "But he still shouldn't have agreed to it."

They are quiet for a long time, and he thinks of what he needs to say, what he has always thought but never articulated. "I know this is going to sound illogical to you," he tells Willem, who looks back at him. "But even all these years later, I still can't think of myself as disabled. I mean—I know I am. I know I am. I have been for twice as long as I haven't been. It's the only way you've known me: as someone who— who needs help. But I remember myself as someone who used to be able to walk whenever he wanted to, as someone who used to be able to run.

"I think every person who becomes disabled thinks they were robbed of something. But I suppose I've always felt that—that if I acknowledge that I *am* disabled, then I'll have conceded to Dr. Traylor, then I'll have let Dr. Traylor determine the shape of my life. And so I pretend I'm not; I pretend I am who I was before I met him. And I know it's not logical or practical. But mostly, I'm sorry because—because I know it's selfish. I know my pretending has consequences for you. So—I'm going to stop." He takes a breath, closes and opens his eyes. "I'm disabled," he says. "I'm handicapped." And as foolish as it is—he is forty-seven, after all; he has had thirty-two years to admit this to himself—he feels himself about to cry.

"Oh, Jude," says Willem, and pulls him toward him. "I know you're sorry. I know this is hard. I understand why you've never wanted to admit it; I do. I just worry about you; I sometimes think I care more about your being alive than you do."

He shivers, hearing this. "No, Willem," he says. "I mean—maybe, at one point. But not now."

"Then prove it to me," Willem says, after a silence.

"I will," he says.

January; February. He is busier than he has ever been. Willem is rehearsing a play. March: Two new wounds open up, both on his right leg. Now the pain is excruciating; now he never leaves his wheelchair except to shower and go to the bathroom and dress and undress. It has been a year, more, since he has had a reprieve from the pain in his feet. And yet every morning when he wakes, he places them on the floor and is, for a second, hopeful. Maybe today he will feel better. Maybe today the pain will have abated. But he never does; it never does. And still he hopes. April: His birthday. The play's run begins. May: Back come the night sweats, the fever, the shaking, the chills, the delirium. Back he goes to the Hotel Contractor. Back goes the catheter, this time into the left side of his chest. But there is a change this time: this time the bacteria is different; this time, he will need an antibiotic drip every eight hours, not every twenty-four. Back comes Patrizia, now two times a day: at six a.m., at Greene Street; at two p.m. at Rosen Pritchard; and at ten p.m. again at Greene Street, a night nurse, Yasmin. For the first time in their friendship, he sees only one performance of Willem's play: his days are so segmented, so controlled by his medication, that he is simply unable to go a second time. For the first time since this cycle began a year ago, he feels himself tumbling toward despair; he feels himself giving up. He has to remind himself he must prove to Willem that he wants to remain alive, when all he really wants to do is stop. Not because he is depressed, but because he is exhausted. At the conclusion of one appointment, Andy looks at him with a strange expression and tells him that he's not sure if he's realized, but it's been a month since he last cut himself, and he thinks about this. Andy is right. He has been too tired, too consumed to think about cutting.

"Well," Andy says. "I'm glad. But I'm sorry this is why you've stopped, Jude."

"I am, too," he says. They are both quiet, both, he fears, nostalgic for the days when cutting was his most serious problem.

Now it is June, now it is July. The wounds on his legs—the old ones, which he has had for more than a year, and the more recent ones, which he has had since March—have not healed. They have barely diminished. And it is then, just after the Fourth of July weekend, just after Willem's run ends, that Andy asks if he can come talk to him and Willem. And because he knows what Andy is going to say, he lies and says that Willem is busy, that Willem doesn't have the time, as if by delaying the conversation, he might delay his future as well, but early one Saturday evening he comes home from the office and there they are in the apartment, waiting for him.

The speech is what he expects. Andy recommends—he strongly recommends—amputation. Andy is gentle, very gentle, but he can tell, from how rehearsed his delivery is, from how formal he is, that he is nervous.

"We always knew this day would come," Andy begins, "but that doesn't make it any easier. Jude, only you know how much pain, how much inconvenience, you can tolerate. I can't tell you that. I *can* tell you that you've gone on far longer than most people would. I can tell you you've been extraordinarily courageous—don't make that face: you have been; you are—and I can tell you that I can't imagine what you've been suffering.

"But all of that aside—even if you feel you have the wherewithal to keep going—there are some realities to consider here. The treatments aren't working. The wounds aren't healing. The fact that you've had two bone infections in less than a year is alarming to me. I'm worried you're going to develop an allergy to one of the antibiotics, and then we'll be really, really fucked. And even if you don't, you're not tolerating the drugs as well as I'd hoped you would: you've lost way too much weight, a troubling amount of weight, and every time I see you, you've gotten a little weaker.

"The tissue in your upper legs seems to be healthy enough that I'm pretty certain we'll be able to spare both knees. And Jude, I promise you that your quality of life will improve instantly if we amputate. There won't be any more pain in your feet. You've never had a wound on your thighs, and I don't think there's any immediate fear you will. The prosthetics available now are so infinitely superior than what they were even ten years ago that honestly, your gait will probably be better, more natural, with them than it is with your actual legs. The surgery is very straightforward—just four hours or so—and I'll do it myself. And the inpatient recovery is brief: less than a week in the hospital, and we'll fit you with temporary prostheses immediately."

Andy stops, placing his hands on his knees, and looks at them. For a long while, none of them speaks, and then Willem begins to ask questions, smart questions, questions he should be asking: How long is the outpatient recovery period? What kind of physical therapy would he be doing? What are the risks associated with the surgery? He half listens to the responses, which he already knows, more or less, having researched these very questions, this very scenario, every year since Andy had first suggested it to him, seventeen years ago.

Finally, he interrupts them. "What happens if I say no?" he asks, and he can see the dismay move across both of their faces.

"If you say no, we'll keep pushing forward with everything we've been doing and hope it works eventually," Andy says. "But Jude, it's always better to have an amputation when you get to *decide* to have it, not when you're forced to have it." He pauses. "If you get a blood infection, if you develop sepsis, then we *will* have to amputate, and I won't be able to guarantee that you'll keep the knees. I won't be able to guarantee that you won't lose some other extremity—a finger; a hand—that the infection won't spread far beyond your lower legs."

"But you can't guarantee me that I'll even keep the knees this time," he says, petulant. "You can't guarantee I won't develop sepsis in the future."

"No," Andy admits. "But as I said, I think there's a very good chance you *will* keep them. And I think if we remove this part of your body that's so gravely infected that it'll help prevent further disease."

They are all quiet again. "This sounds like a choice that isn't a choice," he mutters.

Andy sighs. "As I said, Jude," he says, "it *is* a choice. It's *your* choice. You don't have to make it tomorrow, or even this week. But I want you to think about it, carefully."

He leaves, and he and Willem are left alone. "Do we have to talk about it now?" he asks, when he can finally look at Willem, and Willem shakes his head. Outside the sky is turning rose-colored; the sunset will be long and beautiful. But he doesn't want beauty. He wishes, suddenly, that he could swim, but he hasn't swum since the first bone infection. He hasn't done anything. He hasn't gone anywhere. He has had to turn his London clients over to a colleague, because his IV has tethered him to New York. His muscles have disappeared: he is soft flesh on bone; he moves like an old man. "I'm going to bed," he tells Willem, and when Willem says, quietly, "Yasmin's coming in a couple of hours," he wants to cry. "Right," he says, to the floor. "Well. I'm going to take a nap, then. I'll wake up for Yasmin."

That night, after Yasmin has left, he cuts himself for the first time in a long time; he watches the blood weep across the marble and into the drain. He knows how irrational it seems, his desire to keep his legs, his legs that have caused him so many problems, that have cost him how many hours, how much money, how much pain to maintain? But still: They are his. They are his legs. They are him. How can he willingly cut away a part of himself? He knows that he has already cut away so much of himself over the years: flesh, skin, scars. But somehow this is different. If he sacrifices his legs, he will be admitting to Dr. Traylor that he has won; he will be surrendering to him, to that night in the field with the car.

And it is also different because he knows that once he loses them, he will no longer be able to pretend. He will no longer be able to pretend that someday he will walk again, that someday he will be better. He will no longer be able to pretend that he isn't disabled. Up, once more, will go his freak-show factor. He will be someone who is defined, first and always, by what he is missing.

And he is tired. He doesn't want to have to learn how to walk again. He doesn't want to work at regaining weight he knows he will lose, weight on top of the weight he has struggled to replace from the first bone infection, weight that he has re-lost with the second. He doesn't want to go back into the hospital, he doesn't want to wake disoriented and confused, he doesn't want to be visited by night terrors, he doesn't want to explain to his colleagues that he is sick yet again, he doesn't want the months and months of being weak, of fighting to regain his equilibrium. He doesn't want Willem to see him without his legs, he doesn't want to give him one more challenge, one more grotesquerie to overcome. He wants to be normal, he has only ever wanted to be normal, and yet with each year, he moves further and further from normalcy. He knows it is fallacious to think of the mind and the body as two separate, competing entities, but he cannot help it. He doesn't want his body to win one more battle, to make the decision for him, to make him feel so helpless. He doesn't want to be dependent on Willem, to have to ask him to lift him in and out of bed because his arms will be too useless and watery, to help him use the bathroom, to see the remains of his legs rounded into stumps. He had always assumed that there would be some sort of warning before this point, that his body would alert him before it became seriously worse. He knows, he does, that this past year and a half *was* his warning—a long, slow, consistent, unignorable warning—but he has chosen, in his arrogance and stupid hope, not to see it for what it is. He has chosen to believe that because he had always recovered, that he would once again, one more time. He has given himself the privilege of assuming that his chances are limitless.

Three nights later he wakes again with a fever; again he goes into the hospital; again he is discharged. This fever has been caused by an infection around his catheter, which is removed. A new one is inserted into his internal jugular vein, where it forms a bulge that not even his shirt collars can wholly camouflage.

His first night back home, he is coasting through his dreams when he opens his eyes and sees that Willem isn't in bed next to him, and he works himself into his wheelchair and glides out of the room.

He sees Willem before Willem sees him; he is sitting at the dining table, the light on above him, his back to the bookcases, staring out into the room. There is a glass of water before him, and his elbow is resting on the table, his hand supporting his chin. He looks at Willem and sees how exhausted he is, how old, his bright hair gone whitish. He has known Willem for so long, has looked at his face so many times, that he is never able to see him anew: his face is better known to him than his own. He knows its every expression. He knows what Willem's different smiles mean; when he is watching him being interviewed on television, he can always tell when he is smiling because he's truly amused and when he is smiling to be polite. He knows which of his teeth are capped, and he knows which ones Kit made him straighten when it was clear that he was going to be a star, when it was clear that he wouldn't just be in plays and independent films but would have a different kind of career, a different kind of life. But now he looks at Willem, at his face that is still so handsome but also so tired, the kind of tiredness he thought only he was feeling, and realizes that Willem is feeling it as well, that his life—Willem's life with him—has become a sort of drudgery, a slog of illnesses and hospital visits and fear, and he knows what he will do, what he has to do.

"Willem," he says, and watches Willem jerk out of his trance and look at him.

"Jude," Willem says. "What's wrong? Are you feeling sick? Why are you out of bed?"

"I'm going to do it," he says, and he thinks that they are like two actors on a stage, talking to each other across a great distance, and he wheels himself close to him. "I'm going to do it," he repeats, and Willem nods, and then they lean their foreheads into each other's, and both of them start crying. "I'm sorry," he tells Willem, and Willem shakes his head, his forehead rubbing against his.

"I'm sorry," Willem tells him back. "I'm sorry, Jude. I'm so sorry."

"I know," he says, and he does.

The next day he calls Andy, who is relieved but also muted, as if out of respect to him. Things move briskly after that. They pick a date: the first date Andy proposes is Willem's birthday, and even though he and Willem have agreed that they'll celebrate Willem's fiftieth birthday once he's better, he doesn't want to have the surgery on the actual day. So instead he'll have it at the end of August, the week before Labor Day, the week before they usually go to Truro. In the next management committee meeting, he makes a brief announcement, explaining that this is a voluntary operation, that he'll only be out of the office for a week, ten days at the most, that it isn't a big deal, that he'll be fine. Then he announces it to his department; he normally wouldn't, he tells them, but he doesn't want their clients to worry, he doesn't want them to think that it's something more serious than it is, he doesn't want to be the subject of rumors and chatter (although he knows he will be). He reveals so little about himself at work that whenever he does, he can see people sit up and lean forward in their seats, can almost see their ears lift a little higher. He has met all of their wives and husbands and girlfriends and boyfriends, but they have never met Willem. He has never invited Willem to one of the company's retreats, to their annual holiday parties, to their annual summer picnics. "You'd hate them," he tells Willem, although he knows that isn't really the case: Willem can have a good time anywhere. "Believe me." And Willem has always shrugged. "I'd love to come," he has always said, but he has never let him. He has always told himself that he is protecting Willem from a series of events that he would surely find tedious, but he has never considered that Willem might be hurt by his refusal to include him, might actually want to be a part of his life beyond Greene Street and their friends. He flushes now, realizing this.

"Any questions?" he asks, not really expecting any, when he sees one of the younger partners, a callous but scarily effective man named Gabe Freston, raise his hand. "Freston?" he says.

"I just wanted to say that I'm really sorry, Jude," says Freston, and around him, everyone murmurs their agreement.

He wants to make the moment light, to say—because it is true—"That's the first time I've heard you be so sincere since I told you what your bonus would be last year, Freston," but he doesn't, just takes a deep breath. "Thank you, Gabe," he says. "Thanks, all of you. Now everyone—back to work," and they scatter.

The surgery will be on a Monday, and although he stays at the office late on Friday, he doesn't go in on Saturday. That afternoon, he packs a bag for the hospital; that evening, he and Willem have dinner at the tiny sushi place where they first celebrated the Last Supper. His final sessions with Patrizia and Yasmin had been on Thursday; Andy calls early on Saturday to tell him that he has the X-rays back, and that although the infection hasn't budged, it also hasn't spread. "Obviously, it won't be a problem after Monday," he says, and he swallows, hard, just as he had when Andy had said earlier that week, "You won't have this foot pain after next Monday." He remembers then that it is not the problem that is being eradicated; it is the *source* of the problem that is being eradicated. One is not the same as the other, but he supposes he has to be grateful, finally, for eradication, however it is delivered.

He eats his final meal on Sunday at seven p.m.; the surgery is at eight the next morning, and so he is to have no more food, no more medication, nothing to drink, for the rest of the night.

An hour later, he and Willem descend in the elevator to the ground floor, for his last walk on his own legs. He has made Willem promise him this walk, and even before they begin—they will go south on Greene one block to Grand, then west just another block to Wooster, then up Wooster four blocks to Houston, then back east to Greene and south to their apartment—he isn't sure he'll be able to finish. Above them, the sky is the color of bruises, and he remembers, suddenly, being forced out onto the street, naked, by Caleb.

He lifts up his left leg and begins. Down the quiet street they walk, and at Grand, as they are turning right, he takes Willem's hand, which he never does in public, but now he holds it close, and they turn right again and begin moving up Wooster.

He had wanted so badly to complete this circuit, but perversely, his inability to do so—at Spring, still two blocks south of Houston, Willem glances at him and, without even asking, starts walking him back east to Greene Street—reassures him: he is making the right decision. He has pressed up against the inevitable, and he has made the only choice he could make, not just for Willem's sake, but for his own. The walk has been almost unbearable, and when he gets back to the apartment, he is surprised to feel that his face is wet with tears.

The next morning, Harold and Julia meet them at the hospital, looking gray and frightened. He can tell they are trying to remain stoic for him; he hugs and kisses them both, assures them he'll be fine, that there's nothing to worry about. He is taken away to be prepped. Since the injury, the hair on his legs has always grown unevenly, around and between the scars, but now he is shaved clean above and below his kneecaps. Andy comes in, holds his face in his hands, and kisses him on his forehead. He doesn't say anything, just takes out a marker and draws a series of dashes, like Morse code signals, in inverted arcs a few inches below the bottoms of both knees, then tells him he'll be back, but that he'll send Willem in.

Willem comes over and sits on the edge of his bed, and they hold each other's hands in silence. He is about to say something, make some stupid joke, when Willem begins to cry, and not just cry, but keen, bending over and moaning, sobbing like he has never seen anyone sob. "Willem," he says, desperately, "Willem, don't cry: I'm going to be fine. I really am. Don't cry. Willem, don't cry." He sits up in the bed, wraps his arms around Willem. "Oh, Willem," he sighs, near tears himself. "Willem, I'm going to be okay. I promise you." But he can't soothe him, and Willem cries and cries.

He senses that Willem is trying to say something, and he rubs his back, asking him to repeat himself. "Don't go," he hears Willem say. "Don't leave me."

"I promise I won't," he says. "I promise. Willem—it's an easy surgery. You know I have to come out on the other side so Andy can lecture me some more, right?"

It is then that Andy walks in. "Ready, campers?" he asks, and then he sees and hears Willem. "Oh god," he says, and he comes over, joins their huddle. "Willem," he says, "I promise I'll take care of him like he's my own, you know that, right? You know I won't let anything happen to him?"

"I know," they hear Willem gulp, at last. "I know, I know."

Finally, they are able to calm Willem down, who apologizes and wipes at his eyes. "I'm sorry," Willem says, but he shakes his head, and pulls on Willem's hand until he brings his face to his own, kisses him goodbye. "Don't be," he tells him.

Outside the operating room, Andy brings his head down to his, and kisses him again, this time on his cheek. "I'm not going to be able to touch you after this," he says. "I'll be sterile." The two of them grin, suddenly, and Andy shakes his head. "Aren't you getting a little old for this kind of puerile humor?" he asks.

"Aren't *you*?" he asks. "You're almost sixty."

"Never."

Then they are in the operating room, and he is gazing at the bright white disk of light above him. "Hello, Jude," says a voice behind him, and he sees it's the anesthesiologist, a friend of Andy's named Ignatius Mba, whom he's met before at one of Andy and Jane's dinner parties.

"Hi, Ignatius," he says.

"Count backward from ten for me," says Ignatius, and he begins to, but after seven, he is unable to count any further; the last thing he feels is a tingling in his right toes.

Three months later. It is Thanksgiving again, and they are having it at Greene Street. Willem and Richard have cooked everything, arranged everything, while he slept. His recovery has been harder and more complicated than anticipated, and he has contracted infections, twice. For a while he was on a feeding tube. But Andy was right: he has kept both knees. In the hospital, he would wake, telling Harold and Julia, telling Willem, that it felt like there was an elephant sitting on his feet, rocking back and forth on its rump until his bones turned into cracker dust, into something finer than ash. But they never told him that he was imagining this; they only told him that the nurse had just added a painkiller to his IV drip for this very purpose, and that he would be feeling better soon. Now he has these phantom pains less and less frequently, but they haven't disappeared entirely. And he is still very tired, he is still very weak, and so Richard has placed a mauve velvet wingback chair on casters—one that India sometimes uses for sittings—for him at the head of the table, so he can lean his head against its wings when he feels depleted.

That dinner is Richard and India, Harold and Julia, Malcolm and Sophie, JB and his mother, and Andy and Jane, whose children are visiting Andy's brother in San Francisco. He starts to give a toast, thanking everyone for everything they have given him and done for him, but before he gets to the person he wants to thank most—Willem, sitting to his right—he finds he cannot continue, and he looks up from his paper at his friends and sees that they are all going to cry, and so he stops.

He is enjoying the dinner, amused even by how people keep adding scoops of different food to his plate, even though he hasn't eaten much of his first serving, but he is so sleepy, and eventually he burrows back into the chair and closes his eyes, smiling as he listens to the familiar conversation, the familiar voices, fill the air around him.

Eventually Willem notices that he is falling asleep, and he hears him stand. "Okay," he says, "time for your diva exit," and turns the chair from the table and begins pushing it away toward their bedroom, and he uses the last of his strength to answer everyone's laughter, their song of goodbyes, to peek out around the wing of the chair and smile at them, letting his fingers trail behind him in an airy, theatrical wave. "Stay," he calls out as he is taken from them. "Please stay. Please stay and give Willem some decent conversation," and they agree they will; it isn't even seven, after all—they have hours and hours. "I love you," he calls to them, and they shout it back at him, all of them at once, although even in their chorus, he can still distinguish each individual voice.

At the doorway to their bedroom, Willem lifts him—he has lost so much weight, and without his prostheses is so less storklike a form, that now even Julia can lift him—and carries him to their bed, helps him undress, helps him remove his temporary prostheses, folds the covers back over him. He pours him a glass of water, hands him his pills: an antibiotic, a fistful of vitamins. He swallows them all as Willem watches, and then for a while Willem sits on the bed next to him, not touching him, but simply near.

"Promise me you'll go out there and stay up late," he tells Willem, and Willem shrugs.

"Maybe I'll just stay here with you," he says. "They seem to be having a fine time without me." And sure enough, there is a burst of laughter from the dining room, and they look at each other and smile.

"No," he says, "promise me," and finally, Willem does. "Thank you, Willem," he says, inadequately, his eyes closing. "This was a good day."

"It was, wasn't it?" he hears Willem say, and then he begins to say something else, but he doesn't hear it because he has fallen asleep.

That night his dreams wake him. It is one of the side effects of the particular antibiotic he is on, these dreams, and this time, they are worse than ever. Night after night, he dreams. He dreams that he is in the motel rooms, that he is in Dr. Traylor's house. He dreams that he is still fifteen, that the previous thirty-three years haven't even happened. He dreams of specific clients, specific incidents, of things he hadn't even known he remembered. He dreams that he has become Brother Luke himself. He dreams, again and again, that Harold is Dr. Traylor, and when he wakes, he feels ashamed for attributing such behavior to Harold, even in his subconscious, and at the same time fearful that the dream might be real after all, and he has to remind himself of Willem's promise: *Never, ever, Jude. He would never do that to you, not for anything.*

Sometimes the dreams are so vivid, so real, that it takes minutes, an hour for him to return to his life, for him to convince himself that the life of his consciousness is in fact real life, his real life. Sometimes he wakes so far from himself that he can't even remember who he is. "Where am I?" he asks, desperate, and then, "Who am I? Who am I?"

And then he hears, so close to his ear that it is as if the voice is originating inside his own head, Willem's whispered incantation. "You're Jude St. Francis. You are my oldest, dearest friend. You're the son of Harold Stein and Julia Altman. You're the friend of Malcolm Irvine, of Jean-Baptiste Marion, of Richard Goldfarb, of Andy Contractor, of Lucien Voigt, of Citizen van Straaten, of Rhodes Arrowsmith, of Elijah Kozma, of Phaedra de los Santos, of the Henry Youngs.

"You're a New Yorker. You live in SoHo. You volunteer for an arts organization; you volunteer for a food kitchen.

"You're a swimmer. You're a baker. You're a cook. You're a reader. You have a beautiful voice, though you never sing anymore. You're an excellent pianist. You're an art collector. You write me lovely messages when I'm away. You're patient. You're generous. You're the best listener

I know. You're the smartest person I know, in every way. You're the bravest person I know, in every way.

"You're a lawyer. You're the chair of the litigation department at Rosen Pritchard and Klein. You love your job; you work hard at it.

"You're a mathematician. You're a logician. You've tried to teach me, again and again.

"You were treated horribly. You came out on the other end. You were always you."

On and on Willem talks, chanting him back to himself, and in the daytime—sometimes days later—he remembers pieces of what Willem has said and holds them close to him, as much as for what he said as for what he didn't, for how he hadn't defined him.

But in the nighttime he is too terrified, he is too lost to recognize this. His panic is too real, too consuming. "And who are you?" he asks, looking at the man who is holding him, who is describing someone he doesn't recognize, someone who seems to have so much, someone who seems like such an enviable, beloved person. "Who are you?"

The man has an answer to this question as well. "I'm Willem Ragnarsson," he says. "And I will never let you go."

—

"I'm going," he tells Jude, but then he doesn't move. A dragonfly, as shiny as a scarab, hums above them. "I'm going," he repeats, but he still doesn't move, and it is only the third time he says it that he's finally able to stand up from the lounge chair, drunk on the hot air, and shove his feet back into his loafers.

"Limes," says Jude, looking up at him and shielding his eyes against the sun.

"Right," he says, and bends down, takes Jude's sunglasses off him, kisses him on his eyelids, and replaces his glasses. Summer, JB has always said, is Jude's season: his skin darkens and his hair lightens to almost the same shade, making his eyes turn an unnatural green, and Willem has to keep himself from touching him too much. "I'll be back in a little while."

He trudges up the hill to the house, yawning, places his glass of half-melted ice and tea in the sink, and crunches down the pebbled driveway to the car. It is one of those summer days when the air is so hot, so dry, so still, the sun overhead so white, that one doesn't so much see one's surroundings as hear and smell and taste them: the lawn-mower buzz of the bees and locusts, the faint peppery scent of the sun-flowers, the oddly mineral flavor the heat leaves on the tongue, as if he's just sucked on stones. The heat is enervating, but not in an oppressive way, only in a way that makes them both sleepy and defenseless, in a way that makes torpor not just acceptable but necessary. When it is hot like this they lie by the pool for hours, not eating but drinking—pitchers of iced mint tea for breakfast, liters of lemonade for lunch, bottles of Aligoté for dinner—and they leave the house's every window, every door open, the ceiling fans spinning, so that at night, when they finally seal it shut, they trap within it the fragrance of meadows and trees.

It is the Saturday before Labor Day, and they would normally be in Truro, but this year they have rented Harold and Julia a house out-side Aix-en-Provence for the entire summer, and the two of them are spending the holiday in Garrison instead. Harold and Julia will arrive—maybe with Laurence and Gillian, maybe not—tomorrow, but today Willem is picking up Malcolm and Sophie and JB and his on-again, off-again boyfriend Fredrik from the train station. They've seen very lit-tle of their friends for months now: JB has been on a fellowship in Italy for the past six months, and Malcolm and Sophie have been so busy with the construction of a new ceramics museum in Shanghai that the last time they saw them all was in April, in Paris—he was filming there, and Jude had come in from London, where he was working, and JB in from Rome, and Malcolm and Sophie had laid over for a couple of days on their way back to New York.

Almost every summer he thinks: This is the best summer. But this summer, he knows, really is the best. And not just the summer: the spring, the winter, the fall. As he gets older, he is given, increasingly, to thinking of his life as a series of retrospectives, assessing each season as it passes as if it's a vintage of wine, dividing years he's just lived into historical eras: The Ambitious Years. The Insecure Years. The Glory Years. The Delusional Years. The Hopeful Years.

Jude had smiled when he told him this. "And what era are we in now?" he asked, and Willem had smiled back at him. "I don't know," he said. "I haven't come up with a name for it yet."

But they both agreed that they had at least exited The Awful Years. Two years ago, he had spent this very weekend—Labor Day weekend—in a hospital on the Upper East Side, staring out the window with a hatred so intense it nauseated him at the orderlies and nurses and doctors in their jade-green pajamas congregating outside the building, eating and smoking and talking on their phones as if nothing were wrong, as if above them weren't people in various stages of dying, including his own person, who was at that moment in a medically induced coma, his skin prickling with fever, who had last opened his eyes four days ago, the day after he had gotten out of surgery.

"He's going to be fine, Willem," Harold kept babbling at him, Harold who was in general even more of a worrier than Willem himself had become. "He's going to be fine. Andy said so." On and on Harold went, parroting back to Willem everything that he had already heard Andy say, until finally he had snapped at him, "Jesus, Harold, give it a fucking break. Do you believe everything Andy says? Does he *look* like he's getting better? Does he *look* like he's going to be fine?" And then he had seen Harold's face change, his expression of pleading, frantic desperation, the face of an old, hopeful man, and he had been punched with remorse and had gone over and held him. "I'm sorry," he said to Harold, Harold who had already lost one son, who was trying to reassure himself that he wouldn't lose another. "I'm sorry, Harold, I'm sorry. Forgive me. I'm being an asshole."

"You're not an asshole, Willem," Harold had said. "But you can't tell me he's not going to get better. You can't tell me that."

"I know," he said. "Of course he's going to get better," he said, sounding like Harold, Harold echoing Harold to Harold. "Of course he is." But inside of him, he felt the beetley scrabble of fear: of course there was no of course. There never had been. *Of course* had vanished eighteen months ago. *Of course* had left their lives forever.

He had always been an optimist, and yet in those months, his optimism deserted him. He had canceled all of his projects for the rest of the year, but as the fall dragged on, he wished he had them; he wished he had something to distract himself. By the end of September, Jude was out of the hospital, and yet he was so thin, so frail, that Willem had been scared to touch him, scared to even look at him, scared to see the way that his cheekbones were now so pronounced that they cast permanent shadows around his mouth, scared to see the way he could watch Jude's pulse beating in the scooped-out hollow of his throat, as if there was something living inside of him that was trying to kick its way out. He could feel Jude trying to comfort him, trying to make jokes, and that made him even more scared. On the few occasions he left the apartment—"You have to," Richard had told him, flatly, "you're going to go crazy otherwise, Willem"—he was tempted to turn his phone off, because every time it chirped and he saw it was Richard (or Malcolm, or Harold, or Julia, or JB, or Andy, or the Henry Youngs, or Rhodes, or Elijah, or India, or Sophie, or Lucien, or whoever was sitting with Jude for the hour or so that he was distractedly wandering the streets or working out downstairs or, a few times, trying to lie still through a massage or sit through lunch with Roman or Miguel), he would tell himself, *This is it. He's dying. He's dead*, and he would wait a second, another second, before answering the phone and hearing that the call was only a status report: That Jude had eaten a meal. That he hadn't. That he was sleeping. That he seemed nauseated. Finally he had to tell them: Don't call me unless it's serious. I don't care if you have questions and calling's faster; you have to text me. If you call me, I'll think the worst. For the first time in his life, he understood, viscerally, what it meant when people said their hearts were in their throats, although it wasn't just his heart he could feel but all his organs thrusting upward, trying to exit him through his mouth, his innards scrambled with anxiety.

People always spoke of healing as if it were predictable and progressive, a decisive diagonal line pointing from the lower left-hand corner of a graph to the upper right. But Hemming's healing—which hadn't ended with his healing at all—hadn't been like that, and Jude's hadn't either: theirs were a mountain range of peaks and trenches, and in the middle of October, after Jude had gone back to work (still scarily thin, still scarily weak), there had been a night when he had woken with a fever so high that he had started seizing, and Willem had been certain that this was the moment, that this was the end. He had realized then that despite his fear, he had never really prepared himself, that he had never really thought of what it would mean, and although he wasn't a bargainer by nature, he bargained now, with someone or something he didn't even know he believed in. He promised more patience, more gratitude, less swearing, less vanity, less sex, less indulgence, less complaining, less self-absorption, less selfishness, less fearfulness. When Jude had lived, Willem's relief had been so total, so punishing, that he had collapsed, and Andy had prescribed him an antianxiety pill and sent him up to Garrison for the weekend with JB for company, leaving

Jude in his and Richard's care. He had always thought that unlike Jude, he had known how to accept help when it was offered, but he had forgotten this skill at the most crucial time, and he was glad and grateful that his friends had made the effort to remind him.

By Thanksgiving, things had become—if not good, then they had at least stopped being bad, which they accepted as the same thing. But it was only in retrospect that they had been able to recognize it as a sort of fulcrum, as the period in which there were first days, and then weeks, and then an entire month in which nothing got worse, in which they regained the trick of waking each day with not dread but with purpose, in which they were finally, cautiously, able to talk about the future, to worry not just about making it successfully through the day but into days they couldn't yet imagine. It was only then that they were able to talk about what needed to be done, only then that Andy began making serious schedules—schedules with goals set one month, two months, six months away—that tracked how much weight he wanted Jude to gain, and when he would be fitted with his permanent prostheses, and when he wanted him to take his first steps, and when he wanted to see him walking again. Once again, they rejoined the slipstream of life; once again, they learned to obey the calendar. By February Willem was reading scripts again. By April, and his forty-ninth birthday, Jude was walking again—slowly, inelegantly, but walking—and looking once again like a normal person. By Willem's birthday that August, almost a year after his surgery, his walk was, as Andy had predicted, better— silkier, more confident—than it had been with his own legs, and he looked, once again, better than a normal person: he looked like himself again.

"We still haven't had your fiftieth birthday blowout," Jude had reminded him over his fifty-first birthday dinner—his birthday dinner that Jude had made, standing by himself at the stove for hours, displaying no apparent signs of fatigue—and Willem had smiled.

"This is all I want," he'd said, and he meant it. It felt silly to compare his experience of such a depleting, brutal two years to Jude's own experience, and yet he felt transformed by them. It was as if his despair had given rise to a sense of invincibility; he felt that everything extraneous and soft had been burned off of him and he was left as an exposed steel core, indestructible and yet pliant, able to withstand anything.

They spent his birthday in Garrison, just the two of them, and that night, after dinner, they went down to the lake, and he took off his clothes and jumped off the dock into the water, which smelled and looked like a great pool of tea. "Come in," he told Jude, and then, when he hesitated, "As the birthday boy, I command it." And Jude had slowly undressed, and taken off his prostheses, and then had finally pushed off the edge of the dock with his hands, and Willem had caught him. As Jude had gotten physically healthier, he had also grown more and more self-conscious about his body, and Willem knew, from how withdrawn Jude would become at times, from how carefully he shielded himself when he was taking off or putting on his legs, how much he struggled with accepting how he now appeared. When he had been weaker, he had let Willem help undress him, but now that he was stronger, Willem saw him unclothed only in glimpses, only by accident. But he had decided to view Jude's self-consciousness as a certain kind of healthiness, for it was at least proof of his physical strength, proof that he was able to get in and out of the shower by himself, to climb in and out of bed by himself—things he'd had to relearn how to do, things he once hadn't had the energy to do on his own.

Now they drifted through the lake, swimming or clinging to each other in silence, and after Willem got out, Jude did as well, heaving himself onto the deck with his arms, and they sat there for a while in the soft summer air, both of them naked, both of them staring at the tapered ends of Jude's legs. It was the first time he had seen Jude naked in months, and he hadn't known what to say, and in the end had simply put his arm around him and pulled him close, and that had (he thought) been the right thing to say after all.

He was still frightened, intermittently. In September, a few weeks before he left for his first project in more than a year, Jude had woken again with a fever, and this time, he didn't ask Willem not to call Andy, and Willem didn't ask him for permission to do so. They had gone directly to Andy's office, and Andy had ordered X-rays, blood work, everything, and they had waited there, each of them lying on the bed in a different examining room, until the radiologist had called and said that there was no sign of any bone infection, and the lab had called and said that there was nothing wrong.

"Rhinopharyngitis," Andy had said to them, smiling. "The common cold." But he had rested his hand on the back of Jude's head, and they had all been relieved. How fast, how distressingly fast, had their instinct for fear been reawakened, the fear itself a virus that lay dormant but that they would never be able to permanently dispel. Joyfulness, abandon: they had had to relearn those, they had had to re-earn them. But they would never have to relearn fear; it would live within the three of them, a shared disease, a shimmery strand that had woven itself through their DNA.

And so off he went to Spain, to Galicia, to film. For as long as he had known him, Jude had wanted to someday walk the Camino de Santiago, the medieval pilgrimage route that ended in Galicia. "We'll start at the Aspe Pass in the Pyrenees," Jude had said (this was before either of them had ever even been to France), "and we'll walk west. It'll take weeks! Every night we'll stay in these communal pilgrim hostels I've read about and we'll survive on black bread with caraway seeds and yogurt and cucumbers."

"I don't know," he said, although back then he had thought less of Jude's limitations—he was too young at the time, they both were, to truly believe that Jude might have limitations—and more of himself. "That sounds kind of exhausting, Judy."

"Then I'll carry you," Jude had said promptly, and Willem had smiled. "Or we'll get a donkey, and *he'll* carry you. But really, Willem, the point is to *walk* the road, not ride it."

As they grew older, as it became clearer and clearer that this dream of Jude's would forever remain simply that, their fantasies of the Camino became more elaborate. "Here's the pitch," Jude would say. "Four strangers—a Chinese Daoist nun coming to terms with her sexuality; a recently released British convict who writes poetry; a Kazakhstani former arms dealer grieving his wife's death; and a handsome and sensitive but troubled American college dropout—that's you, Willem—meet along the Camino and develop friendships of a lifetime. You'll shoot in real time, so the shoot will only last as long as the walk does. And you'll have to walk the entire time."

By this time, he would always be laughing. "What happens in the end?" he asked.

"The Daoist nun ends up falling in love with an ex–Israeli Army officer she meets along the way, and the two of them return to Tel Aviv to open a lesbian bar called Radclyffe's. The convict and the arms dealer end up together. And your character will meet some virginal but, it turns out, secretly slutty Swedish girl along the route and open a high-end B&B in the Pyrenees, and every year, the original group will gather there for a reunion."

"What's the movie called?" he asked, grinning.

Jude thought. "*Santiago Blues*," he said, and Willem laughed again.

Ever since, they had referred in passing to *Santiago Blues*, whose cast morphed to accommodate him as he grew older, but whose premise and location never did. "How's the script?" Jude would ask him whenever something new came in, and he would sigh. "Okay," he would say. "Not *Santiago Blues* good, but okay."

And then, shortly after that pivotal Thanksgiving, Kit, whom Willem had at one point told of his and Jude's interest in the Camino, had sent him a script with a note that read only "*Santiago Blues!*" And while it wasn't exactly *Santiago Blues*—thank god, he and Jude agreed, it was far better—it was in fact set on the Camino, it would in fact be shot partly in real time, and it did in fact begin in the Pyrenees, at Saint-Jean-Pied-de-Port, and ended in Santiago de Compostela. *The Stars Over St. James* followed two men, both named Paul, both of whom would be played by the same actor: the first was a sixteenth-century French monk traveling the route from Wittenberg on the eve of the Protestant Reformation; the second was a contemporary-day pastor from a small American town who was beginning to question his own faith. Aside from a few minor characters, who would drift in and out of the two Pauls' lives, his would be the only role.

He gave Jude the script to read, and after he finished, Jude had sighed. "Brilliant," he said, sadly. "I wish I could come on this with you, Willem."

"I wish you could, too," he said, quietly. He wished Jude had easier dreams for himself, dreams he could accomplish, dreams Willem could help him accomplish. But Jude's dreams were always about movement: they were about walking impossible distances or traversing impossible terrains. And although he could walk now, and although he felt less of it than Willem could remember him feeling for years, he would, they knew, never live a life without pain. The impossible would remain the impossible.

He had dinner with the Spanish director, Emanuel, who was young but already highly acclaimed and who, despite the complexity and melancholy of his script, was buoyant and bright, and kept repeating his astonishment that he, Willem, was going to be in his film, that it was his dream to work with him. He, in turn, told Emanuel of *Santiago Blues* (Emanuel had laughed when Willem described the plot. "Not bad!" he said, and Willem had laughed, too. "It's *supposed* to be bad!" he corrected Emanuel). He told him about how Jude had always wanted to walk this path; how humbled he was that he would get to do it for him.

"Ah," Emanuel said, teasingly. "I think this is the man for whom you ruined your career, am I right?"

He had smiled back. "Yes," he said. "That's him."

The days on *The Stars Over St. James* were very long and, as Jude had promised, there was lots of walking (and a caravan of slow-moving trailers instead of donkeys). The cell-phone reception was patchy in parts, and so he would instead write Jude messages, which seemed more appropriate anyway, more pilgrim-like, and in the morning, he sent him pictures of his breakfast (black bread with caraway seeds, yogurt, cucumbers) and of the stretch of road he would walk that day. Much of the road cut through busy towns, and so in places they were rerouted into the countryside. Each day, he chose a few white pebbles from the side of the road and put them in a jar to take home; at night, he sat in his hotel room with his feet wrapped in hot towels.

They finished filming two weeks before Christmas, and he flew to London for meetings, and then back to Madrid to meet Jude, where they rented a car and drove south, through Andalusia. In a town on a cliff high above the sea they stopped to meet Asian Henry Young, whom they watched trudging uphill, waving at them with both arms when he saw them, and finishing the last hundred yards in a sprint. "Thank god you're giving me an excuse to get the fuck out of that house," he said. Henry had been living for the past month at an artists' residency down the hill, in a valley filled with orange trees, but unusually for him, he hated the other six people at the colony, and as they ate dishes of orange rounds floating in a liqueur of their own juice and topped with cinnamon and pulverized cloves and almonds, they laughed at Henry's stories about his fellow artists. Later, after telling him goodbye and that they'd see him next month in New York, they walked slowly together through the medieval town, whose every structure was a glittering white salt cube, and where striped cats lay in the streets and flicked the tips of their tails as people with wheel carts ground slowly around them.

The next evening, outside Granada, Jude said he had a surprise for him, and they got into the car that was waiting for them in front of the restaurant, Jude with the brown envelope he'd kept by his side all through dinner.

"Where're we going?" he asked. "What's in the envelope?"

"You'll see," Jude said.

Up and downhill they swooped, until the car stopped before the arched entryway to the Alhambra, where Jude handed the guard a letter, which the guard studied and then nodded at, and the car slid through the doorway and stopped and the two of them got out and stood there in the quiet courtyard.

"Yours," Jude said, shyly, nodding at the buildings and gardens below. "For the next three hours, anyway," and then, when Willem couldn't say anything, he continued, quietly, "Do you remember?"

He nodded, barely. "Of course," he said, just as quietly. This was always how their own trip on the Camino was supposed to end: with a train ride south to visit the Alhambra. And over the years, even as he knew their walk would never happen, he had never gone to the Alhambra, had never taken a day at the end of one shoot or another and come, because he was waiting for Jude to do it with him.

"One of my clients," Jude said, before he could ask. "You defend someone, and their godfather turns out to be the Spanish minister of culture, who lets you make a generous donation to the Alhambra's maintenance fund for the privilege of seeing it alone." He grinned at Willem. "I told you I'd do something for your fiftieth—albeit a year and a half later." He placed his hand on Willem's arm. "Willem, don't cry."

"I'm not going to," he said. "I can do other things in life besides cry, you know," although he was no longer sure that was even true.

He opened the envelope that Jude handed him, and inside there was a package, and he undid the ribbon and tore the paper away and found a handmade book, organized by chapters—"The Alcazaba"; "The Lion Palace"; "The Gardens"; "Generalife"—each with pages of hand-written notes by Malcolm, who had written his thesis on the Alhambra and who had visited it every year since he was nine. Between each chapter was a drawing of one of the complex's details—a jasmine bush blooming with small white flowers, a stone façade stippled with cobalt tilework—tipped into the pages, each dedicated to him and signed by someone they knew: Richard; JB; India; Asian Henry Young; Ali. Now he really did begin to cry, smiling and crying, until Jude told him that they had better get moving, that they couldn't spend their entire time at the entryway, crying, and he grabbed him and kissed him, not caring about the silent, black-clad guards behind them. "Thank you," he said. "Thank you, thank you, thank you."

Off they moved through the silent night, Jude's flashlight bouncing a line of light before them. Into palaces they walked, where the marble was so old that the structure appeared to be carved from soft white butter, and into reception halls with vaulted ceilings so high that birds arced soundlessly through the space, and with windows so symmetrical and perfectly placed that the room was bright with moonlight. As they walked, they stopped to consult Malcolm's notes, to examine details they would have missed had they not been alerted to them, to realize that they were standing in the room where, a thousand years ago, more, a sultan would have dictated his correspondence. They studied the illustrations, matching the images to what they saw before them. Facing each of their friends' drawings was a note each had written explaining when they had first seen the Alhambra, and why they had chosen to draw what they had. They had that feeling, the same one they had often had as young men, that everyone they knew had seen so much of the world and that they hadn't, and although they knew this was no longer true, they still felt that same sense of awe at their friends' lives, at how much they had done and experienced, at how well they knew to appreciate it, at how talented they were at recording it. In the gardens of the Generalife section, they walked into a room that had been cut into a labyrinth hedgerow of cypresses, and he began to kiss Jude, more insistently than he had allowed himself to do in a long time, even though they could hear, faintly, one of the guard's shoes tapping along the stone walkway.

Back in the hotel room they continued, and he heard himself thinking that in the movie version of this night, they would be having sex now, and he was almost, almost about to say this out loud, when he remembered himself, and stopped, pulling back from Jude as he did. But it was as if he had spoken anyway, because for a while they were silent, staring at each other, and then Jude said, quietly, "Willem, we can if you want to."

"Do *you* want to?" he asked, finally.

"Sure," Jude said, but Willem could tell, by the way he had looked down and the slight catch in his voice, that he was lying.

For a second he thought he would pretend, that he would allow himself to be convinced that Jude was telling him the truth. But he couldn't. And so "No," he said, and rolled off of him. "I think this has been enough excitement for one evening." Next to him, he heard Jude exhale, and as he fell asleep, heard him whisper, "I'm sorry, Willem," and he tried to tell Jude that he understood, but by this time he was more unconscious than not and couldn't speak the words.

But that was that period's only sadness, and the source of their sadnesses were different: For Jude, he knew, the sadness rose from a sense of failure, a certainty—one Willem was never able to displace—that he wasn't fulfilling his obligations. For him, the sadness was for Jude himself. Occasionally Willem allowed himself to wonder what Jude's life would have been like if sex had been something he had been left to discover, rather than forced to learn—but it was not a helpful line of thought, and it made him too upset. And so he tried not to consider it. But it was always there, running through their friendship, their lives, like a vein of turquoise forking through stone.

In the meantime, though, there was normalcy, routine, both of which were better than sex or excitement. There was the realization that Jude had walked—slowly, but assuredly—for almost three straight hours that night. There was, back in New York, their lives, the things they used to do, resuming because Jude now had the energy to do so, because he could now stay awake through a play or an opera or a dinner, because he could climb the stairs to reach Malcolm's front door in Cobble Hill, could walk down the pitched sidewalk to reach JB's building in Vinegar Hill. There was the comfort of hearing Jude's alarm blip at five thirty, of hearing him set off for his morning swim, the relief of looking into a box on the kitchen counter and seeing it was full of medical supplies—extra packets of catheter tubing and sterile gauze patches and leftover high-calorie protein drinks that Andy had only recently said Jude could stop ingesting—that Jude would return to Andy, who would donate them to the hospital. In moments he would remember how two years ago from this very date, he would come home from the theater to find Jude in bed asleep, so fragile that it seemed at times that the catheter under his shirt was actually an artery, that he was being steadily and irreversibly whittled down to only nerves and vessels and bone. Sometimes he would think of those moments and feel a sort of disorientation: Was that them, really, those people back then? Where had those people gone? Would they reappear? Or were they now other people entirely? And then he would imagine that those people weren't so much gone as they were within them, waiting to bob back up to the surface, to reclaim their bodies and minds; they were identities now in remission, but they would always be with them.

Sickness had visited them recently enough so that they still remembered to be grateful for every day that passed so uneventfully, even as they grew to expect them. The first time Willem saw Jude in his wheelchair in months, saw him leave the sofa when they were watching a movie because he was having an episode and wanted to be alone, he had been disquieted, and he'd had to make himself remember that this, too, was who Jude was: he was someone whose body betrayed him, and he always would be. The surgery hadn't changed this after all—it had changed Willem's reaction to it. And when he realized that Jude was cutting himself again—not frequently, but regularly—he had to remind himself that, once again, this was who Jude was, and that the surgery hadn't changed this, either.

Still, "Maybe we should call these The Happy Years," he told Jude one morning. It was February, it was snowing, and they were lying in bed, which they now did until late every Sunday morning.

"I don't know," Jude said, and although he could only see the edge of his face, Willem could tell he was smiling. "Isn't that tempting fate a little? We'll call it that and then both of my arms will fall off. Also, that name's taken already."

And it was—it was the title of Willem's next project, in fact, the one he would be leaving for in just a week: six weeks of rehearsals, followed by eleven weeks of filming. But it wasn't the original title. The original title had been *The Dancer on the Stage*, but Kit had just told him that the producers had changed it to *The Happy Years*.

He hadn't liked this new title. "It's so cynical," he told Jude, after complaining first to Kit and then to the director. "There's something so curdled and ironic about it." This had been a few nights ago; they had been lying on the sofa after his daily, thoroughly draining ballet class, and Jude was massaging his feet. He would be playing Rudolf Nureyev in the final years of his life, from his appointment as the ballet director of the Paris Opéra in nineteen-eighty-three, through his HIV diagnosis, and until he first noticed the symptoms of his disease, a year before he actually died.

"I know what you mean," Jude had said after he had finally finished ranting. "But maybe they really were the happy years for him. He was free; he had a job he loved; he was mentoring young dancers; he had turned around an entire company. He was doing some of his greatest choreography. He and that Danish dancer—"

"Erik Bruhn."

"Right. He and Bruhn were still together, at least for a little while longer. He had experienced everything he had probably never dreamed he would have as a younger man, and he was still young enough to enjoy it all: money and renown and artistic freedom. Love. Friendship." He dug his knuckles into Willem's sole, and Willem winced. "That sounds like a happy life to me."

They were both quiet for a while. "But he was sick," Willem said, at last.

"Not then," Jude reminded him. "Not actively, at least."

"No, maybe not," he said. "But he was dying."

Jude had smiled at him. "Oh, dying," he said dismissively. "We're all dying. He just knew his death would come sooner than he had planned. But that doesn't mean they weren't happy years, that it wasn't a happy life."

He had looked at Jude, then, and had felt that same sensation he sometimes did when he thought, really thought of Jude and what his life had been: a sadness, he might have called it, but it wasn't a pitying sadness; it was a larger sadness, one that seemed to encompass all the poor striving people, the billions he didn't know, all living their lives, a sadness that mingled with a wonder and awe at how hard humans everywhere tried to live, even when their days were so very difficult, even when their circumstances were so wretched. Life is so sad, he would think in those moments. It's so sad, and yet we all do it. We all cling to it; we all search for something to give us solace.

But he didn't say this, of course, just sat up and grabbed Jude's face and kissed him and then fell back against the pillows. "How'd you get so smart?" he asked Jude, and Jude grinned at him.

"Too hard?" he asked in response, still kneading Willem's foot.

"Not hard enough."

Now he turned Jude around to face him in bed. "I think we have to stick with The Happy Years," he told him. "We'll just have to risk your arms falling off," and Jude laughed.

The next week, he left for Paris. It was one of the most difficult shoots he'd ever done; he had a double, an actual dancer, for the more elaborate sequences, but he did some of his own dancing as well, and there were days—days spent lifting real ballerinas into the air, marveling at how dense, how ropy with muscle they were—that were so exhausting that by the evening he had only the energy to drop himself into the bathtub and then lift himself out of it. In the past few years, he had found himself subconsciously drawn to ever-more physical roles, and he was always astonished by, and appreciative of, how heroically his body met its every demand. He had been given a new awareness of it, and now, as he stretched his arms behind him as he leaped, he could feel how every sore muscle came alive for him, how it allowed him to do whatever he wanted, how nothing within him ever broke, how it indulged him every time. He knew he wasn't alone in feeling this, this gratitude: when they visited Cambridge, he and Harold would play tennis every day, and he knew without them ever discussing it how grateful they had both become for their own bodies, how much the act of smacking heavily, unthinkingly across the court to lunge for a ball had come to mean to them both.

Jude came to visit him in Paris at the end of April, and although Willem had promised him that he wouldn't do anything elaborate for his fiftieth birthday, he had arranged a surprise dinner anyway, and in addition to JB and Malcolm and Sophie, Richard and Elijah and Rhodes and Andy and Black Henry Young and Harold and Julia had all come over, along with Phaedra and Citizen, who had helped him with the planning. The next day Jude had come to watch him on set, one of the very few times he had ever done so. The scene they were working on that morning was one in which Nureyev was trying to correct a young dancer's cabriole, and after instructing him again and again, finally demonstrates how to do it; but in an earlier scene, one they hadn't yet shot but that would directly precede this one, he has just been diagnosed with HIV, and as he jumps, scissoring his legs, he falls, and the studio goes quiet around him. The scene ended on his face, a moment in which he had to convey Nureyev's sudden recognition that he understood how he would die and then, just a second later, his decision to ignore that understanding.

They shot take after take of this scene, and after each take, Willem would have to step away and wait until he could breathe normally again, and hair and makeup would flutter around him, blotting the sweat from his face and neck, and when he was ready, back to his mark he would step. By the time the director was satisfied, he was panting but satisfied as well.

"Sorry," he apologized, going over to Jude at last. "The tedium of filmmaking."

"No, Willem," Jude said. "It was amazing. You were so beautiful out there." He looked tentative for a moment. "I almost couldn't believe it was you."

He took Jude's hand and clasped it in his, which he knew was the most affection Jude would tolerate in public. But he never knew how Jude felt about witnessing such displays of physicality. The previous spring, during one of his breakups with Fredrik, JB had dated a principal in a well-known modern dance company, and they had all gone to see his performance. During Josiah's solo, he had glanced over at Jude and had seen that he was leaning forward slightly, resting his chin in his hand, and watching the stage so intently that when Willem put his hand on his back, he startled. "Sorry," Willem had whispered. Later, in bed, Jude had been very quiet, and he had wondered what he was thinking: Was he upset? Wistful? Sorrowful? But it had seemed unkind to ask Jude to say aloud what he might not have been able to articulate to himself, and so he hadn't.

It was the middle of June by the time he returned to New York, and in bed Jude had looked at him, closely. "You have a ballet dancer's body now," he said, and the next day, he'd examined himself in the mirror and realized that Jude was correct. Later that week, they had dinner on the roof, which they and Richard and India had finally renovated, and which Richard and Jude had planted with grasses and fruit trees, and he had shown them some of what he'd learned, feeling his self-consciousness change to giddiness as he jetéed across the decked surface, his friends applauding behind him, the sun bleeding into nighttime above them.

"Another hidden talent," Richard had said afterward, and had smiled at him.

"I know," Jude had said, smiling at him, too. "Willem is full of surprises, even all these years later."

But they were all full of surprises, he had come to learn. When they were young, they had only their secrets to give one another: confessions were currency, and divulgences were a form of intimacy. Withholding the details of your life from your friends was considered first a sort of mystery and then a kind of stinginess, one that it was understood would preclude true friendship. "There's something you're not telling me, Willem," JB would occasionally accuse him, and, "Are you keeping secrets from me? Don't you trust me? I thought we were close."

"We are, JB," he'd said. "And I'm not keeping anything from you." And he hadn't been: there was nothing to keep. Of all of them, only Jude had secrets, real secrets, and while Willem had in the past been frustrated by what had seemed his unwillingness to reveal them, he had never felt that they weren't close because of that; it had never impaired his ability to love him. It had been a difficult lesson for him to accept, this idea that he would never fully possess Jude, that he would love someone who would remain unknowable and inaccessible to him in fundamental ways.

And yet Jude was still being discovered by him, even thirty-four years after they had met, and he was still fascinated by what he saw. That July, for the first time, he invited him to Rosen Pritchard's annual summer barbeque. "You don't have to come, Willem," Jude had added immediately after asking him. "It's going to be really, really boring."

"I doubt that," he said. "And I'm coming."

The picnic was held on the grounds of a large old mansion on the Hudson, a more polished cousin of the house in which he had shot *Uncle Vanya*, and the entire firm—partners, associates, staff, and their families—had been invited. As they walked down the clover-thick back lawn toward the gathering, he had felt abruptly and unusually shy, keenly aware that he was an interloper, and when Jude was just minutes later plucked away from him by the firm's chairman, who said he had some business he needed to discuss, quickly but urgently, he had to resist actually reaching out for Jude, who turned and gave him an apologetic smile and held up his hand—*Five minutes*—as he left.

So he was grateful for the sudden presence of Sanjay, one of the very few colleagues of Jude's he had met, and who had the year before joined him as co-chair of his department so Jude could concentrate on bringing in new business while Sanjay handled the administrative and managerial details. He and Sanjay remained at the top of the hill, looking at the crowd beneath them, Sanjay pointing out to him various associates and young partners whom he and Jude hated. (Some of these doomed lawyers would turn and see Sanjay looking in their direction and Sanjay would wave back at them, cheerfully, muttering dark things about their lack of competence and resourcefulness to Willem as he did.) He began noticing that people were glancing up at him and then looking away, and one woman, who had been walking uphill, had ungracefully veered off in the opposite direction after noticing him standing there.

"I can see I'm a big hit here," he joked to Sanjay, who smiled back at him.

"They're not intimidated by you, Willem," he said. "They're intimidated by Jude." He grinned. "Okay, and by you as well."

Finally, Jude was returned to him, and they stood talking to the chairman ("I'm a big fan") and Sanjay for a while before moving down the hill, where Jude introduced him to some of the people he'd heard about over the years. One of the paralegals asked to take a picture with him, and after he had, other people asked as well, and when Jude was pulled away from him again, he found himself listening to one of the partners in the tax department, who began describing to him his own stunt sequences from the second of his spy movies. At one point during Isaac's monologue he had looked across the lawn and had caught Jude's eye, who mouthed his apologies, and he had shaken his head and grinned back at him, but then had tugged on his left ear—their old signal—and although he hadn't expected it, when he had looked over again, it was to see Jude marching toward him.

"Sorry, Isaac," he'd said, firmly, "I've got to borrow Willem for a while," and off he had pulled him. "I'm really sorry, Willem," he whispered as they moved away, "the social ineptitude on display is particularly bad today; are you feeling like a panda at the zoo? On the other hand, I *did* tell you it was going to be awful. We can go in ten minutes, I promise."

"No, it's okay," he said. "I'm enjoying myself." He always found it revealing to witness Jude in this other life of his, around the people who owned him for more hours a day than Willem himself did. Earlier, he had watched as Jude walked toward a group of young associates who were braying loudly over something on one of their phones. But when they saw Jude approaching them, they had nudged one another and grown silent and polite, greeting him with a heartiness so robust and obvious that Willem had cringed, and only once Jude had passed them did they huddle over the phone again, but more quietly this time.

By the time Jude was taken away from him a third time, he was feeling confident enough to begin introducing himself to the small pack of people who orbited him in a loose ring, smiling in his direction. He met a tall Asian woman named Clarissa whom he remembered Jude speaking about approvingly. "I've heard a lot of great things about you," he said, and Clarissa's face changed into a radiant, relieved smile. "Jude's talked about *me?*" she asked. He met an associate whose name he couldn't remember who told him that *Black Mercury 3081* had been the first R-rated movie he had ever seen, which made him feel tremendously old. He met another associate in Jude's department who said that he'd taken two classes with Harold in law school and wondered what Harold was like, really. He met Jude's secretaries' children, and Sanjay's son, and dozens of other people, a few of whom he had heard about by name but most of whom he hadn't.

It was a hot, breezeless, brilliant day, and although he had drunk steadily all afternoon—limonata, water, prosecco, iced tea—it had been such a busy gathering that by the time they left, two hours later, neither of them had actually had the opportunity to eat anything, and they stopped at a farm stand to buy corn so they could grill it with zucchini and tomatoes from their garden up at the house.

"I learned a lot about you today," he told Jude as they ate their dinner under the dark blue sky. "I learned that most of the firm is terrified of you and think that if they kiss up to me, I might put in a good word with you. I learned that I'm even older than I had realized. I learned that you're right: you *do* work with a bunch of nerds."

Jude had been smiling, but now he laughed. "See?" he asked. "I told you, Willem."

"But I had a great time," he said. "I did! I want to come again. But next time I think we should invite JB, and blow Rosen Pritchard's collective mind," and Jude had laughed again.

That had been almost two months ago, and since then, he has spent most of his time at Lantern House. As an early fifty-second birthday present, he'd asked Jude to take off every Saturday for the rest of the summer, and Jude has: every Friday he drives up to the house; every Monday morning, he drives back to the city. Because Jude would have the car during the week, he'd rented—partly as a joke, though he was secretly enjoying driving around in it—a convertible, in an alarming color that Jude referred to as "harlot red." During the weekdays, he

reads and swims and cooks and sleeps; he has a very busy autumn coming up, and he knows from how replenished and calm he feels that he'll
be ready.

At the grocery store he fills a paper bag with limes, and then a second one with lemons, buys some extra seltzer water, and drives to the
train station, where he waits, leaning his head on the seat and closing
his eyes until he hears Malcolm calling his name and sits up.

"JB didn't come," Malcolm says, sounding annoyed, as Willem
kisses him and Sophie hello. "He and Fredrik broke up—maybe—this
morning. But maybe they didn't, because he said he was going to come
up tomorrow. I couldn't really figure out what was going on."

He groans. "I'll call him from the house," he says. "Hi, Soph. Have
you guys eaten lunch yet? We can start cooking as soon as we get back."

They haven't, so he calls Jude to tell him he can start boiling the
water for the pasta, but Jude's already begun. "I got the limes," he tells
him. "And JB's not coming until tomorrow; some difficulty with Fredrik
that Mal couldn't quite follow. Do you want to call him and find out
what's happening?"

He loads his friends' bags into the backseat, and Malcolm gets in,
glancing at the car's trunk as he does. "Interesting color," he says.

"Thanks," he says. "It's called 'harlot red.'"

"Really?"

Malcolm's persistent credulity makes him grin. "Yes," he says.
"Ready, guys?"

As he drives, they talk about how long it's been since they've seen
one another, about how glad Sophie and Malcolm are to be home,
about Malcolm's disastrous driving lessons, about how perfect the
weather is, how sweet and haylike the air smells. The best summer, he
thinks again.

It is a thirty-minute drive back to the house from the station, a
little faster if he hurries, but he doesn't hurry, because the drive itself
is pretty. And when he crosses the final large intersection, he doesn't
even see the truck coming toward him, barreling into traffic against
the light, and by the time he feels it, a tremendous crush crumpling
the passenger-seat side of the car, where Sophie is sitting next to him,
he is already aloft, being ejected into the air. "No!" he shouts, or thinks
he does, and then, in an instant, he sees a flash of Jude's face: just his
face, his expression still unresolved, torn from his body and suspended

against a black sky. His ears, his head, fill with the roar of pleating metal, of exploding glass, of his own useless howls.

But his final thoughts are not of Jude, but of Hemming. He sees the house he lived in as a child and, sitting in his wheelchair in the center of the lawn, just before it slopes down toward the stables, Hemming, staring at him with a steady, constant gaze, the kind he was never able to give him in life.

He is at the end of their driveway, where the dirt road meets the asphalt, and seeing Hemming, he is overcome with longing. "Hemming!" he shouts, and then, nonsensically, "Wait for me!" And he begins to run toward his brother, so fast that after a while, he can't even feel his feet strike the ground beneath him.

[VI]

Dear Comrade

1

ONE OF THE first movies Willem ever starred in was a project called *Life After Death*. The film was a take on the story of Orpheus and Eurydice, and was told from alternating perspectives and shot by two different, highly regarded directors. Willem played O., a young musician in Stockholm whose girlfriend had just died, and who had begun having delusions that when he played certain melodies, she would appear beside him. An Italian actress, Fausta, played E., O.'s deceased girlfriend.

The joke of the movie was that while O. stared and wept and mourned for his love from earth, E. was having a terrific time in hell, where she could, finally, stop behaving: stop looking after her querulous mother and her harassed father; stop listening to the whining of the clients she tried to help as a lawyer for the indigent but who never thanked her; stop indulging her self-absorbed friends' endless patter; stop trying to cheer her sweet but perpetually morose boyfriend. Instead, she was in the underworld, a place where the food was plentiful and where the trees were always sagging with fruit, where she could make catty comments about other people without consequence, a place where she even attracted the attention of Hades himself, who was being played by a large, muscular Italian actor named Rafael.

Life After Death had divided the critics. Some of them loved it: they loved how the film said so much about two different cultures' fundamentally different approach to life itself (O.'s story was shot by a famous Swedish director in somber grays and blues; E.'s story was told by an

Italian director known for his aesthetic exuberance), while at the same time offering glints of gentle self-parody; they loved its tonal shifts; they loved how tenderly, and unexpectedly, it offered solace to the living.

But others had hated it: they thought it jarring in both timbre and palette; they hated its tone of ambivalent satire; they hated the musical number that E. participates in while in hell, even as her poor O. plinks away aboveground on his chilly, spare compositions.

But although the debate over the movie (which practically no one in the States saw, but about which everyone had an opinion) was impassioned, there was unanimity about at least one thing: the two leads, Willem Ragnarsson and Fausta San Filippo, were fantastic, and would go on to have great careers.

Over the years, *Life After Death* had been reconsidered, and rethought, and reevaluated, and restudied, and by the time Willem was in his mid-forties, the movie had become officially beloved, a favorite among its directors' oeuvres, a symbol of the kind of collaborative, irreverent, fearless, and yet playful filmmaking that far too few people seemed interested in doing any longer. Willem had been in such a diverse collection of films and plays that he had always been interested in hearing what people named as their favorite, and then reporting his findings back to Willem: the younger male partners and associates at Rosen Pritchard liked the spy movies, for example. The women liked *Duets*. The temps—many of them actors themselves—liked *The Poisoned Apple*. JB liked *The Unvanquished*. Richard liked *The Stars Over St. James*. Harold and Julia liked *The Lacuna Detectives* and *Uncle Vanya*. And film students—who had been the least shy about approaching Willem in restaurants or on the street—invariably liked *Life After Death*. "It's some of Donizetti's best work," they'd say, confidently, or "It must've been amazing to be directed by Bergesson."

Willem had always been polite. "I agree," he'd say, and the film student would beam. "It was. It was amazing."

This year marks the twentieth anniversary of *Life After Death*, and one day in February he steps outside to find that Willem's thirty-three-year-old face has been plastered across the sides of buildings, on the backs of bus-stop shelters, in Warholian multiples along long stretches of scaffolding. It is a Saturday, and although he has been intending to take a walk, he instead turns around and retreats upstairs, where he lies down in bed again and closes his eyes until he falls asleep once more. On Monday, he sits in the back of the car as Mr. Ahmed drives him up Sixth Avenue, and after he sees the first poster, wheat-pasted onto the window of an empty storefront, he shuts his eyes and keeps them shut until he feels the car stop and hears Mr. Ahmed announce that they are at the office.

Later that week he receives an invitation from MoMA; it seems that *Life After Death* will be the first to be screened in a weeklong festival in June celebrating Simon Bergesson's films, and that there will be a panel following the movie at which both of the directors as well as Fausta will be present, and they are hopeful he will attend and—although they know they had extended the offer before—would be thrilled if he might join the panel too and speak about Willem's experiences during shooting. This stops him: *Had* they invited him earlier? He supposes they had. But he can't remember. He can remember very little from the past six months. He looks now at the dates of the festival: June third through June eleventh. He will make plans to be out of town then; he has to be. Willem had shot two other films with Bergesson—they had been friendly. He doesn't want to have to see more posters with Willem's face, to read his name in the paper again. He doesn't want to have to see Bergesson.

That night, before bed, he goes first to Willem's side of the closet, which he still has not emptied. Here are Willem's shirts on their hangers, and his sweaters on their shelves, and his shoes lined up beneath. He takes down the shirt he needs, a burgundy plaid woven through with threads of yellow, which Willem used to wear around the house in the springtime, and shrugs it on over his head. But instead of putting his arms through its sleeves, he ties the sleeves in front of him, which makes the shirt look like a straitjacket, but which he can pretend—if he concentrates—are Willem's arms in an embrace around him. He climbs into bed. This ritual embarrasses and shames him, but he only does it when he really needs it, and tonight he really needs it.

He lies awake. Occasionally he brings his nose down to the collar so he can try to smell what remains of Willem on the shirt, but with every wear, the fragrance grows fainter. This is the fourth shirt of Willem's he has used, and he is very careful about preserving its scent. The first three shirts, ones he wore almost nightly for months, no longer smell like Willem; they smell like him. Sometimes he tries to comfort himself with the fact that his very scent is something given to him by Willem, but he is never comforted for long.

Even before they became a couple, Willem would always bring him something from wherever he'd been working, and when he came back from *The Odyssey*, it was with two bottles of cologne that he'd had made at a famous perfumer's atelier in Florence. "I know this might seem kind of strange," he'd said. "But someone"—he had smiled to himself, then, knowing Willem meant some girl—"told me about this and I thought it sounded interesting." Willem explained how he'd had to describe him to the nose—what colors he liked, what tastes, what parts of the world—and that the perfumer had created this fragrance for him.

He had smelled it: it was green and slightly peppery, with a raw, aching finish. "Vetiver," Willem had said. "Try it on," and he had, dabbing it onto his hand because he didn't let Willem see his wrists back then.

Willem had sniffed at him. "I like it," he said, "it smells nice on you," and they were both suddenly shy with each other.

"Thanks, Willem," he'd said. "I love it."

Willem had had a scent made for himself as well. His had been sandalwood-based, and he soon grew to associate the wood with him: whenever he smelled it—especially when he was far away: in India on business; in Japan; in Thailand—he would always think of Willem and would feel less alone. As the years passed, they both continued to order these scents from the Florence perfumer, and two months ago, one of the first things he did when he had the presence of mind to think of it was to order a large quantity of Willem's custom-made cologne. He had been so relieved, so fevered, when the package had finally arrived, that his hands had tremored as he tore off its wrappings and slit open the box. Already, he could feel Willem slipping from him; already, he knew he needed to try to maintain him. But although he had sprayed— carefully; he didn't want to use too much—the fragrance on Willem's shirt, it hadn't been the same. It wasn't just the cologne after all that had made Willem's clothes smell like Willem: it had been him, his very self-ness. That night he had laid in bed in a shirt gone sugary with sandalwood, a scent so strong that it had overwhelmed every other odor, that it had destroyed what had remained of Willem entirely. That night he had cried, for the first time in a long time, and the next day he had retired that shirt, folding it and packing it into a box in the corner of the closet so it wouldn't contaminate Willem's other clothes.

The cologne, the ritual with the shirt: they are two pieces of the scaffolding, rickety and fragile as it is, that he has learned to erect in order to keep moving forward, to keep living his life. Although often he feels he isn't so much living as he is merely existing, being moved through his days rather than moving through them himself. But he doesn't punish himself too much for this; merely existing is difficult enough.

It had taken months to figure out what worked. For a while he gorged nightly on Willem's films, watching them until he fell asleep on the sofa, fast-forwarding to the scenes with Willem speaking. But the dialogue, the fact of Willem's acting, made him seem farther from him, not closer, and eventually he learned it was better to simply pause on a certain image, Willem's face trapped and staring at him, and he would look and look at it until his eyes burned. After a month of this, he realized that he had to be more vigilant about parsing out these movies, so they wouldn't lose their potency. And so he had begun in order, with Willem's very first film—*The Girl with the Silver Hands*—which he had watched obsessively, every night, stopping and starting the movie, freezing on certain images. On weekends he would watch it for hours, from when the sky was changing from night to day until long after it had turned black again. And then he realized that it was dangerous to watch these movies chronologically, because with each film, it would mean he was getting closer to Willem's death. And so he now chose the month's film at random, and that had proven safer.

But the biggest, the most sustaining fiction he has devised for himself is pretending that Willem is simply away filming. The shoot is very long, and very taxing, but it is finite, and eventually he will return. This had been a difficult delusion, because there had never been a shoot through which he and Willem didn't speak, or e-mail, or text (or all three) every day. He is grateful that he has saved so many of Willem's e-mails, and for a period, he was able to read these old messages at night and pretend he had just received them: even when he wanted to binge on them, he hadn't, and he was careful to read just one in a sitting. But he knew that wouldn't satisfy him forever—he would need to be more judicious about how he doled these e-mails out to himself. Now he reads one, just one, every week. He can read messages he's read in previous weeks, but not messages he hasn't. That is another rule.

But it didn't solve the larger issue of Willem's silence: What circumstances, he puzzled to himself as he swam in the morning, as he stood, unseeingly, over the stove at night, waiting for the teakettle to shriek, would prevent Willem from communicating with him while on a shoot? Finally, he was able to invent a scenario. Willem would be shooting a film about a crew of Russian cosmonauts during the Cold War, and in this fantasy movie, they would actually be in space, because the film was being funded by a perhaps-crazy Russian industrialist billionaire. So away Willem would be, circling miles above him all day and all night, wanting to come home and unable to communicate with him. He was embarrassed by this imaginary movie as well, by his desperation, but it also seemed just plausible enough that he could fool himself into believing it for long stretches, sometimes for several days. (He was grateful then that the logistics and realities of Willem's job had, in many cases, been barely credible: the industry's very improbability helped him to believe now, when he needed it.)

What's the movie called? he imagined Willem asking, imagined Willem smiling.

Dear Comrade, he told Willem, because that was how Willem and he had sometimes addressed their e-mails to each other—*Dear Comrade*; *Dear Jude Haroldovich*; *Dear Willem Ragnaravovich*—which they had begun when Willem was shooting the first installment in his spy trilogy, which had been set in nineteen-sixties Moscow. In his imaginings, *Dear Comrade* would take a year to complete, although he knew he would have to adjust that: it was March already, and in his fantasy, Willem would be coming home in November, but he knew he wouldn't be ready to end the charade by then. He knew he would have to imagine reshoots, delays. He knew he would have to invent a sequel, some reason that Willem would be away from him for longer still.

To heighten the fantasy's believability, he wrote Willem an e-mail every night telling him what had happened that day, just as he would have done had Willem been alive. Every message always ended the same way: *I hope the shoot's going well. I miss you so much. Jude.*

It had been the previous November when he had finally emerged from his stupor, when the finality of Willem's absence had truly begun to resonate. It was then that he had known he was in trouble. He remembers very little from the months before; he remembers very little from the day itself. He remembers finishing the pasta salad, tearing the basil leaves above the bowl, checking his watch and wondering where they were. But he hadn't been worried: Willem liked to drive home on the back roads, and Malcolm liked to take pictures, and so they might have stopped, they might have lost track of the time.

He called JB, listened to him complain about Fredrik; he cut some melon for dessert. By this time they really were late, and he called Willem's phone but it only rang, emptily. Then he was irritated: Where could they have been?

And then it was later still. He was pacing. He called Malcolm's phone, Sophie's phone: nothing. He called Willem again. He called JB: Had they called him? Had he heard from them? But JB hadn't. "Don't worry, Judy," he said. "I'm sure they just went for ice cream or something. Or maybe they all ran off together."

"Ha," he said, but he knew something was wrong. "Okay. I'll call you later, JB."

And just as he had hung up with JB, the doorbell chimed, and he stopped, terrified, because no one ever rang their doorbell. The house was difficult to find; you had to really look for it, and then you had to walk up from the main road—a long, long walk—if no one buzzed you in, and he hadn't heard the front gate buzzer sound. Oh god, he thought. Oh, no. No. But then it rang again, and he found himself moving toward the door, and as he opened it, he registered not so much the policemen's expressions but that they were removing their caps, and then he knew.

He lost himself after that. He was conscious only in flashes, and the people's faces he saw—Harold's, JB's, Richard's, Andy's, Julia's— were the same faces he remembered from when he had tried to kill himself: the same people, the same tears. They had cried then, and they cried now, and at moments he was bewildered; he thought that the past decade—his years with Willem, the loss of his legs—might have been a dream after all, that he might still be in the psychiatric ward. He remembers learning things during those days, but he doesn't remember how he learned them, because he doesn't remember having any conversations. But he must have. He learned that he had identified

Willem's body, but that they hadn't let him see Willem's face—he had been tossed from the car and had landed, headfirst, against an elm thirty feet across the road and his face had been destroyed, its every bone broken. So he had identified him from a birthmark on his left calf, from a mole on his right shoulder. He learned that Sophie's body had been crushed—"obliterated" was the word he remembered someone saying—and that Malcolm had been declared brain dead and had lived on a ventilator for four days until his parents had had his organs donated. He learned that they had all been wearing their seat belts; that the rental car—that stupid, *fucking* rental car—had had defective air bags; that the driver of the truck, a beer company truck, had been wildly drunk and had run through a red light.

Most of the time, he was drugged. He was drugged when he went to Sophie's service, which he couldn't remember at all, not one detail; he was drugged when he went to Malcolm's. From Malcolm's, he remembers Mr. Irvine grabbing him and shaking him and then hugging him so tightly he was smothered, hugging him and sobbing against him, until someone—Harold, presumably—said something and he was released.

He knew there had been some sort of service for Willem, something small; he knew Willem had been cremated. But he doesn't remember anything from it. He doesn't know who organized it. He doesn't even know if he attended it, and he is too frightened to ask. He remembers Harold telling him at one point that it was okay that he wasn't giving a eulogy, that he could have a memorial for Willem later, whenever he was ready. He remembers nodding, remembers thinking: But I won't ever be ready.

At some point he went back to work: the end of September, he thought. By this point, he knew what had happened. He did. But he was trying not to, and back then, it was still easy. He didn't read the papers; he didn't watch the news. Two weeks after Willem died, he and Harold had been walking down the street and they had passed a newspaper kiosk and there, before him, was a magazine with Willem's face on it, and two dates, and he realized that the first date was the year Willem had been born, and the second was the year he had died. He had stood there, staring, and Harold had taken his arm. "Come on, Jude," he'd said, gently. "Don't look. Come with me," and he had followed, obediently.

Before he returned to the office, he had instructed Sanjay: "I don't

want anyone offering me their condolences. I don't want anyone mentioning it. I don't want anyone saying his name, ever."

"Okay, Jude," Sanjay had said, quietly, looking scared. "I understand."

And they had obeyed him. No one said they were sorry. No one said
Willem's name. No one ever says Willem's name. And now he wishes
they would say it. He cannot say it himself. But he wishes someone
would. Sometimes, on the street, he hears someone say something that
sounds like his name—"William!": a mother, calling to her son—and
he turns, greedily, in the direction of her voice.

In those first months, there were practicalities, which gave him
something to do, which gave his days anger, which in turn gave them
shape. He sued the car manufacturer, the seat-belt manufacturer, the
air-bag manufacturer, the rental-car company. He sued the truck driver,
the company the driver worked for. The driver, he heard through the
driver's lawyer, had a chronically ill child; a lawsuit would ruin the
family. But he didn't care. Once he would have; not now. He felt raw
and merciless. Let him be destroyed, he thought. Let him be ruined.
Let him feel what I feel. Let him lose everything, the only things, that
matter. He wanted to siphon every dollar from all of them, all the
companies, all the people working for them. He wanted to leave them
hopeless. He wanted to leave them empty. He wanted them to live in
squalor. He wanted them to feel lost in their own lives.

They were being sued, each of them, for everything Willem would
have earned had he been allowed to live a normal lifespan, and it was
a ridiculous number, an astonishing number, and he couldn't look at it
without despair: not because of the figure itself but because of the years
that figure represented.

They would settle with him, said his lawyer, a notoriously aggressive and venal torts expert named Todd with whom he had been on the
law review, and the settlements would be generous.

Generous; not generous. He didn't care. He only cared if it made
them suffer. "Obliterate them," he commanded Todd, his voice croaky
with hatred, and Todd had looked startled.

"I will, Jude," he said. "Don't worry."

He didn't need the money, of course. He had his own. And except
for monetary gifts to his assistant and his godson, and sums that he
wanted distributed to various charities—the same charities Willem gave

to every year, along with an additional one: a foundation that helped exploited children—everything that Willem had he had left to him: it was a photo negative of his own will. Earlier that year, he and Willem had set up two scholarships at their college for Harold's and Julia's seventy-fifth birthdays: one at the law school under Harold's name; one at the medical school under Julia's. They had funded them together, and Willem had left enough in a trust so that they always would be. He disbursed the rest of Willem's bequests: he signed the checks to the charities and foundations and museums and organizations that Willem had designated his beneficiaries. He gave to Willem's friends— Harold and Julia; Richard; JB; Roman; Cressy; Susannah; Miguel; Kit; Emil; Andy; but not Malcolm, not anymore—the items (books, pictures, mementoes from films and plays, pieces of art) that he had left them. There were no surprises in Willem's will, although sometimes he wished there would have been—how grateful he would have been for a secret child whom he'd get to meet and would have Willem's smile; how scared and yet how excited he would have been for a secret letter containing a long-held confession. How thankful he would have been for an excuse to hate Willem, to resent him, for a mystery to solve that might occupy years of his life. But there was nothing. Willem's life was over. He was as clean in death as he had been in life.

He thought he was doing well, or well enough anyway. One day Harold called and asked what he wanted to do for Thanksgiving, and for a moment he couldn't understand what Harold was talking about, what the very word—Thanksgiving—meant. "I don't know," he said.

"It's next week," Harold said, in the new quiet voice everyone now used around him. "Do you want to come here, or we can come over, or we can go somewhere else?"

"I don't think I can," he said. "I have too much work, Harold."

But Harold had insisted. "Anywhere, Jude," he'd said. "With whomever you want. Or no one. But we need to see you."

"You're not going to have a good time with me," he finally said.

"We won't have a good time without you," Harold said. "Or any kind of time. Please, Jude. Anywhere."

So they went to London. They stayed in the flat. He was relieved to be out of the country, where there would have been scenes of families on the television, and his colleagues happily grousing about their children and wives and husbands and in-laws. In London, the day was just another day. They took walks, the three of them. Harold cooked ambitious, disastrous meals, which he ate. He slept and slept. Then they went home.

And then one Sunday in December he had woken and had known: Willem was gone. He was gone from him forever. He was never coming back. He would never see him again. He would never hear Willem's voice again, he would never smell him again, he would never feel Willem's arms around him. He would never again be able to unburden himself of one of his memories, sobbing with shame as he did, would never again jerk awake from one of his dreams, blind with terror, to feel Willem's hand on his face, to hear Willem's voice above him: "You're safe, Judy, you're safe. It's over; it's over; it's over." And then he had cried, really cried, cried for the first time since the accident. He had cried for Willem, for how frightened he must have been, for how he must have suffered, for his poor short life. But mostly he had cried for himself. How was he going to keep living without Willem? His entire life—his life after Brother Luke, his life after Dr. Traylor, his life after the monastery and the motel rooms and the home and the trucks, which was the only part of his life that counted—had had Willem in it. There had not been a day since he was sixteen and met Willem in their room at Hood Hall in which he had not communicated with Willem in some way. Even when they were fighting, they spoke. "Jude," Harold had said, "it *will* get better. I swear. I swear. It won't seem like it now, but it will." They all said this: Richard and JB and Andy; the people who wrote him cards. Kit. Emil. All they told him was that it would get better. But although he knew enough to never say so aloud, privately he thought: It won't. Harold had had Jacob for five years. He had had Willem for thirty-four. There was no comparison. Willem had been the first person who loved him, the first person who had seen him not as an object to be used or pitied but as something else, as a friend; he had been the second person who had always, always been kind to him. If he hadn't had Willem, he wouldn't have had any of them—he would never have been able to trust Harold if he hadn't trusted Willem first. He was unable to conceive of life without him, because Willem had so defined what his life was and could be.

The next day he did what he never did: he called Sanjay and told him he wasn't coming in for the next two days. And then he had lain in bed and cried, screaming into the pillows until he lost his voice completely.

But from those two days he had found another solution. Now he stays very late at work, so late that he has seen the sun rise from his office. He does this every weekday, and on Saturdays as well. But on Sundays he sleeps as late as he can, and when he wakes, he takes a pill, one that not only makes him fall asleep again but bludgeons into obsolescence all glimmers of wakefulness. He sleeps until the pill wears off, and then he takes a shower and gets back into bed and takes a different pill, one that makes sleep shallow and glassy, and sleeps until Monday morning. By Monday, he has not eaten in twenty-four hours, sometimes more, and he is trembly and thoughtless. He swims, he goes to work. If he is lucky, he has spent Sunday dreaming of Willem, for at least a little while. He has bought a long, fat pillow, as long as a man is tall, one meant to be pressed against by pregnant women or by people with back problems, and he drapes one of Willem's shirts over it and holds it as he sleeps, even though in life, it was Willem who held him. He hates himself for this, but he cannot stop.

He is aware, dimly, that his friends are watching him, that they are worried about him. At some point it had emerged that one of the reasons he remembers so little from the days after the accident was because he had been in the hospital, on a suicide watch. Now he stumbles through his days and wonders why he isn't, in fact, killing himself. This is, after all, the time to do it. No one would blame him. And yet he doesn't.

At least no one tells him that he should move on. He doesn't want to move on, he doesn't want to move into something else: he wants to remain exactly at this stage, forever. At least no one tells him he's in denial. Denial is what sustains him, and he is dreading the day when his delusions will lose their power to convince him. For the first time in decades, he isn't cutting himself at all. If he doesn't cut himself, he remains numb, and he needs to remain numb; he needs the world to not come too close to him. He has finally managed to achieve what Willem had always hoped for him; all it took was Willem being taken from him.

In January he had a dream that he and Willem were in the house upstate making dinner and talking: something they'd done hundreds of times. But in the dream, although he could hear his own voice, he couldn't hear Willem's—he could see his mouth moving, but he couldn't hear anything he was saying. He had woken, then, and had thrown himself into his wheelchair and moved as quickly as he could into his study, where he scrolled through all of his old e-mails, searching and searching until he found a few voice messages from Willem that he had forgotten to delete. The messages were brief, and unrevealing, but he played them over and over, weeping, bent double with grief, the messages' very banality—"Hey. Judy. I'm going to the farmers' market to pick up those ramps. But do you want anything else? Let me know"—something precious, because it was proof of their life together.

"Willem," he said aloud to the apartment, because sometimes, when it was very bad, he spoke to him. "Come back to me. Come back."

He feels no sense of survivor's guilt but rather survivor's incomprehension: he had always, always known he would predecease Willem. They all knew it. Willem, Andy, Harold, JB, Malcolm, Julia, Richard: he would die before all of them. The only question was how he would die—it would be by his own hand, or it would be by infection. But none of them had ever thought that Willem, of all people, would die before he did. There had been no plans made for that, no contingencies. Had he known this was a possibility, had it been less absurd a concept, he would have stockpiled. He would have made recordings of Willem's voice talking to him and kept them. He would have taken more pictures. He would have tried to distill Willem's very body chemistry. He would have taken him, just-woken, to the perfumer in Florence. "Here," he would've said. "This. This scent. I want you to bottle this." Jane had once told him that as a girl she had been terrified her father would die, and she had secretly made digital copies of her father's dictation (he had been a doctor as well) and stored them on flash drives. And when her father finally did die, four years ago, she had rediscovered them, and had sat in a room playing them, listening to her father dictating orders in his calm, patient voice. How he envied Jane this; how he wished he had thought to do the same.

At least he had Willem's films, and his e-mails, and letters he had written him over the years, all of which he had saved. At least he had Willem's clothes, and articles about Willem, all of which he had kept. At least he had JB's paintings of Willem; at least he had photographs of Willem: hundreds of them, though he only allotted himself a certain number. He decided he would allow himself to look at ten of them every week, and he would look and look at them for hours. It was his decision whether he wanted to review one a day or look at all ten in a single sitting. He was terrified his computer would be destroyed and he would lose these images; he made multiple copies of the photographs and stored the discs in various places: in his safe at Greene Street, in his safe at Lantern House, in his desk at Rosen Pritchard, in his safe-deposit box at the bank.

He had never considered Willem a thorough cataloger of his own life—he isn't either—but one Sunday in early March he skips his drugged slumber and instead drives to Garrison. He has only been to the house twice since that September day, but the gardeners still come, and the bulbs are beginning to bud around the driveway, and when he steps inside, there is a vase of cut plum branches on the kitchen counter and he stops, staring at them: Had he texted the housekeeper to tell her he was coming? He must have. But for a moment he fancies that at the beginning of every week someone comes and places a new arrangement of flowers on the counter, and at the end of every week, another week in which no one comes to see them, they are thrown away.

He goes to his study, where they had installed extra cabinetry so Willem could store his files and paperwork there as well. He sits on the floor, shrugging off his coat, then takes a breath and opens the first drawer. Here are file folders, each labeled with the name of a play or movie, and inside each folder is the shooting version of the script, with Willem's notes on them. Sometimes there are call sheets from days when an actor he knew Willem particularly admired was going to be filming with him: he remembers how excited Willem had been on *The Sycamore Court*, how he had sent him a photo of that day's call sheet with his name typed directly beneath Clark Butterfield's. "Can you believe it?!" his message had read.

I can totally believe it, he'd written back.

He flips through these files, lifting them out at random and carefully sorting through their contents. The next three drawers are all the same things: films, plays, other projects.

In the fifth drawer is a file marked "Wyoming," and in this are mostly photos, most of which he has seen before: pictures of Hemming; pictures of Willem with Hemming; pictures of their parents; pictures of the siblings Willem never knew: Britte and Aksel. There is a separate envelope with a dozen pictures of just Willem, only Willem: school photos, and Willem in a Boy Scout uniform, and Willem in a football uniform. He stares at these pictures, his hands in fists, before placing them back in their envelope.

There are a few other things in the Wyoming file as well: a third-grade book report, written in Willem's careful cursive, on *The Wizard of Oz* that makes him smile; a hand-drawn birthday card to Hemming that makes him want to cry. His mother's death announcement; his father's. A copy of their will. A few letters, from him to his parents, from his parents to him, all in Swedish—these he sets aside to have translated.

He knows Willem had never kept a journal, and yet when he looks through the "Boston" file, he thinks for some reason he might find something. But there is nothing. Instead there are more pictures, all of which he has seen before: of Willem, so shiningly handsome; of Malcolm, looking suspicious and slightly feral, with the stringy, unsuccessful Afro he had tried to cultivate throughout college; of JB, looking essentially the same as he does now, merry and fat-cheeked; of him, looking scared and drowned and very skinny, in his awful too-big clothes and with his awful too-long hair, in his braces that imprisoned his legs in their black, foamy embrace. He stops at a picture of the two of them sitting on the sofa in their suite in Hood, Willem leaning into him and looking at him, smiling, clearly saying something, and him, laughing with his hand over his mouth, which he had learned to do after the counselors at the home told him he had an ugly smile. They look like two different creatures, not just two different people, and he has to quickly refile the picture before he tears it in half.

Now it is becoming difficult to breathe, but he keeps going. In the "Boston" file, in the "New Haven" file, are reviews from the college newspapers of plays Willem had been in; there is the story about JB's Lee Lozano–inspired performance art piece. There is, touchingly, the one calculus exam on which Willem had made a B, an exam he had coached him on for months.

And then he reaches into the drawer again, most of which is occupied not by a hanging file but by a large, accordion-shaped one, the kind they use at the firm. He hefts it out and sees that it is marked only with his name, and slowly opens it.

Inside it is everything: every letter he had ever written Willem, every substantial e-mail printed out. There are birthday cards he'd given Willem. There are photographs of him, some of which he has never seen. There is the *Artforum* issue with *Jude with Cigarette* on the cover. There is a card from Harold written shortly after the adoption, thanking Willem for coming and for the gift. There is an article about him winning a prize in law school, which he certainly hadn't sent Willem but someone clearly had. He hadn't needed to catalog his life after all—Willem had been doing it for him all along.

But why had Willem cared about him so much? Why had he wanted to spend so much time around him? He had never been able to understand this, and now he never will.

I sometimes think I care more about your being alive than you do, he remembers Willem saying, and he takes a long, shuddering breath.

On and on it goes, this detailing of his life, and when he looks in the sixth drawer, there is another accordion file, the same as the first, marked "Jude II," and behind it, "Jude III" and "Jude IV." But by this point he can no longer look. He gently replaces the files, closes the drawers, relocks the cabinets. He puts Willem's and his parents' letters into an envelope, and then another envelope, for protection. He removes the plum branches, wraps their cut ends in a plastic bag, dumps the water from their vase into the sink, locks up the house, and drives home, the branches on the seat next to him. Before he goes up to his apartment, he lets himself into Richard's studio, fills one of the empty coffee cans with water and inserts the branches, leaves it on his worktable for him to find in the morning.

Then it is the end of March; he is at the office. A Friday night, or rather, a Saturday morning. He turns away from his computer and looks out the window. He has a clear view to the Hudson, and above the river he can see the sky turning white. For a long time he stands and stares at the dirty gray river, at the wheeling flocks of birds. He returns to his work. He can feel, these past few months, that he has changed, that people are frightened of him. He has never been a jolly presence in the office, but now he can tell he is mirthless. He can feel he has become more ruthless. He can feel he has become chillier. He and Sanjay used to have lunch together, the two of them griping about their colleagues, but now he cannot talk to anyone. He brings in business. He does his job, he does more than he needs to—but he can tell no one enjoys being around him. He needs Rosen Pritchard; he would be lost without his work. But he no longer derives any pleasure from it. That's all right, he tries to tell himself. Work is not for pleasure, not for most people. But it had been for him, once, and now it no longer is.

Two years ago, when he was healing from his surgery and so tired, so tired that Willem had to lift him in and out of bed, he and Willem had been talking one morning. It must have been cold outside, because he remembers feeling warm and safe, and hearing himself say, "I wish I could just lie here forever."

"Then do," Willem had said. (This was one of their regular exchanges: his alarm would sound and he would get up. "Don't go," Willem would always say. "Why do you need to get up anyway? Where are you always rushing off to?")

"I can't," he said, smiling.

"Listen," Willem had said, "why don't you just quit your job?"

He had laughed. "I can't quit my job," he said.

"Why not?" Willem had asked. "Besides total lack of intellectual stimulation and the prospect of having me as your sole company, give me one good reason."

He had smiled again. "Then there is no good reason," he said. "Because I think I'd like having you as my sole company. But what would I do all day, as a kept man?"

"Cook," Willem said. "Read. Play the piano. Volunteer. Travel around with me. Listen to me complain about other actors I hate. Get facials. Sing to me. Feed me a constant stream of approbations."

He had laughed, and Willem had laughed with him. But now he thinks: Why *didn't* I quit? Why did I let Willem go away from me for all those months, for all those years, when I could have been traveling with him? Why have I spent more hours at Rosen Pritchard than I spent with Willem? But now the choice has been made for him, and Rosen Pritchard is all he has.

Then he thinks: Why did I never give Willem what I should have? Why did I make him go elsewhere for sex? Why couldn't I have been braver? Why couldn't I have done my duty? Why did he stay with me anyway?

He goes back to Greene Street to shower and sleep for a few hours; he will return to the office that afternoon. As he rides home, his eyes lowered against the *Life After Death* posters, he looks at his messages: Andy, Richard, Harold, Black Henry Young.

The last message is from JB, who calls or texts him at least twice a week. He does not know why, but he cannot tolerate seeing JB. He in fact hates him, hates him more purely than he has hated anyone in a long time. He is fully aware of how irrational this is. He is fully aware that JB is not to blame, not in the slightest. The hatred makes no sense. JB wasn't even in the car that day; in no way, even in the most deformed logic, does he bear any responsibility. And yet the first time he saw JB in his conscious state, he heard a voice in his head say, clearly and calmly, *It should have been you, JB.* He didn't say it, but his face must have betrayed something, because JB had been stepping forward to hug him when suddenly, he stopped. He has seen JB only twice since then, both times in Richard's company, and both times, he has had to keep himself from saying something malignant, something unforgivable. And still JB calls him, and always leaves messages, and his messages are always the same: "Hey Judy, it's me. I'm just checking in on you. I've been thinking about you a lot. I'd like to see you. Okay. Love you. Bye." And as he always does, he will write back to JB the same message: "Hi JB, thanks for your message. I'm sorry I've been so out of touch; it's been really busy at work. I'll talk to you soon. Love, J." But despite this message, he has no intention of talking to JB, perhaps not ever again. There is something very wrong with this world, he thinks, a world in which of the four of them—him, JB, Willem, and Malcolm—the two best people, the two kindest and most thoughtful, have died, and the two poorer examples of humanity have survived. At least JB is talented; he deserves to live. But he can think of no reason why he might.

"We're all we have left, Jude," JB had said to him at some point, "at least we have each other," and he had thought, in another of those statements that leapt quickly to mind but that he successfully prevented himself from voicing: *I would trade you for him.* He would have traded any of them for Willem. JB, instantly. Richard and Andy—poor Richard and Andy, who did everything for him!—instantly. Julia, even. Harold. He would have exchanged any of them, all of them, to have Willem back. He thinks of Hades, with his shiny Italian brawn, swooning E. around the underworld. *I have a proposition for you,* he says to Hades. *Five souls for one. How can you refuse?*

One Sunday in April he is sleeping when he hears a banging, loud and insistent, and he wakes, groggily, and then turns onto his side, holding the pillow over his head and keeping his eyes closed, and eventually the banging stops. So when he feels someone touch him, gently, on his arm, he shouts and flops over and sees it is Richard, sitting next to him.

"I'm sorry, Jude," says Richard. And then, "Have you been sleeping all day?"

He swallows, sits up halfway. On Sundays he keeps all the shades lowered, all the curtains drawn; he can never tell, really, whether it is night or day. "Yes," he says. "I'm tired."

"Well," says Richard after a silence. "I'm sorry to barge in like this. But you weren't answering your phone, and I wanted you to come downstairs and have dinner with me."

"Oh, Richard, I don't know," he says, trying to think of an excuse. Richard is right: he turns off his phone, all phones, for his Sunday cocooning, so nothing will interrupt his slumber, his attempts to find Willem in his dreams. "I'm not feeling that great. I'm not going to be good company."

"I'm not expecting entertainment, Jude," Richard says, and smiles at him a bit. "Come on. You have to eat something. It's just going to be you and me; India's upstate at her friend's this weekend."

They are both quiet for a long time. He looks about the room, his messy bed. The air smells close, of sandalwood and steam heat from the radiator. "Come on, Jude," Richard says, in a low voice. "Come have dinner with me."

"Okay," he says at last. "Okay."

"Okay," Richard says, standing. "I'll see you downstairs in half an hour."

He showers, and then down he goes, with a bottle of Tempranillo he remembers that Richard likes. In the apartment he is waved away from the kitchen, and so he sits at the long table that dominates the space, which can and has sat twenty-four, and strokes Richard's cat, Mustache, which has jumped into his lap. He remembers the first time he saw this apartment with its dangling chandeliers and its large bees-wax sculptures; over the years it has become more domesticated, but it is still, indisputably, Richard's, with its palette of bone-white and wax-yellow, although now India's paintings, bright, violent abstractions of female nudes, hang on the walls, and there are carpets on the floor. It has been months since he's been inside this apartment, where he used to visit at least once a week. He still sees Richard, of course, but only in passing; mostly, he tries to avoid him, and when Richard calls him to have dinner or asks to stop by, he always says he is too busy, too tired.

"I couldn't remember how you felt about my famous seitan stir-fry, so I actually got scallops," Richard says, and places a dish before him.

"I like your famous stir-fry," he says, although he can't remember what it is, and if he likes it or not. "Thank you, Richard."

Richard pours them both a glass of wine, and then holds his up. "Happy birthday, Jude," he says, solemnly, and he realizes that Richard is right: today is his birthday. Harold has been calling and e-mailing him all this week with a frequency that is unusual even for him, and except for the most cursory of replies, he has not spoken to him at all. He knows Harold will be worried about him. There have been more texts from Andy as well, and from some other people, and now he knows why, and he begins to cry: from everyone's kindness, which he has repaid so poorly, from his loneliness, from the proof that life has, despite his efforts to let it, gone on after all. He is fifty-one, and Willem has been dead for eight months.

Richard doesn't say anything, just sits next to him on the bench and holds him. "I know this isn't going to help," he says at last, "but I love you too, Jude."

He shakes his head, unable to speak. In recent years he has gone from being embarrassed about crying at all to crying constantly to himself to crying around Willem to now, in the final falling away of his dignity, crying in front of anyone, at any time, over anything.

He leans against Richard's chest and sobs into his shirt. Richard is another person whose unstinting, unwavering friendship and compassion for him has always perplexed him. He knows that some of Richard's feelings for him are twined with his feelings for Willem, and this he understands: he had made Willem a promise, and Richard is serious about his obligations. But there is something about Richard's steadiness, his complete reliability, that—coupled with his height, his very size—makes him think of him as some sort of massive tree-god, an oak come into human form, something solid and ancient and indestructible. Theirs is not a chatty relationship, but it is Richard who has become the friend of his adulthood, who has become, in a way, not just a friend but a parent, although he is only four years older. A brother, then: someone whose dependability and sense of decency are inviolable.

Finally, he is able to stop, and apologize, and after he cleans himself up in the bathroom, they eat, slowly, drinking the wine, talking about Richard's work. At the end of the meal, Richard returns from the kitchen with a lumpy little cake, into which he has thrust six candles. "Five plus one," Richard explains. He makes himself smile, then; he blows out the candles; Richard cuts them both slices. The cake is crumbly and figgy, more scone than cake, and they both eat their pieces in silence.

He stands to help Richard with the dishes, but when Richard tells him to go upstairs, he is relieved, because he's exhausted; this is the most socializing he has done since Thanksgiving. At the door, Richard hands him something, a package wrapped in brown paper, and then hugs him. "He wouldn't want you to be unhappy, Judy," he says, and he nods against Richard's cheek. "He would hate seeing you like this."

"I know," he says.

"And do me a favor," Richard says, still holding him. "Call JB, okay? I know it's difficult for you, but—he loved Willem too, you know. Not like you, I know, but still. And Malcolm. He misses him."

"I know," he repeats, tears coming to his eyes once more. "I know."

"Come back next Sunday," Richard says, and kisses him. "Or any day, really. I miss seeing you."

"I will," he says. "Richard—thank you."

"Happy birthday, Jude."

He takes the elevator upstairs. It's suddenly grown late. Back in his apartment, he goes to his study, sits on the sofa. There is a box that he hasn't opened that was messengered over to him from Flora weeks ago; inside it are Malcolm's bequests to him, and to Willem—which are now also his. The only thing Willem's death has helped with is blunting the shock, the horror of Malcolm's, and still, he has been unable to open the box.

But now he will. First, though, he unwraps Richard's present and sees that it is a small bust, carved from wood and mounted on a heavy black-iron cube, of Willem, and he gasps as if slugged. Richard has always claimed that he's terrible with figurative sculpture, but he knows he's not, and this piece is proof of it. He glides his fingers over Willem's sightless eyes, across Willem's crest of hair, and after doing so, lifts them to his nose and smells sandalwood. On the bottom of the base is etched "To J on his 51st. With love. R."

He starts to cry again; stops. He places the bust on the cushion next to him and opens the box. At first he sees nothing but wads of newspaper, and he gropes carefully inside until his hands close on something solid, which he lifts out: it is the scale model of Lantern House, its walls rendered from boxwood, that had once sat in Bellcast's offices, alongside the scale models of every other project the firm had ever built, in form or in reality. The model is about two feet square, and he settles it on his lap before holding it to his face, looking through its thin Plexiglas windows, hoisting the roof up and walking his fingers through its rooms.

He wipes his eyes and reaches into the box again. The next thing he retrieves is an envelope fat with pictures of them, the four of them, or just of him and Willem: from college, from New York, from Truro, from Cambridge, from Garrison, from India, from France, from Iceland, from Ethiopia—places they'd lived, trips they'd taken.

The box isn't very large, and still he removes things: two delicate, rare books of drawings of Japanese houses by a French illustrator; a small abstract painting by a young British artist he'd always admired; a larger drawing of a man's face by a well-known American painter that Willem had always liked; two of Malcolm's earliest sketchbooks, filled with page after page of his imaginary structures. And finally, he lifts the last thing from the box, something wrapped in layers of newspaper, which he removes, slowly.

Here, in his hands, is Lispenard Street: their apartment, with its odd proportions and slapdash second bedroom; its narrow hallways and miniature kitchen. He can tell that this is an early piece of Malcolm's because the windows are made of glassine, not vellum or Plexiglas, and the walls are made of cardboard, not wood. And in this apartment Malcolm has placed furniture, cut and folded from stiff paper: his lumpy twin futon bed on its cinder-block base; the broken-springed couch they had found on the street; the squeaking wheeled easy chair given them by JB's aunts. All that is missing is a paper him, a paper Willem.

He puts Lispenard Street on the floor by his feet. For a long time he sits very still, his eyes closed, allowing his mind to reach back and wander: there is much he doesn't romanticize about those years, not now, but at the time, when he hadn't known what to hope for, he hadn't known that life could be better than Lispenard Street.

"What if we'd never left?" Willem would occasionally ask him. "What if I had never made it? What if you'd stayed at the U.S. Attorney's Office? What if I was still working at Ortolan? What would our lives be like now?"

"How theoretical do you want to get here, Willem?" he'd ask him, smiling. "Would we be together?"

"Of course we'd be together," Willem would say. "That part would be the same."

"Well," he'd say, "then the first thing we'd do is tear down that wall and reclaim the living room. And the second thing we'd do is get a decent bed."

Willem would laugh. "And we'd sue the landlord to get a working elevator, once and for all."

"Right, that'd be the next step."

He sits, waiting for his breathing to return to normal. Then he turns on his phone, checks his missed calls: Andy, JB, Richard, Harold and Julia, Black Henry Young, Rhodes, Citizen, Andy again, Richard again, Lucien, Asian Henry Young, Phaedra, Elijah, Harold again, Julia again, Harold, Richard, JB, JB, JB.

He calls JB. It's late, but JB stays up late. "Hi," he says, when JB picks up, hears the surprise in his voice. "It's me. Is this a good time to talk?"

2

AT LEAST ONE Saturday a month now he takes half a day off from work and goes to the Upper East Side. When he leaves Greene Street, the neighborhood's boutiques and stores haven't yet opened for the day; when he returns, they are closed for the night. On these days, he can imagine the SoHo Harold knew as a child: a place shuttered and unpeopled, a place without life.

His first stop is the building on Park and Seventy-eighth, where he takes the elevator to the sixth floor. The maid lets him into the apartment and he follows her to the back study, which is sunny and large, and where Lucien is waiting—not waiting for him, necessarily, but waiting.

There is always a late breakfast laid out for him: thin wedges of smoked salmon and tiny buckwheat pancakes one time; a cake glazed white with lemon icing the next. He can never bring himself to eat anything, although sometimes when he is feeling especially helpless he accepts a slice of cake from the maid and holds the plate in his lap for the entire visit. But although he doesn't eat anything, he does drink cup after cup of tea, which is always steeped exactly how he likes it. Lucien eats nothing either—he has been fed earlier—nor does he drink.

Now he goes to Lucien and takes his hand. "Hi, Lucien," he tells him.

He had been in London when Lucien's wife, Meredith, called him: it was the week of Bergesson's retrospective at MoMA, and he had arranged to be out of the city on business. Lucien had had a massive stroke, Meredith said; he would live, but the doctors didn't yet know how great the damage would be.

Lucien was in the hospital for two weeks, and when he was released, it was clear that his impairment was severe. And although it is not yet five months later, it has remained so: the features on the left side of his face seem to be melting off of him, and he cannot use his left arm or leg, either. He can still speak, remarkably well, but his memory has vanished, the past twenty years deserting him completely. In early July, he fell and hit his head and was in a coma; now, he is too unsteady to even walk, and Meredith has moved them back from their house in Connecticut to their apartment in the city, where they can be closer to the hospital and their daughters.

He thinks Lucien likes, or at least doesn't mind, his visits, but he doesn't know this for sure. Certainly Lucien doesn't know who he is: he is someone who appears in his life and then disappears, and every time he must reintroduce himself.

"Who are you?" Lucien asks.

"Jude," he says.

"Now, remind me," Lucien says, pleasantly, as if they're meeting at a cocktail party, "how do I know you?"

"You were my mentor," he tells him.

"Ah," says Lucien. And then there is a silence.

In the first weeks, he tried to make Lucien remember his own life: he talked about Rosen Pritchard, and about people they knew, and cases they used to argue about. But then he realized that the expression he had mistaken—in his own stupid hopefulness—for thoughtfulness was in reality fear. And so now he discusses nothing from the past, or nothing from their past together, at least. He lets Lucien direct the conversation, and although he doesn't understand the references Lucien makes, he smiles and tries to pretend he does.

"Who are you?" Lucien asks.

"Jude," he says.

"Now, tell me, how do I know you?"

"You were my mentor."

"Oh, at Groton!"

"Yes," he says, trying to smile back. "At Groton."

Sometimes, though, Lucien looks at him. "Mentor?" he says. "I'm too young to be your mentor!" Or sometimes he doesn't ask at all, simply begins a conversation in its middle, and he has to wait until he has enough clues and can determine what role he has been assigned—one of his daughters' long-ago boyfriends, or a college classmate, or a friend at the country club—before he can respond appropriately.

In these hours he learns more about Lucien's earlier life than Lucien had ever revealed to him before. Although Lucien is no longer Lucien, at least not the Lucien he knew. This Lucien is vague and featureless; he is as smooth and cornerless as an egg. Even his voice, that droll croaking roll with which Lucien used to deliver his sentences, each one a statement, the pause he used to leave between them because he had grown so used to people's laughter; the particular way he had of structuring his paragraphs, beginning and ending each with a joke that wasn't really a joke, but an insult cloaked in a silken cape, is different. Even when they were working together, he knew that the Lucien of the office was not the Lucien of the country club, but he never saw that other Lucien. And now, finally, he has, he does; it is the only person he sees. This Lucien talks about the weather, and golf, and sailing, and taxes, but the tax laws he discusses are from twenty years ago. He never asks him anything about himself: who he is, what he does, why he is sometimes in a wheelchair. Lucien talks, and he smiles and nods back at him, wrapping his hands around his cooling cup of tea. When Lucien's hands tremble, he takes them in his own, which he knows helps him when his hands shake: Willem used to do this, and breathe with him, and it would always calm him. When Lucien drools, he takes the edge of his napkin and blots the saliva away. Unlike him, however, Lucien doesn't seem embarrassed by his own shaking and drooling, and he is relieved that he doesn't. He's not embarrassed for Lucien, either, but he is embarrassed by his inability to do more for him.

"He loves seeing you, Jude," Meredith always says, but he doesn't think this is true, really. He sometimes thinks he continues to come more for Meredith's sake than for Lucien's, and he realizes that this is the way it is, the way it must be: you don't visit the lost, you visit the people who search for the lost. Lucien is not conscious of this, but he can remember being so when he was sick, both the first time and the second, and Willem was taking care of him. How grateful he was when he would wake and find someone other than Willem sitting next to him. "Roman's with him," Richard or Malcolm would say, or "He and JB went out for lunch," and he'd relax. In the weeks after his amputations, when all he wanted to do was give up, those moments in which he could imagine that Willem might be being comforted were his only moments of happiness. And so he sits with Meredith after sitting with Lucien and they talk, although she too asks him nothing about his life, and this is fine with him. She is lonely; he is lonely, too. She and Lucien have two daughters, one of whom lives in New York but is forever going in and out of rehab; the other lives in Philadelphia with her husband and three children and is a lawyer herself.

He has met both of these daughters, who are a decade or so younger than he is, although Lucien is Harold's age. When he went to visit Lucien in the hospital, the older of them, the one who lives in New York, had looked at him with such hatred that he had almost stepped back, and then had said to her sister, "Oh, and look who it is: Daddy's pet. What a surprise."

"Grow up, Portia," the younger one had hissed. To him she said, "Jude, thanks for coming. I'm so sorry about Willem."

"Thank you for coming, Jude," Meredith says now, kissing him goodbye. "I'll see you soon?" She always asks this, as if he might someday tell her she won't.

"Yes," he says. "I'll e-mail you."

"Do," she says, and waves as he walks down the hall toward the elevator. He always has the sense that no one else visits, and yet how can that be? Don't let that be, he pleads. Meredith and Lucien have always had lots of friends. They threw dinner parties. It wasn't unusual to see Lucien leaving the offices in black tie, rolling his eyes as he waved goodbye to him. "Benefit," he'd say as an explanation. "Party." "Wedding." "Dinner."

After these visits he is always exhausted, but still he walks, seven blocks south and a quarter of a block east, to the Irvines'. For months he had avoided the Irvines, and then last month, on the one-year anniversary, they had asked him and Richard and JB to dinner at their house, and he knew he would have to go.

It was the weekend after Labor Day. The previous four weeks—four weeks that had included the day Willem would have turned fifty-three; the day that Willem had died—had been some of the worst he had ever experienced. He had known they would be bad; he had tried to plan accordingly. The firm had needed someone to go to Beijing, and although he knew he should have stayed in New York—he was working on a case that needed him more than the business in Beijing did—he volunteered anyway, and off he went. At first he had hoped he might be safe: the woolly numbness of jet lag was sometimes indistinguishable from the woolly numbness of his grief, and there were other things that were so physically uncomfortable—including the heat, which was woolly itself, woolly and sodden—that he had thought he would be able to distract himself. But then one night near the end of the trip he was being driven back to the hotel from a long day of meetings, and he had looked out of the car window and had seen, glittering over the road, a massive billboard of Willem's face. It was a beer ad that Willem had shot two years ago, one that was only displayed throughout east Asia. But hanging from the top of the billboard were people on pulleys, and he realized that they were painting over the ad, that they were erasing Willem's face. Suddenly, his breath left him, and he had almost asked the driver to stop, but he wouldn't have been able to—they were on a loop of a road, one with no exits or places to pull over, and so he'd had to sit very still, his heart erupting within him, counting the beats it took to reach the hotel, thank the driver, get out, walk through the lobby, ride the elevator, walk down the hallway, and enter his room, where before he could think, he was throwing himself against the cold marble wall of the shower, his mouth open and his eyes shut, tossing and tossing himself until he was in so much pain that his every vertebrae felt as if it had been jolted out of its sockets.

That night he cut himself wildly, uncontrollably, and when he was shaking too badly to continue, he waited, and cleaned the floor, and drank some juice to give himself energy, and then started again. After three rounds of this he crept to the corner of the shower stall and wept, folding his arms over his head, making his hair tacky with blood, and that night he slept there, covered with a towel instead of a blanket. He had done this sometimes when he was a child and had felt like he was exploding, separating from himself like a dying star, and would feel the need to tuck himself into the smallest space he could find so his very bones would stay knit together. Then, he would carefully work himself out from beneath Brother Luke and ball himself on the filthy motel carpet under the bed, which was prickly with burrs and dropped thumbtacks and slimy with used condoms and strange damp spots, or he would sleep in the bathtub or in the closet, beetled up as tight as he was able. "My poor potato bug," Brother Luke would say when he found him like this. "Why are you doing this, Jude?" He had been gentle, and worried, but he had never been able to explain it.

Somehow he made it through that trip; somehow he had made it through a year. The night of Willem's death he dreamed of glass vases imploding, of Willem's body being projected through the air, of his face shattering against the tree. He woke missing Willem so profoundly that he felt he was going blind. The day after he returned home, he saw the first of the posters for *The Happy Years*, which had reverted to its original title: *The Dancer and the Stage*. Some of these posters were of Willem's face, his hair longish like Nureyev's and his top scooped low on his chest, his neck long and powerful. And some were of just monumental images of a foot—Willem's actual foot, he happened to know—in a toe shoe, en pointe, shot so close you could see its veins and hairs, its thin straining muscles and fat bulging tendons. *Opening Thanksgiving Day*, the posters read. Oh god, he thought, and had gone back inside, oh god. He wanted the reminders to stop; he dreaded the day when they would. In recent weeks he'd had the sense that Willem was receding from him, even as his grief refused to diminish in intensity.

The next week they went to the Irvines'. They had decided, in some unspoken way, that they should go up together, and they met at Richard's apartment and he gave Richard the keys to the car and Richard drove them. They were all silent, even JB, and he was very nervous. He had the sense that the Irvines were angry at him; he had the sense he deserved their anger.

Dinner was all of Malcolm's favorite foods, and as they ate, he could feel Mr. Irvine staring at him and wondered whether he was thinking what he himself always thought: Why Malcolm? Why not him?

Mrs. Irvine had suggested that they all go around the table and share a memory of Malcolm, and he had sat, listening to the others— Mrs. Irvine, who had told a story about how they had been visiting the Pantheon when Malcolm was six and how, five minutes after they had left, they had realized that Malcolm was missing and had rushed back to find him sitting on the ground, gazing and gazing at the oculus; Flora, who told a story about how as a second-grader Malcolm had appropriated her dollhouse from the attic, removed all the dolls, and filled it with little objects, dozens of chairs and tables and sofas and even pieces of furniture that had no name, that he had made with clay; JB, the story of how they had all returned to Hood one Thanksgiving a day early and had broken into the dormitory so they could have it to themselves, and how Malcolm had built a fire in the living room's fireplace so they could roast sausages for dinner—and when it was his turn, he told the story of how back at Lispenard Street, Malcolm had built them a set of bookcases, which had partitioned their squish of a living room into such a meager sliver that when you were sitting on the sofa and stretched your legs out, you stretched them into the bookcase itself. But he had wanted the shelves, and Willem had said he could. And so over Malcolm had come with the cheapest wood possible, leftovers from the lumberyard, and he and Willem had taken the wood to the roof and assembled the bookcase there, so the neighbors wouldn't complain about the banging, and then they had brought it back down and installed it.

But when they did, Malcolm had realized that he'd mismeasured, and the bookcases were three inches too wide, which caused the edge of the unit to jut into the hallway. He hadn't minded, and neither had Willem, but Malcolm had wanted to fix it.

"Don't, Mal," they had both told him. "It's great, it's fine."

"It's not great," Malcolm had said, mopily. "It's not fine."

Finally they had managed to convince him, and Malcolm had left. He and Willem painted the case a bright vermilion and loaded it with their books. And then early the next Sunday, Malcolm appeared again, looking determined. "I can't stop thinking about this," he said. And he'd set his bag down on the floor and drawn out a hacksaw and had started gnawing away at the structure, the two of them shouting at him until they realized that he was going to alter it whether they helped him or not. So back up to the roof went the bookcase; back down, once again, it came, and this time, it was perfect.

"I always think of that incident," he said, as the others listened. "Because it says so much about how seriously Malcolm took his work, and how he always strove to be perfect in it, to respect the material, whether it was marble or plywood. But I also think it says so much about how much he respected space, *any* space, even a horrible, unfixable, depressing apartment in Chinatown: even that space deserved respect.

"And it says so much about how much he respected his friends, how much he wanted us all to live somewhere he imagined for us: someplace as beautiful and vivid as his imaginary houses were to him."

He stopped. What he wanted to say—but what he didn't think he could get through—was what he had overheard Malcolm say as Willem was complaining about hefting the bookcase back into place and he was in the bathroom gathering the brushes and paint from beneath the sink. "If I had left it like it was, he could've tripped against it and fallen, Willem," Malcolm had whispered. "Would you want that?"

"No," Willem had said, after a pause, sounding ashamed. "No, of course not. You're right, Mal." Malcolm, he realized, had been the first among them to recognize that he was disabled; Malcolm had known this even before he did. He had always been conscious of it, but he had never made him feel self-conscious. Malcolm had sought, only, to make his life easier, and he had once resented him for this.

As they were leaving for the night, Mr. Irvine put his hand on his shoulder. "Jude, will you stay behind for a bit?" he asked. "I'll have Monroe drive you home."

He had to agree and so he did, telling Richard he could take the car back to Greene Street. For a while they sat in the living room, just he and Mr. Irvine—Malcolm's mother remained in the dining room with Flora and her husband and children—talking about his health, and Mr. Irvine's health, and Harold, and his work, when Mr. Irvine began to cry. He had stood then, and had sat down again next to Mr. Irvine, and placed his hand hesitantly on his back, feeling awkward and shy, feeling the decades slip away from beneath him.

Mr. Irvine had always been such an intimidating figure to all of them throughout their adulthoods. His height, his self-possession, his large, hard features—he looked like something from an Edward Curtis photograph, and that was what they all called him: "The Chief." "What's the Chief gonna say about this, Mal?" JB had asked when Malcolm told them he was going to quit Ratstar, and they were all trying to urge temperance. Or (JB again): "Mal, can you ask the Chief if I can use the apartment when I'm passing through Paris next month?"

But Mr. Irvine was no longer the Chief: although he was still logical and upright, he was eighty-nine, and his dark eyes had turned that same unnamable gray that only the very young or the very old possess: the color of the sea from which one comes, the color of the sea to which one returns.

"I loved him," Mr. Irvine told him. "You know that, Jude, right? You know I did."

"I do," he said. It was what he had always told Malcolm: "Of course your dad loves you, Mal. Of course he does. Parents love their kids." And once, when Malcolm was very upset (he could no longer remember why), he had snapped at him, "Like you'd know anything about that, Jude," and there had been a silence, and then Malcolm, horrified, had begun apologizing to him. "I'm sorry, Jude," he'd said, "I'm so sorry." And he'd had nothing to say, because Malcolm was right: he didn't know anything about that. What he knew, he knew from books, and books lied, they made things prettier. It had been the worst thing Malcolm had ever said to him, and although he had never mentioned it to Malcolm again, Malcolm had mentioned it to him, once, shortly after the adoption.

"I will never forget that thing I said to you," he'd said.

"Mal, forget it," he'd told him, although he knew exactly what Malcolm was referring to, "you were upset. It was a long time ago."

"But it was wrong," Malcolm had said. "And I was wrong. On every level."

As he sat with Mr. Irvine, he thought: I wish Malcolm could have had this moment. This moment should have been Malcolm's.

And so now he visits the Irvines after visiting Lucien, and the visits are not dissimilar. They are both drifts into the past, they are both old men talking at him about memories he doesn't share, about contexts with which he is unfamiliar. But although these visits depress him, he feels he must fulfill them: both are with people who had always given him time and conversation when he had needed it but hadn't known how to ask for it. When he was twenty-five and new to the city, he had lived at the Irvines', and Mr. Irvine would talk to him about the market, and law, and had given him advice: not advice about how to think as much as advice about how to be, about how to be a curiosity in a world in which curiosities weren't often tolerated. "People are going to think certain things about you because of how you walk," Mr. Irvine had once said to him, and he had looked down. "No," he'd said. "Don't look down, Jude. It's nothing to be ashamed of. You're a brilliant man, and you'll be brilliant, and you'll be rewarded for your brilliance. But if you act like you don't belong, if you act like you're apologetic for your own self, then people will start to treat you that way, too." He'd taken a deep breath. "Believe me." *Be as steely as you want to be,* Mr. Irvine had said. *Don't try to get people to like you. Never try to make yourself more palatable in order to make your colleagues more comfortable.* Harold had taught him how to think as a litigator, but Mr. Irvine had taught him how to behave as one. And Lucien had recognized both of these abilities, and had appreciated them both as well.

That afternoon his visit at the Irvines' is brief because Mr. Irvine is tired, and on his way out he sees Flora—Fabulous Flora, of whom Malcolm was so proud and so envious—and they speak for a few minutes before he leaves. It is early October but still warm, the mornings like summer but the afternoons turning dark and wintry, and as he walks up Park to his car, he remembers how he used to spend his Saturdays here twenty years ago: more. Then he would walk home, and on his way he would occasionally stop by a famous, pricey bakery on Madison Avenue that he liked and buy a loaf of walnut bread—a single loaf cost as much as he was willing to spend on a dinner back then—that he and Willem would eat with butter and salt. The bakery is still there, and now he veers west off Park to go buy a loaf, which somehow seems to have remained fixed in price, at least in his memory, while everything else has grown so much more expensive. Until he began his Saturday visits to Lucien and the Irvines, he couldn't remember the last time he was in this neighborhood in daytime—his appointments with Andy are in the evenings—and now he lingers, looking at the pretty children running down the wide clean sidewalks, their pretty mothers strolling behind them, the linden trees above him shading their leaves into a pale, reluctant yellow. He passes Seventy-fifth Street, where he once tutored Felix, Felix who is now, unbelievably, thirty-three, and no longer a singer in a punk band but, even more unbelievably, a hedge fund manager as his father once was.

At the apartment he cuts the bread, slices some cheese, brings the plate to the table and stares at it. He is making a real effort to eat real meals, to resume the habits and practices of the living. But eating has become somehow difficult for him. His appetite has disappeared, and everything tastes like paste, or like the powdered mashed potatoes they had served at the home. He tries, though. Eating is easier when he has to perform for an audience, and so he has dinner every Friday with Andy, and every Saturday with JB. And he has started appearing every Sunday evening at Richard's—together the two of them cook one of Richard's kaley vegetarian meals, and then India joins them at the table.

He has also resumed reading the paper, and now he pushes aside the bread and cheese and opens the arts section cautiously, as if it might bite him. Two Sundays ago he had been feeling confident and had snapped open the first page and been confronted with a story about the film that Willem was to have begun shooting the previous September. The piece was about how the movie had been recast, and how there was strong early critical support for it, and how the main character had been renamed for Willem, and he had shut the paper and had gone to his bed and had held a pillow over his head until he was able to stand again. He knows that for the next two years he will be confronted by articles, posters, signs, commercials, for films Willem was to have been shooting in these past twelve months. But today there is nothing in the paper other than a full-page advertisement for *The Dancer and the Stage*, and he stares at Willem's almost life-size face for a long, long time, holding his hand over its eyes and then lifting it off. If this were a movie, he thinks, the face would start speaking to him. If this were a movie, he would look up and Willem would be standing before him.

Sometimes he thinks: I am doing better. I am getting better. Sometimes he wakes full of fortitude and vigor. Today will be the day, he thinks. Today will be the first day I really get better. Today will be the day I miss Willem less. And then something will happen, something as simple as walking into his closet and seeing the lonely, waiting stand of Willem's shirts that will never be worn again, and his ambition, his hopefulness will dissolve, and he will be cast into despair once again. Sometimes he thinks: I can do this. But more and more now, he knows: I can't. He has made a promise to himself to every day find a new reason to keep going. Some of these reasons are little reasons, they are tastes he likes, they are symphonies he likes, they are paintings he likes, buildings he likes, operas and books he likes, places he wants to see, either again or for the first time. Some of these reasons are obligations: Because he should. Because he can. Because Willem would want him to. And some of the reasons are big reasons: Because of Richard. Because of JB. Because of Julia. And, especially, because of Harold.

A little less than a year after he had tried to kill himself, he and Harold had taken a walk. It was Labor Day; they were in Truro. He remembers that he was having trouble walking that weekend; he remembers stepping carefully through the dunes; he remembers feeling Harold trying not to touch him, trying not to help him.

Finally they had sat and rested and looked out toward the ocean and talked: about a case he was working on, about Laurence, who was retiring, about Harold's new book. And then suddenly Harold had said, "Jude, you have to promise me you won't do that again," and it was Harold's tone—stern, where Harold was rarely stern—that made him look at him.

"Harold," he began.

"I try not to ask you for anything," Harold said, "because I don't want you to think you owe me anything: and you don't." He turned and looked at him, and his expression too was stern. "But I'm asking you this. I'm asking you. You have to promise me."

He hesitated. "I promise," he said, finally, and Harold nodded.

"Thank you," he said.

They had never discussed this conversation again, and although he knew it wasn't quite logical, he didn't want to break this promise to Harold. At times, it seemed that this promise—this verbal contract— was the only real deterrent to his trying again, although he knew that if he were to do it again, it wouldn't be an attempt: this time, he would really do it. He knew how he'd do it; he knew it would work. Since Willem had died, he had thought about it almost daily. He knew the timeline he'd need to follow, he knew how he would arrange to be found. Two months ago, in a very bad week, he had even rewritten his will so that it now read as the document of someone who had died with apologies to make, whose bequests would be attempts to ask for forgiveness. And although he isn't intending to honor this will—as he reminds himself—he hasn't changed it, either.

He hopes for infection, something swift and fatal, something that will kill him and leave him blameless. But there is no infection. Since his amputations, there have been no wounds. He is still in pain, but no more—less, actually—than he had been in before. He is cured, or at least as cured as he will ever be.

So there is no real reason for him to see Andy once a week, but he does anyway, because he knows Andy is worried he will kill himself. *He* is worried he will kill himself. And so every Friday he goes uptown.

Most of these Fridays are just dinner dates, except for the second Friday of the month, when their dinner is preceded by an appointment. Here, everything is the same: only his missing feet, his missing calves, are proof that things have changed. In other ways, he has reverted to the person he was decades before. He is self-conscious again. He is scared to be touched. Three years before Willem died he had finally been able to ask him to massage the cream into the scars on his back, and Willem had done so, and for a while, he had felt different, like a snake who had grown a new skin. But now, of course, there is no one to help him and the scars are once again tight and bulky, webbing his back in a series of elastic restraints.

He knows now: People don't change. He cannot change. Willem had thought himself transformed by the experience of helping him through his recovery; he had been surprised by his own reserves, by his own forebearance. But he—he and everyone else—had always known that Willem had possessed those characteristics already. Those months may have clarified Willem to himself, but the qualities he had discovered had been a surprise to nobody but Willem. And in the same way, his losing Willem has been clarifying as well. In his years with Willem, he had been able to convince himself that he was someone else, someone happier, someone freer and braver. But now Willem is gone, and he is again who he was twenty, thirty, forty years ago.

And so, another Friday. He goes to Andy's. The scale: Andy sighing. The questions: his replies, a series of *yeses* and *nos*. Yes, he feels fine. No, no more pain than usual. No, no sign of wounds. Yes, an episode every ten days to two weeks. Yes, he's been sleeping. Yes, he's been seeing people. Yes, he's been eating. Yes, three meals a day. Yes, every day. No, he doesn't know why he then keeps losing weight. No, he doesn't want to consider seeing Dr. Loehmann again. The inspection of his arms: Andy turning them in his hands, looking for new cuts, not finding any. The week after he returned from Beijing, the week after he had lost control, Andy had looked at them and gasped, and he had looked down, too, and had remembered how bad it had been at times, how insane it had gotten. But Andy hadn't said anything, just cleaned him up, and after he had finished, he had held both of his hands in both of his.

"A year," Andy had said.

"A year," he had echoed. And they had both been silent.

After the appointment, they go around the corner to a small Italian restaurant that they like. Andy is always watching him at these dinners, and if he thinks he's not ordering enough food, he orders an additional dish for him and then badgers him until he eats it. But at this dinner he can tell Andy is anxious about something: as they wait for their food, Andy drinks, quickly, and talks to him about football, which he knows he doesn't care about and never discusses with him. Andy had talked about sports with Willem, sometimes, and he would listen to them argue over one team or another as they sat at the dining table eating pistachios and he prepared dessert.

"Sorry," Andy says, at last. "I'm babbling." Their appetizers arrive, and they eat, quietly, before Andy takes a breath.

"Jude," he says, "I'm giving up the practice."

He has been cutting into his eggplant, but now he stops, puts down his fork. "Not anytime soon," Andy adds, quickly. "Not for another three years or so. But I'm bringing in a partner this year so the transition process will be as smooth as possible: for the staff, but especially for my patients. He'll take over more and more of the patient load with each year." He pauses. "I think you'll like him. I know you will. I'm going to stay your doctor until the day I leave, and I'll give you lots of notice before I do. But I want you to meet him, to see if there's any sort of chemistry between you two"—Andy smiles a bit, but he can't bring himself to smile back—"and if there's not, for whatever reason, then we'll have plenty of time to find you someone else. I have a couple of other people in mind who I know would be amenable to giving you the full-service treatment. And I won't leave until we get you settled somewhere."

He still can't say anything, can't even lift his head to look at Andy. "Jude," he hears Andy say, softly, pleadingly. "I wish I could stay forever, for your sake. You're the only one I wish I could stay for. But I'm tired. I'm almost sixty-two, and I always swore to myself I'd retire before I turned sixty-five. I—"

But he stops him. "Andy," he says, "of course you should retire when you want to. You don't owe me an explanation. I'm happy for you. I am. I'm just. I'm just going to miss you. You've been so good to me." He pauses. "I'm so dependent on you," he admits at last.

"Jude," Andy begins, and then is silent. "Jude, I'll always be your friend. I'll always be here to help you, medically or otherwise. But you need someone who can grow old with you. This guy I'm bringing in is forty-six; he'll be around to treat you for the rest of your life, if you want him."

"As long as I die in the next nineteen years," he hears himself saying. There's another silence. "I'm sorry, Andy," he says, appalled by how wretched he feels, how pettily he is behaving. He has always known, after all, that Andy would retire at some point. But he realizes now that he had never thought he would be alive to see it. "I'm sorry," he repeats. "Don't listen to me."

"Jude," Andy says, quietly. "I'll always be here for you, in one way or another. I promised you way back when, and I still mean it now.

"Look, Jude," he continues, after a pause. "I know this isn't going to be easy. I know that no one else is going to be able to re-create our history. I'm not being arrogant; I just don't think anyone else is going to totally understand, necessarily. But we'll get as close as we can. And who couldn't love you?" Andy smiles again, but once more, he can't smile back. "Either way, I want you to come meet this new guy: Linus. He's a good doctor, and just as important, a good person. I won't tell him any of your specifics; I just want you to meet him, all right?"

So the next Friday he goes uptown, and in Andy's office is another man, short and handsome and with a smile that reminds him of Willem's. Andy introduces them and they shake hands. "I've heard so much about you, Jude," Linus says. "It's a pleasure to meet you, finally."

"You too," he says. "Congratulations."

Andy leaves them to talk, and they do, a little awkwardly, joking about how this meeting seems like a blind date. Linus has been told only about his amputations, and they discuss them briefly, and the osteomyelitis that had preceded them. "Those treatments can be a killer," Linus says, but he doesn't offer his sympathy for his lost legs, which he appreciates. Linus had been a doctor at a group practice that he'd heard Andy mention before; he seems genuinely admiring of Andy and excited to be working with him.

There is nothing wrong with Linus. He can tell, by the questions he asks, and the respect with which he asks them, that he is indeed a good doctor, and probably a good person. But he also knows he will never be able to undress in front of Linus. He can't imagine having the discussions he has with Andy with anyone else. He can't imagine allowing anyone else such access to his body, to his fears. When he thinks of someone seeing his body anew he quails: ever since the amputation, he has only looked at himself once. He watches Linus's face, his unsettlingly Willem-like smile, and although he is only five years older than Linus, he feels centuries older, something broken and desiccated, something that anyone would look at and quickly throw the tarpaulin over once more. "Take this one away," they'd say. "It's junked."

He thinks of the conversations he will need to have, the explanations he will need to give: about his back, his arms, his legs, his diseases. He is so sick of his own fears, his own trepidations, but as tired as he is of them, he also cannot stop himself from indulging them. He thinks of Linus paging slowly through his chart, of seeing the years, the decades, of notes Andy has made about him: lists of his cuts, of his wounds, of the medications he has been on, of the flare-ups of his infections. Notes on his suicide attempt, on Andy's pleas to get him to see Dr. Loehmann. He knows Andy has chronicled all of this; he knows how meticulous he is.

"You have to tell someone," Ana used to say, and as he had grown older, he had decided to interpret this sentence literally: Some One. Someday, he thought, somehow, he would find a way to tell some one, one person. And then he had, someone he had trusted, and that person had died, and he didn't have the fortitude to tell his story ever again. But then, didn't everyone only tell their lives—truly tell their lives—to one person? How often could he really be expected to repeat himself, when with each telling he was stripping the clothes from his skin and the flesh from his bones, until he was as vulnerable as a small pink mouse? He knows, then, that he will never be able to go to another doctor. He will go to Andy for as long as he can, for as long as Andy will let him. And after that, he doesn't know—he will figure out what to do then. For now, his privacy, his life, is still his. For now, no one else needs to know. His thoughts are so occupied with Willem—trying to re-create him, to hold his face and voice in his head, to keep him present—that his past is as far away as it has ever been: he is in the middle of a lake, trying to stay afloat; he can't think of returning to shore and having to live among his memories again.

He doesn't want to go to dinner with Andy that night, but they do, telling Linus goodbye as they leave. They walk to the sushi restaurant in silence, sit in silence, order, and wait in silence.

"What'd you think?" Andy finally asks.

"He kind of looks like Willem," he says.

"Does he?" Andy says, and he shrugs.

"A little," he says. "The smile."

"Ah," Andy says. "I guess. I can see that." There's another silence. "But what did you think? I know it's sometimes hard to tell from one meeting, but does he seem like someone you might be able to get along with?"

"I don't think so, Andy," he says at last, and can feel Andy's disappointment.

"Really, Jude? What didn't you like about him?" But he doesn't answer, and finally Andy sighs. "I'm sorry," he says. "I hoped you might feel comfortable enough around him to at least consider it. Will you think about it anyway? Maybe you'll give him another chance? And in the meantime, there's this other guy, Stephan Wu, who I think you should maybe meet. He's not an orthopod, but I actually think that might be better; he's certainly the best internist I've ever worked with. Or there's this guy named—"

"Jesus, Andy, stop," he says, and he can hear the anger in his voice, anger he hasn't known he had. "Stop." He looks up, sees Andy's stricken face. "Are you so eager to get rid of me? Can't you give me a break? Can't you let me take this in for a while? Don't you understand how hard this is for me?" He knows how selfish, how unreasonable, how self-absorbed he is being, and he is miserable but unable to stop himself, and he stands, bumping against the table. "Leave me alone," he tells Andy. "If you're not going to be here for me, then leave me alone."

"Jude," Andy says, but he has already pushed past the table, and as he does, the waitress arrives with the food, and he can hear Andy curse and see him reach for his wallet, and he stumbles out of the restaurant. Mr. Ahmed doesn't work on Fridays because he drives himself to Andy's, but now instead of returning to the car, which is parked in front of Andy's office, he hails a taxi and gets in quickly and leaves before Andy can catch him.

That night he turns off his phones, drugs himself, crawls into bed. He wakes the next day, texts both JB and Richard that he's not feeling well and has to cancel his dinners with them, and then re-drugs himself until it is Monday. Monday, Tuesday, Wednesday, Thursday. He has ignored all of Andy's calls and texts and e-mails, all of his messages, but although he is no longer angry, only ashamed, he cannot bear to make one more apology, cannot bear his own meanness, his own weakness. "I'm frightened, Andy," he wants to say. "What will I do without you?"

Andy loves sweets, and on Thursday afternoon he has one of his secretaries place an order for an absurd, a stupid amount of chocolates from Andy's favorite candy shop. "Any note?" his secretary asks, and he shakes his head. "No," he says, "just my name." She nods and starts to leave and he calls her back, grabs a piece of notepaper from his desk, and scribbles Andy—I'm so embarrassed. Please forgive me. Jude, and hands it to her.

But the next night he doesn't go to see Andy; he goes home to make dinner for Harold, who is in town on one of his unannounced visits. The previous spring had been Harold's final semester, which he had failed to register until it was September. He and Willem had always spoken of throwing Harold a party when he finally retired, the way they had done for Julia when she had retired. But he had forgotten, and he had done nothing. And then he remembered and he still did nothing.

He is tired. He doesn't want to see Harold. But he makes dinner anyway, a dinner he knows he will not eat, and serves it to Harold and then sits down himself.

"Aren't you hungry?" Harold asks him, and he shakes his head. "I ate lunch at five today," he lies. "I'll eat later."

He watches Harold eat, and sees that he is old, that the skin on his hands has become as soft and satiny as a baby's. He is ever-more aware that he is one year older, two years older, and now, six years older than Harold was when they met. And yet for all these years, Harold has remained in his perceptions stubbornly forty-five; the only thing that has changed is his perception of how old, exactly, forty-five is. It is embarrassing to admit this to himself, but it is only recently that he has begun considering that there is a possibility, even a probability, that he will outlive Harold. He has already lived beyond his imaginings; isn't it likely he will live longer still?

He remembers a conversation they'd had when he turned thirty-five. "I'm middle-aged," he'd said, and Harold had laughed.

"You're young," he'd said. "You're so young, Jude. You're only middle-aged if you plan on dying at seventy. And you'd better not. I'm really not going to be in the mood to attend your funeral."

"You're going to be ninety-five," he said. "Are you really planning on still being alive then?"

"Alive, and frisky, and being attended to by an assortment of buxom young nurses, and not in any mood to go to some long-winded service."

He had finally smiled. "And who's paying for this fleet of buxom young nurses?"

"You, of course," said Harold. "You and your big-pharma spoils."

But now he worries that this won't happen after all. Don't leave me, Harold, he thinks, but it is a dull, spiritless request, one he doesn't expect will be answered, made more from rote than from real hope. Don't leave me.

"You're not saying anything," Harold says now, and he refocuses himself.

"I'm sorry, Harold," he says. "I was drifting a little."

"I can see that," Harold says. "I was saying: Julia and I were thinking of spending some more time here, in the city, of living uptown full-time."

He blinks. "You mean, moving here?"

"Well, we'll keep the place in Cambridge," Harold says, "but yes. I'm considering teaching a seminar at Columbia next fall, and we like spending time here." He looks at him. "We thought it'd be nice to be closer to you, too."

He isn't sure what he thinks about this. "But what about your lives up there?" he asks. He is discomfited by this news; Harold and Julia love Cambridge—he has never thought they would leave. "What about Laurence and Gillian?"

"Laurence and Gillian are always coming through the city; so is everyone else." Harold studies him again. "You don't seem very happy about this, Jude."

"I'm sorry," he says, looking down. "But I just hope you're not moving here because—because of me." There's a silence. "I don't mean to sound presumptuous," he says, finally. "But if it *is* because of me, then you shouldn't, Harold. I'm fine. I'm doing fine."

"Are you, Jude?" Harold asks, very quietly, and he suddenly stands, quickly, and goes to the bathroom near the kitchen, where he sits on the toilet seat and puts his face in his hands. He can hear Harold waiting on the other side of the door, but he says nothing, and neither does Harold. Finally, minutes later, when he's able to compose himself, he opens the door again, and the two of them look at each other.

"I'm fifty-one," he tells Harold.

"What's that supposed to mean?" Harold asks.

"It means I can take care of myself," he says. "It means I don't need anyone to help me."

Harold sighs. "Jude," he says, "there's not an expiration date on needing help, or needing people. You don't get to a certain age and it stops." They're quiet again. "You're so thin," Harold continues, and when he doesn't say anything, "What does Andy say?"

"I can't keep having this conversation," he says at last, his voice scraped and hoarse. "I can't, Harold. And you can't, either. I feel like all I do is disappoint you, and I'm sorry for that, I'm sorry for all of it. But I'm really trying. I'm doing the best I can. I'm sorry if it's not good enough." Harold tries to interject, but he talks over him. "This is who I am. This is it, Harold. I'm sorry I'm such a problem for you. I'm sorry I'm ruining your retirement. I'm sorry I'm not happier. I'm sorry I'm not over Willem. I'm sorry I have a job you don't respect. I'm sorry I'm such a nothing of a person." He no longer knows what he's saying; he no longer knows how he feels: he wants to cut himself, to disappear, to lie down and never get up again, to hurl himself into space. He hates himself; he pities himself; he hates himself for pitying himself. "I think you should go," he says. "I think you should leave."

"Jude," Harold says.

"Please go," he says. "Please. I'm tired. I need to be left alone. Please leave me alone." And he turns from Harold and stands, waiting, until he hears Harold walk away from him.

After Harold leaves, he takes the elevator to the roof. Here there is a stone wall, chest-high, that lines the perimeter of the building, and he leans against it, swallowing the cool air, placing his palms flat against the top of the wall to try to stop them from shaking. He thinks of Willem, of how he and Willem used to stand on this roof at night, not saying anything, just looking down into other people's apartments. From the southern end of the roof, they could almost see the roof of their old building on Lispenard Street, and sometimes they would pretend that they could see not just the building, but them within it, their former selves performing a theater of their daily lives.

"There must be a fold in the space-time continuum," Willem would say in his action-hero voice. "You're here beside me, and yet—*I can see you moving around in that shithole apartment. My god, St. Francis: Do you realize what's going on here?!*" Back then, he would always laugh, but remembering this now, he cannot. These days, his only pleasure is thoughts of Willem, and yet those same thoughts are also his greatest source of sorrow. He wishes he could forget as completely as Lucien has: that Willem ever existed, his life with him.

As he stands on the roof, he considers what he has done: He has been irrational. He has gotten angry at someone who has, once again, offered to help him, someone he is grateful for, someone he owes, someone he loves. Why am I acting like this, he thinks. But there's no answer.

Let me get better, he asks. *Let me get better or let me end it.* He feels that he is in a cold cement room, from which prong several exits, and one by one, he is shutting the doors, closing himself in the room, eliminating his chances for escape. But why is he doing this? Why is he trapping himself in this place he hates and fears when there are other places he could go? This, he thinks, is his punishment for depending on others: one by one, they will leave him, and he will be alone again, and this time it will be worse because he will remember it had once been better. He has the sense, once again, that his life is moving backward, that it is becoming smaller and smaller, the cement box shrinking around him until he is left with a space so cramped that he must fold himself into a crouch, because if he lies down, the ceiling will lower itself upon him and he will be smothered.

Before he goes to bed he writes Harold a note apologizing for his behavior. He works through Saturday; he sleeps through Sunday. And a new week begins. On Tuesday, he gets a message from Todd. The first of the lawsuits are being settled, for massive figures, but even Todd knows enough not to ask him to celebrate. His messages, by phone or by e-mail, are clipped and sober: the name of the company that is ready to settle, the proposed amount, a short "congratulations."

On Wednesday, he is meant to stop by the artists' nonprofit where he still does pro bono work, but he instead meets JB downtown at the Whitney, where his retrospective is being hung. This show is another souvenir from the ghosted past: it has been in the planning stages for almost two years. When JB had told them about it, the three of them had thrown a small party for him at Greene Street.

"Well, JB, you know what this means, right?" Willem had asked, gesturing toward the two paintings—*Willem and the Girl* and *Willem and Jude, Lispenard Street, II*, from JB's first show, which hung, side by side, in their living room. "As soon as the show comes down, all of these pieces are going straight to Christie's," and everyone had laughed, JB hardest of all, proud and delighted and relieved.

Those pieces, along with *Willem, London, October 8, 9:08 a.m.*, from "Seconds, Minutes, Hours, Days," which he had bought, and *Jude, New York, October 14, 7:02 a.m.*, which Willem had, along with the ones they owned from "Everyone I've Ever Known" and "The Narcissist's Guide to Self-Hatred" and "Frog and Toad," and all the drawings, the paintings, the sketches of JB's that the two of them had been given and had kept, some since college, will be in the Whitney exhibit, as well as previously unshown work.

There will also be a concurrent show of new paintings at JB's gallery, and three weekends before, he had gone to JB's studio in Greenpoint to see them. The series is called "The Golden Anniversary," and it is a chronicle of JB's parents' lives, both together, before he was born, and in an imagined future, the two of them living on and on, together, into old age. In reality, JB's mother is still alive, as are his aunts, but in these paintings, so too is JB's father, who had actually died at the age of thirty-six. The series is just sixteen paintings, many of them smaller in scale than JB's previous works, and as he walked through JB's studio, looking at these scenes of domestic fantasy—his sixty-year-old father coring an apple while his mother made a sandwich; his seventy-year-old father sitting on the sofa reading the paper, while in the background, his mother's legs can be seen descending a flight of stairs—he couldn't help but see what his life too was and might have been. It was precisely these scenes he missed the most from his own life with Willem, the forgettable, in-between moments in which nothing seemed to be happening but whose absence was singularly unfillable.

Interspersing the portraits were still lifes of the objects that had made JB's parents' lives together: two pillows on a bed, both slightly depressed as if someone had dragged the back of a spoon through a bowl of clotted cream; two coffee cups, one's edge faintly pinked with lipstick; a single picture frame containing a photograph of a teenaged JB with his father: the only appearance JB made in these paintings. And seeing these images, he once again marveled at how perfect JB's understanding was of a life together, of his life, of how everything in his apartment—Willem's sweatpants, still slung over the edge of the laundry hamper; Willem's toothbrush, still waiting in the glass on the bathroom sink; Willem's watch, its face splintered from the accident, still sitting untouched on his nightstand—had become totemic, a series of runes only he could read. The table next to Willem's side of the bed at Lantern House had become a sort of unintentional shrine to him: there was the mug he had last drunk from, and the black-framed glasses he'd recently started wearing, and the book he was reading, still splayed, facedown, in the position he'd left it.

"Oh, JB," he had sighed, and although he had wanted to say something else, he couldn't. But JB had thanked him anyway. They were quieter around each other now, and he didn't know if this was who JB had become or if this was who JB had become around him.

Now he knocks on the museum's doors and is let in by one of JB's studio assistants, who is waiting for him and who tells him that JB is overseeing the installation on the top floor, but says he should start on the sixth floor and work his way up to meet him, and so he does.

The galleries on this floor are dedicated to JB's early works, including juvenilia; there is a whole grid of framed drawings from JB's childhood, including a math test over which JB had drawn lovely little pencil portraits of, presumably, his classmates: eight- and nine-year-olds bent over their desks, eating candy bars, feeding birds. He had neglected to solve any of the problems, and at the top of the page was a bright red "F," along with a note: "Dear Mrs. Marion—you see what the problem is here. Please come see me. Sincerely, Jamie Greenberg. P.S. Your son is an immense talent." He smiles looking at this, the first time he can feel himself smiling in a long time. In a lucite cube on a stand in the middle of the room are a few objects from "The Kwotidien," including the hair-covered hairbrush that JB had never returned to him, and he smiles again, looking at them, thinking of their weekends devoted to searching for clippings.

The rest of the floor is given over to images from "The Boys," and he walks slowly through the rooms, looking at pictures of Malcolm, of him, of Willem. Here are the two of them in their bedroom at Lispenard Street, both of them sitting on their twin beds, staring straight into JB's camera, Willem with a small smile; here they are again at the card table, he working on a brief, Willem reading a book. Here they are at a party. Here they are at another party. Here he is with Phaedra; here Willem is with Richard. Here is Malcolm with his sister, Malcolm with his parents. Here is *Jude with Cigarette*, here is *Jude, After Sickness*.

Here is a wall with pen-and-ink sketches of these images, sketches of them. Here are the photographs that inspired the paintings. Here is the photograph of him from which *Jude with Cigarette* was painted: here he is—that expression on his face, that hunch of his shoulders—a stranger to himself and yet instantly recognizable to himself as well.

The stairwells between the floors are densely hung with interstitial pieces, drawings and small paintings, studies and experimentations, that JB made between bodies of work. He sees the portrait JB made of him for Harold and Julia, for his adoption; he sees drawings of him in Truro, of him in Cambridge, of Harold and Julia. Here are the four of them; here are JB's aunts and mother and grandmother; here is the Chief and Mrs. Irvine; here is Flora; here is Richard, and Ali, and the Henry Youngs, and Phaedra.

The next floor: "Everyone I've Ever Known Everyone I've Ever Loved Everyone I've Ever Hated Everyone I've Ever Fucked"; "Seconds, Minutes, Hours, Days." Behind him, around him, installers mill, making small adjustments with their white-gloved hands, standing back and staring at the walls. Once again he enters the stairwell. Once again he looks up, and there he sees, again and again, drawings of him: of his face, of him standing, of him in his wheelchair, of him with Willem, of him alone. These are pieces that JB had made when they weren't speaking, when he had abandoned JB. There are drawings of other people as well, but they are mostly of him: him and Jackson. Again and again, Jackson and him, a checkerboard of the two of them. The images of him are wistful, faint, pencils and pen-and-inks and watercolors. The ones of Jackson are acrylics, thick-lined, looser and angrier. There is one drawing of him that is very small, on a postcard-size piece of paper, and when he examines it more closely, he sees that something had been written on it, and then erased: "Dear Jude," he makes out, "please"— but there is nothing more after that word. He turns away, his breathing quick, and sees the watercolor of a camellia bush that JB had sent him when he was in the hospital, after he had tried to kill himself.

The next floor: "The Narcissist's Guide to Self-Hatred." This had been JB's least commercially successful show, and he can understand why—to look at these works, their insistent anger and self-loathing, was to be both awed and made almost unbearably uncomfortable. *The Coon*, one painting was called; *The Buffoon*; *The Bojangler*; *The Steppin Fetchit*. In each, JB, his skin shined and dark, his eyes bulging and yellowed, dances or howls or cackles, his gums awful and huge and fish-flesh pink, while in the background, Jackson and his friends emerge half formed from a gloom of Goyan browns and grays, all crowing at him, clapping their hands and pointing and laughing. The last painting in this series was called *Even Monkeys Get the Blues*, and it was of JB wearing a pert red fez and a shrunken red epauletted jacket, pantsless, hopping on one leg in an empty warehouse. He lingers on this floor, staring at these paintings, blinking, his throat shutting, and then slowly moves to the stairs a final time.

Then he is on the top floor, and here there are more people, and for a while he stands to the side, watching JB talking to the curators and his gallerist, laughing and gesturing. These galleries are hung, mostly, with images from "Frog and Toad," and he moves from each to each, not really seeing them but rather remembering the experience of view-ing them for the first time, in JB's studio, when he and Willem were new to each other, when he felt as if he was growing new body parts—a second heart, a second brain—to accommodate this excess of feeling, the wonder of his life.

He is staring at one of the paintings when JB finally sees him and comes over, and he hugs JB tightly and congratulates him. "JB," he says. "I'm so proud of you."

"Thanks, Judy," JB says, smiling. "I'm proud of me too, goddam-mit." And then he stops smiling. "I wish they were here," he says.

He shakes his head. "I do too," he manages to say.

For a while they are silent. Then, "Come here," JB says, and grabs his hand and pulls him to the far side of the floor, past JB's gallerist, who waves at him, past a final crate of framed drawings that are being unboxed, to a wall where a canvas is having its skin of bubble wrap care-fully cut away from it. JB positions them before it, and when the plastic is unpeeled, he sees it is a painting of Willem.

The piece isn't large—just four feet by three feet—and is horizon-ally oriented. It is by far the most sharply photorealistic painting JB has produced in years, the colors rich and dense, the brushstrokes that made Willem's hair feathery-fine. The Willem in this painting looks like Willem did shortly before he died: he thinks he is seeing Willem in the months before or after shooting *The Dancer and the Stage,* for which his hair was longer and darker than it was in life. After *Dancer,* he decides, because the sweater he is wearing, a black-green the color of magnolia leaves, is one he remembers buying for Willem in Paris when he went to visit him there.

He steps back, still looking. In the painting, Willem's torso is directed toward the viewer, but his face is turned to the right so that he is almost in profile, and he is leaning toward something or someone and smiling. And because he knows Willem's smiles, he knows Willem has been captured looking at something he loves, he knows Willem in that instant was happy. Willem's face and neck dominate the canvas, and although the background is suggested rather than shown, he knows that Willem is at their table; he knows it from the way JB has drawn the light and shadows on Willem's face. He has the sense that if he says Willem's name, then the face in the painting will turn toward him and answer; he has the sense that if he stretches his hand out and strokes the canvas, he will feel beneath his fingertips Willem's hair, his fringe of eyelashes.

But he doesn't do this, of course, just looks up at last and sees JB smiling at him, sadly. "The title card's been mounted already," JB says, and he goes slowly to the wall behind the painting and sees its title—*Willem Listening to Jude Tell a Story, Greene Street*—and he feels his breath abandon him; it feels as if his heart is made of something oozing and cold, like ground meat, and it is being squeezed inside a fist so that chunks of it are falling, plopping to the ground near his feet.

He is abruptly dizzy. "I need to sit," he finally says, and JB takes him around the corner, to the other side of the wall where Willem will hang, where there's a small cul-de-sac. He half sits atop one of the crates that's been left here and hangs his head, resting his hands on his thighs. "I'm sorry," he manages to say. "I'm sorry, JB."

"It's for you," JB says, quietly. "When the show comes down, Jude. It's yours."

"Thank you, JB," he says. He makes himself stand upright, feels everything within him shift. I need to eat something, he thinks. When was the last time he ate? Breakfast, he thinks, but yesterday. He reaches his hand out toward the crate to center himself, to stop the rocking he feels within his head and spine; he feels this sensation more and more frequently, a floating away, a state close to ecstasy. *Take me somewhere,* he hears a voice inside him say, but he doesn't know to whom he is saying this, or where he wants to go. *Take me, take me.* He is thinking this, crossing his arms over himself, when JB suddenly grabs him by his shoulders and kisses him on the mouth.

He wrenches away. "What the *hell* are you doing?" he asks, and he fumbles backward, rubbing his mouth with the back of his hand.

"Jude, I'm sorry, I didn't mean anything," JB says. "You just look so—so sad."

"So this is what you do?" he spits at JB, who steps toward him. "Don't you *dare* touch me, JB." In the background, he can hear the chatter of the installers, JB's gallerist, the curators. He takes another step, this time toward the edge of the wall. I'm going to faint, he thinks, but he doesn't.

"Jude," JB says, and then, his face changing, "Jude?"

But he is moving away from him. "Get away from me," he says. "Don't touch me. Leave me alone."

"Jude," JB says in a low voice, following him, "you don't look good. Let me help you." But he keeps walking, trying to get away from JB. "I'm sorry, Jude," JB continues. "I'm sorry." He is aware of the pack of people moving as a clump to the other side of the floor, hardly noticing him leaving, JB next to him; it is as if they don't exist.

Twenty more steps to the elevators, he estimates; eighteen more steps; sixteen; fifteen; fourteen. Beneath him, the floor has become a loosely spinning top, wobbling on its axis. Ten; nine; eight. "Jude," says JB, who won't stop talking, "let me help you. Why won't you talk to me anymore?" He is at the elevator; he smacks the button with his palm; he leans against the wall, praying he'll be able to stay upright.

"Get away from me," he hisses at JB. "Leave me alone."

The elevator arrives; the doors open. He steps toward them. His walk now is different: he still leads with his left leg, always, and he still lifts it unnaturally high—that hasn't changed, that has been dictated by his injury. But he no longer drags his right leg, and because his prosthetic feet are so well-articulated—much more so than his own feet had been—he is able to feel the roll of his foot as it leaves the floor, the complicated, beautiful pat of it laying itself down on the ground again, section by section.

But when he is tired, when he is desperate, he finds himself unconsciously reverting to his old gait, with each foot landing flatly, slabbily, on the floor, with his right leg listing behind him. And as he steps into the elevator he forgets that his steel-and-fiberglass legs are made for more nuance than he is allowing them, and he trips and falls. "Jude!" he hears JB call out, and because he is so weak, for a moment everything is dark and empty, and when he regains his vision, he sees that the flock of people have heard JB cry out, that they are now walking in his direction. He sees as well JB's face above him, but he is too tired to interpret his expression. *Willem Listening to Jude Tell a Story*, he thinks, and before him appears the painting: Willem's face, Willem's smile, but Willem isn't looking at him, he is looking somewhere else. What if, he thinks, the Willem of the painting is in fact looking *for* him? He has a sudden urge to stand to the painting's right, to sit in a chair in what would be Willem's sightline, to never leave that painting by itself. There is Willem, imprisoned forever in a one-sided conversation. Here he is, in life, imprisoned as well. He thinks of Willem, alone in his painting, night after night in the empty museum, waiting and waiting for him to tell him a story.

Forgive me, Willem, he tells Willem in his head. *Forgive me, but I have to leave you now. Forgive me, but I have to go.*

"Jude," JB says. The elevator doors are closing, but JB reaches his arm out to him.

But he ignores it, works himself to his feet, leans into the corner of the elevator car. The people are very close now. Everyone moves so much faster than he does. "Stay away from me," he says to JB, but he is quiet. "Leave me alone. Please leave me alone."

"Jude," JB says again. "I'm sorry."

And he begins to say something else, but as he does, the elevator doors close—and he is left alone at last.

3

HE DIDN'T BEGIN it consciously, he really didn't, and yet when he comprehends what he is doing, he doesn't stop it, either. It is the middle of November, and he is getting out of the pool after his morning swim, and as he's lifting himself up on the metal bars that Richard had had installed around the pool to help him get in and out of his wheelchair, the world disappears.

When he wakes again, it's only ten minutes later. One moment it was six forty-five a.m., and he was pulling himself up; the next it is six fifty-five a.m., and he is prone on the black rubber floor, his arms reaching forward for the chair, his torso leaving a wet splotch on the ground. He groans, moving into a sitting position, and waits until the room rights itself again, before attempting—and this time, succeeding—to hoist himself up.

The second time comes a few days later. He has just gotten home from the office, and it is late. Increasingly, he has begun to feel as if Rosen Pritchard supplies him with his very energy, and once he leaves its premises, so too does his strength: the moment Mr. Ahmed shuts the back door of the car, he is asleep, and he doesn't wake until he is delivered to Greene Street. But as he walks into the dark, quiet apartment that night, he is overcome by a sense of displacement, one so debilitating that for a moment he stops, blinking and confused, before he moves to the sofa in the living room and lies down. He means to just rest, just for a few minutes, just until he can stand again, but when he opens his eyes next it is day, and the living room is gray with light.

The third time is Monday morning. He wakes before his alarm, and although he is lying down, he feels everything around and within him roiling, as if he is a bottle half filled with water set adrift on an ocean of clouds. In recent weeks, he hasn't had to drug himself at all on Sundays: he gets home from dinner with JB on Saturday, and climbs into bed, and only wakes when Richard comes to find him the next day. When Richard doesn't come—as he hadn't this Sunday; he and India are visiting her parents in New Mexico—he sleeps through the entire day, through the entire night. He dreams of nothing, and nothing wakes him.

He knows what is happening, of course: he isn't eating enough. He hasn't been for months. Some days he eats very little—a piece of fruit; a piece of bread—and some days he eats nothing at all. It isn't as if he has decided to stop eating—it is simply that he is no longer interested, that he no longer can. He isn't hungry, so he doesn't eat.

That Monday, though, he does. He gets up, he totters downstairs. He swims, but poorly, slowly. And then he comes back upstairs, he makes himself breakfast. He sits and eats it, staring into the apartment, the newspapers folded on the table beside him. He opens his mouth, he inserts a forkful of food, he chews, he swallows. He keeps his movements mechanical, but suddenly he thinks of how grotesque a process it is, putting something into his mouth, moving it around with his tongue, swallowing down the saliva-clotted plug of it, and he stops. Still, he promises himself: I will eat, even if I don't want to, because I am alive and this is what I am to do. But he forgets, and forgets again.

And then, two days later, something happens. He has just come home, so exhausted that he feels soluble, as if he is evaporating into the air, so insubstantial that he feels made not of blood and bone but of vapor and fog, when he sees Willem standing before him. He opens his mouth to speak to him, but then he blinks and Willem is gone, and he is teetering, his arms stretched before him.

"Willem," he says aloud into the empty apartment. "Willem." He closes his eyes, as if he might conjure him that way, but Willem doesn't reappear.

The next day, however, he does. He is once again at home. It is once again night. He has once again not eaten anything. He is lying in bed, he is staring into the dark of the room. And there, abruptly, is Willem, shimmery as a hologram, the edges of him blurring with light, and although Willem isn't looking at him—he is looking elsewhere, looking toward the doorway, looking so intently that he wants to follow Willem's sightline, to see what Willem sees, but he knows he mustn't blink, he mustn't turn away, or Willem will leave him—it is enough to see him, to feel that he in some way still exists, that his disappearance might not be a permanent state after all. But finally, he has to blink, and Willem vanishes once more.

However, he isn't too upset, because now he knows: if he doesn't eat, if he can last to the point just before collapse, he will begin having hallucinations, and his hallucinations might be of Willem. That night he falls asleep contented, the first time he has felt contentment in nearly fifteen months, because now he knows how to recall Willem; now he knows his ability to summon Willem is within his control.

He cancels his appointment with Andy so he can stay home and experiment. This is the third consecutive Friday he hasn't seen Andy. Since that night at the restaurant, the two of them have been polite with each other, and Andy hasn't mentioned Linus, or any other doctor, again, although he has said he'll raise the subject anew in six months. "It's not a matter of wanting to get rid of you, Jude," he said. "And I'm sorry, I really am, if that's how it sounded. I'm just worried. I just want to make sure we find someone you like, someone I know you'll be comfortable with."

"I know, Andy," he said. "And I appreciate it; I do. I've been behaving badly, and I took it out on you." But he knows now that he has to be careful: he has tasted anger, and he knows he has to control it. He can feel it, waiting to burst from his mouth in a swarm of stinging black flies. Where has this rage been hiding? he wonders. How can he make it disappear? Lately his dreams have been of violence, of terrible things befalling the people he hates, the people he loves: he sees Brother Luke being stuffed into a sack full of squealing, starved rats; he sees JB's head being slammed against a wall, his brain splashing out in a gray slurry. In the dreams he is always there, dispassionate and watchful, and after witnessing their destruction, he turns and walks away. He wakes with his nose bleeding the way it had when he was a child and was suppressing a tantrum, with his hands shaking, with his face contorted into a snarl.

That Friday Willem doesn't come to him after all. But the next evening, as he is leaving the office to meet JB for dinner, he turns his head to the right and sees, sitting next to him in the car, Willem. This

time, he fancies, Willem is a little harder-edged, a little more solid, and
he stares and stares until he blinks and Willem once again dissolves.

After these episodes he is depleted, and the world around him dims
as if all its power and electricity has gone toward creating Willem. He
instructs Mr. Ahmed to take him home instead of to the restaurant;
as he is driven south, he texts JB to tell him he's feeling sick and can't
make it. He is doing this more and more: canceling plans with people,
shoddily and usually unforgivably late—an hour before a hard-to-secure
dinner reservation, minutes after a scheduled meeting time at a gallery, seconds before the curtain rises above a stage. Richard, JB, Andy,
Harold and Julia: these are the final people who still contact him, per-
sistently, week after week. He can't remember when he last heard from
Citizen or Rhodes or the Henry Youngs or Elijah or Phaedra—it has
been weeks, at least. And although he knows he should care, he doesn't.
His hope, his energy are no longer replenishable resources; his reserves
are limited, and he wants to spend them trying to find Willem, even if
the hunt is elusive, even if he is likely to fail.

And so home he goes, and he waits and waits for Willem to appear
to him. But he doesn't, and finally he sleeps.

The next day he waits in bed, trying to suspend himself between
alertness and dazedness, for that (he thinks) is the state in which he is
most likely to summon Willem.

On Monday he wakes, feeling foolish. *This has got to stop,* he tells
himself. *You have got to rejoin the living. You're acting like an insane
person.* Visions? *Do you know what you sound like?*

He thinks of the monastery, where Brother Pavel liked to tell him
the story of an eleventh-century nun named Hildegard. Hildegard had
visions; she closed her eyes and illuminated objects appeared before
her; her days were aswim with light. But Brother Pavel was less interested in Hildegard than in Hildegard's instructor, Jutta, who had forsaken the material world to live as an ascetic in a small cell, dead to
the concerns of the living, alive but not alive. "That's what will happen
to you if you don't obey," Pavel would say, and he would be terrified.
There was a small toolshed on the monastery's grounds, dark and chilly
and jumbled with malevolent-looking iron objects, each of them ending in a spike, a spear, a scythe, and when the brother told him of Jutta,
he imagined he would be forced into the toolshed, fed just enough to
survive, and on and on and on he would live, almost forgotten but not

completely, almost dead but not completely. But even Jutta had had Hildegard for company. He would have no one. How frightened he had been; how certain he was that this, someday, would come to pass.

Now, as he lies in bed, he hears the old lied murmur to him. *"I have become lost to the world,"* he sings, quietly, *"in which I otherwise wasted so much time."*

But although he knows how foolish he is being, he still cannot bring himself to eat. The very act of it now repels him. He wishes he were above want, above need. He has a vision of his life as a sliver of soap, worn and used and smoothed into a slender, blunt-ended arrowhead, a little more of it disintegrating with every day.

And then there is what he doesn't like to admit to himself but is conscious of thinking. He cannot break his promise to Harold—he won't. But if he stops eating, if he stops trying, the end will be the same anyway.

Usually he knows how melodramatic, how narcissistic, how unrealistic he is being, and at least once a day he scolds himself. The fact is, he finds himself less and less able to summon Willem's specifics without depending on props: He cannot remember what Willem's voice sounds like without first playing one of the saved voice messages. He can no longer remember Willem's scent without first smelling one of his shirts. And so he fears he is grieving not so much for Willem but for his own life: its smallness, its worthlessness.

He has never been concerned with his legacy, or never thought he had been. And it is a helpful thing that he isn't, for he will leave nothing behind: not buildings or paintings or films or sculptures. Not books. Not papers. Not people: not a spouse, not children, probably not parents, and, if he keeps behaving the way he is, not friends. Not even new law. He has created nothing. He has made nothing, nothing but money: the money he has earned; the money given to him to compensate for Willem being taken from him. His apartment will revert to Richard. The other properties will be given away or sold and their proceeds donated to charities. His art will go to museums, his books to libraries, his furniture to whoever wants it. It will be as if he has never existed. He has the feeling, unhappy as it is, that he was at his most valuable in those motel rooms, where he was at least something singular and meaningful to someone, although what he had to offer was being taken from him, not given willingly. But there he had at least been real to another person; what they saw him as was actually what he was. There, he was at his least deceptive.

He had never been able to truly believe Willem's interpretation of him, as someone who was brave, and resourceful, and admirable. Willem would say those things and he would feel ashamed, as if he'd been swindling him: Who *was* this person Willem was describing? Even his confession hadn't changed Willem's perception of him—in fact, Willem seemed to respect him more, not less, because of it, which he had never understood but in which he had allowed himself to find solace. But although he hadn't been convinced, it was somehow sustaining that someone else had seen him as a worthwhile person, that someone had seen his as a meaningful life.

The spring before Willem died, they'd had some people over for dinner—just the four of them and Richard and Asian Henry Young—and Malcolm, in one of the occasional spikes of regret he had been experiencing over his and Sophie's decision not to have children, even though, as they all reminded him, they hadn't wanted children to begin with, had asked, "Without them, I just wonder: What's been the point of it all? Don't you guys ever worry about this? How do any of us know our lives are meaningful?"

"Excuse me, Mal," Richard had said, pouring him the last of the wine from one bottle as Willem uncorked another, "but I find that offensive. Are you saying our lives are less meaningful because we don't have kids?"

"No," Malcolm said. Then he thought. "Well, maybe."

"I know *my* life's meaningful," Willem had said, suddenly, and Richard had smiled at him.

"Of course *your* life's meaningful," JB had said. "You make things people actually *want* to see, unlike me and Malcolm and Richard and Henry here."

"People want to see our stuff," said Asian Henry Young, sounding wounded.

"I meant people outside of New York and London and Tokyo and Berlin."

"Oh, them. But who cares about *those* people?"

"No," Willem said, after they'd all stopped laughing. "I know my life's meaningful because"—and here he stopped, and looked shy, and was silent for a moment before he continued—"because I'm a good friend. I love my friends, and I care about them, and I think I make them happy."

The room became quiet, and for a few seconds, he and Willem had looked at each other across the table, and the rest of the people, the apartment itself, fell away: they were two people on two chairs, and around them was nothingness. "To Willem," he finally said, and raised his glass, and so did everyone else. "To Willem!" they all echoed, and Willem smiled back at him.

Later that evening, when everyone had left and they were in bed, he had told Willem that he was right. "I'm glad you know your life has meaning," he told him. "I'm glad it's not something I have to convince you of. I'm glad you know how wonderful you are."

"But your life has just as much meaning as mine," Willem had said. "You're wonderful, too. Don't you know that, Jude?"

At the time, he had muttered something, something that Willem might interpret as an agreement, but as Willem slept, he lay awake. It had always seemed to him a very plush kind of problem, a privilege, really, to consider whether life was meaningful or not. He didn't think his was. But this didn't bother him so much.

And although he hadn't fretted over whether his life was worthwhile, he *had* always wondered why he, why so many others, went on living at all; it had been difficult to convince himself at times, and yet so many people, so many millions, billions of people, lived in misery he couldn't fathom, with deprivations and illnesses that were obscene in their extremity. And yet on and on and on they went. So was the determination to keep living not a choice at all, but an evolutionary implementation? Was there something in the mind itself, a constellation of neurons as toughened and scarred as tendon, that prevented humans from doing what logic so often argued they should? And yet that instinct wasn't infallible—he had overcome it once. But what had happened to it after? Had it weakened, or become more resilient? Was his life even his to choose to live any longer?

He had known, ever since the hospital, that it was impossible to convince someone to live for his own sake. But he often thought it would be a more effective treatment to make people feel more urgently the necessity of living for others: that, to him, was always the most compelling argument. The fact was, he did owe Harold. He did owe Willem. And if they wanted him to stay alive, then he would. At the time, as he slogged through day after day, his motivations had been murky to him, but now he could recognize that he had done it for them, and that rare selflessness had been something he could be proud of after all. He hadn't understood why they wanted him to stay alive, only that they had, and so he had done it. Eventually, he had learned how to rediscover contentment, joy, even. But it hadn't begun that way.

And now he is once again finding life more and more difficult, each day a little less possible than the last. In his every day stands a tree, black and dying, with a single branch jutting to its right, a scarecrow's sole prosthetic, and it is from this branch that he hangs. Above him a rain is always misting, which makes the branch slippery. But he clings to it, as tired as he is, because beneath him is a hole bored into the earth so deep that he cannot see where it ends. He is petrified to let go because he will fall into the hole, but eventually he knows he will, he knows he must: he is so tired. His grasp weakens a bit, just a little bit, with every week.

So it is with guilt and regret, but also with a sense of inevitability, that he cheats on his promise to Harold. He cheats when he tells Harold he is being sent away to Jakarta for business and will miss Thanksgiving. He cheats when he begins growing a beard, which he hopes will disguise the gauntness in his face. He cheats when he tells Sanjay he's fine, he's just had an intestinal flu. He cheats when he tells his secretary she doesn't need to get him lunch because he picked something up on the way into the office. He cheats when he cancels the next month's worth of dates with Richard and JB and Andy, telling them he has too much work. He cheats every time he lets the voice whisper to him, unbidden, *It won't be long now, it won't be long.* He isn't so deluded that he thinks he will be able to literally starve himself to death—but he does think that there will be a day, closer now than ever before, in which he will be so weak that he will stumble and fall and crash his head against the Greene Street lobby's cement floors, in which he will contract a virus and not have the resources to make it retreat.

At least one of his lies is true: he *does* have too much work. He has an appellate argument in a month, and he is relieved to be able to spend so much time at Rosen Pritchard, where nothing bad has ever befallen him, where even Willem knows not to disturb him with one of his unpredictable appearances. One night he hears Sanjay muttering to himself as he hurries past his office—"Fuck, she's going to kill me"—

and looks up and sees it is no longer night, but day, and the Hudson is turning a smeary orange. He notes this, but he feels nothing. Here, his life suspends itself; here, he might be anyone, anywhere. He can stay as late as he likes. No one is waiting for him, no one will be disappointed if he doesn't call, no one will be angry if he doesn't go home.

The Friday before the trial, he is working late when one of his secretaries looks in to tell him he has a visitor in the lobby, a Dr. Contractor, and would he like him sent up? He pauses, unsure of what to do; Andy has been calling him, but he hasn't been returning his calls, and he knows he won't simply leave.

"Yes," he tells her. "Bring him to the southeastern conference room."

He waits in this conference room, which has no windows and is the most private, and when Andy comes in, he sees his mouth tighten, but they shake hands like strangers, and it's not until his secretary leaves that Andy gets up and walks over to him.

"Stand up," he commands.

"I can't," he says.

"Why not?"

"My legs hurt," he says, but this isn't true. He cannot stand because his prostheses no longer fit. "The good thing about these prostheses is that they're very sensitive and lightweight," the prosthetist had told him when he was fitted for them. "The bad thing is that the sockets don't allow you very much give. You lose or gain more than ten percent of your body weight—so for you, that's plus or minus fourteen, fifteen pounds—and you're either going to need to adjust your weight or have a new set made. So it's important you stay at weight." For the past three weeks, he has been in his wheelchair, and although he continues to wear his legs, they are only for show, something to fill his pants with; they are too ill-fitting for him to actually use, and he is too weary to see the prosthetist, too weary to have the conversation he knows he'll need to have with him, too weary to conjure explanations.

"I think you're lying," Andy says. "I think you've lost so much weight that your prostheses are sliding off of you, am I right?" But he doesn't answer. "How much weight have you lost, Jude?" Andy asks. "When I last saw you, you were already twelve pounds down. How much is it now? Twenty? More?" There's another silence. "What the hell are you

doing?" Andy asks, lowering his voice further. "What're you doing to
yourself, Jude?

"You look like hell," Andy continues. "You look terrible. You look
sick." He stops. "Say something," he says. "*Say something*, goddammit,
Jude."

He knows how this interaction is meant to go: Andy yells at him.
He yells back at Andy. A détente, one that ultimately changes nothing,
one that is a piece of pantomime, is reached: he will submit to something that isn't a solution but that makes Andy feel better. And then
something worse will happen, and the pantomime will be revealed to
be just that, and he will be coerced into a treatment he doesn't want.
Harold will be called. He will be lectured and lectured and lectured
and he will lie and lie and lie. The same cycle, the same circle, again
and again and again, a churn as predictable as the men in the motel
rooms coming in, fitting their sheets over the bed, having sex with him,
leaving. And then the next one, and the next one. And the next day: the
same. His life is a series of dreary patterns: sex, cutting, this, that. Visits
to Andy, visits to the hospital. Not this time, he thinks. This is when he
does something different; this is when he escapes.

"You're right, Andy," he says, in as calm and unemotive a voice as
he can summon, the voice he uses in the courtroom. "I've lost weight.
And I'm sorry I haven't come in earlier. I didn't because I knew you'd
get upset. But I've had a really bad intestinal flu, one I just can't shake,
but it's ended. I'm eating, I promise. I know I look terrible. But I promise I'm working on it." Ironically, he *has* been eating more in the past
two weeks; he needs to get through the trial. He doesn't want to faint
while he's in court.

And after that, what can Andy say? He is suspicious, still. But there
is nothing for him to do. "If you don't come see me next week, I'm coming back," Andy tells him before his secretary sees him out.

"Fine," he says, still pleasantly. "The Tuesday after next. The trial'll
be over by then."

After Andy leaves, he feels momentarily triumphant, as if he is a
hero in a fairy tale and has just vanquished a dangerous enemy. But of
course Andy isn't his enemy, and he is being ridiculous, and his sense
of victory is followed by despair. He feels, as he increasingly does, that
his life is something that has happened to him, rather than something

he has had any role in creating. He has never been able to imagine what his life might be; even as a child, even as he dreamed of other places, of other lives, he wasn't able to visualize what those other places and lives would be; he had believed everything he had been taught about who he was and what he would become. But his friends, Ana, Lucien, Harold and Julia: They had imagined his life for him. They had seen him as something different than he had ever seen himself as; they had allowed him to believe in possibilities that he would never have conceived. He saw his life as the axiom of equality, but they saw it as another riddle, one with no name—*Jude* = *x*—and they had filled in the *x* in ways Brother Luke, the counselors at the home, Dr. Traylor had never written for him or encouraged him to write for himself. He wishes he could believe their proofs the way they do; he wishes they had shown him how they had arrived at their solutions. If he knew how they had solved the proof, he thinks, he would know why to keep living. All he needs is one answer. All he needs is to be convinced once. The proof needn't be elegant; it need only be explicable.

The trial arrives. He does well. At home that Friday, he wheels himself into the bedroom, into bed. He spends the entire weekend in a sleep that is unfamiliar and eerie, less a sleep than a glide, weightlessly moving between the realms of memory and fantasy, unconsciousness and wakefulness, anxiety and hopefulness. This is not the world of dreams, he thinks, but someplace else, and although he is aware at moments of waking—he sees the chandelier above him, the sheets around him, the sofa with its wood-fern print across from him—he is unable to distinguish when things have happened in his visions from when they have actually happened. He sees himself lifting a blade to his arm and slicing it down through his flesh, but what springs from the slit are coils of metal and stuffing and horsehair, and he realizes that he has undergone a mutation, that he is no longer even human, and he feels relief: he won't have to break his promise to Harold after all; he has been enchanted; his culpability has vanished with his humanity.

Is this real? the voice asks him, tiny and hopeful. *Are we inanimate now?*

But he can't answer himself.

Again and again he sees Brother Luke, Dr. Traylor. As he has gotten weaker, as he has drifted from himself, he sees them more and more frequently, and although Willem and Malcolm have dimmed for him,

Brother Luke and Dr. Traylor have not. He feels his past is a cancer, one he should have treated long ago but instead ignored. And now Brother Luke and Dr. Traylor have metastasized, now they are too large and too overwhelming for him to eliminate. Now when they appear, they are wordless: they stand before him, they sit, side by side, on the sofa in his bedroom, staring at him, and this is worse than if they spoke, because he knows they are trying to decide what to do with him, and he knows that whatever they decide will be worse than he can imagine, worse than what had happened before. At one point he sees them whispering to each other, and he knows they are talking about him. "*Stop*," he yells at them, "stop, stop," but they ignore him, and when he tries to get up to make them leave, he is unable to do so. "Willem," he hears himself call, "protect me, help me; make them leave, make them go away." But Willem doesn't come, and he realizes he is alone and becomes afraid, concealing himself under the blanket and remaining as still as he can, certain that time has doubled back upon itself and he will be made to relive his life in sequence. *It'll get better eventually*, he prom- ises himself. *Remember, good years followed the bad.* But he can't do it again; he can't live once more through those fifteen years, those fifteen years whose half-life have been so long and so resonant, that have deter- mined everything he has become and done.

By the time he finally, fully wakes on Monday morning, he knows he has crossed some sort of threshold. He knows he is close, that he is moving from one world to another. He blacks out twice while simply trying to get into his wheelchair. He faints on his way to the bathroom. And yet somehow he remains uninjured; somehow he is still alive. He gets dressed, the suit and shirts he'd had recut for him a month ago already loose, and slides his stumps into the prostheses, and goes down- stairs to meet Mr. Ahmed.

At work, everything is the same. It is the new year; people are returning from their vacations. During the management committee meeting, he jabs his fingers into his thigh to keep himself alert. He feels his grip loosen around the branch.

Sanjay leaves early that evening; he leaves early, too. Today is Har- old and Julia's move-in day, and he has promised to go uptown to visit them. He hasn't seen them in more than a month, and although he feels himself no longer able to gauge what he looks like, he has dressed in extra layers today—an undershirt, his shirt, a sweater, a cardigan, his suit jacket, his coat—so that he'll appear a little bulkier. At Harold's, he is waved in by the doorman, and up he goes, trying not to blink because blinking makes the dizziness worse. Outside their door, he stops and puts his head in his hands until he feels strong enough, and then he turns the knob and rolls inside and stares.

They are all there: Harold and Julia, of course, but Andy and JB and Richard and India and the Henry Youngs and Rhodes and Elijah and Sanjay and the Irvines as well, all posed and perched on different pieces of furniture as if they're at a photo shoot, and for a second he fears he will start laughing. And then he wonders: Am I dreaming this? Am I awake? He remembers the vision of himself as a sagging mattress and thinks: Am I still real? Am I still conscious?

"Christ," he says, when he is able to speak at last. "What the hell is this?"

"Exactly what you think it is," he hears Andy say.

"I'm not staying for this," he tries to say, but can't. He can't move. He can't look at any of them: he looks instead at his hands—his scarred left hand, his normal right—as above him Andy speaks. They have been watching him for weeks—Sanjay has been keeping track of the days he's seen him eat at the office, Richard has been entering his apartment to check his refrigerator for food. "We measure weight loss in grades," he hears Andy saying. "A loss of one to ten percent of your body weight is Grade One. A loss of eleven to twenty percent is Grade Two. Grade Two is when we consider putting you on a feeding tube. You know this, Jude, because it's happened to you before. And I can tell by looking at you that you're at Grade Two—at least." Andy talks and talks, and he thinks he begins to cry, but he is unable to produce tears. Everything has gone so wrong, he thinks; how did everything go so wrong? How has he forgotten so completely who he was when he was with Willem? It is as if that person has died along with Willem, and what he is left with is his elemental self, someone he has never liked, someone so incapable of occupying the life he has, the life he has somehow made for himself, in spite of himself.

Finally he lifts his head and sees Harold staring at him, sees that Harold is actually crying, silently, looking and looking at him. "Harold," he says, although Andy is still talking, "release me. Release me from my promise to you. Don't make me do this anymore. Don't make me go on."

But no one releases him: not Harold, not anyone. He is instead captured and taken to the hospital, and there, at the hospital, he begins to fight. My last fight, he thinks, and he fights harder than he ever has, as hard as he had as a child in the monastery, becoming the monster they always told him he was, yowling and spitting in Harold's and Andy's faces, ripping the IV from his hand, thrashing his body on the bed, trying to scratch at Richard's arms, until finally a nurse, cursing, sticks him with a needle and he is sedated.

He wakes with his wrists strapped to the bed, with his prostheses gone, with his clothes gone as well, with a press of cotton against his collarbone under which he knows a catheter has been inserted. The same thing all over again, he thinks, the same, the same, the same.

But this time it isn't the same. This time he is given no choices. This time, he is put on a feeding tube, which punctures through his abdomen and into his stomach. This time, he is made to go back and see Dr. Loehmann. This time, he is going to be watched, every mealtime: Richard will watch him eat breakfast. Sanjay will watch him eat lunch and, if he's at the office late, dinner. Harold will watch him on the weekends. He isn't allowed to go to the bathroom until an hour after he's finished each meal. He must see Andy every Friday. He must see JB every Saturday. He must see Richard every Sunday. He must see Harold whenever Harold says he must. If he is caught skipping a meal, or a session, or disposing of food in any way, he will be hospitalized, and this hospitalization won't be a matter of weeks; it will be a matter of months. He will gain a minimum of thirty pounds, and he will be allowed to stop only when he has maintained that weight for six months.

And so begins his new life, a life in which he has moved past humiliation, past sorrow, past hope. This is a life in which his weary friends' weary faces watch him as he eats omelets, sandwiches, salads. Who sit across from him and watch as he twirls pasta around his fork, as he plows his spoon through polenta, as he slides flesh off bones. Who look at his plate, at his bowl, and either nod at him—yes, he can go—or shake their heads: No, Jude, you have to eat more than that. At work he makes decisions and people follow them, but then at one p.m., lunch is delivered to his office, and for the next half hour—although no one else in the firm knows this—his decisions mean nothing, because Sanjay has absolute power, and he must obey whatever he says. Sanjay, with one text to Andy, can send him to the hospital, where they will tie him down again and force food into him. They all can. No one seems to care that this isn't what he wants.

Have you all forgotten? he yearns to ask. *Have you forgotten him? Have you forgotten how much I need him? Have you forgotten I don't know how to be alive without him? Who can teach me? Who can tell me what I should do now?*

It was an ultimatum that sent him to Dr. Loehmann the first time; it is an ultimatum that brings him back. He had always been cordial with Dr. Loehmann, cordial and remote, but now he is hostile and churlish. "I don't want to be here," he says, when the doctor says he's happy to see him again and asks him what he would like to discuss. "And don't lie to me: you're not happy to see me, and I'm not happy to be here. This is a waste of time—yours and mine. I'm here under duress."

"We don't have to discuss why you're here, Jude, not if you don't want to," Dr. Loehmann says. "What would you like to talk about?"

"Nothing," he snaps, and there is a silence.

"Tell me about Harold," Dr. Loehmann suggests, and he sighs, impatiently.

"There's nothing to say," he says.

He sees Dr. Loehmann every Monday and Thursday. On Monday nights, he returns to work after his appointment. But on Thursdays he is made to see Harold and Julia, and with them he is horrifically rude as well: and not just rude but nasty, spiteful. He behaves in ways that astonish him, in ways he has never dared before in his life, not even when he was a child, in ways that he would have been beaten for by anyone else. But not by Harold and Julia. They never rebuke him, they never discipline him.

"This is disgusting," he says that night, pushing away the chicken stew Harold has made. "I won't eat this."

"I'll get you something else," Julia says quickly, getting up. "What do you want, Jude? Do you want a sandwich? Some eggs?"

"Anything else," he says. "This tastes like dog food." But he is speaking to Harold, staring at him, daring him to flinch, to break. His pulse leaps in his throat with anticipation: He can see Harold springing from his chair and hitting him in the face. He can see Harold crumpling with tears. He can see Harold ordering him out of his house. "Get the fuck out of here, Jude," Harold will say. "Get out of our lives and never come back."

"Fine," he'll say. "Fine, fine. I don't need you anyway, Harold. I don't need any of you." What a relief it will be to learn that Harold had never really wanted him after all, that his adoption was a whim, a folly whose novelty tarnished long ago.

But Harold does none of those things, just looks at him. "Jude," he says at last, very quietly.

"Jude, Jude," he mocks him, squawking his own name back to Harold like a jay. "Jude, Jude." He is so angry, so furious: there is no word for what he is. Hatred sizzles through his veins. Harold wants him to live, and now Harold is getting his wish. Now Harold is seeing him as he is.

Do you know how badly I could hurt you? he wants to ask Harold. *Do you know I could say things that you would never forget, that you would never forgive me for? Do you know I have that power? Do you know that every day I have known you I have been lying to you? Do you know what I really am? Do you know how many men I have been with, what I have let them do to me, the things that have been inside me, the noises I have made?* His life, the only thing that is his, is being possessed: By Harold, who wants to keep him alive, by the demons who scrabble through his body, dangling off his ribs, puncturing his lungs with their talons. By Brother Luke, by Dr. Traylor. *What is life for?* he asks himself. *What is my life for?*

Oh, he thinks, will I never forget? Is this who I am after all, after all these years?

He can feel his nose start to bleed, and he pushes back from the table. "I'm leaving," he tells them, as Julia enters the room with a sandwich. He sees that she has cut off its crusts and sliced it into triangles, the way you would for a child, and for a second he wavers and almost begins to bawl, but then he recalls himself and glares again at Harold.

"No, you're not," Harold says, not angrily, but decisively. He stands up from his chair, points his finger at him. "You're staying and you're finishing."

"No, I'm not," he announces. "Call Andy, I don't care. I'm going to kill myself, Harold, I'm going to kill myself no matter what you do, and you're not going to be able to stop me."

"Jude," he hears Julia whisper. "Jude, please."

Harold walks over to him, taking the plate from Julia as he does, and he thinks: This is it. He raises his chin, he waits for Harold to hit him in the face with it, but he doesn't, just puts the plate before him. "Eat," Harold says, his voice tight. "You're going to eat this now."

He thinks, unexpectedly, of the day he had his first episode at Harold and Julia's. Julia was at the grocery store, and Harold was upstairs printing out a worrisomely complicated recipe for a soufflé he claimed he was going to make. There he had lain in the pantry, trying to keep himself from kicking his legs out in agony, listening to Harold clatter down the stairs and into the kitchen. "Jude?" he'd called, not seeing him, and as quiet as he had tried to be, he had made a noise anyway, and Harold had opened the door and found him. He had known Harold for six years by that point, but he was always careful around him, dreading but expecting the day when he would be revealed to him as he really was. "I'm sorry," he'd tried to tell Harold, but he was only able to croak.

"Jude," Harold had said, frightened, "can you hear me?," and he'd nodded, and Harold had entered the pantry himself, picking his way around the stacks of paper towels and jugs of dishwasher detergent, lowering himself to the floor and gently pulling his head into his lap, and for a second he had thought that this was the moment he had always half anticipated, the one in which Harold would unzip his pants and he would have to do what he had always done. But he hadn't, had just stroked his head, and after a while, as he twitched and grunted, his body tensing itself with pain, its heat filling his joints, he realized that Harold was singing to him. It was a song he had never heard before but that he recognized instinctually was a child's song, a lullaby, and he juddered and chattered and hissed through his teeth, opening and closing his left hand, gripping the throat of a nearby bottle of olive oil with his right, as on and on Harold sang. As he lay there, so desperately humiliated, he knew that after this incident Harold would either become distant from him or would draw closer still. And because he didn't know which would happen, he found himself hoping—as he never had before and never would again—that this episode would never end, that Harold's song would never finish, that he would never have to learn what followed it.

And now he is so much older, Harold is so much older, Julia is so much older, they are three old people and he is being given a sandwich meant for a child, and a directive—*Eat*—meant for a child as well. We are so old, we have become young again, he thinks, and he picks up the plate and throws it against the far wall, where it shatters, spectacularly. He sees the sandwich had been grilled cheese, sees one of the triangular slabs slap itself against the wall and then ooze down it, the white cheese dripping off in gluey clumps.

Now, he thinks, almost giddily, as Harold comes close to him once more, now, now, now. And Harold raises his hand and he waits to be hit so hard that this night will end and he will wake in his own bed and for a while be able to forget this moment, will be able to forget what he has done.

But instead he finds Harold wrapping him in his arms, and he tries to push him away, but Julia is holding him too, leaning over the carapace of his wheelchair, and he is trapped between them. "Leave me alone," he roars at them, but his energy is dissipating and he is weak and hungry. "Leave me alone," he tries again, but his words are shapeless and useless, as useless as his arms, as his legs, and he soon stops trying.

"Jude," Harold says to him, quietly. "My poor Jude. My poor sweetheart." And with that, he starts to cry, for no one has ever called him sweetheart, not since Brother Luke. Sometimes Willem would try—sweetheart, Willem would try to call him, honey—and he would make him stop; the endearment was filthy to him, a word of debasement and depravity. "My sweetheart," Harold says again, and he wants him to stop; he wants him to never stop. "My baby." And he cries and cries, cries for everything he has been, for everything he might have been, for every old hurt, for every old happiness, cries for the shame and joy of finally getting to be a child, with all of a child's whims and wants and insecurities, for the privilege of behaving badly and being forgiven, for the luxury of tendernesses, of fondnesses, of being served a meal and being made to eat it, for the ability, at last, at last, of believing a parent's reassurances, of believing that to someone he is special despite all his mistakes and hatefulness, *because* of all his mistakes and hatefulness.

It ends with Julia finally going to the kitchen and making another sandwich; it ends with him eating it, truly hungry for the first time in months; it ends with him spending the night in the extra bedroom, with Harold and Julia kissing him good night; it ends with him wondering if maybe time really is going to loop back upon itself after all, except in this rendering, he will have Julia and Harold as parents from the beginning, and who knows what he will be, only that he will be better, that he will be healthier, that he will be kinder, that he won't feel the need to struggle so hard against his own life. He has a vision of himself as a fifteen-year-old, running into the house in Cambridge, shouting words—"Mom! Dad!"—he has never said before, and although he can't imagine what would have made this dream self so excited (for all his study of normal children, their interests and behaviors, he knows few specifics), he understands that he is happy. Maybe he is wearing a soccer uniform, his arms and legs bare; maybe he is accompanied by a friend, by a girlfriend. He has probably never had sex before; he is probably trying at every opportunity to do so. He would think sometimes of who he would be as an adult, but it would never occur to him that he might not have someone to love, sex, his own feet running across a field of grass as soft as carpet. All those hours, all those hours he has spent cutting, and hiding the cutting, and beating back his memories, what would he do instead with all those hours? He would be a better person, he knows. He would be a more loving one.

But maybe, he thinks, maybe it isn't too late. Maybe he can pretend one more time, and this last bout of pretending will change things for him, will make him into the person he might have been. He is fifty-one; he is old. But maybe he still has time. Maybe he can still be repaired.

He is still thinking this on Monday when he goes to see Dr. Loehmann, to whom he apologizes for his awful behavior the week before—and the weeks before that, as well.

And this time, for the first time, he really tries to talk to Dr. Loehmann. He tries to answer his questions, and to do so honestly. He tries to begin to tell a story he has only ever told once before. But it is very difficult, not only because the story is barely possible for him to speak, but because he cannot do so without thinking of Willem, and how when he had last told this story, he was with someone who had seen him the way no one had since Ana, with someone who had managed to see past who he was, and yet see him completely as well. And then he is upset, breathless, and he turns his wheelchair sharply—he is still six or seven pounds away from using his prostheses for walking again—and excuses himself and leaves Dr. Loehmann's office, spinning down the hall to the bathroom, where he locks himself in, breathing slowly and rubbing his palm against his chest as if to soothe his heart. And here in the bathroom, which is cold and silent, he plays his old game of "If" with himself: If I hadn't followed Brother Luke. If I hadn't let myself be taken by Dr. Traylor. If I hadn't let Caleb inside. If I had listened more to Ana.

On he plays, his recriminations beating a rhythm in his head. But then he also thinks: If I had never met Willem. If I had never met Harold. If I had never met Julia, or Andy, or Malcolm, or JB, or Richard, or Lucien, or so many other people: Rhodes and Citizen and Phaedra and Elijah. The Henry Youngs. Sanjay. All the most terrifying Ifs involve people. All the good ones do as well.

Finally he is able to calm himself, and he wheels himself out of the bathroom. He could leave, he knows. The elevator is there; he could send Mr. Ahmed back for his coat.

But he doesn't. Instead he goes the other direction, and returns to the office, where Dr. Loehmann is still sitting in his chair, waiting for him.

"Jude," says Dr. Loehmann. "You've come back."

He takes a breath. "Yes," he says. "I've decided to stay."

[VII]

Lispenard Street

ON THE SECOND anniversary of your death, we went to Rome. This was something of a coincidence, and also not: he knew and we knew he'd have to be out of the city, far away from New York State. And maybe the Irvines felt the same way, because that was when they had scheduled the ceremony—at the very end of August, when all of Europe had migrated elsewhere, and yet we were flying toward it, that continent bereft of all its chattering flocks, all its native fauna.

It was at the American Academy, where Sophie and Malcolm had both once had residencies, and where the Irvines had endowed a scholarship for a young architect. They had helped select the first recipient, a very tall and sweetly nervous young woman from London who built mostly temporary structures, complex-looking buildings of earth and sod and paper that were meant to disintegrate slowly over time, and there was the announcement of the fellowship, which came with additional prize money, and a reception, at which Flora spoke. Along with us, and Sophie and Malcolm's Bellcast partners, there were Richard and JB, both of whom had also had residencies in Rome, and after the ceremony we went to a little restaurant nearby they had both liked when they had lived there, and where Richard showed us which part of the building's walls were Etruscan and which were Roman. But although it was a nice meal, comfortable and convivial, it was also a quiet one, and at one point I remember looking up and realizing that none of us were eating and all of us were staring—at the ceiling, at our plates, at one another—and thinking something separate and yet, I knew, something the same as well.

The next afternoon Julia napped and we took a walk. We were staying across the river, near the Spanish Steps, but we had the car take us back over the bridge to Trastevere and walked through streets that were so close and dark that they might have been hallways, until finally we came to a square, tiny and precise and adorned with nothing but sunlight, where we sat on a stone bench. An elderly man, with a white beard and wearing a linen suit, sat down on the other end, and he nodded at us and we nodded at him.

For a long time we were silent together, sitting in the heat, and then he suddenly said that he remembered this square, that he had been here with you once, and that there was a famous gelato place just two streets away.

"Should I go?" he asked me, and smiled.

"I think you know the answer," I said, and he got up. "I'll be back," he said. "Stracciatella," I told him, and he nodded. "I know," he said.

We watched him leave, the man and I, and then the man smiled at me and I smiled back. He wasn't so elderly after all, I saw: probably just a few years older than I. And yet I was never able (and am still not) to think of myself as old. I talked as if I knew I was; I bemoaned my age. But it was only for comedy, or to make other people feel young.

"*Lui è tuo figlio?*" the man asked, and I nodded. I was always surprised and pleased when we were recognized for who we were to each other, for we looked nothing alike, he and I: and yet I thought—I hoped—there must have been something about the way we were together that was more compelling evidence of our relation than mere physical resemblance.

"Ah," the man said, looking at him again before he turned the corner and disappeared from sight. "*Molto bello.*"

"Sì," I said, and was suddenly sad.

He looked sly, then, and asked, or rather stated, "*Tua moglie deve essere molto bella, no?*" and then grinned to show me he meant it in fun, that it was a compliment, that if I was a plain man, I was also a lucky one, to have such a beautiful wife who had given me such a handsome son, and so I couldn't be offended. I grinned back at him. "She is," I said, and he smiled, unsurprised.

The man had already left by the time he returned—nodding at me as he went, leaning on his cane—with a cone for me and a container of lemon granita for Julia. I wished he had bought something for himself, too, but he hadn't. "We should go," he said, and we did, and that night he went to bed early, and the following day—the day you died—we didn't see him at all: he left us a message with the front desk saying he had gone for a walk, and that he would see us tomorrow, and that he was sorry, and all day long we walked too, and although I thought there was a chance we might see him—Rome is not such a large city, after all—we didn't, and that night as we undressed for bed, I was aware that I had been looking for him on every street, in every crowd.

The next morning there he was at breakfast, reading the paper, pale but smiling at us, and we didn't ask him what he'd done the day before and he didn't volunteer it. That day we just walked around the city, the three of us an unwieldy little pack—too wide for the sidewalks, we strolled in single file, each of us taking the position of the leader in turn—but just to familiar places, well-trafficked places, places that would have no secret memories, that held no intimacies. Near Via Condotti Julia looked into the tiny window of a tiny jewelry store, and we went inside, the three of us filling the space, and each held the earrings she had admired in the window. They were exquisite: solid gold, dense and heavy and shaped like birds, with small round rubies for eyes and little gold branches in their beaks, and he bought them for her, and she was embarrassed and delighted—Julia had never worn much jewelry— but he looked happy to be able to, and I was happy that he was happy, and that she was happy, too. That night we met JB and Richard for a final dinner, and the next morning we left to go north, to Florence, and he to go home.

"I'll see you in five days," I told him, and he nodded.

"Have a good time," he said. "Have a wonderful time. I'll see you soon."

He waved as we were driven away in the car; we turned in our seats to wave back at him. I remember hoping my wave was somehow telegraphing what I couldn't say: *Don't you dare.* The night before, as he and Julia were talking to JB, I asked Richard if he would feel comfortable sending me updates while we were away, and Richard said he would. He had gained almost all the weight Andy wanted, but he'd had two setbacks—one in May, one in July—and so we were all still watching him.

It sometimes felt as if we were living our relationship in reverse, and instead of worrying for him less, I worried for him more; with each year I became more aware of his fragility, less convinced of my competence. When Jacob was a baby, I would find myself feeling more assured with each month he lived, as if the longer he stayed in this world, the more deeply he would become anchored to it, as if by being alive, he was staking claim to life itself. It was a preposterous notion, of course, and it was proven wrong in the most horrible way. But I couldn't stop thinking this: that life tethered life. And yet at some point in his life—after Caleb, if I had to date it—I had the sense that he was in a hot-air balloon, one that was staked to the earth with a long twisted rope, but each year the balloon strained and strained against its cords, tugging itself away, trying to drift into the skies. And down below, there was a knot of us trying to pull the balloon back to the ground, back to safety. And so I was always frightened for him, and I was always frightened of him, as well.

Can you have a real relationship with someone you are frightened of? Of course you can. But he still scared me, because he was the powerful one and I was not: if he killed himself, if he took himself away from me, I knew I would survive, but I knew as well that survival would be a chore; I knew that forever after I would be hunting for explanations, sifting through the past to examine my mistakes. And of course I knew how badly I would miss him, because although there had been trial runs for his eventual departure, I had never been able to get any better at dealing with them, and I was never able to get used to them.

But then we came home, and everything was the same: Mr. Ahmed met us at the airport and drove us back to the apartment, and waiting for us with the doorman were bags of food so we wouldn't have to go to the grocery store. The next day was a Thursday and he came over and we had dinner, and he asked what we had seen and done and we told him. That night we were washing the dishes, and as he was handing me a bowl to put in the dishwasher, it slipped through his fingers and broke against the floor. "*Goddammit*," he shouted. "I'm so sorry, Harold. I'm so stupid, I'm so clumsy," and although we told him it wasn't a problem, that it was fine, he only grew more and more upset, so upset that his hands started to shake, that his nose started to bleed. "Jude," I told him, "it's okay. It happens," but he shook his head. "No," he said, "it's me. I mess up everything. Everything I touch I ruin." Julia and I had looked at each other over his head as he was picking up the pieces, unsure what to say or do: the reaction was so out of proportion to what had happened. But there had been a few incidents in the preceding months, ever since he had thrown that plate across the room, that made me realize, for the first time in my life with him, how truly angry he was, how hard he must work every day at controlling it.

After that first incident with the plate there had been another, a few weeks later. This was up at Lantern House, where he hadn't been in months. It was morning, just after breakfast, and Julia and I were leaving to go to the store, and I went to find him to ask what he wanted. He was in his bedroom, and the door was slightly ajar, and when I saw what he was doing, I for some reason didn't call his name, didn't walk away, but stood just outside the frame, silent and watching. He had one prosthesis on and was putting on the other—I had never seen him without them—and I watched as he sank his left leg into the socket, drawing the elastic sleeve up around his knee and thigh, and then pushed his pants leg down over it. As you know, these prostheses had feet with paneling that resembled the shape of a toe box and a heel, and I watched as he pulled on his socks, and then his shoes. And then he took a breath and stood, and I watched as he took a step, and then another. But even I could tell something was wrong—they were still too big; he was still too thin—and before I could call out, he had lost his balance and pitched forward onto the bed, where he lay still for a moment.

And then he reached down and tore off both legs, one and then the other, and for a second—they were still wearing their socks and shoes—it appeared as if they were his real legs, and he had just yanked away a piece of himself, and I half expected to see an arcing splash of blood. But instead he picked one up and slammed it against the bed, again and again and again, grunting with the effort, and then he threw it to the ground and sat on the edge of the mattress, his face in his hands, his elbows on his thighs, rocking himself and not making a sound. "Please," I heard him say, "please." But he didn't say anything else, and I, to my shame, crept away and went to our bedroom, where I sat in a posture that mimicked his own, and waited as well for something I didn't know.

In those months I thought often of what I was trying to do, of how hard it is to keep alive someone who doesn't want to stay alive. First you try logic (*You have so much to live for*), and then you try guilt (*You owe me*), and then you try anger, and threats, and pleading (*I'm old; don't do this to an old man*). But then, once they agree, it is necessary that you, the cajoler, move into the realm of self-deception, because you can see that it is costing them, you can see how much they don't want to be here, you can see that the mere act of existing is depleting for them, and then you have to tell yourself every day: I am doing the right thing. To let him do what he wants to do is abhorrent to the laws of nature, to the laws of love. You pounce upon the happy moments, you hold them up as proof—*See? This is why it's worth living. This is why I've been making him try*—even though that one moment cannot compensate for all the other moments, the majority of moments. You think, as I had thought with Jacob, what is a child for? Is he to give me comfort? Is he for me to give comfort to? And if a child can no longer be comforted, is it my job to give him permission to leave? And then you think again: But that is abominable. I can't.

So I tried, of course. I tried and tried. But every month I could feel him receding. It wasn't so much a physical disappearance: by November, he was back at his weight, the low side of it anyway, and looked better than he had perhaps ever. But he was quieter, much quieter, and he had always been quiet anyway. But now he spoke very little, and when we were together, I would sometimes see him looking at something I couldn't see, and then he would twitch his head, very slightly, like a horse does its ears, and come back to himself.

Once I saw him for our Thursday dinner and he had bruises on his face and neck, just on one side, as if he was standing near a building in the late afternoon and the sun had cast a shadow against him. The bruises were a dark rusty brown, like dried blood, and I had gasped. "What happened?" I asked. "I fell," he said, shortly. "Don't worry," he said, although of course I did. And when I saw him with bruises again, I tried to hold him. "Tell me," I said, and he worked himself free. "There's nothing to tell," he said. I still don't know what had happened: Had he done something to himself? Had he let someone do something to him? I didn't know which was worse. I didn't know what to do.

He missed you. I missed you, too. We all did. I think you should know that, that I didn't just miss you because you made him better: I missed you for you. I missed watching the pleasure you took in doing the things you enjoyed, whether it was eating or running after a tennis ball or flinging yourself into the pool. I missed talking with you, missed watching you move through a room, missed watching you fall to the lawn under a passel of Laurence's grandchildren, pretending that you couldn't get up from under their weight. (That same day, Laurence's youngest grandchild, the one who had a crush on you, had made you a bracelet of knotted-together dandelion flowers, and you had thanked her and worn it all day, and every time she had spotted it on your wrist, she had run over and buried her face in her father's back: I missed that, too.) But mostly, I missed watching you two together; I missed watching you watch him, and him watch you; I missed how thoughtful you were with each other, missed how thoughtlessly, sincerely affectionate you were with him; missed watching you listen to each other, the way you both did so intently. That painting JB did—*Willem Listening to Jude Tell a Story*—was so true, the expression so right: I knew what was happening in the painting even before I read its title.

And I don't want you to think that there weren't happy moments as well, happy days, after you left. They were fewer, of course. They were harder to find, harder to make. But they existed. After we came home from Italy, I began teaching a seminar at Columbia, one open to both law school students and graduate students from the general population. The course was called "The Philosophy of Law, the Law of Philosophy," and I co-taught it with an old friend of mine, and in it we discussed the fairness of law, the moral underpinnings of the legal system and how they sometimes contradicted our national sense of morality: Drayman 241, after all these years! In the afternoon, I saw friends. Julia took a life-drawing class. We volunteered at a nonprofit that helped professionals (doctors, lawyers, teachers) from other countries (Sudan, Afghanistan, Nepal) find new jobs in their fields, even if these jobs bore only a tangential resemblance to what they had done before: nurses became medical assistants; judges became clerks. A few of them I helped apply to law school, and when I saw them, we would talk about what they were learning, how different this law was from the law they had known.

"I think we should work on a project together," I told him that fall (he was still doing pro bono work with the artist nonprofit, which—when I went to volunteer there myself—was actually more moving than I had thought it would be: I had thought it would just be a bunch of untalented hacks trying to make creative lives for themselves when it was clear they never would, and although that was in fact what it was, I found myself admiring them, much as he did—their perseverance, their dumb, hardy faith. These were people no one and nothing could ever dissuade from life, from claiming it as theirs).

"Like what?" he asked.

"You could teach me to cook," I told him, as he gave me that look he had, in which he was almost smiling but not quite, amused but not ready to show it. "I'm serious. *Really* cook. Six or seven dishes I could have in my arsenal."

And so he did. Saturday afternoons, after he'd finished work or visiting with Lucien and the Irvines, we'd drive to Garrison, either alone or with Richard and India or JB or one of the Henry Youngs and their wives, and on Sunday we'd cook something. My main problem, it emerged, was a lack of patience, my inability to accept tedium. I'd wander away to look for something to read and forget that I was leaving the risotto to glue itself into a sticky glop, or I'd forget to turn the carrots in their puddle of olive oil and come back to find them seared to the bottom of the pan. (So much of cooking, it seemed, was petting and bathing and monitoring and flipping and turning and soothing: demands I associated with human infancy.) My other problem, I was told, was my insistence on innovating, which is apparently a guarantee of failure in baking. "It's chemistry, Harold, not philosophy," he kept saying, with that same half smile. "You can't cheat the specifed amounts and hope it's going to come out the way it should."

"Maybe it'll come out better," I said, mostly to entertain him—I was always happy to play the fool if I thought it might give him some pleasure—and now he smiled, really smiled. "It won't," he said.

But finally, I actually did learn how to make some things: I learned how to roast a chicken and poach an egg and broil halibut. I learned how to make carrot cake, and a bread with lots of different nuts that I had liked to buy at the bakery he used to work at in Cambridge: his version was uncanny, and for weeks I made loaf after loaf. "Excellent, Harold," he said one day, after tasting a slice. "See? Now you'll be able to cook for yourself when you're a hundred."

"What do you mean, cook for myself?" I asked him. "You'll have to cook for me," and he smiled back at me, a sad, strange smile, and didn't say anything, and I quickly changed the subject before he said something that I would have to pretend he didn't. I was always trying to allude to the future, to make plans for years away, so that he'd commit to them and I could make him honor his commitment. But he was careful: he never promised.

"We should take a music class, you and I," I told him, not really knowing what I meant by that.

He smiled, a little. "Maybe," he said. "Sure. We'll discuss it." But that was the most he'd allow.

After our cooking lesson, we walked. When we were at the house upstate, we walked the path Malcolm had made: past the spot in the woods where I had once had to leave him propped against a tree, jolting with pain, past the first bench, past the second, past the third. At the second bench we'd always sit and rest. He didn't need to rest, not like he used to, and we walked so slowly that I didn't need to, either. But we always made a ceremonial stop, because it was from here that you had the clearest view of the back of the house, do you remember? Malcolm had cut away some of the trees here so that from the bench, you were facing the house straight on, and if you were on the back deck of the house, you were facing the bench straight on. "It's such a beautiful house," I said, as I always did, and as I always did, I hoped he was hearing me say that I was proud of him: for the house he built, and for the life he had built within it.

Once, a month or so after we all returned home from Italy, we were sitting on this bench, and he said to me, "Do you think he was happy with me?" He was so quiet I thought I had imagined it, but then he looked at me and I saw I hadn't.

"Of course he was," I told him. "I know he was."

He shook his head. "There were so many things I didn't do," he said at last.

I didn't know what he meant by this, but it didn't change my mind. "Whatever it was, I know it didn't matter," I told him. "I know he was happy with you. He told me." He looked at me, then. "I know it," I repeated. "I know it." (You had never said this to me, not explicitly, but I know you will forgive me; I know you will. I know you would have wanted me to say this.)

Another time, he said, "Dr. Loehmann thinks I should tell you things."

"What things?" I asked, careful not to look at him.

"Things about what I am," he said, and then paused. "Who I am," he corrected himself.

"Well," I said, finally, "I'd like that. I'd like to know more about you."

Then he smiled. "That sounds strange, doesn't it?" he asked. "'More about you.' We've known each other so long now."

I always had the sense, during these exchanges, that although there might not be a single correct answer, there was in fact a single incorrect one, after which he would never say anything again, and I was forever trying to calculate what that answer might be so I would never say it.

"That's true," I said. "But I always want to know more, where you're concerned."

He looked at me quickly, and then back at the house. "Well," he said. "Maybe I'll try. Maybe I'll write something down."

"I'd love that," I said. "Whenever you're ready."

"It might take me a while," he said.

"That's fine," I said. "You'll take as long as you need." A long time was a good thing, I thought: it meant years, years of him trying to figure out what he wanted to say, and although they would be difficult, torturous years, at least he would be alive. That was what I thought: that I would rather have him suffering and alive—than dead.

But in the end, it didn't take him much time at all. It was February, about a year after our intervention. If he could keep his weight on through May, we'd stop monitoring him, and he'd be able to stop seeing Dr. Loehmann if he wanted, although both Andy and I thought he should keep going. But it would no longer be our decision. That Sunday, we had stayed in the city, and after a cooking lesson at Greene Street (an asparagus-and-artichoke terrine) we went out for our walk.

It was a chilly day, but windless, and we walked south on Greene until it changed into Church, and then down and down, through TriBeCa, through Wall Street, and almost to the very tip of the island, where we stood and watched the river, its splashing gray water. And then we turned and walked north, back up the same street: Trinity to Church, Church to Greene. He had been quiet all day, still and silent, and I prattled on about a middle-aged man I had met at the career placement center, a refugee from Tibet a year or so older than he, a doctor, who was applying to American medical schools.

"That's admirable," he said. "It's difficult to start over."

"It is," I said. "But you've started over too, Jude. You're admirable, too." He glanced at me, then looked away. "I mean it," I said. I was reminded of a day a year or so after he had been discharged from the hospital after his suicide attempt, and he was staying with us in Truro. We had taken a walk then as well. "I want you to tell me three things you think you do better than anyone else," I had told him as we sat on the sand, and he made a weary puffing noise, filling his cheeks with air and blowing it out through his mouth.

"Not now, Harold," he had said.

"Come on," I said. "Three things. Three things you do better than anyone, and then I'll stop bothering you." But he thought and thought and still couldn't think of anything, and hearing his silence, something in me began to panic. "Three things you do well, then," I revised. "Three things you like about yourself." By this time I was almost begging. "Anything," I told him. "Anything."

"I'm tall," he finally said. "Tallish, anyway."

"Tall is good," I said, although I had been hoping for something different, something more qualitative. But I would accept it as an answer, I decided: it had taken him so long to come up with even that. "Two more." But he couldn't think of anything else. I could see he was getting frustrated and embarrassed, and finally I let the subject drop.

Now, as we moved through TriBeCa, he mentioned, very casually, that he had been asked to be the firm's chairman.

"My god," I said, "that's amazing, Jude. My god. Congratulations."

He nodded, once. "But I'm not going to accept," he said, and I was thunderstruck. After all he had given fucking Rosen Pritchard—all those hours, all those years—he wasn't going to take it? He looked at me. "I'd have thought you'd be happy," he said, and I shook my head.

"No," I told him. "I know how much—how much satisfaction you get from your job. I don't want you to think that I don't approve of you, that I'm not proud of you." He didn't say anything. "Why aren't you going to take it?" I asked him. "You'd be great at it. You were born for it."

And then he winced—I wasn't sure why—and looked away. "No," he said. "I don't think I would be. It was a controversial decision anyway, as I understand it. Besides," he began, and then stopped. Somehow we had stopped walking as well, as if speech and movement were oppositional activities, and we stood there in the cold for a while. "Besides," he continued, "I thought I'd leave the firm in a year or so." He looked at me, as if to see how I was reacting, and then looked up, at the sky. "I thought maybe I'd travel," he said, but his voice was hollow and joyless, as if he were being conscripted into a faraway life he didn't much want. "I could go away," he said, almost to himself. "There are places I should see."

I didn't know what to say. I stared and stared at him. "I could come with you," I whispered, and he came back to himself and looked at me.

"Yes," he said, and he sounded so declarative I felt comforted. "Yes, you could come with me. Or you two could come meet me in certain places."

We started moving again. "Not that I want to unduly delay your second act as a world traveler," I said, "but I do think you should reconsider Rosen Pritchard's offer. Maybe do it for a few years, and then jet off to the Balearics or Mozambique or wherever it is you want to go." I knew that if he accepted the chairmanship offer, then he wouldn't kill himself; he was too responsible to leave with unfinished business. "Okay?" I prompted him.

He smiled, then, his old, bright, beautiful smile. "Okay, Harold," he said. "I promise I'll reconsider."

Then we were just a few blocks from home, and I realized we were coming upon Lispenard Street. "Oh god," I said, seeking to capitalize on his good mood, to keep us both aloft. "Here we are at the site of all my nightmares: The Worst Apartment in the World," and he laughed, and we veered right off of Church and walked half a block down Lispenard Street until we were standing in front of your old building. For a while I ranted on and on about the place, about how horrible it was, exaggerating and embroidering for effect, to hear him laugh and protest. "I was always afraid a fire was going to go ripping through that place and you'd both end up dead," I said. "I had dreams of getting phoned by the emergency technicians that they'd found you both gnawed to death by a swarm of rats."

"It wasn't *that* bad, Harold," he smiled. "I have very fond memories of this place, actually." And then the mood turned again, and we both stood there staring at the building and thinking of you, and him, and all the years between this moment and the one in which I had met him, so young, so terribly young, and at that time just another student, terrifically smart and intellectually nimble, but nothing more, not the person I could have ever imagined him becoming for me.

And then he said—he was trying to make me feel better, too; we were each performing for the other—"Did I ever tell you about the time we jumped off the roof to the fire escape outside our bedroom?"

"What?" I asked, genuinely appalled. "No, you never did. I think I would have remembered that."

But although I could never have imagined the person he would become for me, I knew how he would leave me: despite all my hopes, and pleas, and insinuations, and threats, and magical thoughts, I knew. And five months later—June twelfth, a day with no significant anniversaries associated with it, a nothing day—he did. My phone rang, and although it wasn't a sinister time of night, and although nothing had happened that I would later see as foreshadowing, I knew, I knew. And on the other end was JB, and he was breathing oddly, in rapid bursts, and even before he spoke, I knew. He was fifty-three, fifty-three for not even two months. He had injected an artery with air, and had given himself a stroke, and although Andy had told me his death would have been quick, and painless, I later looked it up online and found he had lied to me: it would have meant sticking himself at least twice, with a needle whose gauge was as thick as a hummingbird's beak; it would have been agonizing.

When I went to his apartment, finally, it was so neat, with his office boxed up and the refrigerator emptied and everything—his will, letters—tiered on the dining-room table, like place cards at a wedding. Richard, JB, Andy, all of your and his old friends: they were all around, constantly, all of us moving about and around one another, shocked but not shocked, surprised only that we were so surprised, devastated and beaten and mostly, helpless. Had we missed something? Could we have done something different? After his service—which was crowded, with his friends and your friends and their parents and families, with his law school classmates, with his clients, with the staff and patrons of the arts nonprofit, with the board of the food kitchen, with a huge population of Rosen Pritchard employees, past and present, including Meredith, who came with an almost completely discombobulated Lucien (who lives, cruelly, to this day, although in a nursing home in Connecticut), with our friends, with people I wouldn't have expected: Kit and Emil and Philippa and Robin—Andy came to me, crying, and confessed that he thought things had started really going wrong for him after he'd told him he was leaving his practice, and that it was his fault. I hadn't even known Andy was leaving—he had never mentioned it to me—but I comforted him, and told him it wasn't his fault, not at all, that he had always been good to him, that I had always trusted him.

"At least Willem isn't here," we said to one another. "At least Willem isn't here to see this."

Though, of course—if you were here, wouldn't he still be as well?

But if I cannot say that I didn't know how he would die, I can say that there was much I didn't know, not at all, not after all. I didn't know that Andy would be dead three years later of a heart attack, or Richard two years after that of brain cancer. You all died so young: you, Malcolm, him. Elijah, of a stroke, when he was sixty; Citizen, when he was sixty as well, of pneumonia. In the end there was, and is, only JB, to whom he left the house in Garrison, and whom we see often—there, or in the city, or in Cambridge. JB has a serious boyfriend now, a very good man named Tomasz, a specialist in Japanese medieval art at Sotheby's, whom we like very much; I know both you and he would have as well. And although I feel bad for myself, for us—of course—I feel most bad most often for JB, deprived of you all, left to live the beginnings of old age by himself, with new friends, certainly, but without most of his friends who had known him since he was a child. At least I have known him since he was twenty-two; off and on, perhaps, but neither of us count the off years.

And now JB is sixty-one and I am eighty-four, and he has been dead for six years and you have been dead for nine. JB's most recent show was called "Jude, Alone," and was of fifteen paintings of just him, depicting imagined moments from the years after you died, from those nearly three years he managed to hang on without you. I have tried, but I cannot look at them: I try, and try, but I cannot.

And there were still more things I didn't know. He was right: we had only moved to New York for him, and after we had settled his estate—Richard was his executor, though I helped him—we went home to Cambridge, to be near the people who had known *us* for so long. I'd had enough of cleaning and sorting—we had, along with Richard and JB and Andy, gone through all of his personal papers (there weren't many), and clothes (a heartbreak itself, watching his suits get narrower and narrower) and your clothes; we had looked through your files at Lantern House together, which took many days because we kept stopping to cry or exclaim or pass around a picture none of us had seen before—but when we were back home, back in Cambridge, the very movement of organizing had become reflexive, and I sat down one Saturday to clean out the bookcases, an ambitious project that I soon lost interest in, when I found, tucked between two books, two envelopes, our names in his handwriting. I opened my envelope, my heart thrumming, and saw my name—*Dear Harold*—and read his note from decades ago, from the day of his adoption, and cried, sobbed, really, and then I slipped the disc into the computer and heard his voice, and although I would have cried anyway for its beauty, I cried more because it was his. And then Julia came home and found me and read her note and we cried all over again.

And it wasn't until a few weeks after that that I was able to open the letter he had left us on his table. I hadn't been able to bear it earlier; I wasn't sure I would be able to bear it now. But I did. It was eight pages long, and typed, and it was a confession: of Brother Luke, and Dr. Traylor, and what had happened to him. It took us several days to read, because although it was brief, it was also endless, and we had to keep putting the pages down and walking away from them, and then bracing each other—*Ready?*—and sitting down and reading some more.

"I'm sorry," he wrote. "Please forgive me. I never meant to deceive you."

I still don't know what to say about that letter, I still cannot think of it. All those answers I had wanted about who and why he was, and now those answers only torment. That he died so alone is more than I can think of; that he died thinking that he owed us an apology is worse; that he died still stubbornly believing everything he was taught about himself—after you, after me, after all of us who loved him—makes me think that my life has been a failure after all, that I have failed at the one thing that counted. It is then that I talk to you the most, that I go downstairs late at night and stand before *Willem Listening to Jude Tell a Story*, which now hangs above our dining-room table: "Willem," I ask you, "do you feel like I do? Do you think he was happy with me?" Because he deserved happiness. We aren't guaranteed it, none of us are, but he deserved it. But you only smile, not at me but just past me, and you never have an answer. It is also then that I wish I believed in some sort of life after life, that in another universe, maybe on a small red planet where we have not legs but tails, where we paddle through the atmosphere like seals, where the air itself is sustenance, composed of trillions of molecules of protein and sugar and all one has to do is open one's mouth and inhale in order to remain alive and healthy, maybe you two are there together, floating through the climate. Or maybe he is closer still: maybe he is that gray cat that has begun to sit outside our neighbor's house, purring when I reach out my hand to it; maybe he is that new puppy I see tugging at the end of my other neighbor's leash; maybe he is that toddler I saw running through the square a few months ago, shrieking with joy, his parents huffing after him; maybe he is that flower that suddenly bloomed on the rhododendron bush I thought had died long ago; maybe he is that cloud, that wave, that rain, that mist. It isn't only that he died, or how he died; it is what he died believing. And so I try to be kind to everything I see, and in everything I see, I see him.

But back then, back on Lispenard Street, I didn't know so much of this. Then, we were only standing and looking up at that red-brick building, and I was pretending that I never had to fear for him, and he was letting me pretend this: that all the dangerous things he could have done, all the ways he could have broken my heart, were in the past, the stuff of stories, that the time that lay behind us was scary, but the time that lay ahead of us was not.

"You jumped off the roof?" I repeated. "Why on earth would you have done such a thing?"

"It's a good story," he said. He even grinned at me. "I'll tell you."

"Please," I said.

And then he did.

Acknowledgments

For their expertise on matters of architecture, law, medicine, and film-making, my great thanks to Matthew Baiotto, Janet Nezhad Band, Steve Blatz, Karen Cinorre, Michael Gooen, Peter Kostant, Sam Levy, Dermot Lynch, and Barry Tuch. Special thanks to Douglas Eakeley for his erudition and patience, and to Priscilla Eakeley, Drew Lee, Eimear Lynch, Seth Mnookin, Russell Perreault, Whitney Robinson, Marysue Rucci, and Ronald and Susan Yanagihara for their unstinting support.

My deepest thanks to the brilliant Michael "Bitter" Dykes, Kate Maxwell, and Kaja Perina for bringing my life joy, and to Kerry Lauerman for bringing it comfort. I have long thought Yossi Milo and Evan Smoak and Stephen Morrison and Chris Upton role models for how to behave in a loving relationship; I appreciate and admire them for many reasons.

I'm grateful to the devoted and faithful Gerry Howard and to the inimitable Ravi Mirchandani, who gave themselves over to the life of this book with such generosity and dedication, and to Andrew Kidd for his belief, and to Anna Stein O'Sullivan for her indulgence, equanimity, and constancy. Thank you too to everyone who helped make this book happen, in particular Lexy Bloom, Alex Hoyt, Jeremy Medina, Bill Thomas, and the Estate of Peter Hujar.

Finally and essentially: I not only never could have, but never would have, written this book without the conversations with—and the kindness, grace, empathy, forgiveness, and wisdom of—Jared Hohlt, my first and favorite reader, secret keeper, and North Star. His beloved friendship is the greatest gift of my adulthood.

ABOUT THE AUTHOR

Hanya Yanagihara lives in New York City.